Matt, to a great scout and better suy, best wishes to you and thank you for your support to trp 61

Godspeed

LTC Michael F. Flick

DRAGON ALLIANCE:
Rise against Shadow

J. MICHAEL FLÜCK

Inspiring Voices®
A Service of **Guideposts**

Inspiring Voices books may be ordered through
booksellers or by contacting:

Inspiring Voices
1663 Liberty Drive
Bloomington, IN 47403
www.inspiringvoices.com
1-(866) 697-5313

Because of the dynamic nature of the Internet, any web
addresses or links contained in this book may have changed
since publication and may no longer be valid. The views
expressed in this work are solely those of the author and
do not necessarily reflect the views of the publisher, and the
publisher hereby disclaims any responsibility for them.

Any people depicted in stock imagery provided
by Thinkstock are models, and such images are
being used for illustrative purposes only.

Certain stock imagery © Thinkstock.

ISBN: 978-1-4624-0357-8 (sc)
ISBN; 978-1-4624-0356-1 (e)

Library of Congress Control Number: 2012918321

Printed in the United States of America

Inspiring Voices rev. date: 11/08/2012

CONTENTS

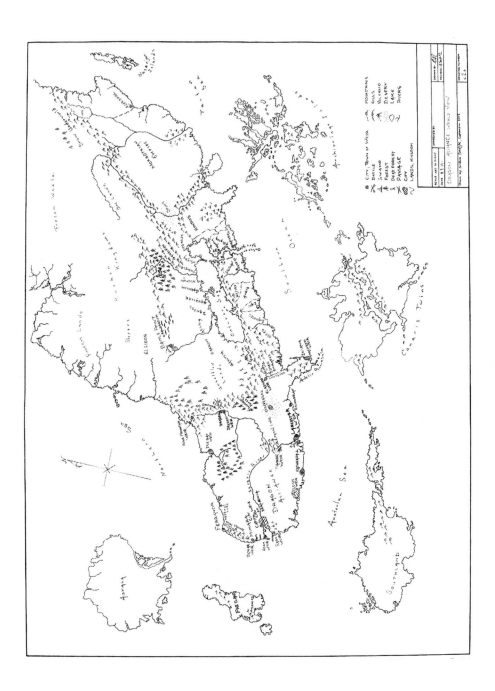

PROLOGUE

It has been said that God created the heavens and the earth in seven days. With the billions of stars and planets in the universe, the beauty and intricacy of this amazing planet cannot be a single creation. With that premise, who is to say that the almighty Creator did not have other experiments? Other worlds with slightly different variables in the mix but centered on the same central theme: mankind's gift of life and the freedom of choice to do good versus evil. According to Scriptures, the angels in heaven fought a brutal war over this principle, resulting in the fall of Lucifer. But what if this conflict was brought to the material world, and the angels and demons took the form of various species of dragons and other assorted creatures that fought each other for the power to guide the human race? This story also attests to the theory of God's constant counterbalance of the dark side of our choices versus the infinite good we can also serve. All of this action and counteraction to slowly move our way toward the shining city on the hill is the ultimate chess game, with a move to correct every wrong decision made.

On this world, this parallel earth, dark forces are already on the move as the Dragon Alliance Republic is slowly awakening to the dark storm on its horizon. Mkel, the Draden Weir fortress leader and gold dragonrider, wakes from his dragon-induced dream of the last horrendous war fought against the Morgathian Empire. His blood bonded dragon, Gallanth, a powerful gold dragon, had been having visions of both the past and a looming darkness that he perceived threatened the very existence of the Alliance. Mkel and Gallanth must ready their soldiers for the war to come, but their enemies are not just the vengeful

Morgathian Empire and their evil chromatic dragon allies; there are also enemies within the Alliance itself. A conglomeration of greedy, power-hungry senators, known as the Party of the Enlightened (POE), is conspiring for the downfall of the Weirs and the republic. Amid this brewing trouble, Mkel and his dragon must lead their friends and the soldiers of their garrison through several pitched battles, with the haunting memory of his father always in the shadows of his mind. The true question he has is, with the odds stacked against them, can his Weir and the Alliance itself survive?

CHAPTER I

DRAGON DREAM

In the ancient times, the kingdoms and nations of man were divided, and chaos plagued the world. The rift between the metallic and chromatic dragons over their opposing views on mankind fomented discourse, resulting in the initial tremors of the rebellion. From the fertile states of the west on the windward side of the Gray Mountains, to the Great Northern Plains of the nomadic Kaskar tribes, to the rough lands of the east, fighting, wars, and skirmishes between all the kingdoms kept those nations divided and weak. The ever-present danger of the insect-like orc hordes constantly threatened all. The elves held the forests, and the dwarves controlled the mountains in the west, but that was the best they could do. Then, at the commandment of the Creator, Michenth, the arch dragon and father to all the dragon races, directed the dragons to bond with human riders and guide the kingdoms of man in uniting the world.

Michenth and a handful of gold dragons were the first to blood bond with human riders. The ritual that joined the souls of dragon and rider also greatly enhanced the dragon's power, cementing the union between the two and strengthening the dragon's oath to protect and guide all of mankind. This, however, was not accepted by Michenth's mate, Tiamat, the dragon queen and mother, or her chromatic dragon disciples. She espoused that man should be subservient to dragons, with their superior power and intellect. The evil arch dragon then led the rebellion that initiated the first Great Dragon War.

1

The five-headed Tiamat and all of the chromatic dragon types (the white, black, green, blue, and terrible red dragons) joined her against Michenth and the metallics (the powerful gold, silver, bronze, copper, and brass dragon species). The Creator then sent his spirit to mend the rift between the warring factions of dragons and men. Legend has said the spirit was dragon, some say man, some say elf, others say dwarf. It was not known anymore, but his message and presence was told to be awe inspiring. Tiamat and the chromatics could not touch him, so she had her dark-hearted human followers take him and break him on the stone square or pyramid: the symbol of the Creator's divinity and the perfection of the universe. This sacrilege, this act of pure evil, led to the final battle of the war.

There were also divisions among the elves and the giants when the battle lines were drawn; surprisingly, however, the race of dwarves did not desert Michenth. The elves split, and over a third of them joined Tiamat, which led to their banishment. Michenth and the elven king Denaris and queen Eladra cursed them, turning them dark as midnight. Now called the drow, they were to be forever envious of the light from which they had turned their backs.

Led by Michenth and his powerful gold dragon Valianth, the metallic dragons and their riders routed the chromatics. Michenth then banished them to the eastern lands of the world, which eventually became the Morgathian Empire. Michenth could have ordered the eradication of Tiamat and her chromatics when they were at their weakest, but he allowed them time to repent the evil they had caused. Instead, she and her dragons seized control of the Morgathian Empire and its people, and they set up a puppet group of magic-using sorcerers to legitimate her position as their god. She gave them lands and dark crystal weapons with incredible magical powers to fortify their control.

The middle kingdoms surrounding the Ontaror Sea slowly began to recover after the devastation caused by the spillover from the protracted war. The metallic dragons settled back into their thirteen Weir fortresses and the provinces that fell under their protection in the western part of the world. All these states were loosely held together by the dragons for mutual protection and trade. Michenth and Valianth coordinated them from the capital city of Draconia, the city of light at the end of Sauric Bay, center of commerce and prosperity in the west.

Eighteen hundred years passed with only minor chromatic incursions and small brush wars, which were stomped out quickly. Then, as a long-awaited answer to the dragons' prayers, a group of astute and incredibly wise men and women arose with the idea of a united land based on freedom and honor. With the guidance and cooperation of the metallic dragons, elves, and dwarves, this Founding Council created the Articles of the Alliance. Upon ratification, this profound document put forth the basis of the new government, and the Dragon Alliance Republic was born. This officially united the thirteen provinces as states of the republic, to form one powerful nation, with Draconia as its capital.

The Alliance now stretched from Rom and Rem, the twin Weirs that guarded the oceanic entrance to Sauric Bay in the west, to the Gray Mountains three thousand miles east, which were guarded by High Mountain Weir in the northeast, Draden Weir in the middle, and what was to become Eladran Weir in the southeast. Ice Bay Weir, which looked across the great northern sea, to the humble Weir at the tip of the Adelif Peninsula almost two thousand miles south, marked the northern and southern extremes of the Republic. From Ferranor and Denar Weirs, which each border the ends of the dwarven Ferranor Mountains in the northwest, to the prosperous port Weirs of Atlean and Lancastra in the southwest, all now formed the borders of the Alliance.

Lastly was Talinor Weir, which was situated in the middle of the republic along the mighty Severic River. It cut the Alliance in half and stretched from Draden to Draconia, emptying into Sauric Bay. This major waterway enabled the earliest of inhabitants to easily traverse the breadth of the nation. The Alliance was found to be the most bountiful and fertile land, rich in precious minerals and metals and many other natural resources. Now all thirteen Weirs bore the Dragon Alliance Republic standard from their massive peaks.

The Alliance flag flew proudly with its gleaming white background, an embossment of Michenth's head in a mithril silver and gold color in the center, to both represent and honor him and all the metallic dragons. A green oak leaf symbolizing the elves appeared in the upper right corner, and a brown and black hammer was in the lower left-hand corner for the dwarves;

both were arranged in a diagonal line. In the upper left-hand corner was a deep blue square field with a circle of twelve white triangles and one slightly larger white triangle in the middle, representing the thirteen Weirs and provinces of the Alliance that protected and bound the republic together, forever linking dragon and mankind.

Two separate kingdoms resided within the great nation: the elves of the grand Allghen Forest that lies over two hundred miles southwest of Ice Bay Weir, ruled by King Denaris and Queen Eladra, and the Dwarven Kingdom in and under the Ferranor Mountains, commanded by King Drekar of the dwarf capital city of Minara. Both kingdoms lived in harmony with the people of the republic. These two great races maintained their sovereignty but pledged mutual support to the Alliance. The small number of thunder and mountain giants that still existed mostly inhabited the mountains above the dwarven cities or the number of floating cloud fortresses that sailed the winds over Alliance lands and seaways. They were loosely allied to the republic, mostly out of respect for the metallic dragons.

In the last two hundred years, the combined might of the metallic dragons, elves, dwarves, and people of the Alliance had rid their lands of evil creatures and made the Alliance a free, safe, and prosperous nation. Its borders were well protected by the Alliance Army's legions and Weirs, which allowed prosperity to bloom.

Jealous and fearful of such a united nation of men, dragons, elves, and dwarves, Tiamat and her Talon Council of dark crystal-empowered sorcerers and overlords, as well as her court of the five most powerful representatives of the chromatic dragon races, known as the Usurper Five, began plans to challenge the Alliance. They forced treaties with the drow and the orcs in preparation for war. The task of increased breeding of chromatic dragons and the raising of huge orc armies, along with conscripting their own divisions and provincial armies, took the Morgathians almost two hundred years. They had also needed time to mine and harvest as much dark crystal as possible for Tiamat to enhance and give to their sorcerers; these crystals, infused with chromatic blood, were used to create weapons of power for their death knights to counter the dragonstone weapons of the Alliance.

A massive attack was launched on the spring equinox, with the Morgathian land armada crushing everything in its path on its trek across the unsettled lands, marching toward the eastern border of Alliance territory. On their rampage, the Morgathian armies and the chromatic dragons conducted large-scale attacks against the northern portion of the middle kingdoms and the Kaskar tribes to keep them off balance and prevent them from aiding the republic. Draden Weir now stood to receive the full brunt of the onslaught, due to its strategic location at the break in the Gray Mountains that formed the eastern border of the Alliance.

Instead of waiting for the Morgathians to strike Draden—or Keystone Weir, as it was now nicknamed—the military command of the Alliance decided on a different plan. Michenth and his rider, General Becknor; Valianth and his rider, Colonel Therosvet; and Jmes, the rider of the young but most powerful gold dragon in the Alliance, Gallanth of Draden Weir, all agreed to go on the offensive in order to dictate the terms of the fight. This was an attack to seize the initiative, a basic tenet of Alliance military operations.

Both armies met in the unsettled lands on a rough plain by a small river, at an infamous place to become known as Battle Point. The Alliance Army came quickly at the Morgathians from the north, threatening to outflank them and forcing them to shift rapidly from their direction of advance. Using the river as a natural obstacle to tie their defensive line, the Alliance legions, the dwarf army, and the elven archers and warriors set the stage for a ferocious fight. Forcing the Morgathians to attack due to the longer range of their archers, waves of orcs, brutish hairy grummish, and Morgathian soldiers fell to the arrows, spears, swords, and axes of the Alliance. However, the republic and its forces were still outnumbered five to one. The battle in the skies above took on an equal ferocity.

In a fury of breath weapons, and the deadly energies of magic spells streaking across the sky, with hundreds of dragons diving and swerving, locked in mortal combat, Michenth finally felled Tiamat. One final blast of the brilliant, golden energy beam of his breath weapon crippled the five-headed demon. His rider, General Becknor, hefted his powerful mithril sword and unleashed a fiery bolt of energy at her, striking the faltering evil dragon and sending

5

her into an uncontrolled spin. Her limp but colossal body, with all five of her chromatic dragon heads flailing, slammed into the ground with an earthquake-like tremor. Whether or not she was dead was yet to be seen, but a wing of red and blue dragons surrounded her seemingly lifeless body, lifted her up, and carried her away, heading due east, back to Morgathia. Six of the largest red and blue dragons were needed to accomplish this, with the others acting as shields to protect her (very uncharacteristic of chromatic dragons).

Although injured, the mighty arch dragon Michenth whirled around to regroup and join the main battle. The skies were still filled with hundreds of dragons and thousands of other flying mounts and creatures, from both the Alliance and Morgathia, diving and swirling, locked in aerial combat. A massive land battle took place below, with armies of tens of thousands of men, elves, dwarves, and their allies, fighting for their lives against a massive force of orcs and other assorted evil creatures, along with their dark-hearted Morgathian masters. The battle raged on, but the tide was turning. The metallic dragons, initially outnumbered six to one by their chromatic counterparts, were now evening the odds. After their evil queen fell, some of the younger green and black dragons began to break, but the Morgathians still had one more trick.

A red dragon, with one of the most powerful Morgathian Talon Council sorcerers mounted on it, charged into Michenth as the sorcerer fired a disruption ray. The deadly beam was stopped by the last strength of the mithril dragon's spell shield. A return blast of Michenth's powerful photon fire breath weapon wiped out the red dragon's and the sorcerer's magic shields, which he then followed up with sunbeam burst beams from his eyes. The beams struck the red dragon square in the upper chest and made him reel back in midair. A follow-on bolt from Becknor's glowing mithril sword struck the sorcerer, almost killing him. The red dragon let loose a blast of fire that hit Michenth, who winced from the impact, but it was minimally effective against the mithril dragon's armored silvery-white hide.

The Talon sorcerer, in a desperate last attempt, fired a barrage of lightning bolts, which hit Michenth with a glancing strike and left smoldering wounds on his shoulder. Michenth then lunged forward, grappled the smaller red dragon with his large claws, and sunk his massive fangs into the dragon's crimson neck, ending its life. Before the severely wounded sorcerer could prepare another spell, Becknor thrust his sword into his chest. At that moment, a demonic rohrlog flew from behind the arch dragon and began to dive on him, raising its huge flaming sword. Becknor pulled his sword from the sorcerer's chest, swung around, and fired a bolt into the half-breed demon's midsection, sending it cascading off its course from the force of the strike.

A blue dragon then came out of teleport with a death knight and another Talon sorcerer mounted upon it. Gallanth immediately sensed the danger, disengaged from the spiraling green dragon he had just flamed, and headed toward the blue chromatic. Blue dragons have a limited power of teleportation, so the sorcerer must have helped phase the trio into battle, which was not an easy task.

Before Gallanth and Jmes could intercept them, the death knight lifted his dark crystal vampire blade and hurled it toward Michenth. Immediately afterward, the sorcerer produced a deadly Orb of Annihilation, a hideous but extremely powerful weapon about the size of a melon. The solid black globe was powered by a large dark crystal and reinforced by numerous death and disruption spells. The orb darted behind the vampire sword, and they both headed directly toward Michenth. Gallanth fired a plasma fireball from his gaping jaws, and a sunburst beam from his eyes that shattered the blue's magic shield.

Jmes lifted Kershan, his single-edged mithril sword, with its glowing ruby dragonstone, and hurled it toward the blue. The intelligent sword streamed toward the sorcerer, who pushed the death knight into its path. The sword pierced his reinforced black iron armor and sunk to the pommel guard, and its curved silvery blade emerged from his back and impaled the sorcerer's shoulder. The death knight grasped the pommel, screaming in pain; blood spurted out of his chest and back, but he could not remove the powerful sword from his armor.

Unfortunately, the vampire blade found its mark and pierced Michenth's armored hide behind his shoulder; few blades could penetrate the mithril dragon's skin. As the arch dragon winced, the black orb exploded just short of the point of penetration of the vampire sword, owing to the Morgathian sorcerer's injury, which had broken his concentration on the deadly device.

7

At the same time, Becknor slew the rohrlog with a final smite from his mithril sword, upon which it exploded in its death throe. Becknor's sword shielded him and Michenth from that blast, but he was not ready for the sphere's destructive implosion. Michenth's magic shield was worn down as a result of his intense battle with Tiamat, which made him vulnerable to this type of attack. The incredible blast knocked him and Becknor unconscious, sending them hurtling toward the ground. If Jmes had not wounded the Morgathian sorcerer, the powerful sphere would have found its deadly mark.

Gallanth whirled around to head toward Michenth, after finishing off the blue dragon and the injured Talon sorcerer with another blast of his sunburst beam, striking them both and sending them on a death spiral. He roared to get the attention of any gold or silver dragons in the immediate area to come to his aid. His brother, Falcanth, another gold dragon, Eagrenth, and the silver dragon, Talonth, answered the call.

Just as he was ready to go into teleport to help Michenth, a black nightmare horse appeared out of nowhere, with a drow sorcerer and a hideous flayer mounted on it. The drow fired a sonic blast from his death staff, which hit Jmes's flying saddle rig. The spell struck its intended target, for Jmes did not have his sword's magic shield, and Gallanth's shield was depleted from the intense combat. The flayer then let loose a thought spell that hit Jmes. The gold dragonrider was suddenly racked with an intense pain, as though his head were going to burst, and he immediately fell from Gallanth's neck, holding his head while screaming in agony.

Gallanth was already in the process of teleporting; the light rays formed a brilliant blue tunnel around him, and he could not stop the procedure once initiated. His large golden frame vanished. He quickly emerged without his rider above Michenth, whom he grabbed immediately, followed up by Eagrenth on Michenth's other flank, Falcanth to his front, and Talonth on his tail. Jmes continued to fall, screaming.

Grab your ring, Jmes, grab your ring! Gallanth shouted telepathically; he also roared out loud to his rider and mind partner. He could feel the pain Jmes was going through but was helpless to stop it. Jmes's dragonstone ring would have controlled his fall, but he could not concentrate on it to enable its power to work. His mithril helmet would also have stopped the flayer's attack, but he had given it to an Enlightened Party senator as a gift of good will to ensure their support of the war effort.

Gallanth and the other three dragons managed to control their dragon lord's descent and set him gently on the ground. Immediately, a female gold dragon and a support corps healer group landed beside them and began to administer aid; they attempted to stem the bluish blood flowing from Michenth's gaping wound. Gallanth was about to jump into the air and teleport to Jmes, when he felt the telepathic connection with his rider sever as Jmes hit the ground and was killed instantly. The other dragons raised their heads as Gallanth's roar shook the ground, for they could feel his intense pain from losing his rider.

Gallanth then launched from the ground and disappeared. "Gallanth, no, you can't attack on your own!" Falcanth roared to his brother, but it was already too late and Gallanth was too enraged to listen. He emerged in front of the midnight black demon steed, which quickly spurred, and started to fly away as fast as its fiery hooves could take it. Gallanth gave immediate chase. Nightmares fear almost nothing, but this demon horse showed fright now. The black beast and its riders attempted to teleport out but were thwarted by Gallanth's vengeful roar, which had the power to dispel and disrupt magic. As he gained on the dodging nightmare, the flayer fired a mind blast at the closing gold dragon. Gallanth felt the invisible impact but shook it off, as adult dragons are immune to these types of attacks. The creature then started to panic and turned to its drow companion to get them out of the area, but the drow screamed back that he could not. The nightmare kept swerving and dodging, but Gallanth was faster and quickly caught up to the black steed. With one swipe of his huge claws, he severed the nightmare's hindquarter along with the flayer's left leg. The evil steed then plummeted toward the ground and crashed in a field.

The drow and the flayer rolled away from their steed. The hideous flayer's leg was bleeding and the drow suffered several broken ribs, but they still managed to get up and attempted to escape. Gallanth back winged and landed on the black steed with a thunderous impact like a hurricane. This knocked the two evil beings back to the ground and crushed their wounded steed.

Gallanth then walked slowly toward them, shaking the ground with each step. He shouted in Draconic with a thunderous tone, "Feel fear, for your death approaches, and your kin will feel my wrath!" The drow raised his staff and cast a lightning bolt. It found its mark, striking the dragon in the chest, but Gallanth took the damage and did not even wince through his rage. He first looked at them directly and forcefully read the drow's mind to discern the underground location of the dark elf city and the adjacent flayer villages. This painful thought extraction caused the dark elf to scream in shear agony.

Gallanth then raised his mighty head and opened his jaws, exposing his razor sharp, eighteen-inch-long teeth and a pair of three-foot-long fangs; fire gathered in his throat and then spewed out, engulfing the evil beings in the searing hot, red-orange plume. Their faces contorted in fear, giving away to the screams of pain as they were incinerated. Their painful deaths did not lessen the gold dragon's rage, but he had avenged his rider. However, he was not finished.

Mkel woke from his dragon-induced dream sweating, with his heart pounding. He reached out and his sword, Kershan, flew across the room to his outstretched hand, the red ruby dragonstone in its pommel glowing brightly. *It is all right, my friend. I was dreaming of your father and the war. You and Michen are all right. No harm will ever come to you or him, I promise that,* Gallanth said to him telepathically in a sincere tone. Mkel had felt this dream before, but it was becoming more common, and more intense. Dragons seldom dream, but Gallanth was doing so more often as of late. He knew the story of the last Great Dragon War, and his father's induced suicide death, and Gallanth attacking the underground drow capital city alone in his rage. He had burnt half the city, killing hundreds of drow as well as two flayer villages. He was only driven off by repeated magical attacks by their most powerful sorcerers and female clerics that had stayed behind while others had been fighting on the plains of the unsettled lands.

Gallanth had then teleported to Aserghul, the Morgathian capital city, and let loose several devastating plasma blasts on the five towers of Tiamat's fortress, wreathing it in flame. He retreated after being hit by multiple lightning bolts, disruption rays, and ballista spears. And that was only at the urgent request of the remaining gold dragons, especially his brother, or he would have been killed himself. The gold dragon then teleported back to the dying battlefield, leaving the Morgathian palace in flames. The single attack of an enraged gold dragon actually distracted the Morgathian leadership and caused a break in the dark army's line, proving the pivotal point in the battle. The orcs, drow, Morgathian armies, and all of their allies were beaten back, both out of revenge for Michenth and by the courage of Gallanth's attack, which boosted the morale of the Alliance armies. However, to this day it is not known how he penetrated the almost invincible magic shield provided by the largest pieces of dark crystal embedded in the five Morgathian towers. It was also not known how he survived the powerful disruption rays from those crystals. Not even Michenth could penetrate the shield with his photon breath weapon. Gallanth himself did not know how he got through it that day.

Mkel also knew of the guilt that Gallanth felt over his father's death, even now almost thirty years later. Dragons, especially gold and silver dragons, display a deep affection for the human race and an intensely close bond with their riders. The loss of a rider can actually drive a metallic dragon that normally is among the most intelligent and wisest of all creatures, temporarily insane.

"I know, my friend. Please do not blame yourself for what happened. It could not have been helped. The Morgathians and the drow are to blame, not you," Mkel said to his dragon partner. His wife, Annan, barely stirred during the episode. *She could sleep through Gallanth's roar*, Mkel thought to himself. So much for the elf half part of her, with all the enhanced senses of her kin, for she was a very deep sleeper. Drake, their elf hound, lowered his head and went back to its watchful sleep at the entrance to the sleeping chamber of Michen, Annan and Mkel's son. Drake weighed in at over two hundred fifty pounds and had incredibly keen senses. He could even see invisible creatures, and he could change the color of his coat, like a chameleon, to match his background. His large head and powerful jaws could rip a grown man's arm off with relative ease.

Mkel was seven years old when his father died. He still remembered his mother and Gallanth waking him up the morning after the battle to tell him. His mother was crying but was still very strong, like always. Even though dragons don't cry, he thought he could see tears in the gold dragon's huge, yellowish eyes. He remembered the promise that Gallanth made to him that day to always look over him and be there for him. Gallanth was a gold dragon, and the biggest one at that. He measured forty-five yards in length, from nose to tail, and had a seventy-five-yard wingspan. He was colossal by a grown man's standard and looked even more immense to a seven-year-old boy.

Mkel also remembered the trip that he and Gallanth took years later to Draconia to see Michenth (on one of the rare occasions that the arch dragon was awake). Even today, thirty years later, the arch dragon was still healing from the wounds he received that day from the vampire blade and dark crystal sphere. Michenth was even larger than Gallanth, being fifty yards long with a wingspan of over eighty-three yards. Mkel remembered entering the great hall in the Capital Weir and walking beside Gallanth and Jodem, the Draden master wizard. Speaking in Draconic, Gallanth introduced Mkel to Michenth as his future rider and soul partner (Mkel did not understand the language at that time but later realized what Gallanth had said to the arch dragon). Michenth raised his huge head from the ground and spoke to Mkel in a soft yet commanding voice:

"You have a large, caring heart and a good soul, young one," the arch dragon said. "You will make a fine dragonrider and leader one day. Remember to always fight the good fight, be honorable and true to yourself, and take care of all in your charge. For with this great power comes greater responsibility, and the lives of many will rest in your hands. Have faith and honor above all else." The mithril dragon finished talking, nodded to Gallanth, and then lowered his head and fell back asleep.

Michenth would sleep for weeks or months at a time, rising only for special occasions, to attend conferences, and to eat. It would take decades for his wounds to heal, for the most powerful evil weapons known to the Morgathians had hit him when he was the most vulnerable. By all rights, he should have been killed.

Mkel walked over to Michen's sleeping chamber and watched his son sleeping soundly in his crib through the lighting crystal's shielded glow. The elf hound did not lift its large head, but Mkel knew he was aware of his presence. The seven-foot-long elvish canine would defend his son to the death, if need be. He then proceeded out of his room into the adjoining landing that served as Gallanth's ledge. He had put his room shoes on, for the gold, silver, and platinum coins and gems that littered the floor were hard to walk on with bare feet.

Mkel knelt beside Gallanth's immense head and leaned against his cheek. "I will always be there for you, my friend," Gallanth told him. Lying beside his dragon was always comforting to Mkel. Gallanth had been his protector, tutor, soul mate, and friend since his father's death. His wisdom was unsurpassed, and the depths of a dragon's emotions were almost beyond human comprehension. "I know, Gallanth. I have always been able to count on you," he replied. Mkel started to fall back asleep lying next to the mighty dragon, as if the rest of the world did not exist.

When morning came, the Weir watch guard blew the warning horn that signaled the arrival of the rangers, returning from patrol on their griffons. Lupek, the ranger platoon commander, had attended this patrol himself; his instincts had made him (and Deless, his elf comrade) wary of some type of problem. They had been patrolling the southern chain of the Gray Mountains for over two weeks, for they had felt that the fire giants were up to something before the onset of the fall season. Mkel got up from Gallanth's side and walked back to his chamber. Annan and Michen were still asleep, so he went into his bathing room and began to prepare for the day.

Using his seeing crystal, Mkel called Lupek to be ready to give the brief from the senior rangers and their men. The rest of the day would consist of training the Weir garrison in preparation for next week's combined exercise with the Draden regiment. He, Gallanth, and Jodem would be taking a trip to Battle Point afterward. The Senior Sergeant of the Weir, Toderan would be in charge of the fortress during his absence. The Battle Point legion's commander had sent a message through his wizard that there was a lot of activity to his northeast and south, and he wanted to have a meeting with him and Jodem.

After Mkel bathed, and while he was shaving, he started thinking about the legion at Battle Point and the frontier city it protected. "A rough life out there," he said to himself. That legion was in the middle of the unsettled lands at the place of the immense battle some decades earlier. The loosely held empire of the Kaskars was to the north, the middle kingdoms (or Northern Ontaror kingdoms) were to the south, and small independent kingdoms were to the east. The Morgathians were much farther east, but within a long striking distance of the fortified city. All the while, they were a three- to four-week ride from any reinforcement from the Alliance, other than from Draden Weir and those that could be sent through the teleportation circles at Draden. The Capital Wing from Draconia was now capable of teleporting an entire legion if needed, along with the incredible power of the wing itself. All could be of quick assistance, but it would be difficult to plan and execute rapidly. Battle Point endured constant skirmishes from Morgathians and its allies and a host of other independent forces.

Mkel finished with his personal hygiene and put on his uniform tunic, riding pants, and boots. He checked his uniform, which the halfling tailors always cleaned and prepared with impeccable workmanship. His captain rank symbol of three silver diamonds was aligned correctly on his right collar, as was his dragonrider symbol (a gold dragon with outstretched wings over a crossed sword and arrow). Dragonriders always wore the symbol of the dragon they were bonded to on their collar. All were treated as Alliance officers, but Mkel also wore the infantry officer insignia in conjunction with his dragon symbol, for he was one of the few dragonriders who also served as a commissioned Alliance officer. Most dragonriders were either wizards or fighters, with no prior military leadership background.

He left Kershan, his sword; hanging in his bedroom chamber with Markthrea, his special crossbow, on the wall in Gallanth's landing. He walked down the winding stone stairs to the ground floor and then to the dining hall. He met Lupek and Deless half way across the grounds beside the Weir's lake, hugging Lupek after a rough salute and a courtesy nod to Deless. "You fared well, my friend," Mkel said.

"Much better than the orc scouts that were making their way across the plains heading to the Weir," Lupek replied. "We killed six of them mounted on dire wolves and hellhounds and let one get away so we could track him. We followed him for over a hundred miles to the outskirts of Lucian Forest, which he skirted to avoid Haldrin's elven patrols. We kept with him until he entered the northernmost fire giant border, where we slew his mount and captured him after he spotted us. After Deless interrogated him in his special way, we extracted some surprising information."

"Hold on, my friend, why don't you get something to eat and see your family, and we'll continue this after lunch," Mkel interrupted, for he knew Lupek's dedication to the mission, and he would have given him the whole briefing right there, but he wanted him to rest up and see his family first. Lupek was the leader of the thirty-six-member griffon-mounted ranger platoon and third in command of the Weir's garrison, after Mkel and Toderan. He was a master ranger of great skill and also carried the rank of senior lieutenant. He oversaw the deployment of the rangers, who performed reconnaissance missions and raids into the unsettled frontier. They also flew over the Gray Mountains as well to ensure no surprises crept into that area. The ranger platoon was based in the Weir along with the rest of the garrison.

Lupek, being a trained ranger, would first put his weapons away. He was an expert with almost all martial varieties, and he could use two weapons simultaneously with great skill. His special elven-made mithril alloy scimitar, given to him by Eldir, the elf clan's best swordsmith, was hanging from his belt. This weapon was capable of dealing incredible wounds from its mithril edge, delivering enough damage to cleave an orc with ease. He also was clutching his powerful dragonstone-powered lightning javelin, which could fell an ogre from over one hundred yards.

Mkel had seen Lupek in action and was always impressed with his ability to fight with two weapons simultaneously, as well as being excellent with the throwing daggers and hand axes he carried on his armor and hips. The ranger leader usually carried at least six daggers and two axes for close-in fighting. He was renowned and feared for his hand-to-hand combat expertise. Lupek's dragon hide-reinforced studded leather armor, as well as a mirrored mithril-lined buckler, did not look overly dirty in spite of being in the field for the last several weeks. This told Mkel that he had not engaged in much fighting, so he was not hiding anything from him. Mkel knew that his friend was very agile and was a whirlwind in a melee, with many an enemy never laying a weapon or hand on him before the ranger finished them. This time Mkel knew that Lupek's excellent tracking ability was his primary mission, as he was as good as or better than any elf (save Deless).

Lupek's rangers all rode the fierce Alliance griffons. These majestic creatures were bred and cared for by the elves in the adjacent Draden Forest with the aid of their riders. They had the foreparts of a giant golden or bald eagle and the hindquarters of a lion, with a plume of feathers at the tip of their tail for flight agility. The average griffon was extremely tough, having twice the constitution of an ogre, and was more maneuverable than an average chromatic dragon, while also being just as fast for short sprints. They were fairly intelligent, being able to understand simple commands, and they could communicate through gestures and croons. Their curved beaks could practically fell an ogre in a single snap, and their claws would tear an orc to shreds. They were also physically powerful, with the strength equal to or greater than that of ogres. Their torsos were as large as or larger than the biggest horses, and they had a thirty- to thirty-five-foot wingspan; their deep eagle-like cry instilled fear in their enemies. Their keen senses also aided the rangers in their reconnaissance missions, making them excellent hunters and fighting mounts; they also defended their riders to the death, being fiercely loyal.

The rangers performed a vital service to the Weir, giving advanced warnings of larger enemy incursions or invasions, providing a presence by constantly patrolling, and keeping enemies off balance with a small but rapid and effective show of force. Many a time, the rangers would sweep down with their griffons, coupled with the power of Lupek and his second-in-command, Deless, a skilled elf fighter/sorcerer, and leave only the bodies of their enemies and other evil creatures in their wake. They were renowned for this quick strike ability; the cry of their griffons and a hail of arrows and spells was a woe to orc war bands. The rangers were all skilled at aerial combat and experts in aerial archery. In intense aerial confrontations, one pair from the ranger griffon squadron usually protected Gallanth's flanks to allow him and Mkel to concentrate on the most powerful enemies and perform strafing runs against opposing armies.

Lupek personally led the strike and recon teams in most missions and major campaigns, for they were the Weir's eyes and ears, especially with the aid of Deless and his magical abilities. This combination made the ranger platoon a powerful force in its own right. Lupek was also a highly trained battle healer, with a mastery of herbal medicines.

Lupek and Mkel attended the Alliance's Military Leader's Guild together, receiving their commissions as Alliance Army officers. They served in the Weir's infantry company together as platoon leaders before Mkel dedicated most of his time with Gallanth and command of the garrison and Weir. Lupek then specialized in ranger training with the elves. They remained best friends and relied on each other, both militarily and for mutual support, considering themselves as brothers.

Lupek himself had a strong constitution, being a tireless runner and hiker while also possessing a great deal of wisdom. He was as tall as Mkel with a very similar build, but he had been very hardened by his life as a ranger; however, he still had a kind heart. His green-gray eyes and short brown hair (it was customary for rangers to shave their heads), along with several scars, gave him a rugged look, but still maintaining a hint of gentleness.

Lupek and Deless gave a quick nod to Mkel and headed to their griffons' stables, to ensure their mounts were settled in, as well as storing away the mithril point extensions on each of their talons. These additions allowed their mounts to inflict a great deal of damage in attacks. They then headed to their quarters and the families' housing area. The rest of the ranger section that had accompanied them had already stowed their gear and put their griffons in their stables to rest and feed.

They all parted but would meet back at the large dining hall in the rear of the Weir interior, followed by a couple of ales at the Weir's tavern. Mkel wanted to get a quick breakfast, for he knew Annan would be waking about this time, and he wanted to see Michen before he became too busy.

He walked into the dining hall and went over to the serving tables to pick up a breakfast cake, fruit mixture, cereal, and milk. Philjen smiled at him in her usual alluring, if not mischievous, way. He had known the tavern keep for years; her smile was always friendly. Philjen was a unique product of a dwarf and a human. She stood about five feet tall and had a very solid build, but she still had a human female's shape. Her large bright blue eyes and short light brown hair added to her appeal. He smiled back and walked over to where Toderan was already sitting.

Mkel sat down beside his tall friend; the paladin was the senior enlisted soldier in the Weir. "Good morning, Senior Weir Sergeant, my friend. You know the rangers are back, and it looks

17

like there is a little trouble brewing from the southeast," Mkel said.

"You talked to Lupek already sir?" Toderan asked.

"Just for a few minutes this morning before I made him go to his family and get cleaned up," Mkel returned. "We will get the full report after lunch. I wanted him to rest before then."

"No problem, I will be looking forward to it sir," Toderan said. "The preparations for the exercise will be finished this afternoon, and the leaders' meeting is on schedule for tonight. Jodem and I already informed Dekeen, Ordin, and Pekram. Is Lawrent supposed to be here for this or not sir?"

"He was supposed to, but I received a short message from him that there was a little trouble in getting to Sauric Bay. He ran into a saragwin raiding party, which he had to take care of," replied Mkel. "I expect him in a few weeks."

"He'll make it up, I'm sure," Toderan replied. Toderan, being a paladin, did not like Lawrent's chaotic ways and the Freilanders in general because of their practices and culture. The senior paladin was a very structured individual, while Lawrent was a sea raider and barbarian, but he had a good heart and good intentions as well as being a dependable and fierce ally. Lawrent commanded his personal dragon or serpent long ship with his hand-picked crew of master mariners and forty or so fierce berserkers. He usually had three to four more that joined him in his raids of the Archipelago Islands, Shidan, Ariana, and parts of the Morgathian Empire. They joined the Weir garrison in battle on occasion, which Mkel used as a reserve counterattack force or a backup raiding group for the ranger platoon. They served on the infantry line but preferred to fight as individuals rather than as a team. Orcs and the Morgathians feared them, for they had a greater ferocity than almost any other warriors known.

Toderan rose from the table. "I have to see to a couple of personnel issues, sir," he said.

"Do you need any help?" replied Mkel.

"No, Captain, just a couple of issues in one of the cavalry squads with two infantrymen."

"No problem; let me know. I will see you at lunch before Lupek's brief in the central meeting room," Mkel finished.

Toderan stood up and walked toward the garrison barracks. Mkel quickly finished his breakfast and took a full tray of food and beverages back up to his chambers. Annan was already awake and taking care of Michen. He set the tray down and they started to eat. Annan asked him what the agenda was for the day. He told her of the brief after lunch and the leaders meeting before dinner, as well as the training exercise scheduled for tomorrow and the trip to Battle Point the next day.

She was upset at that news, and an argument began. Mkel half-heartedly argued back while he played with Michen, knowing she was just worried. He was Mkel's most prized treasure; he loved his son as much as his dragon. Michen's bright blond hair and wide blue eyes only added to his little boy's charm. He picked Michen up and walked out of his chamber to Gallanth after he and Annan came to an agreement.

Michen loved to crawl on Gallanth's tail and claws. "Draagin," he said over and over again as Mkel carried him over to Gallanth.

"Hello, little one," Gallanth replied in a soft tone, for even the average exhalation of the mighty dragon could knock the toddler off his feet. He very carefully moved his huge tail over toward his rider and son; Mkel put Michen on the flat arrow-shaped plate at the end of his tail. Gallanth could amazingly balance the small child on his tail without dropping him, and Michen loved the ride.

Mkel scratched his dragon's ear ridge, which was the most sensitive point on his immense armored head. His watermelon-sized eye closed in pleasure. "Why don't we fly down to the stables and get you something to eat, for tomorrow will be very busy."

"Sounds like an excellent idea," the dragon said as he moved his thick front leg over to Mkel, who climbed on top of it and was lifted to the base of the dragon's neck. The huge tail gently swung the two-year-old over to Mkel after he hooked two of the four flying straps to his belt. He took his son in his arms and nodded to the gold dragon that he was ready. Gallanth stood up and walked over to the edge of his landing, which measured one hundred yards deep and one hundred twenty yards wide. He outstretched his colossal wings and with one gentle leap was airborne. He gracefully sailed down over the Weir lake and landed very gently, with a small whirl of dust, by the stables so as not to unsettle his rider's precious cargo.

Mkel unhooked the riding straps with his free hand. Michen had thoroughly enjoyed the short ride. Gallanth put his massive head and neck on the ground and slightly raised his left front leg for Mkel to slide onto, then lowered it slowly to the ground. Gallanth's arm thickness still put Mkel six feet above the ground, so he sat down on the dragon's arm and slid to the ground, holding Michen firmly. As he carried Michen over to the stable master and his halfling assistants, Gallanth stood up and turned toward the corral. The stable master made a motion to his crew, who went scrambling into the meat storage cold room. He looked up at Gallanth and yelled, "We have three seasoned steer halves for you, Master Dragon."

"I have faith in your culinary skills sir," Gallanth responded.

It always amazed Mkel how much respect Gallanth could command in spite of his gentle reputation, although it was hard not to respect a forty-five-yard-long gold dragon. Gallanth only used a loud commanding voice in battle, when speaking to the Weir garrison and regiment, or when he spoke at a public gathering. Otherwise, his deep voice was gentle to the ear; however, his roar could shake the Weir mountain to its very foundation. This tremendous sound could instill horror in enemy formations while eliminating any fear in the soldiers of the regiment. Other dragons had fearsome roars, but Gallanth's had a deeper, more commanding quality.

When he was fighting chromatic dragons, they would often roar curses or insults at each other in Draconic, the language of dragons, which only dragonriders, scholarly wizards, and clerics could understand (it was very difficult to master, being literally a living language. The reader has to know the intent or emotion of the words). Chromatics, especially red dragons, were relatively easy to goad, being very vain and usually overconfident. Gallanth sent many a red spiraling to their death after foolishly engaging him in battle. Gallanth's spell casting ability was much greater than a red's, which is mostly fire based, as well as his two breath weapons and unique sunburst beams. Gallanth was also stronger, faster, and definitively more intelligent than any chromatic. Added to this was the power of Mkel's crossbow, Markthrea, with its mithril-tipped and exploding bolts, coupled with incredible range, blinding speed, and accuracy; red dragons did not have much of a chance.

As Gallanth and the stable master conversed, Mkel was thinking of the trip to Battle Point coming up and the potential to face the chromatic dragons. Their ancestral enemy depended on sheer numbers when engaging the Alliance metallic dragons for any hope of victory. While almost never allowing themselves to be ridden, they did occasionally permit a powerful Morgathian warlord, death knight, or Talon sorcerer to mount them. This was only done for mutual benefit, and even then they were not blood bonded. This did not make them as effective as the metallics and their riders, for even though both were powerful, they would fight individually and not as a well-coordinated team. Mkel knew that the bonding with a human rider made a metallic dragon's powers greatly enhanced; enabling it to cast more powerful spells and recharge their breath weapons at a much faster rate. This was their major advantage, along with the inherent teamwork that went with a rider and dragon.

The halflings and human butchers wheeled out three slightly cooked steer halves, all sprinkled with a special seasoning. "Thank you for your efforts," Gallanth said and lowered his head while opening his immense jaws, exposing his huge teeth and biting down on one of the steer halves. It was crushed in his powerful jaws and swallowed quickly. Mkel knew the power of Gallanth's bite, for he had witnessed those same razor-sharp, gargantuan fangs rend fire and ice giants to pieces and tear into the hides of chromatic dragons with little trouble.

"I greatly appreciate the fine job you do, Jern," Mkel told the stable master.

"Anything for you and Gallanth," he replied. "He has saved us all time and time again."

It was always nice to hear the appreciation for his dragon, for there was a growing antimilitary movement in the major cities in the Alliance, with a distinct hatred for the dragons. These groups were mostly civilians and not citizens, and their central focus was to blame the dragons for everything from self-imposed poverty to misunderstanding the Morgathians. They even wanted the Alliance to sue for peace with the evil empire.

"Yeah, right," Mkel thought to himself. Ask for peace from a red dragon, orc, or Talon sorcerer. These people were so sheltered by the very security of the organization and protectors they loathed so much that they were ignorant of the hostile world outside the safety and prosperity of the Alliance borders. He had no stomach for them and considered them on the same plane as the insect-like orcs.

Gallanth finished all three steer halves while Mkel was deep in thought. "As always, they were excellent, master butcher," Gallanth complimented Jern. "Mkel, I will go back to my landing for a few more hours of rest before the meeting and our flight afterward," Gallanth continued. "No problem, my friend, I will see you in a couple of hours," Mkel replied.

The gold dragon turned, outstretched his wings, and leapt into the air. Mkel and Michen watched Gallanth fly back up to the ledge of his landing. Mkel went over to the dining hall area to find Annan and drop Michen off so he could go to the council room and his study. Annan had just brought the food tray back with the help of Janta, her halfling nanny. He handed Michen to her and gave her and his son a kiss, and then he walked into the corridor that led to the barracks area and the leaders' council room.

He walked into the empty hall and sat down at the large oaken table to finalize the planning for the training exercise that was to begin tomorrow. It would be a standard regimental attack, putting the Weir garrison in the center and front of the combined Draden regiment, with his company of dwarves in the center of the garrison. The exercise would take place on the large field across the Severic River and from the Weir. The soldiers had been setting up the target frames for the last few days. The Weir garrison would form a battle line with the infantry and dwarves while placing the elven archer platoons directly behind the stout little fighters, to provide intensive arrow fire coverage.

Many times, the only infantry platoon the elf clan could muster acted as a reserve to plug any holes in the line or stem off a penetration, as well as being an exploitation force. The land dragons, toughest and most feared creatures other than the true dragons, would be right behind the infantry to provide the ballista fires at their extended range of a thousand yards or so, followed up by the wingless dragons' fiery breath weapon when they closed on the enemy.

The catapult section, with their thirty-pound stones, would always initiate fire at their range of three thousand yards, followed by their sixty-pound fragmenting stones at two thousand yards, and finalizing with their bursting dragon's fire projectiles at twelve hundred yards, used to attack enemy infantry formations. The Weir's heavy cavalry platoon acted as a mobile attack and ground reconnaissance force; it was also tasked to assail the enemy's flanks. Their charges were always impressive, with their heavily armored knights and paladins in precise formation. The collective resistance of their weapons and mithril alloy armor made them almost immune to a magical attack during their charge, as the collective magical shields of their holy dragonstone-powered swords combined in a synergistic effect. The ranger platoon performed diving attacks, releasing well-placed arrows, bolts, and dragon's fire grenades, not to mention the rending their griffons' claws could do. Gallanth and Mkel would practice their strafing runs before the infantry engaged in a hard fight.

Normally Gallanth and Mkel would eliminate a great deal of enemy ground forces before the garrison or regiment would even get into the battle. Dragon and rider went out of their way to minimize casualties among the regimental ground forces. This was often to the chagrin of the dwarf company, for they lived for combat and were not happy until they saw the grayish black orc blood on their axes.

However, during the exercises, Gallanth and Mkel planned on worst-case scenarios, where they could not provide a great deal of cover from the air, owing to their being engaged with chromatics. Gallanth could decimate enemy ranks with his breath weapons and sunburst beams, which had the ability to wipe out an entire company at a pass. His fireball spells and various other powerful spells could decimate another company sized element at a shot, once per day. His breath weapons and sunburst beams could be fired multiple times, much to the chagrin of their enemies. Gallanth and Mkel would also take care of any giants on the battlefield, but they always initially focused on combating the chromatic dragons, for they could inflict massive damage on the regiment if left unchecked.

Mkel reviewed his plan for the training exercise for the next day. The training event would begin with the garrison on line and the catapults initiating fires at targets twenty-five hundred yards away. The garrison would then move forward in unison to within eight hundred yards, or ballista range, which would trigger their fires. They would initially pick large targets like giants and then concentrate on the infantry columns. When the battle line moved to within three hundred yards, the elven and human archers and crossbowmen would unleash their volleys. This would continue as the line kept advancing. The garrison's Weir company archers and crossbowmen were very accurate and practiced a great deal; however, the elven archers were devastating, capable of wiping out companies at a volley.

As the battle line closed to within throwing range of the target line, the dwarves would initiate with their throwing axes and hammers, and the garrison infantry's first two lines would ready their spears and shields for either an enemy charge or their own slow advance into the enemy ranks. At this point, Mkel would signal to one of the infantry platoon leaders and Senior Company Sergeant Pekram to simulate a breach in the line. The archers would initially move in to stop the break and then fall back. That would give the elf infantry platoon a signal to move in to reinforce the breach. Elves armed with long swords and double-headed pole arms were swift and deadly. The rangers would be performing strafing runs, and the cavalry would be told through the seeing crystals which flank to attack. He and Gallanth would then do one practice strike, which always instilled courage and confidence in the line units.

Mkel also planned for Silvanth to do a diving attack on the Weir garrison and the regiment so they could practice defending against a chromatic dragon attack, simulating that one got past Gallanth. Normally, Jodem, Dekeen, Ordin, or Toderan, the key and powerful members of his Weir council, would face off against a chromatic dragon that made it past him and Gallanth, for their strength could at least hope to match a lone chromatic. Master Wizard Jodem's spell power included major offensive and defensive capabilities, and Dekeen's bow, Ordin's hammer, and Toderan's holy sword, all dragonstone-powered weapons, always confronted the deadliest foes the garrison and regiment faced. Sergeant Pekram also was ever ready to stand against any foe.

Mkel would brief the officers and leaders on the timeline and the battle rhythm later that afternoon. He would need to get Lupek's brief right after lunch to pass the information along to the rest of the leadership, and the ranger leader would brief the regiment commander, Colonel Wierangan, at the planning meeting as well. After he finished up the plan and the conceptual sketch of the battle layout, he decided to go for a run and exercise.

He went to his wardrobe closet in his planning room and started to change out of his Alliance Army uniform and into more comfortable exercise clothes. He normally ran around the Weir lake once or twice, covering two to three miles. He did not like to run but knew it helped him stay on balance when riding Gallanth and it also let him keep up with the infantrymen of his garrison company. They would go on runs three times a week for at least that distance and marches that were three to four times that once a month. The rangers did even more, but he felt that it was up to them.

The ground around the lake was soft and cushioned his steps, and the view of the crystal clear water, as always, was relaxing. After he finished his run, he did a series of push-ups and sit-ups to strengthen his upper body and stomach, again to keep him in shape for flying and for fighting. When he finished with his exercises, he took a quick bath and put his uniform back on. He had at least two hours before lunch, so he retrieved his magic crossbow, Markthrea, and went to the range located at the far side of the Weir landing.

The shooting range held over thirty firing points; archers could shoot to a distance of one hundred yards if they desired, but they could extend that to six hundred yards if all else was cleared from that portion of the Weir grounds inside the hollowed-out mountain. A range was also set up outside the Weir that could be pushed to one thousand yards for Mkel and the elves. He set up at fifty yards first, firing from the prone position. His crossbow had a special sight that was powered by one of Gallanth's dragonstones. The sight had the power of gold dragon vision, which was up to thirty-six times as acute as normal human eyesight; it also allowed him to see clearly at night and estimate ranges as well. The dragonstone was embedded on top of the mithril steel sight, which was fastened to the crossbow just behind string catch. It had a thin crosshair as the aiming point; when shooting at a moving target, a red circle appeared that enabled Mkel to move the crosshair and hit an aerial or fast-moving enemy. The sight also automatically adjusted for distance in regards to the shallow ballistic path of the bolt, which traveled at an unbelievable speed.

The dragonstone also helped him cock and load the bow faster. A lever located behind the trigger cocked the powerful dragon sinew string when it was pushed forward. When the lever was pulled back, a bolt was loaded from the detachable magazine located at the bottom of the stock. The crossbow itself was made of elven dark oak, making it lightweight but very strong. The limbs were made of red dragon bone, with the string made of the same dragon's sinew, taken from a chromatic Gallanth killed in the last war. The dragonstone mounted on the sight pushes the bolt out at lightning-like speeds.

Mkel used three types of bolts. The basic masterwork bolts were made by Dekeen's best fletcher (arrow maker), with the extremely sharp tips made from the strongest steel the dwarves could produce. These bolts were one half inch in diameter and approximately six inches long. They could slice through plate armor at a thousand yards and even cut through demon and black iron armor. These deadly missiles did enough damage to kill two men and were a woe to ogres and aerial foes. Mkel usually carried at least one hundred sixty of these in his flying rig and thirty or more when he dismounted. He also had a select number of mithril alloy-tipped bolts that can penetrate anything, including magic shields, shield spells, and even dragon hide. These bolts did three times the damage as his regular ones and had an even greater range of more than two thousand yards.

He also had bolts tipped with a special formula of wizard-created dragon's fire pitch and Gallanth's saliva. These were made by Jodem and exploded on impact in a fifteen-yard burst, capable of killing all in the impact area; they could also utterly destroy an ogre/troll-sized creature if struck directly. They could inflict a good deal of structural damage to a wall or castle battlement as well. A select number of bolts combined a mithril alloy tip with the bursting bolt for powerful opponents. These first penetrated then exploded, capable of taking out a giant or similar sized creature. Mkel carried sixty of each of these types on Gallanth's flying rig.

Mkel put his first quarrel on the post, put his right arm through the attached sling, and secured it with the hook that was anchored to his dragon hide armor, which doubled as his riding jacket. His dragon hide jacket was made from red, blue, white, and green dragon scales, and the hides taken from dragons that Gallanth slew during the last Great Dragon War. The hide and scales were meshed together with mithril thread, making the jacket as strong as actual dragon hide, and giving Mkel some protection against fire, electricity, acid and frost weapons. The hide-and-mithril-thread combination made the jacket almost impenetrable by all but the most powerful magic weapons, yet it weighed no more than thin leather armor. It had a soft padded interior, making it very comfortable to wear, and fit both his heating and cooling crystals at the top of the back of the jacket just below the neck area.

Mkel lay down on his shooting mat and planted his elbows firmly. His right hand, with his riding glove on, slid up to the sling hook, where it met the steel swivel handstop on the bottom of the stock. He put the elven-oak butt stock of the crossbow firmly into his shoulder and rested his cheek on the raised comb. He leaned into the bow and felt his hand take the pressure. He took a couple of breaths, slowing each one down, until his final exhalation, when he looked through the sight and placed the crosshair on the center of the target (the circle reticule did not appear since the target was stationary). He grasped the contoured firing hand grip firmly with his left hand and rested his finger on the trigger, just in front of the first joint. As his pulse settled to a minor blip, he squeezed the trigger smoothly, taking up the one pound of pressure needed to release the catch, and the string snapped forward, sending the bolt screaming to the target. The bolt struck the target face, cutting the center one-half-inch scoring ring on the right side.

He then pushed the cocking handle forward and pulled it back to its original position, locking the string back, and put another bolt in the ready position. He was loading his bolts one at a time since he was practicing and did not need to rapid fire, and chose to shoot from the sling versus resting the nine-inch magazine on the ground in combat mode instead of target style. Again he squeezed the sensitive trigger, and the second bolt landed directly beside the first. He put his next three bolts in a small cluster, all cutting the small center ring. His next five also put a group in the second target's center ring. He reloaded and proceeded to put five bolts on each target's center rings (his bow could be loaded with ten bolts at a time). His last bolt just slightly missed the center ring, and he teasingly cursed himself for slightly jerking the trigger.

Mkel then got up and fired twenty bolts from the standing position and a final twenty bolts from a sling-supported kneeling position. He walked over to the target line and pulled out all sixty bolts, returned to the firing line, and then reloaded his magazines. He then picked up his crossbow and mat and moved to the one-hundred-yard line. After shooting a twenty-bolt target from the prone position with a sling, he shot with the metal magazine planted on the ground, taking care to firmly put his right hand on the upper front of the magazine, putting slight rearward pressure and firing in a smooth cadence. His next position was to move the crossbow to the supported mount that simulated the firing platform on Gallanth's flying rig. He fired twenty more shots from that position, and after he felt reasonably satisfied, he retrieved the bolts and reloaded. When he finished, he walked back up to Gallanth's ledge and put his crossbow on the wall outside his living quarters.

"Wake up, my friend. We will be taking the brief from Lupek and Deless in a short time," Mkel said to his sleeping dragon. "I am awake, my rider. We can go down to the Weir grounds together, and good shooting by the way," he replied as he stretched his massive front and back legs, jingling the gold and silver coins that made up his bedding. The powerful muscles on his fore and hind legs even showed through his armored hide.

"We will also need to take a flight over the training field before the leaders meeting tonight, just to make sure all the preparations are ready," Gallanth added. "Have you talked to Silvanth yet about her role in the exercise?" Mkel inquired. "Yes, she will be happy to comply, but she is getting close to mating," replied Gallanth. "Then she will be more aggressive for the exercise, and I will feel better about the trips to Battle Point, Draconia, and Freiland that are coming up," Mkel concurred. "Yes, it will be a busy couple of weeks, plus I feel the information we will be getting from Lupek will verify the nagging feeling I've been having about a growing threat to the east in the mountains and beyond. I cannot pinpoint it, but I know something is brewing there," Gallanth added. "We will see, my friend, but we better get down to the planning room, for we don't want to be late for our own meeting," Mkel said.

With that, Mkel grabbed his riding jacket, took his heavy equipment belt and sword, and slung his crossbow over his back. He jumped up on Gallanth's arm, who then raised him up to his neck; he threw the equipment onto the flying rig and harness situated between two of Gallanth's back ridge plates. Gallanth rose up on all fours and lumbered over to the edge of his landing, where he sprang into the air. He gently sailed to the far edge of the Weir's lake and landed with a swirl of dust as he back winged. Mkel slid off of Gallanth's neck onto his arm and was lowered back to the ground, still carrying all of his equipment. He and Gallanth then walked over to the Weir garrison's headquarters. The meeting room held over fifty people, and it had a large opening so Gallanth could lay his head down and face into the big room to participate in the discussions.

Mkel stowed his gear in his planning room, with the exception of his sword, and took his notes to his seat on the huge U shaped table. He placed the notes and sketches he made for the exercise tomorrow on the large oaken table in front of his chair. Gallanth lay down in his normal position so his immense head rested on the ground in front of the thirty-foot opening to the meeting chamber and filled in the top of the U shaped table that faced him from inside the room. *I believe Ordin is approaching from the lower corridor,* Gallanth said to Mkel telepathically.

Gallanth's foresight (his ability to see into the near future) always amazed Mkel. On many an occasion, this ability saved their lives, as well as the lives of thousands that he and his dragon protected. This ability was the bane of their enemies in battle; it always kept any foes from succeeding in a surprise attack. Only gold dragons had this ability. Silver dragons had limited foresight ability, as did brass dragons (to an even lesser degree). This still gave them an advantage over their chromatic counterparts, however.

Sure enough, within seconds Mkel heard the heavy footsteps of a dwarf approaching from the corridor at the far end of the council room that leads from the lower levels of the Weir and the home of the dwarf clan that reside there. Ordin was their leader and one of their toughest fighters. He was the dwarf entrusted by Gallanth to receive Donnac, the dragonstone-powered war hammer made of solid mithril. Its ruby dragonstone mounted on the top gives the war hammer the power of thunder and lightning. Ordin could throw the weapon up to one hundred yards; it would strike one large opponent (or up to ten man-sized targets) and then return to his hand like a boomerang. Upon hitting a single target, it delivered enough concussion and shocking power to kill a full-grown troll. It can also create a spell shield like Mkel's and Toderan's swords were capable of. Upon a successful strike of a giant, it had a 50/50 chance of killing it outright. He also wielded a master-crafted mithril/steel alloy battle-axe in his off hand for balance. Ordin was wearing his mithril-lined dwarven plate armor, likely for the benefit of the regimental commander, as dwarves live for a good fight. In battle, it made him a difficult target to penetrate, but it looked cumbersome, even though it was actually quite light. It also didn't affect his acute dexterity, surprising for his broad but squat frame.

While Ordin was the leader of the dwarf clan that inhabited the lower levels of Keystone Weir, he and his brother Dorin also oversaw the mining operations in the bowels of the mountain fortress. Dorin focused on the mining issues while Ordin worked on making the special dragonstone and mithril weapons, and they led their dwarf infantry company together. Ordin was a key member of the Weir council, as the dwarf clan representative, and also oversaw all dragonstone weapon production and updated the Weir on mining issues.

The burly dwarf stood just shy of five feet tall, but like most dwarves, he was extremely stocky and physically strong. Weighing in at roughly two hundred fifty pounds, he was stronger than most men (save Toderan and Pekram). His well-kept beard and hair were an earthy brown color, and his eyes were a lively light brown-green. He was very jovial and bombastic, but like all dwarves, he could be moody at times and apt to brawl after drinking heavily. Ordin had a good heart though and was usually kind, which sprang from the dwarves' very strong sense of commitment to their friends and allies. He and his clansmen loved to drink ale and eat good food, often frequenting the Weir's tavern as well as their own smaller tavern in their living areas in the deep caves and caverns below the Weir.

Dwarves were extraordinarily tough with high constitutions, which enabled them to stay underground so long. The dwarf clan mined the lower caves of Draden Weir, which was rich in gold, gems, and especially the rare mithril. They kept a small percentage of the wealth, and the rest went to the Weir for its upkeep and pay, with a portion shipped to the capital for the common treasury. The dwarves revered Gallanth and had a great respect for the gold dragon; they owed him their allegiance for his protection, benevolence, and wisdom. While they tolerated elves, they enjoyed the company of humans and halflings more. Most dwarves stood approximately four and a half to five and a half feet tall and weighed between one hundred eighty to two hundred fifty pounds or more. All males wore beards, and even some women sprouted them. Dwarves were adamant in their pursuit of good and to further the cause of the Alliance, but they tended to be loud and bombastic.

Ordin smiled as he walked over to Mkel and said in his low and gruff voice, "Greetings, my young dragonrider friend." He gave Mkel a hug, picking him up in the process. "Ordin is as wide as he is tall," Mkel thought to himself.

"And good to see you too, Master Ordin," Mkel replied enthusiastically, putting his hands on Ordin's shoulders.

"Greetings to you, Master Dragon," Ordin said reverently as he turned to face Gallanth, giving him a slight bow.

"And greetings to you, Master Dwarf. I see you are full of life today as usual," Gallanth replied.

"Aye, Master Dragon; I heard through the rocks that Lupek and the rangers found that the giants are on the move. And in other good news, we struck a solid vein of mithril in the northwest lower cavern. Dorin is working on it now," Ordin stated. The expression of "hearing it through the rocks" was a dwarf phrase that was akin to hearing it through certified rumor. Dwarves had a unique sense about them; their mannerisms, phrases, and customs reflected their underground living tendencies, mining, and soldierly lifestyles.

"How big is the mithril vein, Ordin?" Mkel asked.

"We uncovered the top end of it this morning. Dorin and his miners have been trying to cut away the outer rock, but so far it is at least a foot and a half across. We don't know how deep it goes, but when we get it out, it will be a bounty. Now tell me more of what the rangers found," Ordin replied with a twinge of enthusiasm in his crusty voice. "I have not felled a giant or heard the sweet sound of their large evil bones cracking under my hammer in months."

"All I know is what Lupek blurted out to me after he arrived back this morning, and before I made him get cleaned up and spend a couple of hours with his family. They tracked a scout unit of orcs mounted on hellhounds and dire wolves. After killing most of them, they followed the survivor back across the Gray Mountains to the northernmost fire giant lands. The orc was careful to avoid Lucian Forest but did not escape the elven scouts' watchful eyes as they passed out of our lands. Lupek, Deless, and one of their squads swooped down on the mounted orc before it was able to get to the fire giant encampment. That is all I know at present," Mkel finished.

"Greetings all," stated Jodem from the far entrance of the meeting hall. The Weir's wizard entered the large room, giving his customary greetings. Jodem wore his classic blue and white robe and carried his wizard's staff, which had a sapphire dragonstone mounted on top. He was Mkel's tutor, mentor, and surrogate uncle. He taught Mkel many lessons about leadership, politics, and magic, but especially precision marksmanship. Jodem sported medium-length, unkempt salt-and-pepper hair, and unlike most human wizards, he was clean shaven. He was slightly overweight, for he loved magic, marksmanship, politics, and philosophy, but he especially enjoyed good food, ale, and wine, being able to drink a dwarf under the table.

Jodem was one of the most powerful wizards in the Alliance and served not only on the Draden Weir council, but on the Alliance Wizard Council of Thirteen, which included the top magic users in the republic. He had a mastery of most wizard spells and could route a legion almost by himself if he wanted, with the magic abilities of his dragonstone staff. The power of his spells and magic shield had defended the garrison and the Draden regiment from repeated magical attacks during many battles.

Jodem and Gallanth watched over Mkel until he blood bonded and linked souls with the gold dragon. His laboratory was deep within Keystone Weir behind Gallanth's ledge on the opposite side of Mkel's living quarters. He and Gallanth, Ordin, Dorin, and the elves' best weaponsmiths made arms out of the precious mithril.

One of Jodem's keys to success was that he was very accurate with his wizard's staff, which also doubled as a long, heavy crossbow. It also had the power to deliver a shocking jolt upon a physical strike or a close threat. Jodem aimed his crossbow-like staff to fire most of his offensive spells at ranges over five hundred yards. This gave him the advantage of a much greater range over other wizards in casting spells (and significantly more accuracy). His lighting bolt spells could reach up to five hundred yards, as an example, versus the one-hundred-yard distance of the average wizard or sorcerer. Upon his command, the crossbow limbs sprang up from the side of the thick staff and the dragon sinew string stretched out. As a crossbow, it could deliver a bolt with enough power to fell an ogre in a single shot or fire a regular masterwork bolt that could take down any orc or grummish. He, Mkel, and Dekeen had regular competitions both in the Weir and in open competitions on the plain between the town of Draden and Draden Forest. His staff/crossbow cannot see at night and was not as fast to fire as Mkel's, but it was still powered by a sapphire dragonstone given to him by Gallanth. This dragonstone focused his magical and spell casting abilities and also allowed him to hit an opponent in a close melee, doing enough damage to kill an orc with its intense power. His mithril woven lined robe gave him the same armor protection as full plate, along with heavy magic resistance capable of absorbing several offensive spells.

Jodem had a giant bald eagle named Vatara, which he utilized as his mount. It had a twenty-five-foot wingspan and stood over seven feet tall, with claws that could slice an orc apart and fell an ogre on a diving attack. Its beak could bite for enough damage to almost cut an orc in half, and it was as fast as a dragon for a short sprint and very maneuverable. Several pairs of eagles share a commonality with the elves and both protect the Weir and are protected by it, nesting on the upper ledges of the mountain.

"Yes, greetings, Gallanth, Ordin, Mkel," Jodem said. "Ordin, I hear we got lucky down in the southwest tunnel?"

"Yes," the burly dwarf replied. "It should be a major find and produce many good weapons and tools."

"I hear we might need it soon," Jodem said.

"Keeping a secret in this place is impossible," Mkel thought to himself, but Jodem had a way of finding information out, and keeping secrets from a wizard was very difficult.

"Jodem, are all the preparations for the Battle Point visit in place?" Mkel asked to change the subject until the command group meeting actually started.

"Yes, I talked with the Battle Point wizard on his seeing crystal. He said that he, the legion commander, and the town mayor will be ready for us the day after tomorrow. They have several concerns regarding a great deal of activity on almost all their fronts, as well as trouble between the Kaskar horse clans and the Northern Ontaror kingdoms," Jodem replied.

"Sounds like there is an undertone of great proportions, and a Morgathian or drow plot to destabilize the region," Gallanth added.

"A good point, Gallanth, we shall see when we get out there to address their concerns, for we may have to bring them up to the Dragon Council, and the premier as well as the senate when they convene later this month," Jodem commented.

"Gentlemen, Gallanth, good afternoon," Toderan said as he, Lupek, Pekram, Watterseth, Tegent, and Colonel Wierangan all walked into the room. Mkel got up as Colonel Wierangan entered. Toderan and Lupek walked over to shake Mkel's hand and give Gallanth a respectful nod. As they made their greetings, Dekeen, the elven clan leader, entered the room and gave his salutations to everyone after bowing to Gallanth. The elf clan located in Draden Forest, which lies off of the southern and western slope of Keystone Weir Mountain, had always been protected by the Weir and aided in its defense.

Elves tend to be aloof if not arrogant in some regards, likely because of their long life spans and the way they considered everyone else (save dragons) less experienced. Mkel and Dekeen had attended lessons together in Draden, which elves take on occasion to keep abreast of human ventures. He was actually a young elf, being only three hundred years old, give or take a couple of years, to be in a position of authority.

He was given the leadership of the clan after the former leader was killed in the last Great Dragon War. Dekeen was especially talented with a long bow and had made an almost impossible shot, taking out a death knight before he could deliver a killing blow to an injured brass dragon. In making this shot he had exposed himself to orc return fire and took an arrow in the leg. Gallanth and Jodem awarded him Elm, a dragonstone-empowered bow, as a gift for this act of heroism.

Dekeen stood approximately five feet eight inches tall and weighed one hundred forty-five pounds. He had medium-length dark hair and bronze-silver eyes (rare for an elf), which accented his pointed ears. He has a quiet and pleasant disposition in spite of being a master archer. He utilizes his powerful long composite bow, named Elm, which has a centrally mounted dragonstone located above the hand grip, given to him by Gallanth. This gave the bow great power, enabling it to deliver an energy burst to arrows fired from it when Dekeen desired. Arrows so directed delivered enough damage to fell an ogre with a single shot and could circumvent all but the strongest of magic armor and even magic shields.

The bow was made of elven dark oak, laminated with red dragon bone and sporting the same dragon's sinew for a string. The most feared power of Elm was that once per day, it could empower a slaying arrow of Dekeen's choosing. This deadly arrow, upon a successful hit, could automatically kill the intended target, regardless of the creature's power. While proven on a white and green dragon, it had never been tried on a more powerful blue or red. This also drained the bow's power for a short period of time, however. Elm could also be fired to counter certain spells in midair as well as create a smaller antimagic shield, capable of taking almost the same damage as Mkel's or Toderan's sword. Mkel often witnessed his friend fire ten arrows in extremely rapid succession, stopping an orc charge. Mkel knew Dekeen was almost as accurate as he was with his crossbow, but the magic longbow didn't have quite the same range, being able to consistently hit stationary targets out to five hundred yards. Mkel, Dekeen, and Jodem often had shooting matches in which they pushed each other to strive for more excellence.

Mkel found it puzzling that Dekeen was carrying his powerful bow rather than slinging it across his body. The elf clan leader also had his short mithril alloy scimitar with him, which he utilized for close-in fighting. He was very fast and deadly with the scimitar, being able to cleave a man or orc with a well-placed blow.

Dekeen's wife, Beckann, was herself a powerful wizard, almost as advanced as Jodem. The lady elf was five and a half feet tall with shimmering golden hair and deep violet-blue eyes. Her beauty was only matched by Jennar, the elusive nymph who lived in Draden Forest. Together, they oversaw the elf clan in Draden Forest. The clan consisted of approximately three hundred elves, and they could muster a force of one hundred twenty to complement the Weir's garrison.

Mkel counted on the elven company for the next day's exercise: three platoons of elven archers and one platoon of infantry armed with the deadly double-headed pole arms and long swords. They worked closely with the Weir in providing both local security and trade as partners for goods and services while receiving defense from the Weir. The elves produced fine products of wood, cloth, metal, and magic work, as well as wine and certain fine foods and elvish medicines.

Eldir, the elven master weaponsmith, worked with Ordin, Jodem, and Gallanth on magic items and weapons made with mithril and Gallanth's or Silvanth's dragonstones. Mithril was a very difficult metal to work with and required dwarven strength, elven finesse, Gallanth's intense heat to make it malleable, and Silvanth's cold to cool it down and strengthen it. Jodem's magical abilities made these items among the most powerful known. The weapons they made were given as a reward to those soldiers of the Weir's garrison and the Draden regiment that distinguished themselves in battle. All of the mithril arrow and bolt tips for Mkel's and Dekeen's projectiles were made by them as well.

The elves cared for the giant eagles that inhabited the top of Keystone Weir, and they also trained and bred the griffons used by the rangers. They crafted all the support gear for them as well, including the special saddles and riding equipment. Their forest community was mostly based in the large trees in the middle of the Draden Forest, making it a difficult position to take. It was regularly patrolled by the elven archers and guarded by hidden but strategically placed outposts.

Elves had superior vision, four times more acute than men. They could also see fairly well at night, making it very difficult to surprise an elf, although dwarves could still see better in pitch darkness because of their underground habitat ancestry.

"Are the preparations ready for tomorrow, Senior Sergeant Toderan?" Mkel asked his large friend.

"Of course, Captain," he replied. Toderan was one of Mkel's closest comrades and shared second command authority of the Weir with Jodem; he was also second in command of the Weir's garrison when they did not have an executive officer. He also coordinated on many matters with the Draden regimental senior sergeant or highest ranking noncommissioned soldier, and with

Colonel Wierangan. Toderan was a master paladin of great power and skill, being awarded the highest degree of that order.

Toderan's holy avenger long sword hung from its scabbard on his waist belt. The powerful weapon was forged by the dwarves and elves out of a heavy mithril/steel alloy; it also had one of Gallanth's dragonstones imbedded in the hilt. The sword could smite evil upon every stroke, dealing enough damage to fell an ogre with a single blow. Once per day, it could muster the power to kill a giant or similar creature. The sword also emanated an anti-black magic shield and could ward off evil spells in a one-hundred-foot radius. Its shield could withstand a great deal of spell damage, at least equal to Mkel's sword Kershan, and also gave him immunity to death magic.

When Toderan wielded his magic sword in battle, he instilled courage and strength to individuals around him. The sword allowed him to heal people's wounds; it also enabled him to heal his winged horse. Because of the importance of this meeting, he had left his mithril alloy plate armor in his quarters, but he wore his best uniform. The strong armor he wore was mithril lined, as was his large shield, keeping almost anything from penetrating it. The mithril in the armor also gave him a certain amount of spell resistance.

Toderan's winged horse was named Alvanch. It was intelligent and could fight independently of Toderan if the need arose, as well as being telepathically linked to the senior paladin. This link was not nearly as strong as the link between a dragonrider and his dragon, though. A strong but graceful winged mount, the off-white Alvanch was extremely fast over short distances and highly maneuverable in aerial combat with incredible evasion ability. Its hide was also very tough. Alvanch's attacks were also enhanced; its hoof strikes could kill a grummish in a single blow. Its own inherent constitution gave it the ability to take twice the damage a normal heavy warhorse could take. Winged horses were also immune to certain types of spells.

Toderan often hunted with Mkel, using a repeating crossbow given to him by Dekeen. He was Mkel's confidant on many matters, for the gold dragonrider admired his strength and commonsense wisdom, with a nonyielding determination to fight the good fight. He was a true leader of men. Toderan constantly displayed a cool head, even under the direst of combat situations. His sense of fairness was uncompromising, and he dealt with personnel matters with an even hand. Only Gallanth was closer to Mkel.

Toderan stood tall at six foot three inches and weighed over two hundred thirty pounds. He had a balding head and a well-kept mustache that exuded his forcefulness of leadership. His great physical strength and constitution were equal to that of Ordin. Toderan also served in the Alliance Navy for a short time as a troop transport advisor, bringing his paladin experiences to bear. He has a wife in the support corps company and a young son and daughter.

They all sat at the U shaped table, with Mkel on the left and Colonel Wierangan on the right. Jodem and Toderan sat beside them. Senior Sergeant Pekram, Dekeen, Ordin, Lupek, the Weir cleric Watterseth, and Deless sat in the middle seats, all facing Gallanth's immense head, which was now resting on the ground. "Sir, are you ready to begin?" Mkel said to Colonel Wierangan, as a courtesy for being the highest-ranking officer at the meeting, even though he was the Weirleader and did not have to answer to him.

"At your and Gallanth's pleasure, Captain," Wierangan replied.

"Gentlemen," Mkel said, drawing his sword as all present raised their dragonstone-empowered weapons, "to the Alliance, Draden Weir, Gallanth, the regiment, honor, and each other." They all saluted Gallanth, who gave a small nod with his colossal head, and then laid their weapons on the table, pointing toward the center. The dragonstones in their weapons glowed intensely, indicating the incredible collective power of the swords, bows, javelins, hammers, and staff of the Weir's most powerful members.

This also represented the idea that all Alliance citizens and civilians were granted the right to possess and bear arms and were encouraged to do so. This was the central premise of the Articles of the Alliance, along with personal freedom and freedom of open talk. Misuse of these rights, however, carried a heavy penalty, for freedom without responsibility was a recipe for disaster.

"We will first start with the ranger leader's briefing and will then discuss the exercise tomorrow, followed by a few Weir matters. Lupek, Deless, at your leisure," Mkel directed to his ranger companions.

"Yes sir, Gallanth, Colonel Wierangan," Lupek said, giving the gold dragon, Mkel, and the regimental commander a courtesy acknowledgment. "Deless, if you would," Lupek added, motioning to his elven comrade. Deless placed his bow in the gap in the U shaped table, and a three-dimensional map projected from the centrally mounted dragonstone appeared, representing the terrain of the area between the Weir and the southern chain of the Gray Mountains.

"We first tracked the orc scouts here at the base of the third mountain, just out of sight of Lucian Forest," Lupek began. "They were making good time across the plain at dusk when we attacked. We killed six of the riders and their hellhound and dire wolf mounts and let the remaining one escape. We followed him for eighteen days back across the mountains. He made sure not to get anywhere near Lucian Forest, so we know that the elf clan under Haldrin is alive and well and protecting his borders. We crossed the mountains undetected by the rider while still watching out for any other unfriendly eyes."

Lupek continued, "We finally emerged on the east side of the Gray Mountains and had to track him from the ground so as not to be compromised by them or any other lookouts. Deless used a seeing eyes spell to great effect, enabling us to keep out of sight and still track them. We stopped him just short of the northernmost fire giant kingdom border, when he spotted us. We then killed his mount but managed to keep the orc rider alive long enough to get a little more information out of him. Apparently a large gathering of fire giants is taking place, with a merging of several tribes for some purpose. We scouted a little further and observed a great deal of activity in and around the westernmost fire giant crude mountain castle. We must have counted well over a hundred giants and several thousand orcs, with multiple red and other chromatic dragons. There were also at least three Morgathian death knights and a sorcerer. The orc could not give us any additional information other than that he was to scout the defenses of Keystone and Eladran Weirs and attempt to ascertain our troop strength, our capabilities, and the number and type of dragons that are stationed here," Lupek concluded.

"Yes! Fire giants on the move," Ordin interrupted. "I smell the call to battle." Dwarves have a deep-rooted hatred of evil giants and barely tolerate the good mountain and thunder giants that inhabit the remote areas of the Alliance. This derived from a long-standing conflict between the two groups.

"Over a hundred giants and multiple chromatics," Wierangan repeated with some concern, but you could see in the intensity of his focused steel blue eyes that surveyed the portrayed terrain that he was already working on course of action for a battle plan.

"At least that many, with likely much more," Deless added.

"Smells of Morgathian involvement of some sort, with Keystone and Eladran Weirs as their target," Gallanth stated. "The giants are a concern, but the presence of red dragons with death knights means a Morgathian directive of some sort to control that amount of power," he continued. Metallic dragons had a particular disdain for the evil giant races but little respect for them, for they were not nearly a match in battle. Mkel did have a concern about giants, for even the smaller common giants were very physically powerful creatures, as attested to by the injury he received on his right elbow from an ice giant's axe in a skirmish some years ago.

"Can you sense anything additional, other than what Gallanth feels, Jodem?" Mkel asked.

"No, but I do not like the gathering of that much power that close to our border, and where there is a death knight, there is a Talon sorcerer of some power," Jodem added.

"We must increase our patrols in that area," Wierangan said. "Can we tie them in closer with the Lucian elf clan and Eladran Weir's rangers and centaurs?" he asked Mkel, who nodded a response.

"Yes sir, we will need a couple more seeing crystals, though, for we have three new rangers," Lupek immediately replied.

"We've found several good specimens in the northern mines, which we will bring to Gallanth and Jodem tomorrow," Ordin chimed in.

"We will see to it, sir, and tie in with your patrols on the northern part of the Gray Mountain pass," Mkel said to Wierangan. "Lieutenant Lupek will meet with Haldrin next week when his other patrol comes back from the mountains. Gallanth, Jodem, and I will be going to Battle Point the day after next to talk to

General Daddonan about his concerns on the frontier, at his request. Until then we will have at least one patrol along our border of the Gray Mountains, as well as the flights of the rangers and the Weir eagles over the pass," Mkel finished.

"I will see to the eagles," stated Dekeen.

"Colonel Wierangan, I will speak to Talonth of Eladran Weir after the meeting and have him relay our concerns of the Morgathian and giant incursions along our shared borders to his rider Colonel Lordan and the entire Eladran wing," Gallanth's deep commanding voice added. Dragons can instantly telepathically communicate with each other, like two people can with seeing crystals.

Dekeen spoke up again and said, "I will have Beckann send a message to Haldrin's wife as well and let them know to expect Lupek and Deless. They will be told to closely watch their eastern boundary with the mountains."

Colonel Wierangan stood up. "Excellent, gentlemen. Gallanth, Captain Mkel, we shall bring this matter up to the Colonel's Council next week during the monthly gathering and senate session, as well as any concerns General Daddonan has at Battle Point when you and Master Wizard Jodem return. Captain Mkel, how are the preparations for the exercise going?"

"Excellent, sir," Mkel replied. "They finished setting up the targets this afternoon; the final coordination made by Pekram and your soldiers was a great asset in manpower. All our supporting leaders will be coming in before the evening meal to finalize the plan."

"Good; remember that this operation will focus on the Weir garrison initially being the main effort attack, with the regiment conducting a follow-on attack and exploitation. You all will have a lot of men, equipment, cavalry, and land dragons behind you. It is always good for the regiment to see Gallanth with his abilities and the incredible power that he can bring to bear. To see you in action, Master Dragon, is a definite morale booster for the regiment," Wierangan said, looking at the gold dragon. "Will Silvanth be joining us, Gallanth?"

"She is a little testy at present but will participate in the exercise," answered Gallanth.

"Good, the regiment needs practice in defending against an aerial dragon attack, especially in light of these recent developments. She will only frost our backend a little, I presume?" Wierangan quipped, as all present chuckled a bit.

"Yes, Colonel, I have faith it will not be more than that," Gallanth replied with as much of a smile as a dragon could muster.

"Excellent; gentlemen, Gallanth, the regiment will see you on the practice field tomorrow morning," Wierangan finished. "Bishop Watterseth, a closing prayer," he added.

Watterseth, the Weir's and the regiment's senior cleric, stood up, as did the rest of the leadership. "Let us pray. Creator, we thank you for this circle of friends and comrades, and for your divine leadership. For the dragons that watch over us and for our dwarven and elven brothers, we pray. We also pray for those who currently defend our freedom and way of life and for those in the field right now. We seek your spirit and guidance in all our decisions and endeavors. Faith and honor to all."

Watterseth was not only the senior holy man of the Weir but a powerful cleric and formidable opponent in battle, along with being a master healer. As the Weir's chief cleric and spiritual leader, he was inspirational to all those who served around him, and his talents to heal those wounded in battle were most appreciated. Watterseth was one of the most recognized clerics in the eastern part of the Alliance. He also worked with the support corps group, aiding them in their logistics operations for the Weir garrison, and joined the council members in various missions and campaigns. He was a tall man of six feet two inches and medium build, but he was as tough as he was pious. He had short gray hair and soulful green eyes, and he conveyed a commanding presence, instilling courage in all around him.

In battle, he never wavered, wielding his powerful holy mace. This mithril steel alloy weapon had a sapphire dragonstone, given to him by Silvanth, mounted on the end of the pillar-shaped shaft. Upon a normal strike against an evil opponent, it delivered a crushing blow capable of felling an average ogre and inflicting stunning damage to all evil creatures within ten yards of the hit. Upon command, it could fire a bolt of lightning that delivered enough damage to strike down a troll at a range of up to one hundred yards. Once per day, it could deliver a thunderclap to an opponent that inflicted severe damage, almost able to kill a common giant, and again stun all within ten yards of the strike. The magic shield it can create had the same power as Toderan's holy sword and was especially effective against dark crystal-powered evil magic. His suit of gleaming mithril alloy half plate armor was expertly crafted by the elves and could even reflect certain spells cast at him back to their originator, with the Alliance white triangle of the Creator church over the red Keystone symbol emblazoned on the chest plate.

At the end of the prayer, everyone saluted Colonel Wierangan, and he and Watterseth started to leave the meeting room. *Colonel Wierangan is indeed a remarkable man*, Mkel thought to himself. He was the commander of the reinforced regiment stationed just outside the city of Draden and oversaw the combined units when the Weir's garrison performed joint missions with them. They also defended the Weir and city on the rare occasion when the Weir's garrison was deployed, for Alliance soil had not had a threat since the Great War.

Wierangan held the rank of senior colonel and was an expert tactician and strategist. He graduated from the Alliance Army's senior command school in Draconia and could easily lead an army group if called upon. Draden's regiment consisted of three battalions of six infantry companies each, a cavalry squadron, one reinforced land dragon company, a catapult battalion, a sapper company, a hippogriff wing, and a support battalion. It was a mini strike legion in a basic sense, and with the addition of the Weir's mixed battalion, it was much more powerful than a standard Alliance legion.

Wierangan himself was trained as both a paladin and a ranger, and he attained high degrees of proficiency in both. He was a rare man who had the charisma, strength, and dedication of a paladin and the cunning and fortitude of a ranger. He served in one of the Capital legions as a ranger, in a hippogriff battalion as a platoon leader, and as a ranger company commander. He also served on the High Mountain legion's staff until he was assigned to Draden to command the regiment there and assist in the deployment of the combined forces of the town and the Weir. Mkel worked hand and hand with him as a gold dragonrider and Weirleader, commanding the combined Weir garrison.

Wierangan still enjoyed going out on the occasional patrol with Lupek's rangers, although this was discouraged because of his rank and importance; however, it was hard to say no to a colonel. When not on campaign or battle training, he worked with the town of Draden's mayor as a member of the city's council and was an avid nature scholar.

Colonel Wierangan, while appearing like a modest fellow, was actually quite the combatant himself. Even though he only stood five and a half feet tall, he possessed above average strength and always maintained good physical conditioning. His short blond hair and light blue eyes accented his piercing stare, which always denoted his intelligent and resourceful nature. In battle, Wierangan wielded a powerful holy avenger sword, identical to Toderan's blade. It was given to him by a silver dragon of the Capital Wing for his service and bravery in battle. His assessments and guidance in several fights resulted in many victories for the Draden regiment and Keystone Weir.

Bishop Watterseth escorted Colonel Wierangan to the stables, where Sprinter, his highly trained hippogriff, was waiting. Hippogriffs, being half horse and half eagle, were just slightly slower than a winged horse and not quite as strong as a griffon, combining features of both. The average hippogriff, however, was almost as sturdy as a griffon and slightly more maneuverable. They were somewhat intelligent, were very strong, and served as fierce mounts for their riders. Slightly larger than horses, with twenty-five- to thirty-foot wingspans, they had large sharp beaks and talons that were almost as deadly as a griffon's. While their senses were not as keen as a griffon's, they were slightly faster in the air and much faster on the ground. This came in handy if they were injured and could not fly, for they could easily outpace the average horse for short distances. Hippogriffs were also much easier to train than griffons or winged horses, which must accept their riders and will not yield to another.

"Company Senior Sergeant Pekram, are the platoons ready for the exercise tomorrow?" Mkel asked.

"Of course they are, sir. They'll be ready or I'll put a boot in their backside," Pekram replied with his usual arrogant but still friendly smile. Pekram was a large, imposing figure, as tall as Toderan and just about as strong. The senior sergeant was a devout infantryman, always fighting alongside the Weir's garrison. He had been a friend to Mkel for as long as he had served in the garrison, and he was a powerful fighter who second commanded the Weir's infantry company as the senior sergeant for the Weirleader. He refused to take a commission as an officer, preferring to remain a senior sergeant. Pekram was a very skillful high-level fighter of great prowess. He actually commanded the company when Mkel served within the infantry unit to allow him to gain experience in deploying, maneuvering, and training those men. This enabled Mkel to best employ his and especially Gallanth's power and weaponry to aid them, as well as to just get the infantryman's overall experience.

Pekram led the company in a very tough but down-to-earth manner. His thick mustache and shaven head added to his intimidation, while his piercing light brown eyes were always alive with intensity. His features were rough and weathered, but he had a quick sense of humor, enabling him to handle all personnel matters within the garrison very succinctly. You never had to guess where you stood with him.

In battle, Pekram wielded a massive mithril/steel alloy great sword capable of inflicting horrible damage; he could slice open an ogre with a single stroke. His mithril-lined breastplate armor gave him excellent protection and moderate spell resistance, making it extremely difficult to pierce, and it could even absorb or reflect several spells directed at him.

He was a frontline leader and always went where his men went, personally facing the toughest opponents in battle. Even though he was good and had a kind heart, he was rough by nature, distrusted wizards, and was only lukewarm to dragons, with only Gallanth getting his respect. Even though he and Toderan were friends, his sometimes less-than-professional methods caused some anxiety between them.

The platoon leaders with their senior sergeants then began to make their way into the council room. There was no rush since the evening meal was still two hours away and this coordination meeting only needed to finalize the last details. The Weir's garrison had three infantry platoons of forty men apiece, a land dragon platoon with four of the wingless dragon species, a heavy cavalry platoon, a catapult section, a sapper platoon, and a support corps section. This was all augmented with the ranger platoon, the dwarf infantry company led by Ordin, and the elf company led by Dekeen. All this was reinforced and supported by Gallanth and Mkel as well as Jodem, making it a very formidable force.

The infantry platoon leaders walked in first: Akiser, Paloud, and Howrek, all of whom were commissioned lieutenants. They all wore the standard Alliance tunic and field trousers with their gold- or silver-colored diamonds on their right collar and the gold crossed sword/arrow symbol of the infantry on their left.

Akiser, the 1st Platoon leader, was a hungry young infantry officer with an excellent demeanor and the utmost respect of his men. He stood about the same height as Mkel, roughly five feet eight inches tall and about one hundred sixty-five pounds. His short blond hair and deep blue eyes hid his fierceness in battle. His overall goal was to command either a hippogriff aerial unit or a ranger platoon. While Mkel recognized the young officer's potential and would like to keep him in the Keystone Weir garrison as long as possible, he would not stand in his way either. There would be a slight delay for his transfer until after this new situation could be assessed and the problem resolved.

Paloud, the 2nd Platoon leader, was a senior lieutenant of good wisdom, intelligence, and honor. In fact he possessed an almost impeccable character. He originally started his military career as a catapult crew member and then went to the academy in Draconia to get his commission. He was now the garrison's senior platoon leader and was well respected by his men. He would be the one Mkel selects to be the next infantry company commander once he got a little more experience and a suitable replacement could be found. Paloud stood just shy of six feet tall and was of medium build, with black hair and brown eyes and a deep, commanding voice.

Howrek, the 3rd Platoon leader, was also a senior lieutenant having catapult experience as well. He was the weakest of the three junior officers, which was why Mkel put him in the company's strongest platoon. His platoon's senior sergeant and well-seasoned men were the most experienced in the Weir and could basically lead themselves. Gallanth did not like Howrek, telling Mkel that he felt that the lieutenant had a troubled mind. However, the Weirleader was always willing to give someone a chance, plus with the watchful eye of Pekram, he felt no major problems should arise.

Platoon Senior Sergeant Lenor was the first of the specialty platoon leaders to arrive. He commanded the heavy cavalry platoon and, like Pekram, did not want to pursue a commission as an officer. He was a short but wiry fellow and a formidable, high-level paladin. His midlength stringy brown hair only added to the constant wild look he always had in his eyes. The heavy cavalry platoon consisted of thirty-six paladins of various experience and power under the overall direction of Toderan.

Sergeant Lenor wielded a holy avenger long sword of similar properties to Toderan's but not quite as powerful as this increases with experience. All dragonstones whether mounted in weapons, wizard staffs or healing stones mature with the bonded wielder, gaining power in time, maturity and usage. This mithril alloy weapon had one of Silvanth's dragonstones, a brilliant blue sapphire, mounted on the end of the hilt. He wore mithril-lined half plate armor in battle and had a mithril-lined large shield to give him substantial protection. His paladin's warhorse was armored and much more intelligent than a regular horse, being capable of fighting on its own if necessary, similar to Toderan's winged horse. While he was actually small for a paladin, being just slightly shorter than Mkel, he had an inordinate toughness about him and a natural mentoring type of leadership. Underestimating him had been the woe of many of his opponents. He also resolutely looked out for his men, always leading the cavalry charges personally.

Lenor had three section leaders in his platoon of mid to upper experienced paladins, with the remaining being junior, but hand-picked, knights. All were armed with various magic weapons, making the cavalry platoon a fierce counterattack force backing up the infantry. With all of the paladins of this troop having special mounts and magic weapons, they conferred a great deal magic resistance both individually and synergistically when charging as a unified force, being almost immune to spells until they broke up their formation.

Lieutenant Wheelor walked in behind Lenor. He was a lanky fellow, being just shy of six feet tall with short blond hair and sapphire blue eyes. His easygoing but can-do personality was typical of the Southern provinces of the Alliance. A senior lieutenant, Wheelor commanded the land dragon platoon stationed at the Weir. He and his crews practically lived with their land dragons, overseeing and controlling their movement and deployment in combat as well as their overall training and care. There were four land dragons in his platoon along with a combined crew of twenty. The land dragons were used as a spearhead or breaking force in an all-out land battle or to engage larger opponents of the infantry, such as giants. The wingless dragons used their short-range line of fire breath weapon very effectively. The crews manned armored carriages with ballistae mounted on their dragons' backs, giving them a decimating six-hundred-yard point-blank range and an eight-hundred-yard to a thousand-yard area effective range.

Wheelor was a tough fighter in his own right, always leading his platoon from the front on top of his land dragon, Breigor, a fierce but loyal creature. The land dragons were among the most feared creatures in battle (save the true dragons themselves). The biggest land dragons could even take on the smallest of the chromatics, the white dragons, and had an even chance of winning. Their crew members usually did not like to risk this, preferring to have the metallic dragons deal with their chromatic adversaries.

Mkel had a great deal of respect for Wheelor and his crews. They were very easygoing in general and truly believed in and loved their land dragon steeds. They saved many an infantryman's life and were feared among Morgathian forces. The hybrid creatures were more than a match for any giant or similarly sized creature, who came up very short in a toe-to-toe fight with them. *They will be needed if the giant threat comes to fruition,* Mkel thought to himself.

Senior Lieutenant Willaward then strode in from the other side of the meeting room, likely coming from the Weir's tavern. He was the Weir's catapult section leader. Willaward oversaw the three permanent catapult emplacements on the Weir's defensive wall and the four mobile catapults that moved with the Weir garrison. He specialized in the deployment and operation of these deadly long-range weapons, and his expertise gave the Weir's maneuver forces a distinct edge over any opponent's siege weapons. Each engine of the catapult section had nine to twelve men and six per each supply wagon, totaling seventy-two soldiers. Outwardly, Willaward was a gentleman with an aloof nature, but he had an in-depth knowledge of his machines and could estimate range with an incredible accuracy. He had medium length brown hair and green eyes, always greeting people with a friendly smile.

The last of the specialty platoon leaders finally walked in as the meeting was about to get started. Senior Lieutenant Clydown was the sapper platoon leader. He was a fighter of mid degree experience but a master sapper and engineer that oversaw this unique section of the Weir garrison. His platoon consisted of thirty men who were experts in defensive and offensive earthworks, construction, and siege operations. He also oversaw the Weir's defenses and traveled with the garrison to provide them temporary defensive measures and structures such as earth walls, traps, pits, and ramparts; his platoon built siege towers, operated rams, and developed other siege techniques. He consulted Mkel during planning to determine the best use of terrain to support a fight.

Clydown's men were armed with picks, war hammers, short swords, and weapons that doubled as tools for building and digging or the destruction of structures. Clydown himself was armed with a mithril alloy short sword, along with his special dragonstone staff. This rod, powered by a garnet dragonstone given to him by a copper dragon, enabled him to move large volumes of earth and detect desired minerals or metals with ease.

Clydown routinely said that his men's spades were more important than the infantry's swords, spears, and arrows in winning a fight. While the defensive works that the sappers oversaw were definitely a combat multiplier, he did like to exaggerate.

As they walked in, each platoon leader gave Gallanth a respectful salute (the metallic dragons were the only ones who are honored with a salute indoors) and then shook Mkel's hand. As they were all directed to take their seats, Mkel motioned to Toderan to come over to him. "Weir Senior Sergeant, do you know where Colonel Dunn is?" he asked.

"No Captain, but it is unlike him to be late," Toderan replied. "The senior platoon sergeants will be here momentarily as well."

"Yes, neither he nor Captain Vicasek is here," Mkel added. "Gentlemen, may I have your attention," Mkel said in a loud enough voice to be heard over the conversation. "We will give Colonel Dunn a couple of more minutes before we start. I assume you've all had an unofficial update by either Deless or one of the rangers?" A general "Yes sir" from everyone around the room confirmed his assumption. "Deless, why don't you set up your map image so we can start right away when the support group gets here," Mkel asked the elf.

"Yes, Dragonrider, it would be my pleasure," the elf answered. Deless was Lupek's second in command of the ranger platoon. He was the rare combination of a skilled ranger and a midlevel wizard; few elves and even fewer humans attained such status. This set of skills gave Lupek and his rangers a distinctive edge; Deless used offensive spells such as lightning bolts and fireballs, his defensive spells deflected arrows and missiles, and had other spells such as his surveillance ability with floating or spying eye spells. Lupek and Deless made a very powerful and effective team, which also aided in their other missions of aerial strikes and aerial combat, often deep into an enemy's rear area or homeland. They were very mobile and self-sufficient as savvy trackers, deadly fighters, and well-trained aerial riders on their fierce griffon mounts.

"Captain Mkel," Colonel Dunn called from the corridor, "sorry we're late; we had a couple of last-minute details that had to be addressed prior to your exercise tomorrow. I also kept your platoon senior sergeants to help me plan, so their tardiness is of my doing as well."

"No problem, sir," Mkel replied.

"Gallanth, gentlemen," Colonel Dunn added as he entered the council room with the infantry senior platoon sergeants, Macdolan, Vaughnir, and Gustoug, in tow.

Macdolan, a short but resolute fighter and trained healer, was the 1st Platoon's senior sergeant. While just an inch shorter than Mkel, he was as tough as a wolverine and a devoutly loyal soldier and leader. Vaughnir was also honorable to a fault, almost a frustrated paladin in a sense, but one would be hard-pressed to find another sergeant who cared for his men more. Gustoug was a savvy, wily fighter of good reputation in battle, but there was a small streak of self-centeredness in his character. All three were phenomenal fighters and leaders.

"Good day to you as well, Colonel, Sergeants," Gallanth replied. "Silvanth says that she will be acting as a chromatic dragon tomorrow for the exercise, so she will be delayed in providing teleport coverage for your supply trains," he added.

"Yes, Master Gallanth, we planned for that and it should not be a problem," the colonel replied. "Captain Mkel, please proceed without any further delay." The colonel and Captain Vicasek sat down at the table. Colonel Dunn was the support corps commander for both the Weir's support company and the support corps battalion for the Draden regiment. He stood at the same height as Toderan but was more thinly built with gray hair, sharp features, and an even sharper mind, especially in regards to supply and support missions.

While not known as a fierce fighter, he could take care of himself with his mithril alloy scimitar, which he wielded in an expert fashion. His renowned experience as a master logistician made the difference in several sustained campaigns. The support corps company was a mini version of his battalion; it included a healer platoon; a supply platoon for food, water, heating and cooling crystals, and clothing for the soldiers of the garrison and all their mounts; an armament and repair platoon with caches of spare weapons and arrows, as well as arms smiths and general repairmen; and a wagon platoon for transport. The battalion that supported the regiment was just a larger version of the Weir's support company.

Captain Vicasek was the actual commander of the Weir's support company. She was a lively, hard-drinking woman who was no pushover as a fighter herself. She stood as tall as Mkel and was solidly built but still shapely. She wielded a mithril alloy pole arm weapon with a dragonstone given to her by Silvanth; her long-bladed short spear could strike with incredible power. The weapon delivered a freezing blow in addition to its deadly curved blade head, which was a bane to her opponents. The support company was roughly one hundred twenty strong, almost equally divided into the four aforementioned sections.

"Yes sir," Mkel replied. "As most of you know the results of the rangers' recent scouting mission to the Gray Mountains, we will only briefly review the findings. The fire giants are massing on the western edge of their borders, apparently being reinforced by several battalions of orcs, ogres, and trolls. They are also being visited by several red and blue dragons, Morgathian death knights, and maybe more than one Talon sorcerer. If this does come to fruition, Keystone and Eladran Weirs, as well as Draden itself, are likely their primary targets, so we will have to be ready to move at a moment's notice. The rangers will give us forewarning of any attack, but the giants and mounted orcs could move fast, especially if they are supported by chromatic dragons and other aerial Morgathian forces. We will also be tying our patrols in with Eladran Weir's rangers and centaurs, as well as Haldrin's elves, so we will have a good lead time of any sizable force trying to enter Alliance territory."

"Sir, why don't we assemble all of the Weir on you and Gallanth and take the fight to these vermin in their own lands?" Lieutenant Akiser suggested.

"Lieutenant, you know that under former Premier Bilenton, we were directed not to conduct attacks outside of our borders unless attacked first. General Becknor and Colonel Therosvet fought this with the autonomy we enjoy as the Weirs, but we also have limited resources. Premier Reagresh is still plowing through all of Bilenton's mistakes to correct this, but he has the Party of Enlightened senators fighting him every step of the way," Mkel answered.

"Ahh, to shale with the POE cowards!" Ordin shouted out. "We should attack now."

"I understand your concern and willingness to act, my dwarven friend, but we must be patient to allow the rangers to get the best intelligence on the giants as possible," Mkel said, calming his ally.

"As for the exercise tomorrow, we will focus on a simulated giant attack with chromatic dragon support," Mkel continued. "We will form a standard battle line with the dwarves in the center. Paloud and Akiser, you will be on the dwarves' right. Howrek, you will be on their left, with the elf infantry platoon stationed behind you as a reserve. Line platoon leaders, be ready to mark a break in your battle line to allow the land dragons to pass through quickly. Since we will be facing fire giants, their breath weapons will be only partially effective and they will use them primarily to fry orcs, trolls, and ogres, so they will be pursuing the close fight with the giants." Mkel nodded to Wheelor, who acknowledged his intent with a smile.

"Four land dragons against several hundred giants is not fair odds," Mkel went on, "but we will have the land dragon company from the regiment, as well as Gallanth and Silvanth. Gallanth will be limited to his plasma fire breath weapon and sunburst beams for the fire giants, due to their innate fire resistance. A word to the infantry and rangers: remember that dragon's fire grenades will only have minimal effect on the hellhounds, so save them for the ogres, trolls, and orcs. Willaward, you will also see a minimized effect on your dragon's fire canisters, so you might want to concentrate on your fragmenting stones."

"Yes sir," Willaward replied.

"Gallanth and I will provide cover at intermittent moments and at the end of the exercise, to simulate us being busy keeping the chromatics off of you, then focusing on the giants. You all must think of what you must do if we cannot be there on time, so remember your aerial counterattack drill," Mkel continued. "Jodem will be on the ground to fend off any offensive spells as well as work on the giants for both the exercise and the battle if it comes, depending on the amount of resistance we have in the air. Silvanth will simulate a diving attack by a chromatic dragon so the line company and the dwarves can practice their defensive postures. The archers will be able to fire volleys with practice arrows to hone their skills at aerial targets. She will breathe out a light ice cone, so all those that fail to shield properly will get a little frosted.

"As far as the actual targets," Mkel continued, "the catapults will engage first as the line moves forward, followed by the land dragon ballistae and then elven and garrison archers. The dwarves will put out a final volley of their hand axes and hammers as the garrison approaches the target line. Weir Senior Sergeant Toderan or I will signal the cavalry platoon as to which direction they will charge and attack. Once we reach the wooden targets, we will hold our positions and let the Draden regiment pass us for a follow-on assault. Gallanth and I will finish with a diving attack in coordination with the rangers, prior to the regiment getting to you. The support corps company will then move in to care for the simulated wounded and conduct resupply. Are there any questions from the platoons regarding the exercise tomorrow?" Mkel paused to see if anyone had a comment. "We will be forming on the practice field right after the morning meal."

"Captain," Colonel Dunn spoke up, "the support company will be focusing on quick resupply to the catapult section and the crossbowmen as well as projectiles for the land dragons' ballistae, if desired. We would also like to address casualties with the healer section."

"Yes sir," Mkel replied. "The platoon leaders will provide one casualty per squad for you. Lieutenants, you will have your squad leaders pick those soldiers for the healers to work on and assign wounds to them to be treated. Jodem will supply the illusion to make your selectees' wounds appear real. Senior Sergeant Toderan, anything from your side?"

"Yes sir. According to Jodem and Silvanth, there will be clear skies tomorrow and comfortable temperatures, a good day for a battle exercise. If there are any personnel issues, bring them to me and the captain after the meeting. I will be flying overhead watching the drill and will be the backup signal for the deployment of the cavalry. Make sure you and all your junior sergeants do your pre-battle checks tonight and tomorrow morning. Treat this exercise like we would be actually fighting the giants tomorrow. The more you get things right here, the fewer casualties we will take when we have to do this for real," Toderan explained.

"Gallanth, my friend," Mkel said to his dragon. The gold dragon slightly raised his head and spoke, "I will be teleporting the garrison behind the mountain, enchant their weapons, and then teleport them back to the field. Be prepared to assume the close formation around me and then to quickly disperse after we arrive back to the field."

"I will also add to the enchantment and walk in front of the line," explained Jodem.

Gallanth could teleport anything within the area of his seventy-five-yard wingspan and the forty-five-yard length from his nose to his tail. In other words, he was able to teleport the whole garrison as long as they all gathered around his body and under his wings. This gave the reinforced company a tremendous advantage over an enemy force, in that all its combat power and forces could appear anywhere on the battlefield and also withdraw just as quickly if necessary.

"As usual, the dwarves and infantry will form in front of Gallanth's chest and wings," Mkel said. "The four land dragons will nestle under his massive wings interspersed with the elves, the sappers, and the cavalry. The catapults will pull beside his tail with their supply wagons. The support corps trains will be teleported by Silvanth, who will then transport wounded to the Weir or the wounded collection point, and bring the Draden regiment forward piece by piece."

Gallanth and Jodem could enchant or empower the whole garrison before a battle, which made their armor a little tougher to pierce and their weapons strike with unnatural damage and accuracy. This ability, along with the high level of training and their superior equipment and weaponry, allowed the garrison to take on much larger forces and win. The incredible power of Gallanth, along with the dragonstone weapons of Mkel, Toderan, Ordin, Lupek, Deless, and Dekeen, coupled with Jodem's and Beckann's spells, gave them an amazing combined ability.

"Mkel, will you be going to Battle Point soon?" Lupek asked.

"Yes Lupek, likely within the week," replied Mkel.

"I would like to give you a message for a friend out there," Lupek requested.

"No problem, see me about it tomorrow," directed Mkel. "I will give you all an update of the situation happening around Battle Point when we get back next week. Lawrent and his Freiland raiders will be arriving soon with their ships moving up the Severic River toward the Weir as well, so watch out for them."

"Anything else, Master Dragonrider?" Ordin asked in his gruff voice, for Mkel knew he wanted to go to the tavern.

"Are there any other questions regarding tomorrow?" Mkel asked again. All present did not answer. "Good, gentlemen and lady, see you at the dining hall and tomorrow for the exercise. I wish you all the Creator's blessing, and remember to always keep the faith."

Everyone stood and saluted Gallanth and Mkel, and then they picked up their weapons and began to move to the dining hall. "You better contact Annan to see if she is ready to go to dinner, my rider," Gallanth told Mkel. "Yes, I was just going to," Mkel replied.

"Captain, I will see you in a couple of minutes. I'm going to get my family," Toderan said to his friend as he put his large hand on Mkel's shoulder.

"No problem, see you there," he replied.

"Jodem, what are your plans?" Mkel asked.

"I will be joining you, for we need to talk over dinner about the Battle Point visit," the wizard replied.

"Good, let's walk up to my quarters and get Annan," Mkel motioned.

"Why don't you see if she has her seeing crystal with her?" Jodem suggested.

"Good thought," Mkel commented.

He pulled out the flat-faced quartz crystal from his belt and spoke into it, asking for Annan. These devices were special crystal mirrors made by wizards or elves with the use of a small amount of dragon's blood and a drop or two of the owner's blood. They enabled the holder to see and hear another person who had a connected crystal. The image of Annan appeared on the flat smooth stone face.

"We're ready to eat, my love. Janta and I will bring Michen down to the dining hall," Annan said.

"Tell her that I will come and get them," Gallanth said to Mkel. "Are you sure Gallanth?" Mkel asked. "It would be my pleasure to give Michen a ride," Gallanth added. Mkel spoke back into the crystal, "Annan, Gallanth will come and get you."

"All right, Janta and I will be ready," Annan replied.

"I will be right back with the little one," Gallanth said as he stood up and began to turn around. He quickly scanned the area to make sure there wasn't a griffon ready to take off or land, spread his immense golden wings, and with a leap, a heft of his tail, and a downward thrust of his wings, he was airborne with a strong rush of air heading back to his ledge.

"He really loves that boy," Jodem said to Mkel.

"Yes, I know. I would fear to be the one that would threaten him harm," Mkel replied.

"He feels the same about you, especially since after your father died," Jodem added.

"I know, almost to a fault. I don't know what I would have done without him, my mother and you," Mkel said as he felt the familiar lump in his throat and slight tearing of his eyes as he thought about his father and those he cared about. "You both have been great to me in your teaching, guidance, and caring."

"Never compare me to your dragon," Jodem said. "Your bond goes beyond mere friendship or even family. Yours is the bond of blood, heart, mind, and soul."

Mkel understood his words, for he would never forget the day he and Gallanth blood bonded and thus merged souls. He never felt alone since that day, for no matter where he was, he and Gallanth shared thoughts and emotions. That day, when he was nineteen years old, was perhaps the best day of his life (save the day of his son's birth). Having this kind of bond with a dragon, especially a gold dragon, was beyond what words can describe.

Having a friend and partner that was never more than a thought away had always been the most comforting aspect of being a dragonrider (although having one of the most powerful creatures in the world as your protector and friend also helped).

Dragons were not only incredibly powerful, their wisdom and intelligence even exceeded their strength. The respect for the metallic dragons was almost universal, with the exception of a few minor factions within the Alliance population in the major cities and, of course, the Party of the Enlightened. All elves and dwarves revered the good dragons, as did most men and women.

Gallanth was now gliding down toward the dining hall, with Annan in the rear seat holding Michen in her arms and Janta holding on for dear life in Mkel's saddle. Michen's little face was aglow with a wide grin, and his bright blue eyes were beaming. Gallanth back winged gently before the dining hall so as to not stir up too much dust for those that were already eating. He then crouched down and laid his massive neck on the ground.

"Come on, my friend, let's go help your wife down," Jodem urged Mkel.

They walked past the gold dragon's resting head. "Thank you, Gallanth," Mkel said. "Never a problem to give our Michen a ride," the gold dragon replied. Gallanth thought of the little boy as his own son. Dragon offspring were separated from their parents relatively quickly and sent to the central hatchling training grounds in Draconia. While there was a bond between a mated dragon pair and their offspring, it was understood that dragons had a higher purpose to serve and guide mankind. Therefore they tended to be very affectionate with their rider's children.

Mkel jumped up on Gallanth's thick arm and reached his hands up to Annan. She sat Michen on Gallanth's neck and he slid down the dragon's hide over the smooth tiny teardrop scales into Mkel's arms. He was laughing his irresistible two-year-old giggle, which could mend a torn soul. Mkel helped Annan slide down off of the long saddle, and Jodem caught Janta as she climbed down the notched steps of the thick harness on the immense gold neck. The group walked back past Gallanth's head, and Mkel asked Michen if he wanted to give his dragon a kiss. "Kiss, draaggon," the infant said. Mkel held his son next to Gallanth, and the little boy then leaned his head toward the dragon's upper cheek and touched it with his forehead. The dragon's eighteen-inch-wide eye glowed brightly at the infant's gesture. It always amazed Mkel that such a massive, super intelligent, and extremely powerful creature could derive such pleasure from the most simple of things, but that was what life was about, Gallanth would tell him, and that was what was worth fighting for.

They all walked into the full dining hall and sat down at the head table beside Toderan, Lupek, and the other officers and their families. Mkel always ate last, being the commander and Weirleader, unless necessity forced him to do differently. Dekeen had already left the Weir through the hidden back entrance that led out into Draden Forest to be with his family and clan. The only elves that resided in the Weir itself were the ones in the ranger platoon. Elves did not eat much, for their metabolisms were more efficient than those of humans and dwarves. In contrast, the dwarves that ate at the dining hall could consume vast amounts of food not equal to their short but stout builds.

The Weir cooks were a mix of humans and halflings; the latter were excellent in the diversity of their recipes as a result of their traveling nature. Halflings were restless wanderers, but once they established roots in a particular area, they became a fixture of the community, especially farming communities. They always shared knowledge with each other without a fault, and they were known as excellent small niche farmers and cooks. The kitchen folk had prepared a noodle dish with a spiced tomato sauce, a chicken vegetable stew, and other vegetables and breads.

Alliance farmers of all races were the most productive in the world, taking the best farming techniques of humans, halflings, and elves. No one in the republic went hungry because of a lack of available food as long as they worked for it. Grains and other foodstuffs were a major export for the Alliance as well as finished goods, crafts, and a host of other materials.

As the garrison was finishing the meal, Mkel stood up. "Gentlemen and ladies, may I have your attention?" he announced, raising his wine glass. "To the conduct of a successful exercise tomorrow, to the Weir, and to Gallanth," he toasted.

"To Gallanth," everyone repeated as they turned toward the resting dragon, who raised his immense head and then slightly bowed as everyone toasted. All the soldiers, dwarves, and elves of the garrison knew that the power of the gold dragon had saved all their lives on many an occasion, and everyone had great respect for him.

"To you, gentlemen and ladies, thank you for your service," the dragon replied.

Everyone then sat down as Mkel said a few words of encouragement. "I know your platoon leaders and senior sergeants gave you the briefing regarding the exercise, so I will not go into great details about it. I want you to do is to focus on the coordination with all the members of your squad and platoon and the other specialty platoons. This training ensures that all of our combat power is brought to bear synergistically, which will save lives if the need arises. Even though this is just an exercise, with the giants stirring in the mountains, there may be a real fight soon. I know you will do well, as you always have. Thank you," Mkel finished.

Ordin spoke up, as he usually did. "To our success," he growled.

"To our success," everyone echoed.

"All right, gentlemen, there are some final preparations and last equipment checks to perform before the exercise. I suggest that you see to them and then spend a little time with your families," Toderan finished.

With that, the dinner was officially over and everyone started to get up and leave to go back to their barracks and their quarters.

Mkel shook Ordin's hand and bid him a good night. He headed to the stairway that led to the caverns and tunnels under the Weir that housed the dwarf community. "Good night, my friend," Mkel said to Toderan.

"Just a few things to look after, Captain," he replied.

"No, we can do the final checks tomorrow morning, Senior Sergeant," Mkel chided. "There will time before the exercise; just have to have faith, my friend."

"All right, I'll see you early tomorrow in the meeting room," Toderan said. "Have a good night." He turned and walked toward his quarters.

With that, Mkel picked up his overactive son and gave a nod to Annan and Janta to follow him over to where Gallanth was resting.

"Are you ready, my dragon friend?" he asked. "Let me get a drink first," the gold dragon replied, raising himself up on his four tree-trunk-sized legs. He turned slowly so as to not hit anyone with his huge tail, walked over to the lake in the center of the Weir's ground inside the mountain, and lowered his massive head down to drink. Hundreds of gallons water rushed down his throat, after which he lifted his head and walked back to Mkel and Annan. Gallanth knelt down, and Mkel positioned Annan and Janta, climbed up on the saddle, and held Michen after he secured the flying straps.

"All ready," he spoke to Gallanth. The dragon turned to the far side of the Weir and spread his wings; with three steps and a downward stroke of his wings, they were airborne. In no time, they landed on the platform that housed his sleeping chamber. Gallanth's ledge was basically a huge carved cave that connected to Mkel's living area to the left side and Jodem's quarters and laboratory to the right side. "Thanks Gallanth," Mkel said as his dragon turned around and lay down on his bed of coins and gems.

Gallanth actually slept on the Weir's treasury reserve. First to keep it safe, and second because a dragon's hide is so tough the layers of gold and silver, being very soft metals, actually feel like laying on a comforter or a mattress to the immense dragon. Over the years, the dragon's weight made a nearly perfect imprint of his forty-five-yard-long body on the pile of coins. "Rest well, Gallanth," Mkel said. "Have a good night, my rider, and good night little hatchling," he replied, giving a last wink to Michen and closing his huge eyes.

Mkel carried Michen into their living quarters, with Annan closely following him. They told Janta to go and get some rest. Her room was down the hall from their main chambers. Michen ran to the room and jumped on the resting elf hound. The two-hundred-fifty-pound-dog gruffed slightly with the impact, raised its imposing head, and licked the infant's face as he rolled around on the canine's side. Elf hounds are bred by the elves to serve as fierce, dependable guards. This special breed, aside from having the normal canine alertness and excellent hearing and sense of smell, could see perfectly at night and could detect invisible entities. They could also change the color of their coat to blend in with their environment for a perfect camouflage. Slightly more intelligent than the average dog, they made perfect guardians. Unless an individual was fully armed and armored, one of these large dogs could tear limbs off of the average man, although they were gentle and very tolerant of children.

"Come, little one, it's time for your bath," Annan said.

"Baath," he repeated, getting off of his guardian dog and running into their bathing room.

"Do you have the towels and soap, dear?" Mkel asked.

"Yes, it's all laid out," Annan replied. "What's the news from Lupek?" she continued.

"The fire giants are gathering for something just east of the Gray Mountains, between us and Eladran Weir, as well as many chromatic dragons and other Morgathian types," Mkel explained.

"This doesn't sound good," Annan said with a worried tone.

"Don't worry, we will handle it; Gallanth always looks out for me," he assured her.

"This might produce a lot of casualties; how will this affect your trips to Battle Point and Draconia?" she asked.

"You know we always do everything we can to minimize friendly casualties, but if you don't want to go, you don't have to. You can accompany us to the capital if you want," he said with a smile. "Although you will have to share the seats on Gallanth's rig with Ordin, for he wants to see his cousin from Ferranor." Mkel was teasing, for he knew that she did not like the gruff dwarf.

"He can't go with anyone else?" she said slightly irritated.

"No, you know that he likes Gallanth and has known him longer than both of us have been alive. Besides, he will only fly on Gallanth, for as you know, the only thing dwarves fear is flying," Mkel chided back.

"All right, but he must sit in the rear seat in back of Janta," Annan demanded.

"I'm sure he will not mind," Mkel said, smiling again and lifting his wriggling son out of the bath while he pulled the drain plug. He handed Michen to Annan, who waited with fresh towels to dry him off. "We need to put him to bed now, for tomorrow will be an early day," he added. They put his nightclothes on and carried him to his crib. "Night, night," he said to the infant.

"Night, night," Annan echoed.

"Nigh, nigh," the little boy said, looking at his parents with his wide deep blue eyes as they handed him his bottle.

"Good night, my little hatchling," Gallanth said from his landing.

"I thought you were asleep, my friend," Mkel asked.

"Just wanted to wish the little one a good night; we will be ready for tomorrow morning," Gallanth replied.

Mkel and Annan walked into their bedroom. "How's Silvanth?" Mkel asked.

"She's been gorging and sleeping mostly. I think she will rise to mate in another two or three weeks," she replied.

"Will you will be riding her tomorrow for the exercise?" Mkel asked.

"I'm not sure yet. I will have to ask her tomorrow. I know she will fly for the training, for Gallanth already had her agree to that," Annan added.

"He's hard to say no to," Mkel said.

"You should be so lucky," Annan said with a wry smile.

"I get your point, dear; get some sleep," he replied and gave her a kiss as he lowered the cover on the lighting crystal.

CHAPTER II

WAR GAMES

Morning came quickly. Gallanth stirred and telepathically called Mkel to rise. *Wake up, my friend, or we'll be late for our own exercise*, Gallanth's words echoed in Mkel's head. "I'm up, Gallanth," he answered. "Let me take a quick bath and I'll meet you on the ledge in twenty-five minutes." *All right, I will go down to the lake and be right back*, the dragon replied as he stood up and outstretched his massive wings before flying off the ledge. Mkel walked into the bathing room and turned on the water and adjusted it to the proper temperature.

The infrastructure of the Weir was impressive indeed. The water was supplied from two massive tanks that rested on the top tier of the Weir. The water was heated by one of the quartz heating crystals that Gallanth created by adding a bit of his blood and then blowing a line of fire at it. These heating crystals were placed at the point of use and could heat up the water almost instantly. They lasted for years depending on the type of crystal or stone used, with corundum being the preferred mineral and quartz being second. Gallanth made hundreds of heating crystals a week, and Silvanth made cooling crystals.

These crystals were for the military and also for sale to the general public. The dragon's blood absorbed into the very structure of the crystal and then took the initial energy from their breath weapons, being fire, cold, or lighting. The stone then radiated heat, cold, or light upon contact with a human or other creature. Each crystal was enough to warm a large room, a small house, or a large tank of water, with smaller ones even woven into clothes to warm or cool the wearer. Legion soldiers could wear full armor in the middle of summer and not be overheated, or they could stay warm on the coldest of days.

The tanks that supply the Weir with fresh water held at least ten thousand gallons apiece; they were glass-lined, reinforced-steel vessels. They were supported by large steel beams and connected to the distribution pipes that went to all the Weir's rooms, food preparation areas, bathing facilities, and stables. They were fed by pipes that collected water from the upper tiers of the mountain and by water from the spring that also fed the Weir's internal lake.

Sanitation was handled in a similar way, with all waste transported through copper pipes or stone channels that led to a series of chambers located on the eastern lower end of the Weir. A group of dwarf-bred otyughs resided in these chambers. These nasty, grotesque creatures were disgusting, insect-like beings that fed on refuse, excrement, and offal. They basically ate anything they could get ahold of but prefer organic wastes. Their ovoid bodies had four thick stubby legs; a gaping, sclerotized sharp-toothed mouth part; six long, barbed tentacles; and two small eye stalks. Their bodies averaged six feet in diameter, and they weighed over five hundred pounds. They will only grow to the size of their environment however. These creatures could also draw water up through their legs and body and filter it of all organic and inorganic materials for both food and for their exoskeleton. Their bite inflicted a severe infection, but if they were fed with a steady stream of wastes, they were not overly aggressive.

Overall, the otyughs made very effective garbage disposals. They also treated sewage, excreted oxygen through their integument, and produced small waste briquettes that could be used as a clean-burning fuel or for fertilizer. Great care must be taken when retrieving the briquettes, however. Usually Jodem or a wizard cast a sleep spell over the creatures before any of the Weir's work crews went into their chamber, or several cooling crystals were thrown into their pits, which caused them to go dormant. All of the Weirs and most of the major cities and towns use these creatures to treat sewer flows and to recycle garbage.

The wastewater that flowed into these pits was emptied out of the chambers after it was filtered by the otyughs and then channeled through a series of pipes that collected into a small marshy area to the north of Draden Forest at the base of the mountain. The drinking water was filtered up through the deep underground fissures in the eastern part of the Weir landing. It was treated by several lighting crystals that purified it of any contaminants with a mild electric charge mixed with the air. A filter feeder type of dramite moved the water from the draw wells to the holding tank. These small creatures were another invention of the dwarves; they were created like the otyughs hundreds of years ago and bred for their natural ability to channel and filter water. The dwarves somehow managed to harness these creatures, which were corralled for waste management needs and the creation of breathable air to supplement the natural oxygen-producing molds they cultivated. These subterranean mold growths also produced usable oxygen and emitted small amounts of light. Dwarves even managed to brew a type of ale out of certain kinds of underground molds and fungus (only they could usually stomach this ale, however).

Gallanth landed by the part of the lake that was nearest to the stables. Jern and his work crew were already waiting for him; his team wheeled out two portable ladder platforms. Gallanth knelt down and rested his head on the ground. The stable crew pushed the platforms up to either side of his neck. These ladders were needed, as the girth of the base of the gold dragon's neck was taller than two grown men. Three rigging experts scrambled up each side of the ladder steps and started to unbuckle the straps that fastened the oversized saddle to the three main support straps.

Gallanth's saddle could hold three people comfortably (four with slight crowding). Mkel's front seat held his moveable crossbow firing platform arm, while the back seats just had fastening straps. A small cab could be fastened over the back seats to keep the elements out; it was even equipped with a warming crystal (at Annan's request) when Gallanth or Mkel wanted to preserve the strength of their magic shields, which can keep the wind off of the rider and passengers. This was not normally needed, as the invisible shield that Mkel's weapons created could stop wind and rain with little effort.

Once all the buckles were unfastened, the crews connected the crane hooks to the main support rings and gave the signal that they were ready. The crane crew acknowledged and moved two horses forward, straining on the pulley cables and raising the several-hundred-pound flying rig off of Gallanth's back. The crews then gave the three one-foot-thick leather laminated support straps a quick check and hurriedly moved down the ladder steps, moving the platforms away from the dragon's neck.

Gallanth carefully rose to his feet and walked into the lake until he was totally submerged. The center of the lake was several hundred feet deep but crystal clear and quite cold (not to a dragon's thick hide, though). He emerged and walked back to the shallows by the shore, shaking off the excess water and fanning his wings to dry. Dozens of halflings filed into the water and began to scrub Gallanth's thick hide with a special gritty soap that both cleaned and polished him at the same time. When the workers were done, he dove back into the deep of the lake to rinse off. He then went back to the same position and knelt down, and the saddle was lowered back onto his neck and refastened. Two whole cooked seasoned steer halves were waiting for him upon his return from the lake, which he engulfed quickly. After that, he got back up, thanked Jern and his crew for their efficiency, and flew back to his ledge.

After quickly bathing, Mkel shaved, performed oral hygiene;, and put on a little of the special cream that shielded his face from the wind and sun when flying. He quickly dressed in his Alliance uniform tunic and trousers, gave the still sleeping Annan a kiss, looked in on Michen, and walked onto the ledge where Gallanth awaited.

"You look brilliant, my friend," he said to his dragon.

"Always feels good to take a swim and a bath in the lake. Jern's halflings are very good," he replied. "Is Jodem out yet?" asked Mkel.

"No, but you know he is never late," replied Gallanth.

"You're right, my friend, I'll go and look in his lab," he said as he walked over to the entrance to the wizard's laboratory and opened the thick oaken door to Jodem's work place. The large room was filled with jars, vials, glassware of all sorts containing a multitude of concoctions, and volumes of books, but it was devoid of the Weir's wizard.

"I believe he is already down at the stables with Vatara, overseeing his rigging for the exercise and his flight today," Gallanth speculated.

"All right then, we'll go meet him and the others on the Weir grounds," Mkel said as he donned his dragon scale mithril-lined armor coat that doubled as his riding jacket.

The dwarven-made riding coat was constructed of dragon hide and scales taken from red, blue, white, black, and green dragons that Gallanth killed in the Great War, as well as chest scales that Gallanth and Silvanth shed on occasion. Dragon scales, which only grow on a dragon's ventral side, are the hardest known armor on earth. They are almost impossible to penetrate with non-mithril or black iron weapons and possess a distinct magical-resistant property. This, coupled with the fact that those scales and hide were woven together with mithril thread, made Mkel's jacket very lightweight and flexible, but among the toughest suits of armor known.

Dragon hide itself was basically smooth with small overlapping plates the size of teardrops that when struck immediately spread the impact over a wide area, thus distributing the energy of the blow. The supple quality of dragon skin becomes instantly rigid when some object attempts to pierce it. While flying, it actually helps move air over the dragon's hide and wings, propelling it through the sky and giving the appearance that it is slicing through the air. This enables the large creatures to soar with great ease and hover with little effort.

Mkel made sure to put his uniform collar out over his riding jacket to show his rank and the symbol of a dragonrider with the crossed sword and arrow of an infantry officer. While he was proud of his rank as a captain and his gold dragon insignia, he did not like to show it off. He was ordered by General Becknor to always display them, even over his armor. *Very pretentious but necessary, I guess*, he thought to himself as he straightened his uniform. He put on his soft leather elf-made belt that held Kershan, his powerful mithril sword, as well as several other items such as a canteen, a bandage pouch, several bandoliers of his small but deadly crossbow bolts, and his seeing crystal.

Kershan, his father's pure mithril single-edged sword, was a weapon of extreme power. The dragonstone that was imbedded in the pommel was originally given to Mkel's great-grandfather over two hundred years ago; it was the first dragonstone that Gallanth ever made. The sword has been handed down from father to son since then, which was extraordinary, for most dragonstones died with their blood bonded partner. The dragonstone gave the sword extraordinary powers; through its limited intelligence, it was telepathically linked to Mkel. It could react on its own to defend Mkel, deflecting blows or snapping incoming arrows. It also emanated a defensive spell shield with one fifth of the power of Gallanth's shield. It gives Mkel, an excellent swordsman already, an even greater skill due to its defending ability.

The slightly curved mithril blade could cut through almost any known substance, including rock and steel. Pure mithril had an almost iridescent silvery hue, as if the rare metal had liquid or glass-like properties. All magically empowered weapons were made of some part mithril. Only a precious few, however, were pure mithril, with even Toderan's holy sword just under nine tenths of the rare metal. Draden Weir, with Ordin's clan, mined the richest mithril deposits in all the Alliance and therefore produced the most dragonstone and magical weapons.

After Jmes died and the sword was retrieved from the slain death knight, Gallanth took it and drove it into the rock face side of his landing, only to be drawn again by the next rider he blood bonded with. Mkel looked at the far side of Gallanth's ledge and saw the hole where his sword had been imbedded. This made him remember the blood bonding ritual when he joined with Gallanth.

Thirteen years ago, Jodem led Mkel out of the Weir's Council room with a rope tied to his left arm. He was blindfolded and dressed in the traditional ceremonial blue outfit of a dragonrider candidate. The blue silk half shirt he wore exposed the left side of his chest, with the right pants leg torn off above the knee. Only his left foot had a cloth sandal, which symbolized one's humble beginnings. Candidates touched the ground with their bare foot and then knelt to take the Dragonrider Oath on a bare knee. The portly wizard led Mkel up to Gallanth with Watterseth, Ordin, and Dekeen standing next to the dragon.

All in the Weir were in attendance, gathered beside the Weir lake on the main grounds, with Jodem officiating over the ceremony after he took the blindfold off Mkel. Mkel stood in front of the gold dragon as Gallanth lifted his huge front claw and pierced one of his three front talons with his back claw, forming a small drop of his green-blue blood that glowed with a soft light due to the power it contained. He then reached over to Mkel's exposed left breast and, with a grace amazing for the size of his talon, made a single fine cut over his heart. It did hurt him, but not overly so, considering the size of the dragon's four-foot-long claws. He then put his talon pad on Mkel's chest over his heart, with the large claw almost covering Mkel's whole body. He felt the dragon's blood enter the wound and course through his veins. It seemed to have a life of its own in its directness of travel.

"This will hurt for a few seconds, but then I will be with you forever," Gallanth spoke to him out loud in common tongue. Immediately following the dragon's words and a short directed speech, an intense pain emanating from the center of his mind and chest began to expand like a seed undergoing a rapid germination. It was like something was pushing into his mind and his head was going to burst. His knees buckled, but Ordin and Dekeen were right there to grab his shoulders while Jodem was behind him, waving his wizard's staff over his head, the sapphire dragonstone scintillating in sparking blue light. Jodem uttered an incantation in Draconic to help speed the transition.

This occasionally fatal process was more dangerous with a gold dragon because of their intense power. Right at the point where Mkel thought he was going to pass out, he felt a voice call out to him from inside his head. *Don't worry, my young friend, I am with you now and will be always*, Gallanth gently told his new rider telepathically. "I feel you now," Mkel said out loud in Draconic, the ancient language of dragons and wizards.

Jodem smiled, for only he, Gallanth, the dragons and dragonriders, the elves, and the wizards attending the ceremony could understand what Mkel said, but it signified that the process was successful. Everyone began to cheer and applaud, knowing the bonding was successful and Gallanth now had a rider after ten years of being alone. As wise and powerful as dragons are, they are much stronger when bonded with a human rider, for they are creatures of extremely strong emotions, which can even affect those around them.

"My rider, please kneel." Mkel then repeated the dragonrider oath as Gallanth spoke the words. Gallanth lowered his head and began to speak. "Cemented with blood, well sprung from the heart and soul, you, here in front of all present, your dragon, and the Creator, do you willingly take the oath of a dragonrider, Mkel son of Jmes?"

"I do," answered Mkel.

"Repeat after me, my rider," Gallanth said with an unusual softness in his normally deep and commanding voice. Mkel felt tears roll down his cheeks from the emotion he felt and that which was pulsating from Gallanth. The gold dragon's voice echoed inside his head as well as in his ears, as a strange new feeling and a voice only he could hear.

"I, Mkel," Gallanth started the oath.

"I, Mkel," he repeated.

"Rider of the gold dragon Gallanth and master of Draden Weir," Gallanth continued.

"Rider of the gold dragon Gallanth and master of Draden Weir," he said with a smile past the tears streaming down his cheeks.

"Swear to uphold truth, live with honor, fight with valor; whose heart knows only compassion, whose power you and your dragon are blessed to wield protects the weak, whose wrath brings justice to the wicked, and whose might upholds the Articles of the Alliance with the light of the Creator to guide our way." Mkel repeated the words, with each one burning deeper into his conscious. The power of those words still resonated with him.

After a round of applause, Jodem called Watterseth for a prayer. The cleric raised his glowing dragonstone mace, stepped up to Mkel and Gallanth, and began to speak. "May we all pray," his deep voice boomed over the gathered crowd. All present bowed. "Mkel, please kneel," he stated.

Place your hand on my talon, my rider, Gallanth told him telepathically. Mkel knelt down on his bare knee, as Gallanth lowered his massive head almost touching his nose on the ground. This was repeated by all the other dragons present for the ceremony that were standing behind the crowd. Mkel placed one hand on Gallanth's talon and the other on his snout.

"Creator, we give thanks for the events of today, the bonding of a young rider to our friend and protector Gallanth, and in now knowing that his loneliness is gone and his power to spread good, to vanquish evil is increased tenfold. We all rejoice in the bonding of rider and dragon, remembering the sacrifice of all our comrades that fell defending the Alliance and the Creator's principles of benevolence, love, and freedom. We thank that all assembled here—men, women, elves, dwarves, halflings, and dragons—live in peace and brotherhood for the benefit of all. We wish Mkel and Gallanth a bonding and strength that will last for centuries and pray that the Creator watches over them and guides them, giving them the wisdom and the strength to fulfill their duties. May they always keep the love that they now have for each other and the power which they will derive to dispense justice, as the Creator's love to all of his creatures gives us strength. Amen," Watterseth finished.

Then something that could only be described as mythical happened. As Gallanth raised his head, two iridescent tears rolled down from his huge glowing golden eyes and fell to the ground. The hot liquid crystallized immediately, and the grapefruit-sized teardrops shattered when they hit the ground, splintering into hundreds of small diamonds. It was said by the Alliance historical scholars that when the Creator's earthly spirit was killed by Tiamat's minions, all the metallic dragons shed crystal tears. That was two thousand years ago and has since been known only as an accepted myth. All present, even the normally nonemotional elves, stalwart dwarves, and hundreds of battle-hardened veterans of the Great Dragon War, were wiping tears from their eyes. Dragons' emotions, and especially Gallanth's, could wash over anyone close to him like a tidal wave.

"It is now time to rejoice!" Gallanth's booming voice broke through the silence of the incident. Everyone cheered and moved toward the Weir's tavern.

Mkel remembered this day as one of the happiest of his life. After the ceremony, when he went back to his quarters besides Gallanth's landing, he felt a much weaker tug at his mind.

"That is your father's sword, Kershan," Gallanth said to him. "It is calling to you; reach out your hand." Mkel remembered reaching his left hand toward the sword imbedded in the stone wall. The ruby dragonstone began to shake and glow intensely in a sparkling red light. The powerful sword broke free of the rock and flew to Mkel's outstretched hand. The sword's grip was made of a strong elven dark oak wood rapped with a small piece of white dragon hide and fastened with a smooth twine for better handling. Kershan felt almost vibrant in his hand, and he could feel its presence in his mind. While it couldn't talk, he could sense its emotion and intent. From that moment on, the sword was never far from him. Later he would feel the same connection with his crossbow and his ring, both of which had Gallanth's dragonstones imbedded in them.

Mkel shook himself out of his self-induced daydream and put on his backpack, which contained several essential items including ninety bolts to his crossbow, Markthrea, and many other items for day to day activities and survival tools. He then grabbed his powerful range weapon and began to climb up Gallanth's securing straps. He swung up into his saddle and mounted the crossbow on the firing spindle arm that secured and stabilized it during flight. This setup allowed him to swing it in an almost 360 degree arc and move it up and down to provide Gallanth flank protection fires while still enabling Mkel to attack targets on the ground. "All ready, Gallanth," he yelled to his dragon mate. *Secure your flying straps, my rider,* Gallanth replied. "All right," he answered as he grabbed the remaining two of the four straps and hooked them onto the rings on his belt.

Immediately, Gallanth was airborne, quickly sailing down to the Weir grounds beside the lake; many of the garrison's men were starting to form, and the cavalry's horses and the four land dragons were getting saddled and rigged up. Gallanth gently back winged so as to minimize the dust he churned up and landed with his back feet first.

"You're almost late for your own exercise," Jodem chided Mkel as he walked from the staging area beside the stable.

"Master Wizard, time is a relative concept, plus we still have an hour before the company has to be on the training grounds," Gallanth replied.

"And we are the overseers for this exercise, not to mention the Weirleaders," Mkel added as he slid down Gallanth's neck to his raised forearm.

"Be you the commander or not, Colonel Wierangan would not be pleased if the garrison was late for the exercise, and we don't want to spoil our good relationship with our non-Weir comrades," Jodem said with a slight smile.

"We will be ready. This company has never been late or failed under my command in the past, and this day will not be the first. Have the officers gathered yet?" Mkel asked.

"They are making their way to the council room. Toderan just made his last rounds to inspect the men," Jodem informed him.

"Then I suggest we make our way over to the meeting room," Gallanth said as he started over to his traditional place in front of the huge opening to the council room. "I guess this means 'follow me,'" Mkel said to Jodem as they both started walking toward the hall. As they entered the room and Gallanth settled down on his belly, Toderan walked in closely followed by Willaward, Tegent the Weir's bard, Clydown, and Lenor. Pekram and the infantry lieutenants with their senior sergeants walked in right after them. All gave greetings and sat down. Dekeen, Deless, and Lupek entered from beside Gallanth, and Ordin came up from the corridor that led to the stairs from the lower levels. All gave Gallanth the customary salute and a greeting to Mkel. Wheelor was the last one to arrive, which was customary for a land dragon man. Land dragon crews were never in a rush but still very dependable.

"All right, gentlemen, shall we begin?" Mkel said as they all sat down. Breakfast was brought to them by several halfling kitchen help, to facilitate the preparations for the exercise. They would only meet for a half an hour or less, just to clarify any last-minute details if need be. "Please eat and listen if you all are capable," Mkel said with a smile. "Jodem, if you please," he added, nodding to the wizard. Jodem placed his staff on the stand in the middle of the U shaped table and focused on the dragonstone. The sapphire glowed and emanated a dazzling blue light, which grew and took the shape of the grass field in front of the Weir over the large stone bridge that spanned the Severic River. The plain led to the opening in the Gray Mountains and the Alliance border with the unsettled lands beyond. The legion and settlement at Battle Point lay over five hundred miles to the east; it was the lone outpost between the Alliance and the Morgathian-held lands much farther east.

Mkel spoke as Jodem manipulated the images taking form over the floor. "We shall form the standard linear battle line anchored on Ordin's dwarf company. The infantry will form on both sides of the dwarves as we discussed earlier, 1st Platoon to their left and 2nd and 3rd to their right. We will use the standard formation with heavy infantry up front, two lines deep, and the archers and crossbowmen behind, providing missile coverage. Use the standard attack method of stopping every ten paces, splitting to allow the archers to fire and then re-form the line and move forward with shields locked.

"Two of the elven archer platoons will be positioned in the center to support the dwarves," he continued. "The third archer platoon will support 1st Platoon, and the elf heavy infantry platoon will be held in reserve. I want to practice them plugging a break in the line; I will signal to that platoon leader to simulate the breach through the seeing crystals. The land dragon platoon will split section, with one team on either side of the line. Remember if we face the fire giants, the land dragon's fire breath will be limited in effectiveness against them, so it will come down to a close-in fight. The catapult section will be located in the center and rear of the line, protected by the sappers until they are needed.

"Willaward," Mkel added, "you will initiate fires with your longest range solid stones first. Begin firing on my command or Lupek's, if I become unavailable, launching at your maximum range of two thousand yards. When and if we face them, you would use the spiked ammo to surprise the first couple of giants that would try to catch them. For the exercise, just use solid stones and then switch to the dye canisters to simulate the dragon's fire projectiles intermixed with a couple of real canisters for the spectators' pleasure. Remember, Lieutenant, you fire first, and the more of them you take, the less the infantry and cavalry have to deal with."

"Yes sir, we will bring fire and stone down on them," Willaward replied.

"I have faith, Willaward. Lieutenant Wheelor, you will concentrate your ballista fires on the large targets, simulating giants, trolls, and ogres," Mkel continued as the land dragon leader nodded an acknowledgment. "Lenor, I will signal you as to what side you will lead your paladins to charge, so be flexible. I would normally put you in a heavily contested area with the larger foes or enemy cavalry, which could take the form of orcs on hellhounds or dire wolves. We could feasibly face both. Pekram, I would like you to take the garrison line and Toderan will take over control of the battle if I get too engaged in a fight with the chromatics, which we will assume for the latter part of this exercise. Jodem will be observing from above, mounted on Vatara, to view the operation after walking in front of the garrison line for a couple hundred yards, and Dekeen will provide the dwarves and our men additional cover with his bow. Ordin, you and your brother will take the exact center of the line as usual. I have faith in your ability to handle a couple of giants, but today please take it easy on the wooden targets," Mkel said as he smiled at Ordin.

"I will try, Master Dragonrider," Ordin replied with a smile that showed through his thick brown beard.

"Lupek, take the remainder of your rangers and perform aerial attack missions, but I feel that when we have the actual battle with this army, they will have some sort of winged contingent to deal with, be it manticores, giant wasps, or wyverns, so keep that in mind, my friend," Mkel said. "Lastly, Gallanth and I will be circling above as if we were taking care of any unfriendly chromatic dragons or aerial threats, and we will perform a ground attack as the last event. A reminder to everyone: Silvanth will be conducting attacks against you with a light frost breath to test your reaction to an attacking chromatic dragon in a dive. Remember your shield drill and announcing the direction and type of attack. You may practice your targeting skills as long as all leaders ensure they have practice arrows. Silvanth has an extremely tough hide, as Gallanth knows, but I don't want to risk her any undue pain. She is getting testy, for it is near her mating cycle, and we all know what that does to a female." They all chuckled.

"Captain Vicasek and Colonel Dunn, what is your primary plan of resupply for the exercise?" Mkel asked of his support corps leaders.

"We will focus on an immediate resupply of the catapults," the colonel replied, "followed by arrows and bolts to the elven and human archers and crossbowmen. Afterward, we will practice evacuating and treating the wounded. Watterseth should be with the infantry line if we are to be facing the enemy force that the rangers said we might, plus Silvanth will be able to protect the supply and healer wagons should any giants or dragons slip past you or the line. Additionally, Lady Beckann is only a call away.

That will also allow immediate healing to any who need it right there at the fight."

Support corps units were essential in Alliance military doctrine, for an army without food, healing support, and resupply was not effective over the long haul. This was viewed in such high esteem that the support corps battalion in a legion was commanded by an officer of almost equal rank to the legion commander. He oversaw all logistics operations for the supported unit, which was usually guarded by the female metallic dragons and senior clerics. This usually gave them adequate protection, freeing all combat forces to concentrate on the battle at hand.

Watterseth might be needed in the front line, backing up the infantry, Mkel thought to himself quickly if this fight is against the giants. "That is likely true, sir, especially if there are any liches or beholders," Mkel replied to the senior support corps officer. "Father Watterseth, would that suit you to be with the infantry versus the support corps as long as Silvanth is available?" he asked the cleric.

"It would be my honor, Dragonrider," the cleric stated.

Watterseth was indeed a powerful cleric, with the unique ability to be fierce in close combat and able to cast both strong offensive spells and even more powerful defensive spells. With his special mace, powered with a dragonstone given to him by Silvanth, he was also able to perform amazing feats of healing after a battle. The mace was a standard Alliance weapon of power wielded by clerics. It had a vertical grooved shaft like a pillar with a flattened square between the shaft and the ball head piece. The mace was made of a high-mithril-content alloy with the dragonstone on top of the ball. Each legion and Weir had a senior cleric who not only was the religious leader, but also acted on behalf of the men on many different occasions; they also were the chief combat healers.

"Any questions, gentlemen?" Mkel inquired. Silence indicated the answer. "We'll go down by the numbers and start with the dwarves, Ordin."

"I, my brother, and the dwarves are ready for the drill and for the giants; no changes to our numbers, my dear dragonrider," the burly dwarf replied. Dwarves were very stout and tenacious fighters. The average dwarf was slightly stronger than an average man and had a very tough constitution, capable of taking severe blows. They also had an intense hatred of orcs and giants, which went back for generations. They would be especially valuable in the coming fight with the fire giants.

Their company consisted of one hundred twenty dwarves. It was well known that it was easier to break a wall of reinforced stone than a dwarf battle line. They wore either hardened scale mail or dwarven plate armor and carried large shields. The first rank wielded dwarven war axes or war hammers, with the second rank wielding Urgoshes (an axe/spear combo), and they all had at least two throwing axes or hammers. While they were all resolute fighters, their squad leaders were extra tough; the three platoon leaders answered to Ordin and Dorin, the joint commanders of the dwarf company. The platoon leaders, while not commissioned officers, were the toughest of the lot. The brothers gave the company a heavy knock-down punch, with Ordin's powerful hammer of thunder and lightning and Dorin's pure mithril bladed axe which is capable cleaving through almost anything like Mkel's sword.

"Excellent, Ordin; Dekeen, what say the elves?" Mkel asked his elvish counterpart.

"All four platoons of elves are ready and will meet the garrison on the field. As always, you can depend on us, and the infantry platoon is prepared for the reserve mission," the elf clan leader added.

Elves were very mobile, being able to run faster and farther than humans. This made them very suited as a mobile reserve, for they were also very deft and sure of foot, as well as being able to see and hear better than humans. Elves could cover almost as much ground as a cavalry unit.

The archer platoons of the elves could muster five times the firepower and had a longer range than any other race could hope to produce. Just this company of elven archers could route a battalion. The archers wore either elven chain mail or studded leather reinforced with elven mail; they had long swords as a backup. The heavy infantry had elven chain mail with banded armor, or occasionally light plate armor. They wielded either long swords and large dark elm wood shields or double-bladed spears. The elves that mastered those weapons were extremely dangerous in close battle. It was akin to walking into a round saw. An elven fighter of high experience led this platoon and personally wielded his mithril-edged double-bladed spear. Dekeen was the overall commander of the elven contingent.

"Pekram, are you and your platoon leaders ready?" Mkel said to his senior sergeant of the infantry garrison company.

"No problem, sir, the company is ready. We have two soldiers out, one for a family issue and the other with a fever. Otherwise, the men are ready," he replied in his usual confident but slightly insolent manner.

"Lieutenants, do you concur?" Mkel asked the infantry platoon leaders.

"Yes sir," they all echoed. Even though the three platoon leaders were officers, Pekram was still in charge of the company after Mkel. He was a company senior sergeant and also a fanatical fighter in a melee. The three platoons of over forty men apiece were further divided into three twelve-man squads, consisting of eight infantrymen armed with long spears, large metal or elven elm wood shields, long swords, and daggers. They were issued standard banded or scale armor. The other four men were the range or missile soldiers, armed with long composite bows or heavy crossbows with at least thirty arrows or sixty bolts, backup long swords, and small bucklers; they wore scale armor with chain mail or banded armor.

All the company's weapons and armor were masterwork or better, with an arms and armor smith shops in Draden to support this as well as a similar shop in the Weir itself. The squad leaders were either fighters or senior ranged weapon soldiers of greater experience and usually possessed some sort of magical weaponry. In a usual operation, the range weapon men fired at enemy formations as soon as they crossed the three-hundred-yard mark. The heavy infantry formed an armored buttress with their long spears and heavy shields, until the spears were broken, then they fought with their swords, with the range weapon men and squad leaders filling in with their long swords after they were out of arrows or bolts to plug in gaps in the line. They also had two canisters of dragon's fire, which when thrown, burst into flames in a five-yard radius. This could devastate the front ranks of an enemy line.

The platoon leaders were well-trained commissioned officers, aided by the platoon's senior sergeant. Both had fairly powerful magic or mithril alloy weapons of some sort. Several battle healers were assigned to each platoon, making it approximately forty men strong. While Pekram basically commanded the company, Toderan and Mkel were the overall commander and senior sergeant of the entire garrison.

"Lieutenant Wheelor, how say you of the land dragons?" Mkel asked the tall, lanky officer.

"All four of our dragons are up and ready, as are their crews," Wheelor replied in his strong mountain accent. The land dragon platoon consisted of four dragons, two mated pairs, and their crews made a formidable force in their own right. Land dragons were just slightly smaller than white dragons but just as strong, averaging fifty feet long and resembling a wingless cross between a gold and a bronze dragon. They were of average intelligence, and while unable to blood bond with humans, they grew very attached to their crews. They could speak crude Draconic and breathe a line of fire out to one hundred yards. They had very powerful claws and a strong bite capable of rendering giants and comparable-sized creatures. Their crews, mounted on armored platforms on their backs, fired a ballista to a decimating eight-hundred-yard range (ballistae were either tipped masterwork blades capable of taking out an ogre or manticore on a successful hit or blades topped with a grenade of dragon's fire that burst in a fifteen-yard-sized area). This would do double the damage to a single creature if struck. The land dragons were used as a spearhead or breaking force in an all-out land battle or to face larger opponents the infantry encountered such as giants, which they had an intense hatred of. Giants, on the other hand, had a great fear of land dragons and often retreated at the sight of them.

While they did not possess wings, they moved as fast as horses and could jump short distances. Their hides possessed the same magical resistance as their true dragon cousins, capable of taking several spells or magical damage as well as being tough to penetrate with a sword or spear. The magic shields they generated were weak by comparison to those of metallic dragons but still capable of taking several spells.

In battle, the land dragons could break most enemy formations and were employed to protect the infantry. Land dragons always worked in pairs to give themselves mutual support, especially if facing a chromatic dragon. They coordinated and cooperated very effectively together as teams. Lieutenant Wheelor very masterfully maneuvered them in combat and split them into two dragon pair sections for more flexibility if the situation dictates. While Mkel was a dragonrider and infantryman at heart, he had a great fondness for the land dragon units. The crews had a certain laid-back attitude about them, but they went out of their way to protect the infantry. In land battles, they were hard to match and were the mainstay of the Alliance Army.

"Excellent, Lieutenant Wheelor; Lenor, how about the cavalry?" Mkel asked his senior paladin sergeant.

"We are looking pretty good. We will be four paladins short, though, for we are running two patrols on each side of the break in the Gray Mountains," the wiry, toughened paladin replied.

"Good, my old friend, you'll just have to tighten up your formation. I will give you the signal as to which side you will counterattack from, so keep your seeing crystal handy. Remember during the exercise today that you'll be the ones who will either back up the land dragons against the giants, ogres, and trolls or carve through an enemy cavalry charge, which will likely be mounted on dire wolves or hell hounds," Mkel directed.

"No problem, my boys are ready for a fight," Lenor replied.

The heavy cavalry platoon consisted of thirty-six paladins of various levels of experience, all mounted on special heavy warhorses or paladin's mounts. This constituted the Weir's high mobility ground counterattack force. The paladins all had half plate or full plate armor and large shields. They were armed with long or bastard swords and heavy lances. Most had some type of magical weaponry or armor, with the rest being of masterwork, and half had heavy crossbows. Lenor commanded the platoon, leading with the power of his holy sword. The heavy cavalry platoon usually countered enemy cavalry or Morgathian crimson guards on mounts. They could also keep giants at bay as well.

"Lieutenant Willaward, how is your catapult sections?" Mkel asked.

"All up sir, all four engines ready to go," the catapult leader replied.

"Remember, you fire first after the rangers. You'll need to be accurate, for depending on how long it will take Gallanth and I to take care of the chromatic dragons and how long it will take the Draden regiment to reinforce us, this will be a critical time.

The more you you rain fire and rock, the more of our soldiers will live," Mkel soberly reminded him.

"We will be on target as always," the tall lieutenant replied.

"I have faith," Mkel said with a smile, always impressed by the catapult section's confidence. "Clydown, your sappers will be called out to set up hasty defensive earthworks and obstacles if necessary. I know you all are up to it."

"No problem sir, our men are always motivated to shape the battlefield for our victory," the engineer and sapper lieutenant replied.

The thirty-man sapper section was expert in defensive and offensive earthworks and siege operations. They oversaw the Weir's defensive emplacements and traveled with the garrison to provide them temporary defensive structures such as earthen walls, trenches, traps, pits, and the building of siege towers, rams and various other siege techniques. The sappers were armed with picks, war hammers, field spades, short swords, and weapons that doubled as their tools for building and digging or the destruction of structures. Clydown was the sapper expert and leader of this section. Clydown himself was armed with a lesser mithril alloy short sword and similar banded armor along with a staff powered by a garnet dragonstone given to him by the copper dragon Selenth. This enabled him to move large volumes of earth and rock and could detect desired minerals or metals when directed.

"Lupek, what's your plan for the rangers today?" Mkel asked, although he already knew the answer.

"Deless and I will split sections, with half of us doing aerial sweeps and the other half performing diving runs on the targets. Deless will lead the first flight to simulate us intercepting any aerial threats, for he is more accurate than I am," the ranger leader commented with a slight smile.

"That is an understatement, my friend," Mkel chimed in, bringing a slight chuckle, for it was well known that Lupek was a very dangerous foe in close combat, being able to effectively fight with two weapons simultaneously. He was also accurate with throwing weapons, especially daggers and his lightning javelin, but he left much to be desired as far as employing a bow or crossbow.

"The diving units will exhaust their dragon's fire grenades and then switch to aerial sweeps, while Deless's section will move to diving attacks until all grenades have been utilized. Hopefully, we will have the aerial combat under control between our griffons and you and Gallanth, and then we'll fully concentrate on diving attacks, inflicting as much damage as we can," he concluded.

"Just a reminder to all to remember the signal from the ranger's griffons as they perform a dive to check your arrow fire," Mkel added. "I want no griffon hit with a friendly arrow, for it will bleed just as much from ours as an orc arrow, and I like our griffons very much," he added with a smile, which even got a return grin from Deless, who was usually a very somber individual (even for an elf).

"Colonel Dunn, sir, your focus?" he asked the support corps leader.

"No change from the last briefing," he said. "We will form just over the bridge and have Silvanth teleport the caravan to the far side the Weir and then back again behind the catapults. We will have all of our wagons, for if we are to fight this unholy gathering of evil, we will need to push as much support forward as possible."

The supply caravan was an unwieldy, long train of wagons. They had four armament wagons with caches of arrows and bolts, extra swords, spears, and the like. Four more wagons contained foodstuffs to be able to supply the garrison and its animals for a week and provisions for the dwarves and elves as well. Everything was kept cold by two ice container wagons, with many cooling crystals inside the insulated boxes on top of the wagons. Several other wagons were packed with spare clothing and parts for saddles and so on. Four more wagons were utilized to support the catapults, with ammunition, ropes, and any other necessary parts. Several other wagons were solely dedicated to care for and transport the wounded with assigned healer sections and supplies. These wagons could carry four to eight wounded if necessary. There were also three more spare wagons for any purpose needed or just for replacements.

Colonel Dunn masterfully oversaw the smooth logistical operations of the garrison. Silvanth combined with Watterseth, with Beckann occasionally, provide the heavy protection for this group; a silver dragon of her size and a very high level cleric were a force none too easy to dismiss.

"Silvanth will meet us on the grounds, Gallanth?" Colonel Dunn asked the gold dragon directly.

"Yes, I will make sure of it, my good colonel," Gallanth replied.

"I know you are the only one she listens to, Master Dragon," Colonel Dunn added.

"That is not always accurate, for she shares her mood swings with my rider's mate," Gallanth jokingly replied; everyone present burst out laughing, for even though dragons do have a sense of humor, people were often surprised when they exhibited this trait.

"Toderan, any comments?" Mkel asked.

"I don't think I could top that statement," he said, looking to Gallanth and smiling (rare for him), "but a reminder to all your sergeants and senior fighters to take note of the performance of your new soldiers. This could be the last garrison and regimental exercise we will likely conduct before we face this threat from the southeast. So make sure everyone learns as much as possible and record it in the platoon journals, for it will save lives later," he concluded in his normally somber but commanding voice.

"A good point; I do not want any unnecessary casualties, for when this comes down for real, our soldiers are all we have. Myself, Gallanth, Jodem, and Senior Sergeant Toderan will do all that is possible to provide cover and protection to all of our soldiers, but you must be prepared to fight on your own, just in case. All right, if there are no questions, Gallanth and I will see you on the grounds in one hour. Fall out," Mkel finished as he stood up and saluted. Everyone present stood up and returned the salute to the dragon and rider pair and shouted, "Never a step back!" (the Weir motto).

All the leaders began to leave, with the exception of Toderan and Jodem. "Mkel, I will be observing from the air today after I unleash a spell or two in front of the garrison line, to make sure the coordination between myself, Dekeen, and Declark goes smoothly. I would be doing the same when we do this for real if what the rangers say is true, that they spotted at least two Morgathian Talon sorcerers. I could have my hands full," Jodem commented with a concerned tone.

"I will also be airborne on Alvanch to critique the formation's coordination and to help oversee it. I don't want any mistakes if they can be avoided," Toderan added.

"No problem," Mkel said with a smile. "Between you two, and Gallanth and I, we should get a good picture of what goes on today, just coordinate with Pekram. Gentleman, have faith."

"We both do," they collectively answered.

"Gallanth, are you ready?" Mkel asked his dragon friend.

"Yes; we should go see Silvanth now to make sure she is ready, then we will get in the air," the gold dragon said.

Everyone then walked out of the council room and went their separate directions. Gallanth and Mkel walked over to Silvanth's ground-level sleeping niche at the back base of the interior Weir grounds.

After a brief conversation with Silvanth and Annan, an agreement was reached on their scheme of maneuver for the exercise. Gallanth and Mkel quickly hopped back up to the ledge to finish loading his flying rig. Mkel heard the excited cries of the rangers' griffons and the shuffling of the paladins' horses as well as the roars of the four land dragons.

They are all getting ready, my friend, Gallanth confirmed his thought. "All right then, Gallanth, let's get airborne," he replied as he stepped up onto his dragon's forearm and was lifted up to the main securing strap and climbed to his saddle. He secured the straps and shouted to his dragon he was ready.

Gallanth leaped from the ledge while giving a low intensity roar to signal any creature in the air to immediately go to ground. The whole Weir fell silent for a few seconds as the gold dragon's roar echoed against the thick stone walls of the Weir interior. A cheer erupted from the ground as Gallanth glided toward the one-hundred-fifty-yard-wide entrance. He flew out of the Weir and into the morning sunlight of the late summer day, over the large stone bridge that crossed the Severic River and out over the plain beyond.

With a few flaps of his massive wings, which seemed to make the very air shudder, he rapidly gained altitude. They circled over the field and looked down at the large array of wooden silhouette targets that were set up to simulate the enemy formation. "If it were only as easy to knock off the orcs and giants as these wooden sculptures," Mkel said to his dragon. *No, not as easy, but I have faith that the end result will be the same for both,* Gallanth replied in his usual confident manner.

By this time, the rangers had mounted on their griffons and were starting to stream out of the Weir and began to maneuver into their formations. The cavalry platoon began to trot to the bridge, with the land dragons behind them. The dwarves and the garrison company were next in line. Gallanth pointed down and back winged to a landing on the grass field in front of the bridge. He folded his wings and stood like a statue, waiting for the combined garrison to form.

The thirty-two griffons were now landing by Gallanth, and their ranger riders dismounted and began final checks on their gear and weapons. The griffons on patrol would be missed for the exercise, but Lupek would compensate. *Griffons are magnificent creatures,* Mkel thought to himself: *fierce, loyal and powerful.* They were the second most feared flying creature after dragons, because of their strength, mobility, and intelligence, along with their keen senses and intense fierceness in battle. The golden brown and or white feathers and fur of the half eagle, half lion mounts were just slightly ruffled by the morning breeze. Their alert and intimidating stares caused all who approached them to take caution. While not dangerous to anyone not posing a threat, they were still not overly tolerant.

The rest of the combined company team was now moving over the bridge. The paladin cavalry platoon was across and approaching Gallanth in their tight formation, with the land dragons close behind them. The dwarves were the slowest on the march, just because of their short legs, but they were tenacious and an asset in a battle line. The Weir's infantry company was right behind them, with the catapult section bringing up the rear with the sappers moving with them.

A horn sounded from the edge of Draden Forest, which signaled the elves were on their way. The first thing they would do would be to pack shoulder to shoulder, in a tight formation, next to (and even underneath) Gallanth, to allow him to perform a mass teleport. As long as an individual or creature was within the circle created from the tip of the gold dragon's nose to the ends of his outstretched wings to the point of his tail, he could teleport them anywhere. This was a feat the gold dragons perfected, followed by the silvers. The other dragon races had yet to master this skill. The whole garrison could fit in that circle, but it was a drill that was practiced for exercises like this. Putting all this combat power anywhere on the battlefield, along with the seven Weir council leaders, was a small but extremely powerful force that could enter with surprise, do tremendous damage, and then be gone in an instant. This made the Keystone Weir garrison a feared force among all foes.

As soon as all were across the bridge, they began to assemble in their assigned positions under and around Gallanth. Even though this was a well-rehearsed exercise, it still took several minutes, mainly because of the catapult wagons, for they were only so maneuverable. Mkel knew that this problem was being worked on at Draconia; he was curious to see what they came up with when he visited there in a couple of weeks.

The dwarves moved into a tight rectangular formation under Gallanth's head and neck, with the infantry company split on either side of them. The rangers and their griffons formed under his wings, with the land dragons in pairs behind them. The cavalry also split and formed tightly behind and amongst the land dragons, by Gallanth's back legs. They had to be kept separated from the griffons in case the large avian creatures got hungry. The catapults formed along his tail, and the elven company stood under his belly. The land dragons, being no small creatures themselves at around fifty feet long, were still just over a third the length of the mighty gold dragon.

Mkel spoke into his seeing crystal: "All sections report." The palm-sized, smooth-faced quartz crystal stones were chosen to have a small amount of dragon blood added to them so they could be permanently empowered to transmit images and sounds as if looking into a mirror. The crystals were a very effective means of communication, especially during battle.

Ordin checked in first that he was in place, Pekram was next, followed by Wheelor, Lenor, Dekeen, and Willaward. Toderan and Jodem landed just in front of the dwarves at the last minute and waved to Mkel and Gallanth to go. With that, Gallanth outstretched his massive golden wings, which extended to his full seventy-five-yard wingspan, and he let out a medium-intensity roar to ready all for teleport. His eyes flashed gold and the brilliant streaks of blue light formed in an almost vortex-like tunnel surrounding the compact group. They then disappeared from the grass field only to emerge in the field to the west of the Weir just outside of the border of Draden Forest.

Next, Gallanth quickly enchanted the garrison's weapons and armor. His eyes glowed in a yellowish hue and soft sunburst beams emanated from them, which he swept through the forces gathered all around and underneath him. This action, which the soldiers called "powering up," gave all those who didn't have dragonstone weapons extra damage ability against evil creatures and temporarily strengthened their armor. Soldiers could feel their spears, swords, bows, crossbows, and armor tingle with a warm vibration for a few seconds. This extra power, which lasted all day, sometimes provided the edge that meant the difference between life and death in battle.

Once this was complete, Gallanth raised his head again and prepared to teleport everyone back to the grass field. Before they jumped from the field, Mkel saw the crowds gathering from the town to watch the exercise, and he noticed the Draden regiment marching up to the bridge through the eyes of the Weir dragon head stone carving or sentinel that guarded the entrance to the Weir. The dragonstones placed in the eyes of the sculpture actually gave it limited intelligence, for it controlled the airflow and internal temperature of the Weir as well as being able to defend the mountain in case of invasion. Gallanth could communicate to the sentinel to which Mkel could see what it saw through his dragon's mind.

"All right, gentlemen, we teleport back and immediately go into our assault formations. Are we clear?" he shouted as loud as he could. The combined return cheer of several hundred men, elves, and dwarves told him what he wanted to know. Mkel quickly signaled to Colonel Wierangan with his crystal that they would be there in a few seconds. "Gallanth, shall we?" he said to his dragon. *We shall*, he replied, and with a roar, they entered into teleport and disappeared.

They emerged at the exact place they left from but oriented away from the Weir toward the target field. Gallanth gave a ground-shaking roar, which he would do in battle if immediately facing an enemy to unnerve them. This was also an effective crowd pleaser, for the observers from the town had gathered on the opposite shore of the Severic River in front of the Weir.

The garrison started to deploy into their primary line formation immediately after Toderan took to the air. The dwarves formed the center of the line with a forty-dwarf front, three deep. The infantry company split two platoons on the right side and on the left of the dwarves, effectually doubling the width of the line. The griffons leapt into the air as soon as Gallanth folded his wings, and the land dragons moved to their positions behind the infantry platoons. When the dwarves and infantry were locked shoulder to shoulder, Mkel ordered them to move out. As they started marching, the elves moved into their firing formations behind the dwarves. The paladins spread out their cavalry behind the elves, waiting for Mkel's signal as to which flank they would attack from as well as the overall attack order.

The catapults started preparing to fire as soon as Gallanth leaped into the air with a flap of his huge wings. He soared up over the front line and immediately turned and flew over the river and the town of Draden. The people of the town cheered as he passed over them and then circled back to the practice field. Lieutenant Willaward's crews worked fast; they launched the first volley of solid clay shot, which simulated their stone projectiles, but burst in a cloud of dust on impact for easier marking. The four thirty-pound projectiles sailed over the ground troops high into the air along their ballistic arch, landing in the midst of the standing targets in a thundering impact. Jodem sent an advanced seeing-eye globe over to the crowds, and it began to project an image above the river of the catapults firing and the impacts on the target field.

The crews immediately began to prep the engines to fire again. Their efficiency enabled them to launch one to two shots every minute for an excellent rate of fire. This took the form of cranking up the counterweight while winding the dragon sinew ropes and loading the projectile from the ready rack. They could fire solid stones weighing from thirty to sixty pounds or greater, depending on range restrictions or desired effect. A type of frangible projectile was also used that was constructed with fractures and had spikes running all through its cement structure; when it hit solid ground, it burst, sending the spikes flying in all directions, to the detriment of those affected. Additionally, a giant that tried to catch this type of ammunition would be killed instantly instead of the normal return throw that they were famous for.

Still a third and perhaps most lethal of their projectiles were canisters filled with dragon's fire formula, which burst upon impact, affecting a thirty- to thirty-five-yard area. This inflicted tremendous casualties to tightly packed enemy assault lines. The first volley landed sixteen hundred yards from the river, where the catapults were currently placed. This was a good distance, but they were well within their maximum range of over two thousand yards. The second volley soon was screaming toward the targets. The garrison was still moving at an even pace toward the field, and the ballista crews on top of the land dragons were readying their weapons. They would begin to fire at roughly the thousand-yard mark, which at that range they could hit a giant-sized figure or a densely packed group of infantry or cavalry with their dragon sinew ballistae. They fired either masterwork spear-tipped projectiles that would fell an ogre with one hit or a spear with a small aerodynamically formed canister of dragon's fire that would hit and explode in a fifteen-yard burst.

Silvanth then flew out of the Weir and down flapped her wings rapidly to get up to join Gallanth. Mkel could see that Annan was mounted on the silver dragon's back, for her long gold-streaked brown hair was blowing from underneath her riding helmet. He liked it when his wife joined them in these exercises. *Good morning, my mate,* Mkel heard Gallanth telepathically call to the silver dragon.

Yes my dear, now where would you like me to attack from? she asked, always being direct. Silver dragons were sometimes arrogant but always had good intentions and motives. The female metallic dragons also tended to exhibit a sense of aloofness, but they were always dependable and no less intelligent than their male counterparts. They were usually tasked with defending the support corps supply trains along with teleporting these assets and moving supplies to and from various areas. They also backed up the male metallic dragons in all attacks and in the defense of the ground forces.

Attack from the south against the right flank of the infantry and the dwarves, and please my dear, be nice, Gallanth added. Silvanth looked at him, and with a slight friendly growl, she peeled off and headed south. Her silver toned ventral scales and hide looked brilliant in the warm morning sunlight. Silver dragons had a subtle, more streamlined appearance than most other dragons. Their smooth armored hides had a resistance to cold-based weapons and immunity to acid, as well as an electrical resistance (gold dragons shared in the acid resistance but not the immunity). It was very strong in terms of protection from any form of weapon as well.

Mkel spoke into his seeing crystal. "Good morning, my love, you look radiant on the back of your dragon." Annan looked over her shoulder at her husband, gave him a scowl, and then smiled as Silvanth broke from away from Gallanth.

"Spare me your attempts, my dear; I will need help with your son tonight," she replied.

"Yes, my love, he will join us at the banquet; we will talk later," he told her as Silvanth turned around and started her diving attack.

Silvanth let loose a roar to signal her attack and to simulate a diving chromatic dragon. Her roar, while slightly higher pitched than Gallanth's, was still no less fearsome. Female dragons, chromatic and metallic types, were usually just slightly smaller than their male counterparts. This was not true of the damage inflicted by their breath weapons, or their spells, all of which had the same strength. Overall, though, they were basically as powerful as their male counterparts. The metallic dragons delineated their roles, with the males doing most of the forward fighting and the females serving as transportation and protection for the support corps, as well as teleporting forces to and from the battlefield. They also gave a follow-on punch when necessary. Both saw their fair share of battle, so the female metallic dragons were not being protected or sheltered. They would not allow this to happen anyway.

The chromatic female dragons were just as vicious, voracious, greedy, and evil as their male counterparts. In any event, among dragons there was no quarter given for gender of either side. Gallanth's actual mate was killed in the Great War, as was Silvanth's. Dragons mated mostly for procreation but still mourned the loss of a partner. Only gold and silver dragons could successfully mate outside their own species, while all other types had to partner with their own kind. The offspring between a silver and a gold came out pure; half breeds were never known to have hatched.

As Silvanth swept down on the garrison, Mkel and Gallanth watched their reaction. The calls went out, "Dragon attack, three o'clock," which prompted the front line infantry to half face the direction of attack and raise their shields, as did the dwarves, all in unison. The archer troops raised their bows and crossbows, as did the three platoons of elven archers, fired one volley at the incoming silver dragon, and then quickly moved in behind the infantry's raised shields, going into their defensive posture to hide any exposed skin. All arrows and bolts were blunt tipped in case any got through Silvanth's magic shield, but they all bounced off the invisible barrier by the dozens. She unleashed the blue icy ray of her breath weapon that would have normally frozen anything instantly upon contact, but it was only set to frost for this exercise.

Those that didn't react fast enough or correctly could tell it right away, with a light coat of frost on those exposed areas. The land dragons would normally let loose their line of fire breath weapon at a charging or diving dragon but refrained. Their ballista crews mounted on their backs would fire and help drive the dragon away.

Silvanth frosted the entire front line in her pass. *Their aim is good, I count well over half would have hit her,* Gallanth commented. "That would have likely brought down a white or a black dragon, don't you think?" Mkel responded. *Possibly, it would have definitely driven one off with their true aim. Let us just pray we can make this situation never happen in battle and keep the chromatics away from our soldiers,* Gallanth emphasized. "If anyone can, it would be you, my large friend," Mkel complimented his dragon partner.

Your crossbow is definitely a compliment. We need to get better knowledge on the number of dragons the giants might have. I can feel at least two reds and two or three blues. I don't know how many green and black dragons, and I don't think we have to worry about whites. The fire giants like it too hot for them, Gallanth finished. "You're right, Gallanth," he replied. "We'll have to talk to Lupek and Deless to see how close they can get."

The catapult practice clay stones were striking in the midst of the wooden propped-up targets, as evidenced by the clouds of dust raised by their impacts. The battalion was rapidly approaching the one-thousand-yard mark from the target line as the first round of ballista spears were fired from the land dragon turret weapons. The spear-sized projectiles sailed quickly through the air in their arc toward the targets. The first one struck with a flash of visible fire. The catapults displaced forward and switched to their canisters of dragon's fire ammunition, and larger plumes of fire were seen billowing from the target array. They were on their mark, as usual.

Mkel and Lupek called to Lieutenant Willaward with their seeing crystal to tell him to stop their firing to allow the rangers to perform a strafing run. The ballista fire from the land dragon crews could still fire, for their ballistic arc was not as great as the catapults. He then signaled to Lupek to have his rangers begin their diving attacks.

The rangers began to move into their usual V formation. As soon as Lupek and Deless formed their squadrons together, they oriented on the target field. Lupek's wing dove almost straight down, and as they pulled up, barely fifty feet from the ground, they threw the dragon's fire grenades, which landed in the middle of the targets; all twelve grenades ignited within seconds of each other, to the cheers of the infantry several hundred meters away. Deless's squadron then performed their diving attack from a different direction, to confuse enemy archers. Pekram let the company cheer once and then returned to their focused silence. This unnerved the enemy and instilled discipline.

Lupek swung his wing around and dove on the targets again, but this time they employed their bows and let loose a volley of arrows just before the point where the griffons had to pull up from their dives. Deless's wing performed the same maneuver with an added bolt of lightning from the elf ranger's bow; he always transferred his spell energy into his arrows. The rangers were very accurate with their aerial fire, with the human rangers able to hit a man-sized target six out of ten times and the elven rangers nine out of ten.

The front line of the battalion was now getting within archer range, so Mkel signaled to Lupek and Deless to clear the air above the target area. The griffons broke their formations into their wingman pairs and flapped their golden brown feathered wings to gain altitude. Upon seeing this, Dekeen nocked an arrow and raised his bow. The ruby dragonstone mounted beneath the hand grip glowed, surging with power, and flashed as energy was transferred into the drawn arrow. He let it loose, upon which the white fletched arrow streaked in its low ballistic arch with unnatural speed over five hundred yards toward the center of the target field. It struck one of the giant wooden frames with a brilliant white flash of light, as the explosion of energy sent a dust plume and wooden splinters into the air. He quickly let loose four more arrows toward the field, which all in turn flashed in their mini explosions.

By this time, the infantry line was almost at the three-hundred-yard distance from the targets. Dekeen shouted in elvish to prepare to fire; all three platoons of his elven archers raised their bows, as did the human crossbowmen. He yelled to fire as over one hundred twenty elven arrows streaked toward their targets. Elves had superior eyesight and were an excellent judge of distance. At three hundred yards, they had at least a three out of four chance of hitting a man-sized target. The infantry crossbowmen fired as well. There were sixty missile soldiers in the Weir infantry company, of which well over half were crossbowmen and the rest archers, equipped with long composite bows. The crossbows had a longer range and utilized graduated sights that adjusted for distance in quarrel drop out to three hundred yards. The crossbowmen overall had a longer range and were more accurate but could not fire as fast as the longbow men.

A hail of arrows and bolts streamed from the elves and men as they approached the target line. As the battalion reached the two-hundred-yard mark, the human archers started to fire. They continued to fire their practice arrows until they were within thirty-five yards. By this time, the targets looked like pin cushions. The elves could fire twenty arrows in a minute sustained, while the human archers could put ten to twelve well-aimed arrows out in that time, while the crossbowmen were able to fire five bolts: an overall devastating firepower that could be brought to bear against an enemy army. Mkel was interested in the new crossbows that he was told were being developed at the Capital; he would get to see them during his upcoming visit to Draconia. His archers would be the first to get them.

The dwarves now brandished their throwing axes and hammers and all threw at least one. Driving into the dwarves was like attacking a spiked armadillo. Ordin, in the center of the dwarf line, raised his glowing solid mithril war hammer and hurled it, spinning, toward a larger wooden target. The hammer was pulsating from its dragonstone and hissing with energy. The hammer struck the wooden platform with a loud clap of thunder, pulverizing it and sending wood splinters flying in all directions. The dwarf line then threw a volley of their hand weapons in unison, which struck the first row of targets, and then they threw a second volley. This would decimate an onrushing line of orcs or infantry. They then drew their main weapons and tightened their formation in preparation for what would be an assault if they faced a real enemy.

The infantry company's battle line on either side of the dwarves readied their long spears and raised their shields. The third rank fired one last volley at close range at the targets. The first two ranks of heavy infantry would bear the brunt of an enemy infantry attack, skewering the first rank of attackers and fighting with their spears until they broke. They then drew their long swords and fought shoulder to shoulder with locked shields, thrusting or slicing the enemy ranks. The archers then took shots of opportunity with their bows and crossbows and drew their swords and backed up the heavy infantry. Both the dwarves and the Weir infantry proudly adorned their shields with the head of a gold dragon in the middle of a red keystone, symbolizing their allegiance to, pride in, and appreciation of Gallanth and Draden Weir.

Mkel signaled to Pekram to have the right flank of the infantry line fold between the first and second platoon to simulate a break in the line. Pekram shouted to lieutenants Akiser and Paloud to split their platoons. Mkel then called Dekeen through his crystal to send his elven infantry platoon to fill the gap. Dekeen turned and looked over to his senior fighter and yelled in elvish to follow him. They immediately started to run in unison and quickly filled the gap between the two parted garrison infantry platoons.

The elven fighters were alternately armed with either a long sword and shield or a double-bladed pole arm, which they swung so fast and gracefully that the naked eye could almost not follow it. Elves were not as physically strong as men but were faster and had greater dexterity. They mad poor wrestlers but were deadly with a sword or blade.

At this point in time, the infantry columns were now passing through the targets, so Mkel called Lenor to make his cavalry charge to the left of the front line. Lenor answered into his crystal and drew his holy sword. The paladin platoon raised their lances and spurred their heavy mounts forward. All thirty-four mounted heavy horses charged in two loose V formations past the infantry; Lenor was at the apex of the charge, with his powerful sword pointed to the simulated enemy.

"The formations look good," Toderan said to Mkel through his crystal.

"Yes, it seems very well coordinated," Jodem echoed from his eagle mount as all three circled above the ground formation.

"All we have to do is keep the chromatics and any Talon sorcerers off of them so they can concentrate on the orcs and enemy infantry," Mkel replied to his two friends.

Jodem then waved his staff and thrust it forward, aiming it like a crossbow, and six fiery spheres of his meteor swarm spell rapidly fired out of the dragonstone and screamed toward the earth. All struck in a line about one hundred fifty yards in front of the charging cavalry, detonating in horrendous explosions. This signaled for the paladins to stop their charge and was also a morale booster for the garrison.

"I get your point, my teacher; Gallanth, let's give the rest of the Draden legion something to walk through," he replied.

"It will be a pleasure," the gold dragon replied. Mkel called to Colonel Wierangan that the Weir's attack had culminated and to bring the rest of the legion up to move against their set of targets located another five hundred yards beyond the array where his men now stood.

With that, Gallanth wheeled around and let loose a commanding battle roar as he dove toward the ground. Mkel cocked and loaded his crossbow with an exploding-tipped bolt clip and took aim at a selected target on the ground. A sunbeam burst emanating from Gallanth's now glowing eyes sent two yellowish golden beams down to a target on the grass field, exploding with a tremendous force. Mkel put the crosshairs of his bow sight on the ground next to Gallanth's strike and fired. His bolt darted toward the earth with blinding speed and exploded with an even greater force than Dekeen's arrows commanded. Gallanth then opened his huge jaws, and a glow from within his throat emerged into a ball of brilliant yellowish orange plasma fire. He expelled it out and it then screamed toward the targeted area with the same speed as Mkel's arrow, exploding with incredible power and leaving a crater over forty yards in diameter and ten feet deep at the center.

The men cheered as they stood among the arrow- and axe-riddled targets, and the land dragons breathed jets of flame as Gallanth roared again when he pulled up from his diving attack. This also signaled to the legion's leaders to initiate their movement. Colonel Wierangan called to his catapults and trebuchets to begin to fire, as they were now arrayed only five hundred yards behind the Weir garrison. He then signaled to his hippogriff battalion to take to the air and begin their strafing runs and simulated aerial combat with any enemy aerial forces.

"Now we get to watch the show," Sergeant Tarbellan said to one of his soldiers.

"Yes Sergeant, but I'm sure glad that big dragon is on our side," the young soldier replied as he looked up at Gallanth soaring overhead past them.

"Between Gallanth and Captain Mkel, they have a great deal of power, and it is usually used very wisely. Even though he's an officer, he and his dragon go out of their way to help and protect the company. You'll see that if we have to fight the giants," Tarbellan informed the young soldier, who had not yet been through an engagement.

Gallanth circled around and flew back toward the garrison as the legion's catapult stones were streaming through the air. The sky suddenly became crowded, as hundreds of hippogriffs and several griffons were making their way toward their targets. They passed to Gallanth's left, giving him a wide berth, for they would not fare well ramming into a gold dragon in midair. After they all passed, the immense dragon performed a wing-over-tail maneuver almost over top of the burgeoning lines of the legion formed below.

Gallanth always warned Mkel about this maneuver, in which the forty-five-yard-long dragon almost turned within his own body length. The snap of the maneuver could easily break several of Mkel's bones or his back if he was not ready for it. Mkel locked his crossbow into place and bent down and hugged the security straps on Gallanth's neck to spread out the force of the action. The dragonstones on Mkel's weapons' shields also aided him in protecting from the force of Gallanth's flip. The maneuver took less than a second but was very intense. Gallanth nosed down and curled over as he whipped his tail over and then, with blinding speed, straightened himself out, making the 180 degree turn within his own body length. He then gave a forceful down stroke to gain speed and lift and let out a tremendous roar to get the legion's troops in the battle mind-set. They were also grateful for having him as their ally.

"Captain Mkel, is Silvanth still in the air?" Colonel Wierangan's voice and image came out of the crystal.

"Yes sir, I will have Gallanth call her over," he answered.

Silvanth replied immediately as she swung her sunlit shimmering, silvery body around and glided toward the legion infantry columns. Cries of "Dragon, nine o'clock" echoed throughout the legion formations as they quickly adjusted their shields and assumed a defensive posture. The hundreds of legion archers and crossbowmen quickly took aim and began to fire at the diving silver dragon.

Literally hundreds of arrows struck Silvanth's shield as she breathed a cone of frosty mist onto the legion soldiers. Mkel watched the practice dive run on the regiment through the magnified sight of his crossbow. They reacted well to the attack, although a couple of frosted faces and arms indicated that some were not as quick as they would have liked.

Now the rest of exercise is in the legion's court, Mkel thought to himself. He could now just watch as Colonel Wierangan, Captain Peasem, and Captain Curram worked to keep the regiment formation and coordination running smoothly. So far, they were doing well. Their eighteen catapults were now pounding the target area. The company of land dragons also began to fire their ballistae, and the archers and crossbowmen were readying to fire.

"Keystone Weir, turn right and move to get out of the regiment's way!" Mkel ordered his subordinate leaders through his crystal. The leaders shouted out orders, and the whole garrison, including the land dragons, performed a right face and began to walk out of the way of the approaching regiment's line. They likely did not mind, as there was a great deal of deadly projectiles going over their heads. As the regiment's main force passed the garrison, they yelled out to wish them good luck. The catapults took the longest time to reposition as a result of the weight and size of the wagons that held their siege machines. *This would soon be corrected,* Mkel thought hopefully.

Gallanth flew down and back winged about one hundred yards from the garrison to avoid spraying them with dust and debris from his huge wings, just as Silvanth teleported the support corps train behind him. Gallanth walked to the garrison as the catapult section was arriving. "Excellent job," Mkel shouted from Gallanth's neck twenty-five feet above the ground.

"Yes, excellent job to you all," Gallanth echoed in his deep, commanding voice.

"The first round is on the Weir!" Mkel yelled as a loud response came back from the men and dwarves in particular. "All right gentlemen, I will see you back at the Weir. You're dismissed except for senior leadership and the ones designated to be wounded for the healers to practice their art. I will need the after action report from the leaders by evening," he explained.

Mkel wanted to give them as much leeway as possible with his and Jodem's trip to Battle Point in a couple of days. The battle with the giants and their allies could happen at any time, but he felt confident that they would fare well. However, he did not want to underestimate the enemy either. The garrison and regiment overall had a great deal of strength between Gallanth, the key leaders, and his men, dwarves, and elves, as well as the substantial combat power of the regiment. Together, the Weir garrison and the Draden regiment formed the Keystone Legion, or Strike Legion, as it was known. This combined force was roughly the size of a traditional legion, but much more powerful.

As the garrison started to make its way to the bridge to get to the Weir, Gallanth began to walk toward the regiment. They were getting within archer range, for the catapults were firing their last volley and the company of hippogriffs was finishing their last diving run. As they began to fire with all archers and crossbowmen, Gallanth walked softly, or as softly as a forty-five-yard, sixty-ton dragon can walk, to within a hundred yards of the rear of the regiment's line in between the catapults.

The siege engine battery crews were cranking up the counterweights on their catapults for one last volley. The battery battalion commander was riding back and forth, giving out ranges and directions to his crews. "Range, one thousand paces, converge angles to mass center, fire on my mark, match crystal images," he yelled out to synchronize the catapults' angles and distances with a matching point on the map of the area as seen by his crystal. The image was relayed through either a ground observer or one of the aerial battalion hippogriffs or griffon riders. The catapults were turned on their large wagon platforms by a double crank located on either side of the wagon chassis. It took four men to turn them. Distance was determined by how far the counterweight was hoisted on the throw arm. At full lift with the dragon sinew pulley ropes, the catapult could send a sixty-pound stone over a mile or a thirty-pound stone a mile and a half. The regiment's catapults were larger than the Weir's but not as mobile, nor did they have the same density of dragon sinew as the Weir's.

Once all were loaded and locked into place, the commander lifted his battery banner high and then lowered it quickly, while also giving the command through his crystal. *Always good to have a backup method of communication,* Mkel thought to himself. Within seconds, the commands were echoed and eighteen sixty-pound clay projectiles were hurtling toward the target field. They whistled in unison as they sailed over the heads of the regiment's marching soldiers, and all crashed into the ground almost simultaneously, giving a tremor as if a dragon had performed a crash landing.

The legion was now only one hundred yards from the targets and quickened their pace. As the front row of infantry thrust their spears into the wooden frames and moved through, Colonel Wierangan called to his cavalry troop to charge in from the left. The troop commander acknowledged and raised his lance and spurred his horse forward. All one hundred twenty heavy horses began to gallop into a charge. This was an impressive sight, to see all those heavy barded warhorses move out in front of the infantry line, armor clanking and lances pointed into a projected line of enemy. *Not an easy thing to stop without some powerful magic,* Mkel thought to himself.

The land dragons all let loose a stream of fire. Fourteen of the powerful beasts definitely had the garrison's four beat, but those four under Lieutenant Wheelor were the biggest, fiercest, and most intelligent of all the land dragons in the Alliance. A charge of all fourteen would also be impressive and a definite morale check for an approaching group of giants and their orc underlings.

After the drill culminated, Mkel called to congratulate Colonel Wierangan for the excellent coordination of the exercise and was in turn thanked for the garrison's performance, the work of the dragons, and the overall success of his men and comrades. He told him he would give him a copy of his summary of the event.

"Let's go back, Gallanth," he told his dragon. *All right, but first I have to void,* the gold dragon replied. Interestingly enough, dragon excrement was highly sought after by local farmers. It was highly enriched with minerals and promoted plant growth when spread over their fields; it also kept pest insects away as well. The farmers surrounding the Weir were on a rotating basis to receive either Gallanth's or Silvanth's wastes.

Gallanth launched into the air, and with three strokes of his massive golden wings, he was over six hundred feet above the ground. He then glided past the Weir fortress and pointed toward the farm on the western side of the mountain. It was a co-op farm with several human and halfling families maintaining it, all veterans. *This is the location,* Gallanth said to Mkel. "I'm glad you keep track of this," he replied as Gallanth gave out a greeting roar to notify the farmers. He circled around the farm and then landed in the area beside the cattle stables.

The farmers and their halfling partners came out of the main house at a brisk pace, followed by several of their children. Mkel saw the farmer nodding and pointing that the location he was at was adequate, at which point Gallanth lifted his tail and proceeded to relieve himself. Since a dragon's diet was composed of meat, organic material and minerals (i.e., gems, for their second stomach, or synthensium, which takes the gems and the very matter of the precious stones and transforms them into the power for their breath weapons and spell ability), their wastes had many positive attributes. The size of a dragon's waste was equal to a full-grown steer. He only needed to void approximately once a week, and it did not have an offensive odor. It could be consumed by the otyughs but had better benefits elsewhere, plus it was one of the few things that was almost too rich for them to eat.

The farmers and their older children began to immediately shovel the waste onto a nearby wagon for distribution to the fields. The farmers looked up to Gallanth and Mkel and waived a thank you. Mkel waved back, and Gallanth bowed his huge head and said that they were welcome. These same farmers were among the many that supplied the Weir with its foodstuffs and livestock to feed both the garrison and the meat eaters (i.e., the land dragons, griffons, and of course Gallanth and Silvanth).

With that, Gallanth looked over to the farm house at the children that were gathering in the front of the dwelling. "Good afternoon children," he said as he took several careful steps away from the farmers, and with a leap, a low roar, and one downward stroke of his wings, he was airborne again.

The farmers' children were waving and shouting with great smiles on their faces as Gallanth and Mkel gained altitude. Gallanth loved children and went out of his way to defend them. Although he loved Michen most of all, and with all his colossal Draconic heart, he cared for all children. Woe to those who had committed crimes against the innocent, but especially to children. His goal would be their pain before he granted them final justice.

They flew up and around the Draden Weir Mountain as Gallanth let out a signal roar. The mountain itself rose well over three thousand feet above the waters of the Severic River that flowed in front of the massive Weir entrance. The gate watch blew the warning horn, which resonated inside the Weir to let any flying creature know to go to ground, for Gallanth would be flying through the entrance and onto the grounds inside the mountain. Gallanth's right wing dipped as he made a gentle diving turn and flew into the Weir. He sailed over the large interior lake and back winged onto his landing. As he settled down on his bed of gold and gems, Mkel slid down his neck onto his forearm and then jumped to the ground. He took off his riding jacket and helmet and hung them up on the wall of Gallanth's ledge by the entrance of his chamber, and then he hung up his crossbow.

"You will sleep for a couple of hours?" he asked his dragon mate. *Yes, and I will be in attendance for the review this evening and for the dinner*, Gallanth replied. "Excellent, my friend, get some rest," Mkel said as he patted the gold dragon's cheek. Laying his immense head down, he replied, *Give Michen a hug for me*, as he closed his four eyelids. Mkel smiled as he walked into his quarters.

"Daddy home," his son said as he ran to his father as fast as a two-year-old could and hugged Mkel.

"Hello my son," Mkel said as he grabbed Michen and picked him up. "Thank you, my dear, for helping out today along with Silvanth," Mkel said to Annan as he walked over to her while she was reading a book by their bed.

"It was nice to get out and fly with her, and it is a beautiful day today," she replied.

"How about we go for a walk along the river when Michen takes his nap?" he asked.

"All right, but only this time," she said with a wry smile.

"Yes, I'll have to sacrifice my crossbow and sword practice with Jodem for you," he added.

"It's about time," she replied with a combination of teasing and irritation.

"Captain Mkel, I have some sandwiches and soup for you if you haven't already eaten," Janta said as she walked in with a tray of food and a small cauldron of stew.

"That sounds excellent. Michen, are you hungry?" Mkel asked his son.

"Hungree, meat, bread," the little one answered.

"All right, Michen, let's eat," Mkel told his son as they walked into their small dining room.

Mkel fed his son as he ran around the room, while he hurriedly ate himself with Annan and Janta also helping. Michen's smile and laugh were as good a medicine to Mkel as the best healing abilities that Watterseth or a dragon could muster, for his love for his son was as unconditional as that of a dragon and rider. The little boy looked just like Jmes, with his platinum blond hair and big but lively blue eyes and soft handsome face. Mkel knew Michen would be tall like Jmes, who was just over six feet.

I hope he will be a dragonrider someday, Mkel thought to himself. This was the wish of all dragonriders who had children, for otherwise they would normally outlive their offspring because of the blood bonding, which extended their own life spans. A blood bonded dragonrider lived at least twice the normal human life span, if not three times or more. This was also the curse of the metallic dragons, for they lived to see the riders they loved eventually come to death, as well as their rider's children. This is what tended to keep them somber at times and why they were so protective of their riders.

Gallanth was one of the few dragons whose rider died prematurely. Most times the rider and dragon would fight to the death for each other, but circumstances prevented the gold dragon from saving Jmes. During the Great War, the few riders that had their dragons killed almost always went into a berserking frenzy, unleashing any and all spells or entering into a wild melee with their dragonstone weapons. They continued until they were finally brought down after inflicting an incredible amount of damage to the enemy. Only one rider was ever known to live after his dragon was killed; a brass dragonrider from Lancastra Weir.

"All right, little one, it's time for your nap now," Mkel said to his son.

"Noo, draagon, see draagon," his son said in protest.

"Gallanth is sleeping; Michen," Mkel said, "and you should take a nap too." He and Annan carried the boy to his crib. "Janta, can you fill his bottle for me?" he asked the little halfling nanny.

"Got it already Mkel, sir," she quickly replied.

"Don't call me sir, Janta," Mkel jokingly scolded her.

Janta was a middle-aged halfling widow whose clan's caravan was ambushed by an orc raiding party in the unsettled lands. She was one of the few who weren't killed or taken captive. She stood about three and a half feet tall, which put her just a couple of inches above Michen. A ranger patrol brought her and a handful of others from her clan back to the Weir after they tracked and killed the dire wolf-mounted orcs. They were then offered work either in the Weir or in the town for as long as they needed. She had a very gentle nature about her, and Mkel and Annan needed a nanny for their son, since Annan went with the support corps if Silvanth wanted a rider. She loved to take care of the large two-year-old, even though he could be rough at times.

Mkel put Michen into his crib and handed him the bottle of milk. Drake the elf hound then moved by the entrance to Michen's chamber. He was the ever present guardian of his son. "Do you need to go out on the ledge?" he asked the large canine. The dog shook its head and lay down. Elf hounds could sleep eighteen hours a day if they were allowed, but they were always vigilant, even when asleep. No better guardians existed.

"I let him out right before you came in, sir," Janta explained.

"All right, are you ready, my dear?" Mkel said to Annan as he closed door to Michen's chamber.

"Yes, just need to get my shoes on," she replied.

Mkel grabbed his sword and hooked it on his belt; he also grabbed his crossbow from the wall just inside Gallanth's ledge and slung it over his shoulder, along with a small skin of water.

"You need all that?" Annan snapped.

"Yes dear, just in case. Shall we go out the back and walk through the forest or go down the front entrance?" he asked her.

"Let's go out the front to the river," she replied.

"Hey, why don't we take Michen with us and give him a later nap, that way Janta can get a little break?" he asked.

"All right, that sounds good. Go get him while I finish getting ready," his wife replied.

Mkel walked back into Michen's room and asked him if he wanted to go for a walk.

"Walk, Daddy," his son replied.

"All right, my son, let me get your seat on Drake ready," Mkel said as he grabbed the rig from the wall and called over the elf hound. He fastened the harness on the two-hundred-fifty-pound-plus dog, placed Michen in the seat, and secured him in. "Let's go boys," Mkel said as he directed the large canine out into his chamber. "Annan, are you ready?"

"Yes my love," she said with a sarcastic smile.

They both walked to the ledge and down the stairs into the entrance of the water counterweight-powered elevator, which took them down to the landing level. They then walked over to the archway exit of the Weir and through the one-hundred-yard-deep opening as a pair of griffons with their ranger riders soared in. The riders had their mounts dip their near wings and gave Mkel a salute, which he returned. Michen laughed and smiled at the golden brown creatures slowly soaring overhead. They walked out of the stone entrance of the Weir, and Mkel looked up at the carved dragon head that protruded from the top stone, or keystone, of the archway. The two dragonstones embedded in the eye sockets were giving off a low red glow. These stones provided magical protection for the Weir by emanating a spell shield that protected the mountain from offensive spells and catapult missiles, as well as preventing anyone or anything from teleporting into the Weir. They also set off a loud alarm if any evil creature or humanoid tried to enter, as well as controlling the internal temperature and ventilation for the large mountain fortress as if the Weir itself were alive.

The guards in the two watch towers that stood on each side of the archway waved and saluted Mkel. "Just going for a walk along the river and edge of the woods," he yelled up to them.

"Take care sir," the guards replied.

Mkel and his family headed down the smooth stone path that edged between Draden Forest and the Severic River. The immense doors were opened and closed by the stone dragon head guardian at the request of any member of the Weir council or on its own, if it sensed the Weir was in danger. The head stone had a moderate level of intelligence, basically a small step above Mkel's sword and crossbow. The strength of the massive doors had never been tested in a siege, but they would likely be very difficult to breach if ever attacked.

Mkel and Annan, with Michen on top of the fastened seat on Drake, walked along the smooth stone-faced path that snaked along the river bank at the edge of Draden Forest. The forest was a beautiful old stand of various hardwoods and oak. The river moved at a moderately quick pace at this point, but Draden was the farthest point north and east that the large boats or barges could proceed up the river from the capital. Beyond Draden, the river was too shallow for anything but smaller rafts and canoes. This made Draden an important trading town and distribution point, not to mention the key defensive area in the only substantial break in the Gray Mountains for caravans and ingoing and outgoing armies.

The path was opposite the broader road on the other side of the river which horses, oxen, or even retired land dragons would pull the barges up the river from the towns and cities in the western portion of the Alliance. Sometimes sea elves were paid to pull the ships up the river with their killer whale mounts. The only ships that could make it up the river under their own power were the rowed/sail long ships of the Freiland raiders or the rare ship that had a dragonstone-powered or magical source of a wizard with a gust of wind spell. Another major road was built on the western side of the Weir and Draden Forest for ease of traffic ability and in case the southern road was compromised.

As they walked the path, Annan asked about the trip to Battle Point. Mkel assured her that it was only a routine visit, adding that Jodem was going to be joining them. It was all about keeping contact with the legion garrisoned there and addressing their concerns for the plans of their reinforcement by Gallanth and the Weir's garrison if needed, as well as the whole Draden legion.

The forest was beautiful during the late summer. The tall oak and various deciduous trees offered excellent shade and were very visually appeasing. The river's waters, while not crystal clear, were serene. As they were walking, Drake raised his wide head and looked into the forest. "What's the matter, boy?" Mkel asked the hound.

"Is there something in the trees?" Annan asked her husband.

"It is probably just an elf on a patrol," he replied.

Dekeen always had at least two patrols of two elves that walked his portion of the forest, scouting to make sure there were no trespassers and to gather the many different types of rare plants, herbs, and mosses that the elves made into the many products and medicines that they were famous for.

Kershan's dragonstone was not glowing, so Mkel knew there wasn't any magic or danger in the immediate vicinity. He did hear a feint whistle of air, but it quickly faded. *The elf patrol is sending a message by signal arrow,* he thought to himself. The elves, being rudimentarily telepathic and having excellent hearing and eyesight, could rapidly send signals by arrow and whispers, for an elf could hear a whisper at one hundred paces and actually echo it off an arrow in flight. They did this versus using seeing crystals to keep in practice with this technique.

His curiosity about why the elves were signaling was answered when Kershan's pommel dragonstone began to glow in a low light, which meant it detected another dragonstone weapon, for it didn't signal him of danger. This meant that Jodem, Dekeen, or Beckann was teleporting in. Just then, the air twenty yards in front of them began to shimmer, and Beckann and Dekeen blinked into position, mounted on Desiran, her unicorn. The magical white horse was as impressive a sight as a dragon.

Unicorns were the powerful horned horses that epitomized all that was good and pure. They were gleaming, large white warhorses, with a flowing white mane and a three-foot golden spiraled horn that protruded from their forehead. They were extremely fast and possessed superior magical properties. Their horn did incredible damage to evil creatures, being able to fell an ogre with a single hit. The horn had the same strength as a dragon tooth, capable of piercing any armor, even dragon hide. They projected a strong spell shield with the same strength as that of the most powerful holy sword. They could also teleport at will without error and detect all evil in their presence. They were immune to all charm, sleep, and death spells and to all poisons. They would only let human and elven women of pure heart ride them, defending their riders to the death. Unicorns also had pronounced healing powers and could neutralize any poison.

Dekeen jumped from the magical horse and gave a hand to his wife as she slid down the unicorn's pure white flank. Beckann, wife to Dekeen, was a very distant relation to Mkel from hundreds of years past, when one of his ancestors was married to her grandmother for the short life span of a human.

Beckann was a very powerful elf wizard, being only slightly behind Jodem in magical ability. She was extremely beautiful, with only Jennar, the elusive nymph of Draden Forest, being more stunning. Beckann's long golden hair and blue/violet eyes, along with her stunning features and statuesque figure, all added to her radiance. She and Dekeen oversaw the elf clan in Draden Forest. When she didn't travel with the Weir's forces, she took up the defense of the Weir in the absence of Mkel, Gallanth, and Jodem. Beckann and her powerful unicorn mount made her respected among elves and feared by evil forces.

Her long green and blue silken dress flowed elegantly over her slim figure, and her pointed ears barely protruded from her golden hair. "I heard the son of Mkel and Annan was walking past my woods," Beckann said in her soft but smooth voice as she walked over to Annan and Michen.

"Your elves are getting sloppy, my friend; Drake was aware of their presence," Mkel said as he gave Dekeen a greeting hug. This show of emotion was unusual for elves, but the two were close friends.

"It's hard to fool an elf hound. We breed them too well," the dark-haired, emerald green-eyed elf replied. "The drill today went well; your archers were even loosely accurate," he continued with a smile. "It was an impressive display. I assume Gallanth is sleeping now."

"Yes, you know dragons, either sleeping or philosophizing. You and your elves were on the mark, as usual," Mkel replied.

"Enough with the serious talk, you two. Annan, how is the little sprite?" Beckann asked. After scolding Mkel and her husband, she leaned down to pick up the young boy, and she and Annan walked away from the two men.

"All right, my lady," Dekeen said to his elven wife, as he and Mkel strolled along the river bank. "My friend, I have a couple of things I need to talk to you about before you go to Battle Point. Both Beckann and Eladra have had disturbing images of a growing threat to the east and the plains. With the increased enemy activity around Battle Point and these images they've been experiencing, I just wanted to warn you to be on your guard out there."

"I know, Gallanth has been experiencing increased visions and dreams as well, and they are growing with intensity," Mkel answered.

"These are bad signs, but only time will tell for sure. The sea elves told one of my patrols that they killed three Saragwin about twelve miles downstream, and that they were scouting a cargo barge. This is the farthest up the Severic River that they have ever been seen. Haldrin has also reported greater activity along the Gray Mountain border, as well as more frequent attacks in the non-Alliance villages and settlements in the mountains," Dekeen said with concern.

"Yes, Slidess and Colonel Lordan have reported the same from both High Mountain and Eladran Weirs, as well as raiding parties of orcs, grummish, and gnolls performing probes along our borders. Granted, they're not getting very far with the rangers and Haldrin's elves patrolling there, but that along with what Lupek discovered about the giants says something is going on," Mkel commented.

"Your trip to Battle Point might provide some insight. I give you our prayers for your safe return," Dekeen said.

"Thank you, my friend. I will have the most powerful dragon in the world and a master wizard as companions; how could I be safer? However, I will take extra bolts and gems for Gallanth's synthensium. We also have a backup, just in case," Mkel said with a wry smile.

"You could take an elf with you," Dekeen shot back.

"You are needed here, more so if Haldrin calls for help or if something happens; the Weir can count on you and your clan," Mkel answered.

"One elf would be hardly missed," Dekeen said.

"Yes, but Elm and your leadership would be," Mkel replied quickly.

"I understand, but I would still feel better if I went."

"Next time I will talk to General Daddonan to allow an elven envoy to accompany me on a goodwill visit to ensure the ancient alliances between our peoples are maintained," Mkel said.

"I will hold you to that, my friend. Beckann, have you had enough bothering lady Annan and their son?" he asked as he turned to his wife. The elven couple had two daughters, which was unusual, for elves had an extremely low birth rate. This was likely due to Beckann having a distant human trace in her family, also rare for an elf.

"I must always see my little dragonrider when he passes by my woods," she stated as she handed the toddler back to Annan.

"Dekeen, you are as impetuous as my husband; he is definitely a bad influence on you and your customary elven courtesy," Annan quickly spoke back. "Your wife is welcome to see my son any time she wishes."

"Alas, we must be departing," Beckann said as the great white unicorn walked over to them, her white coat almost gleaming in the sunlight that shown through the overhanging tree branches. *A brilliant creature*, Mkel thought to himself, *rare and elusive*. Once one chose a rider or a companion, they were as resolute in their loyalty as a dragon. Their magical powers were also something to be reckoned with.

"Yes my love, we have matters to attend to back in the forest," Dekeen said.

Their clan's village was set in the heart of Draden Forest, closer to the mountainside. The elves made their homes in the trees and in well-camouflaged wooden structures that could be walked past almost without notice when not lit up by hundreds of lighting crystals. Any force that made it into the forest would face arrows from all sides and from above.

Beckann was always busy instructing the younger elven wizard apprentices or preparing potions and performing experiments to improve upon the products that the elves were famous for.

Dekeen lifted his thin but beautiful wife up onto the large magical horse's back after she gave Michen a kiss on the forehead and Annan and Mkel a hug. Mkel and Dekeen shook hands again.

"Will you be joining us for dinner tonight?" Mkel asked. "I believe Tegent will be entertaining the Weir afterward." Tegent, being the Weir garrison's bard, was very talented with his dragonstone-modified lyre, even by elven standards.

"That sounds like an interesting proposition," Beckann said inquisitively.

"We will be there," Dekeen said.

"Then we will see you there, and we will reserve you two seats at our table," Annan added.

"Until then, my friends," Beckann said, and with that, the unicorn reared back and disappeared.

Dekeen gave a half salute and ran into the wood line to check on his patrols. Mkel and Annan walked another mile or so along the river and then turned around to head back to the Weir. Michen was getting antsy so they knew it was time for his nap. Drake took his fidgeting well. The patience and tolerance of the elf hound was a blessing.

They made their way back to the Weir gates without incident, although Dekeen's warning about the sea devil saragwin did make Mkel watch the water more often then he usually would have. He had confidence in the sea elves, but nobody was perfect. The tower guard again saluted Mkel as they walked back into the mountain. The Weir was surprisingly quiet for an afternoon. Likely everybody was resting, tending to gear after the exercise, or getting ready for the several days off that he gave them prior to the weapons skills and squad drills that were scheduled after he left.

They made their way up to their living quarters and put a very tired Michen down for his nap. Mkel and Annan got undressed and had a moment alone before they fell asleep themselves. Mkel woke up about an hour later, quickly dressed, and gave Annan a kiss on the forehead before he walked out of their bedroom onto Gallanth's landing. He walked past the still sleeping dragon to Jodem's laboratory.

He opened the large oaken reinforced door and walked in. Jodem was at the far end of the large room, gathering papers and poring over a large binder book.

"Come my friend, over here," the wizard said to him without pausing in his tasks. "I'm just getting a few things together for our trip. I have to arrange a meeting with General Daddonan's assigned wizard, Andellion, over a few matters. We are also getting ready to create a dragonstone weapon. Ordin and Dorin have separated a slice off of that vein of mithril that they unearthed. They think it is enough to make a sword and maybe an axe or lance head, with the remainder to be made into a couple dozen bolt tips for us and arrow heads for Dekeen."

"Very good; I assume that will wait until we get back from Battle Point and before we head to the capital?" Mkel asked.

"Yes, that will be the best course of action. The most important issues we have to discuss are the defense agreement with Battle Point and the upcoming senate gathering in Draconia, with the likely issues that will result. General Daddonan will be asking you to agree to a direct defense pact with the Battle Point legion for the whole Weir garrison," Jodem explained.

"Shouldn't that be decided with Colonel Wierangan?" Mkel returned.

"Yes, but even though it is assumed the Weir is responsive to the Draden regiment, the lines of responsibility are still fairly gray. The garrison has a degree of autonomy, although you have always directed it as a combined battalion of the regiment to make the Strike Legion. Other Weirs handle this in different ways. Colonel Lordan and Talonth and his wing basically command the cavalry legion at Eladran Weir, with a regular Alliance army colonel as his deputy ground commander, while Slidess and Trikenth with their wing are a strong air arm of the High Mountain legion under direct command of an Alliance army colonel. This mirrors most Weirs that don't have dragonriders with a military commission and don't directly command troops like you, Lordan, and Sighbolt. Bristurm of Denar Weir will be in this position as soon as he gets his commission. There is no fixed standard or solution, especially until these new Avenger dragons increase their numbers, for there are only a handful of young metallic dragons to come of age anytime soon to be stationed at Battle Point. Plus bronze dragons won't go that far from the sea or a major river or lake," Jodem explained.

"I thought the Avenger dragons were supposed to eventually be stationed in Ian and Freiland?" Mkel asked.

"They are, after the first wing is fully up to strength and the next brood comes of age," Jodem answered.

"Have you seen them yet?" Mkel inquired.

"Yes, they are about the size of a bronze dragon and look like a cross between a bronze and a gold. They have a metallic brown-gold hue to their heavily armored hide. Their mouths are long and lined with powerful teeth and have deep set eyes. Two long, smooth, but sharp horns protrude from the back of their heads. Their bodies are well muscled and powerful; they are almost as strong as red dragons but faster. Their claws are thick and powerfully built, and their wings are rounder or more ovoid compared to other metallic dragons, but each bone support ends in a long talon. This makes the wing strike from these dragons hit with horrific damage. Their long but powerful tails end in a modified plate similar to a gold dragon's but longer like a sword as opposed to a gold dragon's broader arrowhead axe shape; they are capable of slashing or piercing strikes.

"These unique dragons have great optimistic attitudes," Jodem continued, "enabling them to inspire all those around them. While they are not as intelligent as the metallic dragons, their enthusiastic spirit and absolute fearlessness makes up for this. In their presence, they can inspire courage in all around them, giving all creatures a morale boost like Gallanth does, but not to the same extent.

"They are the only successfully created dragon species to date," he said. "This was finally achieved by the top wizards of the Alliance Wizard's Council, along with several of the most talented elven magic users, by taking some of Michenth's blood and that of all other metallic dragon types, with a great deal of other materials. The Avenger dragons are bred to bridge the gap from the more powerful but slower breeding metallic dragons and the faster reproducing chromatics. The successful breeding experiment resulted in these magnificent creatures that are born to battle evil and are masters of the close fight. They have been raised to serve with the highest paladin order of the dragon knights as powerful steeds and defenders of the capital.

"While they cannot cast spells as true dragons can," he continued, "they still have some magical abilities. The magic shield they emanate can defend from as much spell damage as a silver dragon's, and they can also project their shield to protect others up to their line of sight. Their sonic force breath weapon has devastating effects on those that it hits.

"Avenger dragons are born for close combat," Jodem continued. "They can enter into a battle fury once per day; that gives them the strength of a gold dragon for up to half an hour. Normally they possess between silver and red dragon strength, but during this fury, they not only gain in strength but speed and extraordinary evasion and parrying ability. This also allows them to attack very fast with their bite, tail strike, and claw attacks. This ability will make them deadly in close combat. An Avenger dragon will make even a red dragon think twice about engaging them in close quarters.

"The Avengers are also bred to be an extraordinarily tough species of dragon and can shrug off enormous amounts of damage," he said, "being able to completely heal themselves twice per day or spread that healing ability to others. They are immune to death magic of all kinds. The dragon knights are currently training these dragons to wear barding armor made specifically for them. It is mithril lined and extremely strong, giving them an almost impenetrable armor when worn. It does hamper their aerial maneuverability when utilized, which puts them in the flying class of the chromatics. With this armor, speed and agility are wisely traded in when necessary.

"Overall," Jodem concluded, "while they are new to the Alliance and the world in general, the Avenger dragons with their knight counterparts will make a significant impact in future battles. In a larger sense, they are probably the equal to a bronze dragon in a close engagement due to their great strength, speed, and ferocity, as well as their incredibly strong defensive ability. However, their lack of spell casting or general magic ability does not make them as powerful in all other areas, and so far their inability to teleport also limits their deployment. This is why they are to be paired with a powerful dragon knight, or wizard, for their magic ability will make up for the Avenger dragon's limitations."

"So they are meant to serve the dragon knights?" Mkel asked.

"Yes, but also as a mount for a wizard or anyone else deemed worthy. They also seem to only have a limited life span, roughly mirroring a land dragon, which is about that of an average man," the wizard answered.

"Does that mean they can't soul bond?" Mkel asked.

"They are not truly blood bonded with their rider. It is more like the link between a paladin and his dedicated mount, but slightly stronger," Jodem explained.

"Interesting. I am anxious to see them when we go to the capital," Mkel said.

"Please keep this to yourself, for news about them is not official, and the POEs are raising a ruckus lately about the Alliance military expenditures. It is best to keep them a secret as long as possible," Jodem explained.

"Won't it be difficult to hide dragons of that size? And as for the POEs, what a waste of human effort. Do they realize that the shortened name of their movement is the Draconic word for 'weak, traitorous fool,' the worst curse in dragon language. 'People of the Enlightened': hah, nothing more than stealers of air," Mkel said sarcastically.

"The very nature of their philosophy would tend to support that statement," Jodem replied with a smile as he chuckled at Mkel's comment.

"I don't understand how the senators from those areas actually listen to those of that ideology. Most can't even vote because they did not serve," Mkel said.

"You must remember that most of those affiliated senators are former arbitrators from both the army and navy, but mostly the navy. Their views are usually of a more arrogant nature, since they command more power or authority through magistrate law trials and the courts than from the common man. They view the law as a higher ideal or almost as divine, even if it is the citizens of the Alliance who they are supposed to represent, as both arbitrators and senators. This is the unfortunate price that we pay for having a nation based on laws, the dark side of the order we enjoy as part of our society. Those who espouse the antimilitary, antidragon views that can't vote, still donate gold and silver to those senators to fund their elections, and they are gaining strength in the major cities. This is especially true along the coasts in the northwest, and they are gaining converts as they promise more and more entitlements to certain civilians, but especially veterans," Jodem indicated.

"Yes but those laws were derived from the Founding Council of not only humans, but dragons, dwarves, and elves," Mkel said, "who always have more sense than our supposedly learned arbitrators. It was the dragons who united this country two hundred years ago. It was they and the elves who helped forge the alliances we share today, that we depend upon for our very survival as a nation.

"It was the dragons who gave up their freedom at the will of the Creator to soul mate with human riders," Mkel continued, "thus forever tying their fate with ours. They do not need us but we surely need and benefit from them, "a deterrent not only to the chromatic dragons, but to all the forces of Morgathia and the rest of the evil that exists in this world. They must have saved literally millions of Alliance lives, and now they are the target of scorn and ridicule by a group of cowards. These so-called Enlightened thumb their noses at the very instruments of their prosperity and defense, and then insult them by demands to spend less on the military than they already do. We are only at a fifth of the strength that served during the Great War. They seem to actually hate some of the very laws they are sworn to uphold as well as those that protect their very freedom, attempting to twist the law to promote their own self-serving purposes," Mkel said in disgust as he felt his anger grow.

"That is the very reason you might be asked to speak in front of the senate, for your father's sacrifice and unfortunate fate, along with your experience with so many veterans of that conflict and your endeavors to help them. You will need to be heard by those senators who are now indecisive," Jodem said.

"I thought dragonriders were not allowed to be political," Mkel said.

"They are not, except for Becknor, but you could give a nonpartisan speech that addresses veteran issues. Everyone knows of the sacrifice your father made to save Michenth," Jodem explained.

"I understand, but with the growing threats in the east, and the rising Morgathian encroachment, I just don't know how these, again, 'learned' men can come to those conclusions to cut the military budget, to cut veteran retirement pay, and to ask dragons to donate their blood for the heating, cooling, and lighting crystals, rather than sell them to supplement our beleaguered budget," Mkel replied.

"The one thing you must do is to keep your emotions separate," Jodem counseled. "By the nature of you being a gold dragonrider, you will be seen as not being objective. I know you loved and still love your father. This can come out in your speech, but it cannot come out as anger toward those who you feel dishonors his and the military's sacrifices."

"I understand, but it is hard to suppress my hatred toward their ideals and their actions. For it is one thing for those who have not served to espouse their ignorant views and another to have served and then turn on your brethren for nothing more than political expediency. This is nothing short of betrayal," Mkel said.

"We will work on your speech after you get your draft finalized, so it is ready in case you are called. As far as the Avenger dragons, you must not forget the other products of our tinkering with the Creator's work. The horned drakes and the dragon horses are also magnificent, though not as spectacular as a new dragon species. The dragon knights, or mithril paladins as they are now sometimes called, will make an excellent strike force and goodwill ambassadors with a strong arm. They will also take the responsibility of guarding Michenth and the capital from Valianth and Gallanth's brother Falcanth and the Capital Wing as a whole to allow them more flexibility. They will have three components: a wing of Avenger dragons, a wing of dragon horse-mounted knights, and a ground troop of knights on the horned drakes," explained the wizard.

"That will be interesting to see," Mkel thought out loud.

"Yes, and it will give us another, very reinforced dragon wing with which to deal with the increasing Morgathian activity as well as the trouble brewing in the Shidan region and the Southern Ontaror kingdoms. Right now the Alliance and our metallic dragons are stretched very thin. We only have maybe ten young dragons that will be ready to join the adults on the line, and of them there is only one silver dragon, and three bronze dragons, with the rest copper and brass. However, there is a trend of increased mating among the metallics lately, almost as if some part of them knows that their numbers must increase," Jodem explained.

"Do the Avenger dragons mature faster than the metallic dragons?" Mkel asked.

"Yes, they reach maturity in roughly a year," Jodem answered.

"That's a good thing. I just wonder how they will fair against a blue or even a red dragon," Mkel said inquisitively.

"I have faith they will do very well against them. I wonder if the Morgathians are attempting similar experiments," Jodem added.

"I guess we will find out more information when we get to Battle Point. Will we be visiting any of the Northern Ontaror kingdoms?" Mkel asked.

"I don't think we will have time, but it will depend on what General Daddonan has to say. How is Markthrea shooting for you? I saw you basically hit your mark during the practice, but then you were not under pressure," Jodem said with a grin. Jodem and Mkel were always in friendly competition with each other, for the portly wizard was an excellent marksman with his staff/crossbow combination, which is a deadly weapon especially when used in conjunction with his incredible magic ability.

"You don't worry about that. We'll see about my ability when we shoot next time; Markthrea is doing just fine. How is Ordin progressing with the new mithril tips?" Mkel replied.

"They will be making more tips when they get this latest weapon finished and use the shards and leftovers. There will likely be enough for at least a dozen each for us and for Dekeen," Jodem said.

"Excellent, the mithril-tipped bolts always fly just a little straighter," Mkel said with a smile.

"Yes but you still need to have a smooth, reactionless follow through, for without good body and mind mechanics and the synchronizing of trigger control and proper breathing, having a mithril bolt tip or steel will not make a difference," Jodem said with a little more seriousness. "Your accuracy saves lives and means less injury for Gallanth,"

"You know I hit over ninety-nine out of a hundred targets that I aim at, and with the power of Markthrea's energized bolts, I have a lot of confidence in my ability. Not overconfidence, but confidence," he replied.

"Yes, but you do have problems with your release at times, especially when you think of your father. Remember he was not a missile soldier and did not shoot regularly. There is no shadow you live under, and you have nothing to prove but to yourself. Not to me, not to Gallanth, and not to your men other than that you care for them and their well-being," Jodem added sternly, for he was not only Mkel's friend but his shooting mentor as well.

"I know that up here," Mkel said as he pointed to his head, "but I have to incorporate it more completely down here," as he then pointed to his heart.

"I know that your father's death still affects you greatly. He was a good man, but duty and responsibility to the Weir, the families, your men, and Gallanth must be your top priorities. So far you have been able to use your grief and emotion in constructive ways, as strength of your fortitude, but it could easily consume you if you are not careful and Gallanth does not watch closely enough," Jodem said to him with all sincerity.

"Gallanth is overprotective, so I'm not too worried," Mkel replied with a smile, which hid the watering of his eyes.

"Yes, your forty-five-yard-long gold dragon big brother does watch out for you in so many ways," Jodem teased, with a large grin. "On another note, I think that Sergeant Gresh and platoon senior sergeant Macdolan wish to speak to you before dinner about Lieutenant Howrek."

"What is the issue?" Mkel asked.

"I don't know, but it is something to do with the exercise," Jodem added.

"I better go down to the meeting room and read the reports that were submitted. Thanks again for everything; I will see you at dinner. Oh, Dekeen and Beckann are coming and they are bringing their best elf musician to accompany Tegent," Mkel said as he shook Jodem's hand and began to walk out toward Gallanth's landing.

"That will be interesting. I greatly look forward to it. See you then," Jodem finished.

Mkel walked out of the wizard's laboratory, passed Gallanth's huge sleeping frame, and made his way down the winding side stairs to the Weir's main floor and walked across the wide landing to the head council room.

He walked into the large room and found the written reports from his junior officers regarding the drill. Just as Jodem said, there was a special note from Sergeant Macdolan in the drawer as to keep a sense of privacy. Macdolan was an excellent leader with a good sense of proportionality. While he cared a great deal about his men and was a very tenacious fighter in his own right, he could be cantankerous and occasionally mildly self-serving.

The note addressed his concerns regarding Lieutenant Howrek's performance as of late, even questioning his mental state. Macdolan stated that he almost panicked during the exercise when his platoon was tasked to simulate the break in the line for the elven infantry to reinforce. He had to grab Howrek and physically restrain him from running out in front of the whole line when the elves showed up. He expressed great concerns about Howrek leading the platoon into battle if and when the next major engagement came.

There had not been a major fight for a long time, mostly skirmishes of a company or less of orcs, along with a couple of moderately powerful evil creatures that Gallanth and the mixed Weir company handled with relative ease. This was changing now with the news that Lupek and the rangers brought back, and the chance of a serious fight was growing more likely. Mkel knew he would have to address these concerns and counsel the lieutenant tonight after the celebration dinner. *No sense in ruining a man's dinner*, he thought to himself.

Mkel then quickly read through the other assessments from his junior officers from all platoons and sections. Even Ordin wrote a few sentences, which was almost unheard of. The elves and dwarves, while they fought for Mkel, Gallanth, and the Weir, did not truly answer to him. It was a friendly agreement mostly based on the respect for him and especially Gallanth. Dwarves were not known for taking the time for such "frivolous" matters. If it didn't have to do with mining, fighting, eating, or drinking, they usually did not care, preferring to just go back underground to deal with their business affairs, mining, and metal work.

Mkel guessed that Ordin and his clan were hungry for a fight with the giants, for those two races were mortal enemies. In spite of their rumblings and often sour attitudes, a stronger ally in battle you would be hard-pressed to find. This was especially true in a close fight, where they tended to specialize. The elves were almost always on target in any regard, so they did not have much need to critique unless it was of others, save dragons, for which they had great respect. They function and move as one in battle, being slightly telepathic with one another. This ability made their formations and maneuver seemingly flawless. Alone, elves were deadly with a bow or blade; in unison in an infantry line, their swords swung with an almost dazzling synchronized grace.

Mkel made a couple of specific comments regarding the few weak points for the garrison on his report but did not include any direct issues regarding Lieutenant Howrek. *It is better to clean out one's own house before asking for help,* Mkel thought to himself. He was always very accurate with the assessments of the garrison's performance, not berating, but also not aggrandizing their performance or capabilities. He knew their strengths and limitations as well as he knew his own.

When he was done with his report, he called the sergeant on duty for a messenger rider to take the scroll to the regiment's headquarters so Colonel Wierangan could review it. He could have called him directly with his crystal, but this was not an urgent matter, plus Wierangan preferred to read paper rather than view images on a crystal. The messenger arrived in a short time. He was one of the younger hippogriff riders, probably fifteen or sixteen, the son of a soldier who had been killed in battle.

"Sir, Machuen reporting. What is your order?" the young boy asked.

"Just take this to the regiment's headquarters and drop it off for Colonel Wierangan. There is no hurry but for you to get back for the evening meal," Mkel said to the lad with a smile. Mkel was friendlier than most Alliance officers, who tended to be much more serious, or at least take themselves too seriously. *People respect genuine leaders, not bombastic know-it-alls,* Mkel thought to himself. Maybe this part of his personality or leadership style was due to him being a dragonrider, for Colonel

Lordan had a similar style. It could also be in part to his father's death when he was at an impressionable age, for life was too short and precious to be boorish and irritable.

"Now get going, and here's something for your family," he said with a smile as he tossed a shiny gold Drachlar to the boy. One gold piece of Alliance currency was worth than one hundred pieces of silver or Drachmeres; it had the embossment of Michenth's head on one side and the image of Warrenton, the first premier of the Alliance and Founding Council member, on the other side. The boy took the coin and smiled with a nod to Mkel as a gracious thanks. He then turned with the rolled parchment in his hand and started to walk to the stables.

Alliance currency consisted of three primary types of coins and certain gold certificates backed by the Alliance banks. The highest value coin was the gold alloy Drachlar, which was just a little over an inch in diameter. The basic silver alloy coin, the Drachmere, was worth one hundredth of a Drachlar and was about half the size. It had an embossment of Michenth again on one side and Jondam, the second Alliance premier and Founding Council member, over an elven oak leaf emblem. A ten Drachmere piece was a slightly larger silver coin worth ten Drachmeres and was the size of a Drachlar. A fifty Drachmere piece was half again larger than a Drachlar and worth fifty Drachmeres. A rarer but still used one hundred or silver century Drachmere was twice the size of a Drachlar and worth the same.

The third type of coin was a copper alloy piece called the Fenig. It took ten or twenty Fenigs to equal the worth of a Drachmere, depending on which size of Fenig. The smaller Fenig was exactly half the size of the Drachlar and worth one twentieth of the silver piece. The larger Fenig was worth one tenth of a Drachmere and was three quarters the size of a Drachlar. It had the embossment of Jetham, the third Alliance Premier, on one side and the characteristic dwarven arch with a hammer and axe on the other side. Most basic monetary transactions were performed with Drachmeres and Fenigs, with Drachlars usually reserved for more substantial purchases or for the ease of carrying fewer coins. Alliance currency was the most stable monetary system in the known world, with all other kingdoms and states emulating it.

Mkel realized it was getting close to the time for the evening meal and grabbed his seeing crystal from the small holster on his belt. "Annan, are you ready, my dear?" he asked.

"Yes my love, I am just getting Michen ready. I will see you in the dining hall in a little while," she replied.

"I will see you there," Mkel answered. He then got up and started to walk over to the soldiers' living quarters to see if he could find either Toderan or Pekram. Most of the soldiers were getting ready to go to the dining hall or getting their families together. All of them had either their own room or a small complex if they had a family. Each family unit had a small area for food preparation and sanitary and wash area, as well as a central family room and multiple sleeping chambers. Single soldier units also have small wash areas. These were added on for soldier comfort and morale rather than the ones hewn out of solid rock at the right side of the Weir landing. Those were now used for storage and emergency living space in case a larger force was temporarily stationed at the Weir or a large civilian population for emergencies.

Mkel saw Pekram walking out of the company's headquarters room. "Sergeant Pekram!" he yelled to get his attention.

"Yes Captain, what do you need?" he replied.

"I read all the summaries from the lieutenants and the senior platoon sergeants. I just wanted to know if you had anything to add."

"No, they addressed it pretty well. I know about the situation with the first platoon, and I am talking to Sergeant Macdolan about it," Pekram explained.

"I will talk to Lieutenant Howrek after the evening meal tonight before I go to Battle Point," Mkel added.

"He needs to get his head straight or I will knock it off. I will not have him screw that platoon up!"

"I will not let that happen; just leave this scenario to me, I will handle the officers. Any other issues that need to be addressed or any soldier that deserves an award?" Mkel asked.

"No, just a couple of small supply and weapons problems sir, I'll go to Captain Vicasek in the support corps company through Sergeant Sternlan. I will hold off on an award until we have the next engagement. The sergeants controlled the company very well and kept the line moving and intact. Otherwise the company, land dragons, paladins, and catapults did very well. Even the elves were coordinated with us as were you and your dragon," Pekram finished with his typical wry smile.

"Very good, I'll let Gallanth know of your approval," he said, chiding the senior sergeant to let him know he was still in charge but with a hint of humor. "Are you and your family attending the evening meal tonight?" Mkel asked.

"Yes, we will be there, got to hear Tegent perform."

"He will be playing with the elf minstrel as well," Mkel added.

"Looking forward to it, we will be there in a little while sir," Pekram said as he gave a cursory salute and walked back to his quarters.

Mkel started to walk to the dining hall, for the growing noise from conversations from the large hall indicated that the garrison was mostly assembled for the evening meal. As he walked into the hall, a soldier was about to call the room to attention but he motioned to him not to do so; he reserved that honor for Gallanth, Colonel Wierangan, Colonel Dunn, or other officers of similar rank. This courtesy was not important to him. He walked over to his table as the kitchen personnel were starting to bring the food trays out. Beef steaks were the order tonight to celebrate the successful drill today.

Toderan and his family were already there and seated; Annan walked in with Michen almost right after Mkel. Everyone started to be seated when Jodem strode in and walked over to the head table. Ordin and Dorin came up from the lower caverns as Dekeen, Beckann, and the elven minstrel Trilen emerged from the back passage that led in from Draden Forest. The Weir's leaders sat down at the head tables, and Mkel rose with his mug of freshly poured Draden ale.

"Ladies, gentlemen, friends, can I have your attention?" Mkel opened. "I propose a toast. To the garrison, our elven and dwarven allies, Jodem, and Gallanth, for a well-executed drill and our continued success as the foremost Weir in the Alliance. I am, as always, very proud of your performance," Mkel proclaimed.

A large cheer arose in unison before all raised mugs were tipped, especially from the dwarven brothers. They loved the town's own produced ale. The dwarven home brews were made from the special molds and yeasts they cultivated in the lower caverns. These ales were extremely strong and bitter, and only the most devout nondwarf drinkers could stomach them. These molds were also a base for some of the foods they consumed in their subterranean homes and for the air they breathed, being able to quickly convert carbon dioxide and sulfurous gases into breathable oxygen. Dwarves were the inventors of necessity.

Watterseth, the Weir's head cleric and religious leader, rose and said, "My family, let us give our thanks." All present in the vast dining hall bowed their heads. "Great Creator, we give thanks for being allowed to assemble here amongst our friends, family, comrades, and allies. The success of the exercise today and the continued prosperity the Weir and its communities enjoy, we owe to your divine grace. May we always keep your message of right, honor, and caring in all we do and uphold the freedom and justice that you espouse in your teachings. We thank you for Gallanth and the dragons that help us in this quest and promote your spirit. We pray that you watch over all of your children to keep them safe from harm and for the strength to uphold the beacon of light that is the Alliance. Bless all," he finished.

A collective "Bless all" acknowledgment from the garrison resounded softly in the hall. The elves, while not religiously organized, were devoted nonetheless, for they embodied the Creator's perfection of nature. Dwarven clerics, while rare, are very forceful in their devotion. Ordin's dwarf clan of Keystone Weir did not have one, as their own cleric died during the last Great Dragon War, and they depended on Watterseth for their religious needs. This was a rare situation, for the gruff dwarves rarely depended on anybody other than from their own race besides dragons, but Watterseth's power in battle gave him great respect among the dwarves.

With that, the evening meal began and general conversation ensued. Toderan sat beside Mkel, with Jodem across from him, so they could discuss Weir matters. Dekeen and Beckann were at the large head table as well as Dorin, Ordin, and Mkel's and Toderan's family.

"Captain, I heard Pekram talked to you about Lieutenant Howrek," Toderan said quietly.

"Word doesn't take too long to get around here, does it?" Mkel replied with a slightly humorous tone.

"I was going to say something to you in any event tonight if it had not been mentioned to you up to this point," Toderan added.

"I am planning on talking to him after the evening meal and Tegent's performance. No sense in ruining a man's dinner, but I will address the issues that were brought to me. I will not let the vanity of one man affect the training and potentially cost the lives of the men of this company. Depending on what his responses are, I will allow him a chance to redeem himself or I will send him back to the regiment," Mkel explained.

"Yes, but he must be watched, for a fight with this new giant and the Morgathian threat to the east could be just over the horizon," Toderan added.

"You are right, but I trust Sergeant Macdolan to keep things in order, and if he comes to me for help or a concern, it will be addressed right away," Mkel answered.

"I know, I'm just concerned," replied Toderan.

"I would be disappointed if you were not," Mkel answered with a smile. He looked over at Jodem, who gave a smile and a nod in acknowledgment. Mkel knew that the wizard knew what was going on, for very little escaped him in regard to happenings in the Weir. He would seek his counsel after they arrived at Battle Point regarding how he handled the Howrek scenario. Mkel nodded back to acknowledge Jodem's unspoken words. He diverted his attention to help Annan and Janta feed Michen. The little boy was very aggressive at times, so watching him was indeed a full-time endeavor.

Soon the great hall was quieted by Tegent and his apprentices getting up and making their way to the slightly raised platform beside the tavern portion of the dining hall, along with the elven minstrel that was sitting beside Dekeen and Annan. Tegent and the elf musician stepped up and sat on the tall stools at the center of the platform and quickly tuned their lyres. Several flute players and drummers quickly set up behind the two musicians. The familiar chords that harmoniously emanated from Tegent's lyre told the assembled Weir of an uplifting song he titled "Dragon's Wings," which was one of the many tribute songs that he created in Gallanth's honor. Tegent's lyre glowed in its dragonstone light as the accompanying elf minstrel gave the song a new added twist, for elven vocals always added a unique but haunting quality to the melody. This was one of the few songs that he sang that was not meant to be sung along with; however, many still did. He also changed the verses on occasion to reflect events like battles, training exercises, or even social news.

As Tegent and the elf played and sang, even the dwarf brothers listened along with Michen. This was indeed an accomplishment. The songs that he sang could bring a tear to the toughest soldier's heart, even a dwarf. They could rouse the garrison to want to take on the whole of Morgathia. The one central theme of his songs was Gallanth, although he also sang about the elves, the dwarves, the adventures of men, past battles, lost love, hunting, women, and politics. He was one of the most talented bards in all of the Alliance as well as no slouch as a fighter, hunter, and archer. He studied with the elves for several years, which contributed to many of his musical, archery, and swordsmanship techniques.

His sung words were echoed by his elf companion:

> *There's a gathering storm in the east tonight*
> *There's a raging fire from the sky*
> *We'll give them cold blue steel for the right*
> *And make them see the searing light and dragon's eye*
> *Take us on your mighty wings across the sky*
> *They'll feel your fire from above*
> *They'll taste our steel from the heart tonight*
> *They can never defeat us and our love*
> *Take us on your mighty wings for the fight*
> *And Morgathia will feel our wrath and might*
> *The giants are gathering in the east tonight*
> *We will rise on his wings and meet the threat in sight*
> *For all that is good and keep shining the Alliance light*

As he and the elf ended the song, the room erupted in loud cheers. He and his accompaniment immediately started into a lively tune that he took from traveling halflings. Their songs were always upbeat, for they loved good drink, good food, and just having fun.

As they started the song, several of the halflings working in the kitchen started to dance on the floor and bare tables.

Dwarves and many humans stepped to the rhythm and sang with the choruses. A night being entertained by Tegent alone or with company was always a good one.

The duo sang for over an hour before calling it a night and getting some ale themselves. Michen was getting restless, and Annan and Janta took him back to their living quarters. Dekeen and Beckann gave their farewells and walked to the back of the Weir to go out the secret passage to the forest. Ordin and Dorin shook Mkel's hand and went over to the bar keep for more ale. Mkel then motioned for Lieutenant Howrek to come over to him.

"Yes sir, you called?" Howrek asked.

"Let's go to my council room for a little talk," Mkel replied as he got up and started to walk to the planning room and his office. As they entered, he told the lieutenant to sit down at the table he used in his personal office. "I don't like to be anything but direct, Lieutenant, so I will get right to the point. I offered you a position as a platoon leader at the Weir garrison after Colonel Wierangan basically forced you to leave his southern catapult battery. I will give any man a chance as long as he is willing to look out for his men, lead from the front, and always give his best effort. I do not care if mistakes are made, especially in exercises, for they do not cost blood. However, I will not tolerate one of my men, especially one of my sergeants or officers, taking unnecessary risks for personal gain or to chase an award or medal. This is the easiest way to get men killed in battle. Do you understand my philosophy?"

"Yes sir, but I'm not sure what you are getting at," Howrek said pensively.

"It has been brought to my attention through several soldiers that you've been making certain decisions and taking actions that do not have your platoon's best intentions at heart, and that you almost panicked when the elves came to simulate a relief of your platoon. You only want to look good to impress either me or Colonel Wierangan, or Jodem, or whoever else," Mkel said with a serious tone.

"Sir, I would never ..."

"Lieutenant, I am not making any direct accusations or charges against you now. What I am doing is expressing my concerns over what has been brought to me. I do not deal in rumors or innuendoes, but I prefer to correct the problem directly, and this situation is bordering on both. I am not attacking you as a person, but addressing the behavior so corrections can be made. Do you understand my meaning?" Mkel finished with a sincere tone in his voice.

"Yes sir," Lieutenant Howrek responded sheepishly.

"What you have to do is take a long look into yourself and examine your actions and the motives you have. Only when you take this hard look can you grow as a man. As the elves say of griffons and eagles, you only learn when your feathers get ruffled," Mkel added.

"I will look at what I do in a more critical way from now on sir, for the last thing I would want to see is anything happening to this garrison or to offend you or Gallanth," Howrek said apologetically.

"Gallanth and I are not to be worried about, it is the men. To get their respect is very easy. Just look after them, put their well-being above yours, and be true to yourself as well as them. It is an easy formula, just have faith in them and yourself," Mkel finished.

"I will try, sir. Thank you for your honesty and the time you took to counsel me," Howrek answered as he fidgeted slightly in his chair.

Mkel got up and reached over to grab Howrek's forearm and shook it in the Alliance comradeship gesture with a smile. "Remember, always fight the good fight," Mkel said with his natural smile.

"Yes sir," Howrek replied, "and have a good trip to Battle Point, sir."

"Get some rest and think it over. If you have any questions or wish to discuss this or any other matter, my door is always open," Mkel finished. With that, Howrek gave Mkel a quick salute and walked out of the council room and back toward the tavern. *Probably needs a drink now*, Mkel thought to himself. *We will see if what I said to him sunk in, or whether I will need to relieve him.* Mkel then started to walk across the landing toward his living quarter's area.

He walked up the long winding staircase from the landing grounds that led up to his, Gallanth's, and Jodem's chamber rather than taking the counterweight elevator. He stepped onto

Gallanth's landing and looked at his sleeping dragon mate. *It is amazing how peaceful the immense dragon looks when in slumber, compared to the incredible destructive power and incalculable strength he brings to bear in battle*, he thought to himself.

You handled the counseling session with Lieutenant Howrek well, my rider, Gallanth said to him telepathically. "I thought you were sleeping, my friend," Mkel said to him quietly with a smile on his face. *I sensed a little anxiety in your mind so I just listened in*, the big dragon answered back. "Well, I thank you for your comment. It is always hard to discipline one of my men. I want them all to succeed." *Yes, but sometimes you cannot force a rock to move. There are many that nobody can reach or be made to understand or learn. They must hit the wall first and then learn for themselves.* "I understand, we will have to see, but I trust his sergeants to handle the situation." *Yes, but I sense that Lieutenant Howrek's mind is troubled. His jealousy and anxiety are growing, and I do not trust his judgment. I have a bad feeling but cannot pinpoint it*, Gallanth added.

"All right, my large friend, get some rest, the trip to Battle Point is coming up soon and I want you fully rested," Mkel said with earnest.

Give Michen a kiss for me, Gallanth ended with a sincere tone.

"Yes, my friend, good night," Mkel said as he put his hand on the big dragon's nose and then turned and walked into his living quarters. Annan was just getting ready to put Michen in bed. Mkel walked over to them and picked up his son. "It's bed time, my boy," he said.

"Give dragon kiss," he quickly replied.

"All right, let's go give Gallanth a kiss," Mkel said with a smile. This was his son's normal nightly ritual; he had to give Annan, Gallanth, Drake, and him a kiss before being put into his crib. Mkel carried Michen back out onto Gallanth's landing over to the gold dragon's head and leaned him over; he put his little arms on the golden armored hide.

"Good night, my little hatchling," Gallanth said quietly.

"Night, night," the little boy said with a smile.

"All right, let's go to bed now, Michen," Mkel said to his son and walked back to the living quarters. He set the little boy down in his crib after he gave Annan and Drake a kiss, and then he walked back to his sleeping chamber.

"Is everything ready for your trip?" Annan asked.

"Yes, Jodem and I went over everything while you were busy this afternoon," Mkel replied.

"Is there going to be any trouble?" she asked.

"Doubtful; when word of a metallic dragon arriving gets around, the area tends to quiet down, but there has been a lot of activity there. A lot of trouble between the nomadic Kaskar clans in the north and the southern kingdoms, with Morgathian incursions intermixed," Mkel replied.

"Silvanth told me that Jodem, Beckann, and Gallanth have perceived a growing danger in the east," she said.

"Silvanth tends to overexaggerate. Jodem and Gallanth get imprecise feelings this far away from there, and what they feel could be a shadow of the fire giant threat, or some combination of the two areas. In either event, there is a whole legion out there with some of the strongest land dragons in the Alliance. As always, Gallanth is the most powerful dragon in the world, save Michenth and Tiamat, so don't worry. Plus I will be taking extra bolts and gems just in case," Mkel assured her.

"It is my job to worry," she replied.

"Well, you and Silvanth will be the first ones I call if we get in trouble," Mkel said with a smile. "We need to go to sleep, for I have to wake up early tomorrow; remember, Battle Point is a couple of hours ahead of us."

Mkel settled into their large bed. "Good night, my love," he said.

"Good night," Annan replied.

CHAPTER III

BATTLE POINT

Mkel, wake up, my friend, it is time to get ready. Jodem is already up, Gallanth's deep voice resonated in Mkel's head. "I'm awake, you annoying lizard," Mkel replied in a tired but teasing tone. He then got up and went over to take a quick bath and get dressed. When he was finished putting his army tunic on, he kissed the still sleeping Annan and Michen and gave Drake a gentle pat on the head. "Watch over them while I'm gone, Drake," Mkel whispered to the large elven canine, who lowered his head and went back to his watchful sleep. He then walked out to Gallanth's landing, where the gold dragon was waiting.

"Good morning, my friend," Mkel gave a greeting with a smile.

"In a little better mood now, my young friend?" Gallanth replied with as much of a smile as a dragon can muster.

"Yes, I'm awake now; is Jodem already down at the stables?" he asked as he loaded his travel bag and his backpack, in which he carried extra bolts for his crossbow, his ledger for notes, and several other necessary items onto the side security straps of Gallanth's flying harness. He also loaded a sack with several hundred Drachlars and Drachmeres, which he carried just in case Gallanth got hungry or they needed anything when traveling, as well as spare gems and precious stones for Gallanth if he needed it for battle.

"Yes, he went down a short time ago." Mkel grabbed his riding coat off of the wall as well as Markthrea. His sword Kershan

131

already hung from his belt, and he placed his dragon tooth dagger in his boot sheath. He stepped up onto Gallanth's forearm and was hoisted up to his neck, swung his leg over, and sat on the wide padded saddle in between Gallanth's dorsal ridges. After he locked the crossbow onto the spindle, he gave Gallanth the clear signal that he was hooked in and ready. With that, the gold dragon spread his wings and pushed off of the ledge.

As Gallanth quietly glided down over the landing, Mkel thought to himself that Jodem would even be early for his own funeral. If he was late for anything, it meant real trouble. Gallanth landed by the stable side of the lake, and Mkel slid down his neck onto the dragon's forearm and then jumped to the ground. He walked over to the stable area, where Jodem was getting the last of his gear stowed on Vatara's flying saddle rig. Toderan was already there, and they were discussing a couple of matters regarding the Weir's administrative dealings.

"I'm glad to see you're awake and not going to miss our trip," Jodem teased him.

"Right; any issues before we go?" he asked.

"No sir, no real problems, just a couple of accounting issues with payment for the last food shipment from the bakery in Draden and a couple of other minor issues like the last load of heating and cooling crystals we sold to the merchants," Toderan explained.

"Isn't that Captain Hornbrag's area of responsibility?" Mkel asked.

"Yes, but while he is very gifted as a banker and money tracker, his common sense sometimes has to be questioned," Toderan replied.

"I think you don't give him enough credit," Mkel replied; although he knew Hornbrag could be aloof at times, he always had good intentions and his attention to detail in monetary manners was impeccable. Hornbrag also served as a Weir liaison on the staff for the Draden regiment and was a powerful fighter in his own right.

"We're just making sure, for the POE senators will be calling for a review of all the Weir's monetary transactions soon, and they will be looking for any small discrepancy," Jodem stated.

"This Weir will likely be a primary target for them, for the mithril and high gold and gem production we have. You would think they couldn't overlook the one premise in the Articles of the Alliance that states that the Weirs are basically autonomous. Especially since most of them are arbitrators and are supposedly learned in the law," Mkel said with slight sarcasm.

"It is better to be overly cautious than to sit before the senatorial hearing unprepared, plus Premier Reagresh has not yet rescinded Bilenton's coerced decree that the Weirs supply the senate with their financial transactions," Jodem answered. He was also very studied in Alliance laws and procedures and had embarrassed several arbitrators on many occasions.

"I understand that as well, but the law does give the Weirs a degree of autonomy," Mkel re-emphasized.

"That will be a point of contention at the next senate gathering," Jodem said in a concerned manner.

"Well, time will tell, but until then, we have work to do," Mkel answered.

"I will handle matters back here while you two are gone," Toderan said. "We will keep the Weir on track."

"I have faith, my friend," Mkel said to Toderan.

"Well, it's time to go, but first how about a little breakfast?" Jodem asked.

"I arranged for the kitchen personnel to bring sandwiches, fruit, and pastries over to the stables for you," Toderan added.

"How thoughtful of you, like a true support corps sergeant," Mkel said with a teasing smile.

However, as soon as he spoke, several halfling and human dining hall personnel started to stream from the kitchen area with small trays of various food entrees. Toderan and Jodem seldom left any details to chance. Mkel and Jodem quickly grabbed two sandwiches and several small pastries and fruit as well as juices. The group also replaced the provisions on Gallanth and Vatara; Gallanth had just walked back from the other side of the stable area, where he was fed two whole steer halves.

"I see you are full by the size of your belly, Gallanth," Toderan asked.

"Master butcher Jern always does an excellent job on the steers, he puts the other Weirs and town's chefs to shame," Gallanth replied. "Eat your breakfast, my friends, there is time before we have to leave." All three of them sat down and started to eat. The food, as always, was of excellent quality, for the

Weir's cooks took great pride in their work. Both humans and halflings were very skilled at their culinary craft. They finished their food with a little more idle chat regarding Tegent's and the elf's performance the previous night. The issue of Lieutenant Howrek came up; Mkel explained how he counseled him and that Toderan should talk to Sergeants Macdolan and Vaughnir to keep an eye on him. Mkel also wanted any further issues regarding this brought to his attention immediately.

Toderan still did not like giving Howrek a second chance, but he agreed to abide by Mkel's edict. As they finished the food on the table, the stable hands informed them that Gallanth's and Vatara's gear was secured and they were ready to fly. They inspected the flying rigs and straps constantly to avoid malfunctions in the air. The small group all rose and walked over to their waiting mounts.

"I wish you luck, and don't let General Daddonan talk you into anything," Toderan said.

"Don't worry, I will keep the good general from running over our young captain," Jodem teased.

"We will see what he has to say and what is causing him such consternation," Gallanth interjected as he knelt down to allow Mkel to get up on his back.

"I know, Gallanth; best of luck to you all," Toderan said as they mounted and positioned to take off.

"Have faith, good paladin," Gallanth replied, and Mkel waved and shouted a good-bye. Vatara spread his golden brown wings and jumped into the air with a strong downward stroke. The eagle rose and headed toward the entrance tunnel across the landing. Gallanth then crouched down, and with a spring from his four massive legs, a push from his huge tail, and a downward stroke of his wings, he was airborne and following Vatara out of the Weir. They emerged in the morning dawn with the light of the rising sun from the east over the plain coming through the break in the mountain chain facing the Weir entrance. They both performed several gyrations of their wings to gain altitude as they flew eastward toward the distant gap in the Gray Mountains.

They could have flown the whole way to Battle Point, but that would have taken several days, even with the speed of a gold dragon and a giant eagle. Jodem's staff's dragonstone started to glow, and with a bluish mirage-like shimmer of air around him and his giant eagle, they disappeared. Gallanth and Mkel visualized the air space over the walled city of Battle Point, and Mkel saw the familiar blue streaks of light form around them and then blackness. This only lasted a second, but the empty feeling of the inner space between points always reminded Mkel of total nothingness. In any event, they emerged over the city without error and began to circle around as Gallanth gave a greeting roar to announce their presence. This was to assure the tower guards and Battle Point land dragons that he was friendly and not a chromatic dragon seeking battle.

The walls of the city were made of heavy granite and limestone rocks that came from the quarry roughly five to six miles away. There was a smaller wall inside the main city wall, which was hastily built after a momentous battle over thirty years ago. The outer wall was at least sixty feet high, taller in many places. The city itself covered over fifty square miles, making it much bigger than Draden, but still not nearly as big as many of the coastal Alliance cities such as Atlean, Lancastra, and Fathracia, and nowhere near as large as Draconia. The central keep, which held the homes of the mayor and other government officials, as well as the backup headquarters for the commanding general of the legion stationed at Battle Point, now also housed several other key buildings and structures. The troops and various forces of the legion were stationed in barracks that ringed the inside of the city walls. The city itself held two hundred to three hundred thousand at any one time, but could hold much more.

Battle Point sat on the west side of the small river that ran south from the northern plains. It eventually grew wider and deeper as it neared the southern kingdoms and eventually emptied into the large inland Ontaror Sea that lay just north and east of the Fire Mountain chain, over eighteen hundred miles south. It also fed the vast swampland in that region. Battle Point was always bustling with activity. It was the central trading outpost and waypoint between all kingdoms east of the Alliance border as well as those in the north and south. Alliance forces at Battle Point created a degree of stability in the region, which allowed trade to flow freely.

There were three patrols of mounted hippogriffs coming and going in the air above the city besides Gallanth and Jodem, along with dozens of other non-military hippogriffs and flying mounts.

Mkel could see the crowds in the markets below stop to look up at the circling gold dragon and giant eagle. In a couple of minutes, a squadron of hippogriffs rose up from the stables and barracks located in the southern area of the city, which was also the largest landing within the city's walls, to meet and guide Gallanth and Vatara to their landing site. It was customary to escort a metallic dragon down to the landing. The escort was a type of honor or salute to the dragon and rider, for the arrival of a metallic, especially a gold or silver, meant the population would be a little safer and the legion or Alliance forces present had a powerful ally. A visit from a gold dragon also was rumored to mean good luck for that community. There was partial truth to this, for nothing in this world could face a gold dragon in battle and hope to survive one on one. Additionally, the higher metallic dragons, especially golds, inspired courage and uplifted the spirits of those who viewed them or were in the presence of one.

As the twelve mounted hippogriffs gained altitude and lined up with Gallanth and Vatara, the squadron leader waved to Mkel. The hippogriff riders alternated as lancers and missile soldiers, with either short composite recurved bows or repeating crossbows. They flew in pairs or wing mates to complement each other with one lance and one archer. They still wore the traditional banded or scale armor of the Alliance soldier, but it was more padded because of the colder temperatures that aerial riders encountered.

"Captain Mkel, Lieutenant Americ, sir. I am here to escort you, Gallanth, and Master Wizard Jodem to the lower field," the young Alliance officer said to Mkel through his seeing crystal.

"You lead and we will follow," Mkel responded, "but make sure to give us a wide berth, for the draft from Gallanth's back wings when he lands is enough to topple your hippogriffs."

"Yes sir, we will circle the city one more time to give the people one more good look at Gallanth, the mayor's idea, and then you can land in the center of the field in front of the barracks and stables. We will land just after you and behind you," the lieutenant instructed.

"Acknowledged, Lieutenant," Mkel agreed.

The hippogriffs flapped their brownish white wings almost in unison as they tried to move ahead of Gallanth and Jodem for the final circle around the city. Gallanth was a much faster flyer than a hippogriff, but he was cruising at almost a stall speed to allow the half-hawk, half-horse creatures to move ahead of him. It must have looked like an impressive sight from the ground to see the twelve hippogriffs in a V formation in front of Gallanth's immense seventy-five-yard wingspan.

"The crowds do love a show," Jodem said to Mkel through his crystal.

"It is all flattering but totally unnecessary," Gallanth added to both of them.

"Yes, but it is a tremendous morale boost to the city, modest dragon," Jodem responded.

"Yes, wise wizard", Gallanth responded with a slight tint of sarcasm in his voice.

Mkel felt Gallanth's body dip to the right as they followed the hippogriffs around the city's circumference. They swung wide out below the southern boundary of the city to allow a straight flight onto the landing. Mkel looked through his crossbow's sight at the legion's headquarters building at the north end of the landing. He saw General Daddonan and his staff gather outside the building to watch Gallanth and Vatara land.

Gallanth started his approach and quickly began to descend. He flew over the southern wall of the city roughly one hundred feet above the ramparts so as to not knock off any soldiers on the wall from his wing wash. He back winged quickly so as to not stir up too much grass and dirt close to the barracks and headquarters building. If he wanted to, the power of the wind from his wings could knock over an ogre. The bludgeoning power of his wings could kill an ogre or manticore and severely injure a hippogriff or griffon, but he could modify that power to a pretty good degree. The squadron of hippogriffs continued to soar over the legion headquarters building and split to circle back and land by their stables.

The gold dragon landed with a soft but noticeable impact tremor. Gallanth was always careful to land as softly as possible, but weighing dozens of tons does not make this an easy task. He folded his wings and began to walk to the crowd gathering at the headquarters building.

"It looks like they've assembled an entourage to come out to greet us, Gallanth," Mkel said with a smile to his dragon mate. *General Daddonan is always up for a little pageantry, and his staff follows him like a herd of sheep*, the gold dragon resonated again with a slight sense of humor, which was more than usual for him. He must be sensing something wrong, Mkel thought to himself, but still had to laugh out loud at his dragon's joke.

Gallanth stopped short of the legion headquarters building and the gathered staff. General Daddonan gave a cursory bow to Gallanth, after which Mkel saluted the general and gave his greeting of good morning. He put his backpack on, grabbed his crossbow, and slid down Gallanth's neck to his waiting front foreleg. Vatara landed beside Gallanth and Jodem also dismounted.

"Welcome, Gallanth, Captain Mkel, Master Wizard Jodem, welcome to Battle Point," General Daddonan said with a friendly but commanding smile.

"Good morning to you, General Daddonan, gentlemen," Gallanth said with a modest but booming tone.

"Yes General, good morning to you," Jodem added, for it was still morning, but two hours ahead of Draden.

"Sir," Mkel nodded.

"Gentlemen, please come in. We have the council room set up for you. The tea is hot and there are our best sweetbreads there. Come, we have much to talk about," General Daddonan added as he turned to walk up the steps. "Gallanth, you can rest yourself outside the windows of the council room to our right," he added.

Jodem and Mkel looked at each other to acknowledge that they both knew what he was going to propose. A stable hand walked over to Vatara and guided the great eagle to the stables. Gallanth gingerly stepped over to the area in front of the large windows of the council room of the headquarters building and lay down. Mkel could feel this, for the tremor of his massive body settling on the grass made the council room shudder.

"I understand why the Weirs are honed out of solid rock, I don't think our landing could handle him here very often," the general said with a slight smile.

"I could always create my own door to your council room, General," Gallanth said from outside the large room's windowed wall, which he now filled. In laying down, he also took up most of the space in the courtyard in front of the building.

"No, Master Dragon, I think you are fine just where you are, as long as it suits you," General Daddonan quickly replied as Gallanth rested his head on the ground, which still allowed him to look into the council room's open windows. "Now please, Captain, Jodem, sit. You must know why I've asked you to come all the way out here, so I will not insult your intelligence and will get right to the point. There has been a lot of hostile activity in this area in the last several months. Some we can trace to just roving bands of orcs and human marauders from the unclaimed territories in the east, but there is a growing power and organization to the attacks as well as an underlying Morgathian influence.

"The Kaskar clans to the north and the Northern Ontaror kingdoms to the south are also experiencing a great deal of unrest and unprovoked attacks from young chromatics," the general continued. "They are having internal problems as well, but they are blaming each other, and even the Alliance, which makes as much sense as an Enlightened senator trying to find his common sense." The general's joke brought some laughs.

"They blame the Alliance?" Mkel answered with a slight sense of irritation. "We are the ones who provide stability to this whole region. Without this city and your legions to stabilize the area, the trade that takes place here would cease, and open warfare would result. Nobody wins for long if there was no Alliance presence, sir."

"You said that these hostile forces were gaining in both power and organization?" Jodem asked.

"Yes, we are seeing increasingly more powerful creatures accompanying the orcs and human warriors as well as several moderately powerful sorcerers. I will have Colonel Sykes give you a more detailed picture," Daddonan explained.

The colonel stood up and said, "Master Dragon, Jodem, Captain, approximately three weeks ago we became engaged in a skirmish that quickly escalated into a good-sized fight about sixty miles south of here, outside a small river town that is one of the many stops on the way to the Ontaror inland sea. A routine patrol encountered a company of orcs that were being led by a small band of common giants, with a mountain giant in charge. They were threatening the town and claiming that any support to the Alliance would mean their destruction.

"The patrol had to call for reinforcements to deal with the giants," Colonel Sykes continued, "so a mixed task force of land dragons, heavy cavalry, and hippogriffs were dispatched immediately. Our wizard Andellion also accompanied them just in case. A fierce battle ensued, but with the aid of the combined task force, the tide quickly turned to our side. We killed most of the common giants and wounded the mountain giant when a drow wizard teleported in, riding a nightmare. A squadron of orcs riding giant wasp-like hymenoids also entered the fight from the east. The surprise attack took us off guard as the drow unleashed several powerful offensive spells before Andellion could react and eventually counter him. He defeated the dark elf, but the drow was not easy to kill."

The colonel paused.

"Around the same time," Colonel Sykes added, "a group of our rangers on a patrol observed a green dragon attack one of the more powerful Kaskar horse clans to the northwest of us. They eventually drove it back but not before it inflicted a good amount of casualties on the horsemen."

"They drove off a green dragon? With what?" Mkel asked with intense curiosity.

"They have developed a type of arrowhead made from volcanic black stone that is so sharp it can penetrate the hide of certain lesser dragons. It will shatter on metal, though, because it is brittle," Sykes answered.

"Yes, and I imagine it is much more effective on white, green, and black dragons due to their lack of a magic shield," Gallanth added from outside the window. "Precisely, Gallanth," General Daddonan added.

"Tell me more about the drow, Colonel," Jodem said with concern.

"He died in combat, felled by an arrow shot, and finished by the claw of a hippogriff after Andellion depleted his magic power in the exchange. Andellion was injured, though, and is recuperating in the healers' guild now. The drow did not have any Morgathian markings on his cloak, and the orcs did not carry any standard, not even a tribal one," Colonel Sykes added.

"His magical power was derived from a dark crystal, I presume?" Jodem asked.

"Yes, imbedded in his staff, as usual," Sykes said.

"It still smells of Morgathian backing" Gallanth interjected. "While there are rogue drow, a dark elf sorcerer does not usually travel alone, or without at least two or more drow men-at-arms bodyguards; this one was trying too hard to look independent."

"That and the fact that the orcs did not even have a tribal standard, which likely they were attempting to project the image of being just a large raiding party. They are not attacking Alliance forces directly, only neutral, lightly defended villages and caravans that did not want our protection. This is likely some type of deeper plan than simple pillage or want of treasure or food," Jodem surmised. He looked slightly puzzled as a small scowl came across his broad face, and he ran his fingers through his coarse dark gray hair.

"Were you able to take any prisoners, sir?" Mkel asked Colonel Sykes.

"No, the mountain giant managed to dive into the river and make it downstream," the colonel replied. "The orcs were killed outright, for they were not in a surrendering mood."

Mountain giants were excellent swimmers and could hold their breath for almost an hour, with some being able to breathe underwater. *That was an impressive feat for a creature so large to be that nimble*, Mkel thought to himself. They were the aloof but arrogant specimens of the giant races, taking on the very human trait of being either evil or good. Both types, however, considered themselves above all other races of giants. They were large powerful creatures, being second only to the thunder giants in size and strength. They could be up to eighteen feet tall and weighed five thousand pounds or more. They had bluish-white to granite gray skin and silver to bluish hair with clear blue or gray eyes. They were almost as diverse as men and were excellent strategists in war. The unique situation that there were both good and evil mountain giants almost led them to their destruction during the last Great Dragon War, for they attacked their counterparts relentlessly. Many had the spell ability of at least a mediocre cleric or sorcerer.

All mountain giants could throw good-sized rocks out to an effective range of one hundred fifty yards, inflicting great damage. They mostly preferred gargantuan spiked maces or metal clubs that inflicted crushing wounds due to their great strength. These agile brutes were very tough, being three times as resilient as a griffon, and they had a naturally thick skin. Most of the Morgathian or independent mountain giants inhabited crude mountain peak castles. Many of the remaining good mountain giants inhabited the Weirs or lived in mountains close to them and had defense pacts with the metallic dragons of the Alliance. Evil ones usually formed temporary alliances with chromatic dragons, especially red, blue, and greens, but they were careful, for often a chromatic turned on a giant for its treasure or to enslave it. They often headed up war bands of the other lesser giant races and evil creatures such as orcs.

"The drow wizard would have been an excellent source of information. I know this is difficult, but you should have your men try to take a prisoner if they can," Jodem told General Daddonan.

"That drow was too powerful, and Andellion was barely able to defeat him, let alone try to capture him," Daddonan said with authority.

"I realize that, but if drow are involved, this is the beginning of something larger. I'm surprised that you did not encounter a chromatic dragon or two," Jodem said.

"We were lucky, even though nine land dragons could have countered a red dragon," Daddonan replied.

"Yes sir, but you would have suffered heavy losses. Did the Dragon Council in Draconia tell you when you can expect to have a metallic out here anytime soon?" Mkel asked, tipping the hand on what they knew the general was going to ask.

"No, but I did hear it will either be one of the young coppers from Talinor Weir, with a brass dragon, or one of the new Avenger dragons from the capital," the general answered with a raised eyebrow.

"We will feel more comfortable when we get some type of dragon support way out here, Captain," Colonel Sykes said nervously but with a slight indignation. *Again that slight anxiety, almost animosity toward dragons and riders from higher ranking Alliance officers,* Mkel thought to himself, while not displaying any emotion or reaction.

I share your sentiment regarding the good colonel's attitude toward dragons, my friend, Gallanth said to Mkel telepathically as he tried to conceal his smile from his rider's silent comment.

"Captain, you are going to Draconia for the monthly Senate and Dragon Council gathering?" General Daddonan interjected, to redirect the tone of the meeting, as if he could also detect Colonel Sykes's growing attitude but did not want to correct him in front of his guests. He would reserve that task for later.

"Yes sir, Gallanth, myself, Jodem, and the other key leaders of Keystone Weir are going. Do you need transportation?" asked Mkel.

"No, a dragon from the Capital Wing is supposed to come and take me and my adjutant, although our teleportation circle is almost ready," he replied. "I am looking forward to seeing the new Avenger dragons and to make sure that stationing dragons here at Battle Point is a priority. This also brings me up to the point I wanted to talk to you about." He paused. "I know we will be getting a dragon dedicated to our city soon, but until then, I would feel a lot more comfortable if we had an interim defense agreement with a dragon and rider, like one of the most powerful dragons in the Alliance, for example," he said with a smile.

"Sir, you know that Gallanth and I are supposed to be solely dedicated to Keystone Weir, the town of Draden, and its regiment under Colonel Wierangan," Mkel explained with all sincerity. "I would not enter into another agreement unless I talked to the colonel. Now I will tell you that if Battle Point ever needs us or even the whole Weir garrison, we will be more than willing to fight with you and reinforce your legions."

"Yes, and that is both comforting and appreciated, but you also know, as I do, that as the senior dragon and rider and leader of a Weir, you are not totally bound by the Alliance military code. You enjoy a certain limited freedom and autonomy, in that you have flexibility in how you align yourself and those who you command. You are not bound to the Draden regiment," the general said with a softer, more convincing tone.

"I do understand that, sir, but it would not be honorable to make deals behind Colonel Wierangan's back that would leave him high and dry. The forces stationed around Draden are only a regiment, not a legion, like Colonel Lordan and Talonth have at Eladran Weir. The garrison at Keystone Weir is an integral part of the Draden regiment's forces, and I have made a defense allegiance agreement with Draden and its regiment. A dragonrider's word is his bond. I know that if we talk to Colonel Wierangan, we can come to some sort of agreement," Mkel answered.

"We can pursue that course of action, but again there is a simpler solution," Daddonan responded. "The increased trouble we have been experiencing in our region could be abated or put to rest if hostile forces would see a metallic dragon flying and patrolling the skies over our lands, especially a gold dragon."

"While that might be true in the short term, General," Jodem chimed in, "I feel there is a new threat rising, and just a show of force by Captain Mkel and Gallanth would only delay the inevitable. A fight is brewing and likely cannot be avoided, only dealt with and won." Jodem usually sat back and analyzed the situation before weighing into the discussion, but he spoke up sooner here.

"Plus, if my rider and I started to patrol the skies tomorrow," Gallanth added," sufficient force might be brought against us so that we would need to call for reinforcements ourselves. Surprise would be the key in this situation. Also, there is a great threat currently looming in the Fire Mountains that we, Haldrin's elves, and Eladran Weir are currently keeping an eye on. This could pose a significant threat to Alliance territory if left unchecked."

"Master Dragon, being the largest gold dragon, and the most powerful dragon in the world other than Michenth, you would inspire great fear in any chromatic that would dare venture anywhere close to your Weir or our territory," General Daddonan said.

"Yes, General, you would think, and nonaligned or independent chromatics usually respond that way; however, there has been an increased coordination growing in their ranks as of late, and this means a likely Morgathian connection," Gallanth added.

"We have been witnessing an unholy alliance between many of the closer orc tribes and the giants in the southern elbow where the Gray Mountains meet the fire caps," Jodem added. "We are expecting a major battle any time soon. There have been signs that several red and blue dragons have been working in concert in this gathering, along with you slaying a drow sorcerer, as Gallanth said, a dark force is rising under a suspicious cloud. If there is an organization of all the forces we have been discussing, especially chromatic dragons, we along with Gallanth will need reinforcements. The problem is where the next strike will come from and how spread out our forces are. This will determine a great deal. What is the true situation of the northern clans and the southern kingdoms?"

"Master Wizard, I know you know of the growing hostilities between the nomadic clans and many of the southern kingdoms," General Daddonan said. "Ten years ago, the horse clans were striking deep into the eastern lands and Morgathian territory, taking both wealth and resources from those areas. With the Morgathians and their Southern Ontaror kingdom puppets still reeling from the losses they suffered at our hands in the Great Dragon War, they were vulnerable to the rapid quick strikes of the Kaskar clans.

"Lately, however," the general continued, "with the combination of orc and drow pressure, and the ever increasing number of chromatic dragon attacks along with their own internal problems, the Kaskars are on the defensive. They are only organizing small raiding parties into Morgathian-protected lands, which has been only enough to keep them slightly off balance. The orcs and drow are under Morgathian control, with the dark armies led by errant death knights, Morgathian sorcerers, and scattered chromatic dragons. They are attacking deep into the eastern portions of the Kaskar lands but are still being driven back, with both sides incurring heavy losses.

"The Kaskars can drive the white, green, and black dragons away with moderate success," Daddonan said, "due to those types possessing weaker magic shields and the effectiveness of their obsidian arrowheads. Blues and especially reds, however, give them a great deal more trouble. The Kaskars, as you know, are mostly mounted cavalry, using their dismounted infantry as fodder. While their saber-toothed tigers and riders are feared, and the mammoths they employ are like our land dragons, they are not as effective or nearly as coordinated. The giant snow hawks and ravenhawks that make up their aerial wings, while numerous, depend on mass attacks, unlike our hippogriffs, giant eagles, and griffons. They are very mobile on the plains, however, and Morgathian cavalry is too heavy to chase them, and the orc's dire wolves are too slow. They've learned to react well to dragon attacks, being able to scatter quickly to minimize their breath weapons and spell effects. Like I mentioned before, their leaders do not seem to mind taking a great deal of casualties, as long as the outcome is in their favor.

"Lately, King Reshdon, in their capital city Elsidor, is losing his ability to bring the clans together when the situation is required," General Daddonan concluded. "The Kaskar Empire is suffering from a great deal of internal strife and in-fighting. There is an unusually aggressive atmosphere among clan leaders that has weakened the region."

"How are they countering the Morgathian and drow sorcerers along with the chromatics?" Jodem asked.

"They swarm the diving chromatic dragon with a barrage of obsidian-tipped arrows and hundreds of the mounted snow and ravenhawks," General Daddonan explained, "which eventually either drives them off or fells them. The whites usually attack until they are killed or severely wounded, as do the blacks. The greens are more cautious but still are aggressive and sadistic, but they usually retreat. Blues are much more deliberate and will usually fall back after both inflicting and taking a great deal of damage. Red dragons, as you know, are the most dangerous, and it takes several clans in concert to drive one off. The drow and Morgathian sorcerers are just as hard for them to fight, especially if they are on a flying mount. Again, barrages of arrows and spears finally break their magic shields. The Kaskars do have a few moderately powerful sorcerers that have bastardized dark crystals or pieces of a young chromatic's synthensium as a source of their magic. Their crude craftsmen do synthesize weapons from dragon parts of the chromatics that they manage to kill." General Daddonan explained. The general moved to show his guests a large map on the wall.

"It is very dangerous to use a dark crystal," Jodem said with concern, "for its malevolent powers can either seduce or destroy the wielder. Are they getting them through trade or warfare?"

"A little of both," Colonel Sykes interjected, "but their sorcerers don't usually last long enough for their crystals to overtake them."

"This is why now is the time for you, Gallanth, and your whole garrison to come out here. It would be a great bargain, not only for protection but to set up the Alliance for a speedier negotiation to bring the Kaskar clans back into the fold," General Daddonan added.

"It is also well known that the Kaskars are very distrustful of the Alliance and especially dragons. This is not easy to understand, because they and the kingdom of Freiland share a common ancestry, with the Freilanders being our strongest ally," Jodem said.

"Yes, but events are changing," Daddonan said. "It is only a matter of time before some belligerent white or red dragon attacks Elsidor, and then they will beg us for protection. It would be as if you and Gallanth came to their rescue. Gallanth, you are what, over twice the size of a white and a head longer than the biggest red dragon?"

"Yes, General, I can easily defeat six or more white dragons, and it would take three reds to hope to match me, but remember the chromatics breed at a much faster rate than the Alliance metallics. In spite of our power you've seen gold dragons fall right here at Battle Point years ago. The fact that we are soul mated and blood bonded with our riders greatly enhances our power, which is what saved us and the Alliance during the Great War. Recently the chromatics and other evil forces have been getting more aggressive and coordinated, which is unusual for them without Morgathian direction. This is why we suspect that Morgathia has regained her strength and is preparing for something on a larger scale," Gallanth explained.

"Aren't you more vulnerable to a white dragon's icy breath weapon?" Daddonan asked.

"Gallanth is more susceptible to cold-based weapons," Mkel explained, "but not as much as a red dragon is. He is also physically stronger than the most powerful red dragon and more maneuverable in the air, with his spell shield over three times as resilient. A red dragon's fire has a diminished effect against his golden armored hide, while Gallanth's plasma fireball will still inflict a severe injury against them. The sunburst beams he fires from his eyes can even tear into a red dragon's heavily armored hide. His spell casting powers are unmatched by any other dragon except Michenth and Tiamat themselves.

"This is not to dismiss the power of the chromatic dragons, for even a white is a formidable foe. A large red can wipe out an entire battalion in a flash," Mkel added.

"Here is an image of a red dragon that was seen by our ranger scouts last week, flying over the southwest plains from the mountains," Colonel Sykes explained as he directed his seeing crystal to show a good-sized red dragon over the projection of the terrain, soaring and scanning the area in front of him.

Red dragons were the most powerful of the chromatic dragons and perhaps the most cruel, evil, and aggressive. They were very greedy, vain, and covetous, boldly attacking anything they saw with a confidence that many times superseded their intelligence or judgment. Red dragons were extremely powerful physically, with only gold dragons being stronger. They bullied other chromatics and led lesser evil dragons in battle if only to hoard the glory and the treasure, or under the direction of a particularly powerful sorcerer or group of Morgathian nobles, who could mediate them through both their own power and threats from Tiamat.

The reds had a malevolent and threatening appearance, with their scales being a dull crimson red with hints of black on their wings. They slightly resembled silver dragons in their face and head, but their snouts were slightly thinner and narrower in appearance, with black streaks accenting their crimson coloration. Their bodies and wings also resembled silver dragons, with the same large wings and tail length, as well as back ridges. In general, they had a more sinister appearance, with a greater neck frill and narrower eyes.

With their heads not being as broad or powerfully built as a gold dragon's, their bite was meant more to tear than to crush. They had two protruding, twisted horns that swept back from the top of their heads and also spawned a small row of horns that ringed the top of their eye sockets. Chromatics in general had twisted main skull horns as opposed to the smooth horns of metallics. The red dragon snouts were sharp, with several teeth that protruded from their mouths. Their eyes and nostrils also had very sharp edges, adding to their sinister appearance. The red dragons had the longest wingspan of the chromatic types, averaging sixty to sixty-five yards, and they were thirty to forty yards long, approximately the same size as a silver dragon. Their immense size and similar wing outline caused them to be confused with silver dragons when viewed from the ground as they flew overhead at high altitude, for their silhouette was almost identical. This was not a good mistake to make.

Red dragons had a particular disdain for humans and elves but they remotely respect power. While they were as large as silver dragons and more physically powerful, they were slower and much less maneuverable in flight. They were also natural enemies of silver and gold dragons and attacked silvers on sight, even attacking a gold if goaded into doing so. The more intelligent gold and silvers usually played on a red dragon's vanity, for the powerful reds were not used to being challenged. While these evil specimens had powerful magical abilities, the gold dragons always prevailed, and the silvers almost always succeeded in a fight. This was due to their superior intelligence, faster recharging breath weapons, and spell abilities derived from having a blood bonded rider. In spite of this, the red dragons' pride usually provoked them into a fight, which was usually their undoing.

Even with this realization, red dragons still believed themselves to be the epitome of dragonkind, and they resented the superior power of gold and silvers. They were apt to fly into a blind rage in an instant over an insult, a stolen piece of treasure, or a challenge to their strength. These rages often led them to raze entire towns. Their competition amongst themselves also led to conflict. Red dragons loved attacking copper and brass dragons when they could catch them.

They as a species led the charge, under Tiamat's direction, against the dragons' blood bonding with humans. Reds only allowed the most powerful humanoids to ride them. This was done out of fear, mutual lust for destruction, acquisition of treasure, or simple convenience, but always for their best interest, unless they were otherwise coerced. Their temporary riders were not blood bonded, so the telepathic link did not exist, making them a less effective team than metallic dragons and their riders. It also did not increase their magical power or enhance their breath weapon. They worked with the leaders of the Morgathian Empire out of necessity and quest for treasure, as well as hatred of the metallic dragons and their human, elf, and dwarf allies. They were, however, still not easy to rally, with Tiamat being the only creature the red dragons obeyed without question. The five Usurper dragons also helped Tiamat control the chromatics. Only a very powerful sorcerer, death knight, or warlord can control a red dragon.

The red dragons preferred high mountains and caves for their lairs, and they would like nothing more than to plunder a Weir for its wealth and location. While they could swim, they adamantly disliked the water, leaving that realm to the black and green dragons. They would occasionally form pacts with fire giants along with orcs and drow, and occasionally with evil mountain giants. Chromatic dragons and the evil giant races always had an uneasy relationship, however. Many times, fire giants took young dragons and used them as guards and mounts until the dragons became large enough to rebel, then they might become the slaves. The chromatics and mountain, fire, ice, and common giants suffered tremendous casualties during the Great Dragon War, but they all reproduced much faster than their good counterparts. The red dragons were also not known for taking care of their young, but the females protected selected clutches. They preferred fresh meat, with young human or elf maidens and children considered a delicacy due to them also deriving power from their fear. They also consumed sulfur-bearing rocks along with gems, to give them the power for their breath weapons and magic.

Red dragons did not have the ability to create dragonstones; however, they could empower certain weapons, usually made of black iron, with fire ability by adding a drop of their blood. Weapons that were empowered in this way, such as swords, axes, and certain bows, could only sustain their power for a limited amount of time, after which they needed to be recharged by the dragon, who usually only did so at a great price or favor. They can enhance dark crystal, but again the effects are temporary, but with this substance more powerful. Red dragons had the second toughest armored hide, equal to silver dragons, which offered them tremendous protection and fire resistance (with the exception of a gold dragon's plasma fire blast).

They were strong flyers but not as fast or as maneuverable as metallic dragons, preferring to fight on the ground if possible. They only had limited magical ability, which was mostly fire based. This was due to them not being bonded with a human rider, which was also a disadvantage in combat with metallic dragons. Red dragons did have the power of suggestion against weak-minded creatures, which they used to their advantage. Their tails did not have the broadened terminal fin that gold dragons did, but they had large dorsal ridges. They liked to pick fights with coppers, and they usually had the upper hand over the smaller earth dragons. Additionally, their power of teleportation was more limited than that of a metallic dragon, both in the number of times they could use it and in accuracy.

Jodem spoke up, "the important thing to remember is timing. If an attack such as this would occur to either Elsidor or one of the southern kingdoms, we still could not respond or help unless we are asked. I do know there is a planned visit to the northern city. Our ambassadors are currently negotiating this now. Likely Mkel, Gallanth, and I will attend along with Slidess and Trikenth and a contingent from Draconia." Jodem had interjected somewhat forcefully, much to the surprise of Mkel. *He must have been talking to the Wizard Council yesterday*, he thought to himself. "The elf queen Eladra has also had disturbing visions as of late. She sees danger from both the east and the west of the Alliance. Her vision from the east was that the people of the low plains are in danger. This is partially why we are here to investigate," Jodem further explained.

"People of the low plains in the east?" General Daddonan asked. "Could she mean the village of Handsdown? It is a small but growing trading village located about a hundred miles to the east of here at the edge of our territory. We have an infantry platoon there with cavalry and a small aerial contingent as an outpost that we rotate every week or so."

"I would send them reinforcements as soon as possible," Gallanth said, "just as a precaution. I too am feeling a looming danger in that direction."

Eladra was the queen of Allghen Forest, the central elf realm within the Alliance that was treated as a separate nation within the republic. She was more powerful than any wizard or sorceress in the land. Her magical power alone stopped a whole division of orcs during the Great Dragon War, and she felled at least three red and blue dragons herself. While Gallanth as a gold dragon, Jodem, and to a lesser extent silver and brass dragons had a limited power of foresight, Eladra was the most gifted by far. She was so revered, by men and dragon alike, that they renamed a Weir after her: Eladran Weir. Mkel only saw her once, when he bonded with Gallanth. She resembled Beckann to a certain degree but was even more beautiful, with her gold and platinum hair and iridescent aqua-colored eyes.

"I will send a hippogriff squadron to drop off the rest of that company, just to make sure. Colonel Sykes, please see to this immediately," General Daddonan ordered.

"Yes sir, right away," the colonel answered as he nodded to both the hippogriff and infantry battalion commanders that were present.

"I guess I will not be able to convince you to break your defense pact with Draden and Colonel Wierangan," he said again to Mkel and Gallanth.

"As of right now, no sir, but I will contact Colonel Wierangan to see if some compromise can be reached. It is as much a matter of courtesy as upholding my word as an Alliance officer and dragonrider, and is something that must be discussed in person not over seeing crystals," Mkel answered.

"All right, Dragonrider, I will also talk to him when I can arrange a trip back west, as soon as I can break away from here. Until then, I know we can count on you all if we have our backs against the wall. We do have a special treat for you, Jodem and Gallanth. The legion is having an inspection today, in Gallanth's honor, and you are welcome to attend. Afterward, there will be a celebration, feast, and dance to welcome the beginning of the harvest and to honor our hopeful future dragon and rider allies," Daddonan said, giving a nod to Gallanth.

"It is disheartening to see a general grovel like that. Beg to a captain and a dragon," Colonel Sykes whispered to Colonel Ponsellan, the commander sitting next to him.

"We graciously accept your invitation, sir," Mkel said.

"You need not honor me, General. I am always happy to serve the Alliance and help protect its inhabitants and further the cause of light. And Colonel Sykes, it is not considered groveling to ask for help to protect your soldiers," Gallanth added, putting the legion second in command on the spot.

"As you say, Master Dragon," General Daddonan said as he stood up, triggering all in military uniforms to stand up and salute the legion commander as he gave Sykes an evil stare. "Captain, Master Wizard, I will have an attendant see you to your quarters."

"Thank you, General," Jodem answered with a slight smile as they started to walk out onto the landing field to get their gear from their mounts. The day was turning out to be beautiful and sunny, with a slight warm breeze. There would be time before the legion assembly in the afternoon to settle in and walk around. "You handled the general well, my friend," Jodem whispered to Mkel after they were outside. "You didn't cave into his request, but you also did not outright dismiss him either."

"What do you think Colonel Wierangan will say?" Mkel asked.

"There will most likely be a compromise, with Wierangan consenting to have the garrison perform exercises with Battle Point on occasion and come to their aid if needed, until they get a dragon or two from Draconia. Plus, like the general said, we do have a degree of autonomy," Jodem added.

"Time will tell," Mkel responded. "It should not be long before an Avenger dragon or at least a brass or copper can be stationed out here. Freiland should be getting Turanth, the young bronze dragon," Gallanth said as softly as possible.

"That is, if the POE senators do not try to block the move," Jodem answered as he and Mkel moved their gear into their rooms beside the legion headquarters, facing the landing field so he and Gallanth could see each other through the window of Mkel's room.

"The senate has its agenda and we have ours, Master Wizard. The Enlightened senators have only been emboldened from former Premier Bilenton's tenure," Gallanth replied as he lay down and started to fall asleep in spite an ever growing crowd of onlookers. Both legionnaires and civilians gathered to get a peek at the big gold dragon, who looked impressive, even when sleeping. Jodem told Mkel that he wanted to see Andellion before everything started and wish him a speedy recovery, and also to get a little information from him regarding his fight with the drow.

The next several hours passed quickly, with Mkel watching as hundreds of Alliance soldiers, horses, hippogriffs, and land dragons poured out of the barracks and stables. The legion at Battle Point was slightly modified from the standard Alliance legion design, in that it was larger and most of the infantry units were horse mounted, similar to Eladran Weir's legion. Not all were skilled to fight mounted like paladins, but they rode for rapid transportation because of the distances they had to cover out there on the plains of the unsettled lands. The basic legion was composed of roughly six thousand soldiers. This included three medium infantry battalions and a heavy infantry battalion to form the infantry regiment, a land dragon battalion, a heavy horse cavalry squadron, a catapult battalion, a sapper unit, a support corps battalion, and a ranger company. The Battle Point legion had four infantry battalions instead of three, and all were mounted. They had two additional medium cavalry battalions to supplement its heavy cavalry battalion that formed a regiment. This was also done to counter the roving gangs of bandits that plagued the area, preying on the many trade caravans, as well as the Kaskar clans that frequently broke the treaty and raided towns and merchant wagon trains.

As the legion started to assemble, their standard composition started to form with the first medium infantry battalion nearest Gallanth. It had the usual six companies of one hundred eighty soldiers apiece, along with a small staff of ten to twelve with a commander and a senior sergeant for a total of approximately twelve hundred. The soldiers were arranged in twelve-man squads with an eight-man infantry team equipped with a long sword, large shield, long spear, dagger, and either banded armor or scale mail with a helmet. The other four men formed the range weapons team, with two armed with either repeating or heavy crossbows, and the other two with long composite bows. They also had a long sword, buckler, and helmet. They carried forty bolts or arrows, and had the same types of armor. All the Battle Point legion's weapons and armor looked to be of almost Weir quality but more worn.

The squad leaders seemed to be of good quality as they arranged their men, who were fairly well armed with several having either a mithril alloy or magic weapon. There were three squads in a platoon, with the platoon leader being a formally trained commissioned officer, having attended the Alliance military academy or with a field commission, and a senior platoon sergeant of great experience. All officers had to have served at least three years as a line soldier. There was usually one battle healer per platoon, but here at Battle Point, there were two. Each battalion was supposed to have an organic wizard of mid degree with one or two apprentices, all of which provided immediate magic firepower and protection for the battalion, but they were in short supply here in the remote plains.

The heavy infantry battalion formed in the middle of the legion and was structured the same as the medium battalion, but the infantrymen were equipped with either full plate or breastplate over scale armor and were armed with large shields and either long swords, great axes, or heavy maces. The range weapons teams were armed with banded armor, crossbows, and long spears. The heavy infantry battalion was utilized as an anchor for a defense similar to how the Keystone Weir used the dwarf company. They were more focused on the close fight than missile barrages.

The land dragon battalion moved past Gallanth; it was composed of three hundred sixty men working with fifty-two land dragons. They formed three companies composed of fifteen land dragons each, with three platoons of four dragons and the commander's, executive officer's, and senior sergeant's land dragon. There were four land dragons in the battalion headquarters for the battalion commander and his senior staff. The land dragons were utilized by Battle Point like the Draden regiment did, as a spearhead or breaking force in an all-out land battle or to fight larger powerful opponents the legion faced such as giants. The wingless dragons were the heavy hand of the legion and used as much to intimidate potential threats as to help stabilize the region.

The land dragons were among the most feared creatures in the unsettled lands and kept the peace up until recently. The Battle Point land dragons had even slain small white, green, and black dragons, as they always worked in pairs but also worked as a whole platoon.

The heavy cavalry squadron then started to filter in after the land dragons. There were roughly three hundred sixty mounted heavy warhorses. They were arranged in three troops of one hundred twenty cavalrymen apiece plus the commander, senior sergeant, healer, and small staff. The squadron was usually commanded by a powerful and experienced paladin of colonel or senior colonel rank. The heavy mounted cavalrymen were mostly paladins (or horsemen training to be paladins), all equipped with half plate or full plate armor with metal shields, and they were armed with hand and a half swords and heavy lances. Many of the senior paladins had some type of magical weaponry or armor, with the rest being of masterwork. Half had light repeating crossbows.

A very powerful paladin commanded the troop, leading with the power of his holy sword, which was the ultimate weapon for an Alliance knight.

The two medium cavalry squadrons immediately followed. The medium cavalry was organized in the same manner as the heavy cavalry, just lighter armed and armored with more of a focus on speed and mounted archery. Their horses did not wear barding and were runners as opposed to the paladin mounts of the heavy cavalry. The soldiers themselves wore light scale or partial banded armor and were armed with long spears, long swords, small shields, and light helmets, as well as short composite bows or light repeating crossbows. They were meant for fast strikes but could fight on foot as well and operated in the field longer than the heavy cavalry. They trained to have more endurance for covering greater distances faster.

The light archer cavalry worked in conjunction with all the other forces in the legion or performed fast strikes and reconnaissance. Both Battle Point and Eladran Weir took this type of fighting and cavalry style from the northern Kaskar clans, who used mass light cavalry strikes to deliver a hail of arrows and then rapidly withdraw. While they were not as accurate as a stationary archer, they were very effective for these rapid attacks. Their organization seemed different to Mkel, who observed senior archers with very few commissioned officers. He would have to ask General Daddonan about them, for he was indeed curious.

The Battle Point's catapult battalion wheeled in from the opposite side of the field, and Mkel observed them though his crossbow's sight. They consisted of three batteries of three heavy catapults and three trebuchets apiece, mounted on special reinforced spring-equipped wagons with seventy-two men per battery. These siege engines gave the legion a total of eighteen long-range throwers operated by four hundred thirty-two men. The operators were specialized in the deployment of these deadly weapons. Battle Point had extra men and horses to man their catapults to allow more rapid transport over the long distances that they needed to travel to support their soldiers. Their catapults apparently had the same range as his Weir's and utilized the same type of stones, dragon's fire canisters, and the soft clay projectiles that had hundreds of nails imbedded within the sphere.

The sapper unit of the legion consisted of only one hundred twenty men. Mkel surmised that the Battle Point legion was more concerned about their own mobility rather than defensive works, since they were not out to seize opposing enemy fortresses but defended the city and the surrounding areas through a highly mobile force. They were not as concerned with siege towers or battering rams. The sapper soldiers also seemed more armed than the standard Alliance sapper.

The support battalion for Battle Point was also arranged slightly differently, being much more mobile and robust to support the increased number of cavalry; this legion was also more spread out across the broad swath of terrain that they had to cover. They had several senior clerics to help the support battalion commander perform her duties as well as providing a greater magical defensive power to the battalion. Likely also to make up for the fact that they did not have any female dragons assigned to the support battalion. *This would also have to be remedied,* Mkel thought to himself. Again, these support soldiers were also more heavily armed and armored than their standard Alliance counterparts.

The aerial battalion assigned to the legion took off and then quickly landed. It had over seventy-five mounted hippogriffs. They were arranged in a similar fashion to Draden's aerial battalion, with three companies of twenty-five hippogriffs apiece. A soldier told Mkel that they were mainstays of Battle Point, with their flights being a welcome reinforcement to all forces that were hard-pressed. While not at full strength, they were constantly attempting to increase the numbers of their war birds.

Mkel saw the legion's organic ranger company, which was mostly mounted on griffons but had a few giant eagles. This one-hundred-twenty-man unit was composed of all human rangers with one elf to aid them in tracking and dealing with the wood elves that resided in the forests to the northwest. Mkel noticed that he had the markings of Haldrin's clan from Lucian Forest on his cloak. Like the ranger platoon at the Weir, they conducted raids and scouting missions for the legion into enemy and troubled areas.

Andellion, the legion's senior wizard, was a key individual on the legion's staff, being an advisor to the legion commander and teacher to the apprentice wizards. Andellion gave the legion the most magical offensive and defensive capabilities that he could muster and coordinated with the battalion's wizards if a great threat from enemy sorcerers, powerful evil creatures, and chromatic dragons materialized. They also acted as ambassadors for the legion when needed.

Jodem walked out of their lodging and joined Mkel as he made his way over to Gallanth. The gathering legion soldiers were all staring at the sleeping dragon, who even with his tail wrapped around his one side and his wings folded was still just under twenty-five yards long and took up a good patch of ground.

"Hey big fellow, it's time to wake up. The whole legion is gathered to both see you and show off for you," Mkel said to his dragon as he put his hand on his massive cheek. "I am awake. I just wanted to give them a little time to get by and to give me clearance to stand up. Quite a large force compared to the Draden regiment or even a standard Alliance legion," Gallanth replied.

"Yes, but Draden has the Weir garrison and you," Mkel replied.

"It has us," Gallanth said with endearment.

"All right, just get up and raise their spirits," Mkel said with a smile.

Gallanth lifted his head, stood up on all four of his thick tree-trunk-sized legs, and stretched his neck, wings, and tail after ensuring that he would not hit anyone.

"I see General Daddonan and his staff gathering up by his headquarters building, and we don't want to keep the general waiting," Mkel said as Gallanth looked down at him with the best a dragon could do to make a smile.

"No, we can't have that, especially Colonel Sykes and his staff," Jodem echoed as they started to walk to the front of the assembling legion toward General Daddonan and his staff. Gallanth walked slowly behind them, trying not to create too heavy a tremor from his heavy footsteps, for even as big as he was, he could walk relatively quietly when he wanted to. The soldiers of the legion quieted down as Gallanth approached, staring in amazement at the big gold dragon. They probably had not seen a gold dragon for some time, and then to be this close to the largest dragon in the world, save Michenth and Tiamat, must have left a distinct impression. This was especially true since Gallanth was almost three times the size of a land dragon. Mkel's soldiers and even the soldiers of the Draden regiment were used to being around Gallanth.

"Welcome, Draden Weir," General Daddonan greeted them.

"Gold dragon Gallanth, Captain Mkel, Master Wizard Jodem, on behalf of the Battle Point legion, we welcome you and are honored by your presence," Colonel Sykes echoed as the chief of staff and official commentator of the legion. Mkel was used to some Alliance officers having a little animosity toward him for being both a dragonrider and an officer. Only a few like Colonel Lordan and Lieutenant Bristurm were in the same position he was. The only ones who could give Colonel Lordan a hard time were generals, but they did not, because of his stature as a silver dragonrider and Weirleader.

"The legion is anxious for your review, Lord Gallanth," Sykes added, almost biting his tongue. "Commanders, bring your units to attention," he shouted as the subordinate battalion and regiment commanders saluted, turned around, and called their commands to attention. "Sir, Gallanth, gentlemen, if you would follow me." He turned and walked toward the first infantry battalion. The group walked over to the beginning of the infantry regiment. The soldiers were standing tall, shoulder to shoulder, tens of rows deep. Their armor and weaponry looked very well kept, almost to a fault, but still well used. As General Daddonan walked up to the regimental commander, he drew his sword, an impressive mithril alloy broad sword with a dragonstone in the pommel, likely from a bronze or silver dragon. He saluted the general and Gallanth, and the general returned the salute with his sword, and Gallanth lowered his head for a cursory return.

As they walked across the front line of troops, Gallanth spoke in his full voice, commenting on how good the soldiers looked. "Impressive infantry, General. I see courage and spirit in them," he stated. The infantry regiment alone was almost the size of Draden's combined regiment with the Weir's garrison. They then walked past the cavalry regiment. They looked almost as good as Lenor's paladins, but the Weir's knights were slightly better armed. Again Gallanth complimented them, and to the surprise of the cavalrymen, Gallanth did not spook their horses like they've seen chromatic dragons do.

Next was the land dragon battalion. These land dragons were not as big as Wheelor's but were more on par with Draden's company. Gallanth spoke up in Draconic, which only Mkel, Jodem, and the battalion wizards could likely understand.

"Thank you, my little brothers, keep your strength and faith." All the land dragons present, roughly thirty of their total of forty-eight, bowed their heads in unison, much to the surprise of their crews, in deference to Gallanth. This was again the fondness that the metallic dragons had for their smaller land dragon cousins and the inherent admiration that the less-intelligent land-bound fire serpents had for the dragons, especially gold and silvers.

As the group walked in front of the hippogriff squadron, Gallanth stopped and looked directly at a young rider. When any metallic dragon would look at someone, it was as if they could look right into their soul, but especially a gold dragon could make a man shiver. It could be both an uncomfortable and peaceful experience at the same time, for dragons could read emotions as if they were spoken words, and they could always tell if someone was lying.

"Do not worry, young Dackner, rider of Bracks, you will not fail your comrades in battle, and you will find your courage. I have faith, so should you," Gallanth said to the young hippogriff rider, nodding his immense head to convey that an answer was not necessary. Dackner looked at Mkel, who smiled at him as they kept walking. He started to blush with embarrassment as the other riders in his squadron looked at him with an intense curiosity. Even his hippogriff seemed surprised by the incident; they were usually oblivious, being only just slightly more intelligent than dogs. It was well known that gold dragons had the power of foresight to varying degrees, but to be talked to by one was usually a sign of very good luck.

Mkel reminded himself to ask what his dragon meant by his comments. He likely had a feeling of some sort that this particular lad would play a part of something in the near future. *Time will tell*, he thought to himself. They then passed the catapult battalion, sapper unit, support corps battalion, and ranger company. All looked very professional and polished, and they projected good bearing. Their rangers were not all mounted on griffons; some were on giant eagles, and only one of their numbers present were elves, who gave the elven acknowledgment to Gallanth. They at least had two elves, which Mkel considered good. Out here on the plains, they likely didn't feel at home, for a lack of forests. Their dealings with the independent wood elves in the forests of the north made their sacrifice valuable to the Alliance. The wood elves distrusted all and were only slightly friendly to the elves of the Alliance. However, in this far outpost of the Alliance, they came to their aid against the occasional chromatic attack, especially the elf-eating green dragons that tended to inhabit the same areas as elves.

They then made their way back to the front of the legion formation. General Daddonan moved up to the stand and placed his dragonstone-powered sword in the central podium to enable it to amplify his voice. "Gentlemen, ladies, soldiers of Battle Point, please stand at rest. I first want to tell you that all units of the legion look outstanding, and I am very proud of what I see today and the job that you have been doing in the recent months. The fight we recently had south of here showed the enemy our mettle. We suffered only three casualties to a whole company of orcs and a band of giants that were sent to hell. Even the drow sorcerer was taken down fairly quickly. We have a special honored guest here today, in case you missed him," he joked as chuckles reverberated throughout the formations of soldiers in light of the forty-five-yard-long gold dragon sitting directly behind him.

"We want to give the mighty gold dragon Gallanth, his rider Captain Mkel, and the Council Wizard of Keystone Weir, Jodem, a hearty welcome to Battle Point." A thunderous applause came from the six thousand soldiers standing in formation. "I don't want to take any more of your time than I have to, for I will have a meeting with your commanders later. So I now have the pleasure to introduce the most powerful dragon in the Alliance, save Michenth himself," he finished as he turned and walked off of the platform and gave a nod to the gold dragon.

Gallanth raised his immense head as the soldiers of the Battle Point began to cheer again. Mkel was standing with Jodem beside Gallanth and looked up at his dragon. At the Weir and with the garrison, Gallanth did not speak a great deal to the men, other than occasional words of encouragement and during leader meetings. However, when they traveled outside of the Weir or interacted with other non-Weir Alliance units, Gallanth did as much talking as Mkel. Even though he was the rider, he was still a captain, and sometimes higher ranking officers would listen to a dragon, especially a gold dragon, before they would him.

"Soldiers of Battle Point legion, I, my rider Captain Mkel, and the wizard Jodem are all honored to visit your city and our fellow Alliance brothers and sisters of arms. We are extremely impressed with what we have witnessed. I can see the honor and courage that this legion is known for in your eyes and in your hearts. I also mourn with you for the blood you have spilled recently in your battle to the south. You can be assured that the enemy knows who dealt them the blow, for you performed admirably and are a credit to the Alliance. We are entering into uncertain times, and a growing threat is emerging but has not fully identified itself as of yet. Whatever that threat might be, I have faith that this legion will meet this challenge face to face and see it put to ruin. We want you to know that if and when you are in dire need, you can count on the full might of Draden Weir." A loud cheer erupted from all the soldiers assembled on the parade field, for they knew the promise of a metallic dragon was as unbreakable as mithril. The knowledge of a whole Weir, especially Draden, backing them up likely rested a great deal of anxiety and fears of the soldiers of this legion, especially with rumors of chromatic dragons encroaching. Jodem and Mkel looked at each other with an uneasy feeling, for Gallanth had just promised them what he and Jodem had spent hours today avoiding saying to General Daddonan, without consulting Colonel Wierangan first.

Put your mind at rest, my friend. I know Colonel Wierangan will not argue, especially if I tell him it is to his advantage, Gallanth explained to Mkel telepathically. *I hope you are right, Gallanth*, Mkel said silently back to his dragon. *You just have to have faith, my friend*, Gallanth answered back with a trace of humor in his mental reply.

"We will have to trust in your dragon, Mkel," Jodem whispered to Mkel.

"Now my friends, you will need to find your courage, for it will be tested in the coming months. I know you will perform with bravery and honor. Trust in the Creator's divine providence, trust in the Alliance, and trust each other. Faith and strength to you all," he finished as he bowed his head in a kind of Draconic salute and took a step back. He then let out a full battle roar, which could shake buildings to their foundation, which was then echoed by all the land dragons.

General Daddonan quickly sprang back up to the platform and called his subordinate commanders to attention. The clamor of over six thousand soldiers' armor and weapons, and the rustling of beasts reverberated throughout the landing field. He then called for a presentation of arms as a salute to Gallanth. The gold dragon again bowed his head as a return salute. General Daddonan turned back to face the legion.

"Soldiers of Battle Point, I welcome all of you to the celebration feast in honor of our Weir guests and the bountiful fall harvest. Commanders, you may dismiss your men," he finished, saluting with his sword, and the battalion and regimental commanders returned the salute. Gallanth turned to walk back to the landing area in front of the visitors' quarters. Mkel and Jodem quickly turned to walk back as well, for Mkel did not want to hear the slight gloat in General Daddonan's voice.

"Fear not, my friend. Colonel Wierangan will understand. I have an uneasy feeling about this region, now that we are here, in that conflict is just over the horizon. They will need us and likely all the garrison. Maybe even the Draden regiment," Gallanth said out loud to Mkel.

"I always have faith and trust in you, Gallanth," Mkel replied.

"Yes, but how will the Dragon Council react to this?" Jodem asked.

"General Becknor and Valianth will understand. They know that even though the Capital Wing provides overall protection to Battle Point, they take time to mobilize, and time might be critical to these soldiers," Gallanth replied.

"I wish you luck, Gallanth. You know how testy Valianth has been as of late, and remember, he is senior to you," Jodem added.

"Also remember, Master Wizard, that my brother Falcanth is on the council as well," Gallanth replied.

"I guess it will depend on how the other senior Weir dragons and Capital dragons view the situation," answered Jodem.

"How about the Wizard Council of Thirteen?" Gallanth asked.

"I will work on them," Jodem replied.

"I know Eladran, High Mountain, Atlean, Rom, Rem, Denar, and Talinor Weirs will back us up, with Lancastra and maybe Machren Weirs likely agreeing with us as well," Mkel added, knowing the Weir leaders and senior dragons of those Weirs very well. He knew that seven of the twelve Weirs were closely aligned with Draden. Ferranor and Ice Bay Weirs were the other remaining fortresses that rimmed Alliance territory, with the exception of Talinor Weir and the Capitol Weir.

"Just have faith, Mkel my rider, the council will go our way. We do not need permission or funds from the senate either. It is just a defense agreement to support and protect this legion," Gallanth explained.

As they walked back to the visitor quarters, cooks from the legion's support section had already wheeled up two wagons with freshly butchered steers. They were lightly cooked over the large fire pits that were blazing on the south side of the landing field and well seasoned. General Daddonan did his homework, for this was how Gallanth liked his meat.

"I see you've made General Daddonan very happy, my large Draconian friend. I wonder how he acquired the knowledge of your taste in meat?" Jodem asked with a slight hint of curiosity.

"People come and people go through Draden all the time. The caravans that are headed to Battle Point will sometimes stop in the Weir for a weapons fit or trade. We are almost as large a trading center as Battle Point," stated Mkel.

"My rider is correct, Master Wizard, but nonetheless we should address it through Sergeant Toderan and Captain Hornbrag upon our return to Draden," Gallanth added.

"Sir, pardon me, Master Dragon, but your tables, food, and drink are ready," a civilian support staff worker told Mkel and Jodem. While the inspection was taking place, the kitchen workers and halflings had moved all the tables out of the great hall and were bringing food out by the wagon load. Mkel wanted to go back to his quarters and stow his riding jacket.

"Gallanth, go ahead and eat, I'll be right back," Mkel said.

"I can wait, he replied." Mkel hurried to the guest quarters building and put his riding jacket in his room. He was glad to have the dragon armor jacket off and would just wear his uniform tunic and mithril weave undershirt that Ordin gave him. The weather was warm and very nice for a late summer day, with clear skies, for they were on the plains and away from a major body of water and the mountains with forests.

Mkel emerged from the building as the legion was gathering to the hundreds of tables set up on the landing. Gallanth was sitting down by the two wagons that had brought the steer halves; he would have to remain there until the legion dispersed. Even the slightest miscalculation on his part with his tail or his massively clawed foot could kill or maim a man.

The smell of fresh breads, cooked meats, and stews wafted through the air. The kegs of draft ales and wine were tapped, and the bards and minstrels were beginning to play. *An impressive feast*, Mkel thought to himself. Not quite as good of quality as what the Weir put on, but a non-Weir aligned legion did not have the resources or riches that Draden or the other Weirs possessed.

"Mkel, come, sit down; the first course is excellent, and the ale is almost as good as the amber brews of Draden," Jodem yelled over to Mkel.

"I'm coming, I'm coming, just save a few ales for me," Mkel answered.

The melodies of lyres, guitars, flutes, drums, pipes, and the voices of bards could be heard over the low roar of the conversations of a whole legion gathering. These soldiers were a lively crowd but not quite as rambunctious as the garrison or the Draden regiment. The dwarves and halflings that inhabited the Weir and Mkel's brand of leadership tended to make his soldiers more closely tied and less restricted. Dwarves loved to drink, and halflings loved to drink, sing, and dance, and they had a way of drawing all around them into the merriment.

A horn sounded with the legion commander's call. The conversations and music quickly ceased. "Soldiers of Battle Point, a toast," General Daddonan shouted as thousands of glasses and tankards were raised. "To those who fell in battle, to our honored Draconic guest, the gold dragon Gallanth, and to the Battle Point legion. May the Creator grace all of us and give us strength and wisdom," he finished and was repeated by the legion as a whole. Tankards were quickly drained and slammed on the hundreds of wooden tables. Gallanth lowered his head as both an acknowledgment and prayer.

The food trays were now pouring out of the kitchen buildings with the main course and being put on the tables. Seasoned roasted beef, mutton, hearth breads, and several vegetables were the main dishes out here on the plains. There were as many steer and sheep herders as farmers supporting the town and the legion. As far as foodstuffs, Battle Point was more than self-sufficient.

Gallanth was given wide berth to eat the four well-seasoned steer halves. He could later go to the central water fountain, where all the mounts got their fresh water. It was as large as a good-sized pond with the fountain in the center. The water was fed from the central tank that was supplied from a deep spring that provided the whole city with water.

Many soldiers came up to Gallanth to pay their respects. It was not often an Alliance soldier who was not with a Weir garrison or legion got to talk to a dragon, much less a gold dragon. Several soldiers also talked to Mkel and Jodem throughout the meal as well. As the soldiers finished greeting Gallanth, drinking and dancing started in earnest.

The wizard Andellion came over to Mkel's and Jodem's table with difficulty; his arm was bandaged and in a sling, and he used his dragonstone-powered staff to help him walk, because of his leg injury. Mkel sprang up and helped him into a chair. The slightly built wizard looked tired but happy nonetheless. His rust red-colored hair was relatively unkempt and made his light complexion more apparent. He was smiling and very happy to see Mkel and especially Jodem. Andellion had been an apprentice of Jodem's years ago when Mkel was still a lieutenant and a relatively new dragonrider. He was a very intelligent and talented wizard who quickly mastered his dragonstone-powered magical ability. His selection to be Battle Point's senior wizard was due to his quick learning and somewhat aggressive nature, along with his mastery of the magical power of his staff.

"Welcome, my young apprentice," Jodem said. "Sit and have an ale. I have a lot of questions for you since you were still sleeping in the healing hall earlier," he asked with a grin while Mkel shook his non injured hand.

"Let me have a drink first to clear my head from the healer's stones and Aloras," Andellion answered.

"Take your time, my friend," Jodem replied as the red-haired wizard took a long drink from his tankard, grabbed a piece of seasoned beef and bread, and ate it. "I see your appetite hasn't changed," he chided. "You can eat more than a dwarf and still be as thin as an elf. So tell me about your little encounter with the drow."

"He was very powerful and talented with his dark crystal death staff, being at least a master sorcerer. I defeated him, but it was close," Andellion explained.

"I couldn't tell," Jodem again teased the younger wizard. "Give me the details, Andellion."

"Well, we departed here as soon as the ranger patrol told the commanders the situation," Andellion began. "We left with a battalion-sized task force of several infantry companies, one heavy cavalry troop or company, a company of land dragons, and a wing of hippogriff riders, making as much haste as possible. We skirted along the river, for that allowed us to move at a good pace, riding throughout the night and into the next morning until we were just behind a small rise that shielded us from the village.

"The rangers sent a dismounted patrol to get a better look," he continued, "and I sent two seeing eyes from different directions. The enemy had just over a thousand orcs and a band of thirty or more common giants, with a mountain giant as their leader. Several dozen trolls, ogres, and assorted other monsters were also accompanying their group. The leaders and I quickly got together with the colonel in charge and formulated a plan. He and the other officers quickly tightened the troops into a small formation. I put an illusion spell over the whole battalion to make us appear as the background, and we started to move into position behind the enemy. We noticed a couple of mounted manticores and hymenoids flying in from the southwest, but we remained unseen.

"We set up roughly three hundred yards behind them," Andellion said. "One of our land dragons' tails mistakenly swung outside the area of my spell and was seen by a manticore rider. Colonel Sheer quickly ordered the archers, crossbowmen, and the ballista gunners on the land dragons to prepare to fire. I readied a meteor spell, and as soon as I stopped the illusion, I sent the fiery projectiles toward the enemy, followed by a hail of arrows and ballista spears. My spell caught them just as they were turning to face us, and the explosions felled at least two giants and severely wounded three more along with dozens of orcs. The archers' arrows sunk into their ranks as many more fell. Our heavy horse company spurred to the right to attempt to flank them and was met head on by a mixture of mounted dire wolves and regular Morgathian cavalry. The land dragons formed their line in front of the infantry, and our charge began.

"Several volleys of arrows were exchanged before the orc charge hit our infantry line," he continued. "The ballista gunners scored at least fifteen hits on the giants, and one land dragon's shoulder was injured by a boulder thrown by a giant. The land dragons all breathed a barrage of fire, which incinerated the giants' lead charge and took out several of the brutes. Our infantry took the onrushing orcs well, skewering their first line and holding firm as the second wave hit their shields. A basic melee started to break out. Our archers and crossbowmen were dishing out tremendous punishment on the Morgathian reserves. Just as the hippogriff wing entered the fray and started to engage the few manticores and mounted giant wasps, the drow sorcerer teleported in on a nightmare steed.

"He started to make a dive on the rear of our lines when I fired a lightning bolt at him," Andellion continued. "His spell shield took the hit, but it surprised him. As he veered off, I let loose a frost ray, which I knew might do more damage to the nightmare. Again his shield absorbed the spell, but his demon horse did take a frost burn on its hindquarter, which slowed it down quite a bit. I spurred my mount away from the soldiers to draw his attacks. He swung around and cast a disruption beam at me. My shield stopped the dark ray of deadly light, but I felt the powerful shudder to my core.

"I unleashed a barrage of fireballs that bracketed him," the younger wizard explained. "Four of the six fiery projectiles hit their mark, and he reeled back, for his shield was starting to buckle. He let loose a meteor swarm spell back at me, which I tried to outrun, but two of them hit me. My shield was still intact but was weakening. I then fired a chain lightning spell at him; he had cast the same spell at almost the same time I did. His spell shattered my shield and hit me in the shoulder, arm, and hip. My lightning bolts struck the nightmare, almost killing it, and hit the drow hard. I don't know if he was dead or just severely wounded, but a nearby hippogriff rider dove on them and finished them off with an arrow shot and a front claw swipe. I struggled up on my feet and leaned on my staff, for my horse was killed. Colonel Sheer had already sent a hippogriff and rider down to me to take me to a healer."

"The drow didn't have any markings or a standard?" Jodem asked.

"No, he didn't have any markings on his cloak, just the standard drow death staff with a rather large piece of dark crystal on top," Andellion replied.

"A rogue drow," Mkel said.

"There have been a few drow sorcerer and clerics that have attempted to go independent for a wide variety of reasons," Jodem explained, "such as falling out of favor with the spider cult, greed, or even revenge. However, this is rare, and those are usually apprentices or low to mid degree sorcerers or clerics, not one as powerful as the one you tangled with."

"Then what could this mean?" Mkel asked.

"There are too many missing pieces to the puzzle, too many things that do not make sense, like Gallanth's dreams and his feeling of a significant threat. Eladra's visions and these attacks that are growing in strength and frequency are all tied, but we just don't know how. They must be connected to the gathering of giants and dragons in the Fire Mountains to the east of Eladran Weir," Jodem theorized.

"I guess time will tell," Andellion said. "I just hope we are ready for it and have the will to confront it."

"You are concerned with the Enlightened senators and their movement at the capital?" Jodem asked the young wizard.

"Yes, although news comes slow out here, we still hear of the politics," Andellion stated. The way I understand it is they are attempting to convince the senate to cut our budget again and divert most of the weapons-quality dragonstone gems to their projects and other kingdoms as a measure of good will, along with the regular heating and cooling crystals. I understand they want the dragons to just donate them or give them away. That is rather presumptuous, is it not?"

"Yes, but remember they are still a minority in the senate and in the Alliance as a whole. However, they are a very loud minority and gaining popularity among the civilians and some disillusioned veterans. Things will likely come to a head at the next senate gathering at the end of this month," Jodem replied. "Just keep the faith, my young apprentice."

"I will, as always. So Mkel, how is the mighty Gallanth?" Andellion asked to lighten the conversation.

"He is still precocious as usual, but a little more somber as of late. These dreams he has been having about the Great Dragon War, and the foggy, unclear visions of a widening conflict have been plaguing me especially," Mkel answered.

"Well, he is a gold dragon with the power of foresight. That kind of talent can take a toll on anyone, even a metallic dragon," Andellion answered.

"Yes, but it doesn't bode well for a good night's sleep on many an occasion," Mkel answered with a grin.

"I understand, Mkel," Andellion answered.

"Gentlemen, good evening," General Daddonan said as he walked toward the group. Mkel started to stand up to give the general a salute, but Daddonan waved him to keep seated. "Gallanth is keeping busy talking to the men, I see," he stated.

"Yes sir, he does enjoy dispensing out his wisdom on occasions," Mkel answered.

"I can't tell you how happy I am with your decision to support us here at Battle Point, Captain Mkel," the general stated with a large grin.

"Gallanth surprised even me with that statement, sir, but I know we will honor this commitment one way or another. We have to watch this new activity in the south, though," Mkel added.

"Let's hope you and your dragon don't have to be in two places at the same time, son," Daddonan joked.

"General, talking with Andellion, it seems that while your commanders did a brilliant job in outmaneuvering the orcs and their allies last week, you basically were lucky that their forces were not synchronized," Jodem said.

"Andellion did a great job in taking out that drow sorcerer," General Daddonan shot back in an irritated tone, upon which he took a long draught of ale.

"I'm not taking anything away from my old apprentice here, General, but like it or not, that dark elf sorcerer purposefully pushed those orcs and giants forward, knowing that your land dragons and legion soldiers would eventually decimate them. I believe that neither the village nor the soldiers were the target;

I think they were attempting to kill Andellion," Jodem calmly explained.

"How do you draw this conclusion Master, Wizard?" Daddonan asked.

"The drow let him fire several of his most powerful spells at the orcs and giants before he made his attack and then directed his magic at Andellion, not your forces. If the drow truly wanted to attack the town, he would have at least cast some type of spell to injure a land dragon or disrupt your formation. The charge the battalion performed sliced through the orc ranks like a knife. The bottom line is that Andellion was a better shot, and that is how he defeated the drow," Jodem explained.

"Why would they sacrifice so many just to kill our senior wizard?" asked Daddonan with a growing curiosity.

"Morgathia doesn't care how many of its own die as long as the means justify the ends. I'm surprised that they did not throw a chromatic dragon at you. They must have had a coordination problem getting one there," answered Jodem.

"We haven't seen a chromatic this close to Battle Point for years. They have been focusing their attacks on the horse clans and southern kingdoms," the general explained.

"That is likely to just satisfy the intense greed and desire for destruction of those dragon types. There is a purpose for all of this; unfortunately, it still remains unclear," Jodem answered.

"Well then, whatever may happen, my legion and Captain Mkel's Weir will answer the challenge. We will step up our scout activity and extend our range tomorrow, so we will not be surprised," the general added.

"Sir, just to remind you that the rangers of our Weir only two days ago observed a gathering of three fire giant clans and several chromatic dragons along the beginning of the Smoking Mountain chain," Mkel interjected.

"Three clans? With dragons!" General Daddonan exclaimed.

"Yes sir, that would mean over a hundred fire giants, not to mention their own private armies of common giants, ogres, trolls, and orcs. They saw at least four red, green, and blue dragons apiece," Mkel further explained.

"That's hard to believe. There hasn't been that large a gathering since the Great War. Well, I have faith that Colonel Lordan and his cavalry legion can handle that challenge," Daddonan stated.

"Well sir, remember that Keystone Weir is also defensively tied to Eladran and High Mountain Weirs, and if they get in trouble, we must come to their aid," Mkel said.

"I have faith that Talonth can handle the chromatics. He has what, over a dozen dragons in his Weir's wing, and that is not counting their mates," Daddonan responded.

"Yes sir, but that is supposing they are only facing twelve chromatics. Our rangers and Eladran Weir's scouts are keeping an eye on the situation, but if they get hard-pressed, Gallanth and I will come to the aid of Talonth. They are good friends," Mkel explained further.

"What about Machren Weir to the south along the peninsula?" Daddonan asked.

"They are constantly on patrol of our coasts, escorting convoys and providing support to the navy at our trading ports in the island chains," Mkel replied.

"Well then, Dragonrider, let us hope that the Morgathians, if they are indeed behind this increased activity, do not synchronize their attacks well," Daddonan said.

"A hope and a faith," Jodem interjected.

"Master Wizard, just teach young Andellion to be a quicker shot," the general joked as he stood up. "I will see you all tomorrow, late morning in the legion council room. We can work out the details of our first joint exercise, which hopefully will be very soon," Daddonan announced.

"Yes sir, we will see you in the morning," Mkel answered.

"Have a good night, gentlemen; give my regards to Gallanth," Daddonan stated and walked back to his head table for more ale.

"I don't think he understands how much we are overextended," Mkel whispered.

"He is just trying to ensure his soldiers have something to call on in case of the worst or most dangerous scenario. Andellion will do his best to hold off whatever they might encounter, and we will talk to General Becknor and the Dragon Council when we go to the capital in a couple of weeks. We'll see if they can be supplemented with one of the Avenger dragons when they are ready, and a good brass or copper to guide them," Jodem answered.

"We will hold our own until you get here, Mkel, in the event of something major," Andellion spoke up.

"I have faith in you, Andellion. I am just concerned that you'll be counting on us and we will not be able to get to you in time," Mkel explained.

"We'll just have to have faith in each other and in the Creator," Andellion said with a smile on his freckled face.

CHAPTER IV

BATTLE OF HANDSDOWN

Mkel woke up the next morning a little later than usual. He didn't drink too much, but he had a restless night, for Gallanth was having dreams again, and they were very intense. Scenes of pain, suffering, and villages burning dominated these visions. The realism of the images brought Mkel out a deep sleep more than once, sweating with his heart pounding, ready for battle. He had learned to keep Kershan and Markthrea close to his bed, for whenever he called for the mithril sword, it flew directly to him, to the unfortunate circumstance of anyone in its way.

Gallanth was already awake and stretching his long wings as Mkel looked out the window of his room. "You let me sleep a little longer today, Gallanth," Mkel said to his dragon telepathically. *I know I woke you up at least three times last night. Something is wrong, but I cannot place it or discern it, but evil is gathering,* Gallanth replied. Mkel could sense a slight anxiety in Gallanth's voice, again unusual for him.

"Let me get ready. There would be hell to pay for us for being late for General Daddonan's council meeting. Plus I'm sure he will have a good breakfast set up and likely something special for you, now his favorite dragon," Mkel teased. *You should feel honored that General Daddonan has so much faith in us. Besides, I have a feeling that when, and not if, something does happen out here, we will be needed. Unfortunately, I do not think that will be very long from now,* Gallanth added. "The dreams are making more sense?" Mkel asked. *I know the*

174

danger is near and will happen soon, but I cannot pinpoint it. I am drawn to the east, however. We should take a flight out in that direction after General Daddonan's meeting this morning. "We could accompany a hippogriff patrol. I believe one is heading out today," stated Mkel. *I do not think General Daddonan will mind.*

"All right, let me get ready," Mkel replied. "I'll meet you in twenty minutes." He got out of bed and walked out of his room to the bathing facilities. He quickly bathed, shaved, and got dressed in his spare Alliance uniform tunic. He then walked out to Gallanth; where Jodem was already there, talking to the gold dragon.

"It's about time, my young friend. We must be going to the legion's council hall. I'm sure General Daddonan has an excellent breakfast spread for us," Jodem said; he was not one to miss a good meal.

"Well, let us not delay, for orcs, death knights, and chromatic dragons be damned. Do not get in the way of the Master Wizard Jodem and his breakfast," Mkel teased his elder mentor.

"Be careful to mind your elders, young dragonrider, or I might turn you into a goat. Besides, your dragon is hungry as well," Jodem quickly replied.

"Let us go then," Mkel answered as they started to walk toward the legion headquarters building and General Daddonan's council room. As they came up to the complex, three wagons were waiting, filled with food for Gallanth. The good general came out of the large oaken doors to greet them.

"Good morning Gallanth, Master Wizard, Captain Mkel. I tasked my support corps commander to have a special breakfast for our gold dragon guest. He has prepared nine whole pigs, well seasoned of course, along with about two dozen chickens and breads. I hope you find it to your liking, Gallanth," General Daddonan spoke as he nodded a cursory head bow to Gallanth.

"I am sure it will be more than fine, General, but you and your staff should not have gone to the trouble," Gallanth replied.

"Never a trouble for an Alliance gold dragon; come Jodem, Mkel, we've got excellent food awaiting in the dining hall," Daddonan added as he ushered the two into the building and to the hall, where all of the senior legion officers were already eating. There was a table full of fresh fruit, sweetbreads, cereals, and pastries. *They eat very well out here,* Mkel thought to himself. The senior staff and commanders all acknowledged Mkel and Jodem, and they turned to the window to see Gallanth as he started to swallow his specially prepared breakfast.

Sometimes Mkel felt uncomfortable being among these senior officers, all of colonel rank or higher, but it came with being both a dragonrider, especially a gold dragonrider, and an Alliance officer. He wondered how his father felt at such meetings, since he was a soldier, not even a sergeant, although he was a ranger and renowned fighter. Jodem never felt uncomfortable around officers, especially the support corps troops, for he had a mind for logistics.

As they finished breakfast, they moved into the council room and sat down, after a slight break to feed the otyughs, which were located in the lower chamber at the entrance to the sewers. After they were all seated, General Daddonan wasted no time in getting right down to business by asking Mkel when they could schedule an exercise with Gallanth and the legion.

"It will have to be after the end-of-month Senate gathering at Draconia, sir," Mkel stated. "General Becknor and the Dragon Council are also meeting, and Gallanth and I must be in attendance."

"How about next week, for I know that there was just an exercise with the Draden regiment?" Daddonan inquired.

"We have our emissary from Freiland arriving at the Weir next week, sir," Mkel answered.

"Those barbarians, surely a Battle Point joint exercise would take precedence over the raiders," General Daddonan snapped back. Many of the land-locked legion officers and some soldiers of the Alliance legions did not like the Freilanders. The basic cause of dislike was the raiders' lack of discipline, for they fought as individual berserkers, and they were particularly effective and feared. They did not form the disciplined battle lines that made the Alliance legions so successful. The Freiland raiders also did not venture far inland unless there were navigable rivers or inlets. They were seafarers, traders, and raiders, but staunch allies of the Alliance and the metallic dragons who saved their country from an onslaught of chromatics and ice giants during the Great War. They mostly operated with the Alliance navy and the naval infantry.

"Yes General, but we must honor our allies and trade agreements, for these barbarians have come to our aid several times in the past," Jodem explained.

"Yes General, we must be present for Lawrent, the raider leader that is paired with Keystone Weir, but rest assured we will settle on a date that will expedite an exercise between the Battle Point legion and Draden Weir," Gallanth interjected from outside the window with his deep booming voice.

"Of course, Master Gallanth, I always have faith in the word of a gold dragon," General Daddonan said, losing the slight irritation in his voice.

Gallanth then suddenly raised his head, and all the officers present quickly looked over at him. "Mkel, a legion hippogriff rider is approaching from the east, and he and his mount are wounded," the dragon's booming voice echoed in the courtyard of the landing.

General Daddonan and all members of the staff got up and started to rush out of the building; they made their way toward the landing by the stables as they were giving orders through their seeing crystals. The wounded hippogriff and its rider barely made a controlled crash landing by the stables. The poor creature had severe gashes to its hindquarters and left wing. The rider fell off but was caught by two soldiers and a healer. General Daddonan, several senior members of his staff, with and Mkel and Jodem arrived at the landing as the healer was treating the rider's nasty slash wounds. To Mkel's surprise, it was Dackner, the young rider that Gallanth had addressed the day before at the legion's inspection.

General Daddonan knelt down and put his hand on the soldier's uninjured shoulder. "What happened, son?" he said softly.

"They were everywhere, sir," the soldier weakly replied. "My patrol approached the small trading village of Handsdown to drop off the supplies to the infantry company my wing had secured yesterday. It was under attack by a kind of man/dragon-type creature, called spawns. These creatures are a cross between a winged dragon and a man, standing at least eight feet tall and as strong as an ogre. There were also men mounted on manticores, orcs on giant wasps and hymenoids, and death knights on wyverns, with over a battalion or more of orcs and drow on the ground. We dove in to help the infantry company to distract them, but we were quickly overwhelmed. My section leader sent me back to get help. Bracks and I fought through them to get here, but I don't know what happened to the rest of them, sir," the soldier finished with a painful gasp.

"It's all right, son, we'll get them help," General Daddonan replied with conviction and a stern look on his face. "We've got a gold dragon on our side today."

"Sir, how soon can you get a strike force together?" Mkel asked. "We have a small trick now to get you there a little quicker." Mkel assumed that General Daddonan was already formulating a plan.

"Colonel Sykes, go tell Colonel Sheer, Colonel Ronson, and Colonel Dansar that I want at least two infantry companies, a land dragon platoon with cavalry troop, and a hippogriff wing at the landing in fifteen minutes, formed around Gallanth and ready for battle," he snapped at his chief of staff.

"Yes sir, it will be done," Colonel Sykes replied as he gave a quick salute and turned at a fast pace toward the barracks, grabbing his seeing crystal.

"Are you ready, Captain?" the general asked. Gallanth let out a battle roar as he walked over to the landing.

"Any questions, sir?" he replied as he looked up at his dragon mate. "Any time there is a need, we will answer, sir, and I have a score to settle with the drow," he added. "If I may, sir," he saluted as he motioned toward Gallanth.

"Give 'em hell, Dragonrider," the general responded as he returned the salute and started to walk back to his headquarters to get his armor and weapons. Jodem walked over to the stable area to get Vatara ready.

"I tried to get mental images from the hippogriff, but I wasn't able to see any chromatics clearly. Its mind is confused and wracked with pain. If there were any, they would have shown themselves," Gallanth explained.

"I agree with Gallanth, but if drow are present, there could be a sorcerer or priestess of some power, so we should take caution," Jodem explained as he walked his eagle over to the gold dragon and his rider.

"We will handle it," Mkel replied.

"I have faith," he continued.

"As you always should; besides, what is a few lonely sorcerers?" Gallanth added, teasing Jodem, who smiled. "I will enjoy sending a few more drow back to the underworld in ashes. I've not destroyed a dark elf since the Great War, and I will look forward to that privilege soon."

Within minutes, there was a clamor of soldiers getting armor and weapons ready, and soon over a hundred armed men were gathering around Gallanth's feet. They looked up in amazement at the dragon's colossal size. "Thank the Creator he'll be with us on this one," one soldier whispered to his sergeant.

"You are welcome, my lad," Gallanth replied to the soldier, who started to blush with a slight embarrassment from being overheard by the gold dragon. His squad sergeant smiled, as did Mkel. Soon a small cavalry troop was moving from the stables with half a company of land dragons. Mkel saw a colonel walking over to the group.

"Sir, as soon as you have enough, let me know," he yelled to the battalion commander from high on Gallanth's back. Mkel knew it was Colonel Sheer, one of the infantry battalion commanders, just by his size. He stood six feet, four inches tall and was a burly man at that. He guessed he would be the commander on the ground for this fight.

"Right, Captain; there's no time for catapults. As soon as we have at least two line companies and a few more horses, hippogriffs, and land dragons, we can go," Colonel Sheer replied. Sometimes there was a little friction from senior line officers toward dragonriders, who they considered like an aristocracy. It was well known within the Draden regiment and the Battle Point legion that Mkel was an infantryman first and served as a line soldier while a junior dragonrider, and even before he became dragon bonded.

Mkel counted eight land dragons and almost a troop of cavalry and hippogriffs finally gathering around Gallanth's wings and tail. "We're ready, Captain!" the colonel shouted to Mkel.

"All right, gentleman, gather around Gallanth and make sure you are within the circle of his nose, wing tips, and tail," Mkel ordered as Gallanth stretched his seventy-five-yard-wide wingspan and straightened his tail. It was a tight fit, but the whole mixed battalion fit all around Gallanth, with the hippogriffs and cavalry in front of his outstretched wings on either side of his head and neck, a reinforced infantry company under each wing with some cavalry, and the land dragons on each side of his tail. It was very crowded, with everyone, including the mounts, standing shoulder to shoulder. "We will be teleporting just west of the town. The hippogriff wings will need to take off as fast as they can so Gallanth can move away from the infantry and take to the air. Roger, Captain?" he shouted quickly to the hippogriff wing commander, who gave him a nod in acknowledgment.

"You will be a slightly disoriented for a few seconds, but it will pass quickly, my little brothers," Gallanth said to the land dragons in Draconic, for they had never teleported before. "Be ready to move to your flanks. Fear not the transportation magic. We will be fighting for you all. Have faith and may the Creator's strength be with you," he finished with his commanding Draconic voice resonating from the walls of the city.

"Battalion, weapons ready!" Colonel Sheer shouted as hundreds swords and arrows were drawn. "As soon as Gallanth takes to the air, we will form a line directly in front of the land dragons. Hippogriff wing, take to the air and engage any and all enemy flying forces in coordination with Gallanth. Cavalry, be prepared to flank to the best avenue of approach and keep any mounted forces off balance. I will call to you for your attack route. Archers, ready! I will lead the line toward the town, so all stay with me. We will drive these evil demons back. Captain, at your mark," he finished as he drew his dragonstone-imbedded great sword.

Gallanth let out an ear-shattering roar as Jodem took off on Vatara. The giant eagle let out its own war cry, and they both flashed out of sight. Mkel saw the picture of a grass field in Gallanth's mind, which he had gotten from the hippogriff. The brilliant blue light vortex then formed around the gold dragon, and in an instant, they were gone. They emerged on a grass field about three hundred yards from the village, behind a small rise that concealed their position. The fires were immediately visible, and they heard screams from the village. The hippogriffs were spurred forward and took to the air as the cavalry trotted to the left flank. The men of the infantry companies and the land dragons began to move away from Gallanth.

"Colonel Sheer, I see the majority of their forces on the south side of the village, with dire wolves and drow spiders on the north side, Gallanth quickly informed the colonel. Jodem became visible as he and his eagle landed beside Gallanth.

"I concur with Gallanth, Colonel," Jodem agreed. "I haven't seen any chromatic dragons, and I don't know if there are any sorcerers among the death knights and drow, but I feel a magical presence. These new dragon spawn creatures will be difficult adversaries, though, so tell your hippogriffs to watch and keep their wingmen close."

"We will need two hippogriffs as wingmen as well, sir," Mkel told the colonel.

"All right, here's the plan," Colonel Sheer said. "I will take the line companies to the south and engage the orcs directly. Captain Deven, take the cavalry around the north of the town from the west to surprise the worgs and drow and keep them away from us. Captain Javar, split your land dragons, with half reinforcing the cavalry and the other half with the infantry. Captain Salenor, you and your hippogriffs just keep those flying mounts and dragon spawn off of us, and provide Captain Mkel and Gallanth with two wingmen."

"As long as no chromatic dragons show up, we should clear the skies quickly, eliminating the death knights on those wyverns first. Just keep those others off our back for a couple of minutes," Mkel finished.

"Does everybody understand?" the colonel asked. "Good, let's do this and relieve our men." He put his seeing crystal back on his belt, and the officers broke to go back to their units to form their plans. "Mkel, Gallanth, I need you and Jodem to keep the heavy heat off of us."

"We always support the infantry, sir," Mkel spoke with a smile.

"We will protect your men like our own, Colonel," Jodem added

"Have faith, Colonel," Gallanth added. With that, Mkel quickly readied his crossbow Markthrea with exploding-tipped bolts. Gallanth let out an angry battle roar to announce his presence. Mkel felt the dragon's muscles tighten as he leaped into the air, with the hundred twenty mounted hippogriffs falling in behind him to draw all attention to them. Jodem immediately fired a lightning bolt at a nearby mounted manticore, which struck it in the side, killing it instantly and sending its smoldering body plummeting toward the ground. Gallanth fired a sunbeam burst into an orc-mounted hymenoid, almost vaporizing it on the spot. Mkel took aim at a dragon spawn with a proper lead and fired. His bolt struck home, with the missile hitting the creature behind its left arm under the wing. The resulting explosion knocked the spawn out of the air, but barely, Mkel noted. *These creatures are very tough*, he thought to himself, *they will be trouble.*

All the enemy aerial forces immediately began to wing around to meet the new threat of the Alliance hippogriffs and Gallanth; however, several did break and head east at the site of the colossal dragon. The hippogriffs scattered into their pairs and began to engage the giant wasps, manticores, and dragon spawn. Gallanth focused on a wyvern with a Morgathian knight mounted on it. With a roar and a quick turn, he was on the wyvern's tail. The black knight looked back at Gallanth and kicked his mount's side to fly faster. He then called for a nearby orc on a giant wasp to fly interference; Mkel answered with a shot to the orc's chest with a regular bolt that killed him instantly. The wounded insect mount veered off to land, likely to eat its rider.

The knight pulled a wand out of his gauntlet and fired a series of magic missiles at Gallanth. All the small glowing orbs were absorbed by his spell shield like drops of water in a lake. He then threw a spear back at the gold dragon, which snapped off on his shoulder, unable to penetrate his armored hide. As the evil knight drew his sword, Gallanth reared his head up and opened his huge jaws. Mkel felt his dragon's neck tighten as a plasma fireball expelled from his mouth and streaked toward the wyvern. Just as the creature tried to dive away, the fiery reddish-orange energy ball struck it in the lower back and engulfed the pair in a huge explosion, killing the wyvern instantly. Its charred remains fell from the sky. "Colonel Sheer, Gallanth just sent a dead wyvern streaking to the ground with a black guard on it. If he survives the impact, he is yours," Mkel sent the message to the battalion commander on the ground.

"We'll deal with him, Captain," Colonel Sheer replied back through his seeing crystal.

Jodem swung around and dove on the company of drow below and unleashed a meteor storm spell, which rapidly emanated from his staff. The nine fiery reddish black projectiles struck the ground in the midst of the giant spider-mounted drow and exploded in a series of blinding flashes, which killed and injured dozens of the dark elves. As Vatara pulled up, a drow sorcerer fired a lightning bolt at them. Jodem's spell shield held as it took the glancing impact of the bolt.

The hippogriffs were swerving and diving as they fought the hymenoids, spawn, and remaining manticores. A pair of hippogriff riders spurred their mounts into a dive after a dragon spawn and fired their short bows. Both arrows scored direct hits on the large winged dragon/man creature, but it kept flying. It then turned around and came at one of the hippogriffs and hit the rider in the shoulder; the spear pierced his scale armor. His mount whirled around and kicked the dragon spawn in the joint of its right wing, sending it tumbling end over end and allowing his wingman to get another good arrow shot to finish it off.

"Captain Mkel, there is a remnant of a platoon on the far side of the village. They are protecting a group of women and children and are heavily outnumbered. We can't get to them," the hippogriff commander called to Mkel on his seeing crystal with great concern in his voice.

"We'll swing over to them," Mkel answered as Gallanth looked down at the village. There was over a company of orcs surrounding the small wooden fort on the north side of the town. The majority of the Battle Point battalion was on the south side of the village, decisively engaging the bulk of the hostile forces, and the cavalry was in the process of driving off the orc-mounted worgs. Gallanth then banked toward the north and began to dive.

They must be outnumbered five to one; there are at least fifty women and children in the building, Gallanth told him telepathically. Mkel looked through his crossbow's magnified sight. A senior death knight was fighting what he surmised was the platoon leader or platoon senior sergeant, for he was holding his own. The evil warrior was thrusting hard with his black iron sword. The Alliance soldier took a hard hit and wheeled back as the death knight swung around and thrust his evil blade into the soldier's chest.

Gallanth heard a scream as a young teenage boy came running from the building. "That soldier is defending his family!" shouted the dragon. Mkel saw the boy running to his father's side as the death knight pulled the blade from the soldier's chest. He felt his stomach tighten as well as the muscles in his jaws. *Mkel, I cannot*

183

fire, the dragon said, *for they are too close to the building and the boy.* Gallanth roared as his dive increased speed.

Mkel cocked his crossbow and put a mithril-tipped bolt in place and settled the sight on the black knight. In the seconds this action took, all Mkel could think about was the boy's pain in seeing his father cut down in front of him, and his own memories of losing his father. An intense hate and rage began to fill him as he took careful aim, pulled the trigger, and released the bolt, which flew at blinding speed toward its target. The boy had run out and pushed the death knight away from his father as he was pulling his sword from the soldier's chest. He then picked up his father's sword and swung at the knight, who parried his blow and knocked the young boy down. As he raised his sword to smite the boy, Mkel's bolt struck him in the right shoulder, piercing his black iron armor and knocking him off his feet from the impact.

Gallanth landed with an incredible tremor on the west side of the fort, crushing twenty or more orcs in the process and knocking several others off of their feet. He spun himself around with blinding speed, sweeping his tail in a 270 degree arc, sending dozens of orcs flying through the air like a man would flick off ants. The orcs were crushed from the impact of his powerful and immense tail. With an ear-shattering roar, his head cocked back and unleashed a controlled cone of fire that swept through the orc ranks, incinerating over fifty. Most of the remainder quickly began to break and run from the might of the gold dragon.

Mkel unbuckled his riding straps, disconnected his crossbow, and slid off Gallanth's neck, hitting the ground and rolling to cushion the impact. He got up running, swinging the crossbow over his back with its sling, as Kershan sprang from its sheath to his outstretched hand. An orc moved in to intercept him. The hideous brown insect-like orc swung his battle-axe at Mkel, who parried it with Kershan, cutting it in two pieces in the process. He then swung around with dazzling speed and literally cut the orc in half through the chest in a slanting downward stroke. The black grayish blood spilled all over the ground. He was upon the death knight quickly, who had just recovered from the quarrel strike; the fletching of the end of the small arrow was still sticking out from his reinforced black iron armor on his shoulder, a testament to how tough the Morgathian rare metal was to take the incredible penetrating power of Markthrae.

"A dragonrider! Ha, I have not felled one since the Great War," the Morgathian knight scowled at Mkel.

"That would be the last one you ever will, *pogasch*," Mkel angrily cursed at him in Draconic. Mkel swung his sword to the knight's left side, which he knew would be hard to counter. The death knight did parry it but weakly. His sword must have been made of Morgathian black iron as well, for if it had been base iron or steel, Mkel's mithril blade would have severed it. Mkel then swung around with a down stroke that severed the knight's right arm at the elbow, even through his black iron armor. The knight screamed in agony and clutched the bleeding stump.

Mkel swung his sword back around to the left side and low, almost cutting his adversary's leg off at the knee. He was so enraged that tears were streaking down his cheek. The evil knight fell to his right knee and looked up at Mkel, who then lowered his blade to the knight's neck.

"What, no mercy from an Alliance dragonrider?" the death knight said arrogantly.

"Was there mercy for that boy's father?" he shouted. "Now I will send you to the hell your kind so praises," he said coldly but then hesitated, trying to compose himself. The silvery blade then almost launched by itself into the knight's neck and emerged from his upper back. Mkel looked at the death knight's eyes as the pain gave way to shock and finally a blank stare as the life faded from him. He then put his foot on the death knight's chest and pushed him backwards, as he pulled his sword from the dead man's throat. Mkel stood there and stared at the bright red blood dripping off Kershan's mirrored blade until it was quickly all off the mithril sword. He had seen the grayish black blood of orcs and the green to blue blood of chromatic dragons and giants, but he had rarely seen human blood.

He was breathing very heavily, as if he had just run for several miles, but sobered his thoughts as he heard Gallanth's voice in his mind. *Mkel, we have to go. There are chromatic dragons approaching.* Gallanth's voice snapped him back to reality and he turned to the boy.

"I know how you feel, son. I lost my father a long time ago. He did not die in vain. I will be back for you," he told the young boy, who started to tear up but, out of pride, was trying to hide it. Mkel put his hand on his shoulder, looked up to see his mother, and quickly turned and ran to Gallanth as he wiped the tears from his cheek. He jumped onto Gallanth's waiting forearm and was lifted up to his flying saddle. He quickly fastened the four flying straps onto his belt and locked Markthrea back into place.

"How many chromatics are coming?" Mkel asked his dragon.

"I see a blue, a black, and a green, and two strange dragons that I have never seen before. Plus there is something different about the blue and black. I sense a greater power coming from the blue from some source inside him, and an intense almost supernatural anger or hatred from the black," Gallanth explained.

"We can handle them, just be cautious in our approach." Mkel grabbed his seeing crystal. "Jodem, be warned, we have five chromatics inbound, a blue, black, green, and two new strange dragons. Gallanth senses something is different with the blue and black," he warned his wizard friend.

"Yes, I feel something wrong with them as well. I will warn Colonel Sheer," the wizard replied.

Gallanth's muscles tensed and with a powerful heft of his golden wings, they were airborne, rising to meet the new threat. Mkel could still feel the sorrow and emptiness of his and the boy's loss. The anger was rippling through his body. He wanted to scream for blood and vengeance, to curse all evil and charge into battle pouring out all his rage into the fight, but he knew he had to focus or he would be no good to Gallanth in this contest, and his dragon would need him. He would need to focus and rechannel his anger, for the shots he was going to have to make would need his full mental effort. He would need to be here for Gallanth so they could meet this challenge.

Colonel Sheer and the infantry were finally pushing the orcs back. They had inflicted dozens of casualties against them, with only a couple wounded so far in their numbers. The infantry first line was holding, and the Battle Point archers were taking their toll on the orc ranks. The paladin cavalry had routed the orc mounted dire wolves and were now engaging the spider-mounted drow and the dark elves that were on foot. The land dragons, as always, were spearheading the infantry attack, slamming and incinerating the orcs and especially neutralizing the few ogres and trolls that were present.

The hippogriff wing almost had the dragon spawn, hymenoids, and manticores routed, but as soon as the enemy heard the challenging roars of the incoming chromatic dragons, their morale dramatically improved, and they renewed their attack. Gallanth, now at altitude, turned to intercept the incoming evil dragons. He gave a resounding battle roar, much deeper and reverberating than even the large blue.

Blue dragons were the second largest and powerful of the chromatic dragons. This blue was at least thirty-six yards in length with a sixty-yard wingspan, making it very large for its species. It was still a good deal smaller than a gold dragon, especially Gallanth. Its pale sandy blue hide almost blended in with the sky, and its extra large frilled ears were fanned out as it prepared for battle. Its large central nose horn was crackling with electrical energy, for it was preparing its lightning breath weapon.

The smaller bull horned black dragon was roaring and spitting with rage, seemingly eager to engage Gallanth in close combat, which for the much smaller thirty-yard-long swamp dragon would be basically suicide. It was pumping its fifty-yard-wide ragged wingspan as fast as it could to intercept Gallanth. The long-necked, alligator-like green dragon was staying back slightly, but they were the more cautious among the chromatic types. Both the black and green dragons had a superheated fiery acid breath weapon, which while somewhat effective against a gold dragon, had a very limited range and frequency of use.

The other two dragons were only as large as a white dragon. A little over half the size of Gallanth, they were obviously poor flyers but seemed to be very aggressive. Once Gallanth was within a thousand yards, he again let out a tremendous battle roar and fired a sunbeam burst from his eyes at the blue dragon, which struck its magic shield. The blue was pushed off course by the impact, but its spell shield held. He followed up with a barrage fireball spell to make the other dragons veer to the left and then immediately fired his plasma fire breath weapon, which he directed at the green dragon. It struck the green in the lower left flank, shattering its magic shield and inflicting a good amount of burn damage. It quickly veered off to get out of the way.

Mkel shot a mithril exploding tip at the black dragon once they were within his thousand-yard range. Hitting a flying dragon, especially a poorly flying black, was not an overly difficult task, especially for Mkel. The bolt hit the black's invisible magic shield with a good-sized explosion, but the horned dragon took the impact and kept coming. Mkel cocked the crossbow and again fired, hitting the black dragon's shield; he quickly followed up with a third bolt at almost point-blank range that finally decimated the magic barrier. Gallanth and the black dragon traded claw swipes as they passed each other. Gallanth ripped the black's left shoulder, while it caught him on the left leg. Mkel could feel the wound register on his leg, since as a bonded pair, they shared each other's pain. Gallanth started to wheel around to give the black a blast of fire when he suddenly folded his wings and dove to dodge the lightning bolt fired by the blue dragon. The white hot bolt of electricity missed him by only a few feet, for Mkel could smell the ozone in the air. The blue then unleashed a dark beam of tremendous power, which Gallanth could not evade while recovering from his sharp turn from the first bolt. It hit the gold dragon's magic shield hard, causing his large frame to shudder, but his shield still held firm.

Mkel swung his crossbow on the mount swivel and took a quick aim at the blue, which was now veering off; he fired the last exploding-tipped bolt in his bow's magazine. It hit the blue dragon's shield square on its flank. It was weakening and would not hold much longer. "I have to reload," Mkel told Gallanth as he reached for another clip of exploding-tipped bolts from the flying rig quiver. *Watch the flanks. I'm going to take out that blue. I must find his source of extra power, for that last lightning bolt he fired had twice the strength of a normal blue,* Gallanth replied telepathically as he banked to the right and dove after the blue.

Gallanth roared as he quickly flapped his wings to gain air speed to close the distance on the evil dragon. He caught up to within two hundred yards of the fleeing blue and fired a plasma fireball blast, which streaked through the air and struck the chromatic dragon above the tail, smashing through its spell shield and striking its back hindquarter. The blue dragon spun around in midair from the impact and immediately folded its wings in a deliberate high-speed dive to get away from Gallanth.

Just as Gallanth was preparing to dive after the blue dragon, Mkel fired and hit one of the new dragon species coming at them from the left, causing it to veer off, but the other struck Gallanth from his underside, piercing his armored hide with its jagged claws. Gallanth winced from the talon strikes and swung around, hitting it with his front right claw across its back.

"What are you, little horned devil?" Gallanth roared in Draconic at the smaller dragon.

"I am a talon dragon, and I will tear you apart, metallic worm," the heavily armored dragon shouted back, its red eyes almost glowing. Its enlarged scales and hide were grayish in color, and instead of having the small teardrop-sized scales like most dragons, these scales all ended in a jagged point. It also had enlarged claws for a dragon of its smaller size, which was roughly the size of a white dragon at twenty-two yards long. Its tail ended in a wyvern-like stinger that was almost scimitar like. All of its back ridges were sharp spikes rather than the smooth ridges of other dragons, which aided them in flight.

"I do not think so, puny one. Your first lesson from a gold dragon will be a costly one," Gallanth roared as he reared his head back and engulfed the much smaller dragon in a cone of searing hot dragon fire. This was Gallanth's short-range but area effect breath weapon. To his and Mkel's surprise, while it inflicted a good amount of damage to the talon dragon, it was only half as effective as it should have been. This new dragon, while just half of Gallanth's size, seemed to have an extraordinary toughness about it.

"Gallanth, watch its tail," Mkel shouted as the talon dragon reeled back from the searing hot cone of flame and attempted to strike with its tail. Gallanth then spun around in midair, catching its exposed neck with the flat arrow head-shaped plate on the end of his tail, which sliced through even the tough hide of this new dragon, almost severing its head.

The small wings of the talon dragon folded as it gave a departing groan, and its lifeless body plummeted toward the ground. Just then another dark-powered blast from the blue dragon again struck Gallanth's spell shield from his back and rear. His shield still held but was now reduced to half strength. Again the blue dragon dove but Gallanth did not follow, as he turned to face the black dragon now bearing down on him. It opened its darkened jaws and spit a jet of flaming hot acid. Gallanth folded his wings and dove out of the way, just avoiding the virulent, flaming liquid stream. As he stretched his immense golden wings out to begin flying again, Gallanth raised his head and fired a beam of searing light from his eyes, striking the passing black on the left rear leg joint, leaving a decimating wound.

The black dragon then spun around and dove right into Gallanth, wildly raking him with its front claws and attempting to bite his shoulder. Gallanth slashed his right claw across the side of its head, knocking it back with his superior strength. This exposed its neck, into which Gallanth sunk his immense fangs. This normally would have killed a dragon of this size, but it kept struggling.

Mkel loaded his crossbow, cocked it, and took aim at the black's head, but he was distracted by the screeching of the hippogriffs that were acting as their wingmen. He looked up to see the riders fighting with two dragon spawn, as two more were diving toward him and Gallanth. He swung his crossbow around and up on the swivel arm and fired at one of the diving spawn only thirty yards away. The bolt hit it square in the chest, with the resulting explosion blowing the man/dragon apart.

As Mkel cocked the lever to his crossbow again, the remaining spawn hit Gallanth's back, spear first, which partially penetrated Gallanth's heavily armored hide. The spawn then stood up and tried to spear him again, but it did not make it through the golden hide. Mkel could not fire his crossbow, since the spawn was too close for the exploding tips now loaded in his bow. It was too far away for his sword, so he quickly raised his right hand and pointed his fist toward the dragon creature. His ring pulsed in a red scintillating light, and a glowing projectile emanated from the dragonstone gem in the ring and darted toward the spawn. The mini plasma ball struck the dragon/man in the right shoulder, knocking him back and leaving a smoldering wound through its studded leather armor.

It looked at Mkel, gave a nasty hiss from its lizard-like head and pronounced Draconic jaws, and started to move toward him. Mkel followed up with three more plasma balls, hitting its midsection, with the last one finally delivering the killing blow as it slid off Gallanth's back and fell end over end toward the ground.

In the meantime, Gallanth and the black dragon exchanged claw blows; he took another slash to the chest but the black was finally weakening, and one last blow to its neck finally felled it. Normally black dragons will attempt to retreat when mortally threatened, but this one fought to the death, like a wild boar attacking a grizzly bear. The bull horned dark dragon spiraled toward the ground. Gallanth roared the Draconic victory prayer for it to find its soul, which all metallic dragons announce when they kill a chromatic dragon in hope that its spirit will acknowledge the error of its ways.

A lightning bolt from the blue dragon again struck Gallanth's shield, but it had the normal power of a standard blue's breath weapon. *This blue chromatic is getting very annoying*, Gallanth told Mkel as he finally dove forward to give chase to the frilled dragon. It turned and dove to the left to gain speed in an attempt to get away from Gallanth. This was a futile attempt, for gold dragons are fastest of all dragon types. "What is your name, chromatic? I want to know it before I send you back to the underworld," Gallanth roared to the blue.

"I am Evtrix, a demon dragon, which will be your undoing, metallic," the blue yelled back in Draconic.

"Your kind has quickly forgotten the lessons of the Great War. Now you will pay for your ignorance," Gallanth answered the blue as he unleashed a plasma fireball blast, which streaked toward the chromatic dragon, hitting it square in the back. The resulting explosion knocked the blue out of the sky; it hit the ground with a terrific tremor, gouging a huge trench in the earth. Gallanth back winged hard, causing Mkel to grasp the crossbow mount to absorb the jolt. Gallanth then charged the blue as it was attempting to get up on its feet and rammed it with his head at full speed. The big chromatic dragon was almost lifted off of the ground from the force of the larger gold dragon's impact; it landed hard on its left side. Gallanth then followed up with a cone of fire to finish it off, as the flames emanating from his colossal jaws engulfed the blue. He then gave the salutary roar of both deference for and victory over the chromatic dragon before he launched into the air to pursue the errant green dragon.

A loud cheer erupted from the legion soldiers who witnessed the battle between Gallanth and the blue dragon, both in the air and on the ground. The last organized group of orcs was now being broken, partly because of their lower morale from seeing their lead dragon being slain. Most of the giant dire wolf cavalry had been killed by the paladins, and only the drow were still giving resistance. The legion's infantry and land dragons were now bearing down on them as well. The orc chieftain was slain by Colonel Sheer with a final downward smite from his dragonstone-imbedded great sword.

The lead line of infantry had their swords, spears, and shields dripping black with orc blood. So far six soldiers had been killed with thirty wounded, and they were being treated to the rear by several battle healers, who set up a wounded collection point. Their momentum was suddenly halted when the other talon dragon landed in front of the infantry line. The three land dragons that were in range quickly let loose their fire breath weapons on the intruding talon. It took the blasts well but still suffered from the burns. It lunged toward the infantry but was intercepted by a land dragon that jumped over the line of soldiers, knocking the fanged beast to the ground. It whirled back and its bladed tail impaled the land dragon in its side, as it roared in pain. The crew lowered their ballista and fired at almost point-blank range into the horned dragon's back; the spear-like projectile sank into its jagged hide.

The talon dragon pulled back, retracting its bladed tail from the land dragon and poising itself for another attack, when three more ballista spears struck it from both sides. The three large projectiles were fired from the ballista gunners from the injured land dragon's wingman, and another pair was now charging toward the intruder. As the talon dragon recovered from the simultaneous impact, the three land dragons hit it from all sides, sinking their teeth into its spiny hide and raking it with at least one claw.

This was enough damage to kill the creature, but it had enough life left over in it to strike one of the land dragons on its left with an oversized clawed foot, slashing it across the right shoulder. All three land dragons ripped large chunks of flesh from the talon dragon, finally ending its life as it went limp and fell. The land dragon that had been speared got unsteadily to its feet and crashed on its side, spilling its crew on the ground; they rolled away from the reinforced platform. Some type of powerful poison was at work, for nothing else could have affected a creature of this size that quickly.

Jodem had been exchanging spell blasts with the senior drow sorcerer for what seemed like hours, but it was only ten minutes. The drow's hideous twelve-foot-wide spider was now smoldering, leaving the dark elf on foot to fight Jodem. Vatara took a hard bank to avoid another disruption ray from the sorcerer, after which Jodem fired a sunburst beam at the drow that blasted through the last of his spell shield and tore through his midsection, killing him. The giant eagle did take a crossbow bolt to the side, just penetrating its feather layer, but he was in no mortal danger, as the hand crossbows of the drow were underpowered.

The green dragon that Gallanth was pursuing had just taken a diving attack on the paladins; he hit one of the Battle Point knights, killing him and his mount almost instantly with its chlorinated acid breath weapon. Gallanth caught up to the green dragon circling around to the east, cutting off his escape route. This gave him and Mkel a little time to get some information from this last evil dragon. "You should have kept flying, chromatic. You might have lived longer," Gallanth roared at the green.

"I see Evtrix has found his mark several times, gold pogasch," the green dragon swore at Gallanth. Green dragons had a distinct calculated accent when they spoke Draconic, while blues had an arrogant sharp tone and reds a deep angry dialect, but a commanding resonance. Blacks and white dragons were the least intelligent of the dragon races and tended to slur or shorten their words.

"You could compliment him, but unfortunately he has been slain; however, I will now make it possible for you to join him," Gallanth forcefully replied. "What is your name before I save your soul, chromatic?"

"Groncelix, but you sound too confident, Gallanth," the green dragon replied.

"You know my name, puny one?" Gallanth chided.

"All Morgathian dragons know you by sight and your attack on the black fortress. You should have been killed then and now, for how many chromatics have you slain?" Groncelix replied.

"Too many, but there is always room to send one more to judgment, toothy one. Your blue comrade fought like a coward in spite of his added strength," Gallanth said as an insult to keep the green talking.

"Evtrix was a demon dragon, pogasch, consider yourself lucky to have vanquished him," the green replied with increasing anger.

"He must have suckled on Tiamat's under tail to gain the little amount of extra power he possessed. Not that it helped him," Gallanth kept chiding.

"You're lucky the dark crystal that Tiamat put in his heart was not larger, or your oversize frame would be feeding the orcs, gold pogasch," the green angrily responded. This told Gallanth and Mkel what gave the blue his extra power and strength, especially to his breath weapon. The corpse would have to be examined.

"Your Morgathian masters must have underestimated the Alliance again, attacking with only five dragons and a hodgepodge of orcs and drow. It must be comforting to have the drow commanding you. How does the heel of the dark elf boot taste, servant?" Gallanth continued, insulting Groncelix.

"Silence!" he half shouted, half growled.

"How come you and your ilk have been attacking these small insignificant trading posts? Not enough courage or strength to attack Battle Point or a Weir," Gallanth snapped back while keeping his voice level, being careful not to show anger, but with a condescending tone. He and the smaller green dragon kept circling each other in the ritual dragons engaged in before combat. Its fifty-three-yard wingspan, while still very large, looked small compared to Gallanth's full golden wings.

"Why are they just circling each other like that, sir? Gallanth could take that green dragon easily," one of the soldiers asked Colonel Sheer as everyone looked upward at the standoff in the sky.

"I think he is goading him into giving him information," the colonel replied, "but I wouldn't worry about the outcome of this battle, son."

"Colonel Sheer?" Mkel's voice came from Sheer's seeing crystal.

"Yes, Captain," he replied.

"Sir, when things calm down on the ground, the dead blue dragon needs to be secured. Gallanth tricked a little information from this green about it," Mkel asked. He also knew that any slain chromatic dragons were to be taken back to Draconia by the Capital Wing to process all of their parts for weapons and such.

"No problem, Dragonrider," answered Colonel Sheer.

"These villages are just stepping-stones for us. We will piecemeal you from all sides and take your jewels by the sea!" Groncelix screamed back at Gallanth in an almost total rage.

"I am surprised that you don't have a drow sorcerer as a rider to give you direction and courage, worm," Gallanth said with an insulting phrase.

"Pogachhhhhhh," Groncelix's words ended in a roar, and he turned abruptly and started to fly at Gallanth in a direct attack. Gallanth knew he had finally pushed the green over the edge, for its vanity got the best of it. Groncelix opened its long toothy mouth and spit a focused stream of fiery acid. Gallanth quickly banked to intercept the green dragon and answered by breathing a cone of fire to burn the acid before it hit him. After the two breath weapons cancelled each other out, Gallanth then fired a sunbeam burst from his glowing eyes, which struck the green directly in the chest. Mkel fired an exploding bolt at the dragon, which hit it on the front left leg.

Groncelix reeled from the double impact as Gallanth gave a forceful downward thrust of his wings to gain air speed. He roared as the two dragons collided in midair. The green dragon was off balance when Gallanth struck him, and he took the impact from the much larger gold with a tremendous crash that echoed over the plains. Gallanth's outstretched claws pierced the dull forest-colored scales and hide on its chest and side, pushing the green dragon backward in midair. It roared in pain from the impact and Gallanth's claws.

The wounded green was being pushed back and down by Gallanth's more powerful wings and sheer size. In desperation, it swung its long neck around and bit down on Gallanth's left shoulder, but only half of his teeth sunk into the incredibly strong golden hide. Mkel drew Kershan and, with two hands on the long pommel, swung the sword in a forceful downward stroke, which sliced through the green's jaw and upper neck. It reeled back, with bluish-green blood spurting from the large gash from the mithril blade. Groncelix weakly raised his right claw and swiped at Gallanth's side, which caught Mkel's left knee and just penetrated his dragon-skin leg protectors on his riding saddle. The green dragon's claw more bruised than cut his leg because of its sheer strength, but the end result was that it was still incredibly painful. Mkel thrust his sword into the dragon's green forearm as Gallanth roared and turned his large head, biting Groncelix in the neck, which delivered the final blow, slaying him.

Gallanth quickly looked down to see if there was anything below him and released the dead green dragon to plummet to the ground. His victory prayer/roar echoed across the battlefield, and a loud cheer arose from the Battle Point soldiers below. They had just broken the last of the orc organized resistance and were in the process of splitting up into smaller platoon-size units to root out any enemy hiding in the village. "We did it, Gallanth," Mkel said to his dragon mate. *Yes, but that was a much tougher fight than I expected. These new classes and types of dragons disturb me, though. This battle will likely lead to more questions than it will answer,* Gallanth replied.

"I think the paladins and Jodem are still fighting the drow. Want to give them a hand?" Mkel asked. Almost before Mkel finished his sentence, Gallanth had already started to bank around.

"Impact!" the senior soldiers shouted to their more inexperienced comrades as the green dragon hit the ground only two hundred yards from their position. The resulting tremor caused those nearby to be knocked off of their feet. Colonel Sheer ordered a company to secure each of the three dragon carcasses, for they would be made into weapons and armor; they were quite valuable. The bodies of chromatics were always used for these purposes; when a metallic dragon died, they almost always were teleported out of existence. Some say they returned to Heaven, but the dragons said they just went to fight for the Creator and the spirit in the afterlife. In any event, both stories likely had a ring of truth.

The dwarf and elf smiths as well as human master smiths would tear apart the chromatic dragon corpses and use everything from hide to bones for weapons and armor. Even the synthensium was used to empower certain weapons and to create potions with special abilities.

"He did it, outnumbered four to one, and he took them all out!" shouted a young infantry soldier.

"There was never a question in my mind. You should have seen him during the Great War, son. He killed over two dozen chromatic dragons and then attacked the drow and Morgathian capitals alone," a senior sergeant said.

Gallanth had turned and was now flying over the town and the cheering Alliance soldiers as he headed toward the northeastern fields outside Handsdown. The drow were being pushed back by the paladins and Jodem, but there were still some stubborn pockets of resistance. As Gallanth and Mkel cleared the village, they could see Jodem engaging the last drow sorcerer, who was fighting a delaying action for the remainder of their forces to begin a retreat. This was hastened by the sight Gallanth bearing down on them.

Jodem fired a frost ray at the drow, whose shield took the impact but then buckled. The dark elf fired a barrage of magic missiles at Vatara, as the giant eagle passed and was climbing to gain altitude. Vatara flew an erratic pattern to dodge the small glowing projectiles. One hit Jodem's shield, which was weakening, but it still held. Mkel took a careful aim with a standard bolt and fired. The small arrow streaked out of Markthrea with blinding speed, spinning in flight. It was a long shot, over six hundred yards, but Gallanth was holding steady as he was getting ready for an attack run. Amazingly, it hit the dark elf wizard in the abdomen, knocking him off of his black elf horse steed and killing him instantly.

"Need any help, old friend?" Mkel called Jodem through his seeing crystal.

"Hardly, we were just finishing up here, if you don't mind," Jodem replied with a small tone of sarcasm in his voice.

"Good, then you won't mind if I burn a little trash," Gallanth shouted as he gave his battle roar and began to dive. The drow that were still fighting the paladin cavalry now broke and began to run. Most were mounted on their traditional black and gray steeds they bred, but a few were on giant spiders. *Disgusting creatures,* Mkel thought to himself as he cocked his crossbow with an exploding-tipped bolt and fired at one of the spiders. The impact blew it and its drow rider to pieces. Gallanth breathed out a billowing plume of fire, incinerating at least ten drow and their

197

mounts as he cursed them in Draconic, and then he flew back upward after the run.

"You are all weak cowards, shadow elves; I will burn you into extinction!" Gallanth shouted with his deep booming voice. Referring to a drow as a shadow elf reminded them of their fall from grace and also implied that they were mere shadows of their high elf counterparts.

Gallanth demonstrated his particular dislike for the dark elves after their part in the Great War, and he showed them little mercy. The paladins were making chase now as the drow scattered. Gallanth fired a sunbeam burst at two spider-mounted drow, almost vaporizing the pair and their arachnid mounts.

"Mkel, there are two drow escaping to the southeast on spiders. One is a powerful high priestess. I almost had her down, but she retreated before her shield was depleted. She would be very valuable if captured alive," Jodem explained with earnest.

"We will track them down. Gallanth, do you have her scent?" Mkel asked. *Yes, she and her bodyguard took a more southern direction. Likely she sent the others more easterly, so they could mask her escape,* Gallanth added, for in the drow culture, females were the dominate gender, like the spiders they worshipped. *She will not escape us,* he added as he banked to the right to catch up to the fleeing priestess.

Within minutes, they sighted the pair on their giant spiders, moving as fast as they could toward the mountains far to the southeast. Gallanth bellowed out his challenge roar to let them know he was coming and thwart any attempt to teleport away. He also wanted them to feel as much fear as he could inspire. He then dove on them as Mkel sighted in on the priestess's spider and fired a regular bolt, which struck its hairy abdomen, punching a fist-sized hole all the way through the arachnid. The hideous creature reared up from the impact, raising its front two legs. The priestess had another dark elf riding on her spider, likely a bodyguard.

As Gallanth passed just over their heads, the resulting wind draft flattened the male drow's spider to the ground. The drow priestess fired a death ray at the gold dragon, which his spell shield took with ease, in spite of the previous fight with the chromatics. She should have known that gold, silver, and bronze dragons were immune to death magic, but she seemed flustered at having to contend with such a powerful opponent.

Gallanth swung around slowly to start another run at them; there was no need for haste because they could not outrun the flying dragon. He started his dive, aiming at the drow fighter, who had just recovered from the cyclone of air from his first pass. He first fired a sunbeam burst ray at the priestess, which shattered her shield. Mkel immediately fired another bolt at the spider, this time hitting it square in the head segment, killing it instantly. She and the male drow tumbled off of the giant arachnid, rolling onto the ground, her white spider silk robes tasseled all around her, but she still managed to clutch her black iron death staff.

Gallanth then breathed a huge plume of fire, engulfing the other bodyguard and his spider, turning them into ashes. Gallanth back winged and landed with an extra hard thud, knocking the pair off their feet again. His victory roar was ear splitting, for he took great pleasure in the killing of dark elves. Mkel quickly unbuckled the flying straps and slid off Gallanth's neck to his forearm. He left his crossbow mounted on the flying rig and drew Kershan. As he walked toward the evil priestess, she quickly stood up and prepared to face him.

As he moved to within thirty yards of her, she waved her staff and fired a sonic blast at him. He raised his sword, its shield easily taking the impact of the disruption beam. Mkel kept walking toward her, and she fired another blast at him, which was again stopped by Kershan's shield. Mkel could feel the sword almost pulling him toward her, as if it wanted to taste her blood. *It has a good memory*, he thought to himself.

The drow fighter finally moved in front of his master after she yelled at him in the dark elvish dialect; he drew a black iron long sword to challenge Mkel. He raised Kershan to take the drow's down stroke and quickly whirled around, leveling his blade with a swing at the dark elf's midsection. The drow parried it, and Mkel quickly switched angles and delivered a short strike to the drow's right shoulder. Again the black iron blade blocked the mithril sword, but Mkel slid Kershan down the drow's blade, slicing through the pommel guard and cutting into the dark elf's right arm. The drow priestess conjured a death ray and initially attempted to fire it at Mkel, but Gallanth projected his shield in front of his rider, blocking the deadly black ray.

"Make it a fair fight, spider priestess," Gallanth spoke over the combatants. The drow cleric looked up at the gold dragon with a disgusted expression on her face. The elf backed away and flexed his arm to see the extent of his injury, but Mkel quickly pressed his advantage. He attacked forward with a downward stroke, which the drow blocked, but Mkel quickly inverted his sword, pushing his opponent's black blade to the left, and then he sliced down into the drow's right leg, severing it below the knee. As the drow went down, Mkel quickly swung Kershan in a tight circle coming from his right and cut the dark elf's head clean off. The ruby dragonstone on Kershan's pommel glowed more intensely than Mkel had ever seen it, obviously almost happy to taste drow blood.

As Mkel got to within striking distance of the priestess, she raised her black iron staff, which had a dark crystal mounted on its pointed tip, and swung it at Mkel's head. He quickly parried with Kershan, and when the dark staff hit the mithril blade, the energy of both magically powered weapons flashed in brilliant sparks of light. The power of the impact was so great that the drow priestess was forced to take several steps back to keep her balance. Mkel moved toward her, and she again swung her staff, which Mkel once more repelled.

"This game is getting old, priestess, and my sword wants to taste your blood," Mkel said coldly to the drow cleric.

"Don't be so confident, rider of Gallanth the destroyer," she hissed back at him, thrusting the staff's pointed tip toward his chest.

It is time to end this game, Mkel thought to himself, but she knew Gallanth's name, and that was a curiosity. He dodged to the right of the thrust and whirled around, bringing Kershan down in a powerful downward thrust, which severed the hollow black iron staff just behind the dark crystal-mounted tip. A flash and a loud crack emanated from the staff as the black/purple crystal stone assembly was sent tumbling away. She was thrown backwards and landed on her side, unconscious. Mkel walked over to her to investigate.

"Be careful, Mkel, she is still alive. Don't underestimate her trickery," Gallanth told him as he walked over and looked down at her. She was still unconscious as Mkel stood over her. Her spider silk robes and shiny gray dress accented the jet black skin of her smooth, slender legs. Her features were still very much elven, from her thin nose to her pointed ears, all pure ebony in color, almost obsidian-like, not similar to the brown shades of the people of the southern island chains or Canaris Twin Islands, but a true midnight black. She was rather attractive in a dark, seductive way, Mkel thought to himself, in spite of his intense hatred of their race.

Suddenly, she quickly sprang up to her feet. "You are Captain Mkel," she said with a thick sharp accent.

"You know my name, drow witch?" Mkel asked in a commanding manner.

"Your sword and your pet are unmistakable," she hissed.

"Pet? I guess your kind still remembers me, priestess," Gallanth said to her with the best Draconic condescending tone he could muster.

"You destroyed half of our city and killed hundreds of us, including my kin!" the drow priestess yelled back at Gallanth.

"Your kind killed my former rider; you were fortunate I could not do more," Gallanth said with anger reverberating in his deep dragon voice, which almost knocked her over.

"Now tell me why I shouldn't kill you?" Mkel said as he leveled his sword at the drow's slender neck.

"You can kill me if you want, but we will have our revenge," she spat back.

"Doubtful; my dragon burned your city once, and we will see it totally destroyed, I promise you that," Mkel said, but in spite of the rage he was feeling at confronting a member of the race that helped kill his father, he lowered his sword from her neck.

"Maybe you should think of how important your ties to the Alliance are, Captain Mkel, gold dragonrider. You could be very helpful to us, and as a high priestess, I could use a strong mate. I can sense the dragon blood flowing in your veins. Your rage at us is great, as is the sorrow you still feel for the loss of your father. I can take that anger and redirect it, Mkel. I am Vorgalla, a high priestess to Queen Lolth, and you could strengthen us," she said in a soft and seductive voice.

Mkel stared at her pale gray eyes, which became almost hypnotic. He could hear her voice, not just in his ears, but in his head, as if her words were piercing his soul. She had also stealthily moved the robes of her dress aside to uncover her legs and her silken undergarments, accenting her intense sexuality. He could feel himself drawn to her, like a fly enticed into a spider's web. He lost focus for a brief moment until he felt Gallanth snap him back into reality.

Mkel, she is trying to seduce you and cloud your mind, the gold dragon said telepathically. Mkel took a step back and shook his head to clear his thoughts. He then lowered Kershan, stepped forward, and slapped the dark elf across her face, knocking her down. "Nice try, *yvonalch* (the Draconic word for witch), but love and blood are stronger than you will ever know. This is why you and all your kind will never achieve victory."

"You'll never know the pleasure I could have given you, Dragonrider," she said with a slight smile, holding her chin.

"My wife is who I have come to love, you could never fill that role," Mkel answered back, regaining his composure.

"Only a half elf? I doubt it," Vorgalla answered back.

"Again you'll never know, but other than that, you were not good enough," Mkel replied just as Vatara screeched in to a landing. Jodem dismounted from his eagle and walked over to Mkel.

"Mkel, I see you have a new friend," Jodem said with a smile.

"Jodem the Wise, you were lucky Telenkis didn't best you," Vorgalla said.

"Very spirited, my little spider; I assume you are talking about that lesser drow sorcerer I sent back to the underworld earlier," Jodem replied in a coarse manner as he raised his staff and moved the dragonstone head piece just over her. The sapphire stone started to glow bright blue, which became even brighter as the iridescent light enveloped her. Mkel could see her attempt to resist the domination spell, but without her dark crystal staff, her resistance was futile, and her fidgeting soon ended with the dark elf being locked in a still and silent state. Even her natural magical resistance as an elf could not prevent Jodem's spell from taking effect.

"She will be a little more cooperative now," Jodem stated, very pleased with having a live drow priestess as a captive.

"I hope she will give us the information we are looking for," said Mkel.

"We will get what we need out of her, either through magical means or by coercion, whichever works the best, in spite of the famous drow tenacity," Jodem replied.

"Is there any more organized resistance that needs stamping out?" Mkel asked.

"I do not see any more drow or orcs in the vicinity, and all the remaining dragon spawn and other aerial mounts have been killed. I did hear that the spawn took several Battle Point soldiers hostage as well as a couple of civilians," Gallanth said with a distinguishable amount of concern in his deep voice.

"Taken for information, slaves, or food?" Mkel asked.

"That is to be determined. We do not know enough about them yet, their motivations or masters. We will have to get a definitive head count from Colonel Sheer and the commander of the company to know who is missing," Jodem said.

"A search party and rescue mission will have to be arranged then. If that does come to play, we should get the Weir council leaders out here as an enabling force," said Mkel.

"It would be better to send word to Silvanth to get them. That way, you and Gallanth would not have to be absent for any particular time, to aid General Daddonan," Jodem suggested.

"We will have to wait and see what the final count of the missing is, and what Colonel Sheer and General Daddonan will want to do. We achieved a lucky victory today, for they were taken by surprise, but this battle only uncovered more questions than it resolved. We must also look at that blue dragon we slew, for it had considerably more power and strength than a normal member of its kind. I would like to see if it does indeed have a piece of dark crystal in its heart. That new smaller species that called themselves talon dragons, while not particularly powerful, were still somewhat effective in the close fight," Gallanth finished.

"We better let Colonel Sheer know what is going on, and see if they need anymore help in securing the town," Mkel said as he began to feel his left knee start to throb.

"We need to first tend to your wound, my rider," Gallanth said to Mkel.

"What happened?" Jodem asked with a concerned expression.

"That green dragon got a lucky swipe, right before Gallanth delivered his killing blow. His claw hit my leg, more bruising it than cutting through the dragon-skin leg protectors. I will be all right," Mkel answered.

"I will be the judge of that," Gallanth said as he moved his huge front foot toward Mkel. Mkel prepared for the healing process, which from a dragon could be as painful as the initial wound. Gallanth had healed several of his wounds before, which involved a rapid magically enhanced mending process but carried an intense pain. The end result was a scar and stiffness, but the injury was basically healed.

"I think you should tend to yourself first, my friend," Mkel said to his dragon partner.

"My wounds will heal soon enough, but I cannot have you limping around," Gallanth replied.

"You being at full strength is more important, with all that just happened, and what could still be looming out there," Mkel argued back.

"I do not sense an immediate threat, and there will be no movement until tomorrow, when the legion decides on a course of action; now do not argue with me, my rider," Gallanth lightly scolded.

Gallanth's index claw extended toward his rider and gently touched his knee. Gallanth closed his eyes to concentrate; immediately afterward, Mkel started to feel an intense pain grow deep within his knee. It felt like there was a fire inside his leg, and when it almost became unbearable, it quickly subsided, and Gallanth withdrew his claw and placed his foot back on the ground. Mkel's knee felt much better, and he had full range of motion in it again, without any sharp pains. It still felt a little sore but was basically like new.

"Thank you, you big lizard; isn't there any way you can do that without the pain buildup?" Mkel joked.

"Nothing comes without a price, my friend. Life would be too easy if it did," Gallanth answered with a light tone. "All right, I better call Colonel Sheer," Mkel said as he pulled his seeing crystal from its pouch on his belt. "Colonel Sheer?" he called on his crystal.

"Captain Mkel, what is your status?" answered Sheer.

"We just killed the last two drow and captured a priestess. Jodem has her under his control. Do you need any help?" he asked.

"No, we just secured the town and relieved the garrison stationed here. We are setting up a defensive perimeter and camp now, and we recalled the paladins to establish a screen in case they are able to counterattack. I sent the best hippogriff riders to follow those man/dragons to see where they took the ones they captured. I also sent a message back to Battle Point to assemble more forces and prepare our rangers for a rescue mission. None of our men will be left to whatever fate those demon beasts would have in store for them."

"We should talk about that, sir, but how many are missing, and how many wounded are there?" Mkel asked.

"There are at least twelve missing and believed captured. We had nine killed and nineteen wounded, of which four suffered serious injuries. The healers got to them quickly, and I was told all will live. We did lose two hippogriffs though, a sad loss, and a land dragon took a nasty strike from one of those talon dragons' tail stingers and is not faring well. I must say if it wasn't for you, Gallanth, and Jodem, our losses today would have been at least tenfold that amount, and this village would have been razed to the ground. We owe you all a great deal of gratitude, but we can talk of this later. I am setting up my command headquarters at the small keep where you killed that death knight earlier. Tell Gallanth we are still picking up pieces of the orcs he squashed. I will expect you soon," Sheer finished.

"Yes sir, we will be there momentarily," Mkel answered while thinking to himself how quickly information disseminated in this legion.

"We should get back, for we need to talk to Colonel Sheer about how he wants to get those men back," Gallanth stated.

"Yes, and I want to know what this little princess has in her dark mind," Jodem agreed as he awkwardly got back into his saddle on Vatara.

"All right, let's mount," Mkel agreed as he jumped onto Gallanth's waiting forearm to get into his flying seat. As soon as Mkel had fastened the flying straps, Gallanth spread his wings. Vatara took off with his enlarged talons grabbing the drow priestess like he would have picked up a fish. When the giant eagle had gained enough altitude, Gallanth walked approximately one hundred yards from the drow's broken staff.

Mkel cocked Markthrea and placed a mithril-tipped bolt in place. He took careful aim as Gallanth paused to allow him to get an accurate shot. Mkel acquired the dark crystal in his sight and started to time his breathing. The sight's crosshair movement settled onto the crystal, and as he exhaled one last time, he paused and squeezed the trigger. The bolt whistled through the air and struck the darkened crystal just slightly high of center, causing the evil stone to shatter and explode in a violent, blinding flash. Gallanth then leaped into the air, and with three hefts of his golden wings, he was right behind Jodem and Vatara.

They could have teleported back over the town but it was a short flight and they all needed to wind down after the battle; it also saved power of the gems in Gallanth's synthensium, which gave him the majority of the power for his breath weapons, for spells, and for teleportation. The land surrounding Handsdown was relatively flat with grassy plains, a few rolling hills, and small scattered forests as far as the eye could see until the southeastern mountains, which lay well beyond the horizon. A small river bisected the town and eventually rejoined the Milstra River, which flowed past Battle Point.

Vatara could soar for hours without a single flap of his wings, but he still needed to undulate occasionally. Gallanth only needed to heft his colossal dragon wings to gain altitude. To maintain his level of speed, his and all dragons' hides could actually force air to move over them. This enabled them to increase or decrease their speed at will without having to flap their wings. In essence, dragon skin, with its very small overlapping plates, actually had the ability to cause air to flow over their wings and body much like a dolphin can with water. This was also the strength of dragon skin, for when touched gently, it felt smooth, but it would became instantly rigid when struck, spreading the impact out across a wide surface. This and its very composition made dragon hide almost impenetrable, which was why it was so sought after for making weapons and armor. This helped make dragons among the strongest flyers, but not necessarily the most maneuverable. Gallanth could reach speeds well in excess of sixty miles per hour during level flight, and much faster when necessary. His dives attained considerably more speed, which was a woe to an enemy who was struck by him.

Within a short time, they reached the village, which was still filled with many fires; smoke was rising from many destroyed houses and structures. However, most of them were basically intact, as the Alliance reinforcements arrived before too much destruction could take place. Mkel looked through Markthrea's sight to get a better view of the activity below. There was a hub of movement around the small wooden fort where he and Gallanth had crushed those orcs an hour or so earlier and where he killed that death knight. His body had already been removed, and the orc bodies were being put into a pile for burning.

Orcs stank when alive and smelled worse when dead, so the sooner they burned the bodies, the better. Orc weaponry and armor were not worth saving, for they were usually of poor quality. They favored crude swords and scimitars, battle-axes, spiked clubs, and short spears in battle, many of which were stolen or taken from their victims. Some of their ranks employed short bows, but they were not accurate, nor did they have a long range. They also employed very crude crossbows for greater range.

The metal from their equipment was usually melted down for scrap. Orcs were insect-like in their internal structure, having a semi-open circulatory system with grayish black blood. Their skeletal system was also softer than that of humans, but their skin was slightly tougher.

Their insect heritage was why only sterile males were usually encountered. Orc tribes had maybe one or two females, like termite queens, that bred offspring for that particular tribe. They reproduced at an extremely fast rate of one per week (or more, if conditions were right). They had brown, yellow, or almost black skin color, and while usually shorter than humans, some orcs were over six feet tall. Their integument was rubbery as compared to human skin, which made up for their softer skeletal system. Breeding males were up to six and a half feet tall. These specimens were stronger and slightly more intelligent than the average orc. They were usually the chieftains or war band captains of orc companies.

Orcs were mostly substandard fighters, for they were poorly disciplined and did not possess great dexterity. They were very good at massing on an enemy, though, attacking like a colony of termites, and could wreak havoc on lightly protected or undefended communities. It took a strong chieftain, death knight, or sorcerer to keep them in check and focused on an enemy, however. Their leaders, if they were orcs, were usually the strongest and fiercest of the breeding male orcs in that tribe or colony. The orc tribes could be as few as one hundred to more than tens of thousands.

Orcs claimed lands in Morgathia and roamed the eastern unsettled lands, either hunting or pillaging for food and treasure. They warred with anything, even other orc tribes, with the more powerful Morgathian warlords and sorcerers, as well as many giants and chromatic dragons, keeping tribes and even armies of orcs for their service as long as they could feed them. When directed by Morgathia, they banded together to form hoards in the tens to hundreds of thousands. These orc armies were coupled with human forces from Morgathia and its allies, with sections of drow, grummish, lizard men, and gnolls.

As Gallanth approached the village, the Battle Point soldiers started to go into a hasty defensive posture, which was understandable at the sight of an incoming dragon, until several of the senior fighters and sergeants identified him. From the ground, his golden color, his immense wingspan, and the arrow-head-shaped tip of his tail made him very recognizable, even from long distances. Mkel could see that they were preparing a hasty defense by building a shallow trench and short earthen wall around the village and taking steps to flood it. It was being filled with sharpened sticks and was being dug at various depths. In some areas, it was three feet deep, other areas were over six. Once it was filled with water, an attacker could not tell which areas were deep or shallow, and the sticks were always just under the surface. The excess dirt was being compacted into a rampart for elevated defense, so if an attacking force was successful in bridging the spiked moat, they would have to scale the earthen slope and attack uphill into the spears and arrows of the defending soldiers.

A small force could hold here against a much larger invading army when the construction was complete. More sappers would have to be brought in to build the towers and bridge that would be needed for completion of the defenses.

Gallanth circled around the village several times, descending as he turned. He landed just inside the perimeter on the northeast side of the village, as far from the buildings as possible, for the wind generated by his wings could actually flatten small unsecured structures. As the dust settled from Gallanth's downdraft, a cheer erupted from the Alliance soldiers. They knew he had saved many of their lives this day. The dragons that he killed in this battle could have taken out half their numbers, if not completely routed the counterattack.

Gallanth folded his wings and settled down on the grass as Vatara set the drow priestess beside him, and both Mkel and Jodem quickly dismounted. A small squad of heavily armed men then approached them from the direction of the small wooden keep. Mkel could see the one leading them was an officer of senior captain rank. He started to salute, but the officer quickly motioned him not to.

"Captain Mkel, there is no need for military courtesy after what we saw you and your mighty gold dragon do today. You and Gallanth deserve our utmost thanks, for we would not have been victorious without you two and Master Wizard Jodem," the officer said.

Mkel recognized him as Colonel Sheer's second in command of the infantry battalion. "Captain, thank you, this is just what we are sworn to do, protect and support the infantry," he answered with a smile.

"Is Gallanth hurt?" he asked with a concerned expression on his face.

"Just a few scratches, my good captain. They will heal quickly," Gallanth answered, looking down at the squad of men. Gallanth did have several nasty gashes, but Mkel knew he would be almost totally healed by tomorrow morning. All he needed to do was to rest. "Mkel, I will take a short bath in the river and get a little rest after the prisoner is secured," Gallanth continued.

"Be careful, my friend, that river is nothing more than a large stream," Mkel told his dragon mate.

"It will suffice," he said as Jodem walked the drow over to them.

"Good afternoon, Captain," Jodem said pleasantly as the squad of men that accompanied the Battle Point officer surrounded the priestess.

"You might want to have a few paladins guard her as well, for she is very tricky and can easily seduce a man. Your cavalry knights have more of a resistance to this type of manipulation. No offense to your men, but she almost had me under her spell. I would have at least three men with her at all times, and a female soldier from your support corps units wouldn't hurt either," Mkel explained.

"She seems somewhat sedate at present," the captain said.

"That's because she is currently under my control," Jodem stated, "but this will wear off by tomorrow. Her name is Vorgalla, and she is a priestess of the High Aranean order. She should have a little information about what the nature of this attack is all about. Gentlemen, you may escort her. She is harmless in her current state so swords are not necessary," Jodem explained to the soldiers, who looked slightly spooked at being so close to a drow cleric. There was a great deal of lore about the power of the dark elf priestesses. "If it makes you feel better, place her hands in irons," he added as he smiled at the nervous soldiers.

They sheepishly lowered their swords but still did not sheath them, for in spite of the discipline of the Battle Point soldiers, the fear of dark magic was strong. The drow did spill Alliance blood, and she was one of the two most powerful dark elves they faced today, so retribution was also likely on their minds. These top fighters were to not only keep her from escaping, but to protect her from their fellow soldiers.

They walked toward the wooden keep as Gallanth stepped behind them. If there was a plan to kill Vorgalla between Mkel, Jodem, and especially Gallanth, it would not happen now. They were greeted at the keep's gate by Colonel Sheer and the rest of his hastily formed staff with a squad of paladins. Mkel noticed that several riders had arrived on hippogriffs from Battle Point, mostly senior officers with some reinforcements to help relieve the battle-weary battalion; the reinforcements were now preparing the defenses.

"Be careful of the little spider, my friends," Gallanth said. "Even without her staff, she still has a nasty bite." He continued walking toward the river while looking at the group now entering the keep's walls. "Get some rest, you big lizard. We will need you tomorrow," Mkel called to his dragon. He knew Gallanth would fully heal from his wounds in a matter of hours, but he still felt the dragon's pain and did not like his partner to be wounded in any way.

"Master Gold Dragon Gallanth, we owe you our gratitude today," Colonel Sheer spoke up to Gallanth as he walked past the wooden gate from the central building.

"It is my pleasure, Colonel, tell your men that they fought gallantly today and are a credit to the Alliance," Gallanth replied as he kept walking to the stream.

"What do we have here, a little black elf witch?" Colonel Sheer scowled at Vorgalla.

"She can hear you, Colonel, but cannot respond while under my spell," Jodem quickly replied.

"Can we still question her?" he asked.

"Yes, but we need a quiet room where I can concentrate on her," Jodem replied.

"You can use the small dining hall beside the council room in the keep. I will have it cleared of any personnel and leave instruction to not be disturbed and post guards. Captain, see to this," he said to his second in command, who was standing beside Mkel.

"Yes sir, immediately," he replied; he put his hand on Mkel's shoulder in a quick thank-you gesture and briskly walked off into the keep.

"Come, Master Wizard, Dragonrider, let's take the prisoner into the keep. We will be getting visitors both from Battle Point and from Draconia very soon," Colonel Sheer said. "Captain Mkel, are you injured?" he asked as he noticed Mkel limping slightly.

"I just got scratched by that green dragon before Gallanth sent his spirit on to the underworld. He already healed my leg, but it will be stiff for a couple of hours," Mkel replied.

"Nothing a couple of ales won't cure, my son; come in, I will get food and drink for us," Colonel Sheer said with a smile, and they all walked into the battered wooden keep. They filtered through the hallway and into the large council room. The senior captain already had the adjacent dining hall cleared and was making arrangements for food and drink to be brought in. Some of the hippogriffs must have been bringing supplies, and those in the town were now coming out of hiding or from the outskirts, where they fled from the invaders. The storage house next to the keep was made into a temporary healing hall, with all available aloras salve and healers consolidating and treating the wounded there.

Gallanth walked over to the edge of the stream as carefully and gracefully as he could so as to not disturb the soldiers working on the defenses, but all the men in the immediate vicinity stopped working to stare at the gold dragon's immense form. The soldiers by the stream moved aside as Gallanth stepped into the water. It was just over fifty yards across, barely wider than he was long, and as he moved into the middle, it was only twenty feet deep at its center. This was still enough to at least get the bottom half of his torso under water and wash the dried chromatic blood off of his golden hide.

He submerged himself as best he could before turning around to walk back to the point where he entered the river. The soldiers were still staring at him in amazement. Not often would they get an opportunity to stand so close to one of the largest dragons in the world, especially after seeing what he did in battle today. After he fanned his immense membranous wings, Gallanth walked back to the grass field where he landed and settled down.

Jodem placed Vorgalla in the center of the small hall and the rest of the group gathered around her, while several soldiers stood guard at the doors. A few town members came in to place the food and drink on the table at the back of the room. The portly wizard stood in front of the dark elf and raised his staff as the sapphire dragonstone head piece started to scintillate and glow. The drow she-elf reacted abruptly, attempting to fight Jodem's renewed domination spell, but after a couple of seconds, she went back to her calmed state, falling to his magical control.

"She is very stubborn and has a strong resistance to magic," Jodem stated, "but I think this will make her a little bit more amenable."

"What were your objectives at Handsdown?" Colonel Sheer asked her angrily.

"We were to take the town and hold it to draw out the forces from Battle Point," she replied with an unemotional tone.

"Why this village?" he again asked.

"It is a small but important secondary trading post in the unsettled lands, and it is still under protection of the Alliance, but closer to Morgathia, the Kaskars and orc lands," she answered.

"Draw out our forces for what purpose?" Sheer yelled angrily. She did not answer and her face contorted in an attempt to resist the spell.

"What were those new thorny dragons, and what was the source of extra power of the blue dragon that Gallanth killed today?" Jodem interjected to get her off balance.

"The talon dragons are a successful experiment by the drow and Morgathian sorcerers to counter the Alliance Avenger dragons," she replied with less resistance. Jodem was shocked that she knew of the Avenger dragons. "The blue dragon, Evtrex, was a destroyer or demon dragon. His heart was successfully melded with a piece of dark crystal and a drop of Tiamat's blood," she further explained. Looks of surprise and shock came over all the faces in the room.

"How is this done?" Mkel asked, puzzled.

"The strongest dragons volunteer for the ritual for the melding with the dark crystal, but many do not survive," she replied.

"What powers does this bestow upon the recipient?" Jodem asked.

"The successful ritual will affect the destroyer in one of two ways," she explained. "It gives it a tremendous energy boost to its breath weapon, which it can use one to two times per day. The destroyer dragon's spell casting ability also increases. The other way it can affect the dragon is its magic shield will double in strength, and its physical strength increases as well. It can also cast a destruction spell once per day that can shatter castle walls or fell dozens in a single burst."

"How common is this?" Colonel Sheer asked, more inquisitive than angry.

"There are not very many chromatic dragons who have survived the ritual, but the slave miners of the drow have discovered a major vein of dark crystal in a new chamber they unearthed deep below the city of Shanaris, and Tiamat has been empowering it," she further explained.

"Sir, where is Shanaris?" Colonel Sheer's second in command asked.

"It is the drow capital underground city, Captain," Sheer snapped.

"What of the black dragon?" Mkel inquired. "Why was it so ferocious? It was stronger and faster than normal."

"The black dragon was in a fury, like barbarians who go into a berserker rage. This is a skill that we helped the more chaotic species of chromatic dragons perfect. They are given a potion that contains various ingredients, also including a small amount of Tiamat's blood. This allows the dragon to burn up a portion of its own blood for the extra speed and strength. This does exhaust the dragon though and has a longer term effect of shortening its life," Vorgalla answered.

"So Tiamat is still alive?" Jodem asked with some shock in his voice.

"She lives but is still recuperating from the severe wounds that Michenth inflicted on her during the Great War," she replied.

"So she lives, but what does this mean for us?" one of Sheer's officers asked rhetorically.

"It means that there will be another war as soon as she regains her strength," Colonel Sheer answered. "But this time, we are much weaker. We only have a third of the army and one sixth the number of dragons we did during the Great War," he finished. Sheer had been a heavy infantry soldier during the Great War and saw the Morgathian hordes first hand that were eventually defeated, but only after a bitter fight and a great deal of casualties.

"What is the overall plan, priestess? Handsdown is only a small part of Morgathia's goal. What are the objectives you are looking at?" Jodem asked directly while also refocusing the interrogation back to the drow.

"We will attack you by sssseh ..., she ..., destroying your cities in a storm," she yelled, fighting hard to resist the questioning and not reveal any more secrets. Jodem could tell that she was resisting his spell and knew he could not maintain the domination over her much longer.

"She's fighting hard not to reveal anything else," he explained. "I will need help from the Wizard's Council of Thirteen, and maybe Eladra, to get more information. She has vital knowledge of the Morgathian plan but she is still very strong in her resistance to my spell."

"It doesn't matter. I was told that we were to have the prisoner ready to be taken to Draconia for further questioning by the senate," Colonel Sheer said, sounding irritated. "They will be sending a brass dragon sometime tonight."

"How did the senate hear about her and this battle this quickly?" Mkel asked.

"Likely General Daddonan talked to General Becknor when we left. I have been sending him information about the battle from time to time. It is his job to keep the premier and the senate informed of such events. It is the POE senators who are demanding to have the drow brought back to Draconia immediately. Likely so they can defend her position in a tribunal, bastard arbitrators!" Colonel Sheer exclaimed. This sentiment surprised Mkel but he also felt a small sense of relief in that the colonel felt the same way about the Enlightened senators and their arbitrator friends as he did. "I will talk to General Daddonan and see if we can delay sending her back to give you, Gallanth, and Andellion a little more time to get a few more questions answered," he added.

Mkel, danger! Gallanth warned telepathically as a one of the Battle Point soldiers from outside the window raised a small wooden tube and blew a dart at Vorgalla, striking her in the neck. She immediately collapsed to the floor. Even as Markthrea sprang from the wall it was leaning on and flew into Mkel's outstretched hand, the soldier had disappeared from sight.

Mkel sprinted to the window, cocking his crossbow in the process. As he lifted it up into position, he checked to make sure the bolt was a standard nonexploding tip. He quickly scanned the vicinity for the perpetrator while he heard Colonel Sheer yell to not kill the soldier for he wanted him for questioning. The other soldiers in the room ran toward the main entrance to make sure there was no attack coming and to help apprehend the soldier who had fired at the prisoner.

Mkel saw the legionnaire in question face off with one of the soldiers who came running from the river. As they engaged in a melee, he took aim on the assassin's leg and fired. It was a very easy fifty-yard shot, and the bolt caught him on the upper thigh and spun him around onto the ground. Within seconds, four Battle Point soldiers had him surrounded and at spear and sword point. The soldier quickly sat up and bit the ring on his right index finger; within seconds, he was convulsing and twitching on the ground and then fell silent.

The whole group that was in the meeting hall emptied out except Jodem, who stayed with Vorgalla, attempting to neutralize the poison. Mkel was right behind Colonel Sheer, who was surprisingly fast for a man of his size and age, being six foot four inches and well into his upper forties. They crowded around the soldier lying on the ground. "Do not touch him!" shouted the colonel. "He could still be very dangerous."

Mkel thought to himself that he looked pretty much dead, but it was better to err on the side of caution, for whatever he used, both on the drow and on himself, seemed like a very potent poison. Colonel Sheer ordered spears and swords pointed at the now still man's hands, midsection, legs, and throat. With heavy gloved hands, the senior soldier present pulled off the assassin's helmet and face scarf. He had darker features, with thick black hair and a large nose. His deep tan and distinctive tattoos under his armor were not normal for an Alliance legionnaire.

"This man was a Shidanese assassin," Colonel Sheer exclaimed.

"The colonel is correct, the poison blow pipe dart and black scarab tattoo are very telling," Jodem said as he walked up behind the group.

"Is the priestess dead?" Colonel Sheer asked.

"Yes. I could not save her. Maybe if our cleric Watterseth was here or I knew which type of poison he used, but it worked very quickly. Apparently the same poison he used on her, he used on himself. Judging by the purplish black liquid in the small reservoir in his ring and with him likely being a Shidan black scarab assassin, it was either wyvern poison, Death's Dawn extract, or a combination of both to work as fast as it did," Jodem exclaimed.

"Death's Dawn?" Mkel asked.

"It is a rare lotus-like plant that grows in the deserts of Shidan and the Southern Ontaror kingdoms that is used both as a very virulent poison and for medicinal purposes. However, it is favored among their assassin guilds," Jodem expounded.

"Captain, call all of the commanders and tell them what happened here," Colonel Sheer ordered, "Have them check their men for spies and infiltrators. Any soldier not recognized by someone, or doesn't have his identifying seeing crystal, is to be placed under guard until he can be identified. This assassin likely took the armor from one of our captured men to get inside our defenses. Get to it."

"Yes sir," the senior captain replied; he then saluted and turned toward the legion soldiers, grabbing his seeing crystal.

"Who do you think his target was, Wizard?" Sheer asked as he turned toward Jodem.

"It wasn't me or Mkel," Jodem said, "for even apprentice assassins know that a gold dragon and many master wizards have the power of foresight, which warns of such activities. Gallanth, Mkel's sword Kershan, and I did not pick up a threat to us, which is the reason he succeeded in infiltrating this area. His target was the drow."

"Why her?" Colonel Sheer asked.

"I assume that someone was afraid we would get her to talk, and it was only a matter of time before we learned too much, likely about their plan or the overall Morgathian connection. It had to be something they were willing to go to great lengths to protect, for the killing of a drow high priestess must have been ordered by the Morgathian Talon Council itself," Jodem theorized.

"All right, let's get this cleaned up and get back to the keep. We have things to discuss, and I need to talk to General Daddonan," Colonel Sheer explained as he urged all present to move back to the hall.

The colonel started to explain to the general what had happened with the drow and the assassination through his seeing crystal. He replied to Colonel Sheer that he had set out with a regimental size force that would be at Handsdown by nightfall.

"Gentlemen, General Daddonan will be here by nightfall with almost half of the legion," Colonel Sheer proclaimed. "We have to discuss the plan to rescue our captured men." The group sat down at the central meeting table.

"How many total are missing, sir?" Mkel asked.

"At least a dozen; we are still getting final numbers on the missing from the company commanders and the small garrison that was stationed here," Colonel Sheer replied.

"Do you have any information from the rangers and the hippogriff scouts, sir?" Mkel inquired.

"Thank the Creator for the hippogriffs' and griffons' keen eyesight. They are keeping the retreating attackers in sight, because our mounts have better vision than a manticore or an orc, and definitely better than those disgusting hymenoid creatures. So far they are still fleeing toward the southeast," explained the colonel.

"Sir, I can have the whole Keystone Weir garrison here, battle ready, by tomorrow morning," Mkel volunteered.

"I don't know if we need them, Dragonrider," Colonel Sheer replied. "We will have to see what the ranger scouts find, plus since these are Battle Point soldiers that are prisoners, Battle Point legionnaires will want to rescue them or die trying."

"Yes sir, I understand, but we are available to you, as well as my council leaders, who are a very powerful group unto themselves," Mkel added.

"Yes, I know of all of them. Your reputations precede you, and if their talents are needed, believe me I will call. Between the over five hundred soldiers I have here now, and the over two thousand on the march to reinforce us, I have confidence in our ability to handle this situation. Unless there are chromatics or giants, we should have enough strength. However, with you, Jodem, and of course Gallanth with us, I'm not as fearful of them as I used to be," Colonel Sheer answered.

"The planner of this attack did not expect to have a gold dragon and a senior wizard so readily available to help the Battle Point legion," he continued. "The unexpected arrival of you three and all our forces that you teleported in definitively upset their time table and plan. They are reeling but will regroup quickly. I don't think they will hold the prisoners for long. Likely torture them for whatever information they can get and then kill them, or perhaps they will wind up as dinner for those dragon spawn or the orcs. That means we must strike them as quickly as possible. "Jodem, do you think they will bring in any more chromatics?"

"I cannot tell right now," Jodem replied. "Gallanth is asleep and they are out of my range, even for my seeking eye spell."

"General Daddonan also said that a dragon from the Capital Wing will be coming in tonight to aid us in the rescue, as well as several coppers in two days to claim the chromatic dragon corpses. Colonel Lordan will be coming as well, since he shares your border problems," Colonel Sheer added.

"Colonel Lordan? That's good news. Gallanth works well with Talonth, and he will be happy to see him," Mkel explained.

"That will be impressive, to see the largest gold and largest silver dragons in the Alliance fight side by side," Colonel Sheer commented.

"They haven't had the need to since the Great War. Everything since then has been minor skirmishes," said Mkel.

"I had the privilege to witness Talonth and the then Lieutenant Lordan, take on two large red dragons and send them both plummeting to their doom during the fight at Battle Point," Sheer said. "That was after Gallanth went to attack the drow and Morgathian capitals. They both turned the tide for us. I didn't want to bring this up, Captain, but I saw your father fight that day as well. He fought valiantly right up to the end. Michenth would be dead if it weren't for him. You should be proud, as I know he would be of you. Has Gallanth ever determined how he wasn't killed by the death rays from the dark crystals on the Morgathian capital's black spires?"

Mkel was taken aback by this sudden story from the colonel's youth; he didn't quite know how to respond to it. He fought back his emotions enough to clear his throat to answer the Colonel's question. "For some reason, sir, the crystals wouldn't fire on him. In his state at that time, with his magic shield depleted, he would have certainly been killed if only one of the beams had hit him. He doesn't know why, he only remembers being blinded by the rage of the loss of his rider and by the thirst for justice and revenge," Mkel answered.

"Well, maybe one day we'll see the Alliance flag fly over those dark spires," Colonel Sheer stated with a blank look, like he was seeing other events or was in another place. He quickly returned to his normal focused self, as if the very brief interlude never had happened; Mkel could tell he felt bad for bringing that memory to him, knowing that it must be painful to hear about his father's death.

"I hope you are right, sir, but I think some of the Alliance's own people don't want to deal with this problem anymore or don't have the focus for the struggle," Mkel said.

"You're referring to the Party of the Enlightened and their mindless followers," Colonel Sheer snapped. "Since the Great War, life in the Alliance has been made increasingly easy. The proliferation of the heating, cooling, seeing, and lighting crystals from the dragons' own blood and the unprecedented bountiful harvests we have enjoyed with our partnership with the halflings, along with our trade relationships with the elves and dwarves, have made us the envy of the world. The teleportation circles make travel within our borders instantaneous. Our lands are now practically free of evil creatures and have been almost totally safe from any substantial outside threat, until very recently. People tend to forget that just over thirty years ago, we faced a force that almost annihilated us. The short memory of some in our republic is incredible. Thank the Creator that they are still only a minority, a very vocal one, but still a minority. There is a reason that the Founding Council members put in our Articles of the Alliance that you must have contributed to the republic, or be a veteran, to be eligible to vote or hold political office. Anyone who wants to serve is accepted; we find them a place. This all brings stability to our government and the Alliance."

"The POE-aligned senators and other politicians appeal to the worst part of the human mind. They capitalize on emotion and the inherent laziness of many. The fact that they all served at some point in time seems almost like a betrayal," Mkel added with disgust.

"Yes, but this focus on shortsightedness will ensure they will always have some degree of popularity, and it explains why arbitrators are a key part of their movement. They tend to exploit these emotions of the weak minded, self centered, apathetic, and pseudo intellectual types. Their views are counterproductive at best and borderline treasonous at worst," Jodem interjected.

"The one thing that you must remember, young dragonrider, is that wherever the Alliance flag flies, with its the circle of triangles, dragon symbol, hammer, and leaf, truth, honor, and unity reign, hope remains, and tyranny fears," Colonel Sheer said. "Our banner brings strength, justice, and above all freedom. The Alliance is the light, the benevolent force in the world, which especially Gallanth and his fellow metallic dragons help uphold. We all bring men, dwarves, elves, dragons, and an assortment of others together to promote freedom. No other force on this planet fights for the rights of not only its own people, but also for others that are oppressed and threatened. This as well as us spreading the benevolent peace that the Creator and his spirit wish for all, have created an unprecedented prosperity since the Great War and have saved millions of lives.

"As far as anyone who doesn't believe this or in the Alliance's principles," Colonel Sheer continued, "to hell with them! They bask in the very comfort and the light of freedom that the blood of dragons and Alliance soldiers shed to keep. They should be grateful for what they have and not denigrate or castigate the very institution and force that provides them the ability to enjoy their prosperity. These individuals should be grateful they are allowed to even espouse their dissent, for in other lands such as Shidan and Morgathia, they would be either executed or made slaves for their words. These persons who have somehow obtained political office should be held accountable for their words as well."

"I agree and understand, sir. Being mind linked to a dragon gives one a distinct sense of proportionality," Mkel answered earnestly.

"I envy you in that regard, Captain," Colonel Sheer said, "but one only needs to look at that flag flying over the fort with the central embossment of Michenth's head on the white banner to know what freedom means. The triangles, the very symbol of the trinity of the Creator, his earthly spirit, and the Draconic presence, mean order to the universe. For many, especially those who have fought for it, this symbolizes the freedom and the goodness that the Alliance stands for, and for all that who have served and sacrificed in the past."

Mkel understood the colonel's sentiment, for he too always felt pride when he saw the Alliance flag flying over the Weir or being carried by the garrison's standard bearer. Colonel Sheer suddenly grabbed his seeing crystal.

"Sir, we've found their camp. its sixty miles due southeast of Handsdown at the beginning of the hill country," the ranger said in a low tone.

"How many have returned from the battle?" Colonel Sheer asked.

"Not many, sir. I count only three manticores, less than ten of those dragon spawn creatures, and one orc-mounted hymenoid. A very small number of dire wolf and horse cavalry are arriving as well, less than a platoon. They do seem to be getting a slow but steady stream of reinforcements from the east, however," the ranger finished.

"How many?" the colonel inquired.

"I see almost a battalion of orcs filing in from a pass in the hills to the south. There is a scattering of drow and about two companies of human medium infantry with Morgathian armor, but no standards. A troop or so of heavy cavalry with a squadron of manticores and hymenoids is also in the area, and at least a platoon of those spawn. Wait sir, my other scout says he has seen groups of gnolls and grummish with the cavalry, as well as dozens of ogres and at least ten common giants. There are also two or three beholders with the drow," the ranger continued.

"It sounds like they are gathering their numbers, along with a host of other powerful creatures, for something other than a retreat. Keep us apprised of the situation and keep out of sight, especially from the beholders. They literally have eyes in the back of their head. Also let us know if any chromatic dragons arrive," Colonel Sheer ordered.

"No problem, sir, our griffons are back a bit and we have a good hiding spot," the ranger answered.

"Best of luck, son," Colonel Sheer answered as he put his crystal back onto his belt. "Well, gentlemen, we now have at least a small idea of what we are up against."

"Do you think they are preparing for a second battle or just covering their withdrawal?" Mkel asked.

"Likely both, for with the varied types of forces being arrayed, it sounds like they are trying to cover a retreat with a hastily prepared attack," Jodem suggested.

"Excellent conclusion, Master Wizard; if they brought in beholders and more giants, they obviously want those prisoners badly for some reason," Colonel Sheer.

"Yes, but the real threat is still the chromatics," Jodem said. "We can handle the beholders, but if any dragons show up, that will complicate matters. Gallanth and Mkel performed admirably today, but we were surprised by the strength of the blue dragon and the ferocity of that black, not to mention those new talon dragons. By the way, how are your land dragons?"

"One is seriously wounded but will recover. The healers got to it almost immediately. Two more suffered minor injuries, which were also treated quickly, and they will be ready to fight within a short time. I have men and land dragons moving the carcasses of the chromatic dragons back to the village at your request, Master Wizard. It will take two land dragons apiece to move them and another two to tow their wounded cousin back. How big a piece of dark crystal do you think is attached to that blue dragon's heart?" Colonel Sheer asked.

"I don't know, but it must be large just based on the substantially increased power in its breath weapon," Jodem replied.

"Gallanth was victorious, but it fought with an incredible intensity. Its name was Evtrix, and he announced himself as a destroyer or demon dragon. His lightning breath weapon had almost double the power of a normal blue. This would have made it hard for a silver dragon to defeat this evil aberration, and if a red does the same, they will be at the least evenly matched," Mkel exclaimed.

"Well, when the dragon and rider come from Draconia," Jodem said, "we will inform them of the new development to take back to General Becknor and the Dragon Council. I will inform the Wizard's Council of Thirteen upon the conclusion of the operation that will take place tomorrow. Captain Mkel and Colonel Lordan will inform all the Weirleaders and their dragons of this scenario as well." Jodem sat down with a fresh bottle of wine he had just opened.

"Yes, the Weirs and the Dragon Council must be notified of these developments, but we need a tentative plan to rescue our men and attack this camp," Colonel Sheer stated as he placed his seeing crystal on the center of the table. "Last image," he commanded of the flat mirror-like quartz crystal, which immediately glowed and then projected an image of the terrain the rangers were observing above the table for all to see. "You see here, they have set up their camp at the foot of the hills in front of this winding path that leads back to wherever they have come from. You can see at least a thousand strong between the orcs, drow, grummish, and gnolls, not to mention the Morgathian infantry, cavalry, and aerial forces. Only a few survived our counterattack today, so the rest we see here must be fresh."

"I think, sir, that I could insert my Weir's council team, as well as your ranger strike team from Battle Point, behind that taller hill to the north of their encampment," Mkel said. "Jodem can hide my large dragon friend with an illusion spell. The Battle Point rangers can maneuver around to the far side of the camp, with my team coming in from the north. We will wait until you and all of the available men from the legion perform an attack from the southwest, which offers the best concealed route to the enemy, allowing the rangers a more direct egress line to your troops. My team and the rangers will be covered by Gallanth."

"Who would cover the Battle Point troops?" asked Colonel Sheer.

"Sir, you said that a Capital Wing dragon and Colonel Lordan with Talonth will be here soon. Two silvers can make up for a gold," Mkel said with a smile.

"Yes, Captain, I should have faith in Talonth and a Capital Wing silver," Sheer answered. "I think the southern approach is the best. We can get the two silver dragons to teleport us in about a mile or so away in this lower ground here." He pointed to an area in the crystal's image.

"As long as Colonel Lordan and the Capital Wing dragonrider agree, they can lead your hippogriffs into the aerial battle. Gallanth will lie in hiding if any other chromatics appear and ambush them from the rear as they engage the silvers, hopefully after either my team or the rangers have recovered the prisoners," Mkel added.

"You have a lot of faith that the silver dragon and rider from Draconia will cooperate with your plan," Colonel Sheer stated, with a small measure of doubt.

"Yes Colonel," Jodem interjected, "but remember the other dragons have a great deference for Gallanth, even though they ultimately answer to Valianth. There is a slight bit of competition between these two mighty golds, but not animosity. Even though Valianth is the oldest gold dragon in the Alliance, Gallanth was offered the lead of the Capital Wing after the Great War and turned it down to stay at Keystone Weir, in spite of Valianth's wounds."

"I had heard this as a rumor, for it did happen almost thirty ago and I was in the ranks at that time, not privy to such undertakings. I thought metallic dragons were free from these emotions," Colonel Sheer replied.

"For the most part they are, sir, but there are still small quirks from time to time in their dealings with one another," Mkel explained. "It is complicated dance between the Alliance dragon species and riders from time to time, but from an outsider's perspective, it seems seamless. Even riders and those close to them do not see things such as this, for the dragons strongly discourage it. This is a trait they get from us from the bonding."

"Well, hopefully this will not be the case here, my good dragonrider," Colonel Sheer stated, tilting his head in a sideways glance.

"Don't worry, sir, I have faith that the plan will come together," Mkel answered.

"The Keystone Weir council leaders are a powerful group, Colonel, and luck does travel with us," Jodem stated, referring to the half myth, half truth that gold dragons bring luck to those around them. "You will have powerful friends for this fight, and we can bring more if you desire."

"We will see what General Daddonan brings tonight, my good wizard, and then go from there," Colonel Sheer said. "I think we have done all we can do here for now. We'll get back together later when the Battle Point legionnaires arrive. I think that today's victory inflicted a great deal of damage to the enemy, with many thanks owed to you two and Gallanth. General Daddonan will also have a say in what will be implemented for the rescue mission. Captain, go to your dragon and get some rest, for we will all need it tomorrow. That is more of an order than a request, even though I know you are somewhat of an independent operator. I will call you on your crystal when we gather again tonight, for I must let my company commanders and staff know of our plan to give them time to prepare in case General Daddonan wants us for the fight."

"Yes sir," Mkel answered, as even then his knee was still stiff from the healing Gallanth had given him. "Jodem, are you coming?" he asked of his wizard mentor.

"I will be out shortly. I just have a few matters to discuss with Colonel Sheer regarding Andellion," the portly wizard answered.

"See you soon. We still have to talk about the fight today, our own after-battle review," Mkel said on his way out of the room to the large keep door. He walked out of the small wooden fort and onto the gravel roadway that lay beside it, toward the sleeping gold dragon. Several soldiers approached him to give him a salute and to thank him for what Gallanth did in protecting them today. As always, he took the thanks with pride in his dragon and small warmth in knowing that he and Gallanth were appreciated. *I must be the luckiest man in the world to be his rider*, Mkel thought to himself.

He reached Gallanth, who opened his outer eyelid to give him a quick look.

"Go back to sleep, you big lizard," Mkel said, lightly scolding his dragon mate. *I am looking forward to seeing Talonth,* Gallanth said to him telepathically. "You must sleep first, we will likely be in battle tomorrow," Mkel replied. *I am not worried, my young rider.* "Go to sleep. I have to call Toderan and Lupek to give them as much time as I can, so they can prepare."

CHAPTER V

THE GATHERINGS

Lupek and Deless had been skirting around the mountainside all night. The elf scout had been in the lead, for in spite of the senior ranger's woodland skills, elves had superior vision and hearing. This was especially true in the dark, even with the night seeing crystal lenses, which gave the ranger the ability to see in even total blackness. They rounded the last turn to come off of the small ledge, taking care to stop and watch for any enemy presence and not silhouette themselves from anyone in the valley below; they finally saw the large Smoking Mountain rising up over the valley in the predawn light.

"Cover!" Deless forcefully whispered as he dove into a small patch of undergrowth, and Lupek then immediately followed. Both of them quickly covered themselves with their elven cloaks, which turned the same color as the surrounding ground and masked their body heat. Within seconds, a medium-sized green dragon flew over them a couple hundred feet in the air, filling the valley with the bass-like poundings of its fifty-yard-wide wingspan. It sailed past them at a leisure pace, unaware of their presence.

"That was close, Deless. You didn't hear it coming sooner?" Lupek whispered, curious, as they slowly pulled the elven cloaks from their heads. The cloaks were made of a unique blend of special fibers, supposedly spun with a little bit of elf blood. The unique garments will chameleon color change to match the surroundings.

"Green dragons have a special skill at hunting elves, but we have developed an almost sixth sense in feeling their presence," the elf answered. "It comes down to know when they are around or die. Dawn and dusk are the times when dragon sight is more hampered."

"We've got to go," Lupek whispered, "we have to make it down the other side of the valley before full sunrise."

They both slipped down into the wooded valley, but their pace slowed as the trees became less dense and they neared the edge of the plateau that lay before the Smoking Mountain. As they crouched down behind a large tree and a bit of undergrowth, they spotted a small outcropping of rock about fifty yards to the right of their position on the edge of the wood line. They then heard a metal clank of chain mail and quickly crawled to the outcropping.

An orc emerged from the far side of the rock outcropping and peered around, not taking too careful a look into the forest. It did not appear to be very alert or concerned about its mission as a sentry. The orc then turned around at the sound of a war horn announcing the arrival a new battalion of orcs from the southern pass through the mountains. Lupek and Deless slipped from the underbrush and quickly but deftly made their way over to the near side of the large rock.

Lupek nodded at Deless and made a motion to go to the right, and they immediately moved past each other as Lupek drew a hand axe from his belt. Deless nimbly ran to the lower part of the rock and paused. Lupek snuck around to the opposite side of the large boulder and froze. The elven ranger then tossed a small rock to the front and side of the orc, who turned his grotesque brownish red face toward the sound, his yellowish chitin teeth apparent as he snarled.

As the orc lowered his spear to move over to investigate, Lupek emerged from behind the rock face and hurled his hand axe, which was sent twirling through the air. It found its mark, burying itself deep in the back of the orc's neck, killing it instantly. It fell backward, and Lupek and Deless caught it before it hit the ground, to prevent any unnecessary noise from alerting his companions.

They sat the orc down and propped it up with its sword, lashing its spear to its hand. Lupek pried the axe from the back of the orc's neck and wiped the black-grayish blood on its tunic.

"Disgusting creatures," Deless whispered to Lupek.

"Like termites, only much less useful and much more dangerous," Lupek answered as he slid down the back side of the rock to put his body out of view from the gathering armies several hundred yards below at the base of the mountain. Deless slid down on the other side of the dead orc to hide behind the rock as much as possible. Lupek pulled out the two small glass lenses wrapped in a leather tube to get a magnified look at the forces gathering below. Deless did not need this visual assistance, given his enhanced vision.

"Looks like at least ten thousand orcs from three or four tribes," Lupek whispered to his elven comrade.

"Yes and roughly two thousand Morgathian cavalry, and one to two battalions of grummish," Deless continued as Lupek marked the forces they observed in his small log book and the elf captured the scene on his bow's dragonstone. "I see at least four beholders as well, in front of a battalion of drow. They are far from Shanaris. It must be something extraordinary to bring the fallen elves into the sunlight so far from home." He had more than a slight hint of disgust in his voice.

"What's this, overemotion from an elf?" Lupek teased his friend. Deless looked over to his ranger companion and grinned slightly.

"Keep focused, ranger," he quipped back. "There are over one hundred fire giants, with twice that many common giants and ogres, and over a dozen dragons in the caves beside the fire giant castle. I count at least four reds, eight blues, twelve greens, and even more blacks. This is a large gathering of chromatics; it will take more than what Eladran Weir has to counter them.

"Eladran can muster a couple of pairs of bronze, copper, and brass dragons as well as Talonth, his mate, and that young silver. They are a formidable force," Deless continued, "but they are still outnumbered almost six to one with what we can see. We will have to come to their aid when this conglomerated army moves."

"The beholders are powerful by themselves, and I'm sure there are several sorcerers of notable power, as well as death knights," Lupek said.

"Wait, what are those creatures?" Deless exclaimed as Lupek quickly focused his lens on strange, multilegged snake-like dragons that were moving with the cavalry.

"They look like a cross between a blue dragon, an alligator, and a snake. I count at least eight small legs, and their bodies end in a short, stubby tail," Lupek observed. "Can you hear what they are saying?"

"They are calling them 'behirs.' Their riders are having a hard time controlling them and are turning to either one of the several sorcerers or the chromatic dragons to threaten them," Deless said, conveying what his sensitive elvish ears caught from the long distance.

"I wonder what their capabilities are," Lupek said rhetorically.

"The way they are moving this way, we might find out before we want to," Deless answered. A squad of orcs was making their way over to the rock outcropping, likely to relieve the orc they killed with a new guard.

"Let's go, I think our welcome is worn out," Lupek whispered as he slipped down the backside of the rock, quickly followed by his elf partner. They dashed to the wood line and started to move from concealed position to concealed position. Within a couple of minutes, they heard the clamor from the outcropping as the behirs' shrill warbling roars announced the presence of intruders. "Looks like our exfiltration will get a little complicated," Lupek whispered to Deless.

They then heard a crashing of a strange new dragon-like creature entering the sparse woods along with the clang of orc armor and the familiar grunts of their harsh language. As the two were slipping from tree to tree, three manticores flew overhead and began to circle back.

"It looks like we're going to have to fight through this to make it back to our griffons," Lupek whispered.

"These woods are too thin to hide or get around them," Deless agreed.

"We should take out the manticores first, for we can outrun the orcs. As soon as they get above us, you take the lead and trail ones, and I'll hit the one in the middle," Lupek said. Deless nodded as he drew an arrow from his quiver and nocked it onto the string. Lupek repositioned his hand on his dragonstone-imbedded elf wood javelin, its pointed mithril tip glinting in the sunlight. As the manticores approached barely a hundred fifty feet above the trees, Deless drew his bow and whispered a short incantation, upon which the sapphire dragonstone started to glow and transferred energy into the arrow.

Deless's arrow started to crackle with electrical power as the lightning bolt spell fused into it. He gave the manticore a small lead, which for the slow-flying beast was not difficult, and fired. The spell-charged arrow streaked through the air and struck the manticore's enlarged lion-like chest. The evil mount jerked back hard from the impact, let a sharp roar from its grotesque half-lion half-ape head, and then plummeted lifelessly to the ground, its rider frantically trying to loosen the flying straps.

Lupek jumped out from behind the tree and threw the lightning javelin toward the second manticore. It struck the beast on its lower left side, causing it to buckle and spin out of control. Deless quickly drew another arrow as he started another incantation. The arrow started to glisten with frost as he cast an ice ray spell onto it. The third manticore started to bank to the left as it passed over the rangers. Its rider did not know their precise location, but it let loose a volley of six spikes from its tail in their general direction.

Deless swung around as he drew his bow and began to take aim; Lupek jumped in front of him, raising his left arm with the mithril-lined buckler strapped to it, just in time to stop a spike from hitting his elven comrade. Deless loosed the arrow, which had frost vapors coming off of the shaft. It sailed through the air and caught the stubby-winged beast on the underbelly. The ice-empowered arrow instantly froze the manticore almost solid as well as its rider, sending them both hurtling to the ground. When they hit the valley floor, they shattered into thousands of pieces.

Lupek outstretched his left arm, upon which his javelin dislodged from the dead manticore and flew back to his hand. Two orcs then emerged from the brush and charged the rangers. Deless quickly drew an arrow and shot the lead orc in the chest, knocking the chain mail-armored creature off his feet. Lupek drew his scimitar and faced off with the second orc. The rust-colored-skinned orc snarled, revealing his jagged yellow/brown teeth, and raised his battle-axe, swinging down at the ranger. Lupek dodged the pitted axe blade and pinned the back of the weapon down with his javelin. He then swung his scimitar up and cut the orc's arm off at the elbow. The ranger then spun around, thrust the silvery blade into the orc's midsection, and then kicked the mortally wounded creature to the ground.

Ten more orcs took off at a dead run at the two rangers. Deless drew an arrow and took aim. Quickly whispering an incantation, he let loose the glowing arrow, which then split into six glowing projectiles, striking six of the charging orcs in the midsections. Those hit were blown back, with their armor or hide smoldering from the magic missile impact. Lupek stuck his javelin in the ground, dropped his scimitar, and quickly drew and threw two knives at the closest orcs, hitting one in the neck and the other in the chest. They both fell to their knees, grasping the knife handles as their grayish black orc blood spurted from the wounds. He quickly picked up his javelin and scimitar and assumed a defensive stance to meet the two remaining orcs moving toward him.

The lead orc raised his sword just as Lupek dropped down and swung his javelin forward, catching the orc in the legs, causing him to be thrown forward by his own momentum. Lupek then raised his scimitar up and to the right to parry the spear of the second orc. In a fluid motion like water flowing around rock, he spun backward, swinging his javelin around and striking the orc in the midsection, doubling him over. He then continued his turn, bringing the curved scimitar down on the orc's exposed neck below his helmet, easily severing its head.

The first orc had just gotten back on its feet as Lupek thrust his spear, and its pointed mithril tip pierced the orc's breastplate and flesh like a knife slicing a heavy crusted loaf of bread. The orc dropped its axe and grabbed the shaft of the javelin sticking out of his chest in a vain attempt to pull it out. Lupek moved in, grasped the end of his javelin, and sliced down, cutting the orc's leg at the upper thigh. As it fell to the ground, he pulled the javelin out of the orc's chest and moved back to Deless, who lowered his bow.

"What did you think, I couldn't handle a couple of orcs?" Lupek said, smiling at his elf friend.

"Always have your back, my friend." Deless looked over to Lupek and gave a rare smile, but his expression immediately went serious as he shouted, "Down; scutelm!" He raised his bow and spoke the elvish word for shield; the sapphire dragonstone glowed and emanated its invisible magic shield, just in time to take a lightning bolt strike. Deless's screen shuddered with the impact but held.

The behir bellowed a shrill garbled roar from a hundred yards away. "There they are, get the elf vermin," the Morgathian rider yelled to the orcs beside the dragon-like creature. The platoon of orcs began to bellow war cries and charge at the rangers. Deless drew an arrow, powered it with a lightning bolt spell, and released it. The electrically charged arrow sped the one-hundred-yard distance in a blink of an eye and struck the behir square in the chest. The arrow deflected off its dull bluish hide and hit in the middle of the pack of orcs. The explosion sent six of them flying through the air, landing on the ground smoldering.

"That was almost a waste of a spell," Lupek said to Deless.

"I wanted to confirm that these new creatures were immune to electricity, plus I did take out six orcs," Deless quipped back. "Now if you don't mind slowing the others down, I want another shot at the creature to see how tough it really is."

"Just make your shot count, pointy ears!" Lupek yelled back to him as he moved to engage the orcs that were bearing down on them. Deless then drew another arrow, nocked it, and spoke another half-elvish, half-Draconic incantation with a more intense concentration, for he was preparing a powerful disruption spell. Lupek raised his javelin and threw it at one of the orcs in the middle of the group. The javelin impaled a large orc in the lower abdomen and burst with electrical energy, sending out smaller bolts in all directions and hitting eight other orcs nearby. This strike effectively eliminated almost half of the platoon that was bearing down on him.

Lupek then grabbed two daggers from the vest on his mithril-studded leather armor and threw them at the closest orcs, one hitting one in the chest and the other in the shoulder. He then quickly drew his scimitar and a hand axe, wading into the middle of the squad of orc soldiers converging on him. He literally moved right through them, dodging the axe of one while slicing it underneath its armor and hitting another in the knee with his axe. The orcs were clearly taken by surprise at his speed and fluidity in battle, but they wheeled around to face him. He threw the axe at the closest orc, which cut through the leather band on its shoulder and sinking half the blade into its upper chest.

Lupek then outstretched his arm, and his javelin dislodged from the orc it was imbedded in and flew back to his hand. He knew he couldn't power another lighting bolt strike yet but needed the slender five-foot spear to give him reach against his opponents. There were seven orcs remaining to contend with.

He grasped the javelin at the middle of its shaft and held it tight against his forearm, for he could use both ends as weapons this way. He then moved against two orcs in front of him, parrying their swords with his javelin and scimitar. He then thrust the rear end of his javelin backward, hitting an orc behind him in the chest and knocking it back a couple of feet. With a quick thrust forward, he pierced the orc to his front left through the abdomen with the mithril tip. As the other orc swung his sword at Lupek's right side, he again parried with his scimitar, forcing the orc's blade down, then he cut up under the orc's arm pit and through the upper shoulder, the grayish black blood spurting from the wound.

Another orc managed to move up behind the ranger and thrust a spear at the lower right portion of his back. The spear tip caught Lupek's studded armor and slightly penetrated it, but he automatically spun to the left to roll away from the impact. Lupek continued to turn around with amazing speed, hitting the orc's spear with his javelin and following through with his scimitar's curved blade, slicing the orc's exposed neck. He kept the momentum of his spin going, swinging the javelin in a wide arc to temporarily keep the remaining five orcs at bay, to prevent them from converging on him.

In the meantime, Deless had drawn another arrow, which was now almost glowing with power after he finished the incantation, and then released it. The golden-brown fletched elf wood shaft sped toward the behir, which was now moving closer to Lupek and the orcs he was fighting. The arrow struck the bluish, multilegged Draconic creature at the base of the neck and immediately turned into a brilliant streak of energy, cutting through it like a searing hot poker. The behir raised its head in a shrill cry of pain and tipped over on its right side, writhing in agony at the gaping wound the disruption spell the arrow delivered.

Not very magic resistant, Deless thought to himself as he quickly drew another arrow and aimed at one of the two orcs that were bearing down on him. He released the arrow, which found its mark in the orc's face, almost flipping it over. A second arrow, immediately drawn and fired with incredible speed, downed the other orc only five yards away; Deless had to step to the side to avoid the falling creature from hitting him. Lupek killed two more orcs with a quick thrust of his javelin, piercing once orc's shield and continuing through its chest cavity and slicing the other's abdomen with his scimitar. The three remaining orcs rushed him, with the smallest one being shoved onto the javelin as a sacrifice. Another was impaled on Lupek's scimitar, but the third pushed him to the ground. As it raised its axe to deliver a killing blow to the struggling Lupek, an arrow from Deless emerged from the back of the orc's helmet through its forehead. It fell forward, almost on top of the ranger, who rolled away and then sprang to his feet.

"I guess I have to owe you one, pointy ears," Lupek said to his comrade in elvish as he secured his javelin and scimitar.

"Don't worry, I won't let you forget it," Deless replied.

"We'll see, but now we have to go," Lupek said back to him as he looked at the gathering forces that were starting to move toward them. He realized that they would soon be hopelessly outnumbered, so they started to run through the remaining part of the sparse woods back toward the mountain pass to get to their griffon mounts. As they made it through the woods and were running through the boulder-strewn path around the rocky mountain, they could hear the pounding hooves of the Morgathian heavy cavalry stop at the edge of the forest, where it was too rocky for horses to traverse and too narrow for the behirs.

Lupek wondered if they would send a chromatic after them, for once the senior sorcerers and warlords learned that three manticores, a platoon of orcs, and a behir were killed, they would figure that someone of power had been encountered. They might send a dragon to investigate, if anything just for an opportunity for a budding young red or green to show off its power. He knew that all they could do was delay a blue or red. Even a big green or black would give them a very hard time. He quickened his pace, as Deless kept up with him.

They stealthily moved through the rock formations, keeping ahead of the pursuing orcs and out of sight of the aerial patrols of manticores that were flying overhead. The elf-made cloaks definitely aided them in avoiding detection from the manticores and their riders. They moved for several hours around the mountains until they finally came to the rock outcropping and cave where they left their griffons.

The statuesque creatures were nestled inside, still waiting for their masters. Lupek and Deless could tell that they were unsettled, though, in that they could sense their mortal enemies, the manticores, nearby. They moved to their mounts to quickly calm them down. The shallow cave hid them from aerial view, but the orcs would not be too far behind. Deless was starting an incantation as they both mounted and secured themselves in their flying saddles.

"I am preparing the teleportation spell to get us back to the Weir, but it will take a couple of minutes once we are airborne to focus to allow both of us to go. You must be within wingtip distance when I give the mark," Deless told Lupek as they both waited on their griffons for the manticore patrol to fly around the mountain.

"If we run into trouble, you just go and I will get back the hard way," Lupek answered.

"No, that would be unwise. First, Captain Mkel told us not to go out; second, you are the ranger platoon leader and therefore too valuable to be left behind. Third, I won't do it, for you are my friend," Deless replied.

"Remember, elf or not, I still outrank you, and this information is more important than either one of us. You have a better chance of making it back, so I will run interference for you," Lupek answered.

"Just keep close and I will get us both home as soon as I can," Deless said.

"I'll run cover for you if we encounter anything; let's go," Lupek ordered. They urged their griffons forward. The large golden brown feathered mounts stood up on all fours and walked out of the cave, their white feathered heads peered out of the entrance. They separated enough to spread their wings, and with a short sprint and a leap, they were airborne. Griffons were powerful flyers, and they gained altitude rapidly. As they continued to make their way up the narrow valley, a muffled roar came from behind them. A pair of manticores were attempting to pursue them but were several hundred yards behind. They didn't concern the rangers, since manticores were much slower than griffons and did not possess seeing crystals to call for help.

The manticores were beating their bat-like wings hard in an attempt get within range to use their spikes. Lupek knew that they could only shoot accurately out to fifty or so yards hence why they loosed volleys of six or more at a time. They usually had up to twenty four that grew back rapidly after they were used. Even with the griffons ascending, they would not get to within three times that distance. Their luck then changed as a lone manticore emerged to their front from around one of the steep narrow mountains, heading to intercept them.

Foolish rider, Lupek thought to himself: a lone manticore against two griffons. "Razor Claw, let's answer his challenge," he said to his mount. He veered right, away from Deless's griffon. Razor Claw let out a deep piercing war cry as a challenge to the manticore and stretched out its sharp front talons. The manticore moved to intercept them and raised its spiked tail, bristling with over twenty pointed hollow spikes at the tip. Lupek's griffon was swerving from side to side so as not to give the manticore a stationary target.

When they closed to less than one hundred yards, the manticore whipped his tail, sending a shower of a dozen or so spikes darting toward the ranger and griffon. The powerful golden wings immediately folded, and they dove hard. One spike hit the griffon on the right rear haunch, causing it to wince from the black thorn, and Lupek stopped another with his buckler. The griffon immediately unfurled its wings and used its downward momentum to shoot back up with a forceful acceleration.

Razor Claw struck the manticore from the underside, tearing into the creature's hide with its talons. Its beak tore a deep gash in the manticore's chest, and it ripped the base of one wing with the other talon, almost disemboweling it. Lupek thrust his javelin at the rider, who was human and wearing the typical Morgathian leather armor of an aerial soldier, striking his midsection before he could parry with his own spear. The mithril tip cut through the blackened leather armor like going through air. Manticore riders couldn't wear very heavy armor because their mounts were not strong flyers, so weight must be conserved.

Lupek pulled his javelin out of the rider's chest just as his griffon let the dying manticore go. Both were mortally wounded, but their end would come quick at the conclusion of their fall. He looked back at his griffon's hindquarter and saw that the spike had gone in at a shallow angle, so the wound would not be serious.

"Lupek, we are ready to teleport," Deless shouted at his ranger comrade. Lupek yelled a command to his griffon to turn left and rendezvous with Deless. The other three manticores were closing the distance on them, and then they heard the challenge roar of a dragon in the distance. A red dragon then flew around the mountain about a mile and a half back, making its way toward them. This would not be a fair fight; Lupek thought to himself and quickly flew to Deless's griffon.

As the elf raised his bow and whispered the spell, they were immediately surrounded by blue streaks of light and then disappeared. Just as they dematerialized, a shower of dozens of manticore spikes whistled through the air in the spot they had just occupied. The manticores let out warbled roars in frustration and split off, turning around to head back to the fire giant's stronghold. The red dragon had just caught up to them and roared in a deep, sinister, angry voice, "Fools, you let them get away! You will pay for your incompetence". He then opened his crimson-colored jaws, filled with jagged teeth, and breathed out a cone of fire, engulfing one of the manticores and its rider, instantly incinerating them. The other two immediately dove and scattered to try to escape the dragon's wrath.

Lupek and Deless emerged over the plain in front of Keystone Weir. "That was closer than I would have liked," Lupek called to his elven comrade.

"Are you and Razor Claw all right?" Deless asked with a concerned tone in his voice.

"I'm fine, but Razor Claw has a spike in his hindquarter. Looks worse than it really is, for the angle of penetration is shallow. He will be fine after a healer removes it and puts a little of your clan's aloras salve on it." This opaque cream was derived from a particular plant that the elves harvested; it acted as both an anesthetic and an antibiotic, and it healed most wounds very quickly. Alliance soldiers and healers carried small jars of the salve, which could instantly stop blood flow from a wound and numbed tremendous pain at the same time. It formed a protective type of second skin over a wound or burn, which fell off once the skin was healed. This gave the Alliance Army a distinct advantage, for a soldier could return to fight in minutes instead of weeks, saving literally tens of thousands of lives.

The two griffons soared around the Weir Mountain and gave their greeting cry to announce their intention to enter and land. The gate watch blew the warning horn to announce the griffons were going to enter the opening into the mountain. Lupek called through his seeing crystal to the tower watch to have a healer ready by the stables. They sailed in at great speed and immediately veered toward Lupek's and Deless's stable perch, where their griffons called home. A healer was waiting for them with a pack full of bandages, aloras salve, and stitching kit, and a worried look on his face.

Lupek and Deless's mounts both back winged onto their adjacent landings. The healer ran over to Lupek to see who was wounded. "Sir, are you or Deless hurt?" the young healer asked.

Lupek pointed to the black spike still half buried in the griffon's hindquarter. "That little spike, sir; it's only a splinter for Razor Claw," he said with slight smile. The griffon's large white eagle-like head turned toward the young man and stared at him with a small hiss. The healer's expression quickly turned serious with a slight twinge of worry. "I will get on it right away," he said with a slightly nervous tone.

"A good idea, son. I'll hold his head steady so he won't eat you if you miss a stitch," Lupek said in a serious tone, which gave way to a smile as he turned away from the healer and faced Deless to hide his chuckle. The elf smiled back and began to unpack his flying rig. The healer quickly applied the aloras salve to the wound and prepared his healing kit. The great white head of the golden brown griffon eased a little as the salve quickly numbed the pain.

"Whenever you are ready, lad, I have his beak," Lupek told the healer.

"All right, sir, I'm pulling it out now." He gave the spike a good yank and barely got it out as Razor Claw jerked up with a deep screech. Lupek quickly spoke to his mount in elvish to calm him down. The large majestic creature quickly settled and lowered its head to allow Lupek to scratch the white feathers above its sharp eyebrow crests. The healer put another layer of aloras on the puncture and began to fasten the silver staples to close the wound, which he accomplished with surprising skill for someone so young. He finished quickly and applied one more layer of salve.

"Sir, it should heal quickly. His hide is very tough," he said.

"Thank you, lad, you did a good job," Lupek answered. "All right, you big vulture," he said in elvish to his griffon, "let's get you something to eat so you can rest and heal." They started to walk down the ramp to the Weir landing and the stock pens on the far side of the grounds.

Razor Claw wasted no time in moving over to the herding area and snatched a sheep, quickly snapping its neck and devouring it. The great war bird would take at least two more sheep before he would be satiated. Griffons only bathed occasionally, unlike dragons, which swam regularly. Being part eagle, they preened the feathers of the upper body and were actually very clean creatures.

After the griffon satisfied its hunger, Lupek walked him back to its loft to sleep. He then went back to his living quarters to clean his weapons and equipment, and to see his family.

"Toderan, are you about?" Mkel called through his seeing crystal.

"I'm here, Captain, just tending to a couple of small matters this morning," the Weir senior sergeant replied.

"Sorry, I forgot the time difference from here," Mkel said. "It's late afternoon, and we just completed a pretty substantial battle with a good-sized force of orcs, Morgathian soldiers, and drow. Gallanth and I also tangled with several chromatics."

"Are you all right?" Toderan asked with a concerned tone in his deep voice.

"A small wound for me and a couple of scratches on Gallanth," Mkel said. "About two dozen casualties for the Battle Point legionnaires and seven killed in action; may the Creator watch

240

over their souls. There were also several who were captured by these new creatures called dragon spawn, a kind of half-man, half-dragon. Some abomination created by a Morgathian sorcerer and the drow, most likely. This is why I called you. We will be conducting a raid to rescue the captured men, and I need our Weir council mates to assist."

"I will muster them immediately, although I think Lieutenant Lupek and Deless just got back from a long patrol from the Smoking Mountains," said Toderan.

"What? I told him to stay with his family and take a couple of days off. I will talk with him later," Mkel said with a modest irritation.

"Before you get too set on scolding him, he has some very valuable information that must be disseminated."

"I'll have him brief me when I see him," Mkel answered. "I'll need the council leaders here before evening, and unfortunately I will need Lupek, for we will be conducting a mission behind the enemy encampment in coordination with the Battle Point rangers. I wanted him to rest with his family for a couple of days, ahh. Tell the council as a warning order that we will be conducting a raid to rescue the captured Battle Point men, as the legion conducts a frontal attack to distract the enemy."

"Yes sir, I will let all of them know immediately to prepare; how are we getting out there?" Toderan asked.

"Gallanth had a tough fight today and must sleep in case we run into more chromatics tomorrow, so Silvanth will have to bring all of you here," Mkel answered. "I also want Jodem's staff to fully recharge. I'm sending you the map of the area through the seeing crystal, as well as a brief summation of the battle."

"Thank you, Captain, we will be ready," Toderan said with his usual business-like confidence.

"I look forward to seeing you all later," Mkel said as he concluded his message. Toderan immediately called for a runner to send word to Ordin in the lower levels, for the dwarf routinely forgot where he put his seeing crystal. He picked up his crystal and spoke Dekeen's name into its lighted surface. The elf's image quickly appeared in the smooth crystal face.

"You called, my good sergeant?" Dekeen answered.

"I just talked to Captain Mkel. He requested that the council leaders meet him at a small town outside Battle Point. There was a surprise attack of substantial force along with several chromatic dragons."

"Is he all right?" Dekeen asked with a concerned tone in his voice.

"He and Gallanth had a rough fight but held the day," Toderan replied. "Gallanth is resting now but there will be another fight tomorrow, and they need us to be there by nightfall."

"How are we getting there?" the elf asked.

"Jodem will be coming back to guide Silvanth to teleport us," Toderan answered.

"I will be at the Weir shortly. Just have to gather a couple of things, since we are going into battle," Dekeen exclaimed.

"I will see you and Lady Beckann then," Toderan said as he blanked his crystal. When the Keystone Weir council members were away on a mission or traveling, Annan and whatever senior officer from the garrison that remained would be in charge of the Weir. Beckann and Watterseth would help if need called for it and if they weren't traveling with the rest of the council. However, this time, the situation required both of their magical abilities to be brought to bear.

Toderan thought to himself that Tegent and Watterseth would be very useful for this mission. Tegent, the Weir's bard, was also an excellent hunter, warrior, and expert archer. He made up for Deless staying behind to oversee the patrols that were still being conducted to watch the gathering army in the fire giant lands. Watterseth would be needed with his combined healing power and combat prowess, for the condition of the prisoners would likely not be good, and he could defend himself quite well, while a normal healer would need protection. Minimizing the size of the group would also keep them from being discovered.

He then picked up his crystal and spoke both their names into it. Within seconds, both their faces appeared side by side on the mirror surface.

"Yes, my good sergeant?" Tegent's smiling face appeared.

"You called, my son?" Watterseth answered.

"Captain Mkel needs our assistance for a rescue mission of several Battle Point legionnaires, who ran into some trouble in a big fight they just had," Toderan explained.

"I'll be there in a couple of hours," Tegent said.

"Likewise, my son," the cleric answered.

"Excellent; see you all this afternoon," Toderan replied and blanked his crystal. He got up and walked back to his living quarters to get his armor and gear ready, and let his family know that he would be leaving for a day or two.

All the remaining members of the Weir council gathered later that afternoon in Mkel's leader's room. "Gentlemen and my lady," Toderan said as soon as they were all gathered, giving a slight bow to Beckann. "As per Captain Mkel's request, we are to take part in a rescue of a dozen captured Battle Point soldiers that were taken during a battle that took place earlier today in the village of Handsdown. This is a small but busy trading town located approximately one hundred miles east of Battle Point." He put his crystal down and spoke several keywords, and the image of the enemy encampment appeared, along with a glowing map of the area. "Here is a view that Captain Mkel sent me of the enemy camp where the prisoners are held. We will be teleported by Silvanth to Handsdown, which is now back in Alliance hands, and get more details then. Any questions?"

"Was the fight today a big one?" Ordin asked.

"Yes, a large force that included several chromatic dragons, drow, a new type of creature called dragon spawn, a half breed of man and dragon, and several hundred orcs and men," Toderan explained. "Gallanth and Mkel teleported a mixed battalion from Battle Point, and their combined strength, along with Jodem, drove the invaders back and decimated them. Several new and disturbing events unfolded, however. Two of the chromatics had an extraordinary power, and a new breed of dragon made its appearance. While Gallanth and Mkel defeated all five dragons and helped route the enemy air and land forces, it was still a tough fight."

"Jodem is coming to teleport us to the battle?" Ordin asked.

"Yes, he should be here to guide us, but Silvanth will teleport our group ..." Toderan began to answer but was interrupted by the sound of the tower watch horn blowing, followed by a distant screech.

"That is Vatara's cry; Jodem has arrived," Dekeen spoke out.

"He is weary and concerned over the events of today," Beckann added. Her powers of foresight almost rivaled Gallanth's, and

243

as far as elves were concerned, only Queen Eladra herself had a greater ability to see the future and be aware of the events around her. Vatara streaked into the Weir and flew directly over to the council room. The great eagle back winged and landed. The portly wizard slid down from his feathered mount and walked over to the group.

"Gentlemen, and my lady," he said with a quick head nod to Beckann, "are we ready for a rescue, my friends?"

"I understand there was a heavy drow presence at the fight today," Beckann asked.

"Yes, news travels fast, I see. A priestess and a male sorcerer of mid power led the dark elf company. I had to slay him, but Mkel and Gallanth were lucky enough to capture her. We questioned the priestess back at the village, but then a Shidanese black scarab assassin killed her. We started to get an interesting picture from her, in spite of her resistance. She did, however, tell us about the extraordinary power of the blue and black dragons that Gallanth and Mkel slew, and the origin of these new talon dragons as well as the man/dragon spawn. Apparently the Morgathians and drow are experimenting with cross breeding and introducing dark crystals into the mix," Jodem explained. "She also alluded to some impending threat but was killed before I could get it out of her."

"I will have to let Eladra and Denaris know of this, Master Jodem," Beckann spoke up. "We must link dragonstones before we depart." The dragonstones in both wizards' staffs and in weapons had memories that can be shared just by the gemstones touching each other or by a directed message. The latter takes more time, however, and drains energy from the powered gems. These images can then either be projected or accessed telepathically, just as with the seeing crystals, only in greater detail.

"No problem, my lady," Jodem replied. "Now are all of you ready to go, in say one hour?" All nodded in agreement. "Good, Ordin, why don't you ride with Toderan; Watterseth, you can ride with Tegent on his griffon," he delegated. "Let us go, there is a long night ahead for us, followed by an even longer day."

"Yes, Master Wizard, I am looking ever forward to felling giants," Ordin said, "but can't we just teleport from the Weir grounds?" The dwarf tried ever so tactfully to hide his fear of flying.

"Master Ordin, Gallanth can perform teleportation from the ground much easier than I or Silvanth, and it takes more energy from my staff to do that. You will be fine on Toderan's Alvanch," he said with a slight smile, seeing through Ordin's bravado.

"Yes, of course, Master Wizard. I just thought that it would be faster to just leave from the ground," he courteously replied in a shallow attempt to hide his anxiety about flying on something besides Gallanth.

"No worries; we need to prepare to leave. I will meet you all back here in an hour, agreed?" Jodem asked the group. A rounding yes came from the assembled, after which he turned and started to walk to his quarters to gather more materials for his spells and two old books he needed for background on the potential fight they were facing.

They all met back at the landing with all their gear ready for a several-day fight, in case they could not get back to the Weir for a while. They all mounted up, with Ordin grudgingly climbing onto the white winged horse. He secured himself very tightly with the flying straps and grabbed Toderan's belt. Toderan looked at Jodem and smiled at Ordin's trepidations. Annan mounted on Silvanth's back, and the statuesque silver dragon moved in front of the group.

"After you, Master Wizard!" Toderan shouted to Jodem.

A smile came over the stout wizard's face. He then nodded to Silvanth and gave Vatara a small nudge with his heels, and the giant eagle spread its wings and sprung into the air. Toderan's winged horse galloped and launched off the ground, followed by Dekeen's eagle and Lupek's and Tegent's griffons. Beckann closed her eyes and spoke a small incantation in Draconic, after which a soft glow enveloped her and her unicorn, which she had charmed with a flying spell. Silvanth let out a low roar to announce she was taking to the air and then gracefully took off. Once they were all airborne above the plain past the Severic River, Jodem waved his staff to signal them to form up to within wingtip distance of Silvanth. The two eagles, two griffons, unicorn, and winged horse all angled to where they were almost overlapping wing lengths under and around the great silver dragon.

"Get close, my friends," Silvanth explained. The dragonstone in Jodem's staff started to glow brightly to give the silver dragon a picture of the teleportation point. The familiar blue field surrounded them, and they disappeared. They emerged over the village of Handsdown. Toderan looked down to see the Battle Point soldiers still digging in and building the new defenses of the town, with Gallanth laying on the grass field on the north side, looking up at them. He gave them his greeting roar, which was acknowledged by their mounts and his mate, who answered his challenge.

Mkel looked up as Gallanth was peering to the sky. An image of the Weir council group formed in his head. *Jodem and my wife brought our friends*, Mkel thought to himself. The Battle Point soldiers immediately dropped their shovels and grabbed their weapons. They were not accustomed to the deep dragon roars of the metallics, not yet able to distinguish a dragon's greeting versus a challenge roar. Once they saw the Weir group's mounts and recognized a silver dragon, they knew they were Alliance flying creatures and lowered their weapons, resuming their duties, but they were all still on edge. Jodem led the group in a descending circle around the village so all the legionnaires could tell they were friendly, then back winged to land beside Gallanth in the field.

Silvanth did not land; she stayed in her lazy circular pattern around the town and wished her mate the best of luck, along with an invitation in case she was needed for the fight to come. Annan did the same to Mkel through her seeing crystal. Mkel was touched by the sentiment from his wife and told her to give Michen a kiss for him before the silver dragon teleported away.

All of the Draden Weir council dismounted; Ordin was the first one off of Alvanch, grabbing the ground in his normal ritual to thank Jevya, the dwarvish word for the Creator, for his safe return to land. As they all walked over to Mkel and Gallanth, the great gold dragon slightly bowed his head in a welcome salute. Everyone in the party returned the salute to both Gallanth and Mkel.

"Welcome to Handsdown, my friends," Mkel greeted his comrades.

"You and Gallanth look like you went through hell," Dekeen said as he embraced Mkel.

"A tough fight, Captain?" Toderan asked as he also gave Mkel a quick hug.

"Slightly tougher than we anticipated," Mkel said. "We were doing well until those five dragons arrived. We flamed all of them, but the black and especially that blue dragon put up one hell of a fight. Its extraordinary power was based on a piece of dark crystal imbedded in its heart."

"Amazing; that is what the drow priestess stated as well?" Watterseth asked.

"Yes, and believe me and Gallanth, it made that blue dragon a much more formidable opponent, so I have no reason not to believe her, even though the blue's carcass has not been examined yet," Mkel answered.

"Yes, I see the damage on Gallanth's hide. My large friend, let me take care of these for you," Watterseth told Gallanth.

"No, my good cleric, there are several Battle Point soldiers who need your attention more than I. These wounds will be healed by tomorrow," Gallanth answered.

"I have plenty of healing power to go around, and I will attend to them with undue haste," Watterseth said. "Right now we need our Draconic benefactor in top shape if we are to repatriate our unfortunate brothers tomorrow, especially if we run into something like you did today. Their lives and ours will likely depend upon your strength, my good dragon." Watterseth spoke to Gallanth in a lightly scolding manner. He was one of the few people who could convince Gallanth to change his mind. Mkel, Beckann, Silvanth, and sometimes Jodem were the only others who enjoyed this privilege.

"Yes, my good priest, I will obey your holy command," Gallanth said back with a bit of sarcasm.

Watterseth looked at Gallanth with a slight expression of admonition and a furrowed brow at his teasing. He raised his mithril alloy mace, with its sapphire dragonstone glowing in a brilliant blue. He then whispered several prayers in Draconic, which was considered by many clerics as a holy language, even though all but the oldest of the scripture books were written in common tongue. Draconic was an extremely difficult language to decipher, for it was written in three-dimensional symbols, which can take on different meanings depending on who wrote it and who reads it. As his mace glowed intensely, he lowered it and touched Gallanth's armored hide. The whole of his colossal body was immersed in faint blue light. The great dragon lowered his head slightly and closed all of his protective eyelids.

As the light subsided, Watterseth pulled his mace away, and Gallanth raised his head. The deep gashes that were well on their way to being healed were now nothing but faint scars. Even these would be gone in a couple of days. "Thank you, my good priest, that does feel better, but now you have several brave soldiers to attend to," Gallanth stated.

"Yes, let's all go to Colonel Sheer's temporary headquarters in the keep, so we can solidify our plans," Mkel said after embracing Ordin and shaking Tegent's hand in a lion's grip. Just as he turned, Gallanth looked skyward and let out a greeting roar. *Talonth and Strikenth arrive,* Gallanth told Mkel telepathically. "Good," Mkel said, "I am looking forward to seeing Colonel Lordan and Lieutenant Padonan," referring to the respective riders of the large silver dragons that had just teleported in.

"The biggest gold and two biggest silver dragons in the Alliance gathering in one place at the same time; I feel much safer now and see the workings of a good song in the making," Tegent said with his normal lively smile. The two silver dragons had teleported in close to each other, but they were coming from very different locations. Their combined roars echoed across the plain as they returned Gallanth's salute. The glimmering silver hides of the pair showed brilliantly in the early evening sun. The two big metallic dragons quickly matched their flight pattern and circled around the village, eventually landing on the east side to minimize the amount of debris and dust they kicked up with their mighty wings.

The two riders slid off of the silvers' necks and onto the waiting forearms of their dragon mounts. Mkel knew the rider on the left was Colonel Lordan right away, from both the slightly larger size of Talonth and his couple of inches over Padonan. Lordan also carried his characteristic dragonstone-imbedded lance, a very powerful weapon in his hands that sent many a foe to their doom. The mithril-tipped tribladed head could pierce any armor or dragon hide and fire deadly bolts of energy for incredible damage.

Padonan was a nimble but resolute fighter. He wielded a glaive, a unique weapon that was a star-like mithril alloy disc with six fingers, each ending in a pure mithril blade. The central mounted dragonstone gave it the power of guided flight, like Ordin's hammer, but it could fly much greater distances and slice through almost any armor, including dragon hide, with ease. It could also block unfriendly spells and smash magic shields. He also was equipped with a small mithril alloy dragonstone-powered shield, given to him by Strikenth, that could project a powerful magical defensive field that enabled his dragon to have the shield strength of a gold. Padonan utilized this defensive weapon to protect himself and Strikenth when he threw his glaive. He also had a backup short sword, just in case. Overall, this made Padonan a formidable character, and with Strikenth the second largest silver dragon in the Alliance, it was no wonder that Valianth chose them to be one of his wing seconds.

Lieutenant Padonan saluted Colonel Lordan after they both dismounted and greeted each other with an arm grasp, and then they walked over to Mkel and the Keystone Weir group. Mkel saluted Colonel Lordan a hand salute bringing his right hand to his eyebrow out of custom.

"From the heart, Dragonrider," he said with a smile as Mkel slid his right hand from his head to a fist over his heart. Dragonriders saluted each other with this gesture, since they knew that being a dragonrider was a matter of the heart and of the soul.

"Yes, Colonel, sir," Mkel said with a smile in return, and then they reached out for Colonel Lordan's hand as they grasped each other's forearms in a lion's grip, putting their left arms around each other and touching the right sides of their heads.

"*Onaba haam*, good to see you, laddy, and how is the mighty Gallanth?" Colonel Lordan asked, using the sacred Draconic word meaning "greetings" to an honored friend and comrade who was dedicated to fight evil, a standard dragonrider greeting.

"A bit worse for wear, for today was a tough fight; is Talonth up to wing?" Mkel answered.

"He's fine, but we heard about your battle today. Very interesting, this blue and black you two fought, as well as this entirely new breed of talon dragons, as I understand them to be called," Lordan exclaimed.

"Yes sir, they are. Good to see you and Strikenth, old friend," Mkel answered Colonel Lordan and gave Padonan the dragonrider embrace. "I still see you carry that little pinwheel of yours," Mkel teased Padonan about his dragonstone-imbedded glaive.

"You still shoot that mutated crossbow, sir," Padonan quipped with his normal mischievous smile.

"Worked for me today there, Capital boy!" Mkel teased back.

"All right, enough with the Weir/Capital wing rivalry bit; what is the plan for tomorrow?" Colonel Lordan asked with his usual humor-laden brevity.

"We all should move to Colonel Sheer's temporary headquarters at the wooden keep to ensure everyone is keyed into the plan, gentlemen," Mkel replied. "I'm sure Gallanth, Talonth, and Strikenth have a lot to talk about." He looked up to the two large silver dragons that had now walked up behind the group and were in telepathic conversation with Gallanth.

"Those three always did get along well," Colonel Lordan said as he leaned on his upright dragonstone lance. "Captain Mkel, I have heard that your rangers found a major gathering in the southern chain of the Smoking Mountains just southeast of my Weir."

Mkel looked over at Lupek, who had a guilty smile. "Sir, my Weir's lead ranger will inform us all of his findings when we go over the plan for tomorrow," Mkel answered.

"We should get over to the keep, sir," Toderan spoke up.

"Yes, I think Colonel Sheer will be expecting us, for he likely knows that Talonth and Strikenth have arrived. It's hard to hide two silver dragons," Jodem stated. Strikenth and Talonth walked up to Gallanth and lowered their heads in a sign of deference to the gold dragon. Gallanth acknowledged the salute from the two large silver dragons and began their dialogue in Draconic. Mkel and Jodem ushered the two dragonriders and the Keystone Weir council to the wooden keep. As they walked up to the side gate, Colonel Sheer met them.

"Dragonriders and Draden Weir council, welcome to my temporary home," he said with a slight sense of sarcasm. "Come in; we have much to discuss." They all walked into the hall, where hours earlier Jodem had interrogated the drow priestess. All of his officers and senior fighters were already gathered there.

"Gentlemen, let us begin with an update from my ranger commander, Captain Decray," Sheer stated.

"Yes sir," the lanky but tough-looking ranger started as he placed his seeing crystal on the large table in the center of the room; his brown eyes possessed both a fierce determination and a subtle kindness at the same time. "You'll see the enemy encampment at the base of these small hills in the scrub. They have been getting a steady stream of reinforcements all afternoon. A wide variety of forces that include three battalions of orcs, one grummish, one gnoll, a Morgathian infantry regiment, and a Morgathian heavy cavalry battalion are gathering for a total of at least five thousand in strength. We have seen at least a wing of manticores and hymenoids landing. There is also a strange new land dragon type of creature, somewhat resembling a blue dragon but looking like a snake as well."

"They are behirs, sir," Lupek spoke up. "Myself and my comrade had an encounter with them earlier this morning in the Smoking Mountains." Mkel's expression indicated that he was slightly irritated but still approving of his actions. "They seem to be some type of offshoot of a blue dragon and snake. They have a blue dragon's lighting breath weapon, but not nearly as powerful, and their hide is less than half as strong as a blue."

"How many did you encounter?" Colonel Sheer asked. "Since you are still here, I assume you either killed them or escaped."

"My elven counterpart killed one of them with one of his more powerful spells," Lupek answered, "for they weren't very magic resistant, but they seemed to be able to recuperate their breath weapon quickly. A land dragon would not have too much trouble handling this creature on a one-on-one fight, but I would recommend that you take as many as you have available for the battle tomorrow, to counter their power."

"The two of you killed it by yourselves?" inquired Colonel Sheer.

"Yes sir, myself and my elven ranger friend have a bit of experience in handling matters like these sir," Lupek answered.

"Our rangers are well trained Colonel," Toderan spoke up.

"I have faith, my good senior Weir sergeant. I know General Daddonan has at least half a battalion of land dragons on their way here as we speak, and they should arrive anytime now. They will be utilized heavily as they always are, but this time we have three of the most powerful metallic dragons in the Alliance fighting with us," Sheer stated.

"We must be cautious, Sheer," Lordan spoke up, "this new enhanced chromatic dragon threat has me somewhat concerned."

"We don't know how many chromatics have successfully completed this ritual, but the drow priestess's memories indicated that there weren't very many," Jodem explained, following a roar that by the deepness of the bellow they knew came from Gallanth. All eyes focused on Mkel.

"The lead elements of the Battle Point legion are arriving. That was Gallanth's greeting roar to the land dragons," Mkel explained; the roar was soon followed by the more distant and less bass roar of a land dragon. The senior dragon in a group was always the one who gave the challenge or greeting.

"Excellent; gentlemen, our reinforcements are arriving," Colonel Sheer said as he started to walk out of the room toward the entrance of the keep. All in the room followed him and walked out of the front gate. The lead land dragon platoon, flanked by cavalry, was just outside the village, entering from the west. A long column of infantry in wagons were trailing them, with more land dragons and supply corps wagons intermixed in the train. The sky was filled with at least half a battalion of hippogriffs crisscrossing above the length of the column, providing flank security. A hippogriff accompanied by two griffons flew ahead of the column and landed in front of the keep. Mkel could tell it was General Daddonan and his personal guards. All present except for Jodem rendered a hand salute, which he returned as he dismounted.

"Gentlemen, well done, I monitored the fight on my crystal. Mkel, congratulations to you, Gallanth, and Master Jodem, for without you this village would now be burnt to the ground," General Daddonan said with an appreciative smile. "My welcome to the Keystone Weir council; Colonel Lordan and Lieutenant Padonan, your presence and help is most appreciated," he continued. "Now we have much work to do in preparation to repatriate our fellow soldiers from their bondage and torture."

"Sir, my executive officer will see to the stationing and camping of the legion," Colonel Sheer stated.

"We only have about half of the legion, Colonel. We are spread too thin to bring all of them here with the limited time we had. There are two land dragon companies, two hippogriff wings, two cavalry troops, and one reinforced battalion of infantry. This is all we could spare and muster for this fight. This is why we need at least one dragon," General Daddonan explained as he looked to Mkel, Lordan, and Padonan.

"Point taken sir," Mkel acknowledged as he gave Colonel Lordan and Padonan a quick side glance.

"All right, let's get this plan together. We have a lot of work to do," General Daddonan said as he walked into the keep, quickly followed by all present. As they assembled around the central meeting table, Colonel Sheer and Captain Decray placed their crystals down in the center of the table and uttered several commands. The stones projected the image of the terrain and the current view of the enemy encampment as conveyed through the rangers who were on their reconnaissance mission.

"Sir, I will let my ranger commander give you the latest update on the enemy situation," Colonel Sheer exclaimed. Decray thoroughly explained the scenario, including the most recent enemy troop breakdown.

"General, Colonel Lordan and I have surmised two possible courses of action," Mkel said. "I'll address my portion first, followed by the senior silver dragonrider. We will insert my council team and Captain Decray's remaining rangers with Gallanth at this point here, roughly a mile from the encampment in this draw. Jodem will camouflage Gallanth, and the team will approach from northeast of the camp. The Battle Point rangers will skirt around to the southeast to this position that offers us both the maximum cover and concealment. We will attack when your forces draw out and fully engage the majority of the enemy from the west along this field. Both our groups will then move in to repatriate the captured soldiers, with the rangers taking them back to safety as fast as possible. My team will take any prisoners we can and wait for any enemy reinforcements or chromatics to arrive to ambush them from the rear. Colonel Lordan, sir."

"Sir, Lieutenant Padonan and I, with Talonth and Strikenth, will teleport your forces approximately to this location," Lordan explained, "roughly two miles from the encampment in this lowland, to hide our dragons and the entrance of the legion. You can align your forces with your two land dragon companies on line forward of the infantry, flanked by the cavalry."

"I will need to keep at least a platoon of the land dragons as a reserve," the general said.

"That is our normal procedure as well, sir, but if you put them all on line up front, the enemy will think you have a bigger force and hopefully deploy all of their behirs. As the two lines approach each other, Padonan and I will launch and knock out as much as we can until they call for their chromatics, if they have any. They will only attack after the ground forces, for that is their way. We will then engage them to keep them off of you, as you start to cut the enemy apart. We have an idea of the strength of these behirs but have not yet fought them. In the meantime, Captain Mkel and his council and the remaining ranger teams will attack and eliminate their reserve forces and cover the rescue of the prisoners, who are likely in this tent," Lordan said, pointing.

"Then who will be our reserve?" Daddonan asked.

"Sir, Gallanth and my council will be your reserve. If any chromatics are called, they will be focused on Strikenth and Talonth, and should not see Gallanth. We will then attack them from the rear in a surprise that hopefully will break them, for they will soon realize who and what they are dealing with," Mkel added.

"Sounds good, Dragonrider, but I will keep a troop of cavalry back for a mobile reserve," Daddonan added with a wink. "Colonel Sheer, what were your casualties today, and what damage did we inflict on the enemy?"

"Sir, among the relief forces, we had seven men killed, fourteen seriously injured, and twenty-nine with minor wounds. We lost two hippogriffs and four horses. Only one land dragon suffered significant injuries, but he is expected to recover. Our garrison company here at Handsdown suffered much greater. They had over twenty-four killed, and almost all of the remainder of their numbers wounded. If you hadn't sent the bulk of their company here at the warning from Gallanth, the platoon that was on watch would have been decimated to the man. There are also a total of twelve soldiers officially missing.

"We killed—actually, Gallanth and Mkel killed—three chromatic dragons and two of those new talon dragons," Sheer continued. "Our forces eliminated another of those new types, almost a battalion of orcs, a company of cavalry that was human and orc mixed, a wing of manticores, twenty-nine drow with spider mounts, and roughly twenty of those dragon spawn creatures. They were particularly tough but not invincible."

"Today held a number of firsts: chromatic dragons with increased power, a new dragon species, a new unholy hybrid of a chromatic and a man, as well as an unusual assassination of a drow priestess by a Shidanese assassin. I am no oracle or elf, but I sense something larger brewing here; why was a little trading town that just came under our protection so important to them?" General Daddonan asked rhetorically.

"The information that we pulled out of the drow priestess lends to even more questions," Jodem added.

"Even more puzzling was an immediate request from several ranking Enlightened senators that the drow be turned over to them before either the Wizard's Council or the elves," the general added. "This interest, as with most of what the POEs say, was almost bordering on the fanatic, as was their response to accusations that this attack was of Morgathian origin."

"They never care much about the military unless they are trying to divert funds away from it, or have it do their bidding, and never do they react this quickly to any event," Colonel Sheer said with irritation. "But why would they be so intent on not asking, blaming, or even inquiring whether this attack was Morgathian orchestrated?"

"It is all puzzling," General Daddonan said, "but we will not solve it here. Colonel, gentleman, dragonriders, as long as all the crystals are synchronized, we must finalize preparations for tomorrow and still get our soldiers enough rest. Let us work one more run through the plan with all commanders moving their forces on the crystal image field."

Immediately, all the officers present made sure that their seeing crystals touched Colonel Sheer's so they would all have the same information, and their unit symbol appeared in the three-dimensional terrain representation that emanated from all the crystals. The general's chief of staff, Colonel Sykes, oversaw the turns that each unit commander took in moving his piece to synchronize the legion's plan and operation.

Colonel Sheer, Colonel Magallan, the infantry battalion commanders, Colonel Ronson (the land dragon battalion commander), and Colonel Dansar (the hippogriff commander) were all confident and competent battle leaders. As they finished the exercise on the crystal projected map field, General Daddonan turned to Colonel Tomslan, the support corps battalion commander, and asked him if he could support this battle. The support corps commander told the general that he had a steady stream of supplies moving toward Handsdown on a day and night basis. The method of support that logistics officers in the Alliance conduct resupply operations was amazing. The bottom line was that an army could only move so far on an empty stomach, with no arrows and broken swords.

All the commanders again touched their crystals to ensure that all information captured was shared. Seeing crystals were impressive devices. They could not only give instant communication to other crystals, they could also project images of what both it and its blood bonded owner had seen; they could even manipulate and add to those images. This capability was due to the melding of a small amount of dragon blood and the blood of the crystal's owner. Much of the Alliance military doctrine and operations now depended on using these devices, which were derived in much the same way as a dragonstone but much simpler. The owner of a seeing crystal was the only one who could operate it, which made it a very secure means of communication. This bonding between the owner and the crystal was accomplished with a drop of the owner's blood at the time of purchase.

After the officers present acknowledged that they had the information, they all rendered the general a salute, which he returned and wished them all luck. Mkel gestured to Captain Decray to come with him as he walked back to where Gallanth, his council members, and the two silver dragons were staying. "Just wanted you to meet the group you are going into battle with tomorrow, Ranger Captain," Mkel told Decray, who in turn gave a greeting to all of the Keystone Council and then looked up at Gallanth and saluted him.

"Not necessary but the sentiment is appreciated, Captain Decray," Gallanth replied to the ranger's salute.

"It will be an honor to fight beside you tomorrow, mighty Gallanth. I saw what you and your rider did in battle today against the chromatics and their minions, and it was an awe-inspiring sight. Without you, your rider Captain Mkel, and Master Wizard

Jodem, the tide of this fight would have gone against us," Decray said with reverence to Gallanth.

"You do not give your land dragons enough credit, my good ranger," Gallanth said back to him.

"They are indeed a tough lot and have seen us to victory on many an occasion, but only against a single chromatic dragon or an enemy army, not the combined force you faced today," Decray explained.

"Then let us pray that our luck holds for tomorrow. You have a good soul, Ranger Captain, and are an honorable man, now raise your swords." Captain Decray looked puzzled but Mkel nodded for him to comply.

"Gifts from dragons are to be just accepted and not questioned my friend," Mkel whispered to Decray. He drew the two short swords he preferred to fight with.

"Cross your swords," Gallanth ordered as Decray touched the points of the two swords together. Gallanth raised his massive foot, and with his four-foot-plus-long front claws, he deftly and ever so slightly punctured the thick hide of one of his own toes and placed a single drop of his greenish blue blood on the sword points. The blood immediately absorbed into the low mithril alloy blades, which made them almost hum with energy. Decray could barely hold on to them, and then suddenly the vibrations subsided.

"They will not have the power of a dragonstone weapon, but you will find they strike harder and faster and cooperate in battle better now," Gallanth said. "Ordin, the next two stones we find of quality are now earmarked," Gallanth told the dwarf.

"As you wish, Master Dragon," Ordin quickly replied. Decray was deeply and visibly touched by Gallanth's generosity and acknowledgment, as the expression on his hardened face was almost childlike.

"No words need be said, Captain, just continue to fight the good fight and watch over your men," Gallanth quickly spoke up.

"Now that we are done with all the pleasantries, I would like to get our plan synchronized so we can rescue those soldiers tomorrow," Mkel spoke up as he put his hand on Decray's shoulder. "Gather around," he continued as he drew Kershan and stuck the gleaming pure mithril blade upright into the hard earth. He spoke a command in Draconic to the dragonstone, and the image of the enemy encampment emanated from the glowing red gemstone.

"This is the present look of the enemy encampment," Mkel began. "You'll see the gathering forces in front of this series of large tents at the base of the hills. There are several battalions of orcs, humans, gnolls, and grummish, with a scattering of drow. These new creatures are the behirs, like the one that Lupek and Deless killed, along with several common giants. We are not worried about them, however, but are focusing on this tent in the center, where the Battle Point rangers think the prisoners are. Captain Decray, correct me if I get anything wrong. The legion will perform a frontal attack to draw all their forces out onto the plain. Strikenth and Talonth will teleport them here, then they will march toward the camp. Jodem will accompany them to deal with any Morgathian or drow wizards, as well as the beholders. If any chromatics appear, the two silvers will engage them first, with Gallanth and I weighing in only if necessary.

"We will teleport here, in this slight depression," Mkel continued, "to keep Gallanth as hidden as possible. Captain Decray's rangers will circle around to this location, and the Weir group will go here. When we are in position and the main attack begins, we will move closer to the camp. Dekeen, Tegent, and I will take out any guards with arrow fire. We all will then rush the tents, secure the Battle Point soldiers, and move them to the mounts. From there the Weir group will support the main effort of the legion in destroying their supplies at this camp and defeating any reinforcements that arrive. Gallanth and I will join Talonth and Strikenth if any chromatics arrive in force or provide support to the legion in the main fight. All signals and communication will be performed with seeing crystals, with a flaming arrow as a backup signal for the assault. Watterseth, Beckann, I would like for you to accompany the support corps trains to provide them magical power in case any dragons or other threats get through, but be ready to reinforce us in case things go bad. The depression we teleport into will be our rally point in case something goes terribly wrong. Let us make them think about who they dare to fight. Any questions?"

"No, the plan looks sound, Captain, but what if we run into heavier resistance at the camp?" Toderan asked.

"Then we will hold them off while the rangers take the prisoners back to their mounts to get them to safety. Worst case scenario, I will call Gallanth up, but we want to keep him out of the fight unless the chromatics appear. I have confidence in our council's ability to hold its own," Mkel said with a smile, which Dekeen and Ordin echoed. Mkel could tell Ordin was itching for a fight.

"Just point me toward the giants," the dwarf stated with a large grin.

"You will get your chance, my friend, but it must be coordinated. We can handle a lot but not a whole army," Mkel said to his dwarvish companion. "Once the prisoners are clear and we eliminate their reserve, we will join the general fight and squeeze those vermin like a grape between two anvils."

"Sounds like an agreeable arrangement," Dekeen spoke up.

"Then we shall meet in the morning, Dragonrider," Decray asked.

"Yes, we will depart after a quick breakfast at first light, for the Battle Point legion will not strike until midmorning. I know Lordan and Padonan will try to get them out in one teleport jump, but it could take them several trips. Then they have to form and march over a mile to the enemy encampment," Mkel replied.

"Understandable. I am honored to be fighting beside you all," Decray finished with a hand salute, which Mkel returned with the others echoed or nodded in acknowledgment. He then walked back to the keep to make further preparations.

"All right, gentlemen, let's grab something to eat and drink and settle into our deluxe accommodations," Mkel said as he walked over to the satchel bags on Gallanth's flying gear. He always packed five gallons of the Weir's spring water, wine, ale, and enough food for a week, just in case. The others walked to their mounts and returned with portions of rations and drink. Dekeen brought a couple of scrap logs, which he placed in front of Gallanth's massive head, as Mkel was setting down the ale tankard from the saddle gear.

"Master Gold Dragon Gallanth, if you would be so kind," the elf courteously asked the dragon in elvish. He opened his huge jaw and blew a small jet of flame onto the logs, which immediately caused them to burst into flames. "Thank you, my large friend," Dekeen added.

As they all gathered around the fire and started to eat their various rations of salted and dried meats and breads, the ale was passed around, and Ordin took his normal generous portions. Just as well, for dwarves could always fight better a little drunk.

"Captain, how tough was the fight today, really?" Toderan asked.

"To put it truthfully, if Gallanth, myself, and Jodem were not visiting Battle Point when we were, this village would have been razed and the relief force would have walked into a trap. We were lucky, but tomorrow we have surprise and audacity on our side, and we will use it," Mkel answered.

"So many drow and then a high priestess slain; this is very convoluted. You say Jodem killed a drow wizard of power?" Dekeen asked.

"Yes, he fought him while we were busy with the chromatics," answered Mkel.

"There is some sort ill wind here. An attack of chromatics here in the plains, on the edge of our area of influence, also led by drow, but no Morgathian standards. In addition, a gathering of many more along our southeastern border, also without banners. Too much organization to be independent endeavors," Tegent spoke out loud.

"I have to agree with the bard on this one, plus the giants in the south; even fire giants cannot hold onto large coalitions for long, beyond simple raiding parties," Ordin added.

"You are correct, Master Ordin," Jodem spoke as he walked from behind Gallanth. "We don't know what the connection is, or if they are connected at all, but there are far too many similarities to not be masterfully orchestrated. The question is by whom and for what purpose?"

"Ah, Master Wizard, so good for you to grace us with your presence," Ordin said. "We even saved you some ale." He raised his tankard in a salute to Jodem, with Dekeen giving his salutary nod of deference, for elves have as deep a respect for magic users as they do for dragons.

"I think I need a glass of wine instead, but this will do for starters," Jodem answered as he took the tankard from Mkel.

"Long meeting with the legion officers?" Mkel asked.

"The third battalion commander, Colonel Ponsellan, who arrived late after you all left, is a self-centered, egotistical politician, not a soldier or warrior. If it were not more apparent that he wanted all possible glory in tomorrow's battle, and did not seem to care if he suffered an inordinate amount of casualties, then I am a wizard apprentice," Jodem complained.

"Let me take care of the shale head," Ordin said, slurring his words as he drained his tankard again.

"He is General Daddonan's problem," Jodem said, "but unfortunately he will affect us as well in our support to Battle Point. At least it is just us, the council here, and not the whole garrison or the Draden regiment.

"Why doesn't General Daddonan relieve him? I thought you were just staying to inform the commanders of your magic ability for tomorrow, not to rehash the whole battle plan. Should I have been there?" Mkel asked.

"Because Ponsellan is very friendly with one of the Enlightened senators, and Daddonan dare not touch him unless he and his legion suffer the consequences," Jodem explained. "You must remember that the non-Weir aligned legions are at the mercy of the senate for their funding. This is one of the dark sides to the checks and balances of our system that insures that neither the Weirs nor the central government becomes too powerful. You didn't miss anything, but that colonel wanted the whole plan explained to him."

"I still don't understand how the POEs, a minority in the senate, can wield so much power," Mkel said.

"They mostly pontificate and stall, and perform a great deal of political maneuvering, for they are overridden on most occasions, but they can wield their power very judiciously. Many a time, the rest of the senate basically placates them by letting them get their way."

"Politics as usual, and for some reason, the Enlightened party always seem to be at the bottom of things, like the scum on the bottom of an otyugh's foot," Toderan interjected.

"All too much intrigue; you humans are too complicated," Dekeen stated.

"Consider yourself lucky that elves do not engage in such practices," Mkel countered.

"Yes, but there are still subtle nuances that the elvish hierarchy wrangles with; remember, elves are not perfect, just look at the drow," Dekeen explained. "We just hide it better." he said with a slight smile of elvish sarcasm.

"Well, as long as we hold up our end of the operation and back the Battle Point legion up after our mission is accomplished, we shouldn't have any problem," Mkel said in an encouraging tone. "While the enemy always has a vote on events, I have faith in my friends and in our ability to get the job done. Plus Gallanth is always with us." Mkel said with an encouraging tone.

"Yes, we have confidence in ourselves, but still, this will not be a walkthrough tomorrow. However, I, like the captain, have faith," Toderan echoed.

"Again thank the Creator that the Weirs have a degree of autonomy from the senate," Mkel added. "I see that the master dwarf is asleep already; did he have a rough trip?" Mkel said with a mischievous smile.

"You know that he hates to fly on anything but Gallanth, and he turned a lovely shade of forest green on the back of Alvanch by the time we landed at this village," Toderan said with a chuckle. Normally dwarves can drink twice as much as an average man, but the flying sickness really knocked it out of them. "Just as well, it will be an early morning tomorrow and we have to have our wits about us. The legion is manning the village defenses, so we will have ample warning if anything dares to attack tonight, and if they know that Gallanth, Strikenth, and Talonth are here, they wouldn't even think about it. Good night, gentlemen," Toderan finished as he got up and walked over to his sleeping winged horse.

Normally they would all sleep in close proximity to Gallanth, for both shelter and security, but it was a perfect night with just a slight coolness to the air. Insects did not come near dragons for unknown reasons, which was another added benefit to sleeping near one. Dekeen said good night and walked to his eagle.

"Jodem, Gallanth, I need to talk over what happened today," Mkel said with a change in his normally jovial tone of voice.

"You are troubled over the Morgathian death knight you killed today?" Gallanth asked him in a surprisingly low but audible tone, not communicated telepathically.

"Yes and no. The black hearted *pogasch* deserved what he was given. He killed that boy's father in cold blood. He was defeated and could have been bypassed, but he brutally killed him anyway, and in front of his family. I have no remorse for letting Kershan's blade go through him, although the sword almost seemed to act on its own. Until now, I have only killed orcs and their associated allies, no more than insects. They are born to be evil and know nothing else," Mkel explained.

"But you still have a small sense of remorse?" Jodem asked.

"Again yes and no, it was just different. I have not felt that kind of anger before. If you hadn't snapped me back to my senses when the chromatics appeared, I don't know how much of a help I would have been for you, my friend," Mkel answered as he put his hand on Gallanth's large clawed front toe.

"Remember that a metallic dragon's true strength comes from his soul bonding with his rider. Your emotion and love give me as much strength as the purest of gems that Ordin supplies. Without it, we would be only slightly better than the chromatics. The Creator intended this as a balance to the evil that the world can dish up," Gallanth explained.

"But then why does he let this evil exist, since he created all of this? Why not stop it?" Mkel asked.

"In his immeasurable wisdom and boundless love, he gave all his creatures with even the remotest level of logical thought the power of choice and free will. Dragons, elves, and giants did choose as whole races and species. From this decision there is usually only one turning point, and that can only occur just before death. Humans, which he loves most of all, were given individual choice as to which path they choose to follow. This is what also makes mankind so fascinating," Gallanth explained. "We dragons were put here to guide humans and protect them. Unfortunately, the chromatics, led by Tiamat, resented this subordination to what they considered a lesser species. That is why they call men Sapsprech, or talking monkeys"

"Yes, I understand, but that still doesn't explain why good must suffer so under such tyranny and evil," Mkel said.

"Mkel, while there is much evil in the world, there is also much good. Acts of evil do not go unpunished, for while it is free will that allows men and creatures to commit evil, it is also the same for those who do good," Jodem commented to his young friend.

"The Creator is constantly adjusting or guiding events to make up for the evil that is done by those who would perpetrate it. Like the death knight you killed today, it was not your fault that he killed that boy's father, but by you felling the pogasch, he will not kill any more innocents or good men. No, it will not bring back that boy's father, and I know you very much identified with the boy's pain, but it was not your fault. I know you thought of your father today and of your loss, and I know it is never easy for you. Remember that I will always be here for you, my friend, and take comfort in the fact that we saved hundreds of lives today and delivered a major blow to the enemy, as we will do tomorrow," Gallanth explained with an unusual display of emotion in his voice, which he lowered to as much of a whisper as a dragon could do.

"And remember that the Creator also sacrificed his earthly spirit by letting him attempt to bring the chromatics and their followers back into the light, and correct the error of their ways," Jodem explained." "That is the true love he has for all of his creations, even the five-headed evil arch dragon herself."

"I understand; it is all part of an immense balancing act that the Creator is constantly juggling," Mkel said, trying to control his emotions, for he could feel the inner pain and sorrow welling up inside him, and he knew Gallanth could sense this as well.

"Yes, but remember the overall balance has always slightly tipped to our side," Gallanth said in a slightly comforting and confident tone, trying to tell Mkel that everything was all right.

"Again I understand a bit more, but it is still difficult to forget that boy's face. I saw him through Markthrea's sight when that Morgathian killed his father right in front of him. All I wanted to do was eviscerate him, make him suffer, no capture, no trial, no mercy. Yet after I cut off his leg and sword arm and had Kershan's blade pointed at his throat, I hesitated until I saw something in his eyes. Without flinching, Kershan effortlessly trust into his exposed neck. I can't describe it; it was like I was outside myself watching and unable to affect the scenario," Mkel explained, sounding very emotional and slightly confused.

"You are just tired, my young friend. Tired and upset. We should be getting some sleep now, for tomorrow will come very quickly," Jodem said to him with a sympathetic smile as he gave Gallanth a quick sideways glance.

"Yes, it is time for rest now, my rider; you need to lay down under my wing and sleep. Like Jodem said, we have important work tomorrow, and I will need at least two gemstones prior to the fight and you riding with me, ready for battle," Gallanth added as he stretched out his right wing slightly to cover Mkel's bedroll. Mkel could feel he was getting very tired quickly and knew that either Gallanth or Jodem were casting a minor sleep spell over him, but he did not fight it, for he was tired. The ground mat he used felt comfortable, and he fell asleep within seconds.

"He is very troubled about what happened today, Gallanth," Jodem said to the gold dragon in Draconic.

"I know, but he will overcome it. While his emotions run high, so does his strength and courage. Tomorrow we will be too busy to dwell on this, and we will be there for him when we return to Draden and the Weir," Gallanth answered as he lowered his huge head on the ground, and curled around to almost face Mkel. "I want Watterseth to stay back here, just in case something slips around us tomorrow and Lady Beckann needs help. Andellion is still too weak to come out here to fight, or even to defend this town from anything, and they could use the good cleric's healing ability as well. I will tell him tonight before I sleep."

"I agree, even though he will protest," Jodem answered.

"I gave into him this evening by allowing him to heal me, it is his turn now," Gallanth replied.

"I wish you luck, my old friend," Jodem quipped.

"No luck involved; good night, my good wizard," Gallanth finished, which was a strange saying for a gold dragon, who were considered by many the luck dragons.

CHAPTER VI

REPATRIATION

"Mkel, wake up. The legion is getting ready, and we must not be late," Jodem said to his dragonrider friend, while gently shaking his shoulder.

"I'm awake. I'll be ready in a couple of minutes," Mkel answered as he sat up from his bedroll and pulled his blanket off. He quickly shaved, cleaned up, and dressed. The members of the Weir council, except for Ordin, had already gathered when he walked over in front of the still resting Gallanth.

"I guess the local grog is a little stronger than Ordin expected," Mkel said to the group while he finished fastening his belt and shoulder strap that held his crossbow, sword, quiver, and other equipment.

"I will wake him up," Dekeen said with a mischievous smile, as he took his water skin from the saddle harness on his eagle and poured it over Ordin's head. The dwarf immediately jumped up, brandishing his powerful war hammer, Donnac, and whirled around, only to see his friends laughing.

He smiled as he lowered his hammer and asked, "Well, are we finally ready to fight?"

"I guess the Battle Point grog is a little stronger than you're used to, my good dwarf," Toderan said pointedly.

"No, I was just resting from a full day's mining," he quickly answered.

"Well, Ordin, I have faith you are always ready for giants," Mkel interjected.

"Let them feel the power of my hammer," Ordin growled.

"The Battle Point rangers are approaching," Mkel said as he looked behind his group. Twelve rangers were walking behind Decray and Lupek as they approached. *The two seemed to be working together well already, which is a good sign*, Mkel thought to himself.

"Sir, gentlemen, welcome," Toderan greeted Captain Decray and his team. "We look forward to drawing swords with you today."

"Likewise," Decray answered and looked toward Gallanth with a slight bow in a sign of deference.

"And draw swords you will do," Gallanth answered over the gathered soldiers as he raised his head.

"General Daddonan wants us to move to our position as soon as possible, Mkel," Decray said as he shook Mkel's hand.

"Understandable. Do your rangers watching the enemy encampment have the plan?" Mkel asked.

"They have two scouts waiting beside the gully as we speak. It is roughly a mile from the camp and affords good concealment from the ground. From the air is a different story, though, with the sparse vegetation there," Decray explained.

"Gallanth and Jodem will take care of that with a little illusion. The site sits north and east of the enemy camp, so it is so far not in the direct flight path of any reinforcements that have been flying in. And that includes chromatics. They are and likely will continue coming from the southeast," Mkel surmised. "Hopefully the appearance of Colonel Lordan and Lieutenant Padonan with Talonth and Strikenth will keep the chromatic dragons focused on them and not looking around their camp," Mkel continued. "Well, speak of the silvers," Mkel noted as Strikenth and Talonth walked up with their riders. Gallanth stood up to accept the silvers' head bows in their gesture of deference. "Colonel, I wish you good luck today. And could you be so good as to keep them busy and share a little of the work load we've been experiencing lately?" Mkel jested to the senior silver rider as he rendered him a salute.

"Have no worries there, Captain. The good lieutenant and I, with our dragons, will deal with anything we encounter. So you and Gallanth can do your little hide-and-seek game," Lordan said with a smile.

"Plus two silvers definitely equals a gold," Padonan added in his usual joking manner.

"Well, what a momentous occasion, a Weirleader and a precocious Capital dragonrider actually cooperating on a joint attack. This is truly an event to remember," Mkel quipped back, and all three dragons snorted in their unique form of a short laugh.

"Point well taken, Captain; we must go and coordinate with General Daddonan while they are getting their troops ready," Colonel Lordan smiled and answered, while gripping his powerful lance.

"Yes sir, and Padonan, don't lose that pinwheel of yours," Mkel said with a smile.

"Well, just shoot straight for once, Captain," the silver dragonrider quipped back, as he pulled his glaive from its lanyard. The center sapphire dragonstone glowed, with the six mithril blades all extending at once, brilliantly shining in the predawn morning. With a flick of his wrist, he sent the deadly star-like weapon streaking past Mkel, spinning so fast that it looked like a blur. The weapon made a wide arc around Mkel and Gallanth, quickly finding its way back to Padonan's outstretched hand. It flew much faster than Ordin's hammer but was also much smaller, and it was a cutting weapon, while Donnac was a large crushing instrument.

"Impressive, my friend, but more importantly, strength and luck to both of you," Mkel saluted with his fist over his heart, which they both returned. Saluting was not just a military courtesy among the dragonriders that were actual Alliance officers or soldiers, but a gesture of acknowledgment and kinship among the riders themselves. The two silver dragons walked away toward the eastern side of the keep, where the Battle Point legion was gathering. It would take both of the large silvers to teleport the partial legion at once, and even then it would be tight. Gallanth gave Talonth and Strikenth a luck prayer in Draconic, which they acknowledged. Luck wished by a gold dragon was prized, even by a silver dragon.

"All right, gentlemen, let me call General Daddonan and let him know we are going to leave," Mkel said to the assembled men, as he pulled out his seeing crystal. "General Daddonan, sir."

"Yes, Captain Mkel," the general answered.

"We are going to be teleporting momentarily, sir; any last-minute directives?" Mkel asked.

"No, I have faith in your men and mine. Keep me informed, as will I, and the strength of the Creator to you all. Bring our brothers home," General Daddonan espoused.

"Yes sir," Mkel answered. "Sir, the elf wizard, Lady Beckann, will be moving with your supply trains for added protection, and our cleric Watterseth will be staying here, just as a precautionary measure." Mkel put his crystal back into its pouch on his belt. "All right, gentlemen, mount up," Mkel ordered, and everyone moved to their mounts. "Decray, do you have the current image in your crystal of our destination from your men on the ground?" he asked.

"Yes," he replied as he pulled his seeing crystal out.

"Good, can you hold it up so Gallanth can see it?" Mkel asked. The ranger captain held up the crystal, which still carried the image that was transferred from his men's crystals at the site.

"I have a clear picture of where we are to go. Captain Decray, tell your men to stand clear," Gallanth spoke as he transferred the image telepathically to Mkel.

"Gentlemen, please gather as close to Gallanth as possible," Mkel instructed. "When we teleport in, make sure to control your mounts to keep them quiet."

Ordin secured himself into the third seat behind Mkel, just in front of Gallanth's larger back ridges. He had a smile on his face; Mkel didn't know whether it was for the upcoming fight, or from the fact that he was mounted on Gallanth, and not Alvanch, or another smaller mount.

Gallanth spread his wings to begin the process. Jodem waved a salutatory good-bye, along with Beckann, who raised her palm to her husband in an elvish gesture of luck and fondness. Mkel wished they could accompany them, for wizards of their power were always welcome in a fight, no matter what the odds, but the Battle Point legion needed them more. Andellion was still recuperating and would be too weak to put up an effective fight, especially if the enemy had a sorcerer of some power or several beholder creatures. They would save many lives today by fighting alongside the legionnaires.

The familiar blue light streaks surrounded them, and in an instant they were gone. They reappeared in the shallow gully surrounded by small trees and scrub. Gallanth quickly folded his wings and lay down. The spell Jodem cast over the gold dragon before the teleportation was taking effect, making Gallanth appear like a rock outcropping if you looked at him from a distance. Up close, the illusion was apparent do to the distance from Jodem, but from overhead and from a quick glance, as long as he remained still, his immense body blended in with the countryside. Having Jodem cast the spell made it harder for another dragon or sorcerer to detect the magic than if Gallanth had done it himself.

Mkel made sure to secure all his gear, slung Markthrea over his shoulder, and began to climb down, with Ordin immediately following him. All the others dismounted and gathered their arms and gear. Mkel and Decray then signaled for everyone to meet in front of Gallanth after they secured their mounts. As everyone gathered, Decray and Mkel both placed their seeing crystals together, along with the ranger that had guided them there. An image appeared from the crystals that imitated the terrain, as the ranger spoke up.

"This is where we are currently," the ranger explained. "The camp is just under a mile to our southwest. We have a squad of rangers holed up here, to the south of the camp, waiting for us. Our scouts have found a concealed path that will lead the rest of you to this point just north of the encampment. We will leave one of our rangers here to guide you to this assault position. We have been watching the enemy and believe that the Alliance soldiers are being held in this tent that is currently surrounded by orcs and those two beholders."

"Good report, ranger; Captain Decray, you will take your men around to the east and link up with the rest of your platoon," Mkel stated.

"Yes, we'll move around to the right, cross this make-shift road, where the enemy has been receiving reinforcements, and link up with my men. It will take us at least two hours, for we must remain undetected," Decray explained.

"Understandable; we will wait here under Gallanth's illusionary camouflage until you are close to your assault position. We will then move into our over-watch position and let you know when we are ready. Hopefully the attack by the legion will drive most of their forces out onto the plain. Once this happens, we will see what is left over and decide who is going to take who. Once all remaining enemy are killed, we will then move in, repatriate the prisoners, and head directly back here to the mounts. Captain Decray, I assume you will still fly the prisoners back to friendly ground?" Mkel formulated the plan and then asked the senior ranger a question.

"Yes; what if we run into heavier resistance than expected?" Decray asked.

"My team will hold off any powerful creatures encountered, while your rangers rescue the prisoners. If we get too heavily pressed, I will call Gallanth up, which anything short of three or more chromatics, I am not too worried about," Mkel answered.

"I understand, Dragonrider," Decray replied.

"Any questions?" Mkel asked as he looked around to all gathered.

"How far is our final position from the encampment?" Dekeen asked.

"About one hundred fifty to two hundred yards, Master Elf," the ranger answered. "Sorry we couldn't get you in closer."

"That is perfect," Dekeen answered. "That is an easy shot for me and Mkel, and out of their effective range."

"Good, then best of luck, Captain Decray," Mkel said in parting.

"May your swords serve you well, and a dragon's luck to you all," Gallanth said in his softest tone possible.

Decray and all his men nodded in thanks, for he definitely wanted to test his pair of short swords, with their added power bestowed by Gallanth.

"Rangers, follow me," Decray spoke up and very stealthily led all but one of his men into the scrub hills.

"All right, my friends, let's gather close to Gallanth and wait for our signal," Mkel said as he loaded his crossbow with a magazine of ten master-crafted bolts and leaned back against Gallanth's front leg. The rest of the Weir council group followed suit, with only Dekeen moving up to the crest of the hollow to take watch. Between Dekeen's elvish eyes and ears, and Gallanth's foresight, he was not worried about being surprised. Now it was just a matter of waiting.

Colonel Lordan and Lieutenant Padonan walked over to the legion's gathering place, with Talonth and Strikenth right behind them. The legion's soldiers had already been astonished when Gallanth teleported out with the Keystone Weir council group and the rangers. They now watched in amazement as the two large silver dragons approached. Strikenth and Talonth stopped just shy of the gathering legion and settled down on their bellies. The land dragons all looked over to the silvers and bowed their heads in a type of Draconic salute.

The Battle Point land dragons did not see metallics often. They usually only witnessed the Capital Wing dragons on special envoys, but even then they almost never operated directly with them. Until now there hadn't been a need for much metallic dragon support, for the most powerful enemy the legion had to deal with were giants or a very rare errant young chromatic. This was usually a single white, green, or black, with the worst being a young blue dragon, which several land dragons from the assigned battalion working in teams could easily handle. Those that were alive during the Great War worked with the metallic dragons to a greater degree, but there were only two left that old still serving. Land dragons had basically the same life span as their human crews.

Lordan and Padonan walked into the bustling crowd of soldiers that were getting their weapons and gear ready for battle. The soldiers closest to the dragonriders quickly stood up and saluted them.

"Soldier, do you know where General Daddonan or Colonel Sheer are?" Lordan asked the nearest legionnaire while he returned the salute.

"Sir, I think they are over passed the land dragons and hippogriffs," the soldier answered, sheepishly staring at Lordan's mithril-headed dragonstone lance.

"Thanks, my boy, and good luck today," Lordan replied as he walked past the group of soldiers toward the hippogriffs. There were thousands of Battle Point soldiers moving about, making last-minute checks of their armor, weapons, and mounts. *This legion is similar to mine*, Lordan thought to himself; the legion under his command at Eladran Weir was a pure cavalry-based force, with a combination of land dragons; heavy, medium, and light cavalry; hippogriffs; and a ranger company mounted on griffons similar to Keystone Weir. All this accompanied with a battalion of centaurs. The difference at Eladran was that he commanded the whole legion, as opposed to Mkel commanding just his Weir garrison, which was the equivalent of a large battalion and was reinforced by the Draden regiment.

The Battle Point legion also had heavy war wagons pulled by large, well-barded draft horses. These armored wagons brought the infantry forces to the battle, but they then dismount to fight. While they could fight from the turreted wagons if necessary, they usually formed the base around which the cavalry maneuvered and were supported by the power of the land dragons. "A different concept, but effective out here in the flat plains of the unsettled lands surrounding the city," Lordan surmised. He sighted General Daddonan and his command group looking over the images of several seeing crystals and headed over to join them. Padonan walked with him, observing the detailed preparations taking place.

"General Daddonan, good morning sir," Colonel Lordan greeted him while rendering a salute.

"Colonel Lordan, Lieutenant Padonan, welcome this morning. Glad to have you here. We were looking at the point of entry that your dragons will take us to. There are two of my rangers waiting for us at this location, in concealed hiding positions. How will you want us arrayed for the trip?" the general asked.

"Sir, we will have Talonth and Strikenth stand wing tip to wing tip over there on the field," Lordan explained. "We can take one land dragon company apiece, but I recommend that they are placed in front of our dragons in line under the fore part of their wings. Behind them I would put the infantry, which will have to be dismounted. Your war wagons will take up too much space. Each silver dragon can take a battalion, but the men will have to be packed tightly, shoulder to shoulder, several deep. The cavalry will be split, with half straddling Talonth's tail and half behind Strikenth's. There will be room for only one battery of your catapults though, sir, and we will have to see how many of the hippogriffs can be squeezed in."

"Well, we'll get everyone formed up around your dragons and see what else we can fit. I would like at least one catapult battery per battalion and two companies of hippogriffs. The rest will go by conventional travel and act as our reserve once they arrive," General Daddonan answered while thinking out loud. "Once we get there, we will align our forces for battle and attack to draw out their army to give your friend Captain Mkel and the rangers time to rescue our men."

"Yes sir, we'll get Strikenth and Talonth up and ready," Colonel Lordan replied.

"Excellent; gentlemen, you heard Colonel Lordan. Let's get formed around the two silver dragons in the order he just discussed," Daddonan told the colonels assembled around him: Colonel Sheer, Colonel Magellan, and Colonel Ponsellan, the infantry commanders; Colonel Reddit, the cavalry commander; Colonel Dansar, the hippogriff commander; Colonel Ronson, the land dragon commander; and Colonel Tomslan, the support corps commander. "Colonel Sheer, I want you to be my second on the ground since you know this enemy the best," Daddonan added.

"Sir, I feel …," Ponsellan started to interrupt but was stopped by General Daddonan raising his hand to silence him. *Good,* Lordan thought, *he whines way too much,* as Daddonan did not want to hear his complaints or grandstanding. Lordan turned and motioned to Padonan to follow him back to their dragons.

"You just witnessed a *dacul* being silenced," Lordan whispered to Padonan.

"You would call that colonel a fool?" the younger dragonrider asked.

"I have dealt with him before and have seen his kind too many times. He is more interested in his own career and advancement than his men's welfare. Those kind of officers crave power above all else and do not care who gets hurt or is crushed to get it," Colonel Lordan explained. "Make sure that you never become a leader like that."

"Have no fear, sir," Padonan replied. "I don't think Strikenth would let me anyway."

"We do have that advantage of having a very active, larger-than-life conscience always present," Lordan smiled as he spoke.

"Wouldn't have it any other way," Padonan smiled back. They walked over to their dragons, who both raised their heads and looked at their riders.

"Is it time to go, my good rider?" Talonth asked Lordan. "Yes, my large silver friend, I hope you are ready for a fight," Lordan replied.

"They won't know what hit them," Strikenth replied. "I have faith, my friend," Padonan replied, as they directed both silver dragons to stand up and move apart until they were exactly touching wingtips.

The land dragons then started to form in front of their outstretched wings. Both of them conversed with the land dragons, easing their anxiety over both teleporting and the fight to come. They also gave them a description of the behirs and an assurance that they and Gallanth would handle any chromatics that would be encountered. The land dragon crews were amazed at how easily their mounts could converse with their larger winged cousins. Land dragons in general could understand common tongue but cannot speak it well. The crews worked out a series of commands with their mounts that were easily understood but were nowhere near the level of communication that existed between a metallic dragon and its rider.

Both companies of land dragons lined up, almost touching side by side under the front part of the silvers' wings to their outstretched heads, in a wall of greenish brown/bronze dragon hide. Their crews readied the ballistae on the platforms. *This would be an impressive first onslaught,* Padonan thought to himself.

The three partial strength infantry battalions gathered behind the land dragons, standing in tight formation from the beginning of their tails to beyond the tips. All twenty-four hundred infantrymen gathered with weapons ready, in spite of being foot mounted rather than in their war wagons. The cavalry then formed behind them. Almost six hundred horses were attempting to form a dense line, but the mounts were skittish around the large dragons. Both Strikenth and Talonth turned their heads around and spoke Draconic in a surprisingly calming tone for such large creatures, which settled the horses immediately. The medium-type Battle Point cavalry stood up in their saddles in awe at the calming affect the silvers had on their horses.

There wasn't a lot of room for the hippogriffs; only half of the four hundred total creatures could fit. "That's all we can get, General," Colonel Lordan spoke into his seeing crystal.

"I understand, Colonel Lordan. Colonel Dansar, you'll have to get the other half of your battalion to meet us there," Daddonan ordered.

"Yes sir," the aerial battalion commander replied and then ordered his other two companies to take to the air and fly to the teleportation point, after confirming the location with his crystal. The hundreds of hippogriffs all took to the air; the sound of their wings beating to gain altitude all at once was very loud. General Daddonan then ordered his six catapults to the back of the silver dragons' tails, and his support corps commander started for the battle location as well as the remaining cavalry troop. They would be his reserve along with the hippogriffs; the winged mounts would arrive in an hour or so.

"Whenever you are ready, dragonriders," General Daddonan said into his seeing crystal. Both Strikenth and Talonth gave out a low but still very deep roar to get everyone's attention.

Talonth then spoke up for Lordan, who could not yell loud enough for all to hear and didn't want to power up his dragonstone lance to amplify his voice. "When we teleport in, you will feel slightly disoriented, but it will pass in a few seconds. It is imperative that you do not move outside the span of our wings or past the tip of our tails. If you do, you could be lost forever." The whole formation slightly tightened. "If you are all ready, we will go," the senior silver dragon finished and looked over to Strikenth. They both focused on the same image together, and the familiar blue light streaks started to surround them and the thousands gathered all around their massive silver bodies and under their wings. In a blink of an eye, they were gone.

"They have left Handsdown," Mkel whispered to all of his comrades, and then he told Captain Decray through his seeing crystal. They all got up and did a last check of their weapons and armor, after which Mkel gave the ranger a nod. They moved out, following him closely, with Dekeen on their flank for security. Elves were almost impossible to detect and moved ever so stealthily. They then came to a small rise and stopped.

"We have to crawl over this small ridge. There is a drop on the other side, and then we will be able to see their camp, for we will be within two hundred fifty yards of most of it. The only problem is that when we crawl over this rise, we will be exposed to the camp's view for a second or two," the ranger explained.

"Understood; Dekeen, go ahead and get over to get eyes on the camp. Let us know when it is clear to send someone over to you," Mkel stated. Dekeen nocked an arrow and crouched down, wrapping his elvish cloak over his head and back. The cloak turned a yellowish brown color within seconds, matching the surroundings. He quickly slid over the rise and went down the other side. "Toderan, you and Ordin will go over last, for you have the heaviest armor and will make the most noise, so it will take you the longest. Tegent, you go next," Mkel ordered. Everybody nodded as Tegent slowly crawled over the rise after Dekeen gave the clear signal from his crystal. One by one, they all made it over into the slight depression. They used Dekeen's cloak over top of both Ordin and Toderan, and Tegent's underneath them, for camouflage and to dampen the sound of their armor.

Mkel, Dekeen, and Tegent took positions to overwatch the camp. Dekeen's elf eyes and Mkel looking through his crossbow's sight could ascertain the enemy situation. The camp was littered with the still burning cooking fires, tents, and the thousands of orcs, grummish, gnolls, and Morgathian soldiers moving about finishing meals and getting ready for something. He saw a large tent toward the back of the encampment, roughly two hundred yards from them, and a smaller tent beside that one. "Dekeen, what do you make of that large tent, and the smaller one to the left?" Mkel asked.

"There are several guards and a beholder in front of the large tent," Dekeen answered, "which tells me that someone of magical power or a warlord is in there. I can hear screams from the smaller tent. Screams of men."

"I guess that is where our soldiers are, or if it isn't, it is a good place to start. Wait, I can see the heat signatures of eleven men against poles, and several other figures around them. Let me tell Captain Decray," Mkel answered, for Markthrea's sight could also see the heat given off by warm-blooded creatures like a dragon can. This ability, which he can choose to use or not, allowed him to look through light materials like a cloth, vegetation, and thin wood to see what was inside, as well as being able to see in the dark. "Decray, are you and your men doing all right?" he asked.

"Yes, Mkel, we just got into position. There was a great deal of traffic on the road through the valley. We could only get across one at a time, and it took almost an hour. I assume you are in position and the legion teleported in," Decray answered.

"Yes, and Dekeen's elf ears hear screams from the small tent by the largest one, and I confirmed it with my crossbow. That should be our target," Mkel replied.

"I see it. You will take out the guards, and we will seize the tent," Decray asked.

"Yes, hopefully the legion's attack will drive most of them to the battle. Strikenth and Talonth will let the legion attack first to lure this army out onto the plain, away from the encampment. They'll then attack and will quickly even the odds for your comrades. I estimate well over five thousand here, and that is probably low," Mkel surmised.

"Yes, I'll give General Daddonan the revised enemy troop strength," Decray added.

"Listen, Alliance battle horns," Dekeen whispered to Mkel and the rest of their company. "The Battle Point legion is on the attack."

"I see them moving. They are about three thousand yards from the edge of the camp," Mkel said as he looked through his crossbow sight, barely able to make out the line of Alliance forces over the horizon from the depression they were concealed in. A flurry of activity started among all in the encampment. Leaders and warlords started to shout orders to get their troops up and ready to meet the advancing legion.

"What is going on out there?" the black robed sorcerer demanded of the guard.

"I don't know, my liege. I will find out immediately," the guard quickly answered.

"I will go to see as well and get the orcs and those dog grummish up," the death knight growled.

"Fellaxe, make sure that oaf of an orc warlord, Barlog, gets his vermin to fight in the front," the sorcerer ordered. "This is likely just a Battle Point cavalry troop or reconnaissance force."

"Yes, Lord Ashram," Fellaxe answered as he grabbed his black iron battle-axe and walked out of the tent.

"Now, my good Alliance soldiers, there are more questions to be asked," the sorcerer declared to the chained and bleeding

Battle Point legionnaires in an evil and condescending manner. "What are these Avenger dragons that the Alliance is breeding?" he demanded.

"We don't know!" the senior legionnaire screamed back at the sorcerer.

"Not the answer I wanted to hear. Vetness, if you would," Ashram replied and directed the drow sorcerer to inflict pain on the soldier. The small piece of dark crystal on top of the drow's staff glowed purple and crackled with electrical energy. He walked over to the soldier and touched the man's shoulder with his staff. The electrical energy transferred into him, and he then twitched and screamed in agony.

"Now, another question: how many metallic dragons are stationed at Battle Point, and who was that dragon that fought our forces yesterday?" Ashram asked again.

"It was just some dragon from back west," the legionnaire screamed back at him.

"Some dragon? Just some dragon that took on a destroyer, a demon, and three other dragons, single handed, and won. I highly doubt it. Vetness, if you would please," the sorcerer said coldly as the drow shocked all twelve of them, with their collective screams echoing from inside the tent.

"It was a big gold dragon," one of the younger soldiers yelled out, after the drow pulled his staff away from them.

"Now that is more like it. What was the name of this dragon and its rider?" the sorcerer asked again.

"Keep your teeth together, soldier," the senior legionnaire yelled at him.

"Silence!" Ashram sternly ordered the sergeant as he slapped him across his face with the back of his hand, leaving a nasty scratch from his ring. "Now, who was the dragon, and how many are residing at Battle Point, and all the coastal Weirs of the Alliance?" he screamed.

"Lord Ashram!" the death knight cried, bursting into the tent.

"What, Fellaxe?" the sorcerer snapped back in an angry tone.

"Our gnoll scouts say there is almost a whole legion with an Alliance council wizard, and at least two companies of land dragons are on the march barely two miles from here. All of

Battle Point must be bearing down on us," Fellaxe said with a worried tone.

"How did they get so many here so fast and undetected?" Ashram asked. "It doesn't matter; get the behirs to the front. They will take care of the land dragons, and I will deal with this Alliance wizard. Slave, see to my mount," he ordered his servant, who rushed out of the tent. "We shall continue our conversation when I get back," he told the chained legionnaires. "Vetness, stay here with them and my guards. We will get information out of them, even if I have to eradicate their minds," the Talon sorcerer stated to the drow and walked out of the tent to where his nightmare steed was stabled.

"Look, they are forming up. I count at least thirty of those behirs that you and Deless dealt with yesterday," Dekeen whispered to Mkel and Lupek.

"They will soon find out that they will need at least three or more times the advantage in numbers to fight land dragons," Lupek stated.

"There is also a whole clan of giants down there, behind that small hill," Dekeen continued.

"Giants! Where?" explained Ordin.

"Quiet, my bearded friend. You will get your chance. Until then, we must be patient," Mkel said to the dwarf.

"My hammer is growing hot in my hands, Dragonrider," Ordin said back to him with a smile.

"A sorcerer of great power is emerging from the small tent and walking with a death knight," Dekeen reported.

"We must let Jodem know of this," Mkel said as he pulled his seeing crystal. *I already told him, my rider,* Gallanth told him telepathically. "Thanks, Gallanth," Mkel answered out loud, but still in a low tone.

"It looks like the sorcerer is ordering all of their army out into formation now," Lupek noted.

"He is riding a nightmare, so he must have some connection to the drow," Dekeen theorized out loud. "I have only seen one sorcerer and the death knight, who wields what looks like a black iron battle-axe, as characters of power. The orc warlord looks somewhat menacing as well, but he is still an orc. It appears like they will be using the behirs in the front, interspersed by the grummish in the center, then surrounded by orcs."

The grummish were large brutish humanoid creatures averaging seven feet tall, covered with grayish black to yellowish brown hair. They had pointed ears and protruding fangs, like some hideous cross between a bear, ape, and a man. They usually armed themselves with large spiked wooden clubs, maces, or crude axes, and wooden shields. They rarely used armor of anything stronger than leather. Orcs hired them to act as line breakers in an attack, for they had no fear and fought ferociously until killed. Their main motivation was devouring their victims, as much as the pay they received.

"The gnolls are assembling as flankers. This warlord and sorcerer are somewhat knowledgeable in tactics. Those foul wolf/ man-like creatures, while dull witted, are fast and cunning. Ideal flank infantry given their two-legged speed," Dekeen said, for he knew that gnolls were the only two-legged humanoid creatures that were faster than elves, though not as nimble.

"Yes, it seems that they are starting to imitate Alliance tactics," Mkel answered. "The problem they will have is that we are better trained at it; we have superior equipment, a professional sergeant's corps, better archers, and stronger forces, not to mention our metallic dragons. We also have to have faith in Daddonan and Jodem to deal with them until we can get into the fight. Remember that two of the biggest and most powerful silvers and their riders are with them," Mkel answered.

"No sign of chromatics yet, Captain?" Toderan whispered.

"No, but that could change quickly, as Deless and myself found out yesterday," Lupek chimed in.

"We still have to talk about that, my brother, but for now we have other things to attend to," Mkel whispered back.

"Their army is finally moving out," the ranger said. "Their manticores and hymenoids are taking to flight. I count at least two wings," he continued.

"The Battle Point hippogriffs will keep them busy until Talonth and Strikenth take to the air. Which should be soon," Mkel suggested. "Then once these poor souls are rescued, we will join the main fight," he continued. "Dekeen, how many are left behind?"

"I see one man and three orcs outside the tent, and I hear at least four more inside, along with a stealthy figure I can't identify," the elf answered.

"Decray, did you hear that?" Mkel asked quietly into the crystal.

"Yes, we will handle those in the tent, for we are within a hundred yards and can rush it quickly, as long as you can take out those guards," the ranger captain answered.

"Consider it done. Dekeen, you take the one on the right by the entrance to the tent; Tegent, you hit that orc with the small shield, for he's the closest. I'll silence the one farthest away. Dekeen, I have a bottle of your cousin's best wine that says I will get the last orc guard before you," Mkel said with a smile, for the farthest orc was approximately one hundred fifty yards away, which would be an easy head shot for Mkel with his special crossbow.

"The bet is on, my friend," Dekeen answered as he drew and nocked an arrow.

"Decray, when you see the four fall, we will both rush in," Mkel whispered into his seeing crystal as he steadied Markthrea on the berm and took careful aim at the orc's head.

"Understood, Dragonrider," Decray whispered back through the crystal.

"Fire," said Mkel as he pulled the sensitive trigger of the crossbow, which sent the bolt flying at amazing speed, finding its mark in the back of the orc's head, killing it instantly. Dekeen's arrow pierced the base of the other orc's neck, severing its windpipe and bringing it to its knees. Tegent's seventy-five-yard shot found his arrow deeply imbedded into the man's chest, spinning him around and knocking him to the ground. Mkel immediately cocked the crossbow, shifted his sight to the midsection of the last orc, and fired. Both his bolt and Dekeen's arrow found their mark in the orc's chest as he spun around to see what had happened to his comrade that was beside him. The double strike lifted him off of his feet as he fell dead.

"We'll call that a draw," Dekeen said with a smile.

Mkel smiled for a second before shouting, "Go!" to all in his party, and they all scrambled over the berm and sprinted toward the tents. The rangers sprang up from the scrub brush they were hiding in and were at the tent in a matter of seconds. Decray was the first in, with both his short swords drawn. The first orc in the tent didn't know what hit him, as his blades made two deep cuts to its neck and midsection. He spun with surprising speed and grace and had both his swords imbedded in the second orc's chest. They sunk in surprisingly easy, even through the orc's breastplate armor. *The blades almost swing themselves*, Decray thought to himself as he noted the increased effectiveness of his swords since Gallanth empowered them. His men quickly dispatched the remaining two orcs, but a sonic blast from the drow's staff knocked two of his men out of the tent.

"Alliance rangers, how nice of you to drop in," the dark elf sorcerer said in a dry cool tone, as he began to power up his staff for another shatter spell blast, which he then fired at the rangers. Dekeen burst into the tent and blocked the spell with Elm's defensive shield, and then he drew an arrow.

"Would you like to take this outside, fallen elf, or should I just kill you here?" Dekeen taunted the drow.

"It would be a pleasure to see you die in the sunlight you so praise," the black elf replied as they faced off and maneuvered to exit the tent, never breaking their locked and intense stare. As the two walked out of the tent to continue their duel, Mkel and rest of the Keystone Weir council had just caught up to them. They all raised their weapons to smite the drow sorcerer with one massive blow, but Dekeen told them to stop.

"This is between me and the fallen elf!" Dekeen shouted surprising his friends at his unusually loud outburst.

All of them understood and proceeded into the tent with Tegent remaining outside, likely wanting to see the duel for a future poem or song. *The prisoners look horrible*, Mkel thought to himself, as he surveyed the poor wretches, bruised and bleeding from the torture they had received.

"Mkel, my men will carry them back to our griffons and get them to Handsdown and the healers," Decray stated.

"We will cover your withdrawal," Mkel spoke quickly, catching his breath from the long sprint he just performed. Outside, Dekeen and the drow were beginning their deadly winner-take-all duel. Elm's dragonstone was pulsating in a red scintillating glow, which reflected its master's anger toward the drow, for elves consider drow as the ultimate betrayers. The drow sorcerer's dark crystal was also glowing, emitting a dull black-purplish light.

"So drow, I would like to hear your name before I put you to judgment," Dekeen said calmly to the dark elf.

"My name is Vetness, high elf, and this sorcerer will silence that insolent tongue of yours," the drow snapped back.

"I am Dekeen of the Draden Clan, which is the last name you will ever hear," Dekeen answered.

"The master arcane archer?" Vetness quipped back.

"What, is that fear in your voice, dark elf?" Dekeen chided.

"Salvinesh!" Vetness shouted in the elvish drow dialect, as he raised his staff and fired a bolt of lightning at Dekeen, who nimbly dove to the side to dodge the main blast of the charged jagged beam. His bow's spell shield did have to take the secondary energy of the deadly bolt. He rolled and instantly sprang to his feet, firing an arrow. The speed of Dekeen's arrows surprised Vetness, who was normally quick enough to dodge such missiles. The dragonstone-empowered arrow hit the drow's spell shield with a thundering explosion that made him step back. As the dark elf sorcerer prepared another spell, Dekeen had already nocked and fired a second arrow. The concussion forced Vetness back again, as he felt his shield weakening.

The drow sorcerer focused with all his might and managed to conjure a fireball spell from his staff and hurled it at Dekeen. The third arrow he had drawn was let loose, after Dekeen whispered a quick elven command phrase. The arrow sped through the air and directly intercepted the glowing fireball with a collision, resulting in a blinding explosion. This did not mean good bidding for Vetness, for he was not a master sorcerer yet, and was limited in the amount and strength of his offensive spells. He could not believe the power of the high elf's bow.

Another arrow struck the drow's invisible shield as he was trying to gather power for a return spell. The explosion and transfer of energy broke the drow's shield and knocked him to the ground. Vetness raised his hand and fired a series of magic missiles in a barrage to attempt to keep Dekeen from firing another arrow. The Draden elf quickly moved to dodge the first two missiles. The next four were absorbed by his shield, but the last one slipped though his shield and glanced off his mithril chain mail vest. He winced at the slight burn that made it through the armor, but his mail saved him.

Dekeen then fired an arrow with a quick aim, which struck Vetness in the chest, piercing his sorcerer's robes, with half the shaft emerging from the drow's back. The dark elf grabbed the arrow's golden brown fletching in tremendous agony, dropping to his knees. Dekeen drew another arrow and took aim at the dark crystal mounted atop the drow's staff.

"What, fire while your opponent is down, High Elf?" Vetness gasped out as his dark green blood was oozing from both ends of the arrow shaft.

"Just making sure that your evil crystal does not enslave another fool and wreak more destruction," Dekeen answered. *"Rescula se Solrela,"* Dekeen spoke a similar prayer that metallic dragons give when they kill a chromatic to save their souls, and then he released his arrow. The glowing tip of his arrow struck the crystal, resulting in a small but blinding explosion that consumed the drow.

"Dekeen, you didn't think that would attract attention?" Mkel shouted over to his elven comrade.

"My fight already compromised us, and anytime we can destroy a piece of dark crystal, it makes the world a safer place," the elf said nonchalantly.

"Fellaxe, what was that back at the camp?" Ashram yelled over to the death knight.

"I don't know, but I'll send one of the manticore riders back to check," the warlord yelled.

"No, go back yourself," the sorcerer ordered. "I don't want anything happening to our backs while I have to deal with a whole legion to our front. And by the looks of those two land dragon companies bearing down on us, and an Alliance wizard, this will be a challenge."

"It's probably Vetness getting those giants moving to join our fight," Fellaxe answered.

"That was not a request, warlord," Ashram demanded.

"Yes, my liege," the death knight replied with a scowl on his scarred face, as he swung his wyvern around to head back to their encampment.

Ashram spurred his nightmare steed forward to motivate his army. "I will see that sorcerer grovel before me one day," Fellaxe grumbled to himself, as his wyvern mount veered to the right to head back to their encampment.

"Mkel, a rider on a wyvern is coming back from the enemy army. And I hear giants approach from the hills," Dekeen spoke quickly.

"Decray, we are expecting company any minute. You need to get those men to your mounts," Mkel relayed.

"Giants! Finally a fight worthy of my hammer. The earth tells me they come from the east," Ordin said with glee, for dwarves were very in tune with ground vibrations, being a race that lived a good portion of their lives underground.

"Lupek, Toderan, go with Ordin and Tegent and head off the giants. Dekeen and I will take this wyvern down," Mkel quickly directed.

"Yes, Captain, good luck," Toderan replied as Lupek and Tegent nodded an acknowledgment.

Mkel, there are at least three giants coming down the valley, with more following several miles behind, along with ogres and more orcs, Gallanth told Mkel telepathically.

"Toderan, Lupek, there are at least three giants, with more to follow, so be careful," Mkel shouted as he loaded an exploding-tipped bolt magazine into his crossbow.

"Mkel, the wyvern carries the death knight," Dekeen spoke as he drew an arrow from his quiver.

"Not for much longer," Mkel answered as he cocked the lever behind the trigger, which loaded and readied it to fire. "Wait until he dives toward us," Mkel spoke to Dekeen as he dropped to a knee and lifted his crossbow to his shoulder, carefully taking aim at the approaching wyvern.

Who are these insolent invaders of our camp? Fellaxe thought to himself as he spurred his dragon-like mount to dive on the two closest foes, who were daring to take aim at him. His wyvern would slice those two to shreds with its talons, and then he would deal with the others in turn. The black iron axe he wielded had felled many a foe, and he attacked the small group with confidence. He surmised that any Alliance soldier or warrior of strength would certainly be heading the legion that his forces were marching to meet, not here skulking in their encampment.

The brownish gray steed brought up its raptor-like talons and raised its tail with its enlarged poisonous stinger. Wyverns did not have front legs like true dragons, and without an antidote, the poison from their tail stinger was deadly to all but dragons. The wyvern let out a warbled roar, tilting its wings to initiate its dive. These creatures were minute compared to a true dragon, even smaller than a white, and were just larger than a manticore. Their roughly fifty-foot wingspan was just over half of a white dragon's. They did possess a long tail, making them appear bigger than they actually were. In a close fight, a land dragon would tear one of these creatures apart, and a good-sized griffon could beat them, as long as it could avoid its deadly tail.

"Fire!" Dekeen shouted as he released his arrow, which was immediately followed by Mkel's bolt. Both missiles streaked toward the diving wyvern. Dekeen's hit the creature on the base of the neck, easily piercing the wyvern's relatively lightly armored hide, as compared to a dragon's. The energy of the dragonstone-enhanced arrow transferred into the wyvern, as Mkel's exploding-tipped bolt struck it in the left front region of the chest and burst in a brilliant flash. The resulting double impact from the powerful weapons' missiles actually interrupted the wyvern's dive, pushing it up and to the left of its flight path. The mortally wounded creature crashed into one of the larger tents, sending its black armored rider tumbling to the ground.

In the meantime, three common giants emerged from around the small hill on the left side of the shallow valley behind the camp. When they saw Ordin, they shouted something in their crude simplistic language and raised their huge clubs as they rapidly moved toward him. Ordin smiled, raised his thunder hammer, Donnac, and hurled it at the lead giant. The powerful double-headed hammer whirled end over end, with its ruby dragonstone glowing and crackling with energy, as it sped toward the giant. The large brute did not think of it as a threat and kept advancing toward the brown-bearded dwarf. The hammer struck the giant square in the chest, with a loud thunderous clap, knocking the fourteen-foot-tall, two-and-a-half-thousand-pound creature off its feet. It gasped, as it slammed on its back in a muffled thud. The hammer flew back in a wide arc to Ordin's outstretched hand.

The giant that was hit was not killed but must have had several broken ribs and likely a crushed diaphragm, for it was barely able to roll over and get to its knees. The other two did not even acknowledge their companion's plight and continued to advance on Toderan, Lupek, and Tegent. Toderan faced off the giant on the right and drew his holy sword while firming his grip on his mithril shield. Lupek raised his javelin and threw it at the giant that was rapidly bearing down on them from the left. The lightning javelin streaked through the air and easily pierced the giant's hide armor on the right shoulder, with the electrical energy blast spinning it around and bringing it down to one knee. Tegent fired two arrows in rapid succession, one hitting it the stomach and the other in its back, as it was twirled around by Lupek's javelin.

Toderan moved toward the third giant as it raised its five-foot-long club and swung at the knight. The paladin ducked and raised his shield, making the club only score a glancing blow. Even with that, the burly paladin was pushed back a step but quickly recovered with a downward thrust of his long sword that sliced through the giant's hide armor and cut into its side, transferring the energy of the sword into the brute. It winced at the blow, which left a nasty and deep gash in its side. The giant had received wounds from a long sword before, but never like this, as the pain from the gash was intense.

As it raised its club again, Toderan moved in and struck the giant's right leg with his blade, cutting the thigh to the bone. The giant crumpled but did manage to hit Toderan with his club, which he again blocked with his shield, but was thrown back, landing on his side. He quickly got up, as his mithril plate armor was much lighter than steel, and in three strides he was on the giant. As it was attempting to get to its hands and knees, the paladin thrust his holy sword into the base of its thick hairy neck. The shimmering mithril alloy blade sunk almost to the hilt. The giant let out a gurgling groan as it fell dead.

Ordin had moved up to the giant he first hit and struck it in the calf, as it just had gotten back on its feet, with one hand still clutching its club and the other grasping its chest. The giant's lower leg snapped with a loud crack, bringing it back to the ground. It swung its club in a powerful downward stroke as it fell. Ordin deftly rolled away from the huge club, which struck only earth. He then sprang back up on his feet and swung his hammer, hitting the giant square in the forehead, killing it instantly.

"Ahhaahahh!" Ordin shouted in a victory cry. Tegent fired another arrow, which struck the third giant in the chest as it attempted to get up and pull the mithril javelin out of its shoulder. Lupek quickly closed in on the giant while drawing his scimitar and sliced a wide but thin and deep cut along its side, then he whirled around and plunged the curved blade to the hilt in its back. The giant's distorted face reflected the pain of the deep wound as another arrow from Tegent pierced its neck, finishing it off as it fell forward with a thud.

Fellaxe had finally recovered from being thrown from his wyvern when it crashed; he grabbed his axe and moved to meet this insolent threat. As he rounded his dead mount, he faced Mkel and Dekeen, who had drawn arrows trained on him. He grasped his black iron double-headed axe, with its bronze skull head in the center of the spiked circle that both blades of the axe originated from. "A dragonrider and an elf?" he shouted as he noticed the dragon symbol on Mkel's collar. "Where's your dragon? Too afraid to fight?" he attempted a weak insult.

"No, you're just not worth the bother, death knight," Mkel answered back, matching his insult. "Now it's time for you to surrender, or die," Mkel quipped as he and Dekeen aimed their bows on him.

"No, Captain. He's mine," Toderan shouted as he walked over to them.

"An Alliance paladin; I will enjoy splitting your skull with my axe," Fellaxe replied, as Mkel and Dekeen lowered their bows. Toderan's holy sword was still dripping with the last of the dark reddish-purple giant's blood, its ruby dragonstone glowing brightly.

The two armies were now converging on each other. When the lines were within one thousand yards, all six small catapults that had managed to squeeze into the group that Strikenth and Talonth teleported in started to fire. The ballistae gunners on the land dragons also initiated firing with their dragon's fire-tipped spears. The catapults that the Battle Point legion had taken with them were smaller than what Jodem was used to seeing but slightly more mobile. This did limit their range to a thousand yards as opposed to the mid to large size catapults that had a two- to three-thousand-yard range. The largest trebuchets of the Alliance Capital heavy legions could throw a sixty-pound projectile over two miles.

One of the two fragmentation stones hit directly in the center of the orc lines, sending out nails and sharp metal fragments in a deadly twenty-yard circle. Nineteen orcs fell dead and twenty-four more were wounded by the secondary projectiles. The other stone hit just behind the lines, which only killed four and wounded twelve. The gunners quickly adjusted their catapult throw strengths to correct for the distance and the orc forward movement.

"Down hundred yards and left fifty," the second catapult crew leader shouted, as his men wound the throwing arm to a specific tension and loaded a dragon's fire canister, as did the other engine. "Fire!" both crew leaders shouted to their men to let the arms fly forward. This time both hit their marks, with fireball bursts exploding in the middle of the orc and human infantry ranks, killing scores, coupled by the two dozen smaller bursts from the land dragon ballistae.

"Damn that dragon's fire of theirs. Why can't our alchemists or the drow find the formula for that material?" Ashram grumbled to himself as he just reached his army, flying on his black demon horse steed. "We'll see to that later." He spurred his mount on toward the legion, preparing a spell, as the dark crystal on his staff started to glow. Suddenly an arrow sailed dangerously close to him, and then another struck the nightmare in the hindquarter, just penetrating its tough pitch black hide. The sorcerer looked up to see two squadrons of mounted hippogriffs bearing down on him. He quickly raised his magic shield, which stopped eight more arrows from finding their mark as the hippogriffs started to dart past him on their way to strafe his army below. He did manage to fire a lightning bolt, which struck one of the hippogriffs, sending it end over end toward the ground, but the rest had all passed out of his range before he could prepare another spell.

"Where in Tiamat's name are those manticores?" he shouted to himself, then looked over and saw them slowly approaching at mid altitude from the east. In the meantime, the first wave of hippogriffs dove on his mixed army below, letting loose a hail of arrows and dragon's fire grenades, many of which found their mark. They then pulled up just as the second wave of two squadrons dove on the army from the opposite direction. The two squadrons of hippogriffs unleashed a hail of arrows and dragon's fire grenades on the sorcerer's army, resulting in over a hundred casualties. Several hippogriffs received arrows hits, mostly to the hindquarters as they flew by and pulled away. Orc archers were notoriously inaccurate and depended on pure numbers to achieve hits. The usual Morgathian army makeup had only a quarter of the number of archers the typical Alliance legion deploys.

"The manticores will keep them busy for a while, it's the land dragons that I have to worry about," Ashram said to himself as his black steed dove down toward his own lines, looking for his key leaders. He saw Barlog moving behind the line of grummish and the behirs, shouting at the orc battalion he led. "Barlog!" he shouted as his nightmare steed reared up in midair just over the orcs' heads. The land dragon ballistae were bursting in regular order all around them, accented with the occasional larger explosion of a catapult canister. This was playing havoc on the orc and human infantry lines.

"Keep your scum in order!" the sorcerer screamed. "You are facing a reinforced legion; they somehow got here through your scouts." Ashram was furious that the Battle Point legion had gotten so close without being detected, especially with nearly a battalion of land dragons. He estimated that this portion of his army still had them outnumbered, but not by as much as he would have liked. "And don't let those grummish outdistance the behirs, or they will be burnt to ashes in the cross fire between them and the land dragons."

"Yes, my lord," the large muscular orc shouted back.

"Dog orc, we will not be told when we can kill," the grummish leader growled in half common and half his own tongue.

"You heard Lord Ashram," the hierorc yelled back at him in orcish, "you are to stay in line." Barlog brandished his black iron axe in a threatening posture.

"You are food," the hairy, brutish grummish leader snarled as he moved to engage the orc chieftain, raising his spiked morning star.

"Enough!" Ashram yelled, and he fired a magic missile, hitting the grummish chieftain in the head, killing it instantly. "Now get back in line," he continued as Barlog echoed the command and pushed several of the larger grummish back in their skirmish line; they all obeyed with little less hesitation. Grummish did not fear anything, but they respected power, especially magically originated power.

A ballista spear then struck one of the behirs in the neck, piercing it straight through. The creature reared up, gave a muffled roar, and then collapsed. Three more were then struck, killing one and severely injuring the other two.

"These snake dragons don't have very thick skin," Colonel Ronson said. "Pour it on boys," he ordered through his seeing crystal, as all his ballistae gunners were loading and firing as fast as they could. "Drop as many as you can; that will make less work for your dragons."

"Damn those ballistae!" Ashram screamed. He counted almost thirty land dragons, and he surmised there must be another company in reserve, so he flew down and yelled to the remainder of his behirs to move to the front line, to hit them as hard and as fast as possible, then prepare for their reserve forces. He would soon join the behirs with his own destructive spells but couldn't right now. He knew better than to take on such an assembled force, especially with the wizard that was moving with them. He had over ninety of these new creatures, and he felt confident they would match the Alliance land dragons.

As the front lines of the legion and Ashram's army closed to within three hundred yards, the Battle Point archers and crossbowmen began to fire in volleys. Hundreds of arrows arched over and rained down onto the ranks of the evil sorcerer's troops. Many were finding their mark, for the orcs and grummish in particular were not that heavily armored. Some of the arrows were actually penetrating the behirs' hides as well. The orc and Morgathian archers began to fire back, but their short bows, weaker limbed crossbows, and iron or soft steel arrow tips did not have the distance and power of the Alliance long composite bows and crossbows. The sorcerer's army also lacked leadership in coordinating their archers.

Scores of orcs and regular infantry were falling to arrow wounds, as the both armies continued to close the gap between them. Once they were within one hundred yards of each other, both the land dragons and the behirs began to gather power to unleash their breath weapons. The ballistae and catapult crews continued to fire and wreak heavy damage to the enemy lines, as well as hitting more behirs with greater consistency and effect.

Jodem saw Ashram on his nightmare take to flight, and he responded by nudging Alvanch to launch into the air to meet him. The Talon sorcerer started the close melee by firing a series of lightning bolts at the legion. Jodem raised his staff and stopped the six chain lighting bolts with his shield, but the energy of Ashram's spells did strike hard. "A sorcerer of some power," he shouted to Ashram. "You might actually present a challenge before I vanquish you." he chided.

"I wouldn't be so confident if I were you, Alliance magician," Ashram countered.

"Fool, you don't know what you have just entered into," Jodem said as he fired a disruption ray at Ashram. The Morgathian sorcerer's shield held against the spell, but the blast pushed the nightmare back several yards in midair. Jodem then sent up a prismatic ray, which burst in brilliant colors several hundred yards into the sky. With that signal, the land dragons all breathed fire at the onrushing behirs and the line of troops moving with them. Strikenth and Talonth then took to wing from back where they had originally teleported the legion into the area, issuing their challenge roars.

Ashram's eyes opened wide in both shock and amazement at the presence of the two silver dragons, and he spurred his pitch black demon horse to the rear. The legion's hippogriff wings were heavily engaged in fighting the manticores and hymenoids, along with the remaining dragon spawn. The numbers were about even, with both sides having approximately two hundred aerial forces, but the hippogriffs and their riders were slowly gaining the advantage.

"Padonan, we'll do an attack on the sorcerer's ground forces, then sweep through and give the hippogriffs a little help, and repeat that until either they are destroyed or chromatics appear," Lordan yelled over to the junior dragonrider.

"Yes sir," he answered. "Did you get that, my friend?" he asked Strikenth.

Talonth already let me know, we will hit the right side of the Morgathian columns, concentrating on the behir creatures, his silver dragon answered.

"Excellent, my friend; follow Talonth in his dive," Padonan explained as he grabbed his glaive, springing the mithril blades open from its six curved arms. The two silver dragons began to dive on the leading edge of the sorcerer's army. Both roared before simultaneously firing their freezing breath weapons. The icy blue beams had a cold that was beyond imagination, and they struck two of the lead behirs and any orc or grummish standing within fifteen yards of the creatures. The orcs and grummish caught in the icy blast instantly froze solid and shattered as they fell. The behirs that were hit roared a high shrill warble as their long sinuous bodies were partially froze and fell over on their many legs, which shattered from the intense cold. The combined strike left both behirs severely wounded and over sixty or more orcs and grummish dead, with as many injured from partial freezing. Lordan fired an energy bolt from his powerful dragonstone lance, which burst in the middle of the orcs, sending a dozen flying through the air.

As the two silver dragons pulled up from their diving attack, the behirs switched from firing lightning bolts at the land dragons to them. Twenty or more bolts were directed at the pair of metallics, of which four struck Talonth's shield and three hit Strikenth's. Their shields took the impacts of the bolts without much trouble, as the snake-like dragon creatures had a fraction of the power of a blue dragon. As they pulled up and ascended, the downdraft from their wings almost knocked a section of the ranks of orcs and men over, and they both unleashed a flame strike spell on the troops in the back of the army's column. Sheets of flame engulfed three dozen orcs and Morgathian fighters in a combined area of forty square yards.

Padonan looked back as Strikenth flew up and away from the sorcerer's army and threw his glaive, which streamed toward the rear columns. The mithril star-shaped weapon hit the trailing orc, cutting him in half in a blink of an eye, and continued slicing twenty more before ascending to return to Padonan's waiting hand. Both dragons roared a challenge to let the Battle Point hippogriffs know they were coming and to clear a path for them to attack any enemy in front of them.

The two armies were almost on top of each other now. The legion had three land dragons injured to the point that they could not continue the attack in the exchange in breath weapon fire from the behirs. Two had taken three or more direct hits in the chest and neck from the lightning bolts, with the third being hit in the front leg after their magic shields had depleted. They fell back to the rear of the advancing legion, and their crews immediately started to apply Aloras salve to their wounds. The behirs were not faring well, with the combination of the land dragons' fiery breath and their ballistae gunners taking out half of their numbers. Over twenty had fallen so far, along with hundreds of orcs and grummish caught in the blasts. The magic shield that the land dragons can project, while only a fraction of what a metallic dragon can produce, was still more than what the behirs had; which was minimal.

"Sergeant, tell all the crews to ready for close combat," Colonel Ronson ordered. "Thank the Creator these creatures don't have shields, or we might have been in trouble, for they can fire their lightning bolts very fast. Let's see how they are in a fang and claw fight."

The land dragons started to issue their challenge roars, which the behirs returned weakly. The remaining grummish and orcs started to break into a charge from about fifty yards out. The heavy infantry line in the front, three deep, lowered their spears and raised their shields in preparation for the assault. The two rows of archers and crossbowmen fired as fast as they could to maximize the damage on the rushing creatures. One grummish took six arrows to bring it down.

"Arms!" the sergeants shouted to the front line infantrymen as they locked shields and readied for the orc and grummish charge. "Archers, fire at will!" Colonel Sheer shouted as the two ranks of bowmen and crossbowmen began firing as rapidly as they could at the onrushing creatures. In spite of the damage inflicted by the archers, ballistae, land dragons, Strikenth, and Talonth, the legion was still outnumbered, but the odds were now better.

The first wave of orcs and grummish were skillfully impaled on the legionnaires' long spears, with the wall of locked shields taking most of the blows. The discipline and coordination of the Battle Point soldiers was impressive. They were a well-drilled team, with the second and third infantry ranks spearing, hacking, or thrusting any enemy that was giving the first line a great deal of trouble. The first line soldiers knew their lives depended on this until the formations were completely broken, when the fight would then go into individual melee. Additionally, this coordination went on with the aid of the two ranks of archers directly behind them, either taking close shots of opportunity or drawing their short swords and entering into the combat directly.

The Battle Point line held the initial assault, with only a handful of the most tenacious grummish breaking through. These were quickly met with a several arrows fired at point-blank range or as many swords thrust into them as possible to bring them down. The land dragons had moved just ahead of the infantry to take the behirs on directly. In a tooth to claw fight, the blue snake-like creatures proved to be severely overmatched by the powerful land dragons. They were not nearly as strong or as tough. One of the larger land dragons almost picked up the behir it attacked, as its fangs sunk into the softer blue hide, knocking it to the ground and then raking it with its two front claws, bearing all of its weight onto the slender blue torso.

The ballistae gunners were firing at their wingman's opponents if they could not get a shot at the one their land dragon was fighting with. Land dragons always fought in pairs for mutual support. This added to their effectiveness, especially against larger opponents such as giants or chromatic dragons.

General Daddonan called to Colonel Reddit for the cavalry to charge on both flanks to prevent the numerically superior enemy from flanking them, especially the nimble gnolls and the Morgathian cavalry. Reddit ordered the horns to be sounded and called his cavalry commanders to split troops and charge up both sides of the enemy battle line, with the order to keep any enemy cavalry and the gnolls from moving behind the legion. The medium-type cavalry split and thundered past the right and left side of the line, cutting the gnoll scouts apart with their deadly tribladed lances in their wedge formations, which did not allow the hyena-like creatures to single out riders and jump them. This was a favorite tactic of the man/wolf creatures.

Ashram's cavalry had to re-form after Strikenth's and Talonth's attack, which delayed them. Now Colonel Reddit's horsemen had the initiative, and they charged headlong into the disorganized black armored cavalry, dashing any hope of them using their slightly greater numbers to their advantage. As a whole, the Battle Point horse soldiers rivaled even Colonel Lordan's own cavalry of his mounted legion, taking many lessons from the northern Kaskar horse clans.

As the battle raged behind him, Ashram was cursing the giant clan that was supposed to support his behirs. Now with two silver dragons to contend with, he was starting to panic. "Lodar, I need at least two wings of chromatics, and I need them now!" the sorcerer shouted into the dark crystal on the end of his staff, as his nightmare was racing back to the encampment. "And where is that incompetent Fellaxe?"

"Ashram, are you having a little problem?" the warlord sarcastically responded.

"There is no time for your insolence, Lodar, send the dragons now," Ashram snapped back.

"I'll see what I can do, sorcerer," the senior death knight and warlord answered back, with a sinister smile on his scarred face, obviously enjoying Ashram's predicament. "Ashram, I'm sending Thurex and Krekon, with their wings, to relieve you. That will give you two red dragons and the combined twelve additional dragons in their squadrons. Again it has to be me to rescue the mighty Talon sorcerer, what a pity," Lodar chided. These reinforcements would be coming from his northern most outpost along the Morgathian border.

"I will see to his attitude later," Ashram said as he began to approach his camp, only to see three dead giants lying beside his now collapsed tent. "What is going on here?" he shouted at Mkel and his group on the ground.

"The Talon sorcerer!" Dekeen shouted as he drew and fired an arrow. The empowered arrow from Elm struck Ashram's magic shield with a huge explosion. The impact pushed the sorcerer's nightmare back in midair. Mkel quickly followed up Dekeen's shot with an exploding-tipped bolt that burst on the sorcerer's shield, again pushing his mount back from the resulting impact.

Who are these individuals, and what powers do they possess? The source must be dragonstone in origin, Ashram thought to himself as he whirled his staff to focus on a fireball spell, which he hurled at Dekeen and Mkel. The glowing fiery projectile hurtled toward the two, which impacted on their combined magic shields from their three dragonstone weapons.

"This sorcerer is powerful," Dekeen said to Mkel as he drew another arrow and prepared to fire.

Mkel, there are chromatic dragons inbound, at least two wings, Gallanth's words echoed hard in Mkel's mind. Both Dekeen and Ashram almost simultaneously refocused as if they both heard Gallanth's telepathic message.

"Does Gallanth know how many chromatics are coming?" Dekeen asked as he read the concern on his friend's face.

"At least two wings," Mkel replied to his friend.

"Two wings? There hasn't been that many chromatics fighting together since the Great War," Dekeen said with a slight tone of anxiety, very unusual for an elf. Mkel had never heard his lifelong elvish friend express concern like this before.

"Hah! I have a few friends coming, so I will have to deal with you later, Alliance vermin. You will pay for this intrusion. Fellaxe, I leave you to your own fate," Ashram shouted to his second in command as he spurred his steed back toward the two armies fighting. The downdraft beats of over a dozen dragon wings began to echo up the shallow valley.

Mkel, you must fall back, Talonth and Strikenth will be calling for our aid soon, and the rangers have the Battle Point soldiers secure on their mounts, Gallanth told Mkel. "Dekeen, I must fall back, Gallanth is calling me. Toderan, I must go," Mkel spoke to his companions.

"I will not be long, Captain," Toderan replied. "This puny specimen here will not be much of a challenge. Now go, for they will need you and Gallanth with the chromatics coming."

"Call through your crystal if you need help. Dekeen, Lupek, I must go. Tegent, you stay with Toderan to watch his back. Ordin, let's move," Mkel called out.

"Mkel, there are many giants approaching from up the valley," Ordin announced.

Mkel had to quickly rethink how he was to rearrange his personnel, for the giants had to be delayed. Lupek, Ordin, Dekeen, Tegent, and Toderan could do that, but he needed Ordin or someone else in the rear seat on Gallanth's saddle to watch his back with the fight that will take place soon.

"Ordin, how many giants are there in this group?" Mkel asked.

"At least a dozen, if not more," Ordin said, grinning with excitement. Mkel knew his friends were powerful fighters with powerful weapons, but four against a clan of giants, even common giants, without Jodem or Gallanth would be a tough fight indeed. He would take Tegent and leave his four powerful friends to fight a delay against the giants.

"All right; Tegent, you come with me. You and your griffon will be my wingman, so I hope your bow is accurate today. Dekeen, Ordin, Lupek, when Toderan finishes with that death knight, go and delay those giants. If you get hard-pressed, fall back through the scrub to your mounts and join us in the air. Gallanth and I will come back for Ordin if we can break off from the aerial fight; otherwise, don't forget him," Mkel spoke quickly with a slight smile, but then he was interrupted by the challenge roars of the approaching chromatic dragons. Dekeen looked up at the ridgeline to the east as the dragons appeared.

"I count two reds leading at least three blues, four greens, and four black dragons," the elf spoke out loud. Elves with their keen eyes were experts in identifying dragons flying overhead by the silhouette or outline of their wings, torso, and tail, along with their size. The challenge roars that the different dragons emitted were also distinctive. A gold dragon like Gallanth or Valianth had the deepest and most commanding roar. A silver dragon's was similar, just not quite as deep. A red dragon's roar was shriller, with what was best described as an angry tone to it, for red dragons were by far the most sinister and vicious, if not the most arrogant, of the chromatic types. Blue and bronze dragons had a slight hiss to their roars, likely due to the electrical nature of their breath weapons, but blues sounded slightly more evil or raspy. The roars of the green and black dragons were very shrill and had a shallower quality to them, while white dragons were the shrillest with the most tenor, likely because they were the smallest of the true dragons.

"Thirteen chromatics with two reds; bad odds for Talonth and Strikenth. Gallanth, can you tell if any of them are demon or berserker dragons?" Mkel asked. *The red dragon on the right is a demon dragon. The aura of power emanating from him is immense. Talonth and Strikenth will need our help.* "Dekeen ..." Mkel started to say.

"I know even with my elf ears, I can't hear Gallanth talking to you through your mind, but by your expression, I can guess the answer," Dekeen interjected.

"The red on the right is a demon dragon," Mkel answered, "and if the blue we killed yesterday was any indication of the extra powers these dragon types have, this red will give Talonth and Strikenth a terrific fight."

"Mkel, go, we will be able to hold off the giants until you come back," Toderan yelled as he swung his shimmering holy sword at Fellaxe. The death knight parried the blow with his black iron axe blade, but the sword's energy knocked it back into his hands.

"What is this, a holy sword, an Alliance master paladin?" Fellaxe bantered. "I thought they were only legendary."

"Too bad it is the first and last you'll ever see," Toderan answered back as he swung his sword to the right, aiming at Fellaxe's midsection. The death knight barely blocked it with the handle of his axe, which split off from the impact. He then gave a downward thrust with the large axe blade, which Toderan blocked with his shield.

His shield took the blow and did not buckle or splinter, Fellaxe thought to himself. He was used to his opponents' shields being torn asunder from his axe blows. *It must be made of mithril, this will not be an easy fight,* he said to himself.

"I'll see you all soon; die well, death knight!" Mkel shouted. "Tegent, let's go," he continued, nodding to his friends before he turned and ran back into the hills to meet up with Gallanth, with Tegent sprinting right behind him.

Fellaxe knew he had to get around the large mithril shield, or he had no chance of winning this fight; he swung his axe to the left, aiming at Toderan's right side, where he thought he could get negate his shield arm and find a weak point in his strong armor. Toderan arched back and dodged the axe swing with a surprising grace and speed that one would not think possible with plate armor. This attested to the extreme lightweight property of his mithril suit, being tenfold as strong and a fraction the weight of steel.

Toderan then moved in quickly, bashing Fellaxe's left arm with his shield and delivering a downward stroke that sliced into the black iron armor on his opponent's shoulder. Fellaxe let out a gasp of pain as he moved back away from Toderan. He felt the blood trickle down his shirt inside his armor. The pain was excruciating, much more than just the cut; it was as if a devastating energy had been also delivered by the blade. He also could not believe his black iron armor had been compromised.

With his left shoulder wounded, he had to switch hands on his axe, putting him at a disadvantage. He moved slightly to the right to attempt to get Toderan off guard and then swung the axe back to the left. Toderan blocked the axe with his sword under the blade and smashed his shield into Fellaxe's chest and face, making him stagger back several steps to maintain his balance.

This paladin has great strength, Fellaxe said to himself; the blood began to run from his now broken nose, as the face guard on his skull shaped helmet was dented in from the blow. He then leveled the axe, with its protruding point on top of the double-headed blade, and aimed at Toderan's neck with his charge, hoping the longer weapon would give him reach over the paladin.

Toderan quickly moved to the left, deflected the axe with his shield, and used Fellaxe's momentum as well as his own to spin himself around and deliver a hard backhand angled blow to Fellaxe's shoulder blade between the black iron plates, cutting deeply into his back. The death knight fell forward onto the ground, gasping in pain. He did get back to his feet surprisingly quickly, given the severity of his wounds. "Do you wish to yield?" Toderan asked.

"The renowned paladin mercy? I would rather die," he spat back, again charging and swinging his battle-axe with one hand. Toderan raised his shield, blocking the weakened swing of the axe, and thrust his sword into Fellaxe's side, with the blade sinking deeply into the death knight's chest. This was the killing blow; Fellaxe gasped, looking at Toderan, and then fell to the ground. Breathing heavily, Toderan turned to Dekeen, Lupek, and Ordin, who nodded in an acknowledgment of his victory, and walked over to them.

"All right, we better devise a quick plan of attack to deal with this giant clan," Toderan spoke to his friends.

Talonth and Strikenth had just made a return pass on Ashram's army, freezing solid dozens of orcs and Morgathian infantry in the rear ranks, so as to not endanger any Battle Point soldiers currently engaging the enemy. Lordan and Padonan targeted a behir and a beholder, as their silver dragons ascended from their aerial strike. The fire bolt that emanated from Lordan's lance struck one of the behirs in the back of the neck, knocking it forward and to the ground.

Padonan's glaive whirled through the air, making a direct path to the beholder who had hit Strikenth's shield with a disruption ray. The star-bladed weapon cut through the vile multitentacle, orb-like creature's spell shield with a thunder-like crack and sliced into its large central eye. The glaive emerged from the back of the creature's spherical body, spun up, and quickly changed direction to go back to its wielder's hand.

The dying beholder fell to the ground, which their kind never touched, preferring to hover several feet from it at all times. While magically powerful in their own right, a beholder was still no match for the spinning mithril-bladed glaive, which was renowned for slicing through magic shields and almost anything else. Jodem was currently engaging the other beholder from behind the front line of clashing troops and orcs.

"Good hit, Lieutenant," Lordan said to Padonan through his seeing crystal.

Lordan, Gallanth just told me that two wings of chromatic dragons are inbound, and the lead red is a demon dragon, Talonth quickly informed his rider.

"Padonan, we must gain altitude quickly, for we must attack them from above and draw them away from the legion. Two red dragons can wreak havoc on an army, much less than one of those demon dragons," Lordan said again through his crystal.

"Yes sir, Strikenth already relayed the message," Padonan replied as both dragons hefted their silvery wings with deep strokes to gain altitude as rapidly as possible. Normally a silver dragon can handle a red with slight effort, for they have stronger defensive magic shields and greater spell casting ability, along with being faster and more maneuverable in the air. Red dragons were physically more powerful, however, with only gold dragons having greater strength.

As Talonth and Strikenth flew upward, both opened their jaws and emitted a cone of cold mist that started to form a dense fog cloud in the clear sky. As the shrouding mist started to form in front of them, they split and began to circle within the white plume to expand it. They would attack from this concealed position.

"Krekon, send Voltex and one of your green and black dragons with the same from my wing to attack the Alliance legion and their wingless dragons; the rest will follow me to destroy the silvers," Thurex commanded, for not only was he a senior red, but a demon dragon as well.

"Yes, Lord Thurex. Voltex, take Batuul and Kakol from our wing, and Slyvar and Saarex from Lord Thurex's wing to attack the legion," the junior red dragon commanded.

"Yes, Krekon. You four, follow me!" the large blue roared back to the smaller green and black dragons when he split off to the left. The two red dragons and the other eight chromatics of the now combined squadron veered right and headed toward the large cloud.

"Krekon, Arathus, Klaxtor, fire into the cloud to flush these cowards out," Thurex ordered as a billowing cone of fire cut into the mist, followed by the two lightning bolts from the blues to couple with Krekon's fire. Just as the breath weapons extinguished, Talonth and Strikenth emerged from teleport above the chromatic wing and unleashed two ice rays, along with a barrage of spells.

Talonth cast his powerful lightning storm spell on the red dragons; the main bolt hit Thurex's shield, followed by a rapid barrage of twenty smaller bolts, striking with blinding succession on both the crimson dragons' invisible barriers. He simultaneously breathed a deadly icy beam at the closest blue dragon. All three chromatics had their shields rocked and faltered in flight, being forced to veer off because of the impacts.

Strikenth fired his lightning storm spell at the four black and green dragons hovering behind the reds and blues. Black and green dragons had comparatively weak shields and did not stand up well against the metallic dragons' attacks. Strikenth's main lightning bolt struck the largest green, with the follow-on twenty bolts hitting all four remaining chromatics in rapid succession. He then breathed his freezing ray at the other blue; its shield barely contained the powerful silver's breath weapon.

Lordan followed his dragon's attack on the blue with a fire-bolt from his lance, which struck the beast's shield with full force.

Padonan threw his glaive at the nearest dragon. The spinning blade sliced the black dragon's tough skin on its right wing, cutting a long swath in the thin armored membrane. It then proceeded to gash the thick blackish hide on its lower back. The combined strikes took the chromatic squadron by surprise, putting them all off balance. The two silver dragons then dove into the middle of the group and delivered claw slashes and tail strikes to several chromatics on their way through the pack.

This was a good first strike; Talonth and Strikenth delivered devastating blows to the chromatic dragons' shields to help even their odds. They dove fast, partially folding their wings to get away from the chromatic wing and avoid a breath weapon to their backs. Silver dragons were extremely fast in the air, being second only to gold dragons, and were also very agile for their size.

"How did they teleport so fast? Thurex roared. "They never did that during the Great War. Don't just hover there licking your wounds, go after them!" he bellowed to his squadron, which all turned and dove after the two silver dragons.

Voltex dove on the legion's formation, with the four blacks and greens close behind them. Cries of "Chromatics incoming!" rose from all the Battle Point legion's soldiers that were not actively engaged against the orcs and Ashram's infantry. The behirs were being beaten back and taking heavy losses in the tooth and claw fight with the land dragons. Being smaller and much weaker, they could not stand against them for very long. The orcs and Morgathian infantry had started to swarm past the land dragons to fight the legion but were stopped by the intense and accurate volleys of arrows and the many long spears of the heavy infantry. The tide was starting to turn until the chromatics appeared.

Colonel Ronson pulled half of his land dragons that had any shield strength left slightly back and oriented them skyward to meet the incoming chromatics. The land dragon crews oriented their ballistae skyward to add to their dragons' breath weapons, to meet the new threat. Jodem quickly landed Vatara and raised his staff, uttering a quick incantation in Draconic. Eight of the land dragons were too injured to continue the fight, which left Ronson with twenty. The ten he pulled back prepared to breathe their fire breath weapons in unison.

Voltex opened his large pale blue jaws, as his large thick nose horn glowed and fired a lightning bolt, which had greater range than the green and black dragons' fiery acid breath weapon. Jodem's magic shield took most of the impact, with the largest land dragon exhausting the last energy of his shield taking the remainder of the deadly energy. He then aimed his staff and fired a meteor swarm spell at Voltex. Six glowing balls of energy streaked in rapid succession at the blue dragon, striking his shield with tremendous force, causing it to alter its diving flight path from the successive impacts. The four trailing chromatics spewed their jets of hot acid as the ten land dragons breathed their fire skyward, along with ten ballista spears fired by their crews. The archers and crossbowmen that could shoot did so, sending hundreds of arrows at the chromatics.

One land dragon was hit by a green dragon's acid stream in the back hindquarter, causing it to wheel around, roaring in pain. One black dragon's acid struck beside a land dragon, killing ten archers standing next to it. The other two acid strikes were stopped by the barrage of the land dragons' fire. The searing hot jets of flame not stopped by the acid struck the four chromatic dragons with a terrific collective force. The fiery strike caused their weakened magic shields to rupture all at once, allowing the ballista spears to freely penetrate. Each chromatic was struck by at least two projectiles. The Battle Point land dragon crews were used to this kind of team fight against the occasional wandering chromatic dragon, which proved very effective against them, as long as they had the better odds. The thick armored dragon hide was too tough for most of the arrows, but at least half a dozen did pierce each of the chromatics.

As Ashram was about to fire a lightning bolt at one of the land dragons, he heard Thurex roar to Voltex to join them in the pursuit of the two silver dragons. This enraged him, for he needed them to continue to attack the legion; he spurred his nightmare steed to intercept the large red dragon. Voltex roared a command for the other dragons to follow him, begrudgingly, for his attack did not have the desired effect he wanted.

Jodem concentrated intensely while uttering a quick Draconic incantation; he aimed his crossbow-like wizard staff and fired a chain lightning spell at the green and black dragons. The twenty-one bluish-white bolts streaked upward in rapid succession and pounded all four dragons as they attempted to ascend following Voltex. Without their shields, and from the rear, Jodem's powerful spell inflicted a tremendous amount of damage to the lesser chromatic dragons, as noted by the burns on their tough hides and violent reactions to the hits.

The black dragons started to turn to exact revenge on this painful strike, but Voltex roared, "Stay in formation, or you'll have to deal with Thurex." The devil or bull horned blacks grumbled but then turned back to follow him. Usually black dragons, being very chaotic by nature, did not listen to orders, especially when angered, but the fear they had of the large demon red dragon forced their obedience.

Talonth and Strikenth were flying as fast as they could to lure the chromatic dragons away from the legion. "Padonan, we will have to break and turn to attack them soon," Lordan said through his crystal. "We are far enough from the legion now, and I want to keep them busy. The demon red dragon has only a small amount of shield power left, and the other red's shield is gone. The blues' shields are at half strength, and the shields of the greens and blacks are gone. We'll split horizontally and come back around to get them in a cross fire, and then split vertically. If we're lucky, they'll hit themselves more than they will hit us."

"Right, sir; which way do you want to break?" the younger dragonrider asked.

"We'll let our dragons decide," the colonel replied with a smile; immediately afterward, they both banked in opposite directions. As the two metallics turned hard, the two blue dragons fired their lightning breath weapons. They were just over three hundred yards behind the silvers and took a long shot. Both bolts sizzled past the silvers' tails, barely missing them, but then Thurex fired his dark crystal-enhanced breath weapon, and the purplish fiery beam streamed out and struck Talonth's shield with a terrific force. Talonth and Lordan felt the powerful blow to the silver dragon's shield.

"Gallanth was not misleading about the enhanced power of these demon dragons," Talonth exclaimed to his rider.

"We will still take him, my friend, but the range he has with this dark crystal melding worries me," Lordan answered his dragon as he banked hard to come around and engage the pursuing chromatics. The faster silvers turned in a tight arc and came back into the opposite sides of the chromatics from their oblique.

Both breathed their icy beam breath weapons at the nearest dragon within range. Strikenth hit the green dragon, Kakol, solidly in the lower left flank. His green hide instantly froze, with pieces of flesh cracking and splitting off the dragon's left leg, side, and tail, severely injuring it. Kakol retaliated by spitting its hot stream of acid, which hit Strikenth on his left wing, but merely splashed off, barely leaving a mark.

"Fool, silver dragon hide is immune to your acid," the blue dragon Klaxtor roared, as he tried to turn to face the attacking silver. Padonan threw his glaive, which hummed through the air and struck the black dragon Batuul, slicing another long gash on his already wounded wing, further making his ability to maintain flight more difficult.

Another hit like that and he will go down, Strikenth said to his rider. Talonth then breathed his icy beam at the black dragon Slyvar, catching it on the right upper shoulder and neck. It reeled from the icy blow, knocking it off course as chunks of frozen black hide shattered and fell off its body from the wound. Lordan fired an energy bolt at the smaller green dragon Saarex, hitting it in the chest as it squared off against Talonth.

The two silvers flew right at each other, and then Talonth dipped slightly and nosed almost straight upward. Strikenth rolled completely over and pulled into a hard dive. Klaxtor fired a chain lightning spell at the two silvers as they performed their separation maneuver. Seventeen white hot lightning bolts shot out from the blue dragon. These were smaller and less powerful than Talonth's and Strikenth's spell, but deadly nonetheless. The first and largest bolt missed both of them, literally streaking in between the two and striking Batuul in the back. The injured black jerked violently up as it absorbed the energy of the bolt. Klaxtor immediately tried to adjust by spreading the other bolts up and down in an attempt to bracket them but only managed to hit Talonth with two and Strikenth with three.

The blue dragon Arathus immediately dove after Strikenth and fired his chain lightning spell. Seventeen bolts shot out of the dragon's outstretched front claws fractions of a second apart. The first several missed the silver dragon, who was agilely twisting and weaving to make a difficult target to zero in on, but four of the bolts struck his shield. Saarex also nosed down to pursue the diving Strikenth. He quickly fired a prismatic burst spell, and six multicolored beams darted out of his long clawed foot. Three beams hit the silver's shield, which still held firm, being at just over half strength.

Strikenth was faster in the dive and quickly outdistanced his pursuers. He pulled up at the last moment to maximize his speed in regaining altitude and doubled back on the chromatics. He unleashed a blast of his icy breath at Arathus; the bluish white beam of pure cold struck the blue dragon's shield, smashing the last amount of its strength and slightly frost burning its indigo blue hide. Padonan threw his glaive, which spun through the air and sliced Saarex's left shoulder and back, causing him to wince from the wound.

Slyvar dove to pursue Strikenth, for with his injured wing, it was easier to dive than to climb. As Strikenth flew past the green and blue dragons he had just attacked, the bull horned black dragon fired a barrage of magic missiles. Fifteen small glowing projectiles streaked out in rapid succession, six of which were absorbed by the silver dragon's shield. The magic missile spell, while effective against humanoid targets, was just an annoyance to a silver dragon. Black dragons, however, had very weak magical abilities and did not possess more powerful spells. This, coupled with the fact that they could only fire their acid breath weapon two to three times a day, put them at a severe disadvantage in a fight with the metallics.

Strikenth was flying too fast to turn and attack the black dragon directly, and his breath weapon needed a few more moments to recharge. As soon as Padonan's glaive reached his hand, he sent it flying back toward Slyvar. The spinning blades tore into the black dragon's injured wing, ripping another hole and slicing into the actual wing arm. This injury was too much, and Slyvar began to lose altitude; he made a barely controlled glide toward the ground.

Talonth kept flying almost straight upward, quickly outdistancing his pursuers. "We've got the two reds and the blue below us; let's attack, my friend," Lordan said to his dragon mate. *I agree, but we must avoid direct combat with the reds as long as possible,* Talonth replied telepathically. *Hold on,* he continued as he prepared for a wing-over maneuver, and Lordan quickly laid his lance across his lap, locked it in on his saddle, and leaned forward to grab the riding straps. Talonth hefted his wings forward, tucked, and rolled over in midair, whipping his tail over to aid the maneuver. The pressure exerted on the rider was intense, but as long as he was prepared for it with the aid of his dragonstone weapon, he could tolerate the move.

The big silver dragon emerged from the wing-over facing straight down, and with one flap he was in a full dive. Letting out a challenge roar, he breathed an icy beam at Thurex, shattering the red dragon's remaining shield strength. The fast maneuver took the chromatic dragons by surprise, as Talonth flew past the demon dragon and swiped Krekon's right shoulder haunch with his front claws, slicing the armored crimson hide. Lordan fired an energy bolt at Klaxtor, hitting his shield, which now was below half strength.

Talonth then flew toward Kakel and collided with the green dragon in midair, sinking both of his front talons into its chest and left side. As the green attempted to reel back and break Talonth's clawed grip, the large silver sunk his massive jaws into the green's long neck. Talonth was almost forty yards long, with a wingspan of sixty-five yards, which made him ten yards longer with a fifteen-yard-wider wingspan than the smaller green dragon, as well as possessing much greater physical strength. Kakel let out a garbled gasp of a roar and tried to swipe Talonth with his right claw, but Lordan leaned over and thrust his mithril-bladed lance into the green dragon's upper neck, finishing him off.

Talonth let the green dragon's limp body go ensuring no one was below, and after it plummeted to the ground, he let out his victory roar. "One down, my friend!" Lordan yelled to his dragon, as a blast of fire from Krekon hit his shield. He immediately folded his wings and dove to evade, as a lightning bolt from Arathus glanced off of his magic shield. The diving silver turned slightly to fire a multispectrum prismatic spray; eight beams then shot out of his left claw. He missed with two, but the other six struck both pursuing dragons equally. This combined spell slowed down the chromatic pair's pursuit enough to allow Talonth to dive out of range and pull up just to face Thurex.

Both dragons immediately fired their breath weapons at each other; the fire and ice would have normally struck in midair and exploded, canceling each other out, but the enhanced power of the dark crystal forced energy back at Talonth's shield. "Move, Talonth!" Lordan yelled. "There are too many to face him directly yet." Lordan's dragon quickly veered right and dove away from the demon red. Just as Thurex moved to pursue Talonth, the silver dragon cast a rainbow shield spell directly behind him, which the large red dragon hit before he could change his direction. The power of the pulsating rainbow shield forced the colossal crimson dragon to glance off his flight path.

As Thurex reeled from the impact of Talonth's prismatic shield, he roared to Krekon and Voltex, who had just arrived with the other injured chromatics. "Voltex, take the squadron over to Arathus and Klaxtor," Thurex ordered, "and keep that other silver dragon busy. Krekon, go now and attack the legion."

"Thurex, if I break from this fight to attack the Alliance soldiers, that silver will pursue and hit me from behind. And with my shield gone, I am especially vulnerable," Krekon roared back at him angrily.

"That is the idea. If we continue this aerial dance, they will pick us apart one by one. We must force them to slow down, or to be decisively engaged, and then jump them," Thurex replied.

"It is not your hide that will be ice burned!" Krekon angrily roared.

"Either ice blasted by him or slashed by me, now go!" Thurex roared back.

Krekon snarled at his larger counterpart and winged toward the armies fighting on the ground several miles away.

"Talonth, the smaller red is heading toward the legion," Lordan quickly exclaimed. *We must intercept him. An unchecked red dragon will wreak havoc on the unprotected legion. The fire from the land dragons will not even slow him down,* Talonth replied as he veered sharply toward the red.

He took the bait, Thurex said to himself as he winged to pursue Talonth, who was now in full speed flight to intercept Krekon. While red dragons were fast flyers, they still fell short of the speed and agility of most metallics. This was especially true of a silver or a gold. Cries of "Chromatic!" rose up from the rear ranks of the legion, as those few soldiers not in active combat prepared for the terrific onslaught from the red dragon.

Talonth caught up to Krekon just before he reached the legion and unleashed an icy bluish beam of pure cold at him, striking his lower back. The red dragon arched violently from the impact and turned to face his attacker, as cries of relief and gratitude from the Alliance soldiers rose from the ground. Talonth hit him before he could breathe his cone of fire, slamming into the red dragon with outstretched claws that sunk into Krekon's left flank and chest. The red dragon roared in pain but did manage to get a quick but powerful counterswipe on Talonth's left shoulder, before the silver could deliver his bite on Krekon's neck. The greenish blue blood oozed from the cuts on Talonth's silvery hide.

Krekon then tried to maneuver his jagged-toothed, gaping jaws at Talonth's left wing, but instead of biting the silvery membrane, he met Lordan's lance, which punctured the tough crimson hide behind his jaw. Just as Talonth was about to hit Krekon with a sunburst beam, Thurex's purplish fire blasted his shield. The large silver dragon had barely recovered from the impact when Thurex slammed into his lower back, delivering a nasty bite to the lower left portion of his haunch. He did not slash Talonth with his claws but rather grasped his upper tail and rear left leg instead, to force him to the ground. Lordan quickly turned around and fired an energy bolt at almost point-blank range into Thurex's neck and shoulder area.

The blast on the crimson hide made Thurex jolt his head back and roared, "You will pay for that, Dragonrider!" Talonth then fired a sunbeam ray from his silvery eyes at Krekon to keep him away. The bright yellow-orange beams partially hit Krekon's underbelly, doing half the normal damage, for it was hard for Talonth to be accurate with Thurex dragging him from the sky. Strikenth and Padonan saw Talonth's predicament and turned to help their friend, but they were met by Voltex's squadron. The blue dragon directed his wing of dragons to send a barrage of spell-based lightning bolts and the blue chromatic's breath weapons to stop him. He had to veer away, being struck by at least ten of the forty bolts directed at him, after he hit one of the greens with an icy beam, which finished it off. His shield was almost gone from the onslaught of fiery bolts, and he now faced eight chromatic dragons.

CHAPTER VII

COUNTERSTRIKE

"Mkel, Talonth is in trouble! We must go," Gallanth said out loud to his rider. Mkel looked over to Tegent, sitting on his griffon, and nodded as he bowed his head in prayer.

"Dear Creator, I pray for the courage to confront this evil; grant Gallanth the strength to answer this challenge," Mkel whispered, as he grabbed the mithril silver triangle on his neck chain, the symbol of the Alliance Triad religion. *Don't worry, my friend, we have his blessings*, Gallanth answered. His gold dragon's confidence always had a soothing effect on Mkel's prebattle anxiety. "Time to spring the trap, my friend," Mkel answered and then scrambled up to his saddle.

Gallanth rose up on all fours and stretched out his wings as Jodem's illusion spell disappeared. With two forward steps and a powerful heft, they were airborne. Tegent's griffon rose up behind and to the left of the gold dragon, to use the upward rushing air ricocheting off of the ground from Gallanth's downdraft to catapult him into the sky. Tegent was accustomed to taking off beside a dragon, which if done in the wrong location could slam even a griffon to the ground.

Strikenth tried again to fly through the phalanx of chromatics and exchanged breath weapon fire with the blues. He struck Voltex's shield with a direct hit from his icy breath weapon, almost blasting him out of the sky. Padonan's spinning glaive sliced the right shoulder of Arathus's indigo blue hide. Klaxtor

312

did manage to hit Strikenth in the side with a lightning bolt that left a nasty burn on his silvery hide. The undeterred silver dragon dove, turning away quickly, and maneuvered around for a second attempt.

Strikenth and Padonan swung up and around to try to break through the wall of chromatic dragons blocking their way. As he charged down into the fray, he fired a sunburst beam that hit and seared through Voltex's shield, striking him in the chest and pushing him back off course. Arathus and Klaxtor fired lightning bolts at him once he was in range; one overshot him, and the other just singed his tail. The silver's speed was greater than the chromatics were used to trying to hit in midair. An icy blast response hit Klaxtor's shield, smashing the remnants of its strength, and struck him with its remaining power on his neck and left shoulder. The blue dragon emitted a high-pitched squeal and veered off.

The determined silver then streaked past the reeling blues and attempted to break through the attacking greens and blacks. A black dragon flew directly in Strikenth's path, and was met with the silver dragon's open talons, which tore into him. One claw grabbed the smaller black's neck, and the other struck its shoulder, with both sinking deep into the rough dark hide. The black dragon was already severely wounded and could not take the impact from the larger and much stronger silver; he was finished.

As Strikenth let the dead black dragon go and roared the Draconic prayer, Padonan threw his glaive at an advancing green dragon, which cut deep into the evergreen hide on its left side, causing it to veer off. A green dragon and a black dragon then hit Strikenth from both flanks, swiping at him with their front claws. The agile silver immediately turned 180 degrees in a split second, slashing the black dragon with his talons and pounding the green with his large dorsal finned tail. This quick action pushed both attackers away, but Strikenth had to back wing quickly to avoid the diving attack from the other two black and green dragons. By this time, the three blues had re-formed and were bearing down on him, so he had to break contact and dive away to come back at them again.

A powerful sunburst beam hit Thurex hard on his flank, knocking him away from Talonth. Gallanth followed up the strike

313

with a deep challenge roar that echoed across the plains. Mkel followed his dragon's attack with an exploding-tipped bolt that struck Krekon's left wing, blowing a good-sized hole in it in spite of its heavily armored density, and forced the red dragon to break away. Talonth shook off the painful wound from the bite and quickly flew away from the reds. "You've entered into the eye of the storm, demon dragon," Gallanth roared.

"Where did you come from, gold dragon?" Thurex snarled defiantly to Gallanth.

"All that matters is where I am going to send you," Gallanth roared back as he moved incredibly fast to intercept him.

"We shall see, monkey servant," the red dragon growled, as he unleashed his last enhanced fire breath at the charging gold dragon. The purplish line of fire partially struck Gallanth's shield as he veered to avoid the full impact, but this didn't even slow him down as he hit Thurex in midair with a resonating thud, as the two colossal bodies collided. Gallanth's front two talons penetrated deep into the red dragon's thick hide, but he couldn't connect with a follow-up bite, as Thurex managed to push himself free of the gold dragon's grip. Gallanth was surprised at his increased strength, for even though red dragons were second only to gold dragons in physical strength, the melding of the dark crystal made this one almost as powerful as him.

Thurex was also not used to aerial wrestling with a dragon that was as strong as he was, so brute force alone would not work.

"Your dark crystal heart gives you great strength, Thurex; too bad it will be of no use to you after I send you to your repentance," Gallanth taunted. "You couldn't even handle a silver dragon on your own. So much for the theory of the all powerful Morgathian selvachs."

"I am no servant, gold dragon. I answer to no one", Thurex roared back angrily.

"Then who sent you here, the death knight overlord? I share a bond with my rider. You are just a pet to serve a human's will, so go back now and cower your head to your master, selvach," Gallanth said, continuing to insult him. The infuriated Thurex roared and lurched forward, hefting his wings down with all his might to charge the hovering gold dragon. This is what Gallanth was hoping for, to play on the renowned red dragon vanity and make him attack, thus throwing him off balance in his rage.

Thurex charged Gallanth with his huge pointed jaws gaping open. Mkel fired a well-aimed exploding mithril-tipped bolt, which struck the red dragon on the top of its head, blowing off one of the two main eye horns at its base above the left eye socket. This was not an easy feat, considering that red dragon hide and horns are the third strongest armor known. The blast knocked Thurex's head to the right and, coupled with a plasma fireball from Gallanth that blasted the red's shoulder, sent him slightly off course. This allowed Gallanth to move up slightly and come down on the charging red dragon, delivering a devastating bite and claw attack on its neck, shoulder, and side.

Gallanth's powerful jaws sank into the base of Thurex's neck, with his thirty-six-inch fangs tearing into the dark crimson hide. Its neck vertebrae were crushed, along with deep claw strikes inflicted on the red dragon's upper neck and side. Nothing can stand up to a gold dragon's powerful crushing bite. It could tear a giant in two, or even snap dragon bones like twigs. The combined strike was too much for Thurex, and he was finished.

Gallanth let out a resounding combined victory roar and prayer for the soul of the red. The deep bellow echoed across the plains, which distracted Krekon in seeing the elder dragon fall. Talonth had banked around hard and came back at the stunned red dragon, hitting him with an icy blast, which was combined with a fire bolt from Lordan's lance. The well-placed strikes seared off his left wing, deeply penetrating the dark red hide, and killed him instantly. He immediately was sent plummeting after his master.

Talonth's roar emanated almost immediately after Gallanth's died down. Both metallic dragons slowly glided toward each other, as Lordan raised his lance in a sign of victory and thanks. Mkel quickly disconnected his crossbow and raised it in a return salute. "Thank you for the help, Gallanth," Talonth spoke out loud to his friend in Draconic.

"For the master of our sister Weir, Eladran, I am glad to be of assistance. Now let's help that young Capital dragon," Gallanth replied with an almost upbeat tone, showing his respect for the fight the two silver dragons had given. They both turned toward the wing of chromatics, with Strikenth still struggling to break past them. They roared to signal their attack and cast a negation spell at their enemies to prevent them from teleporting away. This way, they would have to stay and fight.

"Tegent, we are moving to attack the remaining chromatics. Watch our backs, but keep clear of them, for they will be infuriated at the death of their master," Mkel said through his crystal.

"I'll watch your backs and mine," Tegent said back with a smile as his griffon turned around and began to follow the two metallic dragons.

"I have faith, my minstrel friend," Mkel answered. *Talonth, fall in behind me, for my shield still has strength,* Gallanth conveyed telepathically to the silver dragon, which he immediately maneuvered behind his tail. Voltex and the other three blue dragons instantly moved to intercept the attacking metallic dragons.

"Batuul, come with us. We need at least a two-to-one ratio with this gold dragon. Saarex, lead the other two against the silver, Voltex commanded the black dragon.

"What? I need all the help I can get with this silver, desert dweller, I cannot spare him and we can't teleport out now," the green dragon angrily replied.

"We all have our challenges, now do as you're told or you will have me and the metallics to deal with," Voltex roared back and turned to charge into the fast approaching Gallanth, who then fired a sunburst beam. The powerful light rays struck Arathus directly in the chest and shoulder. The deadly beams penetrated deep into the blue dragon's shoulder, almost flipping him over in midair. The wounded blue squealed in pain and then opened his jaws, firing a lightning bolt at his attacker. Gallanth dodged the electric blast by diving and then quickly rose to avoid the bolt fired by Klaxtor, but a third one from Voltex hit his shield as if they had bracketed him. The invisible barrier still held strong as he continued his attack.

Mkel, fire an exploding bolt at the blue on the left to force him up, Gallanth told his rider. Without hesitation, Mkel took aim and fired the bolt, aiming just under Klaxtor's belly. The small projectile struck the dragon on the left front foot. While this did not do much damage, only injuring the blue's talon, it forced Klaxtor up from the explosion. Gallanth then opened his massive jaws and fired a plasma fireball. The glowing fiery sphere of energy streaked toward Klaxtor and struck him squarely in the base of his neck. The blue dragon immediately fell out of formation from the impact; he was severely injured but was not yet felled.

Talonth emerged from behind Gallanth and fired an icy beam that struck Arathus on the right shoulder and flank, finishing him off. The dead blue nose-dived toward the earth, still smoldering from the hit from Gallanth, and the parts of his hide that were frozen solid by Talonth shattered and flew off of him as he fell.

Voltex immediately attempted to veer away from Gallanth before they met in midair for a tooth and claw fight, but Gallanth caught him and they exchanged slashes. Batuul took advantage of this and dove on Gallanth. The gold dragon's unique power of foresight sensed this, and he tried to maneuver his hindquarter and tail away from the stream of fiery acid the vile black dragon spit at him. Only a small portion of the flaming virulent liquid hit his upper tail, which only circumvented Gallanth's shield because Batuul flew within a couple of yards from him, but it still made him wince.

Getting this close to fire his acid cost the black dragon a high price. Gallanth whirled his huge tail around and struck the attacking chromatic with the hardened plate bone on the end of his tail, which both sliced into its lower back and flank and broke the smaller dragon's rear right leg. Mkel quickly turned his crossbow's swivel mount and fired an exploding-tipped bolt, striking Batuul's right wing and side. Tegent, who had yelled to warn of the attacking black dragon, fired an arrow from his enhanced bow, which struck it on the opposite side. The arrow burrowed deep, transferring the energy given to it by his silver dragonstone into the evil beast.

Mkel quickly cocked his crossbow and fired another exploding-tipped bolt at the injured and fleeing black dragon, which hit it in the center of its lower back. The explosion finished Batuul off, and his power dive turned into a death fall.

Ashram observed the dragon fight, and to his horror, he saw the demon dragon and the other red fall. He had witnessed the power of gold and silver dragons as a young apprentice during the Great War, but they now seemed even stronger. Thurex did not even kill any of the silvers. He knew it was only a matter of time now until the other chromatics were vanquished, and this gold dragon seemed particularly powerful as well as huge. *The dragonriders give them a distinct edge. That must be their weak point. Kill them, and metallics won't be quite as strong,* he thought to himself. "Togar!" he screamed into his dark crystal staff at the dragon spawn chieftain.

"Yes, my lord," the man/dragon creature responded with its deep but raspy hissing voice.

"Bring your entire company to me, and tell that cowardly mountain giant to lead his pod to attack the legion's right flank," the sorcerer ordered.

"Ashram, their land dragons are not vanquished, and Grummel's tribe has not arrived," the mountain giant replied in an irritated tone, as he was beside Togar when Ashram signaled.

"Do as you're told, or I will kill you myself," Ashram ordered.

The giant grumbled and yelled over to the seven common giants congregating behind him, as he picked up his huge spiked mace and shield. The hundred or more dragon spawn creatures launched into the air, following their chieftain, who headed toward the hovering sorcerer's nightmare steed.

Jodem had just finished off the last beholder. The sunburst ray from his staff blasted through the tentacle orb creature, sending it falling to the ground behind the line of soldiers, who were fighting for their lives. Just as he called over to Vatara, the sky erupted in the wing beats and war cries of the company of dragon spawn as they flew over the raging battlefield. *Why didn't they attack the legion?* Jodem said to himself. *They must be going to help the chromatics. The dragonriders!* "Mkel, beware," he said into his crystal. "There is a company of dragon spawn heading your way, and I think they are targeting you, Lordan, and Padonan."

"Thanks for the warning, Jodem," Mkel quickly answered through his seeing crystal.

Then deep echoes of the attacking giants rippled from behind the southern hills, signaling their advance. Jodem started to walk toward the point where the giants were going to come from, when Colonel Ponsellan ordered his reserve to commit and pushed his battalion forward in his personal attempt for glory in winning the battle. General Daddonan screamed through his seeing crystal for him to move back and re-form the line. Before the battalion could readjust, over forty orcs poured through the temporary seam between Ponsellan's men and the adjacent battalion.

The orcs streamed through with weapons raised, screaming and running toward Jodem. The wizard turned and raised his staff, his ruby dragonstone glowing brightly. He uttered a few words in Draconic, and his staff emanated a light pulse that enveloped and stopped the first forty orcs that came through the break in the line. Their dark, sullen, insect-like eyes immediately unfixed, almost as in a trance. Jodem spoke in orc and commanded them, "Protect your sorcerer." As the spell was taking effect, six other orcs from the back of the group ran around their charmed comrades and moved to attack the concentrating wizard.

General Daddonan and Colonel Sheer met them with swords drawn. Daddonan, in spite of being in his late fifties, was surprisingly spry, meeting the first orc with a swift blow to its side. His dragonstone-powered long sword crackled with electricity, which blew the orc to the ground, killing him instantly. Sheer swung his large mithril alloy two-handed sword hard down on the next orc, breaking his raised rusty scimitar and carving through its tattered chain mail vest, sundering the creature. The other four soon fell to their comrades' swords.

"Thank you, gentlemen," Jodem spoke to them as soon as he could break from the concentration of his spell.

"Master Wizard, you need a bodyguard for this fight in facing the giants," Colonel Sheer said with concern.

"I have forty at present," he said looking at the orcs, with the legionnaires fighting their comrades just behind them. "Now I must deal with the giants," he continued.

"Colonel Ronson, send a land dragon team with the Draden wizard and his orcs to halt these big brutes," General Daddonan ordered through his crystal.

"Your help is most appreciated, General," Jodem said.

"Orcs?" Ronson said.

"Relax, Colonel. They belong to the Weir wizard now. Just send your dragons," Daddonan said with a quick smile. "Now Master Wizard, I must deal with an errant, self-serving battalion commander." He then walked over to the battle line. Colonel Ronson called through his seeing crystal to two land dragon crews, who immediately disengaged from the battle. They moved back and to the right to join Jodem and his newly acquired orc platoon as the squad of giants, along with a couple of gnolls and orcs, emerged from behind the small hills to the south. The remaining land dragons readjusted to close the gap in the Alliance line. The Battle Point infantry were finally pushing the orcs and Morgathian infantry back. The odds were now more than evened up, in spite of three points in the line that had broken into open melee.

"Fight, you dogs!" Barlog screamed at his last line of orc reserves as he pushed them forward at the point of his axe. At twenty years old, he was considered middle aged for an orc, but he was very combat experienced in fighting other orc tribes and the human kingdoms of the south and eastern areas that bordered Morgathia. However, he had never fought against so disciplined and well trained a force. Each soldier of the Alliance had the same armor and arms that only chieftains or knights had in all other armies.

Barlog then charged into battle, swinging his axe down on the first Battle Point soldier in front of him. The young legionnaire raised his shield, which was broken by the orc's black iron battle-axe. The pitch-colored axe blade split the metal shield and cut into the soldier's arm. He swung his sword in response to this hit and struck the large orc in the side. His blade did not pierce Barlog's breastplate armor, but it still did not feel good.

The large orc struck the soldier in the face with the handle of the axe, knocking him to the ground. As he raised his axe to finish the wounded soldier off, an older sergeant quickly disengaged his fight and moved in to protect his wounded comrade. He blocked the downward stroke of the black axe with his long sword. The force of the parry made the sergeant step back to keep his balance. Barlog quickly followed this intrusion with a strong swinging blow from the left. The senior legionnaire again blocked it with his sword, and the black iron axe took a chunk of steel out of the blade and almost knocked it out of his hand. The large orc then smashed the terminal end of the axe against his shield, pushing him to the ground.

As Barlog raised his axe to cleave his opponent, the legionnaire spun around and struck his adversary in the leg with his sword. The damaged blade managed to cut through the hierorc's armor and into its thigh. Barlog screamed and brought the axe down onto the sergeant's shield, cutting through it and pushing the soldier back down to the ground as he was attempting to get up. The legionnaire's arm was cut badly, and Barlog stepped on his sword arm, pinning it to the ground. With a quick thrust, the hierorc's blade sliced through the metal strips of the sergeant's banded armor and cut deep into his chest. A normal axe blade would not have been able to do this, for Alliance steel was of the best quality in the world, but black iron had almost the strength of mithril.

Decray and his rangers had just flown back to the battlefield after dropping off the rescued soldiers with the support corps wagon train that was en route from Battle Point; the healers went right to work treating their injuries. The ranger captain observed the dragon spawn company flying toward the dragons fighting off to the north. He ordered his rangers on their griffons to pursue the spawn, when he saw Barlog breaking through the Battle Point line, knocking down several legionnaires in the process.

"Keep those spawn creatures away from the metallics, I'll join you in a couple minutes," Decray spoke into his seeing crystal and then pulled on the reins of the flying rig and directed his griffon to dive toward the battle. The powerful eagle/lion creature pulled up just behind the battling troops, where Barlog had broken through the line. Decry quickly unbuckled his fly straps and jumped off his mount, while drawing his two short swords.

"Orc chieftain," Decray shouted in orc language to Barlog, "raise your axe if you dare!" Barlog ordered three orcs that were with him to attack the ranger. As the first orc met Decray, it raised its sword in an overhead swing. Decray quickly blocked the orc's sword with his left and, in an elf-like quick motion, crouched down and brought his right hand sword over and cut through the orc's leather armor, slicing deep into its abdomen, doubling it over. He then jumped forward, tucked, and rolled, coming up just to pierce the next orc in the chest with both his blades, stopping its advance cold.

Decray's griffon jumped with amazing quickness and slashed the third orc with its front talons, grayish black blood spurting from the three very deep wounds. "Thank you, my lady," Decray quickly said to his mount. Barlog then moved in to engage Decray with a sideways swipe from his axe. The ranger jumped back to avoid the axe blade, which missed him by inches. He then tried to move in and thrust with this short sword, but he had to duck and roll away from Barlog's return axe swing. *Surprisingly quick, this orc is,* Decray said to himself. Instead of going for a killing blow, Decray quickly decided to change his tactics.

Barlog moved in again with a slightly angled downward cleaving stroke. Decray half jumped to the side and parried with his short sword, which took the glancing blow. He deftly aimed an upper cut swing with the short sword in his right hand, landing a well-aimed blow in between armor plates and slicing into the orc's blackish arm. He leaped away as the axe blade cut empty air where his head used to be. Gallanth's enhancement of his swords the day before had paid off, for his blade would have been broken by that huge axe if it had not received the gold dragon's gift.

As he moved around to gain an advantageous position against Barlog, another orc attacked him from the rear. Decray raised both his swords above his head, stopping the downward stroke of the orc's scimitar. He then turned around quickly, disarming the orc, and cross slicing both blades, decapitating the foul insect. As he turned back around, he raised his right sword just in time to parry Barlog's axe. Even the drop of dragon blood could not make the sword strong enough to stop the heavy black axe head from breaking the twenty-inch blade in half. The ranger tried to roll out of the way, but the axe sliced through his studded leather armor, slightly cutting into the skin on his chest.

Decray peeled away from the strike, which saved him from a deeper wound. As he moved, he swung his remaining sword down and sliced into Barlog's left leg, continuing to spin away to get out of his axe's reach. Growling in pain, Barlog raised and swung his axe toward the ranger's head. Anger had gotten the best of the hierorc, for this was a clumsy strike. Decray moved to the right of the blow, stepped on the base of the axe head to both block a return swing and boost his leap, and came down on Barlog's shoulder area, driving his blade to the hilt in between the shoulder and neck plates of his armor.

Barlog screamed in pain and immediately grabbed the hilt, punching Decray in the chest, which knocked him back. The large orc then tried to pull the blade out, but Decray had sprung back to his feet and deftly side kicked the orc on the shoulder, which had the unintentional effect of snapping the sword blade inside his chest. This brought the orc chieftain to his knees, as the grayish black blood spurted from the wound. With a final loud anguished cry, the hierorc fell forward, dead.

A loud cheer rose from the Battle Point soldiers near the scene of the fight. The orcs viewed the death of their chieftain and began to fight more defensively. This would prove to be the turning point in the land battle. Without weapons, Decray knew he would be of limited use, so he grabbed a short spear and an orc scimitar that were lying on the ground and jumped back on his griffon. He quickly strapped himself in, and the large beast spread her brownish tan wings, took a short run, and leaped into the air, heading to rejoin his rangers in the fight with the man/dragon creatures.

Mkel, I need a gem. My synthensium is growing empty, Gallanth said to Mkel, who immediately reached into the small pouch that he kept in his thigh pants pocket. He pulled out the good-sized rough diamond that Ordin had given him for Gallanth. "Here you go," he said, reaching up as far as he could. The gold dragon curled his head back toward his rider and flicked his huge tongue out, taking the precious stone and swallowing it.

It is a good stone, well rounded, it will produce great power, he said. It still amazed Mkel how dragons could produce such immense power from so small an object. Gallanth explained to him that in their second stomach or synthensium, dragons can convert the gems into pure energy of various forms, one minute piece at a time. This was the source of the dragons' incredible magical power and the power for their breath weapons.

They both suddenly heard the hundreds of war cries and roars of the dragon spawn, closing in on the aerial battle between them and the chromatics. Mkel looked back through Markthrea's sight. He saw the company of the creatures coming toward them like a small plague of locust. "Tegent, be on guard, we are about to have a great deal of company from those dragon spawn creatures," Mkel warned the warrior minstrel.

"I'll keep them as busy as possible until you can knock all the chromatics out of the sky," Tegent replied.

"Just be careful, those creatures put up quite a fight the last time we dealt with them, they are very tough," Mkel added as

Gallanth veered slightly left in pursuit of the lead blue dragon. Talonth and Lordan turned right to pursue Klaxtor.

Talonth caught up to Klaxtor quickly because of his wounds. *Finish him off, my rider,* Talonth told Lordan. As soon as he was in range, Lordan took aim and fired an energy bolt at the stuttering blue dragon. The light beam struck the blue in the middle of its back, and with a dying muffled roar, Klaxtor started to spin out of control toward the ground. The big silver then veered toward Strikenth and his fight with the remaining two greens and black. Gallanth moved fast to intercept Voltex, who had dove and turned sharply to evade the pursuing gold dragon.

"A little disheartening, Voltex, usurper of the plains, to see your comrades fall from the sky," Gallanth roared to the fleeing blue dragon. Mkel was lining up a shot at the blue, when he heard the crack of Tegent's arrow striking a spawn to his right rear flank. He quickly turned to see two of the dragon/man creatures bearing down on him from above. He quickly sighted in on the lead spawn and fired. The exploding-tipped bolt struck the creature in the chest, literally blowing him out of the air. He quickly reloaded and killed the second one before it reached Gallanth's wing span. Six more now dove from the left, aiming directly at him with their spears drawn.

Mkel swung his crossbow's swivel mount a quick 270 degrees off of Gallanth's back ridge, took quick aim at the first spawn in his sights, and fired. The creature's left wing was blown off from the resulting explosion, which also injured the spawn immediately beside it. He cocked Markthrea and fired again, almost vaporizing a second spawn. When he cocked the crossbow again, his magazine was empty. "Gallanth, reload!" he shouted. Gallanth turned his head to the left and unleashed a cone of fire that engulfed the four diving dragon spawn, turning them to ashes.

Just as Mkel began to thank Gallanth, the dragon interrupted. "To your back!" he shouted as he raised his tail and smashed the leading spawn in flight. Another was struck by Tegent's arrow and forced out of formation. The trail man/dragon was cut in half by Gallanth's return tail sweep. The three remaining spawn landed on Gallanth's back and began to run toward Mkel. He grabbed the first nonexploding bolt magazine his hand found and quickly loaded it in the bottom of Markthrea. He cocked it and while awkward in trying to twist around to face behind him, he still quickly fired off three bolts at the lead spawn. Mkel was amazed, for it only took one or two shots to down an ogre. *These creatures are tough*, he thought to himself. The fourth shot struck the second spawn in the chest, stopping his advance as his dead kin slid off Gallanth's back.

Mkel raised his right hand, making a fist, and fired a small plasma ball projectile from his dragonstone ring. The explosion blew the injured spawn off of Gallanth's back, killing him in the process. The last spawn rushed Mkel, pointing its large spear at him. Kershan sprang from its scabbard and barely deflected the spear, which glanced off of Mkel's dragon hide-armored jacket. He grasped the sword and swung it back, cutting the spear in half. As the spawn threw the severed spear shaft down, it raised its oversized clawed hand to swipe at Mkel. The thick muscled brown-green arm came down, only to be severed by the mithril blade. Mkel returned the swing and cut the creature from the lower abdomen through its upper rib cage. The dark green blood spurted from the spawn's long deep cut, which ended its life with a gurgling roar as it fell off of Gallanth's back.

Mkel sheathed Kershan and put Markthrea to his shoulder. He took careful aim and shot one of the spawn that was attacking Tegent's griffon in the back. A claw swipe and bite to the neck by the griffon's powerful beak finished another one off. His mount then had to immediately dive to get out of the way from four more that were diving on them.

At least eight squadrons apiece were attacking Strikenth and Talonth, forcing them to break off their attack against the remaining chromatics. Lordan was firing energy bolts as fast as his lance could reenergize, while Padonan's glaive was slicing the wings of several dragon spawn at a throw. The two silvers were also freeze shattering several with each breath weapon unleashed. The chromatics, however, took advantage of the distraction and started hit-and-run strikes against the three metallic dragons. They were getting smarter, for the green and black dragons were moving to attack Gallanth, while Voltex attacked Strikenth and Talonth, trying to take advantage their preoccupation.

As Gallanth was weaving and swerving in the air to not allow the dragon spawn to mass on him, the younger green dragon tried to get too close to spit her acid stream. Her aerial charge was met by a plasma fireball from the gold dragon, which struck her in the neck and chest, killing her instantly. Gallanth's triumph roar was shortened by Saarex's angry reprisal at the death of his mate, and he charged headlong into him.

Gallanth and Mkel were surprised at the speed and rage of the charging green dragon, for the gold dragon was only able to hit him with one of the two sunburst beams from his eyes. A rare occurrence, for Gallanth almost never missed. This angered attack was also unusual, for most chromatic dragons had no emotion or ties to their mates, as did metallic dragons. Saarex's headlong charge was met by Gallanth's claws, and they exchanged swipes. Gallanth rammed his horned head into Saarex's jaw to prevent him from biting his neck. Even though Saarex was large for a green dragon, he was still only two thirds the size of Gallanth, being roughly thirty-three yards long, with a fifty-five-yard wingspan. The gold dragon pushed Saarex back in midair and lunged forward, with his huge jaws ready for a crushing strike.

The injured green tried to push Gallanth out of the way with a claw swipe, but the gold dragon was too big and too strong. Gallanth's jaws clamped down on Saarex's long neck and left shoulder, sinking deep into the forest green armored hide. He shook the green dragon violently, like a doll, demonstrating his sheer strength. This was the death blow for Saarex, with Gallanth's deadly fangs penetrating deep into the green hide, also crushing the strong dragon bones in his neck and shoulder. Gallanth let the dead green dragon go, and it fell end over end as his victory roar echoed across the plain.

"That's another chromatic dragon vanquished," General Daddonan said to the young soldier beside him. "We definitely needed them on our side today."

The remaining black dragon dove on Gallanth from behind, spitting his acid stream. The vile, hot, caustic liquid was blocked by the gold's magic shield, and he quickly whirled around to face the attacking black, smashing four attacking spawn with his wings in the process. Mkel was firing his crossbow as fast as he could, just to keep the man/dragon creatures from massing on him, but their attacks were getting more coordinated. Just then, they heard the war cries of the Battle Point rangers' griffons as they moved in to join the aerial melee.

Mkel always liked griffons. Next to dragons, he thought they were the most majestic creatures in the air. Now he was glad they were here to distract the dragon spawn. The rangers immediately split into five six-man squadrons, with one group flying to in to cover each dragon, and the other two to hunt and intercept the spawn. "Decray has to be rewarded for his bravery and battle prowess," Mkel said to Gallanth. *I agree,* Gallanth replied.

The rangers were firing arrows and crossbow bolts as their griffons sought out direct fights with the dragon spawn. Several griffons flew into the spawn and grappled with them. Their talons could do horrific damage, and their curved, razor sharp beaks could rend an orc in half. Even with this, the spawn still proved formidable foes, although several of the man/dragons started to fall from the sky, with slashed wings and deep wounds from griffon beaks.

The black dragon now facing Gallanth quickly conjured up a shatter spell and charged his bull-like horns with energy. He then launched forward in an attempt to gore Gallanth. His charge bounced off of Gallanth's shield like a ram hitting a stone wall, with the spell energy transferring into the shield.

"If you want a fang and talon fight, chromatic, you cannot magically empower your horns, fool," Gallanth roared at the reeling black dragon, as he summoned up his plasma fireball breath weapon and unleashed the powerful blast, hitting his foe in the chest and underbelly at point-blank range, killing it instantly. Gallanth's roar was also echoed by the six griffons, who in conjunction with Mkel's crossbow were taking a toll on the dragon spawn.

With their reinforcement of the griffon squadrons, Talonth and Strikenth immediately moved to pursue and attack Voltex. While the blue dragon did get a lucky hit on Talonth that took out the last of his shield, he was now fleeing for his life. Blue dragons were reasonably fast in the air, but they were no match for the swift silvers. Voltex knew he could not outrun his pursuers and finally turned around to face them, firing another lightning bolt.

Strikenth and Talonth split to let the bolt pass between them; they came back together and simultaneously breathed their icy beams at Voltex. The bluish white frost rays struck the blue dragon, freezing large portions of his hide and burning deep into his flesh. A final energy bolt from Lordan's lance finished Voltex off. The two silver dragons roared simultaneously in victory and crisscrossed in flight to head back toward the battle.

They both quickly caught up to Gallanth and the griffons. The dragon spawn were almost all vanquished, with only three griffons receiving injuries that forced them to retire and one slain by a mass attack of four spawn. The three metallic dragons, with the aid of the rangers, quickly cleared the sky of the remaining spawn. "Talonth, Strikenth, go and help our Weir wizard with that giant pod that emerged from the south. We will help our Weir mates with the clan that is attacking from the east," Gallanth ordered his two silver dragon friends. In spite of Colonel Lordan outranking Mkel, Gallanth was a gold dragon, therefore senior in status to the two silvers. A unique situation that while slightly tenuous was understood by the dragonriders.

The two parties split, with six griffons following Mkel and Gallanth, and the other twenty trailing Talonth and Strikenth as they all headed to their respective destinations on the battlefield.

The lead two giants had taken the bait. They charged Toderan and Ordin with their clubs raised, ready for what they thought would be an easy victory. When they got to within fifty yards, Ordin raised and threw his hammer. "Seek Donnac," he whispered to his war hammer as it twirled end over end toward the lead giant. It struck the hide-covered common giant directly in the chest with a deafening clap of thunder, literally lifting the thirteen-foot-tall behemoth off its feet. The grotesque monster landed on its back, dead from the impact. Its companion barely had a moment to look back at the fate of its clansmen, when both Dekeen's empowered arrow and Lupek's lightning javelin struck it from opposite sides of the trail.

The power from the arrow and the javelin spun the fourteen-foot giant around and brought it to its knees. Toderan rushed the creature and, with a quick thrust of his holy sword into its heart, felled the beast. This victory was very short lived, for as soon as the second giant slumped to the ground in front of Toderan, four melon-sized rocks were hurled through the air toward the paladin and dwarf. One overshot the duo, and another landed just short, but the other two had to be stopped by their weapons' magic shields. When the rocks hit the invisible force fields, they shattered to dust and debris, but shook the knight and dwarf.

The four giants that threw the rocks then charged from one hundred yards away, fumbling to get another boulder out of their sacks. Dekeen responded by firing an arrow, which hit one of the giants on the left shoulder, causing it to drop its rock and twirling it around from the impact. He followed with another arrow, which hit the grotesque creature in the midsection, causing it to double over. A third arrow hit it right in between the eyes, killing it instantly.

The other three giants continued to advance rapidly, closing the distance between themselves and Toderan and Ordin. Two of the rocks they threw were directed at Ordin, likely because of their intrinsic hatred of their ancestral dwarven enemy. He nimbly dodged the first rock with surprising speed for his stout frame. The second rock he stopped cold with his hammer's shield, as did Toderan with his, but both force fields were starting to weaken.

"Try to catch this, giant!" Ordin shouted as he threw Donnac. The double-headed mithril hammer spun through the air, crackling with energy, and struck the middle giant on the left shoulder, literally flipping him over in midair from the tremendous impact. He landed on his side with a huge thud.

Lupek, having recovered his javelin, threw it at the giant on the right. The pointed spear pierced the giant in the center in its torso, transferring the electrical energy into its barrel chest. The giant gasped in pain and grasped the shaft of the javelin that was sticking out of his side. Lupek then quickly drew his scimitar and moved from his hiding position onto the valley floor.

The third giant ran right at Toderan and Ordin, raising his club over his head. Toderan moved forward to engage the giant, sword and shield in hand. The brute swung its club in a downward stroke; Toderan half dodged and half blocked the six-foot-long thick weapon as it glanced off his shield and hit the ground. The paladin quickly raised and swung his sword down on the giant's right arm. The shimmering blade cut into the giant's thick matted and dirty arm, while also transferring its energy into the beast.

The giant winced, twitching its protruding brow in pain as it dropped its club. It then hit Toderan's shield with its left fist, sending him flying backward. Ordin caught Donnac on its return, jumped and rolled to avoid the brute's swing, and then sprung back up and struck the giant in the left leg. The force of the hammer broke the giant's lower leg, instantly bringing it to its knees. Toderan quickly recovered, moved back to the giant, and delivered a fatal blow to the back of its thick neck. It slumped to the ground, lifeless.

The giant that had been hit by Lupek's javelin now moved to attack his assailant. He swung his club wildly at the ranger, who dove and rolled out of the way, springing up and slashing the beast in the hip with his scimitar, and continued to move to avoid the counter swing. As the thirteen-foot monster turned to face his nimble adversary, Lupek extended his hand, and his javelin tore from the giant's chest and flew back to his awaiting grasp. He twirled it to shake off the dark reddish-purple giant blood and assumed a ready stance to face the large creature.

It then roared and growled, charging the ranger with its club ready to strike. The giant lunged forward and brought its club down hard, trying to crush Lupek. He feigned a move to the right and then jumped to the left just in time as the thick wooden club smashed the ground beside him. He then spun around, slicing the giant's club arm with an upper swing and stabbing the giant's side with his javelin in a backward, overhand thrust. It took two steps back, grasping the wound as the electrical energy burned deep into its side. It began growling and uttering a slurred but deep and raspy curse in the crude tongue of giants.

"You're welcome," Lupek said back to the giant in its own language, with a dubious smile. This enraged the wounded brute, and he charged again, both seven-foot-long arms extended to grasp the ranger. Lupek preempted this charge by diving forward and rolling underneath the giant's grasp, coming up and thrusting his javelin deep into its abdomen, bracing the end of the weapon on the ground to take the brute's weight. As the giant's feet almost came off the ground from its momentum and from being impaled by the javelin, Lupek ducked under its legs, came back around, and thrust his scimitar into its broad back, almost to the hilt. The giant tensed and then went limp and fell. Lupek quickly recovered his weapons and hurried over to Toderan and Ordin.

The giant that Ordin had knocked flat finally got up and started to slowly advance toward the three Draden Weir council members with its left arm dangling, likely broken at the shoulder. Dekeen drew an arrow and shot the giant in the center of its chest, finishing it off. Ordin grumbled, "Pointy-eared elf, that one was mine to finish off."

"I have a bad feeling you will have more opportunities," Dekeen quipped back as the bulk of the giant clan was gathering at the edge of the draw.

"I think they will all charge at once, for even those dim-witted creatures should now realize that sending small groups at us will only lead to them to be piecemealed apart," Toderan said.

"Toderan, you are correct, I count twenty-four remaining in their clan, along with at least that many ogres behind them," Dekeen said calmly, observing the scene with his elvish eyes and maintaining his composure in spite of the impossible odds they were facing.

"Those are not good numbers, even for us," Lupek said as he jogged up to the group, slightly winded.

"Ahh, kill them as they come," Ordin grumbled, holding his hammer ready for battle.

"Mkel, look through your crossbow; our friends are in trouble," Gallanth spoke out loud to his rider. Mkel looked through Markthrea's sight and saw the giant clan ready to attack the small Keystone council group. "Toderan, we're on our way with friends, get out of there now," Mkel spoke into his seeing crystal.

"We will be all right for a short time and should be able to hold them off," Toderan replied, even though there was a hint of relief in his voice. *Stubborn fools*, Mkel thought to himself as he felt Gallanth hasten his wing beats and his hide draw air over it faster to gather speed. This was too close to teleport, and they had to get there fast. It would still take them a minute or two to get there, however, for it was several miles away. Mkel loaded a magazine of explosive-tipped bolts into Markthrea's stock, pre-positioned several more magazines, and took up a good firing position to shoot as soon as they were in range.

Dekeen drew an arrow and fired at the closest giant. The arrow's speed covered the three-hundred-yard distance in the blink of an eye; it struck one of the giants in the chest and exploded, leaving a deep wound. The giant roared and started to charge, quickly followed by his clan. Another arrow found its mark in the center of the same giant's chest, exploding with a precise force that likely crushed his heart. He fell to the ground and was quickly trampled by his compatriots as they advanced, killing him if he wasn't already dead. Dekeen fired another arrow as they rushed to within a hundred yards, and he hit a second giant in the upper thigh, knocking him to the ground, and tripping two others in the process.

Almost simultaneously, the clan began throwing rocks as Ordin's hammer crackled through the air, striking one in the head and crushing its thick ape-like sloped skull. Toderan's and Dekeen's weapons' shields were raised to stop the dozen or more melon-sized rocks that were heading their way. Both of their shields took the multiple impacts as Ordin and Lupek dodged several thrown boulders and raised their magical shields for protection against the hail of hundred-pound stones.

The four looked at each other with an unspoken exchange, knowing that they would soon be overwhelmed, the dragonstones on their weapons glowing intensely for their last stand. The giants were nearly upon them when Gallanth's plasma fireball burst danger close in front of them, keeping the Weir group at the edge of blast radius. The first three giants were killed by the explosion, and ten more were blown off their feet. An exploding bolt from Mkel struck one of the giants in the arm, blowing it off at the shoulder. The gold dragon back winged hard as he landed on one of the giants, claws extended, both stabbing it and crushing it beneath his colossal body, killing it instantly. He raised his head quickly and let loose an ear shattering challenge roar to the giant clan.

The giants that were not knocked down began to move around Gallanth at the command of Grummel, the clan chieftain. The other half of the clan began to move toward the sounds of the ongoing battle. Ten of the remaining nineteen giants immediately obeyed and started to move away toward the armies fighting on the plain. This was likely at the order of Ashram to reinforce his army, which was almost on the verge of defeat. The other nine giants and twenty ogres, including the giant chieftain, who was at least sixteen feet tall, began to encircle the gold dragon and his rider. The chieftain had used this technique to slay a white dragon in the north once, and he wrongly surmised that it would work on this larger gold. Another small group of giants then arrived from the valley as the final part of their clan.

Gallanth coiled his tail and smashed the first giant that moved in range of his back quarter. The flattened arrowhead-shaped plate hit the giant like a huge battle-axe, cutting deep into the giant's side and lifting the large-framed brute off of the ground, throwing it into another giant, knocking both down. He took two steps forward and lunged with his massive jaws open, sinking them into another giant, lifting it up and shaking the huge creature like a doll, and then throwing it thirty yards onto an ogre. Two more giants moved to attack the dragon from each side, clubs raised, but Gallanth stretched his wings out and struck them hard in their faces, knocking them onto their backs. Mkel quickly sighted on the nearest giant and fired, hitting it in the chest with a huge explosion that blasted it to the ground.

Two giants and an ogre then charged in from Gallanth's left rear, their clubs ready to strike. The gold dragon's huge tail swung back around, with the flattened plate decapitating one of the giants. The other two struck Gallanth with their clubs on the base of his tail and side, causing him to wince from the blows. Mkel swung his crossbow on its swivel and fired at the closest ogre, blowing it off its feet and killing it instantly. Gallanth lifted his left rear leg and slashed one of the attacking giants across its midsection, leaving deep wounds and knocking it to the ground with his great strength. Mkel hit another ogre with a bolt, sending the six-hundred-pound scraggly creature thirty feet back, landing burnt and disfigured.

Three other ogres then threw their spears at Gallanth's armored hide near his chest and shoulder. Two bounced off, snapping in half, unable to pierce the gold dragon. The third barely penetrated, doing only slight damage. Gallanth reared back and breathed a billowing cone of fire that incinerated two giants and three ogres. He then did a complete whirling strike with his tail, smashing or slicing all within the forty-five-foot radius that his tail length made spinning in a circle. This devastating maneuver, which few dragons can master, killed four ogres and two of the wounded giants that could not move out of the way, along with injuring two more. It was also done to keep them all from converging on him at once.

Dekeen readied an arrow to fire at the ten giants that were fleeing from the battle with Gallanth and Mkel, but Toderan stopped him. "We will finish the fight here first. Help Mkel and

Gallanth, then join the main fight." They all nodded and began to sprint to the ongoing fight between their friends and the giants and ogres.

Gallanth finished his tail sweep and prepared for the next assault as the energy for his breath weapon recharged. Mkel took advantage of the distance Gallanth achieved by his tail maneuver and fired his crossbow rapidly. He hit two ogres in the midsection, taking body shots rather than aiming for their heads, then shifted his aim to the one of the wounded giants and fired two shots as rapidly as he could. The giant was finished off by the two blasts. He then shot his remaining bolt at the other giant that Gallanth had wounded with his tail strike. The explosion slamming it to the ground, severely wounded.

A blast from Dekeen's arrow struck one of the giants in the back, forcing it to its knees. "Gallanth, our friends are coming," Mkel yelled to his dragon as he quickly reloaded his crossbow. Grummel, seeing the four giants he had previously sent to kill the gold dragon felled, growled another command for all his clan to attack Gallanth. The remaining giants and nine ogres all began to charge at once, with even the large chieftain joining.

Gallanth again breathed out a billowing plume of fire that engulfed two giants and two ogres, burning them to ashes. Mkel fired two bolts before the brutes reached his dragon, striking one giant twice in the chest, forcing it to stop its advance, wounding but not killing the creature. Gallanth brought his tail down on another giant, delivering a fatal blow. The tail plate cut through its shoulder, crushing its clavicle; the dark blood spurted from the deep wound.

The giants and ogres that were not struck by the combined attacks reached Gallanth and started to strike him with their clubs and spears. Gallanth swiped one giant with his left front claw, spinning it to the ground with deep slashes across its shoulder and chest. The other giants and ogres continued to strike Gallanth, with two ogres jumping up and grabbing the dragon's flying harness.

Five giants hit Gallanth with their clubs at points on his neck, side, and tail. The ogres had less luck with the gold dragon's tough hide, breaking most of their spears. The two that jumped up on Gallanth were doing their best to get to Mkel. The ogre that was climbing up Gallanth's left side got to him first. Just as he was about to strike him with his club, Mkel drew Kershan and delivered a backhand downward swing, cutting the ogre's head off just below the chin. Its headless body fell backward onto another ogre climbing up behind it. He then switched the sword to his right hand and thrust it down into the approaching ogre on Gallanth's right side, the point of the blade silencing the creature's rough growl by piercing its forehead and coming out the back of its skull. The creature fell as Mkel pulled the blade from its head.

Gallanth was ready to strike again when the thunderclap of Ordin's hammer struck one of the wounded giants in the back, snapping its vertebrae like a twig. An arrow from Elm hit a second giant in the side, knocking him away from Gallanth. Another crackle of lightning echoed as Lupek's javelin struck still another giant in the shoulder. Toderan was running as fast as his mithril armor and shield allowed, with sword drawn to engage the first enemy he could get to. The gold dragon roared, spreading his wings, striking a giant and an ogre, sending the broken body of the ogre flying through the air and almost flipping the giant over. He then turned to face the chieftain.

Mkel fired a bolt at one of the ogres with too quick an aim, just winging it, but it was still enough to kill it. A follow-up arrow from Dekeen slew one of the wounded giants, which fell with a huge thud. Toderan had finally reached one of the giants, who turned and faced him. Ordin was just behind the group, not being the fastest runner with his short stubby legs, but managed to catch his hammer and move to fight another giant. Lupek reached the giant his javelin struck, recovering his weapon to the discomfort of the brute, and moved in to finish it off.

Gallanth faced the chieftain with a loud growl. The giant started to step back but then stopped, realizing there was no running now. He yelled and charged the dragon, swinging with his club. Gallanth raised his head, avoiding the club swing, and then lunged down in a blinding strike, biting down on the giant's right arm. He crunched the bone while picking the brute up and flung him through the air, also tearing his arm off above the elbow in the process. He slowly walked over to the screaming giant as it rose to its feet. He deftly swiped it with his left claw, leaving deep slashes across its shoulder and chest.

He was now toying with the chieftain, as he knew giants liked to torture their victims. "Does it not feel good, giant chieftain, to be on the receiving end, like so many of your innocent victims?" Gallanth roared in giant tongue. The chieftain scowled through his pain in a last defiant expression, and then Gallanth struck forward with his huge jaws open. His thirty-six-inch-long fangs sunk deep into the giant's chest and abdomen; the brute briefly struggled as he left his parting groan and gurgled as the purplish dark blood spurted from its hideous mouth. Gallanth lifted its lifeless body up and spit it to the ground.

Mkel turned and shot another ogre in the side; the explosion tore it in half. Ordin's hammer fell heavily on a wounded giant's knee, snapping it back with a sickly noise. Once it fell, he finished it off with a blow to its skull. Lupek thrust his javelin into another giant's chest after it weakly missed him with its club. It fell back dead as Dekeen's arrow struck one of the two ogres that was trying to attack Toderan from his back, easily slaying it, while a bolt from Mkel almost took the other ogre's head off.

Toderan moved in and smote the giant he was facing with a powerful overhand swing that sliced his foe from its diaphragm to its pelvis. A paladin's smite with his holy sword can be very deadly. The giant reeled back, grasping his deep wound as the dark blood poured out, but then it raised its club and moved to attack the paladin. His club rang down on Toderan's shield, knocking it from his arm. If it had been anything but mithril, it would have crumpled under the incredible strength of the brute. Toderan then moved to the right, ducked the next swing from the giant's club, and thrust his sword into the beast's side between its ribs. The giant screamed and then fell with a dying gasp.

"Excellent job, gentlemen. Toderan, are you all right?" Mkel yelled.

"Just a little sore, that giant hit hard," the paladin replied with a smile as he picked up his shield and sheathed his sword after wiping the giant blood off of the blade.

"Glad to hear it; take a breath before we go and help the legion. Ordin, I want you to come with me, I need someone to help Tegent watch my back," Mkel said with a smile, for he knew Ordin only liked to fly on Gallanth, versus a griffon or winged horse. The dwarf smiled, walked over to Gallanth, and started to climb up to the rear seat on his flying rig. "I need a drink," Mkel said as he pulled the canteen from his flying gear. The cooling crystal-chilled water was what Mkel needed, although a tankard of ale would have been good too. "Thanks for all your help," Mkel continued.

"No, thank you and Gallanth," Dekeen said with a smile, "there were a lot of giants, and we would not have fared well against so many." Mkel gave a quick half salute as Gallanth bowed his head and shook off the injuries from the giants' clubs.

"Gallanth, are you hurt?" Ordin asked the gold dragon as he climbed up to his saddle.

"I am fine, my good dwarf," Gallanth replied.

"The fight against the chromatics went well then?" Lupek asked Mkel.

"These demon dragons have incredible strength. That unnaturally enhanced red was almost as strong as Gallanth. I don't think that we could have handled that wing by ourselves without Talonth and Strikenth. This increased cooperation among the chromatics is also disconcerting, for they were organized and fought with a ferocity that Gallanth hasn't seen since the Great War," Mkel replied.

"No time to contemplate it now, I want that Morgathian sorcerer captured after we see his army crushed," Gallanth said with an angry tone to his normally deep commanding voice.

"All right, my friend, I'm loaded up and Ordin is ready," Mkel answered his dragon. "Gentlemen, I'll see you in the air."

"Hold on, Master Dwarf," the dragon spoke as he stretched his wings and launched into the air. Toderan, Dekeen, and Lupek then called for their mounts, who emerged from behind the ridge line and landed beside them.

"I was on my last two arrows. Mkel and Gallanth arrived just in time, thank the Creator. We owe them our lives," Dekeen said to his companions who all agreed as they mounted their flying steeds.

General Daddonan dispatched a land dragon team to finish off the wounded black dragon that had crash landed some distance from the battle. This, along with the two he sent with Jodem to deal with the giant pod, had caused him to delay his order for a final push to break the enemy line. The behirs were falling fast in direct fang and talon fights with the land dragons, but with taking out four from the line, he did not have the strength for an all-out assault. He then called Colonel Reddit through his crystal and redirected his cavalry to head off this new giant threat from the east. He looked into his seeing crystal to view the battle between the Draden Weir crew, and now Gallanth and Mkel, with the giant clan. They let ten of the brutes get through but were in the process of killing the bulk of the beasts. Again he was glad they and the two silver dragons were here, or this battle would have been a certain defeat.

The cavalry commander had rallied his remaining forces, having just defeated Ashram's cavalry and gnolls. He had almost all of his battalion minus the few that were killed or wounded from the first fight. His horsemen did not suffer very many casualties thanks to their speed and prowess along with the aid of the coordinated attacks by the dragons and hippogriffs. Daddonan then ordered Colonel Ronson to send two more land dragons to aid the cavalry with this new giant attack. Begrudgingly, the land dragon commander readjusted his remaining forces and sent another pair around to the left to join the cavalry to head off the giants. This stretched his forces even thinner, but they still had the upper hand.

As soon as the two land dragons joined the cavalry, they all oriented and charged toward the onrushing giants. They were immediately met with a hail of thrown rocks from the beasts, which seemed to focus on the land dragons; one took two hits, and the other took one. Four of the other seven rocks struck horses, killing or injuring them and their riders. They all continued their advance to rapidly close the distance between them and the giants to give the beasts minimal time to throw their boulders.

The cavalry flanked the two land dragons in their headlong charge toward their enemy. In spite of being up to fifty feet long, the well-muscled land dragons could keep up with horses for a short distance. Once within one hundred yards, they breathed jets of flame, striking two giants and engulfing them in the searing hot fire. The beasts roared as they fell to their knees and then collapsed. Five of the remaining giants managed to throw more rocks, two of which overshot the charging cavalry, one hit each dragon, and another hit a rider, killing him instantly. Two giants were then struck by ballistae spears from the land dragon crews; immediately afterward, they quickly secured the large crossbow-like weapons and grabbed their spears and short bows to prepare for a close fight.

The two groups collided, with the land dragons lowering their heads and delivering well-placed bites on two giants, pushing them to the ground. Two hundred cavalry riders streamed through the attacking giant pod, thrusting spears and lances into the forward giants. The lead brute received almost twenty spears, piercing his thick hide before he fell dead. All the remaining took at least five successful hits each as the cavalry thundered past them, for these horsemen were veterans at fighting giants. The large brutes did manage to hit five cavalrymen in the charge, killing one and wounding four, who were immediately picked up by their comrades and taken to safety.

The giants reeled from the shock of the cavalry charge but managed to regroup and attempt to attack the land dragons. Each dragon was rushed by three giants wielding their large clubs, while the seventh was headed off by a cavalry platoon. The remaining beasts were pulling the multiple spears sticking from them with their free hands. The first giant to reach the side of one of the land dragons was met by the point of a long spear from one of the crewmen along with an arrow in the chest from another. It snapped the spear in half, leaving one end stuck in its shoulder, and struck the dragon in the side with a thud against its greenish brown hide.

Another giant met the same treatment on the other side of the land dragon while the one attacking from the rear was hit with dragon's tail, smashing it in the side and knocking the twelve-foot-tall brute to the ground. The dragon turned quickly to the left and sunk its jaws into the giant's shoulder and threw it to the ground while striking the other giant with its tail, snapping its neck and killing it. The third giant had gotten up and struck the dragon in the hip with its club, causing it to roar in pain. One of the land dragon's crewmen hit the giant with another arrow as the land dragon limped back a couple of steps away from it, to gain distance for a counterattack. Just then the cavalry came back, attacking the giant from the rear and finishing it off with multiple spears and arrow hits. The other wounded giant met the same fate.

The giants attacking the other land dragon met similar demise, with one being killed by the dragon and the other two finished off by the cavalry's lances. The last standing giant was surrounded by the cavalry and the land dragons. It looked all around at the dozens of spears pointed at it and the two enraged land dragons. The lead paladin called in its own tongue for it to surrender. The protruding brow crumpled in a brief moment of contemplation. Being very cruel but cowardly by nature, the giant laid down its club and lowered its head in a sign of surrender. The injured beast was then escorted to the rear by the land dragons and the troop of cavalry.

The pod led by the mountain giant moved quickly toward the legion, weapons ready to crush anything in their path. Jodem raised his staff and fired a disruption ray at the mountain giant. The clever giant quickly pulled a smaller common giant in front of him to take the spell blast. The bright ray struck the common giant in the chest, wrenching his thick frame before it went limp. The mountain giant towered over his dead common giant type cousin, standing at least five feet taller. He then shrugged it to the ground with ease—attributing to his great strength, for only thunder giants and dragons were stronger than these creatures. He raised his nine-foot-long studded mace and continued the charge with the remaining six common giants.

When the two groups got to within a hundred yards of each other, the giants began to throw rocks and the land dragons breathed their line fire. Six rocks hurtled through the air as one common giant was struck by the cone of fire, searing him over half his body and killing him instantly. The other land dragon hit the mountain giant's huge metal shield, which blocked the fiery blast, but both knocked it out of his large hands and partially melted it. Three rocks glanced off the land dragons, with the other three squashing five of the charmed orcs.

The land dragon crews fired two ballistae spears, which struck two of the lead common giants. Both grabbed the shafts and pulled them out of their midsections with roars of pain. As the two forces came together, the land dragons quickly struck two common giants with deadly bites, lifting them in the air and throwing them aside. The charmed orcs moved in and began to attack three of the other common giants with spears and swords. The mountain giant sprinted in quickly and struck one of the land dragons in the head with his mace, knocking it on its side. The four-man crew spilled out and quickly tried to recover themselves as their dragon roared in pain.

The giant raised his morning star to hit the injured land dragon again, but Jodem beat him to the strike and fired a sunburst beam at the evil brute, so as not to cause any collateral damage to the land dragon or its crew. The mountain giant raised his hand, enacting his spell shield and absorbing some of the power of the wizard's light ray, but it knocked him back several feet as his magic force field gave way, and the remainder of the beam hit him in the chest.

The other land dragon turned to face the mountain giant, who just managed to roll away from its jaws, which clamped down on empty air. Mountain giants were not only incredibly strong, they were also very nimble for their size, making them very dangerous as compared to the common giants or even the ice and fire giants. He moved in and struck the attacking land dragon with his mace, just missing the crew's fighting carriage. Nimble or not, the giant did not dodge the land dragon's tail strike, which hit him in the hip and sent him tumbling to the ground.

A common giant then lumbered in to attack the land dragon, only to meet a claw swipe that slashed the giant's abdomen, forcing it back. The injured land dragon got back up on its feet and shook its head to clear it from the hard hit, with the greenish blood oozing from the wound. Its crew scrambled to get up into the armored carriage on its back. Jodem powered his staff and unleashed a freezing ray at one of the common giants. The icy blast hit it in its upper midsection, freezing a good part of the creature's body solid, which then cracked and burst. Jodem had used several spells fighting the chromatics and beholders, and he was getting down to his last few before his staff would need to fully recharge itself.

The orcs were swarming two of the common giants, who were smashing one with each club strike, but it was like beating crazed hornets away; they were taking their toll on the large brutes. The remaining common giants were now focused on attacking the land dragons, with the mountain giant sprinting toward Jodem. The wizard quickly waved his staff and created an ice wall that encircled the giant, which it ran into and bounced back covered in an icy frost. Enraged, the creature got up roaring, raised his mace, and struck the twenty-inch-thick wall. It cracked but did not give. As he struck it again, Jodem prepared a spell to greet the angered creature.

With a final blow, a portion of the ice wall gave way and the mountain giant stepped out and yelled to Jodem in his dialect, "Wizard, you will now meet your fate."

"Be careful when you play with fire, for you might get burnt, my overconfident brute," he yelled back to the giant, casting a fireball at him. The mountain giant attempted to dodge the large flaming sphere that streaked toward him. He was only partially successful, with the fiery blast hitting him in the side as he jumped away, throwing his large frame farther than he expected. He slowly got up, his right side and back smoking from the flames of the spell blast. Jodem was amazed at the speed of the twenty-foot-tall giant and quickly started to prepare another spell to finish him off.

The mountain giant got up smarting from his burns, with a look of pure ferocity across his smudged bluish white skin. He lifted his mace with his blackened arm and limped toward Jodem. The wizard was preparing another spell, but it would likely be too close to being able to cast it before the giant got to him. Just then an icy beam from above struck the giant, freezing him solid as his final deep shout of pain faded, and then he shattered into hundreds of pieces. Talonth quickly back winged and landed beside Jodem. Strikenth dove and hit a common giant with his icy breath, turning it into a frozen statue before it cracked and shattered under its own weight.

"Thank you for your assistance, Talonth," Jodem nodded to the pair.

"No thanks needed, Master Wizard, your fight with the chromatics earlier and the wounds you inflicted on them greatly helped us in battle. We are just returning the favor," the large silver responded.

"Your wounds are deep, Talonth, you should retire and tend to them with Aloras salve," Jodem responded.

"There will be time for healing later, Master Jodem, but for now there are still enemy on the field," Talonth replied.

"Master Wizard, you know of the dedication of silver dragons," Lordan yelled down to Jodem with a smile. An audible thud distracted them as Jodem's charmed orcs finally felled one of the giants, who had killed all but four of the twenty that had attacked him. The other giant had just crushed the twenty orcs that were fighting him, but evidenced by the multiple broken spears sticking from him, and dozens of bleeding sword and axe slashes, they had not died without taking their toll on the brute.

The wounded giant limped over to the remaining orcs and began to swing sluggishly. It crushed one of the orcs with its club, with the other three attacking it with the same mindless ferocity that helped them kill the first giant. The brute managed to kill the remaining orcs after taking several more hits to its legs and midsection. As it turned, it looked at the silver dragon with an almost fearful expression, which Lordan then hit it with a blast from his lance, finishing it off.

"Those orcs did come in handy after all," Jodem said to Lordan and Talonth.

"Too bad you couldn't do that to the entire army," Lordan quipped.

The land dragons quickly felled the other two giants with almost point-blank blasts of fire. "Gallanth and Mkel just finished off the large giant clan," Talonth explained as he looked to the east.

"Now is the time to destroy this army," Lordan spoke up. "Jodem, we will have to work together to cut off their retreat eastward."

"Gallanth has taken to the air, along with his Weir companions. We must join him," Talonth added.

"We must also not let this Morgathian sorcerer escape. I will meet you by Mkel and Gallanth," Jodem said as he closed his eyes and whispered in elvish into the dragonstone at the end of his staff, calling for Vatara.

"See you in the air," Lordan said, looking down at Jodem and saluting as Talonth took a couple of steps away from Jodem and the land dragons and launched into the air, a cloud of grass and dust rising from the downdraft of his wings.

"Good fight, my little brothers, now take your rest to heal," Talonth spoke in Draconic to the two injured land dragons as he slowly flew a slow circle above them, who then bowed their heads in response. Vatara swooped down and landed beside the wizard. Jodem climbed onto the flying saddle and nudged the giant eagle to take off.

"Excellent job, Lieutenant; you, your men, and your dragons fought well," he yelled to the land dragon crew leader as Vatara took off into the air.

Slyvar was attempting to limp away toward the southwest when the pair of land dragons caught up to him. The injured black chromatic turned to face them, knowing he could not outrun the land-bound Alliance dragons, and there was no lake or river in sight to dive into. He was only seven or eight yards longer than the land dragons and not much stronger, especially being as wounded as he was from the fight with the metallics. He was just about to spit a stream of his vile burning acid when two ballistae spears struck him in the side and upper back. Both spears penetrated the armored black hide, being fired at not more than one hundred yards; close range for the large weapons.

The black dragon then rose up and unleashed a stream of fiery acid at the land dragon on the left. He fired it at the extreme end of his range and was surprised to see the wingless dragons react quickly, with both breathing their jets of fire to block the acid stream. The land dragons then closed in on him in seconds, with their crews holding on hard from the rapid movement. They were bounced around by their mounts running at their top speed, which was just over what a good horse can do. They then split and went to opposite sides of the chromatic to bait it and keep it off guard.

"Come, wingless worms, and face the ferocity of Slyvar," the black dragon boasted. Then one of the land dragons made a false lunge and backed off just as the black dragon attempted to strike with its jaws and sharp bull-like horns. The land dragon on the opposite side then quickly moved in and clamped down on the chromatic's dark shoulder. As Slyvar turned his head around to counterstrike the land dragon, its wingman then lunged quickly and bit down on the black's neck. The two land dragons shook the chromatic, forcing it to its belly and raking it with their front claws. This was enough to finish off the wounded black. Both land dragons raised their heads and bellowed out their victory roars, with a tinge of pride at bringing down a chromatic, most of which referred to their breed as inferior.

"Excellent job, my little brothers," Strikenth roared down to the victorious land dragons, as he and Padonan circled back toward the fighting. The pair had quickly flown to intercept the fleeing Slyvar and help the land dragons defeat him, but they happily did not need their assistance. Gallanth had flown toward the dwindling aerial battle and fired a sunburst beam, killing one of the last manticores that the Battle Point hippogriffs hadn't caught yet.

Below, Ashram's army was starting to break. All the behirs were now slain, as were all the giants, save the one that was captured. The Talon sorcerer himself was finally deciding to get involved in the fight by firing a lightning bolt at a land dragon. The searing charged beam knocked it down from the impact but did not kill it. Upon seeing the destruction of two wings of chromatics, including a red demon dragon, the whole giant clan, and his entire battalion of behirs, he was also having second thoughts. His cavalry was also crushed, as he apparently underestimated the prowess and coordination of his Battle Point opponents. The orc and Morgathian infantry were being routed as well. He now stood alone and rationalized to himself that it was time leave versus actually fighting the Alliance forces to attempt to save the remainder of his army.

The two silver dragons joined Gallanth and the Draden Weir group in the air above the battle, as the remaining hippogriffs began to perform diving attacks against the remnants of Ashram's army. "Talonth, Strikenth, help the hippogriffs cut off the sorcerer's army's retreat, and destroy it if they don't surrender. The sorcerer Ashram is still very dangerous, and your shields are down," Gallanth directed the two silvers as they nodded in acknowledgement. "Jodem, shall we have a talk with the good Talon sorcerer?" he continued with a more upbeat tone. Jodem nodded and smiled at the gold dragon's invitation. Mkel could tell that Gallanth was getting tired. Two major battles back to back, and against such formidable foes, were taking a toll on the large gold dragon. He knew Gallanth wanted this battle over.

Mkel cocked Markthrea and loaded a mithril-tipped exploding bolt to deal maximum damage to the sorcerer's magic shield. "We're going after the Morgathian sorcerer," Mkel shouted back to Ordin.

"Good, I enjoy seeing sorcerers crushed almost as much as giants. No harm intended to Master Jodem," Ordin said with a smile as Mkel looked back at him.

"No harm taken, my friend," Mkel said back. Toderan, Lupek, and Dekeen were following Gallanth and Jodem on their mounts, as they all streamed toward the hovering nightmare. Ashram saw the approaching group and quickly summoned up a spell from his dark crystal-powered staff. Just as Gallanth fired a sunburst beam, Ashram let loose a meteor storm spell. The powerful, glowing fiery projectiles and the intense light beam passed each other with blinding speed. The sunburst beam struck Ashram's shield with a terrific explosion.

Ashram's fiery meteors streaked toward the gold dragon, who took the first hit with his shield and then began to turn, roll, and twirl in the air to dodge the eighteen follow-on fiery projectiles. Only five more hit his shield, with the rest sizzling past him. His magical barrier still held firm.

"Toderan, Tegent, bank to the right; Dekeen and Lupek, go to the left. We will slow him down and prevent him from teleporting out," Mkel said into his crystal to his comrades. He knew they couldn't catch a nightmare, but a winged horse and a giant eagle could at least match its speed and prevent him from turning away from his dragon. Gallanth was gaining on him, however.

"Mkel, we need to take him alive if possible. We must get to the bottom of this increase in aggression," Jodem's voice came through Mkel's crystal.

"If we can, my friend," Mkel answered.

As Gallanth was gaining on the sorcerer's nightmare, he roared an antimagic spell to prevent him from teleporting, although Ashram might be powerful enough to overcome this spell lock, given enough time. Ashram looked back at the pursuing gold dragon, who was now only one hundred yards away. Gallanth summoned up his barrage fireball spell and raised his left front talon, opening his claws, upon which six fireballs formed and streaked out in succession.

Ashram's nightmare dodged the first one by veering hard to the left. He could feel the heat from the flaming projectile as it streamed past him. He couldn't move too far to either side, for he saw the two mounted flyers on both his flanks start to box him in. The second fireball barely missed the demon horse, but as Gallanth was leading the banking nightmare, the third projectile hit the sorcerer's shield with a glancing blow. The fourth fireball struck the magic shield directly, and Ashram shuddered from the impact. The fifth fireball hit his shield and shattered it, bursting through the invisible force field and striking the hindquarter of the nightmare and singeing Ashram's robes. Nightmares possessed very tough hide that was very fire resistant but not fireproof.

"Mkel, down the demon horse with Markthrea," Gallanth said to him.

"No problem, my friend," Mkel answered as he removed the exploding-tip magazine from the crossbow and loaded his standard bolts. He took aim through Markthrea's sight and locked onto the undulating nightmare. The demon horse was very agile and a difficult target. He lined the crosshair in the lead aiming circle and fired, but at the last second, he slipped the sight reticule just outside the circle in his scope. The bolt launched from the crossbow and streaked by the right side of the black steed, missing it by a couple of inches. *Take your time, my rider, I know you can hit it,* Gallanth encouraged Mkel telepathically.

Mkel cocked the crossbow and bore down on the comb of the stock, ensuring a good cheek to stock weld, and acquired a good sight picture with Markthrea's reticle. He moved the crosshairs into the circle to adjust for the lead, carefully gripped the stock with his left hand, and put the pad of his trigger finger on the surface of light trigger. This time he kept the crosshair still and let the black demon horse veer into his sight picture. He then pulled the trigger back in a smooth even motion and fired, taking extra precaution to extend his follow through. The bolt struck the nightmare's hindquarter, burrowing deep inside the tough pitch-colored hide. The sorcerer's steed was flipped sideways from the impact of the lightning fast quarrel, which apparently did a great deal of damage.

Mkel cocked Markthrea and took aim again, giving it a little more lead, and fired. In spite of being wounded, the nightmare was still fairly maneuverable and fast. He had better luck this time, however, and the bolt struck the nightmare's left rib cage after going through the calf of Ashram's left leg. He could hear the sorcerer scream in pain immediately following the roar-like whinny of the nightmare, as the bolt likely punctured its lungs. It immediately began a forceful descent, with the dying demon horse barely maintaining controlled flight. They then crashed onto the grassy plain, with the Talon sorcerer being thrown from his mount and tumbling head over heels before coming to a halt.

Ashram raised himself to his knees by leaning on his staff. Blood was rushing from the wound on his left calf, and the bolt likely had broken one or both of the bones in his leg. Gallanth back winged hard and landed with a terrific thud, almost knocking the Morgathian sorcerer back to the ground. Jodem's eagle landed beside Gallanth, as soon as he furled his wings. Mkel and Jodem dismounted. Gallanth watched the sorcerer with a careful eye, in case he tried to cast a spell. As soon as Mkel slid off of his dragon's front forearm, he leveled his crossbow on Ashram.

Their comrades landed within seconds as the two griffons, eagle, and winged horse set down. "What's the matter, sorcerer? I'm still waiting for you to take care of us. Amazing how the mighty fall," Mkel mocked Ashram's threat from the beginning of the battle. Ashram scowled as he leaned against his staff. "Now that you are a little subdued, what was your objective for this attack? You come here with so powerful a force, although not so much anymore," he taunted the sorcerer.

"Ashram, if you cooperate with us, you will be treated fairly according to Alliance justice," Jodem said, stepping in with his staff slightly glowing to cast a counterspell if necessary.

"Alliance justice? I want none of your mercy or your republic. You will only feel our wrath," the sorcerer lashed back.

"Then it is justice you shall receive for the death and misery you caused today," Toderan spoke as he raised his holy sword, dragonstone glowing.

"Hah, I dismiss your intent, paladin," Ashram spat back, preparing to cast a spell.

"You will be persuaded to help us before justice is administered to you, dark sorcerer. We will see to it," Gallanth's booming voice emanated from above the group. The sorcerer's expression suddenly changed after Gallanth's words. He knew no one could lie in the presence of a gold dragon.

"Death is coming soon to you all," he quipped as he drew a dagger from his robes, sliced his own hand, and grabbed the dark crystal mounted on top of his staff.

"Mkel, fire!" Jodem yelled. Mkel quickly took an instant sight picture, putting the crosshairs on the black robes of the sorcerer, firing as they filled his sight picture. The bolt struck the sorcerer's shoulder just as he vanished.

"Jodem, how did he break Gallanth's spell?" Mkel asked.

"Dark crystal can be temporarily empowered by the sacrifice of a part of the user's life force. It wasn't just blood that Ashram offered the stone. It was years off of his life. They can only do this on extreme circumstances, for it will eventually lead to their early death or worse. The conversion into an undead lich, for Tiamat's blood that empowers the dark crystal stones is as evil and demanding as the arch dragon herself," the wizard explained.

"He and his ilk are only concerned about the present and their own power, wealth, and influence. They do not care about the future," Dekeen lamented.

"One step closer to shaking the talons of Tiamat, or becoming a lich or shadow, dependent on blood to sustain their tortured life," Tegent said with his normal cheerful smile, referring to the sorcerer's hastened path to his own demise by selling his life force to his evil crystal.

"I just hope he didn't see how we teleported the legion in. I don't want our edge compromised to the Morgathians. I know he witnessed the defeat of the behirs by the land dragons as well as the sudden appearance of three of the most powerful dragons in the Alliance," Mkel said.

"I think he was mostly attempting to direct his forces by himself during the battle, and they were taken by surprise by the Battle Point legion. I'm sure he did not see Talonth and Strikenth teleport them here, for he was too busy torturing those legionnaires," Lupek chimed in.

"You're right, but I just wish we could have let Gallanth and Jodem work him over for the information he likely had, regarding these scaled-up operations as of late. Maybe he knew something about the gathering you saw in the Smoking Mountains," Mkel explained.

"In either event, all we can do now is help General Daddonan and our dragonrider friends complete the destruction of the sorcerer's army," Toderan spoke up, always with his no-nonsense comments.

"As always, my good paladin, you are correct. Let's get in the air," Mkel directed. They all gave him a quick nod and moved back to their mounts. As soon as they were ready, the others moved away from Gallanth, and they took to the sky. When all was clear, the big dragon took a couple of steps and launched into the air with a whirlwind of dust, grass, and debris in the wake of his immense wings. They quickly caught up to their friends, and Gallanth and Mkel led them back to the dwindling battle.

Ashram emerged from teleport in the courtyard of his and Lodar's shared fortress on the northwestern border of Morgathia. He collapsed from his wounds and the energy that his dark crystal took from him to break Gallanth's antimagic spell. At his pain-ridden call, several servants rushed to his aid, for the hole in his lower leg was still bleeding and the crossbow bolt that Mkel fired as he teleported out had pierced his upper right shoulder. Another inch or two to the left, and it would have likely killed him.

The slave servants carried him into the fortress hallway and laid him down on the large dining table. A Morgathian cleric came over to him and began to treat his wounds. Lodar soon came into the hall and over to the injured sorcerer. "Ashram, I see you ran into a little trouble," the warlord said with a sinister smile across his scarred face.

"Careful, death knight, I am not so injured that I couldn't cast you into oblivion," Ashram snapped angrily.

"I guess this means that you lost the fight with the Alliance legion," Lodar chided.

"They were heavily reinforced!" the sorcerer yelled back at him through his pain.

"I sent you two wings of chromatics, almost a third of our total dragons, led by a demon red no less, and what returns with you," Lodar chided back.

"They had two large silvers and a huge gold dragon that came out of nowhere, along with an Alliance wizard of considerable power. There were a strong group of allies that had dragonstone weapons. It is as if they knew we were coming, and the legion appeared right in front of my army. A whole legion, well rested and ready to fight," he rambled on. "Ahhhhhhhrrrr, fool!" he screamed as the cleric pulled the bolt out of his shoulder; the sorcerer responded by firing a magic missile into his chest, blowing him back against the wall and killing him instantly. He looked at the other two clerics and scowled, "You'd better be more careful, and get my private stock of Alliance aloras." The two remaining clerics cautiously cast a healing spell over the sorcerer, stemming the blood flow, and then gingerly placed bandages on the wounds.

"Get me wine now," he shouted at one of the dozen or so slaves in the room, who immediately ran out toward the pantry.

"We will have to modify our methods for our plans along their eastern border," Lodar surmised.

"Yes, we have much to talk about, but I need rest first, so leave me now," the sorcerer ordered.

"The whole army, giant clan, and two wings of chromatics, Ashram; the Talon Covenant will not be pleased at your incompetence, and I guess your little back-scratcher Fellaxe did not perform to measure. I also see your dark crystal is taking its toll," Lodar sniped, referring to his skin, which was showing signs of mummification, as Ashram weakly raised his staff, the dark crystal glowing. "All right, I'm leaving, heal well, my lord. I must tend to what army we have left," he said sarcastically as he hurriedly exited the room.

"I will see him eat those words, arrogant warlord," Ashram said to himself as his servants nervously escorted him to his chambers.

Talonth and Strikenth were performing crisscross strafing attacks, freeze shattering dozens of orcs and Morgathian infantry, aided by the blasts from Lordan's lance. Padonan's glaive was also slicing through the ranks with each pass. The Battle Point legionnaires had broken their lines, and they were in a hasty retreat, with some still fighting, and others fleeing.

Colonel Ronson yelled to the fleeing human troops in Morgathian to surrender, adding that they would be spared. Morgathian soldiers were indoctrinated from childhood that Tiamat was their god, and the members of the Talon Council were her high priests. The way of servitude, and unquestioned obedience, was what they demanded to maintain their power to keep the Alliance at bay. They were also told that those who surrendered to the Alliance were fed to the metallic dragons or tortured to death, and that their souls would be forever lost. This, for them, was easy to believe, for that was what was done to most prisoners taken by Morgathia. The families of those soldiers who surrender were also threatened and usually treated with enslavement and sacrifice to the chromatics. However, those who believed in the arch dragon queen that were sacrificed were immediately granted access to paradise, or that was what they are told from a young age. What problem this brought to the Alliance was that there were not many that readily surrendered, with most fighting to the death or usually taking their own lives.

Orcs, however, never surrendered, having a more insect-like obedience to their chieftain and queen, like a termite colony. Quarter was rarely given for prisoners, who were usually eaten but occasionally sold as slaves. The exception to this rule was the hierorcs, who possessed greater intelligence, or at least greater cunning, and surrendered on a rare circumstance.

As their lines broke, the Battle Point archers were quickly re-formed and began to hail arrows and bolts down on the sorcerer's retreating forces. This was aided by the diving attacks from the hippogriffs, griffons, and their riders. The combined attacks, especially from the silver dragons, were quickly decimating their remaining numbers.

The coordinated strikes were keeping most of the fleeing forces contained, along with the cavalry attacks on their flank, but several were making it to the scrub woods at the beginning of the hill country to the south. Gallanth and his group arrived as Talonth and Strikenth had just completed an attack on the forces below.

"Victory!" Colonel Lordan yelled to Mkel with his usual exuberant smile. Mkel quickly drew his sword in a return salute. "We accomplished a great deal today, Captain," he continued. "Two chromatic wings sent to their repentance in the afterworld. A giant clan eliminated along with a rogue mountain giant, and a whole army bent on destruction was crushed and sent fleeing."

"Unfortunately, their sorcerer leader managed to escape," Mkel yelled back.

"No one is perfect. Especially in our business," Lordan replied.

"Is anyone surrendering?" Mkel asked.

"Colonel Ronson offered them surrender in their tongue, but only a couple of takers. The infamous Morgathian propaganda and coercion at work again," Lordan answered.

"I wonder why they didn't carry any banners or regimental colors. They have always done so," Mkel asked rhetorically.

"I don't know, it doesn't make sense to me either," Lordan replied. "Well, let's make another run and finish off whatever strength they have left."

"Sir, you and Talonth, please lead," Mkel stated; it was a gesture of honor for a gold dragonrider to allow a lesser metallic dragon to lead an attack.

"I am honored, Captain; Talonth, let's dive," he yelled to his dragon as the big silver banked and dove, immediately followed by Strikenth and then Gallanth. The sorcerer's army, which numbered over eight thousand at the beginning of the battle, was now down to only a few hundred, as they fought a retreating battle against the Battle Point legion. The three dragons unleashed their breath weapons almost at once, with two icy beams freezing dozens, and Gallanth's cone of fire incinerating even more along a thirty-five-yard-wide, one-hundred-yard-long swath of destruction. Mkel fired two exploding-tipped bolts, Lordan blasted a shot from his lance, and Padonan threw his glaive, slicing many along its deadly course.

"That was the last clump of resistance, sir. We should let the Battle Point cavalry handle the rest, plus you know the Enlightened want us to not waste our gems," Mkel said with a smile.

"Good idea, Mkel. Padonan, we'll land behind the legion," Colonel Lordan ordered.

"Good fight, my brothers," Gallanth's booming deep voice resonated in the air. The two silver dragons slightly bowed their heads in acknowledgment.

The three dragons, followed by Mkel's friends, soared over the legion line as the cavalry charged into the scrub forest in pursuit of the fleeing enemy, with several platoons of infantry right behind them. Mkel could hear loud cheers from the Battle Point soldiers as they back winged and landed. General Daddonan and his small entourage started to walk over to the dragons and their friends that landed just as the dust settled from the three pairs of massive wings that had filled the air in the immediate area.

"The diplomacy will begin after the congratulations," Lordan whispered to Mkel after they slid down to their dragons' forearms. As the general and his staff came up to the dragonriders and their companions, Gallanth and the two silvers did something that no one had seen before. Talonth and Strikenth bowed their heads to Gallanth, who then returned the Draconic salute. All three dragons then bowed their heads to their riders.

"Gallanth, what is this for, my friend?" Mkel asked as a small crowd of the Battle Point soldiers also looked at the unique sight.

"Talonth and Strikenth thanked me for my help in this tough fight, and we all honor our riders for the enhanced strength you give us. For this separates us from our chromatic enemies," the great gold dragon said with a slightly reverent tone in his deep voice. "The power we derive from your love and emotion translates into the fury that the chromatics experienced today. This, for me and for my brothers here, was enough to turn the tide against their numbers and their hatred," Gallanth explained to the surprise of all within earshot of the dragon's booming voice, including their riders.

"I never knew that about the dragons," a seasoned sergeant said out loud as his young soldiers gathered beside him. "I thought that they only derived their great power from eating gems and gold; so much for the POE propaganda. I know the Alliance dragons are renowned for their compassion, but I did not know to this extent."

The support corps wagon trains were almost to the location of the current battle that Gallanth had given telepathically to Desiran, Beckann's unicorn. She was riding up and down the long column that stretched hundreds of yards, to both check on their progress and to give them a little encouragement and confidence in knowing an elven wizard of power was guarding them. Plus the sight of a unicorn was almost as awe inspiring and morale strengthening as a metallic dragon.

Beckann was also watching both the battle that Gallanth and the silvers had just completed and the fight her husband was in with the giants through her staff's dragonstone and her seeing-eye spell. She almost teleported out to join Dekeen, but she knew that would have left the wagon trains defenseless against a powerful opponent. Luckily that did not come to fruition, or that is at least what she thought. Then something started to make her anxious. There was a feeling of evil and magic nearby as they approached the final couple of miles from the battle scene. She spurred Desiran forward to the head of the column, where she felt the presence.

As Beckann rode at full gallop, she began to prepare her staff for a possible fight, muttering several words in Draconic. As she sped by the columns of wagons, all the support troops began to draw their weapons and ready short bows and crossbows for firing. The unicorn had just made it to the head of the column and the cavalry platoon that was also escorting the convoy when she noticed a subtle depression in the ground and vegetation that seemed out of place. She raised her staff and cast an antimagic spell at the depression. Her spell was absorbed by a distortion in the air, causing the area around the depression to flash and then shatter, like the breaking of a mirror. This revealed an assembled force of orcs surrounding a twelve-foot-tall, deep red colored balor in the center, flanked with three trolls. A young Talon sorcerer stepped from behind the demon half-breed creature and yelled out a command to prepare to attack, and then he fired a lightning bolt at Beckann. The deadly bolt was readily absorbed by her spell shield. Desiran then spurred, fiercely gazing at the hybrid demon, her horn glowing in an anticipation of a fight

"Surprised, apprentice?" she asked the younger sorcerer, who crumbled his tanned forehead over his thick black eyebrows. He quickly composed himself and gave the command to attack in Morgathian, at which the balor spread its bat-like wings, brandished its oversized flaming axe, and took to flight. The orcs charged toward Beckann and the wagons. She immediately cast a flame wall spell that forced the orcs to go around. The cavalry behind the elf wizard charged the attacking orcs, even though they were outnumbered at least three to one.

The Morgathian sorcerer whirled his short staff over his head, dark crystal pulsating, and cast a fireball at Beckann. She spurred her unicorn forward, almost launching from its position, the flaming sphere hitting their combined spell shields in the back half of the unicorn, inflicting only a portion of its energy on them. The sorcerer knew from the way she absorbed both spells without much effort that he was facing a powerful wizard. His master Ashram told him the attack on the Battle Point support corps wagons would be a massacre. This was now going to be a tough fight, especially without a mount.

Beckann unleashed a meteor swarm spell, firing six large projectiles of fiery energy at the standing sorcerer. His shield took the impact from all six, but it shook him mightily. He called for the balor in Draconic to aid him in the fight with the elf. The demonic creature immediately turned from his attack on the wagons and headed back to the sorcerer.

Beckann knew she could handle the apprentice sorcerer or the demon, but both at the same time would be a challenge, and all the while also trying to defend the support corps soldiers. She raised a small vial, touched it to her staff, and quickly formed the viscid liquid in the shape of an arrow. She then sent it darting toward the nearest troll, which was trying to catch up to Desiran. The acid arrow sped toward the hideous nine-foot-tall green and brown creature. The missile struck the charging troll, covering it in the caustic liquid, which quickly started to dissolve the creature. Troll skin, while tough and rubbery, was very susceptible to acid attacks. It let out a shrill cry as it fell, with its skin smoking as it dissolved.

Desiran galloped fast around the sorcerer as Beckann prepared another spell; three orcs then ran toward the charging unicorn. The large brilliant white mount lowered its head and speared the first orc, slicing it through its side, killing it instantly. Beckann whirled her staff over her head, bringing it down on the second orc as they galloped past. The power from her dragonstone staff blew the orc off its feet, sending it flying. The large unicorn trampled over the third orc like it wasn't even there.

A large fireball struck the ground in front of Beckann, causing Desiran to rear up from her charge. While the blast was a miss, the secondary effects of the spell were absorbed by their magic shields. The balor then dove on the elf, his flaming axe poised to strike, but Beckann parried the powerful blow with her staff.

An amazing feat, the junior Talon sorcerer thought to himself at how a thin female elf could parry such a mighty blow from the balor's oversized axe, not knowing that she had hastily cast an energy sword spell on her own staff. As Beckann stopped, her blonde silvery hair blew in the rush of hot air from the fireball explosion, and her blue-violet eyes glared skyward as she extended her staff and cast a chain lightning spell. Bolts of white hot lightning fired in rapid succession from the dragonstone, as she bracketed the balor. It attempted to evade but the fourth bolt found its mark as well as the next several. The demon was knocked off of its flight path as Beckann's bolts slammed into its magic shield.

The fifth hit smashed the balor's shield, and two more sent it spiraling out of the sky, crashing with a good thud behind the apprentice sorcerer. She then turned Desiran toward him and prepared another spell as a lightning bolt struck their shield. The unicorn lowered its head and charged. Beckann pointed her staff forward like a paladin's lance and uttered a few words in Draconic, as a disruption ray beamed toward the sorcerer. The bright beam hit his shield, shattering it, causing him to be knocked on his backside. Just as he got up, he barely ducked in time as the unicorn's horn sliced into his shoulder, twirling him around and onto the ground, clutching the bleeding laceration.

Beckann edged Desiran toward the balor as it just started to rise from its crash landing. The unicorn lowered its horn again as it charged, with the demon raising its flaming axe to strike. Beckann knew that the balor was on its last legs; she didn't want to waste a more powerful spell on it, so she quickly spoke the Draconic word for sword. At once her staff's dragonstone projected an image of a sword made of light energy in front of her, which then solidified. She sent the energy blade forward and directed it to strike the balor from its left. As the demon parried the blow from the glowing sword, Desiran charged headlong at it and gored it in the center of its chest. The yellow-white horn easily sunk into the dark reddish dragon-like hide, its magical energy transferring into the evil creature. Desiran pulled back quickly to avoid a claw slash or a swing from the demon's large axe; the dark purplish blood dripped from her horn and poured from its chest. It fell to its knees, one oversized clawed hand clutching its wound, the other driving the axe into the ground, its flames extinguishing.

"Back to the underworld, demon spawn," Beckann confidently scowled at the dying balor; it fell forward, vanquished, but then it exploded. Her shield held against the blast, but the tremor was ferocious. A disintegration ray then hit her spell shield from the rear. The deadly beam was stopped but did a great deal of damage to the elf's and unicorn's magic shields. They turned around to face the sorcerer, who had a look of surprise in not getting the effect that he quite desired by his most powerful spell.

She then spurred Desiran forward toward the sorcerer, the light sword staying right with them.

Without his shield, the sorcerer knew he was now almost defenseless, but he quickly prepared another spell, even though the dark crystal in his staff was nearing the end of the power he could summon from it. Beckann wanted to capture this young upstart rather than vanquish him for whatever knowledge he might possess, but she would not endanger her unicorn either. As she bore down on him, he managed to conjure up a freezing ray spell and fired it at her at the last second before she was upon him, but his quick aim and the nimbleness of Desiran caused the icy beam to only glance the shield of the powerful unicorn.

She then directed her conjured sword to move in and strike him; he parried the first blow with his black iron staff. The hovering light sword struck at him again, and again, until a final cleaving strike severed the staff in half, knocking him to the ground. "Yield, dark sorcerer, and your life shall be spared," she commanded.

"Never, I know what you Alliance vermin do to prisoners. And I will not have my family put in the dungeons of Aserghul," the sorcerer spat back at her.

"Surely, even though you are young, you do not believe the Morgathian propaganda and lies they spew about the Alliance?" she asked him.

"I know what I am told," he said, "and I know what happens to the families of those that surrender. They are sacrificed to the chromatics to pay for our cowardice and regain honor from Tiamat."

"Your loyalties are misplaced, and as for your surrender, you will be protected and kept in secrecy by the elves and the Weir. That you have my promise," she offered to him.

"I can only offer this, elf!" he screamed as he took the half of his staff that had the dark crystal and thrust it into his chest. The pointed end of the staff pierced his heart, and the black purplish crystal absorbed into his body. He fell back convulsing as the dark energy transferred into him, as he repeated an incantation in the chromatic dialect of Draconic. His whole body became immersed in a dark light that drew in the two closest orcs, and then he burst. When the debris from the explosion subsided, two balors appeared; he had transformed the orcs in his dying move, and they now stood in front of Beckann and her mount. Just as the demon on the left raised his dark crimson claw to cast a spell, a powerful bolt of lightning struck it, as the holy Draconic word uttered by Watterseth echoed like a clap of thunder across the plain. The tall Weir cleric cast his most powerful smiting spell, and coupled with the power of his holy mace, it utterly destroyed the demon, shattering it, while also containing its death throes explosion.

"Thought you could use the help, my lady, plus I live to smite demons," the cleric shouted to her as he galloped up on a borrowed Battle Point warhorse.

"Any help is always appreciated, my dear holy man. Now we still have this one last problem to deal with," Beckann said, turning to the other balor, who was just getting up from being knocked down from his companion's dying implosion. The demon raised his non-sword hand and spoke in Draconic, as he cast a fire storm spell, which unleashed a torrent of flames that engulfed the riders and their mounts. Both their spell shields held firm, especially Watterseth's, for his defensive power against evil magic rivaled Jodem's.

Watterseth cast a powerful dispel ray that eradicated both the flames and the balor's shield. Beckann then sent her light sword to attack the demon. As it was parrying the blows from the spell sword, Watterseth prepared another spell from his mace. "I'll give him a sonic blast to injure him, then you send him back to hell," Watterseth told Beckann, who nodded an acknowledgment.

As the balor thrust the spell sword away, he took to the air to gain some type of advantage on his powerful adversaries. The Draden Weir cleric tapped his mithril mace against his breastplate armor to give it a slight vibration and then directed an intense and focused beam of sonic force at the demon. He struck the balor in the torso, which sent it reeling back to the ground. Beckann's light sword immediately flew over to engage the demon, who barely parried the first blow but was unsuccessful at blocking the second thrust, which burrowed deep into its midsection, expending its last energy into the vile creature, killing it. Its death throe explosion was far enough away from anything that it had no effect.

"That's one for the Weir and the support corps, my dear," Watterseth said.

"The Battle Point cavalry and their support soldiers have handled the orcs. That spry little female soldier even felled two," Beckann said, but she was interrupted by the screams of two troll as they charged at them, claws raised. "I will take care of this one," she stated as she raised her staff, the dragonstone glowing as she cast a domination spell over one of the trolls. "Protect your master," she spoke to it in orcish, upon which the charmed troll immediately turned on its companion and a fight to the death ensued. The two trolls then started to tear each other apart. The cavalry would finish off whatever was left. A cheer arose from all the Battle Point soldiers as a sign of victory and thanks for the assistance Beckann and Watterseth gave them in defeating the powerful foes.

"I have to tend to their wounded, my lady," Watterseth said as they started to ride over to the wagons where they had collected the wounded soldiers from the fight with the orcs.

"No one on our side was killed, but they have ten wounded, my dear holy man," Beckann informed him as she quickly surveyed the support corps wagons and the cavalry platoon.

"That will be solved soon, and bless you, my lady," Watterseth replied. The support corps captain in charge of the train started to get the wagons moving again to facilitate the supplies getting to the village, but a small contingent remained behind to get his own wounded back as well. Beckann nodded to him to let him know that she would accompany the wagon train the remainder of the way to battlefield.

"Dragonriders, Master Wizard, Weir soldiers; many thanks for a job well done. You have saved countless Alliance lives and defeated a powerful force bent on our destruction. Please let me call for healers for your dragons," General Daddonan stated.

"Have your healers tend to your wounded first, General Daddonan, we dragons heal quickly," Gallanth spoke out.

"I understand, my good Gallanth, but Talonth's wounds look deep," the general replied.

"I will be all right, General. Your healers can apply aloras after all your men are treated," Talonth explained.

"Yes, but if it weren't for you all, there wouldn't be many of my men left to attend to," Daddonan lightly argued back.

"It is our honor to serve your brave legion," Strikenth said to ensure solidarity among the dragons.

"I understand, my good dragons. I underestimated the stubbornness of dragonkind," General Daddonan said with a half smile as he turned his head toward the three dragonriders standing beside him, all chuckling slightly. "The cavalry and the hippogriffs riders are chasing down the fleeing remnants of the sorcerer's army. My men are now collecting anything of interest in their encampment and cleaning up bodies for burning and burial."

This was a standard Alliance practice, to burn all but human corpses, which were buried. It was as much a guard against disease as a final deference to your enemies. The chromatic carcasses would be taken back to the capital and several other Weirs to be skinned and processed for armor and weapons. The bones, organs, and hide would all be utilized. Their synthensiums will be transformed into powerful components for the Alliance wizards to be made into potions and other elixirs. This was also done so that they could not be made into weapons for those who could not control them or those who would use them for evil or selfish purposes.

"General, we could use a couple of men to help us apply the aloras salve we carry with us, if you could spare a few. They do not need to be healers," Mkel said. General Daddonan immediately pulled his seeing crystal and spoke Colonel Ponsellan and Colonel Sheer's names. Both responded very quickly.

"Gentlemen, I need a platoon to help the dragonriders apply aloras to their noble mounts," Daddonan requested.

"Sir, I have to reorganize my men and tally enemy killed ...," Ponsellan started to whine, but Colonel Sheer interrupted him: "I will send a platoon over immediately." He knew that Ponsellan was attempting to claim more of the Morgathian and orc dead as credited from his battalion, as much to make up for his almost fatal mistake during the battle as for his own sense of personal glory.

He may have it, Sheer thought to himself, as he called to one of his company commanders who had the most strength left after the battle to send over a platoon to the dragons. The infantry captain had to almost shout to his men to be quiet for the exuberance of getting a chance to get that close to a dragon. He quickly picked one of his platoons and sent them off.

The platoon jogged over to the metallic dragons with surprising speed, considering they had just finished a tough battle and were all still in full armor. The lieutenant yelled to his men to fall into line and turned to face the dragonriders. "At your service sir," he spoke plainly to General Daddonan but with a hint of excitement as he rendered a hand salute.

"Lieutenant, have your men ground their weapons and armor and break into three sections, one for each of the dragonriders," General Daddonan ordered.

"Yes sir," he replied, saluted the general again, and then turned to his men. "First squad to Gallanth, second squad to Talonth, and third squad to Strikenth," he ordered. His squad sergeants replied with a salute and immediately started to have their men stow their equipment in a line, and then they moved toward the respective dragons. Mkel, Lordan, and Padonan walked them to their mounts and handed the large jars of the healing salve while giving them instructions on how to apply the aloras and how to take care while they were climbing on the dragons.

One young soldier had just applied an aloras-soaked cloth onto one of Talonth's wounds, when he noticed the greenish-blue blood almost grab the cloth and drain the salve from it. "Sergeant, did you see that? Its blood is alive," the startled soldier yelled.

"It is, lad; dragon blood carries its own life force. How do you think they make dragonstone weapons, or even heating and cooling crystals? This is also how they heal quickly and derive much of their power," the sergeant explained to his charge.

"Your sergeant is correct," Talonth spoke to the startled and slightly embarrassed young legionnaire.

"We thank your men for their help, sir. This will allow them heal even faster. They will be back to full strength in a day or two now," Colonel Lordan told General Daddonan.

"Anything for our Alliance dragons; speaking of that, which one of you will be staying out here until we clean this mess up and get everyone back to Handsdown, and eventually to Battle Point?" he asked.

Lordan gave Mkel a quick wink as if to say he knew this was coming. Jodem then spoke up, "General, all three of these mighty dragons have been injured in this great fight. They need to take their leave to return to their Weirs to rest in case of another conflict. I will request a Capital dragon to stay behind for a day or so to help cover your clearing out of any leftover resistance, and I will stay as well if necessary."

"Master Wizard, I am honored by your offer of assistance and both know of and have seen your power, but I am concerned about the return of more chromatic dragons and fear you would be overwhelmed without metallic support," General Daddonan expressed his concerns.

"General, Gallanth and I have to return to Draden, for our envoy from Freiland is expected to arrive any day now," Mkel responded, "and we must prepare for the monthly senate meeting in Draconia. I might be requested to testify regarding the POE senators calling for a reduction in veteran benefits and budget decreases for the military. You have my word, sir, that if a chromatic threat arises, Gallanth and I will be by your side in the blink of an eye. Plus Gallanth doesn't sense any impending attacks, especially from chromatics, and he has a sense of these things." Mkel was attempting to avoid an argumentative situation while also giving a promise based on the renowned gold dragon power of foresight.

"Sir, I talked to General Becknor a couple of minutes ago on my seeing crystal. He is sending Bagram and Tigrenth from the Capital Wing to stay with the legion until you return to Battle Point," Padonan said. "They will be arriving within the hour with an entourage to view the battlefield and talk to you and your senior commanders, as well as to pick up the chromatic carcasses."

"That is good news; I look forward to seeing General Becknor, and I have confidence in your Capital Wing brother lieutenant, Strikenth," Daddonan acknowledged as he nodded to the silver dragon. Lordan met eye contact with Padonan to acknowledge a good call.

"General, as soon as the aloras salve is applied to our dragons' wounds, we must take to the air to collect the chromatics' treasure hoards. We will divide it when we get it back at Handsdown," Mkel explained.

"Dragonriders, I would ask that you bring it back here first, so my men can see it with their own eyes. Then you can take it back to Handsdown, where I will have my legion's money managers meet you. They will have containers for you to take your portions back to your Weirs. The question now is, how will we divide it?" Daddonan asked.

"Sir, with Colonel Lordan's and Lieutenant Padonan's concurrence, I suggest that whatever we bring back, Battle Point keep half, with the other half split three ways between us," Mkel suggested.

"I concur, your men have fought hard and well today, but I must insist on you personally ensuring that the families of the slain legionnaires be given a bonus over the normal pension due to a veteran's surviving family," Lordan insisted.

"I will personally see to it, my good colonel," Daddonan replied with a determined smile.

"Padonan, is Strikenth strong enough to gather treasure?" Mkel asked.

"The chromatics fought fiercely, and he is injured, but between our dragon's healing powers and the aloras salve, my friend will be up to collecting the spoils of victory," Padonan answered with his usual half smile.

"Let's redistribute a little treasure. I almost feel like an Enlightened senator," Lordan joked; all those around him started to laugh at his sideways insult to the Enlightened senators' misguided and false premise of wealth distribution. They feigned their concern for the poor and pushed to give free welfare to those that did not deserve it, in exchange for votes. All three dragonriders remounted, as the Battle Point soldiers backed away from the dragons.

"Good hunting, my friends," General Daddonan yelled to them. They all waved as their dragons turned and took a couple of steps to get the forward momentum to take off without knocking the soldiers on the ground off their feet with the downdraft of their wings.

"Where are they going, sir?" one of the soldiers standing close to General Daddonan asked.

"To bring back a little gold and treasure for the legion," Daddonan explained. "They are going to collect the slain chromatics' treasure hoards. It is a kind of battle spoils for a victorious dragon to take their opponent's treasure; for chromatics prize their accumulated wealth almost above their own lives. It is also a final insult to them to have their stolen treasures used for good, and especially for the people of the Alliance."

Gallanth emerged from teleport in the low mountain ranges that lie over the border of the northwestern Morgathian lands. He sharply veered to the right and descended toward a particularly strange rock outcropping on the side the lower mountain. He took the mental picture from Thurex of the location of his lair before he died to ascertain the general location. *I smell his lair on the south side of this mountain,* Gallanth said to Mkel. "This land is desolate, and the farm fields look poorly maintained in the valley," Mkel stated as he looked through his crossbow sight. *It is the sign of oppression and collectivism,* Gallanth answered as he banked around the rocky mountainside. Mkel was surprised to not hear the beating of chromatic wings to challenge their presence in the evil dragons' own territory. *I think that the demon dragon was not challenged in these lands, even by his chromatic kin. This would also explain the desolation of the area,* Gallanth explained, answering his rider's mental question, *and we likely killed all the chromatics in this portion of the region, for even under the service of Tiamat and the Morgathian Empire, they still need a large expanse of territory, and Morgathia stretches three thousand miles by three thousand miles. This will create many openings for younger, hungry chromatics to take their place.*

This would also mean that his lair would likely not be guarded, Gallanth continued, *for chromatic dragons, especially reds, are extremely protective over their hoards and do not trust anyone or anything around them.* Gallanth started to back wing and hover just in front of a large outcropping that opened to a huge cave. "It isn't very well hidden, my friend," Mkel stated.

"He did not fear anything save Tiamat herself, or the Usurper Five, and I am surprised he was serving under that Morgathian sorcerer. While he was a Talon sorcerer, he was not powerful enough to subjugate a dragon of that strength. There must have been something else motivating him. A possible pact with the Talon Council in exchange for the ritual of his demonization process with the dark crystal," Gallanth surmised.

"Yes, this with what Vorgalla told us at Handsdown lends to a great deal of intrigue with the list of recent events. We will have to see what the General's Council's advisors and the Wizard Council of Thirteen can piece together, as well as Eladra if she is willing to help," Mkel theorized.

"It will also make this month's senate gathering interesting. Now let us see what Thurex used to guard his treasure, Gallanth said. As he hovered closer to the landing, a force wall spell repelled him.

"Simple but effective; let us see how powerful his legacy spells are," Gallanth said as he backed off and fired a sunburst beam from his golden eyes and followed it up by a plasma fireball. Mkel fired an exploding-tipped bolt at the same time. The magic shield glowed and shook from the combined impacts and then gave way as its magically derived light disappeared. Gallanth then landed on the outcropping and furled his wings. He walked into the large cave, in which he barely fit, being slightly larger than the vanquished red dragon. Dragons can cast legacy spells that will remain intact with their power by using a drop of their blood to give it energy. *Stay mounted, my friend. It is not uncommon for chromatics to place multiple traps in their lairs.*

Mkel lowered the mithril alloy crystal visor on his helmet, which also allowed him to see in the dark, as it was powered by a small dragonstone, and made sure the two spell shields from his dragonstone weapons were at full strength. The cave was scarred with several scorch marks on the walls and littered with hundreds of blackened bones on the ground. Mkel guessed they were sacrifices given to the red dragon as tribute, for they loved the taste of human flesh, especially young maidens and children. All of a sudden, Gallanth's head and neck were engulfed in flames. His quick reaction, magic shield, and tough, almost fireproof hide kept the flames from causing him any injuries, but it would have killed or severely injured a chromatic dragon. Mkel's shields from both Markthrea and Kershan protected him from being burnt. Gallanth backed away from the wall of flame and raised his left talon, invoking a freezing ray spell. The icy beam extinguished the flames, and he then proceeded deeper into the mountain.

The cave opened up to a larger chamber, approximately one hundred fifty yards across, with a roof that rose fifty yards above the floor. A huge mound of gold and silver coins was piled in the middle of the chamber, along with various artifacts and precious gemstones. Gallanth scanned the hoard quickly and was just about to step into the chamber when he backed off. *Mkel, fire a bolt at the treasure,* he said telepathically. Mkel quickly replaced his exploding-tipped bolt with a standard one and fired. Just as the projectile streaked into the large room, an icy beam shot across the chamber entrance and was reflected multiple times throughout the cave. It finally subsided and froze the whole inside of the cavern.

"Clever Thurex, he had the ice trap focused from one side of the cave and reflected it off the mirror polished opposite side to strike an intruder multiple times if they entered and did not know the command to nullify it. This was meant for a rival red dragon in particular, not very trusting of their own kind," Gallanth surmised. "I estimate just over a half a million gold, silver, and platinum coins, and at least one hundred fifty good quality gems. A sizable hoard, but not quite what I expected him to have. If you look over here, there are marks in the stone floor that indicate he removed over half of his treasure very recently, which doesn't make sense for a red dragon. Especially a demon red, for they do not part with their hoard easily; this is curious."

"Well, in any event, the remainder is the Alliance's now, save several of those gems for us and Silvanth. What do you say about giving that fortress at the entrance of the valley a little visit, my friend?" Mkel asked.

"I think a small dose of retribution is in order. We'll make one pass to give them something to think about and then return with the treasure." Gallanth perked up, liking the idea. He walked back through the cave to the flat rock outcropping and spread his wings. "We will strike them hard and fast, coming in low, flying only a few dozen yards above the river."

"I will hit the right tower with an exploding bolt, you hit the left tower with a fireball, and we'll fly over the wall, knocking off anyone defending it. Maybe you can give them a spell to choke on when we pass over the fortress?" Mkel suggested as he proposed a quick plan as Gallanth leaped from the ledge and nose-dived toward the river far below. He dove almost straight down to gain speed and pulled up barely a hundred feet above the river. The speed of the maneuver forced Mkel to brace himself against his crossbow mount, but he recovered and prepared Markthrea to fire.

As they got to within a half mile from the fortress, he could see the defenders on the wall and towers finally recognize the threat that was coming their way. *Not much they can do about it now*, Mkel thought to himself as he lined the crosshairs of Markthrea's sight on the right tower. He could feel Gallanth's neck and body tense up as he gathered the plasma fireball together from deep in his synthensium. The large gold then unleashed the glowing fiery ball of energy, which streaked toward the left tower. Mkel waited a few seconds and fired. Both projectiles impacted within a second of each other, blowing great holes in the towers and actually crumbling the top of the left tower that Gallanth had struck.

The soldiers on the wall did not have time to load their ballista, and the archers who did manage to fire arrows either missed Gallanth or bounced them off his heavily armored hide and magic shield. The gold dragon streaked just over the parapets, sending several Morgathian soldiers hurtling toward the ground from the windblast. As Gallanth flew over the fortress courtyard, he cast an incendiary cloud spell over the barracks building. A dark reddish black cloud of sparking vapor emanated from his mouth and descended on the stone building and enshrouded it, causing it to enflate. Dozens of Morgathian soldiers began running out choking and then succumbed to the flames. Gallanth lowered his tail, hitting the opposite wall with his rounded arrowhead-shaped plate, taking out a five-yard by ten-yard section of the blackened stone face.

"Lord Ashram, an Alliance gold dragon is attacking the fortress; you must come out and help us defend the castle." Ashram's apprentice sorcerer ran into his master's bedroom chamber with Lodar close behind him.

"I am in no shape to do anything now; go and face it yourself," Ashram screamed back to the young dark-haired sorcerer.

"Ashram, you are the cause of this attack by not dealing with it in the unsettled lands, the castle is getting pounded!" Lodar shouted back.

"Then get your cowardly men to fire the ballistae and chase it away. If it is attacking alone, it is here for a simple raid, now leave me to my rest," the sorcerer commanded as the two hurriedly left before Ashram could cast a spell at them.

"What are we going to do?" the apprentice asked Lodar.

"You are going to face that dragon while I get my men mobilized to mass ballistae fires on it," he scowled at the young sorcerer, who gulped in fear.

Gallanth soared away from the fortress and began to turn back for a final return strike. "I wonder if Ashram will come answer our challenge to his home fortress," Mkel said.

"I smell his presence, but he is still deep within the castle," he responded. Gallanth made a lazy turn and headed back toward the fortress. A lightning bolt came from the middle of the courtyard in front of the keep, striking his shield.

"An apprentice sorcerer of Ashram, foolish to engage us," Gallanth spoke as his golden eyes glowed in preparation to fire a sunburst beam. Mkel quickly loaded a mithril pointed bolt in his crossbow and began to acquire a good aim on the sorcerer. Gallanth fired the sunburst beam before he even flew over the fortress wall, striking the apprentice sorcerer's shield and smashing it. As Gallanth flew over the wall, Mkel fired his bolt, which streaked toward the sorcerer. The bolt sunk into the black-robed sorcerer's chest just above his heart. He gasped in pain and then sunk to his knees and doubled over, dead. The mithril tip also nicked the dark crystal on his staff, which started to vibrate and then erupted in a violent explosion, killing several soldiers near him.

Gallanth roared, and a billow of searing hot dragon fire emanated from his open jaws, engulfing the stables, dozens of Morgathian soldiers, and several wagons on the riverside of the courtyard in flames. The remaining Morgathian soldiers on the wall had managed to ready two ballistae and fired as Gallanth streaked over the wall. The first spear missed altogether, and the second managed to strike him in the upper tail but barely penetrated his tough hide and fell out. It only was able to get past his shield because it was fired at extremely close range. He gave two flaps of his great wings to gain altitude above the range of the remaining Morgathian ballistae, and then he roared an insult, calling them cruel cowards and headed back to Thurex's lair to gather the treasure.

Mkel swung his crossbow around, took aim at one of the ballistae, and fired an exploding bolt. He hit it just left of center, blowing it apart and sending its crew flying. "That will keep them thinking for a while," Mkel said with pleasure.

"It will serve as a reminder that their lands are still susceptible to our attacks. Hold on, my rider," Gallanth added as he inverted in flight and sent a meteor swarm spell, with its six fiery projectiles hurtling toward the fortress wall. Each struck the side of the fortress, blowing three large holes in the wall. This coupled with the structural damage already done to the two towers collapsed a good section of the castle wall. Mkel grinned at the results as they flew back up the steep valley.

They landed back on Thurex's ledge and walked into the cave and the red dragon's treasure chamber. He stood in the middle of the pile of gold, silver, and gems, and spread his wings.

"First I'll make it hard for another chromatic to use this lair," he said to Mkel, casting a shatter spell through an enhanced roar on the cave entrance that likely echoed down the valley. The spell caused the rock over the entrance to shake and begin to crack. He and Mkel then focused on the plain by the fresh battlefield. Gallanth could see no one was in the vicinity through the general's seeing crystal, and in a flash, they and the treasure were gone.

They emerged back at the rear of the battlefield, surrounded by the demon dragon's treasure. General Daddonan's chief of staff ordered guards posted around it immediately, so as to not tempt the legionnaires. Talonth emerged almost beside Gallanth, with a slightly smaller pile of booty.

"Good strike on the sorcerer's fortress, my brother. We would have joined you, but I sensed at least two wings of chromatics inbound to challenge us for their kin's treasure, the silver dragon said to Gallanth.

"We have seen enough killing among dragons today, but there is always tomorrow," Gallanth replied with the best sense of humor that a dragon could muster. Both dragons then leaped into the air and disappeared simultaneously, just at Strikenth appeared with another pile of treasure. Within time, all thirteen chromatics' treasure hoards were returned, with Strikenth and Padonan dripping wet from the last mission.

"Get a little wet, Lieutenant?" Mkel yelled over to Padonan.

"The black dragon had his hoard underwater, vile chromatic stench," Padonan replied with a smile, as he tried to wipe the swampy water off of his dragon hide riding armor. "A bath we will need, my friend," he told his dragon.

"I agree," Strikenth replied.

"How much do you think you all collected?" General Daddonan asked as the dragonriders dismounted.

"Gallanth estimates that there is over three and a half million coins, of which a tenth are platinum, a third are gold, and the rest equal amounts of silver and copper. He has also sensed over eight hundred gems of worth," Mkel conveyed his dragon's assessment. "The dragons will consolidate the piles, and they want each legionnaire to grab one hundred drachlars, or the equivalent of that amount," Mkel explained. "Plus we still must collect the treasure from that demon blue dragon, along with the black and green that we killed over Handsdown. That will only add to the booty we have gathered."

"Captain, I understand that, but do the dragons realize that there are over three thousand soldiers on the field, and several hundred more back at Handsdown and on the support corps wagons heading here now?" General Daddonan inquired.

"Yes sir, they do, and they estimate that it will take almost four hundred thousand drachlars to give that amount out, which will leave roughly three million or more for us of to divide four ways. As for the gems, we will also divide them in four parts as well, sir," Mkel explained, although he could clearly see that the general was not overly excited about this new plan for the redistribution of the booty. But since the dragons had fought for it, and collected it, he did not have much choice. Mkel knew that this was like giving the soldiers a year's pay as a bonus, which after this fight; they all felt they deserved.

"Well, if that is what the dragons want, we will comply. Colonel Sykes, make this transfer happen in an orderly manner," the general ordered.

"Yes sir," the senior colonel replied with a salute, turning to organize the transfer with the commanders on the ground. The dragons began to push the piles of coins and treasure together as the Battle Point soldiers began to stir and line up for their bonus. The dragonriders then quickly remounted, and after Gallanth gave Talonth and Strikenth the image from the black and green dragons from the previous battle, they took off. Their treasure was quickly collected and brought back to the field without incident, besides the normal spells and traps that protected the hoards. The demon blue dragon had a fairly substantial treasure, being just over three hundred thousand coins, and a good crop of gems. The other two dragons had very small hoards, with barely one hundred thousand from each of them.

The soldiers were very happy as they lined up and collected their coins, each legionnaire either bowing or verbally thanking the three dragons and riders for the gift. "Now those are happy soldiers, and out here the Enlightened senators won't know to tax them on it," Padonan said to his fellow dragonriders and the Draden group standing with them, who laughed at his joke.

"They deserve it after this fight. This is probably the biggest battle the Alliance Army has fought since the Great War. There have been skirmishes of battalion strength, but not a whole legion committed. The dragons have been the Alliance's hammer for the last thirty years," Lordan explained.

"You are right, Colonel, but with the incidents of the last two days, I think that trend is unfortunately over. I am concerned about the recent events, plus what that drow sorceress told us, as well as the appearance of these demon, berserker, and talon dragons. I feel the Morgathians are up to something big," Jodem further surmised.

"Well, time will tell, but you all know that the Enlightened senators will attempt to explain this as an anomaly. If not just to justify their latest budget cut proposals to the military," Toderan said with disgust. "Especially that imbecile Senator Tekend from Ferranor and that wolf-bitch Senator Hilrodra from Atlean." Toderan almost spat the words.

"Tell us how you really feel, my friend, but I wholeheartedly agree with you and would rather fight another demon dragon than have to testify in front of them at the end of the week," Mkel lamented.

"You will do fine, my young friend. We will go over your speech when we get back to Draden," Jodem said confidently to his charge.

"Yes, we all wish you luck with the likes of them, Captain," General Daddonan said, giving a nod of encouragement.

"We all know you will do well, for you will be talking from the heart," Lordan added.

"It seems strange that I am invited to speak in front of the senate, just because of my father and his sacrifice," Mkel asked.

"It is really for your work for veterans' rights and your research with the University in Draconia and their scholars for war effects on veterans. It was instrumental in getting more funds from the senate for their benefits and medicines," Lupek gave his friend an encouraging comment.

"Well, for the wife of a former premier, Hilrodra seems to forget that her inept husband is out of power. It does astonish me that the POEs are as popular as they are, with their anti-Alliance and antidragon views and attitudes," Padonan added.

"I agree with Toderan's words regarding the nature of the two prominent senators and their seemingly fanatical devotion to their political causes, along with their desire for the dismantling of the military and the redistribution of the Weir's earned wealth to all of their mindless followers," General Daddonan said.

"At least we still have the majority in the senate to trump the black iron tongues of the Enlightened, and Premier Reagresh is on our side," Tegent said with a smile.

"It's hard to understand how a veteran can have that much hatred for the very organization that they served and gave them the ability to become a public official in the first place. It's almost as if the arbitrator guilds are involved in a conspiracy against the very country that they represent, and they have the majority of the magistrates with them. Since they can't win with an open forum of their ideas and policies at the ballot, they are attempting to match and usurp the good will and prestige that the dragons promote through gifts of other citizens' gold, court rulings, and legal actions," Mkel theorized.

"There seems to be a trend in the way your magistrates have been conducting their rulings in your courts that is definitively anti-Alliance and antidragon," Dekeen said. "You humans are strange beings, in that some members of your species not only do not appreciate what gives them freedom and prosperity, but actively plot and scheme against it. Their attitude would be a mystery, but it is easily explained by a false sense of guilt from their success, and an intense emptiness they have in their souls." Dekeen surmised with his normal elven objectivity and rapier-like perception.

373

"As always, your analysis of the situation is as penetrating as your arrows," Mkel agreed with his elven friend.

"Something will eventually yield. The Alliance can't continue on the course that was set by former Premier Bilenton," Toderan theorized.

"Yes, our problems definitely began under Bilenton's tenure in office," Mkel said, "and we are still feeling his unique legacy today: less than a third of the legions we had during the Great War, and less than half the warships for the navy. We are lucky that he or the Enlightened senators could not touch the Weirs' treasure accounts and that we have a degree of independence from the senate and the rest of the Alliance military, as far as funding and action." Mkel expressed his feelings regarding the former premier and the current internal political fight that the Alliance was embroiled in. "I know that Premier Reagresh has been attempting to correct these issues and a great deal more, but it is an uphill battle with the Party of the Enlightened causing so much trouble in the senate."

"You all should feel grateful for your independent status that your Weirs enjoy," General Daddonan said. "Being at the mercy of the senate for funding can be a problem at times. Luckily, here at Battle Point, we do have a small amount of autonomy being a thousand miles from the Alliance border. However, it is not as much freedom as the dragons and Weirs maintain. I envy you on that point."

"Well, sir, it looks like most of your men have had their fill of dragon booty," Colonel Lordan said to General Daddonan. "All we have to do now is divvy up the quality gems."

"Gallanth senses just over eight hundred gems that could be used for either dragonstones or the dragons' synthensiums. I know your land dragons have used many in this battle, but so have our mates. We will have to separate them judiciously, sir," Mkel said to General Daddonan.

"You're correct, Captain. I trust your dragons have already identified all the gems they would like," Daddonan inquired.

"Yes sir, they are very vital to our efforts. Gallanth burnt through three in just this fight alone," Mkel answered.

"It still amazes me how the dragons can derive so much energy and power from such a small object," Daddonan rhetorically asked.

"It's all about their synthensium, sir. That special organ they possess, coupled with their unique blood, gives them this ability; thank the Creator they can, or we would all be dead men," Lordan explained.

"All magic is derived in some way from dragons," Dekeen commented.

"You are right there, Colonel," Daddonan said. "Their power has defended us time and time again. From the great gold and silver metallics, to our humble land dragons, we owe them much."

"I wouldn't underscore the land dragons too quickly, sir. They have been the mainstay and backbone of the Alliance Army since the Great War. They can take on almost any opponent, save chromatics, and usually come out on top," Mkel said, defending the land dragons' contribution.

"Don't get me wrong; I truly appreciate what our land dragons have done for us," Daddonan stated quickly, "especially those we have in service here at Battle Point. The threat of them, our hippogriffs, and cavalry keep this region in check, between the nomadic Kaskar horse clans to the north, and the constantly warring middle kingdoms to the south and east. Their strength has allowed us to be the true middle ground and the center of trade, which greatly contributes to our prosperity out here in the frontier of the unsettled lands."

"We understand, my good general; wait," Jodem started to speak when he suddenly turned to the west, at the same time Gallanth raised his head and turned in the same direction.

"Valianth is arriving, with Lionoth and Tigrenth right behind him," Mkel said, getting the thought from Gallanth.

"Their power of foresight is amazing," General Daddonan exclaimed. "Valianth, who is with him, Captain?"

"General Becknor and Colonel Therosvet are mounted on Valianth. Bagram and Delker are alone on their dragons, sir," Mkel answered with a half smile, for he was glad to see Delker, as well as his mentors and leaders. Delker had been a soldier and a young sergeant in the Draden Weir's infantry company under Mkel's command. He then was chosen to soul bond with Lionoth after his rider died of old age, at two hundred twenty. He was sorry to see him go, but the Alliance and Lionoth gained a good dragonrider.

The three Capital dragons emerged from teleport and then circled around the battlefield, eventually landing behind Gallanth and the two silvers. General Becknor and Colonel Therosvet sprung off Valianth quickly, very spry for their age, Mkel thought to himself. Bagram and Delker were also quick to dismount their silver dragons. They walked over to the assembled group at a brisk pace. Gallanth nodded to give his respectful salute to the second most senior dragon in the Alliance, second only to Michenth himself, even though it was widely known that he was slightly stronger and larger than Valianth.

"Sir," Colonel Lordan and Captain Mkel quickly put their right fist over their heart, giving the dragonrider salute to General Becknor, being the highest ranking military officer and dragonrider. General Daddonan walked over to meet Becknor and shook his hand.

"Becknor, my friend, good to see you out here in the middle of nowhere," General Daddonan greeted his comrade.

"I heard you have had a tough fight out here in the last three days. Valianth relayed the messages from Strikenth and Gallanth that you fought two full wings of chromatics. There were also these new demon dragons and a talon dragon type? We also saw images of the Morgathian behir snake dragons, the man/dragon creatures called dragon spawn, and a whole army led by a Morgathian sorcerer. Master Wizard Jodem reported the presence of drow and Shidan assassins. I'd say you all were busy," Becknor stated in his greeting. "Captain Mkel, the good Battle Point general was lucky you and Gallanth were visiting when you did, or there might have been a drastically different outcome of the events of the last several days." Becknor shook Mkel's hand with his normal warm but quick smile. He then shook Lordan's and Padonan's hands and acknowledged the rest of those assembled, congratulating them for their successful fight.

"Master Wizard Jodem, your service is again appreciated. Master Hestal is eager to talk to you about the events here when you come to Draconia. Toderan, my favorite paladin, I see you are no worse for wear," Becknor greeted Toderan, who had worked with General Becknor years ago, before he came to Draden Weir to be the senior Weir sergeant.

"The giants were slower than I was, sir," Toderan replied to Becknor.

"That dent in your armor tells me that at least one wasn't too slow. Just be careful next time," Becknor replied. "Gentlemen, I want to congratulate you all for your victory. You took on great odds and prevailed, for this was the biggest fight since the Great War." Mkel noticed the dragonrider general rub his left hand where a scar from an annihilation sphere was still visible. It amazed Mkel that the wound from over thirty years ago would still bother him, but he understood that those dark spheres had an unnatural and evil energy. This was how it could still affect Michenth to this date. "I expect all here to touch crystals so I and Colonel Therosvet can review what happened," the general requested. All present gave a quick acknowledgment. "Daddonan, what was your final casualty count?"

"We had twenty-four killed and fifty-two wounded; unfortunately sir," General Daddonan replied. "We also lost four hippogriffs and had ten more wounded, along with nine land dragons with serious injuries and five more with lesser wounds. The support corps wagons are now en route to move the dead and wounded back to Handsdown and then to Battle Point. The more serious wounded were carried out by hippogriff as soon as the battle subsided. While we mourn our dead, we could have lost the whole legion today if it wasn't for our friends and allies from Draden, Eladran, and Capital Weirs."

"We will transport your wounded land dragons and those hippogriffs that cannot fly back to Battle Point," Becknor offered. "Delker with Lionoth and Bagram with Tigrenth will remain here to provide protection to the legion as you move back to Handsdown, in case the Morgathians decide to attack again. Your honored dead will be given full military burials, with the Capital Wing performing an overflight in their honor."

"That would be of great help, my friend," General Daddonan told Becknor. "Those nine wounded land dragons could use a lift to Battle Point, as well as several of our hippogriffs. We also thank you for Lionoth's and Tigrenth's service and your sentiment."

"We are pleased to support those in the eye of the storm," Therosvet stated, "and more pleased to deliver the hammer if we are called upon," he continued as he grabbed his mithril mace with its large diamond dragonstone mounted on the top of the weapon. Mkel knew of its power; it could deliver destructive blows like Ordin's hammer and fire sunburst beams like Lordan's lance and Becknor's sword. During the Great War, Therosvet was said to have personally killed a dozen giants and even a few chromatics almost single-handedly.

Becknor's sword was also a legendary weapon. It was pure mithril like Kershan, but a straight blade or long sword. It mounted a huge diamond dragonstone from Michenth in the pommel, which gave it amazing power. It could either fire a sunburst beam or empower the blade with that same energy for a devastating strike. This sword was the most feared in all of the Alliance and, likely, the world.

"All right, gentlemen, we shall talk more at Draconia next week when the Dragon Council and I, with the Alliance generals, can review all the events of the last few days. We will also discuss what your rangers uncovered in the Fire Mountains, Captain Mkel, so we can determine courses of action there. And Mkel, I need to talk to you before you depart," Becknor stated.

The general motioned Mkel away from the gathered group. "Mkel, I wanted to tell you that the Enlightened senators are preparing to confront you on your testimony to the Senate next week," Becknor said. "There are rumors that they will specifically go after you in any way they can to discredit you. I know Gallanth and Jodem will be by your side, but I also suggest you bring your Weir's arbitrator as a precaution."

"No problem, sir, Captain Fogellem is very learned in the law, and in spite of that, he's still a good guy," Mkel said with a smile, to which Becknor gave a quick laugh.

"I know you and Gallanth have been through a lot the last few days, and I want you and your fellow Weir council members to stand down for the week," the general said with a warm but concerned smile. "I am afraid that the fight you could have with the POE senators could be just as challenging as the one you had with the chromatics."

"I understand, sir, but I will be all right, and I will have Gallanth and Jodem behind me as well as the arbitrator in front of me to take their arrows," Mkel again said with a grin.

"I have faith, young dragonrider, and we will see what tricks they have in store for us this time. I will be there as well, but remember to have your council get some rest, as well as your garrison, for I have fear they will need it all too soon with the forces gathering in the Fire Mountains. Tell your rangers they did a good job in scouting out that area, and get Toderan to rest even though that will be a challenge unto itself," Becknor stated with his toothy smile.

While Becknor was of medium height and thin build, he eloquently managed to inspire both respect and authority with his demeanor. His short brown hair and green eyes added certain gentleness to his determined persona.

"I will try, sir, and thank you for the warning," Mkel answered.

"Dragonriders must look out for each other, Captain, for if the POEs had their way, we would all be sent flying across the western ocean, never to be seen again until they realized how much our society depends on us. And then they would blame us for leaving in the first place," Becknor joked.

"Again understandable, sir," Mkel answered.

"I understand you and Gallanth tentatively agreed to a defense pact with Battle Point?" Becknor asked.

"I still have to give Colonel Wierangan a chance to hear the proposal, since he is the Draden regiment commander. It is a matter of courtesy," Mkel replied.

"I have faith that he will not give you a difficult time about it, for I already talked to General Craigor, who agrees to the idea. Especially after these last two attacks," he said with a wink. "We are making arrangements to get a few dragons out here very soon, which would alleviate your duel defensive role. All right, get on your way, and get some of the land dragons back to Battle Point. Then you, your friends, and your treasure, go back to Keystone Weir."

Mkel gave the general the dragonrider salute and walked back to the group. General Becknor walked off with General Daddonan to discuss matters on the Battle Point situation. Mkel walked back to the group of his friends and fellow dragonriders.

"What did he say?" Lordan inquired.

"He just wanted to talk about the senate gathering next week and my testimony, and told us to get the injured land dragons back as soon as possible," Mkel answered. "Gentlemen, let's get ready to go. Gallanth and I have to take one of the wounded land dragons back to Battle Point first, then we will take the treasure to Handsdown, then back home to Draden. General Becknor told us to stand down until the Honors Day games and the senate assembly in Draconia next month. This shouldn't be a problem, with Lawrent arriving soon with his pirates," Mkel said with a smile. Ordin and Tegent seemed very pleased with this, for they knew the drinking and festivities that would take place at the Weir to celebrate the transfer of goods that the Freiland raiders always had to trade. They also just enjoyed the general celebration and camaraderie with their allies from the island kingdom to the west.

Most of their trading with the Alliance dealt with gems and foodstuffs, of which the latter were rare fish and seafood as well as spices and other exotics wines and ales. They kept perishables from spoiling with the cooling crystals that they received from the Alliance in trade. It was known that they sometimes dealt in the prisoner slave trade, even though this practice was illegal in the Alliance and in Freiland. This was a part of the treaty that the kingdom of Freiland agreed to in their defensive pact with the Alliance, but on the high seas and in their raiding of Morgathian lands, the Southern Ontaror and eastern island kingdoms, and other unfriendly lands, many practices were hard to enforce and were overlooked. The Freiland raiders were excellent mariners and taught the Alliance Navy many lessons. They were generally loosely banded privateers preying on Morgathian, Shidanese, and non-Alliance-aligned kingdoms that supported the Blood Wolf pirate packs. Even the Alliance Navy looked the other way with their dealings with those nefarious groups.

Mkel always looked forward to Lawrent coming to Draden Weir. The raider captain had the typical Freiland outlook on life: it was to be lived to the fullest. He had served with Mkel on and off for several years and was made the official Freiland ambassador to Draden Weir. This was a special title for a scoundrel such as he. In any event, the Weir always livened up when the Freiland raider sea serpent ships were docked by Draden Weir along the Severic. The Weir was the farthest point that was navigable up the Severic River from the sea and Sauric Bay in Draconia. Up to High Mountain Weir, it was too shallow for anything but barges and small boats.

"Mkel, go ahead with Gallanth and take the wounded land dragon on the far left back to Battle Point. We will watch over the treasure and secure the gems before you get back," Jodem told him.

"No problem, my friend, we will be back quickly," Mkel replied.

"I think this gem here," Jodem said, pulling out a good-sized ruby, "will make an excellent dragonstone. We'll have Gallanth inspect it to make sure. These gems will refill our coffers for Gallanth, for in spite of the two Ordin gave you a couple of days ago, we are running a little low, and we can't have Gallanth be out of precious stones. Where would he get the energy to power that bad breath of his?" Jodem joked.

"It is just a little more than that, but if any good has come out of these last several days, besides a little more stability to this region, it is that we will go home with a little to offer the Weir and Draden," Mkel replied.

"We'll give Mayor Guilored a little token of our hard-fought reward. I don't think the chromatics will mind," Jodem said, again with a small smile.

"As long as the mayor appreciates it," Mkel quipped back.

"Gold and silver are the universal gifts to a politician, my young friend, and our good mayor is a consummate politician," Jodem answered, "but at least he is not a POE."

"I will take your word for it," Mkel stated back as he fastened his dragon hide riding jacket and slung Markthrea over his shoulder in preparation to mount Gallanth.

He along with Lordan and Padonan climbed up on their dragons and gave General Becknor and General Daddonan a salute. Gallanth, Talonth, and Strikenth bowed their heads to Valianth and walked over to where the wounded land dragons were gathered. It was only three hundred yards away from where they had landed, so it wasn't worth flying over and kicking up all that dust and debris with their huge wings. The land dragon crews, along with several other soldiers from the legion, were working on applying layers of aloras salve on the injured creatures, and the battle healers were introducing dramites to the ones with internal injuries.

"Ah, dragonriders, General Daddonan called me on my crystal and told me you were coming to take our wounded dragons back to Battle Point," Colonel Ronson yelled up to the dragonriders as they approached. "We arranged the land dragons into two groups of wounded, and the injured hippogriffs and one griffon have been gathered as well. We put our more serious wounded with the hippogriffs to get them back to the healers, so haste is important."

"We will get them back momentarily, Colonel Ronson," Lordan yelled down to the land dragon battalion commander.

"Talonth, I will take the larger group of land dragons. You take the other, and Strikenth take the men and their feathered mounts," Gallanth directed the two silvers as he moved over toward the group of five land dragons. "Have no fear, my little brothers," he comforted the wounded land dragons. "We will have you all home soon." He moved carefully into a position where he could cover all of them with his wings for the teleport back to Battle Point.

Mkel looked down at one of the land dragons, who obviously had a broken front leg and severe burns from the behirs' lightning bolts. He felt bad to see them and the soldiers in pain, but as long as they could get them back to Battle Point, he knew their chances of survival were very good. Alliance healers were the best known, utilizing their inherent skills, and the healing crystals, aloras, interefron, dramites, and their great knowledge and experience derived from the elves. They could save lives and ease suffering in a manner that was unheard of before the Great War.

The severe internal injuries of some of the men and hippogriffs would have to be healed using the dramites. The incredibly small creatures were derived from the dwarves' skorts, which were insect-like and almost too tiny to see. The dwarves and the Weirs used the skorts to clean their underground dwellings. The skorts resembled small headless armadillos that silently crept along the ground, walls, and ceilings, eating small bits of organic matter such as hair, dust, bits of food, mold, and even small insects. The elves took these creatures and, utilizing dragon blood and a little magic, created the incredibly small dramites. A hundred could fit on the head of a pin. They were combined with a drop of blood from the intended patient and then introduced into the body and the blood stream via the nose or a wound, going to the affected or damaged area to heal or fix it. Once they were finished, they remained for a short time before they naturally died and were passed out of the body.

Mkel took a long drink of cold water from his canteen. The cooling crystal kept it just above freezing. He needed that but looked forward to drinking an ale back at the Weir. Gallanth lifted his right claw and reached over to the wounded land dragon next to him. A light emanated from the palm of Gallanth's claw and literally transferred into the land dragon's body. As the light faded, the wingless dragon's leg straightened out, and the burns were half healed. "Do not put weight on your leg yet, my little brother. I have healed it, but it is still tender and needs further attention," Gallanth directed the land dragon. "Are you ready, Mkel?

"Yes, Gallanth," Mkel answered. "Let's get these poor lads back to Battle Point."

Gallanth spread his wings, and Talonth and Strikenth followed suit. With a last warning from the dragons and coordination with the healers on the parade grounds at Battle Point, the dazzle of blue light enveloped all around them and they blinked out. Mkel was accustomed to this but he knew it could be disconcerting to those who had never teleported before. Within seconds, they emerged in the middle of the grass landing at Battle Point. They were immediately surrounded by dozens of healers and support soldiers, as well as the few infantry that were left behind to man the city's defense. Gallanth and the two silver dragons furled their wings and aided the more injured land dragons back to their compounds. Gallanth even supported one with his tail, almost lifting the fifty-foot land dragon off the ground as he helped it into its stable.

Healers began to crawl all over the land dragons, spreading generous amounts of aloras over their wounds. Mostly what the land dragons needed was more salve, for their natural healing powers were almost as good as true dragons. They were a tough lot. The wounded men, horses, and hippogriffs were also being treated as fast as the healers could get to them, attending the most seriously injured first. Several men and beasts needed dramites, for their wounds were deep and would be fatal if left untreated for very long. As soon as the healers formulated the tiny creatures with the patient's blood, they quickly introduced them to the wounds for faster healing and immediately applied aloras to stop blood flow.

"Gallanth, we should get back," Mkel said. "They will attend to their own, plus I think you used up your remaining healing power on that land dragon."

"You are right, and Talonth and Strikenth agree with you as well. It has been a long day," Gallanth replied as he carefully walked away from the wounded and those treating them. Talonth and Strikenth followed the gold dragon, and as soon as they were a couple hundred yards away, they launched into the air while emanating a salutary roar in deference to the wounded. Within moments, they were back over the battlefield.

The three dragons circled and landed almost in unison. "Jodem, Toderan, is our crew ready to go?" Mkel asked through his crystal.

"Yes, we're all assembled and ready," Jodem replied. "Ordin just needs to get up onto Gallanth. You know his whole flying trepidations, and Tigrenth and Lionoth transported the treasure back to Handsdown while you were gone."

"Send the good dwarf over," Mkel shouted as Ordin quickly sprinted over to Gallanth and jumped onto his forearm and crawled up the riding straps. "Good to see you are still fit, my stout friend," Mkel yelled back to the dwarf.

"You know I only like to fly on mighty Gallanth's back, Dragonrider," Ordin replied with a smile through his haggard brown beard.

"It is always a pleasure to convey you, Master Dwarf," Gallanth said, turning his head to Ordin, who was securing the flying straps on the rear seat of the saddle rig. "Best of luck, General Daddonan, General Becknor. Colonel Lordan, Padonan, thank you," Mkel said into his crystal. Gallanth spread his wings and, with a not overly loud roar, took to the air and quickly disappeared with the blue flash of light; he and their companions emerged back at the north end of Handsdown, where they had spent the night before. There was a flurry of activity going on from the support corps personnel, making the evening meal, getting enough water purified, and setting up the amenities, for the lion's share of the legion that would be returning from the battlefield by nightfall.

Mkel quickly dismounted and was met by Colonel Tomslan, the leader of the Battle Point legion's support corps. "Welcome back," the colonel said, "and thanks to you and your dragon. We will have your treasure packed in bags and loaded on slings in a short time, for we know you and your comrades as well as the other two dragons want to get back to your Weirs as soon as possible. Until then, we have hot food and spirits for you and your men, and a steer and several pigs for Gallanth and your fellow dragons."

"That would be excellent, Colonel; I know my men and I are hungry, as is Gallanth," Mkel answered.

"Have your men come over to the village hall; there are tables set up there," Tomslan said, pointing over to the large building in the center of the village. "I will send over food and water for your mounts."

"We'll be over in a couple of minutes, sir; thank you for your hospitality," Mkel answered. He gave Colonel Tomslan a salute and the colonel turned to attend to the camp area.

Mkel and the Draden group walked over to the large wooden hall after the stable crews came over with food, meat, and water for their mounts and a freshly butchered steer and two pigs. Gallanth already had the steer down before they got to the hall, after he cooked it a little more with his fiery breath. Inside there was a huge fire pit with two steer halves roasting and pieces of beef and pork being barbecued on grates over several fires and heat crystal ovens. Huge cauldrons of vegetable stew were steaming beside that, and there were several large tables full of breads and pies.

They all sat down and ate almost without words; given how hungry and tired they were from the battle. Ordin went back for seconds and thirds, not unusual for a dwarf. After they all had their fill, they thanked the support corps cooks and left the hall. They walked back to their mounts to see them fed, watered, and ready to go. Razor Claw chirped up loudly, his deep eagle-like warble indicated to Lupek that he was anxious to get to his den.

"Been a long couple of days, Razor Claw," Mkel said softly to the griffon as he reached up to scratch the feathers above his eye crest.

"Yes, I think he's looking forward to several days off," Lupek answered.

"That's good you said that, for the entire Weir council will stand down for a month or more until we go to Draconia for the Honors Day games and the senate gathering, with only select ranger patrols. Is that understood?" Mkel asked, looking pointedly at Lupek. All in attendance acknowledged. "Plus Lawrent and his raiders will arrive in a day or two, and that means the Weir will be alive and rowdy for several days and weeks following. You all finish preparations to go. I have to look for someone."

"Who are you seeking out?" Jodem asked.

"The boy whose father was killed by that death knight I sent to the underworld. I want to talk to him and his mother," Mkel answered. "I won't be long, plus we have to collect Beckann and Watterseth, or else you know he would be left behind as focused as he gets on healing and giving his ministries." He walked toward the wooden keep, where he had fought the death knight days earlier. Neither Jodem nor any of his comrades said anything to him as he left. They all knew how he felt about situations like this.

He walked to the keep's open gate; the two guards immediately saluted him, seeing the rank and especially the dragonrider insignia on the collar of his uniform over his dragon hide armor jacket. He returned the salute and asked them if they knew where the families of the keep's defenders were. They told him to go over to the family housing area at the far end of the small fortress. He walked over to the large structure on the west side of the wooden fort's wall.

"Captain, oh, excuse me, Dragonrider, may I help you?" a soldier asked him as he gave a quick salute.

"I am looking for a boy and his mother, whose father was a senior legionnaire here," Mkel asked as he waved off the salute.

"I know of whom you speak," the soldier stated. "I will get them for you. The boy's name is Tylorn."

"And then will you please go and tell the cleric Watterseth that the Draden Weir crew is ready to go?" Mkel asked. "He can meet us as soon as possible on the north field by the gold dragon."

"Yes sir," he answered and turned around to go into the building. Mkel knew he would have to drag the Weir cleric to the field to get him back home. He sincerely dedicated himself to ease the suffering of the innocent and to spreading the word and spirit of the Creator. The Battle Point legion had its own cleric, and one of some power, but Watterseth would spend days here if he was allowed.

"Sir, here is the boy and his mother," the soldier said.

"My lord dragonrider, my name is Debesora, and you've already met my son Tylorn," the beautiful women introduced herself.

"My lady, my name is Mkel. I am the rider of the gold dragon Gallanth, but I am no lord," Mkel answered her.

"I am sorry, Captain Mkel," she replied.

"There is no need for any apology, my lady," Mkel quickly corrected her while trying to make her feel more at ease. Her crystal blue eyes were stunning and accented by her tanned skin. Mkel guessed her to be in her midthirties, but she looked much younger.

"I want to thank you for saving Tylorn's life yesterday," she said with emotion. "I don't know what I would have done if I had lost my husband and him."

"I apologize for not being there sooner to save your husband. The battle was chaotic, and Gallanth heard your son when he cried out. He has a soft heart for children, and I for a boy who has lost his father," Mkel said with increasing emotion in his voice.

"Please, Captain, do not blame yourself, you did the best you could, and again, you saved Tylorn," Debesora told Mkel in a very caring manner as she reached up and touched his cheek to catch the single tear that came rolling down. His eyes met hers for only a few seconds, but it seemed like an infinite flow of emotion transferred between them.

"I still failed you, but I will make it up. I have this for you," Mkel said, handing her a small bag containing over one hundred Drachlars and half as many platinum coins.

"Captain, I cannot accept this," she said, pushing the satchel back.

"No, my lady, I insist," Mkel insisted. "That is enough money to last you for years, over top of the pension you will get for your husband. The Alliance does not forget the widows and the children of its soldiers, and the dragons and Weirs definitely do not. As for you, my boy, the courage you showed in taking on that death knight was impressive. You deserve this, and you would have made your father proud." Mkel reached up and unfastened the gold dragon emblem on his collar and gave it to the boy, and then he took the dragon tooth dagger from his calf. "This dagger is from one of Gallanth's teeth that was broken off when he killed a chromatic dragon in battle. It will cut through anything, so take care."

"Thank you, sir," Tylorn managed to get out, even though he was on the verge of tears.

"I know how you feel, trust me," Mkel told him. "I must be going now and return to my Weir with my friends and my dragon. If you need anything, and I mean anything, just get a hold of me through your seeing crystal, or have someone in the legion get ahold of me by one of the officer's crystals. I will look in on you from time to time, and whenever you want to visit Keystone Weir and Draden, you and your family are more than welcome." Mkel finished as he saw Watterseth emerge from the hall, and he touched his seeing crystal to Debesora's to ensure the connection was made.

"It is time to go, sir," Mkel told the Weir cleric.

"I understand and am ready," the cleric replied.

"We must take our leave, my lady; remember what I said," Mkel told the well-mannered woman, and he and Watterseth walked out of the keep.

"That was a very nice gesture, my son. I talked to several of the wounded from this town's garrison and comforted their families. They all said you and Gallanth got here just in time. The orcs you killed that were led by that death knight were almost ready to break the gate of this keep, and most of the defenders were wounded. It would have been a slaughter, and you know the orcs would not have taken prisoners," Watterseth explained.

"You know that's our job," Mkel answered the holy man. "If it was any other dragon but Gallanth or a gold, they would not have known what was going on. A gold dragon's sense of foresight does come in handy at times. Unfortunately, we were too late to save that boy's father."

"Do not diminish your accomplishments these last several days. You and Gallanth saved hundreds of lives, and the people here are very grateful to you both. One woman said that when Gallanth streaked in and landed in the middle of that company of orcs, he looked like the Creator's own vengeance and was the answer to her prayers to save her family. Do not trouble yourself about the boy's father. You did not kill him, that death knight did, and you ensured that he is now facing judgment for his sins. Trust me, no one here finds you at fault for killing that evil warlord," Watterseth explained.

"Again I understand, Father, but it still bothers me. I don't want any son to go through what I went through, it's not fair. The pain he will feel will haunt him for the rest of his life," Mkel explained while he felt the memories of his father well up inside him.

"Again, my son, even you and your mighty dragon can't prevent all evil from happening; this is beyond you both. Leave these things to the Creator. There is a reason for everything in the balancing act of life," Watterseth continued, comforting Mkel.

My rider, are you all right? Gallanth asked him telepathically. "Yes, my friend. Watterseth and I are walking over to you now," Mkel answered him back telepathically.

"Tell your giant overprotective lizard that I won't make you upset anymore," Watterseth interrupted, "but I want you to think of what we've said."

"How did you know Gallanth was talking to me?" Mkel asked quizzically.

"First, it is my job to know all in my flock, and that includes you and the big gold dragon," Watterseth answered in a slightly stern but friendly tone. "Second, when Gallanth talks to you through your mind, your face immediately changes expression, and many times your eyes fixate on a distant point."

"I guess I have to be more cautious," Mkel said.

"No, your emotion is your strength, and his. Well, all my cantankerous sinners, I see you actually did a little of the Creator's work today," Watterseth called over to the Draden crew as they walked up to them.

"Hah, our favorite holy man; nice to see you, Taloshj," Ordin said, calling Watterseth the dwarven word for respected cleric.

"Master Ordin, I will save your wretched soul yet," Watterseth jokingly replied.

"Your grace, I want to thank you for aiding my wife in battle today." Dekeen nodded with his usual sign of deference, for elves did not have clerics or priests. This was because they were all totally comfortable with their beliefs, and in the Creator's plan and divinity. They knew their place in the grand scheme.

"I live to serve, and I would never see our Lady Beckann harmed. Toderan, Tegent, Lupek, I am glad to see you made it through this fight relatively unscathed," Watterseth jubilantly exclaimed as he gave each a lion's handshake. "Gallanth," the cleric said, giving the dragon the sign of the triad. Watterseth believed that even dragons were just creatures looking for the truth, just as all others, seeking the truth in faith, truth in friends, and truth in life. They were just immensely more powerful and wiser than the rest of us. He also knew that in spite of the fact that they were the Creator's agents on earth, they possessed more human emotion than they were even aware of, and Gallanth especially was no exception.

"Bless you as well, my friend," Gallanth answered the kind gesture. "In spite of you upsetting my rider," the gold dragon continued, with a slight tone of sarcasm.

"My good dragon, you don't give your rider enough credit for his resiliency," the cleric chided Gallanth back.

"I have a slightly greater insight than even your wisdom can see, my good cleric," Gallanth answered.

"Then I defer to your greater wisdom, mighty dragon," Watterseth concluded with a wink.

"It's time to go home, gentlemen; mount up," Mkel interjected with a command to his Weir mates and Beckann, who had just ridden up on her unicorn. All smiled and began to climb up onto their mounts. Jodem and Toderan could tell that Mkel wanted to get into the air. Still, they all gladly secured themselves into their flying rigs, for they were all looking forward to going back to the Weir for a little rest. The battle, while short, had been intense, and they were also thankful that none of their friends had been wounded or worse. When they all gave Mkel the word that they were ready, he gave them the signal to take to the air. Beckann cast a flying spell over Desiran, to enable her to join the others in flight. She and Dekeen gave each other a nod and a wave, which was a great show of emotion for elves.

Mkel liked to watch the combination of the giant eagles, griffons, winged horse, and now unicorn take off in unison and soar in formation. As soon as they gained a little altitude, he told Gallanth to take off. The big dragon grabbed the reinforced, oversized sacks in his front and rear talons, and with a powerful heft of his colossal wings, and a push from his tail, he was airborne. The bags full of precious metals were heavy even for Gallanth's strength, but he was still able to catch up to his friends once they rose to soaring altitude. They could all hear the cheers behind them of the Battle Point legionnaires and townspeople, as a final thanks for saving their town and their lives.

They all maneuvered in closer to Gallanth, and as soon as they were in formation within the gold dragon's wingtips and tail, he and Mkel focused on the Weir, and in a second they were gone. They emerged over the plain immediately to the east of the Severic River and gently dove in unison toward the Weir entrance, which was open and awaiting them. Word had quickly gotten back to the Weir, and the garrison was out in force to meet the leaders for their return. Gallanth slowed his speed slightly to allow the others to go through the entrance tunnel first, for it would be harder for the dragon to land with all the weight he was carrying.

Mkel could hear the welcome of the Weir horns from the towers, a good sound to his ears after the events of the last several days. His friends flew into the Weir landing, with Gallanth right behind them. They all diverted toward their landings and stables, while Gallanth back winged and landed between the lake and the main housing complex of the Weir. The gold dragon dropped the large sacks of treasure and stepped away from them. Captain Hornbrag moved in immediately with an armed platoon and surrounded the sacks, for he was the one responsible for the tracking, storage, and managing of the Weir's wealth.

Mkel waved to the soldiers of his garrison who had assembled and quickly dismounted. Gallanth lowered his head in a greeting to the Weir's soldiers. Janta walked over with his little Michen, who smiled and toddled over to his father. Mkel knelt down and grabbed him as Gallanth lowered his massive head just beside his rider. He gave his son a big kiss on the cheek.

"Daddy," the little boy said, adding, "Dragon," as he turned his head to look at Gallanth's imposing frame.

"Hey, my little boy. Daddy's so happy to see you," Mkel said to his son.

"As am I, little hatchling," Gallanth added.

"Give Daddy a kiss," Mkel told his son, who leaned forward and kissed him on the cheek. "Thank you; how about Gallanth?" he asked his son. The toddler leaned toward Gallanth, putting his hands on the side of the dragon's nose and gave him a kiss. Gallanth's golden eyes glowed in response to the loving gesture.

"I wouldn't want to be the one who hurt or even threatened that little boy," Pekram said to a garrison soldier he was walking with. "To incur the wrath and fury of a gold dragon is not something you'd like to have on your shoulder, and they won't rest until a blood debt is paid. Captain Mkel, good to see you all back," the senior company sergeant's booming voice echoed over the general conversation.

"Pekram, good to see you!" Mkel exclaimed as he gave his company's senior legionnaire a lion's grip handshake and hug.

"Sir, it was only three days," the big man replied.

"Yes, but it was a long and tough three days," Mkel commented.

"I heard one hell of a fight. You should have called for Silvanth to bring the rest of the garrison, or at least the company," Pekram commented.

"Events unfolded very quickly, plus General Daddonan is a stickler about requesting non-Battle Point aid, at least other than dragons," Mkel explained.

"Pride is a bad thing for an officer, especially a legion commander," Pekram commented.

"I know, but there is nothing as close to divine as a general in command," Mkel said with a smile. "I have to go with Gallanth to let him void and have given the rest of the Weir council off until the Honors Day games and senate gathering in Draconia. Captain Hornbrag and the lieutenants will be here. I want the men to concentrate on weapons skills and squad training on fighting giants, for I think we will be doing so before too long. A mountain giant led a pod of common giants that almost put an end to our good Weir wizard. Let me transfer the events of the battles to your seeing crystal so you can review them and determine what other tasks you want the men to train on. You should also look at what Lupek and Deless saw in the Smoking Mountains, for that army is likely what we will face." Pekram pulled his crystal from his belt and touched it to Kershan's dragonstone.

"One last thing, tell the men the first round of ale is on me tonight, just because I'm glad to be back and see their ugly faces," Mkel said again with a smile. "Oh, tell the lieutenants I will meet with them tonight, an hour before dinner."

"I will let them know, now take that big lizard out to relieve himself," Pekram said with his normal sarcasm.

"I heard that, Sergeant," Gallanth chided the senior fighter. "Mkel, Michen wants to ride," he told his rider. "Janta, do you have ...," Mkel started to ask the halfling.

"Michen's seat is right here, sir," the diminutive halfling said, moving the boy's carriage over to him with its padded seat.

"Thanks, my dear," Mkel said, taking the seat and putting Michen on Gallanth's huge head. He would hold onto one of the gold dragon's two head horns and play. Gallanth would make sure he would not fall by his limited telekinetic ability and careful manipulation of his tail. Mkel then waved to all assembled and to Jodem and Toderan; he then climbed up Gallanth's arm and onto the flying rig. He fastened the padded cloth and wooden seat onto Markthrea's mount and asked Gallanth to lift Michen up to him. Gallanth responded by shuffling the boy onto his tail and then lifted him up to Mkel. He grabbed his giggling son, and placed him into the seat, and secured him in.

Gallanth then moved over to the lake, took a quick drink, and launched into the air. He soared over the lake and out of the Weir to the sound of the warning horns, as well as Gallanth's own roar. They sailed over the Severic River, and Gallanth banked to the left as he gained altitude. Michen was giggling and laughing, thoroughly enjoying the ride. Gallanth was flying at a very leisurely pace so as not to whip too much wind at the little boy, for Mkel didn't want to use the shield that one of his dragonstones could emanate, for it was a comfortable evening and Michen liked the wind in his face.

"Enjoying yourself, little hatchling?" Gallanth asked Michen as he turned his head briefly around to look at the boy. Michen smiled and yelled, "Gallyanth, flying!" Mkel could almost make out a smile on the dragon's huge jaws.

"I know you need to talk, my friend. I can feel your mind is busy and slightly troubled," Gallanth spoke aloud to Mkel.

"I still have consternation about the happenings of the last several days," Mkel explained. "Never before in battle have I had these feelings. I do not fear death for my own sake, but with Michen now, I am scared of leaving him like my father left me. As for the men I killed, including that death knight, I guess that bothers me slightly as well. That *pogasch* deserved to die for what he did, but I can't help feeling a slight remorse. At the same time, I feel I failed by not protecting that boy's father as well."

"I understand your fear of leaving Michen," Gallanth said in a comforting tone. "Our job is a dangerous one, in spite of all our advantages. I also noticed that you fought these last two days like a ghost was looking over your shoulder. Remember that you do not need to prove anything to anyone, even your father's memory and especially to me, only to yourself. Up until now, you've only had to fight orcs and their allies; killing them is akin to squashing an insect. Remember evil exists in many places and can take many forms. The men we killed today, including the death knight, deserved what happened. This does not mean you can't pray for their souls, however.

Gallanth's words hit him hard and made him think. His wisdom and brotherly tone always comforted him, especially now. "I understand your words, my friend, and they do make sense. It is just I still see that boy's face in my mind, and I can't stop thinking about Michen and my own memories of my father," Mkel replied.

"Again I understand your feelings. It is the true facet of humans that makes you unique in this world. It is also what gives you strength and the ability to love. In regards to your thoughts that we did not do enough, you must remember that as powerful as we are together, we cannot save every soldier or every innocent life. We do not have the power of the Creator and cannot be held to that same level of responsibility. All we can do is the best we can, maintain our honor, look out for our friends and those we are responsible for to the best of our ability, and above all love those who love us. Remember the oath you took when you became a dragonrider. One of the many themes of that oath is that the Creator makes us only strong for a certain period of time, to enable us to defend the weak.

"This is also the curse of the metallic dragons," Gallanth continued, "in that the very soul bonding we do with our human riders, the very thing that makes us more powerful, is still a temporary endeavor. Dragons are immortal unless killed in battle. We almost always outlive our bonded rider. This means we will face the loss of our soul mate many times, and dragon emotions are extremely powerful, like the pulsating of an erupting volcano." As Gallanth spoke, Mkel felt the surge of emotion from the dragon come over him like a tidal wave. Immediately tears welled in his eyes and started to run down his cheeks before the wind whipping around his mithril crystal visor dried them.

"The love you feel for Michen is the same as the love I feel for you and all my riders. But even this is infinitesimal compared to the love the Creator feels about all of his creations, and the loss of his earthly spirit at the hands of Tiamat and her drow, orc, and Morgathian minions, which he also created. He bore all the evil of mankind, elf, dwarf, halfling, and dragonkind, in an attempt to bring the world back into balance. All of the power that dragons bring to bear is nothing compared to what power of love that he and his spirit brought. This is true power. He keeps the world in balance through the deeds of those who are good, to counter the deeds of those who do evil or are evil. This constant give and take keeps the world in its present balance. Imagine trying to orchestrate all that, and still allow all those involved to have free will for the power to do good or evil, Gallanth said.

"It is just amazing how he has the fortitude to allow such things to happen," Mkel thought out loud to Gallanth.

"It all comes back to his gift of free will. Dragons chose by species, as did the elves. Humans have an individual choice and continue to do so. You, as all men, have two dragons fighting inside of you for the control of your soul, one good and one bad," Gallanth told Mkel, much to his surprise. Mkel, slightly startled, asked, "Which one will win?"

"The one you feed," he answered.

Mkel's seeing crystal vibrated. He picked it up and said, "Yes, my dear?" answering the image of Annan in the mirror face.

"Where are you? You fly in from a huge battle in the east, land, then take off on that oversized gold lizard with Michen," she yelled at him.

"Just wait, we have been through hell in the last several days and Gallanth needed to void," Mkel answered her, slightly irritated.

"How do you think I feel back here dealing with all the Weir matters, worrying about you? And Michen has been very difficult as well, as if he knew you were in danger. Janta and I could hardly handle him at times. You should have let me and Silvanth know more of what was going on," she continued.

"There wasn't much free time, Annan. We were involved with two major battles and had to fight dozens of chromatics," Mkel answered, getting more irritated.

"I know you weren't fighting for three days straight, and I know there's a dragon gypsy cult in Battle Point. I'm pretty sure you had many drinks offered to you along with other things, but most importantly, we were worried about you and should have joined you in the fight," Annan continued her worried rant.

"Enough! I will talk to you later when sense has returned to your head. I missed you greatly and look forward to holding you," he spoke back and made the crystal go blank, ending the conversation.

"I will have Silvanth talk to her. She is just worried, if not a little tired," Gallanth interjected.

"I understand, but she can be a little trying at times; lady dragonriders," Mkel explained.

"We should be getting back soon. I'll drop down to the small farm east of the Weir and quickly void, to not make you a liar, and then circle back. Michen is a little cold," he added.

Mkel reached down to the back of his son's neck and tapped the heating crystal on his jacket twice to make it warmer, as Gallanth banked and flew east. He didn't even touch the ground to void, and they flew back over Draden Forest, hugging the mountain base of the Weir, and darted into the large entrance. Michen was laughing and talking the whole time.

"He does like flying," Gallanth said with a warm tone to his deep voice. Mkel knew how fond his dragon was of his son, which made him feel more relaxed. He was glad to be home.

CHAPTER VIII

THE ARRIVAL OF LAWRENT AND THE RAIDERS

The sound of a ranger's griffon's cry woke Mkel a week after the Weir council group returned from Battle Point. He had spent the last several days trying to relax and spend time with Michen and Annan. Gallanth mostly slept, only rising to make a large batch of heating crystals, since he was behind in his production quotas. They both needed a little time off. Now he wondered what was going on to make the griffon give an alarm screech; had the fire giants started to move? He hoped that there would be at least several weeks before another battle.

Nothing to worry about, my friend, the griffon and his rider were on patrol and sighted Lawrent and his ships slowly heading up the Severic River. They must be heavily laden, for they are apparently moving at a crawl pace, Gallanth told Mkel telepathically.

"I thought you were supposed to be asleep, my friend," Mkel replied to his dragon through their mind link.

You know I have different levels of slumber. I am asleep to a point, but I wanted to maintain a certain level of awareness, for I knew that the raider was coming soon. I have also been concerned about the gathering in the fire giant lands with Lupek and Deless telling of chromatics. Just making sure my power of foresight was still on alert, Gallanth explained.

"You'll need your strength both to control Lawrent's berserkers and for a possible fight with the chromatics, so go back to sleep, my friend," Mkel scolded Gallanth.

I slept at my deepest level the last two days, in which I do my fastest healing. I would like to greet the good pirate and his raider ships, and maybe give them a little boost getting up river to the Weir, Gallanth stated to him with an unusual mischievous hint. "All right, Gallanth, as long as you promise to get more rest this week, only being available to converse during the evening meal and the laudations that will follow with this crowd," Mkel conceded. *As you wish, my rider,* Gallanth answered almost sarcastically.

Mkel smiled and said, "Let me get ready." He quietly got out of bed and went into his bathing room. He quickly bathed, shaved, and dressed, then gave the sleeping Michen a kiss in his crib as well as Annan, but gently so as to not wake her up. As he walked out of his chambers onto Gallanth's landing, he asked, "Will Silvanth join us?"

"She actually will, even she likes the barbarian," Gallanth answered. Lawrent, while brash and sometimes obnoxious, was a very humorous and personable individual.

"Excellent, my friend," Mkel answered as he pulled his seeing crystal and called the watch tower to sound the horn to announce that Gallanth and Silvanth would be exiting the Weir, warning others to clear the airspace in front of the entrance.

They both heard the resonating of the warning horn from outside the Weir's guard towers, and then Gallanth launched off of the ledge. Silvanth was right behind them from the adjacent ledge. Mkel tipped his riding helmet to Silvanth as they sailed above the Weir lake and into the large tunnel opening. They emerged into a gorgeous late summer morning with the sun just above the Gray Mountain chain. The air had just a tint of autumn as Mkel tapped the heating stone once on the back of his riding jacket by his neck to warm him. He would not need this soon, as it would get warm quickly but didn't want to power one his weapon's shields, for he wanted to feel most of the wind in his face.

Silvanth moved up beside Gallanth, almost on his wing tip. Both her and Gallanth's metallic hides almost glimmered in the morning sunlight, a beautiful sight as they turned to the right and began to follow the river downstream at a leisurely pace. Mkel loved to feel the air literally pulled over the dragon's small scales as they glided through the air. The dragons' secret to flight was both the small scales on their hide and wings that would actually force air over them and their limited ability to manipulate gravity, making them lighter for flight. This and the fact that the dragons weighed proportionately much less than other creatures with the mithril content of their bones and musculature.

Mkel could even see some of the elves come out of their posts along the shore line with Draden Forest as they flew overhead to wave. Elves above all others had a deep respect for the dragons, recognizing that they were the source for most magic in life. It took just under a half hour to cover the thirty miles of shore line of the elven-controlled portion of Draden Forest. There was no need to teleport the short distance, and sometimes a nice, slow, lazy flight is good for the soul of both dragon and rider. The small tributary that separated Dekeen's part of the forest with the remainder of the woods was also kept under watch by his clan. This portion of Draden Forest would end in another thirty miles. Sometimes both he and Gallanth just needed to soar, for on his mighty wings, the relaxing flight made all of life seem better.

The griffon sighted the ships on his long swing to the Draden Forest borders, at the last port town of Columbrian, that lies on the southern edge of Draden Forest along the Severic River. Many times the griffons and hippogriffs would swing north or south and fly along the river and its tributaries to catch any large fish they would spot. They liked to dive for fish in the river; they could spot them from over a mile high with their keen eyesight. Gallanth liked the occasional fish as well but needed to catch the larger oceangoing types or sharks. He did this occasionally when they visited Draconia and especially when they went to Freiland to see the raiders.

"I see their ships about a couple of miles ahead," Gallanth announced, "just past Columbrian." Mkel quickly looked through Markthrea's sight. He could see Lawrent on the ship's bow and his men rowing the many oars on each side. The other two ships in his small fleet were just behind his flag raider. The carved wooden dragon's head in the image of Gallanth was freshly painted. He then reached for his seeing crystal and said with a lively but joking tone in his voice, "Hey you scurvy pirate, it's about time you showed your ugly face."

"Mkel, you son of dog, is that you and Gallanth bearing down on us up there, or have the chromatics been told of our arrival?" the tall barbarian answered in the seeing crystal he had been given by Mkel.

"It could be an angry red dragon that finally found you to exact revenge for stealing its treasure, but in this case you're lucky, even Silvanth wanted to see your arrival. Still carrying that frozen ice cycle of a sword?" Mkel again teased Lawrent.

"Are you still carrying that stumpy crossbow and little curved dagger sword of yours?" Lawrent joked back.

"I'm looking at you through its sight right now, I could shave that mustache off if you want," Mkel good-naturedly answered.

"No, that's all right," Lawrent answered. "I heard you both had a hard fight recently?"

"My lord, you will let him threaten you like that?" the barbarian's young crewmen asked him in a surprised tone.

"Fool, he could put an arrow in your eye from a thousand paces, not to mention that he rides the most powerful dragon in the Alliance, which has saved this ship dozens of times," Lawrent quickly snapped at his underling.

"News travels fast, my friend; could have used you and your crew," Mkel told him. "We faced a formidable force of chromatics and giants, not to mention the orcs and drow. No need to talk about business now, have your men unfurl your sails and Silvanth will give you a little breeze to get you upstream and save your strength for the drinking later."

"You are too kind, Dragonrider. Men, recover the oars and unfurl the sails, we will have a good wind soon!" In a commanding voice, he bellowed orders to his men, who immediately secured the oars and began to lower their main sail. Gallanth and Silvanth dove and circled around the ships only a couple hundred yards above the river. The raiders cheered and waved at the two dragons. Silvanth then made a strong breeze funnel over the river, which caught the raider ships' sails and began to propel them forward at a good pace.

"A little breeze for the last leg of your journey," Silvanth said as she dove down and over the raider ships, her great silver wings glistening in the morning dawn.

"Sorry we're late, but we were attacked by a saragwin hunting party a day's sail from Sauric Bay," Lawrent began to tell Mkel.

"That close to our shores? I'm surprised the sea elves didn't find them first," Mkel said. "I'll have to ask Dekeen if he has heard of anything from his ocean-dwelling cousins."

"I think their war is escalating. We've been noticing a lot of bodies floating about, both sea elf and saragwin as well as their mounts. It's been disturbing the fishing and commerce in the several sections of ocean between the edge of Alliance waters to our shores and as far south as the Canaris Twins," Lawrent explained. "Our kingdom has even lost several ships in the process, and several of our smaller coastal villages have been attacked. Our ambassador will be addressing your senate at this next gathering for assistance from your navy and the bronze dragons, as well as for information you might have from the sea elves."

"That shouldn't be a problem, you just have one major obstacle, and that is the Enlightened senators," Mkel explained.

"Dogs, cowardly scum!" Lawrent exclaimed. "I should address the senate and challenge them to personal combat."

"Your temper is what keeps you as Draden's emissary, for I am the only one that can control you," Mkel teased the tall raider, for he could see through the crystal that his face was turning red with anger that was immediately changed with a smile at Mkel's joke.

"Well, I could have worse places to go. In any event, we have a lot of goods and foodstuffs for trade. I hope you have enough heating and cooling stones for barter; are your local women ready for us?" he asked with a smile.

"I don't think they are ever ready for you and your merry men," Mkel quickly replied.

"That's all right, for we've brought some of our own, just in case," he answered.

"You should think more carefully how you treat women, my good barbarian," Silvanth interjected in her usual condescending tone.

"Yes, my lady dragon, and you do look radiant in the morning sunlight, Silvanth," Lawrent quickly complimented her. He has always been grateful to her for bestowing on him the dragonstone that empowered his frost sword.

"Flattery will not get you another dragonstone, Lawrent," she half chided, half teased him.

"Then I'll have to try harder, my lady. I do, however, have several gems of excellent quality and several of those rare fish you and Gallanth like," Lawrent quickly added.

"Bribery might get you somewhere, Freiland raider, but it had better be good," Silvanth answered.

"My lady dragon, I always deliver what I promise," Lawrent continued to quip.

"Gallanth, my mate, I think the good barbarian and his pirate friends need a bath before we allow them into our Weir," Silvanth told Gallanth, which made Mkel smile, for he knew what this meant. Both dragons veered away in opposite directions and started a wide opposing circle to come around and fly at each other.

"Mkel, what did she mean by that?" Lawrent asked.

"I think you will all find out in a minute," he answered into his crystal. Gallanth did a lazy turn and took a headlong course directly at Silvanth, who was flying at him. Once they were within one hundred yards, they both unleashed their breath weapons; Silvanth's icy beam hit Gallanth's fiery breath head on. The two extremes struck with a continuous clap of thunder, but the result of this tremendous amount of energy colliding was a simple but heavy localized rain. The torrent immediately began to fall on the three raider ships.

"Had to open your mouth, Lawrent," the barbarian leader's ship second Kerlaw said as he drew his sword and commanded it to start flaming. Immediately the steel mithril blade was surrounded by flames, which he used to dry his clothes. None of his men were wearing their armor since they had sailed into Sauric Bay, no need for it while in Alliance internal waters.

"You whine like an old woman," Lawrent said teasingly to Kerlaw with a grin. "All right, you dogs, while we have his water, clean the decks and prepare the cargo for transfer," he bellowed, which immediately started the crews of all three ships into a flurry of activity.

"Well, my pirate friend, we'll leave you and your men to your preparations. I'll have the Weir ready for you at the docks with wagons to unload your goods, and the tavern keeps to ready more barrels of ale," Mkel said to Lawrent through his crystal.

"Yes, Dragonrider, we will see you in a couple of hours," Lawrent responded.

"Remember to keep your barbarians under control, my good Lawrent, or I might get hungry," Silvanth's deep but still feminine voice carried over the three ships.

"And a welcome to you on behalf of Draden Weir, Freilanders, the first draft of ales will be courtesy of me and my rider, for I have to spend some of the spoils of our victory over the chromatics, Gallanth said, softening Silvanth's tone to the result of cheers from the raiders. With that, Gallanth and Silvanth again broke their lazy circular flight pattern over the ships and began to fly upriver toward the Weir. "And Lawrent, remember to keep your men from venturing into the forest past the tributary stream or Dekeen's elves might stick an arrow in their backside," Mkel teased the raider one more time.

"Consider the warning heeded," Lawrent replied, for he and his men knew of the legendary accuracy of the elven archers, especially when firing from concealed positions from within their own forest.

"Looking forward to having an ale or two with you, my friend, and seeing what you brought us," Mkel further added.

"We have good surprises for you," Lawrent replied.

"I have faith; see you on the docks," Mkel said, ending the conversation with a wave from atop Gallanth's back. He could see Lawrent give him a half wave, half salute; it was actually a sign of deference or honor for a Freiland raider to make such a customary Alliance military gesture. Freilanders were by their nature pure attacking berserkers in a fight. Not that they didn't plan battles or develop strategy, for they were masterful tacticians, but in actual battle, once committed, they did not form disciplined ranks like Alliance soldiers did. They preferred to fight as individuals; their prowess in this type of fighting was feared throughout many lands. Even the brutish grummish recognized their fighting ability and wildness in melees, and they were especially feared by the Shidanese, who were better braggarts and assassins than soldiers. Most of the raiding that the Freiland dragon ships performed was on Shidan and their allies as well as Morgathian-controlled areas.

Gallanth and Silvanth soared back over the forest, making a straighter line toward the Weir, which looked like a small hill on the horizon. They were flying at a faster pace but nowhere near their top speed, arriving at the mountain in twenty minutes. They could have flown even faster, but Mkel asked Gallanth to fly just a few hundred feet over the treetops. It was an exhilarating and breathtaking sight to sail over the forest, so lush and serene. Mkel also liked just flying for the sake of flying. It was exhilarating just to soar on the back of his mighty dragon above the tall trees of the pristine Draden Forest.

Gallanth gave a muffled roar to announce his arrival, which was echoed by the tower's warning horns. Mkel called to Hornbrag to let him know that Lawrent's ships would be arriving at the docks in front of the Weir in a matter of hours. "You don't give a man any rest, do you?" Hornbrag said as his image came across Mkel's crystal, the smile offsetting the protruding brow of his forehead. "My staff and I have not yet completed categorizing the treasure that you and Gallanth brought from Battle Point, but I will see that preparations are made and ensure Lawrent's ill-gotten booty is correctly off-loaded and categorized. We don't want that pirate claiming he brought more than he actually did to get more crystals and goods from us," he said with his normal boyish laugh.

Hornbrag also knew Lawrent for years and had fought beside him on a few occasions. They were almost the same size and strength, and he enjoyed the camaraderie of the Freilanders' visits as well. Mkel knew Hornbrag had a good soul and was his trusted Weir clerk and money tracker as well as the Weir's financial manager. While he was very good natured, he was still a very powerful fighter and had a keen mind in money matters. Mkel knew he would have the wagons with the necessary personnel to get the ships off-loaded and that Lawrent could not pull any tricks over him, not that he expected any.

Gallanth sailed into the Weir and landed on his ledge, nestling back onto his pile of gold and silver coins and gems that made his bed. "It's time for you to uphold your end of the bargain and get some more sleep, my friend," Mkel chided Gallanth.

"Yes, my rider, I as always will uphold my word, but if Silvanth gets more proddy and takes off on her mating flight, I must give chase," Gallanth replied.

"Maybe you'll have more luck catching your mate than I have with mine," Mkel answered.

Gallanth snorted, which was a dragon form of a chuckle.

"You wrong yourself at times, my friend," he retorted as he laid his gargantuan head down into the proper indentation in his treasure bed. Mkel smiled back as he hung his dragon hide armor riding jacket up on the hook beside the entrance to his quarters. "Sleep, my friend," he said as Gallanth closed his eyes and he walked into his chamber. Annan had just gotten up and was bathing. Janta was still waiting beside Michen's chamber.

"Still sleeping?" he asked the little halfling.

"Yes sir," she replied with a smile across her small but broad face.

"All right, I'll fetch us something for breakfast. Tell Annan not to worry, I'll be back in a few minutes," he continued. She nodded and he walked out of the far side of the quarters and into the loading platform. He pulled the lanyard to allow it to lower. It was made to go up and down by the addition or subtraction of water in a counterweight container. He lowered himself to the floor level of the Weir landing and walked over to the feeding hall beside the tavern.

The rest of the morning and early afternoon went quickly. Mkel walked Michen around the lake and let him play in the Weir's nursery with the other children after breakfast. News of the Freiland raider ships docking along the Weir's landing at the Severic traveled fast. Their arrival meant a new shipment of goods, rare foods and spices, and especially the ales that they were famous for brewing that were popular among the garrison soldiers. This would kick off a feast and drinking celebration that would last for several days, which they knew Mkel would authorize.

Mkel knew his men needed to relax, for the stories of the fight at Battle Point and the news of the fire giants had everyone on a slight edge. This would relieve some pressure and worry he knew many of them had, and they could forget their duties for a short period of time. He knew it would take Hornbrag's men several hours to unload the ships, for they would be thorough. The masts of the raider ships were in plain view from the entrance of the Weir as the wagons were steadily streaming in, heading for the temporary market area by the Weir's tavern.

Mkel watched as the wagons pulled by, loaded with rare fishes in containers with cooling crystals to keep them preserved, other foodstuffs, furs, barrels of Freiland ale, locked boxes (which he knew contained gemstones that were no doubt obtained by pirating), and other trading materials. There was one wagon with chests that had soft skins stuffed in them, but he did not know what they contained. It must have been the surprise Lawrent was talking about. Who knew with that barbarian, but he would find out before too long for Lawrent could not keep a secret.

"Speak of the devil," Mkel said; he could see Hornbrag and Lawrent walking into the Weir entrance past the watch towers. Their large frames were unmistakable, as was Hornbrag's lumber and Lawrent's swagger. He started to walk toward them past the Weir lake. Lawrent looked no worse for wear. His reddish blond hair was still kept short, unusual for a raider, and his mustache still neatly groomed. The raider captain was about as tall as Toderan and likely just as strong. His wide toothy smile was always welcome, even though it hid a fierce warrior behind it. "Well, look what the sea washed upriver!" he yelled to the pair.

"Dragonrider!" Lawrent yelled back as he walked up to Mkel and gave him a friendly embrace.

"I'm glad Gallanth and Silvanth decided to give you a bath, even though you still smell like a whale's backside," Mkel said with a smile. "Good to see you again, Lawrent; let us have a drink. I've had the Weir tavern's keeps bring up our better ales," he continued.

"What, not your best ales?" Lawrent smiled.

"We like you Freiland raiders, but not that much," Mkel quipped back with his normal happy grin.

"First I want to show you something that you'll like," the tall berserker said as he walked over to the last wagon and pulled the cover from an insulated chest. He took a key from the pocket of his tunic, put it in the keyhole, and turned it. He opened the large lid to expose an egg, about half the size of a dragon egg, warmed by a single heating crystal. "Our visit to the Canaris Twin Islands was an interesting one. The civil war there is intensifying. The northern island has been getting aid from some outside source, which we know is Morgathian and Shidanese, for we have personally sent several of their ships to the bottom in our raids.

"Do you have any ship flags or solid proof of this?" Mkel asked.

"The ships didn't fly flags, and several crews actually scuttled their own vessels rather than have us capture them; others fought to the death. Their armor was Morgathian or Shidanese for both the men and the orcs, and they fought like them as well: poorly. Some of the gold and treasure we took had the Morgathian or drow seal on it. We have also seen larger quantities of platinum, which is definitely drow," Lawrent added with a smile.

"That won't be good enough for the Enlightened senators," Mkel said, "for they could say that it was just stolen by another faction. You couldn't take any prisoners?"

"Usually that is what we want," Lawrent explained, "for we always need more prisoners to row, but even those that didn't want to fight us jumped into the sea. In the three weeks we were hunting about the north island, my raiders sent eight of the badly damaged ships to the bottom and took the cargo of eight more. We were only able to actually capture two totally intact. Many of my fellow countrymen have joined us, for the hunting is good; however, there has been increasing numbers of warships and galleys escorting them, so our raids have had to be more coordinated. The Morgathian and Shidanese ships are not as fast as Alliance vessels, nor are there crews as well trained, and our ships still have an advantage in speed over all of them. In ship to ship fighting, as long as they only have three-to-one odds on us, we can usually win pretty easily."

"What is going on with the civil war there?" Mkel inquired.

"The fighting is mostly in the middle of both islands where the narrow straights separate them," Lawrent said. "Both the northern and southern tribes are using their giant dragon-like lizards in the fighting, kind of like the metallic and chromatics do here on the main continent. Their conflicts are bloody affairs, with the giant two-legged sharp-tooth predator lizards tearing each other apart, and the four-legged horned ones with incredibly powerful charges smashing into each other along with all the rest. We obtained these eggs only after we agreed to go along with one of their raiding parties and help the southern and western tribes in a battle, as well as ferrying over a small army to the north island. We towed over barges loaded with their giant lizards. It was very intense, and I had two of my men killed and five wounded. They don't have very good armor or weapons, but they fight with a savagery almost like my berserkers, just not as skilled."

"What has fueled this civil war?" Mkel asked.

"Some type of tribal squabble. The leaders we spoke to said that for no reason, the tribes in the north and eastern part of the islands started to raid their villages for gemstones, giant lizard eggs (especially the long-neck ones), and the berries they use to make the concoctions that can control the lizards," he answered.

"Why would they want to steal the eggs if both sides have these giant lizards?" Mkel asked.

"The lizards they use for fighting are both the two-legged meat eaters and a wide variety of four-legged horned herbivores," Lawrent explained. "The ones that provide food for the meat eaters are these incredibly large long-necked lizards with long tails and heavy but streamlined bodies. They use these like cattle, but they can grow to over one hundred twenty feet long. They are very docile and grow very quickly, eating almost any type of plant food. They also use them to carry war bands into battle, like our land dragons. That is why I brought you a few; I thought that Gallanth might try one when it gets full grown and lessen your costs of buying all those cattle. A full-grown long neck is almost as long as a Silvanth, and I don't think even both of them could down one of these in a sitting."

"Interesting, but I'll have to ask Gallanth if he wants to try one of these creatures and then check with Dekeen and the sea elves to see if introducing this foreign species will hurt the rivers and lakes or not," Mkel answered.

"The elves worry too much about the trees and the dirt; these longneck lizards eat almost anything and grow like weeds, much faster than cattle, and those two-legged sharp tooth lizards surely liked them. The tribes herd these in the many rivers, swamps, and lakes on the islands and use them to feed themselves and the predators," Lawrent countered.

"The elves help maintain the balance in nature here," Mkel answered. "Many of the medicines you trade for, aloras, interefron, and the dramites, are all derived from natural products and a little dragon blood, along with a little magic that they developed. They will know what, if any, effects these creatures will have on Alliance lands."

"Whatever," Lawrent said. "I'll have to slap old Dekeen around tonight if the master archer graces us with his presence." He rolled his eyes and gave his normal mischievous toothy grin. "I know how much he and his kin love to be around me and my men."

"Lawrent, you piece of whale dung," Jodem spoke to the raider leader as he and Toderan walked up to the Freilander and Mkel.

"Ah, Master Wizard Jodem, the wise and powerful, a pleasure as always," Lawrent replied, still smiling.

"A pleasure indeed; you lost another wizard, how careless and inconsiderate. I would guess you already have another candidate?" Jodem said with a slightly scolding tone.

"He fought bravely but was just not quick enough to avoid the saragwin spear. He died a raider's death, brave and honorable, taking many foes with him as well as defeating two Morgathian and Shidanese sorcerers," Lawrent said, defending his position.

"The Morgathians are putting sorcerers on their ships now?" Jodem asked.

"Yes and the Shidan ships are also starting to do the same, but they are usually inexperienced," Lawrent answered.

"They must have unearthed more dark crystals to be actually stationing magic users on their own ships, not to mention the mongrel Shidanese," Jodem said with both disgust and curiosity. "I wonder why there has not been news of this from any Alliance warships or merchant ships."

"That's because they have been avoiding all ships flying the Alliance flag. We are even hunting those ships that are taking maneuvers to get out of the way of any of your vessels," Lawrent stated.

"This is very curious and doesn't make sense," Jodem said, puzzled.

"Well, I am glad to see your undisciplined brawlers take down any Morgathian ship on the seas; you do serve some purpose, at least," Toderan said, reaching to grasp Lawrent's arm.

"Good to see you too, paladin," Lawrent replied with his normal smile to the somewhat stone-faced Toderan, even though he did have an ever so slight smirk at the corner of his mouth that Mkel noticed. Toderan, while he didn't overly like many of the facets of the Freiland raider life style, did respect their fighting ability and seamanship, and liked having them as an ally. "I've got some of our best stag meat for you as well as that smoked river fish, along with a cask of Shidanese ale," Lawrent added; with that, Toderan's eyes slightly widened, for both meats that Lawrent said he had were particularly succulent. The Shidanese, who didn't consume wine or ale made from grains, because of their religion, made a very potent and sought-after concoction. However, their less devout consume this very thick but sweet ale, usually at sea. Shidanese ale was made from special types of beans and sweet stalks that grew in that region of the world.

"I look forward to having a small taste, but now I believe I owe you and your men the first barrel of our best ale," Mkel interjected as he ushered the group to the Weir's tavern. "Plus I know Sternlan is waiting to see you, for I think you owe him something," he continued.

"Ah, the Canaris leaf I promised him," Lawrent said.

"You do have it, don't you?" Mkel asked as he led the group from the wagons to the tavern.

"I would never forget a gift for the crotchety old curmudgeon," Lawrent replied.

Mkel knew he had great respect for the old warrior, who fought along with the raiders in the Great Dragon War to repel the Morgathian incursion in the swamps of the Adelif Peninsula. The 9th Legion had saved a Freiland battalion from annihilation but suffered heavy casualties of its own. Sternlan had been with his platoon in a battle where he alone walked out alive.

They all proceeded into the tavern, where Mkel ordered the first barrel to be tapped. Lawrent's men began to stream in after the ships and the cargo were secured. The trading would all happen over the next several days and weeks, although some exchange in foodstuffs would go on tonight, with the raiders supplying rare seafood and foreign delicacies for Alliance beef and steak, and the many other dishes that the Weir's cooks were known for.

Soon after the kegs were tapped, almost like a griffon tracking its wounded prey, Ordin, Dorin, and dozens of their dwarven clansmen started to filter up from the lower levels of the Weir. *They could smell ale through rock*, Mkel thought to himself as the five-foot-tall stocky dwarves shuffled into the tavern.

"You scurvy sea dog, a lot of nerve to show your ugly face here," Ordin shouted to Lawrent. "You piece of slimy flotsam!" Dorin added.

"Hah, an invasion of the ill-tempered short people!" Lawrent bellowed. "Raiders, raise your tankards. To our dwarven brothers, may your beards always grow and your courage never falters." Over one hundred fifty of Lawrent's men stood and raised their drafts and yelled in a salute to the dwarves. A big smile came over all the dwarves' faces, especially Ordin's. All present took a big drought from their tankards, including the dwarves, who were quickly given full mugs. The Freiland raiders and the dwarves shared a common fondness for drinking and carousing, along with their almost fearless way of fighting.

"Let the drinking begin," Mkel said to Toderan, Jodem, and Lawrent, who were standing at his table. He knew that the raiders and the dwarves would now be attempting to outdrink one another with several of Mkel's men also joining in, and by the end of the night or early the next morning, there might be trouble. "I have five drachmeres that Ordin's dwarves and two of my bigger fellows over there outlast your raiders, my friend," Mkel wagered Lawrent, for he knew he couldn't resistance a challenge.

"Five drachmeres it is, Dragonrider," Lawrent smiled back as he drained the contents of his mug. "Well, brother elf?" Lawrent shouted across the room, as Dekeen walked into the tavern with several of his elf clansmen.

"Spare me the pleasantries, barbarian, we heard you had brought cloths and wines from the south islands and a new type of lizard egg," Dekeen said with his usual sarcastic bent, for the elves, while they valued and honored all their allies, did not particularly like the Freilanders' chaotic ways, with their kind being the epitome of nature's order.

"Elf Clan Master, I have rare treats I bring just for my elven allies," Lawrent said. "The cloth of the rare sheep from Southland as well as the Shidanese wine, and several gems of dragonstone quality that we know you and the noble dragons of Keystone Weir will find very useful. In regards to these thunder lizard eggs, I explained a little about them to Mkel earlier today. They are not dragons, for they do not have any magic to speak of; they can't breathe fire or cast spells, and are not any smarter than a horse or dog, but the natives of the Canaris Twins use them as beasts of burden, food, and ferocious weapons of war. I've also included some of the berries and poison extract from a certain type of fish that the tribes use to make the concoction that can control the lizards," Lawrent explained.

"Mkel, with your permission I want to take the eggs, potions, and the rest of the materials for my clan to study them," Dekeen asked.

"Please feel free," Mkel replied.

Dekeen said, "Raider, I will arrange payment for you through my negotiator."

"As always, I can trust your elven generosity," Lawrent said with a smile. "I've included the instructions on a parchment roll that is with the cart that has the eggs in it." Lawrent stated with a complimentary smile. Lawrent's men saw the unusual manners of their barbarian leader but did not question them, for above all the many types of humanoid creatures they fought and did dealings with, they respected the elves the most, because of their superior archery skills and deadly speed with a sword, not to mention their innate magical ability. This more than made up for their lesser physical strength, which the Freilanders prized.

"Well Sternlan, you old curmudgeon, good to see you're still alive," Lawrent burst out at seeing the aged warrior come up to Mkel's table.

"Ah, still just as stupid as you are ugly, pirate," Sternlan shot back as he walked up and gave Lawrent a lion's grip greeting. "My son, I am glad you're all right after your fight in the east. The supply chief for the Draden Regiment had me busy until now, I thought I would never get back to the Weir," he added, turning to Mkel and giving him an embrace. "I see Gallanth saved your tail again." Sternlan had served as the garrison supply chief since Mkel started training with the company when he was nineteen. He also knew his father well, fighting beside him on many occasions during the last Great Dragon War after he transferred out of the 9th Legion. He subtly took it on himself to look after Mkel after his father's death.

"Never a problem, my friend," Mkel answered the older legionnaire. Sternlan was a highly decorated Alliance soldier. His platoon, along with several Freiland raiders, held a critical pass in a swampy region in the southern Gray Mountains up the inlets from the Adelif Peninsula against terrible odds to prevent the legion and a Freiland battalion from being flanked. He was one of the few that made it out of that pass alive, but their sacrifice saved hundreds.

"Now, you scurvy pirate, where is the Canaris leaf you promised?" Sternlan said, turning back to Lawrent.

"Relax old man, I have it right here." He pulled out a pouch from his tunic. "Now what do I get for this and the case that is waiting for you on my ship?" Lawrent inquired.

"Me, not putting you in your place in front of your miscreant crew," the middle-aged soldier snapped back with a smile. "I have a couple of items for you, but we will haggle tomorrow," he replied. Sternlan was a renowned scrounger, and through his many contacts, he could get many items that were both rare and sought after, from dwarven weapons to exotic spices. Although the Canaris leaf, which he rolled and smoked, was very rare, the calming effects it had when smoked were appreciated by a few older fighters; it also eased aches and pains. "Now, tell me of your journey across the seas and up the Severic as well as how your old chieftain is doing?"

"Where is that lumbering hulk of pirate?" Curram shouted over the crowd. The short but stout Draden regiment senior captain walked over to the raider and shook his hand.

"My half-dwarf friend, how are you?" Lawrent greeted Curram with a slight jab at his short stature. Curram was two inches shorter than Mkel but built like a dwarf, being very stocky, scrappy, and solid. He was one of the two senior captains that aided Colonel Wierangan in commanding the Draden regiment. A good leader, strong fighter, and better drinker someone could not be.

"By the Creator, what slimy ocean creatures have you been eating, you stinking son of a worg? Every time you and your raiders come to Draden, our otyughs get bellyaches," Mkel said, chuckling at the heinous scent Lawrent unleashed, upon which all at the table burst into laughter after they temporarily scattered.

The night was kept lively by the combination of Tegent's music, the flowing ale, and the tall tales from all parties present. The raiders traded with the Weir's garrison company, along with the dwarves and elves that stayed after Dekeen departed to collect the items he and Lawrent discussed. They had all fought and shed blood together at some point in time, except the new members from the garrison and those on Lawrent's ships for the first time. Invariably, trouble started with these new soldiers and sailors after sufficient spirits were consumed.

Mkel was beginning to feel the effects of the ale, but he was still not drunk. He was not permitted by Gallanth to become totally inebriated unless the dragon was there. He, Lawrent, Toderan, and Ordin quickly became aware of shouting above Tegent's music and the singing and laughter. Several young raiders had started to argue with two dwarves over a trade, and they were soon backed up by four of Mkel's new soldiers. They then drew weapons and prepared to fight when Mkel and Ordin rose and drew their dragonstone weapons. Mkel whispered, "Kershan, disarm them," to his sword, which flew from his hand toward his men and deftly knocked their swords to the ground. Ordin's hammer twirled through the air and struck the ground in between the young raiders and his two clansmen, knocking them off their feet. Lawrent moved surprisingly fast and grabbed two of his men by the shoulder and shoved them back to the ground. Jodem also cast a small prismatic burst spell in the center of brawlers, which temporarily blinded and disoriented them.

Before anyone could say anything, Toderan moved to the center of the group with his holy sword drawn, blade glowing, and shouted, "There is no trade or drunken insult that can cause brothers in arms, comrades, to draw blood from each other. Young tempers are quick, but a fight stirs in the east and we will all need each other for it, I promise you of this. Now say your peace to each other and go back to enjoying your ale and the music. All is forgotten." His large frame, plus the attention of the now quiet tavern, along with the several dragonstone weapons separating all the aggressive parties, quickly cooled all tempers. Tegent and his group immediately began to play again, and within seconds all was normal. More maidens and working girls from Draden and the surrounding villages began to arrive as well to get their share in the commerce as well as possibly sell their wares, and they were also a welcome relief to the women of the Freiland ships.

The party lasted almost all night and was without further incident. Mkel had left the Weir tavern roughly two hours after midnight. In spite of his desire to sleep in, morning came just too soon, so he got up, dressed, and took the lift to the Weir landing. Gallanth was still in his deep sleep, which was good, for he would need all the rest he could get for the senate gathering in Draconia at the end of the month and especially for the Honors Day games.

Mkel walked over to the wagons containing all the goods from Lawrent's ships to get a better look at them, for there had been no time last night between ales. To his surprise, Lawrent was already up and inspecting the goods for today's trading. "Well, surprise to see you up this early, raider," Mkel yelled over to Lawrent as he walked up to him.

"You get enough sleep when you're dead, my friend," Lawrent smiled with life in his bloodshot eyes. "The ride back down the Severic is a lazy one and enough rest can be gotten then."

"I understand, my old friend, it was good to unwind last night, especially after the last several days in Battle Point," Mkel replied.

"A tough fight, I heard; wish me and my raiders could have been there."

"There will be others, and likely sooner than later. Lupek and Deless witnessed a large gathering of fire giants and orcs in the Smoking Mountains after they tracked an orc raiding party that my cavalry routed. Something big is coming, the question is when," Mkel explained.

"Ahh, you sea dog, where is the gold you owe me for the bet," Ordin shouted over to Lawrent as he emerged from the staircase from the lower levels.

"What gold? Two of your dwarves passed out before my men," Lawrent answered with a smile.

"Yes but there were more dwarves left standing at dawn's first light than pirates," Ordin responded.

"So what I am hearing is a draw for now and a rematch to follow, as I will defer my bet as well," Mkel interjected. Ordin scowled but seemed to accept this mediation.

"Well, for now. Dorin finally freed a sliver of mithril off of that vein we've been working on and has been heating it for a good high alloy sword. The gem that we gave Gallanth last week would make a good dragonstone weapon, which could be ready by tonight," the dwarf suggested.

"That is excellent news, I know who deserves this," Mkel said, grabbing his seeing crystal, "Silvanth, are you awake, my lady dragon?"

"Yes, Master Mkel," Gallanth's mate answered.

"I was wondering if I might ask a favor of you?" Mkel inquired. "We have two gems of quality that are ready to be made into dragonstones by tonight, one for you to give the Freiland wizard apprentice and one for Gallanth. The recipient of Gallanth's will be the ranger captain named Decray from Battle Point. Could you fly out to the walled city and bring him back here? Gallanth is still sleeping from the long fight we had in the east."

"He is the one who led the griffons to your aid?" Silvanth asked.

"Yes, and he is also the one who Gallanth empowered his swords before the battle. Unfortunately, both of those blades were destroyed in a fight with a powerful orc warlord, but he saved many lives in the process," Mkel explained.

"Anyone who comes to the aid of my mate is worthy to me," she agreed; "tell him I will be over the city in exactly three hours, I have other matters to attend to first." Mkel knew she had many cooling stones to make and then eat and bathe.

"Remember, my dear Silvanth, it is midday there now," Mkel teased his dragon's mate.

"Then they will have their afternoon interrupted," she replied in her normal nonchalant tone.

"At your pleasure, my dear Silvanth," Mkel politely replied as he cleared his crystal and spoke General Daddonan's name to connect it to the Battle Point general's seeing crystal. He quickly but respectfully requested the general to have Decray ready to be transported to Draden Weir. The general was very pleased to see to the ranger captain's upcoming award, not only for the honor but for the additional power a gold dragonstone weapon would bring to the legion. After Mkel ended the conversation, he went back to looking over the goods in the wagons and tables.

Silvanth sat in front of several bushels of quartz crystal stones, with one basket having mirror polished specimens. At each container, she took one of her front talon claws and, after piercing her hide ever so slightly, placed a gallon-sized drop of her blood onto the crystals. Immediately the bluish blood began to seep around and absorb into the crystals. Once all the blood was gone, she breathed a line of cold frost onto the stones. At once, all began to slightly glow, and then frost started to emanate from them. With the last bushel of the mirror-faced crystals, she spoke several words in Draconic over the basket after putting her blood onto them; they then started to glow intensely before subsiding. This was the process for making the cooling crystals and the seeing crystals, which drove the Weir's economy and allowed for the Alliance way of life in providing cooling for comfort and food storage, as well as instant communication over long distances. Gallanth made the heating crystals in the same fashion, and the bronze dragons made the lighting crystals.

Mkel, a Draden arbitrator has just entered the Weir, Gallanth told him telepathically, *and he brings evil with him. The Draden constables have captured the three responsible for the death of that orphan child from the fallen Draden regiment soldier. I will be down there in a moment.*

"What does the mighty Gallanth have to say?" Lawrent asked. "I can always tell when you talk to him through your mind."

"You are more perceptive than you let on to be," Mkel noted. "There will be a quick trial with those three being escorted toward us from the Weir entrance." Mkel turned toward the lake to see the group coming toward him with several guards; Jodem, Toderan, and Fogellem were also walking toward him from the council room. By the time they got to him and Lawrent, Gallanth had flown down from his landing and now towered over the group.

Mkel looked at the three who stood before him with utter contempt. The killing of an innocent, of a child, he could barely keep his rage intact. He wanted to slice them apart there and then. The gemstone on Kershan was glowing bright red, almost scintillating, reflecting his anger. Gallanth felt this and spoke up. "Bring the accused closer," he said with a deep and angry tone. None that stood in judgment by gold dragon could tell a lie, and the three men began to tremble before him.

"Look into my eyes," he demanded of them; they all turned their heads away, as if trying to avoid staring into the sun. "I said look at me now!" His deep voice grew almost to a roar, with the force of the dragon's words almost pushing them back, echoing throughout the Weir landing. They tried to resist Gallanth's order, but their faces wrenched against their own will and turned toward him as he lowered his massive head, putting his chin close to the ground to look at the men at eye level. "You, Bashier, I see evil in your heart, you held the little boy down. Gremker, you also took part in this heinous crime, laughing at the horrific act as it was taking place and aiding Bashier. And you, Salas, what you have done can only be mirrored by the darkest of the chromatic dragons. I find you all guilty by your own thoughts and memories, and you will suffer unimaginably for this crime against the innocent."

"Wait, I demand a civilian trial for my clients in the magistrate of my choosing," the defense arbitrator from Draden said before being interrupted by Mkel.

"Dragon justice applies to a crime against an Alliance soldier or their family, which supersedes civilian law, arbitrator. You and your other guilt-ridden Enlightened *scheilsach* have no jurisdiction here," Mkel snapped at the arbitrator.

"I will not be insulted by a dragonrider or any other ..." the Enlightened arbitrator started to argue.

"Silence!" Gallanth roared. "Your warped sense of justice and misplaced guilt does not hold credence here. No creature can tell a lie in my presence, and these vermin are all guilty. The Articles of the Alliance bear truth to this even if you are foolish enough to doubt my word, arbitrator," Gallanth scolded him.

"This is Alliance law as stated in the third clause of Article 13, you as an arbitrator should know this," Fogellem, the Weir's own arbitrator, spoke up.

"These men are civilians and not subject to Weir jurisdiction, for that child was not a veteran or active veteran's family member," the arbitrator argued. "I demand that ..."

"You demand nothing! They fell under Weir law when they killed an Alliance soldier's child, now leave this Weir before I have you in chains for contempt," Gallanth demanded as he moved his slightly opened jaws toward the arbitrator; a low threatening throat growl emphasized his displeasure, and in an instant, the Enlightened arbitrator became overwhelmed with fear at the close proximity of the dragon. He ran away screaming at his frightful presence.

"Now vermin, you shall know your fate. Bashier, you shall join the raiders as one of their guests. If you survive the trip back to the sea, you will likely fill the bellies of the saragwin as a sacrifice if you are not worked to death at their oars. Gremker, for your role in this crime, I sentence you to death at next dawn by the dwarf axe. Ordin smiled at that statement, knowing his brother enjoyed dispensing justice. When the prisoner heard this, he pushed one of the guards away, knocking him down, but he was stopped cold when Kershan sprang from its sheath in a flash, flew into Mkel's open hand, and then was thrust into his midsection. The large man stood there stunned at both the speed and pain. Mkel then sliced him down through his groin. The mithril blade cut so neatly and cleanly that the long wound did not bleed for a couple of seconds. As the man grabbed his abdomen and crotch, Mkel lifted his blade over his head.

"When you get to the underworld, tell Tiamat a gold dragonrider sent her another soul to feast on," upon which he deftly sliced him from the left shoulder through the chest and out the opposite rib cage. Gremker stood emotionless for a second before his body fell into two pieces.

"Salas," Gallanth continued as if nothing had just happened, "for what you have done you will be cast into the pit of the otyughs, where you will be eaten alive over the course of several days. This will cause you excruciating pain as they rip out chunks of your flesh and then cauterize it with their acid spittle."

"Guards, take them away, their very presence disgusts me," Mkel could barely gather the words as he seethed in rage, still gripping Kershan, its dragonstone ruby pulsating with power.

Mkel's anger must be calmed, Jodem thought to himself. Toderan called for several soldiers and Weir servants to remove the pieces of Gremker's body and clean up the blood.

"His body is to be cast into the otyughs pit," Jodem ordered. "Salas will have the pleasure of his company while the foul creatures tear him to shreds."

"Mkel, it is over now; breathe easy." Gallanth's words caused him to refocus and lower his mithril blade.

"Justice has been served; it's time to move on," Jodem said as he walked over and put his hand on Mkel's shoulder.

"I will see to the boy's funeral and to his relatives, Captain," Toderan interjected.

"Stellaynan, Jorgest, take our guest to his new home," Lawrent ordered two of his men, who grabbed the criminal, punching him in the stomach and the head as they dragged him to one of their ships.

"Are you all right, my friend?" Jodem asked Mkel.

419

"Yes, just not use to killing a man before breakfast," Mkel answered with a slight quiver in his voice.

"I understand, but just remember that the blood of the guilty and the evil doesn't stick to mithril," Jodem said in a comforting tone. Mkel looked at the gleaming blade of Kershan and saw that there was not a drop of blood on it. All had quickly dripped off.

"My rider, ease your mind, justice has been served today. Jodem's words ring true. Those men can no longer hurt anyone, and their evil dies with them. Go with your friends, get something to eat, and let this unpleasantness pass into history. We have a celebration today in the merging of man and dragonstone, Gallanth said lovingly to Mkel.

"You're right, my dragon," Mkel replied as he sheathed his sword.

"Ordin, I will meet you at the central hearth by the noon hour," Gallanth said.

"Yes Lord Gallanth, I'll have Dorin and the mithril there. It is almost heated to its peak now and is ready for your fire. Master Mkel, can you call Dekeen to bring Eldir and a good elf wood staff for the other dragonstone?" Ordin asked.

"Consider it done," Mkel answered with a smile. After he called Dekeen, they all went to breakfast. Several hours later, Ordin and Dorin walked up from the lower levels, with Dorin holding the glowing piece of mithril. Gallanth, Mkel, Jodem, and Toderan were already assembled at the central hearth located by the main entrance to the dwarfs' lower levels. Dekeen and Eldir had just arrived and were prepared for the arduous task ahead.

Mithril, being the hardest known substance in the world, was also the most difficult to work with to create tools and weapons. In its pure form, it was even harder than most dragon teeth and bone but had almost a living quality, making it tricky to form. Silvanth had not yet returned from Battle Point yet, so only the initial heating and forming of the metal could be done. Dorin placed the rough mithril rod in the center of the hearth on a blackened stone pedestal and backed away immediately. Gallanth moved closer to the hearth and, with a controlled blast, engulfed it in flame. He kept the stream of dragon's fire billowing for several minutes. When he stopped, the mithril was glowing so bright that dark glass was needed to observe it directly.

Dorin and Eldir picked it up with special mithril-tipped tongs and placed it on a mithril-plated anvil just in front of the hearth. Everyone near the hearth had to activate their cooling stones to take the intense heat emanating from the special metal and the dragon fire.

Ordin walked up to the anvil with Donnac in his hand. He spoke in dwarvish to his brother and Eldir, who moved the metal to a particular angle, which he then struck. The resulting thunderous clap and shower of sparks was like a small but brilliant explosion. He, his brother, and Eldir had performed this ritual many times, for it was they who created Toderan' s holy avenger sword, Dorin's axe, Lupek's javelin, Pekram's great sword, and Lawrent's frost sword, just to name a few. It was a very arduous and delicate process, but incredible to observe. This was the ultimate in arms smithy. Ordin's hammer rung throughout the Weir's landing with every calculated blow.

Silvanth's roar announced her arrival. Mkel took out his seeing crystal and spoke directly to the Weir sentinel itself, the dragonstones that were the eyes of the dragon head statue that looked over the archway of the Weir entrance. He asked it who was accompanying Silvanth and to show what it saw over the Weir lake. The image of the brilliant silver dragon appeared over the calm water, with twelve griffons flanking her, all heading for the entrance.

Without interrupting his gaze at the trio working on forming precious metal alloy, Gallanth spoke out, "I see Captain Decray brought friends; General Daddonan is accompanying him, along with several of his rangers."

"I better let Colonel Wierangan know," Mkel said. "Maybe they can hash out this whole support pact issue while they are both together."

Silvanth soared in from the entrance, flew over the lake, and back winged next to the group, just in time as Dorin and Eldir picked up the still glowing piece of mithril and moved it back to the hearth. Annan dismounted, gave Mkel a sideward look and smile, and proceeded to their quarters. Mkel knew she had no interest in the whole weapon making process and ceremony, but she would come back as soon as she changed, if not just to be by her husband. Mkel was surprised she had left with Silvanth for Battle Point without him knowing.

As Dorin and Eldir backed away from the hearth, Silvanth reared back and breathed a narrow icy beam onto the forming sword. The sword quickly cooled, with a billowing cloud of steam rising from the metal. Gallanth then moved in and engulfed the blade in his searing hot dragon's fire again. A gold dragon's fire could melt iron and steel in seconds, depending on its quality, but this heat only made mithril malleable. Ordin quickly placed a steel rod into the rough mithril sword blank to increase its mass. With the intense heat, the steel only took seconds to melt into the mithril.

The rapid heating and cooling of the mithril both sped up the forging process and strengthened the metal itself. Once mithril was actually brought up to forging temperatures, it would take hundreds of gallons of water to cool the metal and a fair amount of time. A silver dragon can do this in seconds. Dorin and Eldir moved the glowing mithril back to the anvil, where they and Ordin again proceeded to make coordinated and successive blows with Donnac.

A crowd began to form to watch the delicate and brilliant display of teamwork in the forging of this new weapon of power. Decray and General Daddonan walked through the crowd to Mkel and Toderan. Mkel gave the general a quick salute and motioned them over.

"I hope your trip with Silvanth was a pleasant one," Mkel whispered.

"Your silver dragon is very precocious," General Daddonan said with a smile.

"Females are females, sir, regardless of the species," Mkel smiled back, as everyone around him muffled their laughter. "This is something that should not be missed," he added, confident that Decray did not know that this weapon was being formed for him. Ordin's hammer strikes rang again and again as the blade of the sword began to take shape. The process took almost three hours before Ordin's final blow signaled the sword was ready for finishing. Gallanth and Silvanth had to heat and cool the weapon over a dozen times. Ordin had mixed about 20 percent steel with the mithril in the sword, for 100 percent mithril weapons were reserved for dragonriders only. Plus with mithril being such a rare metal, that the other 20 percent of the left over metal would be mixed with dwarven steel to make stronger weapons for several soldiers or arrow and bolt tips for Mkel and Dekeen.

As Silvanth gave the bare blade one last quick cooling, Eldir then went to work preparing the pommel with a tight and intricate wrap of dragon hide from one of the many chromatics that Gallanth had felled, interwoven with mithril-laced twine. As he was preparing this, all that had gathered moved to refresh their drinks and eat some of the food on the trays that were brought out from the Weir's tavern as snacks. Jodem had the gems that were to be made into the dragonstones and was preparing the spell he needed to aid Gallanth and Silvanth for the ceremony.

After a short time, Jodem spoke up in a slightly enhanced voice for all to gather and be silent. "Please all gather for the merging ceremony," the wizard called out. By now, Dekeen and Beckann had arrived. Beckann was always present at the creation of a dragonstone weapon, for she also aided Jodem in the process.

Jodem raised his staff, and the dragonstone at its top glowed brightly, at which all grew quiet. "This merging of a dragonstone and man is a momentous occasion," he began. "Every time a new instrument of power is created, this not only brings dragon and man closer, but also springs forth new power to fight for justice, freedom, and the Alliance. These brothers in arms that have been chosen to accept this trial and responsibility will be rewarded with the newfound strength to bring light to the world by vanquishing darkness. This bonding will yield a new extension of themselves and create a powerful ally in their ability to protect the weak, bring justice to the wicked, and further the righteous cause of the Creator in his benevolence. Cleric Watterseth, please grace us with a prayer." Jodem finished as he looked to the Weir cleric.

The tall cleric moved beside Jodem and raised both his hands as he said, "Let us pray; Great Creator, may your grace through your ever living spirit shine upon these candidates and their hearts be pure enough to accept this gift. May they pass your trial to serve you for the greater good and enable them to demonstrate your power and mercy. We pray they will remain your faithful servants and honor all those who have sacrificed in your name for the good of the Alliance and the light that it sheds, as well as our thanks for our dragon protectors and the wisdom and strength they bring to the world. Amen." As Watterseth finished, everyone raised their bowed heads.

"Lord Gallanth, I yield to you," Jodem said, stepping back from the dragon pair for the actual performance of the ceremony.

"My mate, please proceed," Gallanth said, letting Silvanth perform her ceremony first.

"Rainebard, step forth," she said in her feminine but deeply commanding voice. Lawrent's young wizard apprentice cautiously walked toward the silver dragon. "Raise your right hand and echo my words. Do you, Freiland raider, ally to the Alliance and friend of this Weir, accept this trial of your own free will, which if successful will bestow upon you a heavy responsibility to pursue justice, confront and vanquish evil, and protect the weak for the rest of your years?"

"I do and enter the trial of my own free will," Rainebard replied.

"Then prepare yourself, young wizard," she finished. With her final words, Jodem and Beckann both raised their staffs, dragonstones glowing. The well-cut sapphire gently rose from the dwarf's hand and levitated in front of the Silvanth. She raised her right front foot and deftly pierced her one toe with her opposite talon. She then placed a sizable drop of greenish blue blood on the gem, which immediately soaked into the sapphire and began to glow. "With my blood does this consecrate. Raise your hand, Rainebard," she requested.

The young man raised his right hand, upon which she very deftly cut his palm with her huge talon. This was the critical moment in that when he grasped the suspended gem, it could either accept him or kill him. Swallowing hard, he reached forward and grabbed the swollen, glowing sapphire. He immediately felt his whole body start to tremble as if he were about to be struck by lightning; the stone glowed in his hand with an intense brightness. Just when he thought he was going to pass out from the pulsating energy emanating from the palm of his hand, the sensation ceased and he felt a distant but noticeable presence in his mind. Dorin and Eldir moved in quickly and began to fasten the new dragonstone to the elven oak staff with tiny mithril-woven bands, aided by magic from Silvanth, Jodem, and Beckann.

They finished very quickly and together handed Rainebard his new wizard's staff, which he quickly grasped, for dragonstone weapons will defend themselves and their bonded wielder. At this point, the crowd erupted into applause at the successful union of dragonstone and its wielder as well as for another wizard to join their ranks.

"Welcome to the order, brother," Jodem whispered to the young wizard as he released his grip from the new staff.

"Thank you, Silvanth, and your entire Weir for this," Rainebard answered with a tear in his eye. All mentioned gave a slight bow in acknowledgment.

"My mate," Silvanth said, looking to Gallanth and taking a couple steps back as the gold dragon moved forward.

"Captain Decray, ranger leader of Battle Point, step forward and prepare for the trial of blood and stone," Gallanth said to the ranger, who looked puzzled. "This is long overdue, my friend, and may the Creator be with you," the smiling Mkel whispered to Decray as he walked over to him and then led him up to face Gallanth. With a quick shake of his right hand, Mkel walked back over beside his dragon.

Jodem and Beckann released the emerald gemstone and levitated it directly between Gallanth and Decay. "Decray, do you, as an officer of the Alliance, enter this trial of your own free will, which if successful will bestow upon you the enhanced power to pursue justice, confront and vanquish evil, liberate the oppressed, and protect the Alliance and all her citizens in accordance to the Creator's merciful decree?" Gallanth said in a firm yet almost hopeful tone.

"I do, of my own free will, enter this trial," Decray replied. The ceremony then began. Just as Silvanth had done, Gallanth raised his left front foot and made a small puncture of his toe with the opposite talon and placed a large drop of glowing blood on the gem. The blood, which was almost pure blue with a hint of green, quickly absorbed into the emerald, increasing its mass.

"Decray, raise your right hand. With my blood does this consecrate," Gallanth said to the senior ranger. Just like his mate, the point of his long talon made a small thin cut on Decray's palm. Without hesitation, Decray reached out and grasped the glowing emerald. He felt its power immediately course through his hand and up his arm, rapidly progressing throughout his shoulder and chest. The energy emanating from the stone started every muscle in his body to tremble. Just when he thought he would shake apart, it suddenly ceased. Like Rainebard, he then felt an echo or a subtle presence in his mind as if something were communicating to him through notion or urges, not a distinct voice but a remotely intelligible presence nonetheless.

He then released the newly complete dragonstone, which was again levitated by Jodem and Beckann. Ordin, Dorin, and Eldir quickly walked to the floating, glowing gem and prepared to finish the weapon. Dorin lifted the mithril alloy sword, and then Eldir grasped the dragonstone with the clasp, for even now it could defend itself from being touched by someone other than its master. The elf smith put the gem into its final resting place in the bottom of the hilt of the sword. Dorin then grasped the hilt and pommel with both hands and braced himself. Gallanth looked down and fired a very thin sunburst beam at the mithril bands that surrounded the gem. This heated the metal along a narrow part, and Ordin then struck it with his hammer, sealing the emerald in the hilt. The strike forced the blade partially into the stone floor of the Weir landing.

The three moved away from the new weapon and looked toward Decray. "Go and call for it, my friend," Mkel whispered to the ranger. He nodded with a smile and walked over to the gleaming sword. He reached out, grasped the hilt, and with a heft called it by its name: "Palador, the Anvil of Light, arise," Decray said, upon which the long sword almost leapt from the solid stone floor. He held his new weapon of power aloft as the gathered crowd erupted in applause. Gallanth's and Silvanth's roars drowned out even the collected shouts and clapping of the throng. The ceremony was now complete.

"It's time to celebrate!" Ordin shouted as he wiped the sweat from his crumpled brow. It was rare to see a dwarf perspire from just forge heat, but the high temperatures needed to make the mithril malleable made even him break a sweat.

"I agree," echoed Toderan. Jodem and Beckann were visibly exhausted from their part in the process and bid their retirement, but not before talking to Rainebard and giving him instructions on how to begin his training and journey into his newfound power in creating spells and magic through his staff. They basically warned him not to try anything too ambitious until they could properly instruct him, lest he hurt himself or someone else.

"You will learn your sword's abilities in time," Mkel said to the ranger captain. "It is an art to learn to listen to it, but I have faith you will master it quickly. Now we need an ale, this is your and Rainebard's night." Decray was looking forward to exploring the powers that Palador possessed, but he was still surprised and honored at being chosen to accept this gift.

The celebration lasted well into the night, adding on to the already festive mood from the Freilanders being at the Weir. This was the first time the Battle Point rangers had dealt with the raiders, and like all Alliance soldiers, they found them good natured but very undisciplined and rawdy. Their reputation for ferocity, however, was still widely known.

A week later, Silvanth woke very early and went down to the stables, taking an early meal of a live steer. This was unusual, for both she and Gallanth preferred their meat slightly cooked when they were at the Weir, but she quickly devoured the lone steer. She usually ate at least twice that, which puzzled Jern, the master butcher. She then started to pace all around the Weir lake, seemingly very agitated. Annan also got up early and was anxious, even somewhat catty.

"Mkel, you must wake," Gallanth said. "Silvanth will fly at any minute, she is in season and ready." The gold dragon's voice woke Mkel up from a sound sleep. "I'm getting up now," Mkel said. "I thought something was amiss, with Annan waking early and in a mood. We'll meet you in fifteen minutes to go down to the landing." Mkel got up and walked into his bathroom.

As soon as he was ready and dressed, Mkel directed Annan over to Gallanth, who was waiting on his landing to fly down to the lake. They quickly mounted, and Gallanth pushed off the ledge and glided down to Weir lake, where Silvanth was still pacing. Her eyes were almost glowing and she seemed very agitated. A crowd started to gather, and it was apparent that the female dragon's emotions were affecting the Weir, especially all the women present.

"Gallanth, are you recovered enough to catch her?" Mkel asked.

"She has not been able to outdistance me yet, my friend," he quickly answered. The last mating flight they had was over ten years ago, which was before he was married to Annan, and before she was soul bonded with Silvanth. Jennar, the nymph from

Draden Forest, had stepped in as a temporary consort for Mkel during that mating flight. It was the only time she ever appeared in the Weir and in front of so many non-elves, for the mere sight of her could cause men to almost go mad.

"I don't understand these feelings I have, as if I am being washed over by a huge wave," Annan said to Mkel.

"It's your dragon, my dear, you are feeling her mating call," he answered as he helped her dismount Gallanth. Silvanth looked at Gallanth as if to say, go ahead and catch me if you can. With that glance, she spread her brilliant silver wings and took off toward the Weir entrance with a challenge roar. Gallanth quickly walked away from the gathered crowd and with a hurried sprint, jump, and heft of his huge wings was airborne in pursuit of his mate. His answering roar echoed throughout the Weir. Jodem raised his staff and a seeing eye orb emanated from it and darted after the dragons. He then directed a large image to appear over the lake, which showed the dragons in flight.

Silvanth veered hard to the left as she emerged from the Weir and worked to gain speed and altitude. She hugged the Severic River and then kept banking left to fly over the town of Draden. Gallanth streaked out of the Weir in hot pursuit of his mate, but she had the jump on him. While gold dragons are the fastest flyers in the world, silver dragons are better sprinters, capable of getting to their top velocity very quickly. Mkel and Annan were watching the chase on Jodem's projection as well as seeing it through their dragon's eyes.

Mkel heard, through Gallanth's ears, cheers coming from down below in the town as he chased Silvanth. For those who were patriotic and cared about the Weir, this was a momentous occasion, for it meant another dragon would be born in nine months, as long as Gallanth could catch his mate. On rare occasions, a female metallic could outpace her mate, resulting in a strange sense of disappointment. This was one of the very few times that the metallic dragon intellect was dulled. Silvanth darted over the southern part of Draden city and started to round the Weir Mountain. Gallanth was only a mile behind her and slowly gaining.

The hollowed mountain was over three thousand feet tall and at least three to four times that wide at the base. Silvanth was hugging the side of the mountain as she tried her best to gain speed. Gallanth cleared the city and started his hard turn to follow her. She rounded the far side and began to streak over Draden Forest. As Gallanth flew over the forest, the elves below, in an unusual display of emotion, cheered from the tops of the trees and the shore of the Severic as he roared past them. They, above all, knew that every new dragon born into the world brought more magic with it. It was almost a holy occasion for the elves, who respected all of dragonkind and magic itself. They would be celebrating tonight, especially in the forest.

The nymph Jennar looked up as Gallanth flew overhead. Her radiant beauty shimmered like the crystal pool behind her. Her iridescent blue eyes looked skyward, and she thought of the last mating flight of the two dragons when Gallanth let her stand in as Mkel's mate. Gallanth would not permit her to continue as his rider's lover, for he had to marry a woman who could both bear him children and soul bond with Silvanth. As an immortal creature, she could not. She did defy the gold dragon for a time, for Mkel was smitten by her supernatural beauty. Her union with him was intense, even for her, a nymph, the embodiment of nature's beauty and passion. The mating flight in which she was present in the Weir was the only time she had ever ventured out of the forest and had been in the presence of so many humans. However, she enjoyed the adoration and lust that she inspired in mortal men.

"Well, mighty Gallanth, a good chase to you, but let it be known that I am not done with your rider," she said out loud, then with a sigh she disappeared into the pool. The griffons and giant eagles that were sunning themselves on the south side of the mountain all took to the air and started to follow the two dragons in a simple gesture of deference.

"Sergeant, why don't they just mate in the Weir like the land dragons?" a young soldier asked Sergeant Tarbellan.

"Be they a good looking lass or a lady dragon, women love the chase, son. You'll understand this in time," the old infantryman told his young charge as he smiled at his own comment.

Back on the Weir landing by the lake, Mkel and Annan had drawn themselves together in a tight embrace; the dragon-inspired passion was overtaking them, and they were almost oblivious to all around them. Mkel began to almost tear off Annan's dress as they kissed each other deeply. In spite of this personal display, all in attendance barely noticed the couple, for all eyes were locked on the image of the pursuit emanating from Jodem's staff projected above the lake.

As Silvanth rounded the mountain from the forest side and emerged over the Severic River, she suddenly pulled almost straight up, flying nearly vertical. Gallanth streaked over the Severic and nosed up as well, still gaining on the fleeing silver dragon.

"Catch me if you can, my mate," Silvanth roared to him.

"You are bragging like a chromatic, my dear," he chided back as he closed in. She took them almost out of sight from the ground before he finally caught up to her. They locked talons and intertwined tails as they began to spiral back toward the ground, which began the mating process. Mkel could hardly think, in his arousal, as he grabbed his wife in a hard embrace, kissing her neck. Jodem knew that it was time to get them back to their quarters, and with a quick incantation in Draconic, he flash teleported them there. Gallanth and Silvanth continued to plummet at an incredible speed as they mated; the assembled crowd was feeling the effects of the dragon emotions, which was making all anxious and forcing a wanting desire among all assembled.

Mkel threw his wife on their bed, and they quickly disrobed, compelled to imitate their dragons. Gallanth and Silvanth were now only a couple of hundred feet from the ground when, at the last minute and at the termination of climax, they released each other and veered apart. The two large dragons skimmed barely a few feet above the surface of the river before they pulled up, turned back toward each other, and started a slow glide over the training grounds across from the river and back toward the Weir. Mkel and Annan lay beside each other, both breathing heavily. The tension in the crowd at the Weir broke, with the group taking a collective sigh as if they were all coming out from the control of some spell. Dragon emotions can have a dramatic effect on all those that are in close proximity to them; there is always a corresponding spike in births later as a result.

The dragon pair lazily flew back into the Weir. Silvanth went directly back to her ledge, while Gallanth flew to the stables for something to eat. "Congratulations, my friend," Mkel said to Gallanth out loud from his room. "We will see a dragon egg on the hatching ground in a couple of months and a hatchling shortly after that." *We will also see a new child of Mkel and Annan at that time as well, my rider,* Gallanth replied. "What do you mean?" Mkel asked. *Annan is now with child. You must remember that Silvanth knows everything about your wife, including the addition of the two new lives now growing within them.*

"What does Gallanth say?" Annan asked him.

"You are with child, as is Silvanth," he answered.

"Why didn't Silvanth tell me directly?" she wondered.

"She is very tired after the flight and all that has happened the last several weeks and likely didn't want to interrupt us. You can talk to her later; as of right now, she needs rest. We are going to be parents again. The Creator has blessed us," Mkel told her as he pulled her close to him. She smiled and put her head on his shoulder. This event sparked a new round of celebrations, not only at the Weir but in the town of Draden itself. The drinking and feasting went on for several more days.

The festivities did not go without some tensions, however. General Daddonan and Colonel Wierangan engaged in a rather heated discussion regarding the defense pact that Gallanth made with Battle Point. They were both at the head table in the Weir tavern the second evening after the mating flight when the subject was breached.

"General, Gallanth and Captain Mkel as well as his combined garrison are already tied to support the Draden Strike Regiment. This unit needs the mobility and power that they bring to the table. They are the regiment's hammer and anchor," Wierangan stated.

"Colonel, I understand your need for the dragon and rider as well as his unique garrison with his elven and dwarven allies," General Daddonan said. "However, as a Weir commander, he is not singularly bound to any one Alliance unit. They traditionally operate independently, and Battle Point has been under significant pressure. Just look at the last two battles we fought at Handsdown. If Gallanth and his Weir mates had not been there, we would have lost the whole village and at least two battalions of legionnaires. The Morgathians are up to something. A whole wing of chromatic dragons and a sorcerer of power with a company of drow conducted a coordinated attack against us, and our land dragons could not have stemmed that tide if we had been without metallic support. Even the nature of the chromatics that Gallanth and Mkel killed, and the presence of a new type of evil dragon, indicates that a dark dawn is on the horizon."

"General, I do sympathize with you and understand your position," Wierangan countered, "but as you've heard from Captain Mkel's ranger leader, there is a large gathering of forces in the fire giant lands. Dozens of giant clans, several thousand orcs, grummish, gnolls, and Morgathian infantry, as well as over a dozen chromatics, were seen; there has not been such a gathering of this magnitude since the Great War. Captain Mkel and Gallanth's garrison company with its land dragon, cavalry, catapult, and sappers, along with their dwarven and elven allies, are a unique force in the Alliance; only Eladran Weir, with their greater numbers of cavalry and centaurs, are as effective."

"Colonel, I see we will not come to an agreement here," Daddonan said. "I suggest that we bring the matter to both Generals Becknor and Craigor. Until we can arrange for a meeting with all parties, we should agree that Draden will come to Battle Point's aid if required, unless the Capital Wing is available or we finally get a dragon or dragons permanently assigned to the city. This will be tough, for bronze dragons will resist coming out there, for we have no major lake, and the river that flows by the city is not deep enough for a bronze. There is no silver or gold currently of age, and a copper or brass would not likely be powerful enough, given recent events. I have heard that there may be something else coming soon, so I don't think this pact will need to stand long, and General Craigor has tentatively signed off on this already." Daddonan finished, and Wierangan nodded in agreement.

When Mkel was told of the temporary agreement between the two leaders, he could finally dedicate himself to preparing for the trip to Draconia for the senate gathering and the Honors Day ceremonial games. He did feel a slight bit irritated about being argued over, especially without his or Gallanth's input. *Maybe I shouldn't support either one of them,* he thought to himself. Mkel knew he and Gallanth could never turn down an Alliance soldier in need, but this meant that he, his dragon, and the Weir would likely get a great deal busier in the near future, which brought an increased risk to his soldiers.

The trip to Draconia was only a couple days away, and Mkel had to finalize all the preparations. He had his testimony almost ready, in case the issue was brought up before the senate regarding his initiative to give benefits to families of veterans who saw a good deal of fighting then later suffered from wounds of the mind that would not heal and had taken their own lives. He was also proposing a program through the Alliance churches to help prevent such occurrences. Mkel had seen the beginning of this with his father before he died in the Great War and several men throughout the Alliance Army after they retired or left the military. The Enlightened senators were vowing to fight this, of course, stating that those costs could be used for more useful endeavors and claiming there was no proof of this phenomenon. He also wanted to get the Alliance Church of the Three Spirit to start to train their clerics in recognizing those who suffered from this mind wounding and to start helping those veterans. *The Healing Guilds should also be a part of this*, he thought to himself.

The Enlightened senators, who espoused to represent and champion the plight of the downtrodden, veteran and civilian alike, were actually going to fight this. Likely because they wanted to allocate that amount of gold to some useless project or subsidize alms for those who did not have the initiative to care for themselves and would rather live off of others' generosity. The Enlightened were very generous with other people's tax money but definitely would not be caught dead giving to charity or the church themselves. This is yet another example of their hypocrisy.

"I was just thinking, my old friend, that I would rather deal with the chromatics than the POEs sometimes, for at least they are honest in their espousal of evil, rather than disguising it like the illustrious band of Enlightened senators do," Mkel said to Jodem as he walked into the council room.

"Don't worry," Jodem replied. "Remember, we have allies in this endeavor. The sister of the hippogriff squadron commander and the son of Admiral Zewal will also be giving testimony to the senate. We will also have the majority of the senators with us on this as well, but the Enlightened could stall the vote for weeks if they have the stamina to continue to talk it to death. Key senators from Machren and Lancastra will be pushing for your initiative, as well as one of our own senators from Draden."

"I hope they can contain the flow of poison that the Enlightened senators will spew forth. Their words are akin to the vile acid of a black dragon," Mkel said with disgust. "For if they can't, I will," Mkel answered with a fierce determination.

"Be careful, my young friend, politics is a whole different fight than engaging chromatics and the Morgathians. This battlefield is constantly shifting, and alliances can switch faster than a dragon can teleport," Jodem explained. "I also think you need to see Father Watterseth before you go to Draconia. Your soul needs a little cleansing."

"I will see our good cleric before we leave for the capital, but I must talk to Wheelor first to see how his land dragons are doing and if they are ready for the games. We must also verify by tonight who is going and who is not. The teleportation circles will be getting full soon, and I want to get everyone there in one jump if possible."

"Wheelor and his crews have been training heavily and have a good chance to win at the games this year. Is Gallanth ready for the dragon contests?" Jodem asked.

"I'm pretty sure, for he has been sleeping heavily since the dragonstone weapon ceremony and his mating flight. The experience we gained during the fights at Battle Point will be invaluable, although Strikenth and Talonth also learned from the encounter."

"You all should do well, but remember it is the spirit of the games and the demonstration of their power to defend the Alliance and its citizens that is the ultimate goal. No matter how ungrateful some might seem, above all, it is to honor all the Alliance veterans," Jodem replied with a smile on his broad face. Mkel smiled back and shook Jodem's hand as he walked out of the Weir council room toward the land dragon stable area. The wingless dragons were housed close to the hatching grounds that Silvanth would soon use to lay her precious egg. Originally bred to protect metallic dragon eggs and young, the land dragons evolved into the most formidable earthbound creatures. Unless opposed by chromatics, they remained the strongest creatures faced by any army attempting to fight the Alliance. When they marched in formation in the attack, the very ground shook to warn those that would challenge them.

Wheelor and his crews were attending to the two mated pairs of land dragons that comprised Draden Weir's contingent. "Lieutenant, how are your crews this lovely morning? Breigor, Valkuran, Strongst, Shantor, my greetings to you," Mkel spoke in Draconic and nodded in a customary greeting usually reserved for true dragons, giving it to the Weir's land dragons under his charge as a sign of deference. The four land dragons of Draden Weir were among both the largest and most intelligent in the entire Alliance. Breigor had seen many battles as his brother Strongst, and they had taken down several smaller chromatic dragons with the aid of their mates. A stronger land dragon platoon would be difficult to find.

The four dragons nodded their return greeting to Mkel. "Sir, we're ready for the games," Wheelor said. "My crews have studied the shooting tips you left them, especially regarding follow through, hold, and consistency of their trigger pull and grip, and steady extended release. As for our dragons, I have no doubt about them."

"I don't know, the Battle Point land dragon crews were pretty good at holding the line against those new behir creatures, and their ballistae gunners scored a lot of hits," Mkel teased his lieutenant.

"Well, we will just have to see in Draconia, plus most of the Battle Point land dragon crews were either injured or are out on patrol," Wheelor quipped back.

"A bad way to win, but as long as you get a good practice out of the games, it will be worth it. I fear your skills and strength will be put to the test very soon," answered Mkel.

"We will be ready, sir."

"I have faith. I'll see you at the council meeting tonight and then at the teleportation circle the next morning. Thanks for you and your platoon's good work. Have a good day; Breigor, *preitoras*," he added, using the Draconic word for guardian or sentinel as a compliment to their wingless dragon cousins. He nodded to all four land dragons and walked out of their stabling area.

Mkel then checked in with all his Weir soldiers that were picked by their leaders to attend the games in Draconia, which would precede the senate gathering. He would be sending one of his catapult crews, four of his heavy cavalry paladins, four rangers with griffons, and several of his best crossbowmen and heavy infantry for marksmanship, dueling, and other weapon competitions. Mkel himself was not allowed to compete in the archery contests because of his distinct advantage with Markthrea, but he competed in the dragonstone matches.

He, Dekeen, and Jodem would compete in a special category of range dragonstone weapons, which he always looked forward to. Jodem had also told him that there were two new inventions awaiting them in Draconia for the Weir to try out. One was a new type of repeating crossbow, and the other was to be kept a closely guarded secret, but he was told it would have a dramatic impact on the way the Alliance Army fought. His curiosity was piqued.

He and his handpicked teams were to meet with their counterparts from the Draden regiment to travel together to Draconia. Mkel knew that his men could field the whole team for the games, but they had to partner with the regiment because of the relationship they had. *A small matter*, Mkel thought to himself, but he still had to remind his men anyway.

The next day went quickly, with all in the Weir either in preparation for the games or still celebrating with the Freilanders. Lawrent told Mkel that he wanted to accompany him to Draconia, so the numbers on Gallanth's back were getting tight. This meant that the big raider, Ordin, and Dorin would practically be sitting on top of each other. "Hopefully the flight will be a short one, with those two fighting like antagonistic siblings," Mkel chuckled to himself, but he knew that Annan wasn't going with them, for the mating flight knocked it out of her.

Mkel made it a point to go to the Weir's barber to get his hair cut prior to leaving. All the Weirs and most of the senior general officers would be attending the senate meeting, so he knew he had to look presentable. Dodom's shop was empty when Mkel walked in. The portly old barber looked up and smiled as he grabbed the cape he put around his customer. "Captain Mkel, welcome. Please have a seat; a little early this week?" he asked.

"We leave for Draconia tomorrow, so I just wanted to get a jump on things with everything else to do," Mkel replied.

"Well, Weirleader, you can relax now for a couple of minutes and leave everything in my hands," the jovial barber said, still smiling as he put the cape around Mkel as he sat in the raised chair. He then grabbed his finely made mithril hand blade he used to cut hair. "Will it be the usual?" he asked.

"Yes sir," Mkel replied. Dodom put one of the guards on his small hand blade and began to neatly cut the hair on the top of Mkel's head. The mithril blade with its guard cleanly cut his brownish blond hair for a smooth, even look. He then changed the guard and cut the hair on the side and back of his head closer down to skin above his ears and back of his neck. All dragonriders wore their hair short but not totally shaven, and all Alliance soldiers kept their hair short as well. Human rangers many times would completely shave their heads to make it easier to wear the different head garments used in stalking. This requirement of the Alliance for its soldiers to have short, well-kept hair, as well as maintaining personal cleanliness, symbolized the Alliance order and law over the chaos of evil of the less organized armies and self-serving kingdoms in the rest of the world.

"Thank you, my friend, an excellent job as usual. Here's a little something for you," he said as he tossed him a ten Drachmere coin, double his normal payment.

"Dragonrider, this is too much," he explained.

"You worry too much, and I know you give some older veterans and some of my younger men a break at times. It is much appreciated," Mkel replied.

"Thank you, and may the Creator bless you, sir." Mkel nodded a reply and walked out of Dodom's shop.

He then went back to his quarters to spend the rest of the evening with Michen and Annan. He would have to gather his things for the trip before they all went to sleep, for tomorrow would be a long day. He was always a little sad to leave his son behind, but it would be very busy in Draconia with the games and the senate gathering, and with Annan not able to go now, it would be just too hard to have him there even with Janta helping.

Lieutenant Ablich had arrived the day before, which Mkel considered a fortunate event. He was a fellow platoon leader with Mkel at the Weir's infantry company years ago and had moved to Machren Weir for a short time to attend a learning guild. Mkel had requested that he come back as his second in command of the garrison infantry company. He worked well with Pekram, which was no easy task, and had his complete confidence. He was a tall, slender man, with a somewhat ruddy complexion, receding hairline, and gentle smile, but a warrior through and through. This made Mkel more comfortable in leaving his men on the frequent trips that he had to make for his duties as a dragonrider.

Mkel gave his final instructions on what was to be done in his absence. He was only leaving for a couple of days and could be back in minutes if the need arose, but it was always good to leave a contingency. After handing off the gauntlet to Ablich and Pekram, he told all his men to gather at the Weir entrance. He agreed to allow Lupek and Deless to stay back because of the increased movement of the fire giants to the southeast and to coordinate their patrols with Colonel Lordan's legion's second in command. Both of the ranger units from these two Weirs would perform joint patrols to ensure this gathering army did not slip past them or any of the border outposts in the Gray Mountains.

Lupek and Razor Claw usually either won or placed in many events in the games, but there were more urgent matters to attend to, and his two ranger leaders needed to be here, not three thousand miles to the west. Jodem, Dekeen, Toderan, Ordin, Dorin, Wheelor, Willaward, Tegent, Fogellem, and Watterseth from the Weir council would join him in going to Draconia. Lenor would also stay behind to aid Lupek in the ground patrols on the border. He knew he would need Fogellem with him at the senate session, just in case. Mkel then had all that were going with him to Draconia assemble by the Weir lake for a quick speech. Besides the mating flight, Annan also needed to stay behind for Michen and also for Silvanth if she was needed immediately for any reason. He always liked to take her and his beloved son to the games, but these were different times.

"My friends, I wanted to just take a couple of minutes to talk to you about our trip to the capital before we leave," Mkel began. "The Honors Day games are important spectator events for the citizens of the Alliance and are good military skills practice. Gallanth and I will be with you all for as many of the events as possible, but we will be also engaged in a difficult fight of our own in the great halls of the Alliance senate to ensure the rights of our honored veterans.

"With that said," he continued, "I want you all to know of the threat that is materializing to the east and what we could be facing soon. The army that Battle Point defeated, with a little help from Keystone Weir, was just the beginning. The fire giants gathering with chromatic dragons in the southern Smoking Mountains are a growing and significant threat to both our Weir and Eladran, not to mention the whole eastern part of the Alliance itself. Use these next several days to pursue excellence and hone your skills while putting your mind in proper perspective, which is to be as proficient as possible in your particular area of expertise. This will in turn save lives, the lives of our brothers and sisters in battle, if it should arise. I still want you to have fun in the competitions. Do your best and reinsure the confidence of the people of the Alliance in your ability to defend their freedom. As I trust this Weir, our garrison company soldiers, and our dwarven and elven brothers to always be victorious in battle, I trust you will do your best and be true to your Weir and yourselves. Gallanth and I wish you all the best. Honor above all," he finished.

"Honor above all," Gallanth reinforced with his booming deep voice, which was then echoed by all gathered.

"Land dragon crews, make your way to the teleportation circle as per the march order. Lieutenant Wheelor, lead them out. All others follow Gallanth and me to wing as soon as they clear the Weir entrance." Mkel moved over to Gallanth to help Lawrent, Dorin, and Ordin get strapped into his dragon's flying harness. Lieutenant Wheelor quickly mounted on Breigor and gave the hand signal to all the ground crews and soldiers to move out of the Weir behind his land dragons. Even the proportionately slow catapult crews were moving at a good pace as they brought up the rear of his column.

Once they had moved out of the Weir, Mkel nodded to his companions and the rangers with them, and then Gallanth turned and walked to the entrance of the Weir. With a couple of short strides and one mighty heft, he was airborne, followed by the host of large feathered mounts. The land component quickly made it to the nearby teleportation circle, which was just on the north side of the Weir between the mountain and the city of Draden. This teleportation circle was the second biggest in the Alliance, being three hundred yards in diameter. A regiment could teleport into or out of this circle if needed. The entire floor, the surrounding three-foot wall that lined its circumference and the dragon head sculpture on the tall archway at the circle's entrance were all made of a low-grade mithril ore. This material was rock that the dwarves could not extract any more of the precious metal out of, but it would still conduct magic. It was powered by the two dragonstones in the eyes of the gold dragon embossment at the keystone of the arch. This was what gave the circle its power to teleport. It also kept the elements out the circle and could, if need be, defend itself. Normally the circle was divided in half with those departing and those coming in, but when the military used it, they would routinely utilize the whole area at once.

There were teleportation circles at each of the major cities and all the Weirs. These were opened shortly after the Great War. First created to allow the Alliance to shift troops and supplies rapidly throughout its large expanses, it then led to immense travel to all points within the republic for commerce and general movement for the population. The latest one to be opened was at Battle Point, which would be finished within a couple of weeks, and one was being considered in Freiland. Draconia itself had three, with one beside the Capital Weir and the other two on either side of the city. These were also the size of the Draden circle. The circles at Eladran and Machren Weirs, as well as the ones at Lancastra, Atlean, Ice Bay, and High Mountain Weirs, were roughly half the size of Draden's. A second circle was also being planned for Atlean as that thriving trade and sea port city was expanding at a good rate. Both dragons and entire legions could muster at any Weir or city in the Alliance in hours or less. The circles communicated with each other to ensure transport was instantaneous and incident free, with their dragonstones giving them limited intelligence like the Weir sentinels.

The Weir's crews and soldiers were met at the circle by their counterparts from the Draden regiment to travel together. Mkel and his companions flew a lazy pattern just a few hundred feet above the circle and were soon joined by the regiment's chosen hippogriff riders, led by Colonel Wierangan. Mkel guessed he wanted to talk to the council of generals regarding the developing situation in Battle Point and the southern Gray Mountains with the fire giants. Also he was likely to complain about the pact that Gallanth made with General Daddonan to General Becknor and ask for a speedy assignment of a dragon or two to the walled city. *It's all about territory*, Mkel thought to himself, but it was Wierangan's regiment, and the Weir was his main fighting power and anchor.

Lieutenant Wheelor deferred to the regimental forces and let them enter the circle first, as a sign of politeness and comradeship. They matched the Weir teams with a platoon of land dragons and equal counterparts to the cavalry, catapult, and infantry, all for the games. As soon as the regiment's soldiers were through the arch and settled toward the back of the teleportation circle to make room for the Weir's forces, Lieutenant Wheelor told the senior sergeant to lead their troops in behind the two land dragons. The combined group didn't even fill up half of the circle, so there was not the crowding that the soldiers were used to. Lieutenant Wheelor and his land dragon was the last to enter the archway, and he then announced to the head stone their destination. He looked up toward the slowly circling Gallanth and waved to Mkel. The dragonrider waved back, and in a second, the invisible dome shimmered and the whole group was gone.

Mkel then called to Colonel Wierangan through his seeing crystal to form up around Gallanth. Within a minute, all the flyers from Draden and the Weir were tightly packed in formation around Gallanth's massive wings. In a blue flash of light, they disappeared and reappeared over Sauric Bay just to the side of the massive carved mountain, which was the Capital Weir.

CHAPTER IX

CITY OF SHADOW

There was a low haze over the Morgathian capital city of Aserghul and the five dark spiraling towers of Tiamat's fortress. The sun was barely piercing through the clouds, and the sea surrounding the city seemed angry in spite of no storm on the horizon. The five immense, twisted, grayish black towers rose sharply above the sprawling city and the trash-strewn harbor. The inhabitants of Aserghul were scurrying about, conducting the daily trade and business of the large densely packed city, but with a certain hesitancy, almost like they were constantly watching over their shoulder, and with the ever present Talon guards constantly patrolling, their caution was warranted. Most of the wooden and cheaply made brick houses were dingy and smudged as a result of their use of the black fire rock to heat their homes. While chromatic dragons can make heating and cooling stones, they only do so for a very high price, which only the Morgathian party officials and a few merchants, sorcerers and warlords could afford.

Many of the lower districts by the harbor were shanty, made of bamboo and light woods with hastily patched roofs. The streets were mostly dirt or thrown down rock, with brick streets only seen in the areas around Tiamat's fortress or in the military districts and the sorcerers' guilds. The city was not overly destitute or severely poverty stricken, but the oppression of the Talon Covenant, the chromatic dragons, and the magitocracy severely limited opportunity.

442

The bustle of the markets by the shipyards was interrupted when a very large red dragon emerged out of teleport over the harbor and swung toward his perch on the crimson-topped tower. A black dragon then erupted from the choppy waters of the harbor, capsizing a small fishing boat, and worked hard to gain altitude as he flew toward the fortress. People would quickly make the streets less crowded when a chromatic appeared, just as a precaution.

Shortly afterward, large specimens of the other three chromatic types teleported in and glided toward their respective towers. These were the strongest of each of their species and served as Tiamat's personal guards; they were known as the Usurper Five. They enjoyed any amount of plunder from others of their species and were given enhanced magical powers from Tiamat. These positions of privilege were decided by a ritual combat tournament every one hundred years (or sooner if that particular dragon was vanquished).

The fortress of Aserghul was an immense structure; its five thick towers were made from grayish black brick. They rose up from the center hub and terminated hundreds of feet in the air at their colored apexes, representing the five chromatic dragon types and each of Tiamat's heads: white, black, green, blue, and red. They were all connected in the center to an immense, dimly glowing dome with a huge dark crystal at its center. It constantly emanated a purplish light, as did the crystals at the apex of each of the towers. This structure resembled a sharp talon hand, with its fingers turning in toward the center. From the air, the fortress took the appearance of a colossal clawed hand, defiantly reaching up from the underworld to the heavens.

The winds were blowing the fifty-foot Morgathian flags straight from each tower. Each flag was of the color of the dragon the tower belonged to, with the outline of a talon in the center of the standard in blazing white. The exception was the tower belonging to the white dragon, which was all a dull white with the black outline of a talon, simple but imposing, like the chromatics themselves. The openings next to the base of each tower, where they met the central structure like a finger joint, were just large enough to accommodate a large type of that particular chromatic dragon.

A great black stone wall surrounded the towered fortress and was manned with hundreds of troops with dozens of ballistae trained on anything that approached. The stronghold overlooked the harbor, which was lined with catapults and ballistae along its heavily fortified docks and shore line. The dilapidated lower parts of the city almost breathed out its frustration in the oppression of the Morgathian autocratic magitocracy, ruled by the sorcerer elite with the guise of stern protective oversight. The empire itself was ruled with an iron fist by the powerful sorcerers and warlords of the Talon Covenant, along with their chromatic dragon allies, under the strict confederation of Tiamat. The Talon sorcerers each lorded over a province of the empire with almost unchecked power. Almost all of these warlocks had a second in command or deputy that was a powerful death knight and warlord, who vied for power and territory themselves.

The twenty most powerful of the empire's sorcerers, with their death knights or death lord companions, formed the Talon Covenant. These ruthless tyrants controlled their provinces through fear, oppression, false propaganda against the Alliance, and their sycophantic religion of worshiping Tiamat, as well as the threat of chromatic dragon retribution. They heavily taxed their people under the guise of service to the state, requiring at least one child sacrifice per family to the local ruling chromatic. Additionally, mandatory service in the army of their particular province for two years or more was required. The Morgathians maintained a strong-armed reign over the orc tribes that inhabited the vast lands to the north and west of their empire. This was accomplished mainly by the pure brute force of the Morgathian army and especially by the power of the chromatic dragons.

There were, however, many chromatics that operated independently of the empire or just gathered plunder from outside the Morgathian borders. They preyed on the northern Kaskar horse clans; the Eastern, Middle, and Western Ontaror kingdoms; and the islands of the Southern Sea. However, they were reined in by Tiamat's powerful crew if they got out of line.

More dragons started to teleport in above the harbor and the spiral towers. The provisional lords also started to arrive on a wide variety of mounts. Nightmares were the preferred steed for Morgathian sorcerers, but manticores and wyverns were also utilized. All the dragons arrived without riders, for chromatics only consented to be ridden when going into battle, and even then it was rare. Their anti-subjugation mentality was a strong emotion with them, along with their fierce independence in not being tied to anything but themselves. Only the senior dragon from each province was allowed to attend, by the permission of Tiamat's five minions, and even then they were only allowed to view the meeting from the ground through magic eye spells.

The Usurper dragons were all keeping a watchful eye from their tower entrance perches, as the other province dragons arrived with their respective sorcerer and warlord flying with them. A feared group of death knights, called the Talestra, were standing guard at the heavy reinforced gate to the base of the fortress. They were watching all who entered the imposing opening. Statues of the five heads of Tiamat protruded from the top of the gate and looked down menacingly at anyone entering. The massive doors were several feet thick and had to be opened by the four common giants chained to the side of the entrance. The Talestra death knight guards were chosen for their strength, ferocity, and cruelty in battle, but not their intellectual prowess. They were heavily armed, each with a dark crystal sword or battle-axe, or black iron weapon magically enhanced by one of the Usurper dragons. They also all had demon armor with its imbedded dark crystal, clawed gauntlets, and skull-shaped or jagged-toothed demon face helmet. These formidable guardians also accompanied the lead warlock of the Talon Covenant as his personal bodyguard when he ventured out of the fortress.

Stalenjh, the prefect of the Talon Covenant, had these death knights trained well. They stared intently at the provincial sorcerers of the Covenant and their warlord companions, as if to entice them to a fight. This, however, was not unusual, for succession of power in the Morgathian Empire was merely a feat of strength, cunning, and favor with Tiamat herself. Even though this was usually a chaotic method of government, the arch dragon Tiamat maintained order. She did so even in the face of armed conflict among the members of her own inner circle. The same was true of the chromatics dragons among the Usurper Five and the provincial hierarchy.

All of the nine provinces and eleven sub-provinces had this type of hierarchy as well. A red, blue, green, black, and even a white dragon were senior dragons of a particular area and worked with that particular sorcerer or warlord. It was a very uneasy relationship, considering the chaotic tendencies of the chromatic dragons; however, this was maintained through mutual respect for power and benefit. They knew they had a better chance of maintaining control of their provinces and in obtaining treasure and lands by begrudgingly working together.

Many of the provincial sorcerers had now arrived, and their mounts were being taken to the stables at the far end of the walled compound. The dragons present gave a salutatory bow to their Usurper Five counterparts and began to settle down on the stone and gravel grounds surrounding the fortress.

Most of the Covenant that arrived began sitting in the one-hundred-yard-diameter stone circle located in the large center of the fortress that surrounded Tiamat's personal lodging. The immense dragon queen lay curled up asleep in the center of the large chamber, her bedding of broken and crushed bones lay neatly underneath her, and all five of her colored heads rested on the floor. Her actual lair was underneath this meeting chamber, where she had her immense pile of hoarded treasure. The resting place here was for gatherings only. She was still recuperating from the wounds she received from her defeat by Michenth at the last fight at Battle Point during the Great War. She, like the mithril dragon and her formal mate, would only wake to feed and for Covenant gatherings and the like.

"Well, our queen mother is still in slumber," one of the death knights said in a loud and boisterous manner as he walked into the chamber.

"Hold your tongue, talking monkey, or I will do it for you," Uthrex, the red dragon of the Usurper Five, answered in his normal angry but now even more irritated manner.

"Uthrex, my dear dragon, in a good mood as usual," the Morgathian overlord said with a smile on his ruddy, scarred, and weathered face.

"I warn you, warlord, I will not tolerate insolence," the red dragon growled.

"Well, demon dragon, a little demanding considering your fellow Thurex was felled by a metallic as of recent. I guess this means that you dark crystal-enhanced hybrids are not the war gods that you proclaim to be. But since he has been vanquished, it does ensure you will remain here as Tiamat's senior dragon handmaiden." Uthrex let out another deep growl at the death knight.

"We should not wait anymore for these overgrown lizards to grow in numbers. Ashram's defeat on the plains told us not that the Alliance is strong, but they had to get Capital dragons to reinforce them. They are spread too thin, their numbers are still small, and the time to strike is now. Tiamat is either dying or too weak to control the chromatics, for more and more are defying our plans and going on independent quests for treasure and conquest," the warlord shouted out as he walked about the gathered group.

"The defeat at Handsdown was just a temporary setback. The master plan in still intact," Yveshra, the drow countess, weighed into the argument.

"Ha, your kin didn't do much better than the chromatics. I heard that the Alliance wizard and a gold dragon wiped out a whole company of spider-mounted drow, killed one of your more powerful sorcerers, and captured a queen court priestess. I think you've been underground too long!" the death knight quipped back. "The fleet and the army are ready now; we must strike, or maybe we should seize control from our five-headed dragon god and her minions. The giants are ready, along with dozens of chromatics and the growing armies of orcs. We can bring the Alliance to its knees now, but not by waiting."

"You will take your place now!" Stalenjh stood up, shouting at the errant dark knight; the dark crystal skull-shaped head of his sorcerer's staff was glowing in an eerie purplish color, indicating he was angry and possibly ready to cast a spell.

"Hold your tongue, sorcerer!" he shouted back. "Your leadership has been knuckled under by your obedience to these lazy lizards here at Aserghul and their weakened queen."

"Enough, your lead dragon puts too much ambition in you empty head!" Uthrex roared back.

"Go kneel before your master, Uthrex, so much for our living god!" he yelled back and spit in Tiamat's direction. With this, the demon red dragon roared and moved toward the warlord, who drew his dark crystal sword and prepared to defend himself. Faster than the eye could see, Tiamat's scythe-bladed tail struck out and pierced the knight's black iron armor back plate and emerged out of his chest. He dropped his sword and grasped the blade-like tail as blood poured from the wound. Even if he could have survived the injury, he would not have been able to cure the incredibly potent poison delivered by her tail stinger. Tiamat lifted him off of the ground as she raised all five of her heads.

"The only one to kill in my house is me! Enough of this trivial nonsense!" her blue head roared as she flung the impaled knight against the far wall of her chamber, killing him. Uthrex lowered his head and moved back to his place in the room. "If there is any doubt to my power, anyone else is welcome to challenge me!" Tiamat shouted with all five heads as they scanned the gathered crowd and her dragon minions.

"No one challenges your power, Queen Tiamat," Stalenjh quickly stated. "He was just a fool drunk with power and overly ambitious."

"For all of your sakes, I hope you are correct," her green head commented as she started to set herself back down.

"My queen, if I may, we should discuss our plans," Stalenjh interjected to regain control of the Covenant gathering.

"You may proceed, sorcerer," Tiamat's blue head replied.

"Thank you, Queen Tiamat. We all know of Ashram's defeat on the plains. While we knew they would have been pushed back anyway, the complete destruction of his northern army's excursion force came as a surprise. The eradication of the two wings of chromatics and the death of two demon dragons also was unexpected. Thurex fell without even killing a metallic, as they were taken off guard. Our informants within the Alliance have had their families executed for their failure to warn our forces," Stalenjh explained.

"He and his wing were ambushed by two large silvers and a huge gold dragon. There was also an Alliance wizard of considerable power with a group of strong warriors with dragonstone weapons," Uthrex spoke up, defending the efforts of his rival.

"The three metallic dragons had dramatically increased magical power as well as very short recovery times for their breath weapons. Their antimagic shields were also extremely strong, much more so than we encountered during the Great War," Zythor, the demon blue dragon, added.

"The Battle Point legion appeared out of nowhere, as if from thin air, or they teleported in all at once, which is impossible, and there was not supposed to be any metallics at Battle Point at all," Xylest, the male sorcerer/fighter accompanying Yveshra, explained. "We should hold off on our planned attacks until we can ascertain the source of both the metallics' increased power and the new mobility of their legions. So much for the information we are supposed to be getting from our enlightened spies in the Alliance."

"No, we must keep the pressure on the Alliance, to keep them off balance, or our grand scheme will be compromised. Besides, our allies in their senate will falter if we back away now," Stalenjh stated strongly.

"Ashram and Lodar lost half their northern army in just this small fight alone, when they were supposed to roll over the garrison at Handsdown and then ambush the reinforcements. I also understand that adding insult to injury, the three metallic dragons even teleported into our lands and took the slain chromatics' treasure hoards. The gold dragon actually had the audacity to attack their fortress and inflicted heavy damage," stated Tbok, an overlord sorcerer of one of the western provinces of the empire.

"Lodar and Ashram still have the majority of their army left, but if they need a little reinforcement in their province, I would be happy to send over troops to maintain order. At least until poor Ashram heals, of course, or until you repair your damaged fortress," offered Dreadleg, a death knight overlord of the Eastern province; he had an impetuous grin across his black and gray bearded chin, in a very sinister but poignant expression.

"Our fortress only suffered minor damage before we drove the gold metallic off. We still have most of our army intact and several more wings of chromatics, vermin," Lodar spat back as he began to stand up and grasp his dark crystal vampire sword in a show of force against Dreadleg.

"Their dragonriders are the key," stated Rexkald, the green dragon of Tiamat's court. "When attacking a metallic you not only have to deal with a dragon's normal breath weapon, spells, fangs and claws, but they strike you with a dragonstone weapon or powerful spell from their rider that hits you from where you can't defend yourself. Again, their riders are the key, their familiars, and their focus of magical power. We must separate them first, but the metallics guard them like a treasure hoard."

"There is a plan to address this soon," Tiamat's blue head said. "As for your forces, you all can lose half or all of your armies if I see fit. The time for our revenge is coming. Stalenjh, Uthrex, contact the fire giants and the dragons we have reinforcing them, and tell them to attack with undue haste. Wvythresher, have the ice giants prepare for their attack in the north as well. Tbok, I want the Shidanese fleet to increase its attacks on all non-Morgathian-aligned ships heading for trade with the Alliance to force them to disperse their navy to a greater degree. We must also pull more dark crystal and giant longnecks lizards from the Canaris Islands to power our fleet with weapons and feed our growing numbers of chromatics and orcs. I demand more gemstones from Shidan and Ariana, as well as more strikes against Southland and Freiland." The demon, berserker white dragon, and sorcerer nodded an acknowledgment.

"My queen mother, Shidan, has been losing many ships to the Freiland raiders and the Alliance warships," Tbok interjected, "and they do not possess the ability to build ships quickly to replace their losses."

"Then we must give the desert mongrels a dozen or so of our ships to fly under their standard or a pirate flag and get them more timber from Canaris," Tiamat's green head dictated. "We will also force either the Shidanese or their neighbors to attack Ian, either in concert or alone. It doesn't matter how many of them die, convince them their false god decrees it, and send them a wing of our younger but hungry dragons to reinforce them. Tell my minions that they can have any treasure they kill for or usurp. The Kallysh infantile cult makes the desert vermin easy to manipulate. Their ignorance is our bliss, for they and their mindless devotion to their religion will allow us to make them bleed for our cause."

"My queen, the Shidanese, while ready for battle, might not want to risk all out war with Ian. Especially in conjunction with our plan with them for the Alliance operation, and their fear of an Arianan attack from across the strait is always worrisome for them," Tbok countered.

"Tell that spineless cleric king, Ibliss, that either he does our bidding or he faces Morgathian retribution, and he then won't have to worry about the Alliance or the Arianans, her white dragon head countered. "Send a messenger to the Arianan king, that there will be no aggressive move against Shidan while these actions take place or we will send in wings of our dragons to seize their gemstone mines," her black dragon head added in its raspy hissing voice.

"Yes, my queen," Tbok quickly acquiesced, knowing this would be a difficult task. He would have to enlist the most powerful blue dragon of his wings, with maybe the aid of Zythor, the demon blue dragon of Tiamat's court, if necessary. He could use him to just ride herd over the wing of chromatics that were to be sent and over the ones already in that kingdom that were getting ideas of their own.

"I will be suspending the trials this turn, so we can have as many of our dragons alive for the upcoming battle," Tiamat also added.

"Queen Mother, won't this bring dissent among the chromatics?" Stalenjh asked.

"If there are any questions, any dragon can always bring their grievances to me," her red dragon head quickly responded. Every one hundred years, Tiamat conducted a tournament to determine who would represent their species in her court. Many of these contests were fatal, with dozens of chromatics killed in this event. This was a loss that the multiheaded queen dragon did not want to happen at this time. This was especially true with the number of dragons currently dying as a result of the attempted demon ritual and their melding with a dark crystal to their synthensium.

"There is also resistance growing at the increased conscription for this massive army we are building, as well as getting the numbers of experienced sailors we need," one of the Talon sorcerers said, with hesitation.

"Reinforce to the people of your provinces that service to the queen and the empire is their duty, as well as to provide defense against the threat and oppression of the metallic dragons. You must also remind them of the penalties of disobedience," Stalenjh replied with a smile seen through his thick gray/black mustache. "Those that continue to resist will be given the opportunity to sacrifice more of their children to our queen mother and our chromatic dragons or offer themselves as an alternative."

Service with the Morgathian army was mandatory for two years for all men upon reaching seventeen years of age. The

Empire did not believe in a strong non-noble professional soldier like the Alliance, likely from a fear of revolt. The Morgathians also did not elect provincial overlords, telling their people that they were chosen by Tiamat to best serve the empire and protect them from the Alliance and the metallic dragons, as well as from their orc allies. Despite the mandatory conscription, Morgathians were not allowed to own or practice with weapons, again another form of population control.

"In either case, we should continue to allow the orc tribes to increase in numbers, but we must provide food for them or they will turn on each other and likely attack the Northern and Western provinces," said Reigngrim, one of the most feared and powerful Morgathian death knights.

"That is why we need to keep the supply of lizard meat flowing from the Canaris Twins. Our peasant farmers and herders can barely keep the dragons, giants, wyverns, and manticores supplied in meat," Dreadstone emphasized to the group.

"The Freilanders are sinking or capturing as many of our merchant ships as the Shidanese are of other kingdoms," Tbok explained.

"This means that the Shidanese and their immediate allies must declare open naval war on all Alliance-bound ships," Dreadstone suggested, "and we must release at least a squadron of our warships to act as independent pirates on the high seas." He was notorious for his ruthlessness and cruelty, with his power almost being unmatched in the empire, save Stalenjh himself. His tall lanky appearance, with his long curved nose, long dark gray beard, and deep sullen blackish eyes, gave him a menacing appearance. His sorcerer's staff had a black iron halberd head surrounding the fist-sized dark crystal. Dreadstone's cruelty was so respected among the chromatics that they allowed him to mount them when going into battle. Mostly he rode the blue, green, and black dragons in his wings, but even red dragons allowed this occasionally.

Dreadstone was renowned for his massacre of an Alliance settlement in the unsettled lands and his bringing down of a copper dragon during the Great War. Many a metallic would like to see him dead, but even a bronze dragon would have to be cautious in engaging him. He and Stalenjh had an uneasy relationship, with the lead Talon sorcerer always keeping a careful eye on him. Dreadstone and his warlord partner Reigngrim made a very dangerous duo, commanding a large army, and three to four dozen squadrons of chromatics.

"Yes, the orc tribes to my north are already venturing over into our lands, looting for food, so we must shift more of these large lizards to keep their appetites in check," Tbok said. "I don't want to get into a skirmish with them yet or enforce their obedience by using our dragons."

"The problem is that they grow faster in the Southern and Eastern provinces, which have more swamps and vegetation, and herding them to your borders is arduous. Plus they are picked off as we move them west by roaming dragons and even some manticores," Karnack blurted out defensively.

"Keep the orcs in check by force if you have to, and send at least two tribes to the north to reinforce the ice giants. That will alleviate some pressure on our borders without having to sacrifice some of our own pawns to keep the rest of them in line. If you have to, send another colony to the fire giants through the mountain pass route," Tiamat's blue dragon head directed, at which all nodded.

"We have our spies and provocateurs working in the Northern Ontaror kingdoms from within their criminal and elite classes, trying to subvert their parliaments and armies. While we have not been as successful in the Alliance itself, our allies there are gaining in political power. We will help them in their endeavors to subvert their governments, but this will take skill in their provocation. We also must keep our agents in the dark of our real intentions. Their own sense of self-righteousness, greed, and lust for power is their weakness that we will exploit. The fools don't know what is really in store for them, and it will be too late once they realize our true purpose," Tiamat's black head's raspy voice explained.

"We are even staging several of the fire giant clans' raiding parties in parts of the kingdom of Gransaulf, just to the east of the Gray Mountains from the Alliance's border," Tiamat's green dragon head said. "This is arranged by some of their towns who harbor ill will toward the Alliance. Those in that area who don't actively support us at least exhibit duplicity. The fools don't realize that they are contributing to the doom of the very agent of their freedom and prosperity."

453

"We will play on the inherent weakness of the Alliance and their cursed metallic dragons. Their foolish sense of honor, fairness, and the idea of freedom they so idealize can be used very effectively against them. The Alliance value of the individual and sense of right over wrong, as well as their sensitivity to their children, demonstrate their failing. Our official philosophy of egalitarianism, total equality through submission to the empire as the pabulum for the masses, when really it is about our ruling class and political elite, this Covenant, and most importantly me, your queen and living god," Tiamat's white head angrily said

"The metallic dragons also show their weakness in their misguided love of these talking monkeys and in the way they actually pray for our redemption to the cursed Creator when they are lucky enough to slay one of my minions. Remind all your kin what could happen to them if any consider a conversion from whom they serve. The chromatics serve us, they serve me both in this life and my mirror in the afterlife. They are to fight for me on both planes, for if they don't, I will eat their souls," Tiamat's red head said, looking around the gathered to bring home her point more forcibly.

"We have an issue with this year's harvest, my queen," Tbok stated. "Our collective farms across the empire are failing. The only thing that is keeping the people fed, are the small private plots that the peasants are allowed to keep. This is proving difficult in feeding both our people and the orcs."

"The collective farms are one of our methodologies in controlling our population and keeping them dependent on the Covenant and the provincial rulers. We must continue to emphasize to the peasants that it is the collective that is the most important, not themselves; we must destroy their individualism. Order must be maintained by fear and provocation, and by keeping the population ignorant," Stalenjh stated.

"I agree, Stalenjh, we must maintain respect through fear. They must know that their protection from the perceived threat of the Alliance, the Kaskars, and orcs comes at a price," Tiamat's blue dragon head stated. Therefore, there will be punishment for lack of production from these serf farmers. We will also send our captured slaves under control of the army to aid them in the coming harvest.

"My Usurper Five, I want you to enforce to the dragons of the provinces, that these insolent insects are to be made to respect our power and authority over them or there will be consequences, Tiamat's red dragon head angrily spoke up, at which all the demon dragons of her court nodded quickly.

"Karnak, you and your errant death knight are to push the Arianans to increase their piracy on the high seas as well," her green head added.

"Queen Mother, they are not as easy to manipulate as the Shidanese, and we don't have a dragon presence there," the Talon sorcerer stated.

"Then tell their theocratic rulers that we will stop buying gemstones from them and simply take them by force," the arch dragon's black head hissed. "We can and will stop the shipment of dark crystal to them and seize what gem wealth they have. It is their choice, and if they choose wrongly, then one of their cities will be annihilated as a demonstration of our power and authority.

"Yes, Queen Tiamat, I will take an envoy with one of my dragon squadrons to enforce your decree," the apprehensive sorcerer replied.

"Stalenjh, I want you to start extracting more grain from the Kaskars, the Indus, and our pawns in the northern Canaris Twins to supplement our food stores; by force if necessary. This should be enough to satisfy the whining of our subjects," the blue dragon head of Tiamat stated. Her blue head was the most calculating of her five and usually formed all her plans.

"Yes, my queen mother, I will make arrangements immediately," Stalenjh quickly replied.

"It is now time to feed. Vasterlan, take your former death knight's sword and contest it among your top warriors, and remind them of how it came to be available if anyone else should decide to challenge me," she finished as the massive doors from one side of the colossal room swung slowly open. Black-hooded men ushered in several dozen children dressed in white. They were to be sacrificed to the queen dragon; she derived healing and strength from their screams and terror. Similar to the way the metallics drew power from their riders' love and emotion, the chromatics extorted a lesser degree of energy from the fear and screams of the victims they devoured.

455

The worship of Tiamat was the state-enforced religion of the Morgathian Empire, for she, like Michenth and the other dragons, extended themselves both on this world and into the afterlife at the same time. The worship of the multiheaded dragon was considered to be communal, because she had five different colored heads representing all facets of life. This was supposed to embody the ultimate equality or egalitarianism of society, like the burden shared by sorcerer, warlord, and peasant alike to defend and serve Morgathia. It was supposed to be considered an honor for a family to sacrifice a child to a dragon, especially Queen Tiamat, plus the money they received was usually a month's wages. This once popular sentiment was slowly changing, for no child of a Morgathian Covenant member or a noble from the provinces had been sacrificed to a chromatic in many years. Morgathians were encouraged to have many children for this purpose and for more fodder for their overlord's armies.

"Members of the Talon Covenant, this gathering is now concluded," Stalenjh stated. "The feast and entertainment are in the lower halls. Let us move there now." He ushered the gathered group out of the chamber as the sacrifices were herded in; there were similar horrible attractions waiting for the council below.

The Covenant had their marching orders now and started to leave the large room. As the group of powerful warlords and sorcerers exited the hall, the screams of the children being devoured echoed off of the stone walls. The evil of the chromatics knew no bounds.

CHAPTER X

CITY OF LIGHT

Gallanth soared toward the Capital Weir with all from Draden right behind him. The sky over the immense mountain fortress was fairly crowded with dragons, hippogriffs, griffons, eagles, and even the new dragon horses flying about and around the monstrous gleaming white and gray carved mountain. It always amazed Mkel when he saw the grandeur of the Capital Weir, literally an entire mountain that was sculpted and reinforced by thousands of dwarves and human workers centuries ago. Those dwarves still continued its upgrades and repairs in the constant battle with the elements. The three immense openings to the ten-thousand-foot-tall mountain were large enough to allow two gold dragons to fly into and out of the Weir side by side and still leave enough room for several griffons to accompany them. At one time before the Great War, the Capital Weir alone had more dragons than currently existed in all the Alliance.

The docks and the waters of Sauric Bay were very busy, with a wide variety of merchant, passenger, cargo, and warships all going about their business. The immense Alliance flag mounted atop the snow-capped mountain was standing almost straight out. At night, hundreds of lighting crystals were set up with polished mirrors that illuminated the huge flag, which stretched one hundred yards long and sixty yards wide. This served as a symbol of the Alliance's might but also as a beacon for incoming ships, knowing that they were entering a free, protected, and safe port. The blue, white, gold, brown, and green of the large flag showed brilliantly in the morning sun.

Mkel could see the legions training their formations in the huge field to the north of the Capital Weir. They swung wide in their descent toward the northern entrance to the mountain. He also saw his and the regiment's soldiers and mounts exit from the teleportation circle and move toward the barracks and stables at the base of the north face of the Weir. It would be an hour or so for them to settle in and then move to the training grounds. He waved his and the regiment's hippogriffs and griffons off, as they peeled away toward their respective landing sites and the visiting stables by the barracks. Gallanth, with the Weir staff and Colonel Wierangan still following, flew into the north entrance of the Capital Weir. Mkel and Gallanth didn't get to the Capital often, but that didn't bother him. *Much too busy here*, he thought to himself, but its sheer size always impressed him. Almost all of Keystone Weir could fit inside this great interior.

They did one circle around the inside of the Weir space, with Gallanth giving a greeting roar to all the Capital Wing dragons, but especially his brother Falcanth, who he liked to visit whenever he got the chance. His roar was echoed by all the capital dragons currently in the Weir. The thunderous noise of the combined roars filled the huge interior space of the mountain. This was usually only done for the senior dragon of each Weir, but Gallanth was honored since he was a gold dragon and also for the fight in Battle Point.

Falcanth's rider, Lloydell, had a special fondness for Mkel, for he served with his father in the Great War as a newly bonded dragonrider. He knew and respected Jmes as the Draden wing's leader and mentor. His death had a profound impact on the now veteran dragonrider, but he was very pleased to see Mkel become bonded with Gallanth and become the Draden Weirleader. Mkel looked forward to talking to him, but he also knew that he and Gallanth had to see either Therosvet or Becknor and Michenth as soon as possible. As he made the complete swing around the interior circumference, he nosed down and landed by the entrance to Michenth's chamber. The huge opening that went deep into the mountain was familiar to Mkel, for he remembered when he was seven and Gallanth and Jodem brought him here to see the arch dragon.

458

He and his Weirmates, along with Colonel Wierangan, dismounted and were met by Lloydell, Colonel Therosvet, General Becknor, and several other Capital Wing dragonriders. "Mkel, always good to see you, lad," Lloydell quickly spoke up as Mkel rendered a salute to Becknor.

"Good morning, Captain Mkel. I trust you and Gallanth have recovered from your fight in the east?" Becknor inquired with a smile.

"We're just fine, sir; Gallanth has been resting as much as possible, even with the visit from our Freiland brothers and his and Silvanth's mating flight. Sir, this is Lawrent, Draden's official Freiland representative," Mkel answered as he introduced the raider and gave Lloydell a wink to acknowledge his greeting.

"Good to have your acquaintance, raider. We look forward to having your countrymen talk to the both the senate and the Dragon Council," the general said as he reached out his right hand. Lawrent grasped the dragonrider's smaller hand with a big smile.

"Always a pleasure, General, as it is working with Captain Mkel, Gallanth, and Keystone Weir," he returned the greeting.

"Good to see our Freiland brothers with us, Raider Captain," Becknor replied. "Toderan, good to see you here, my friend; Master Jodem, Dekeen, Ordin, all of Draden, welcome to the Capital Weir." General Becknor shook their hands after taking a salute from Colonel Wierangan.

"Mkel, Gallanth, great to have you here, especially after what we heard happened out at Battle Point. Good job, by the way," Lloydell said as he gave Mkel a hug.

"Always good to see you as well, Lloydell; how is my brother?" Gallanth asked of the senior gold dragonrider.

"He is back with Valianth and Michenth, waiting to do the official greeting; Eagrenth is on a ferrying mission for the senate," Lloydell answered. "We have some surprises for you, my lad; after we meet with Michenth, I will show them to you and your Weir mates. You will be impressed."

"Let's go see my still healing dragon. Michenth has been asking about you and Gallanth," Becknor said to Mkel, as he motioned them all to follow him into the great hall that led to Michenth's chamber. He had not seen Michenth since he was nineteen years old, just after he bonded with Gallanth, and that was only for a couple of minutes. That was the second time in his life he had been in the presence of the great arch dragon.

Becknor led all of the party into the great hall entrance from the Weir landing. The immense hall was on the east side of the carved mountain, which was the only direction where there was no other dragon perch or landing. This hall directly led to Michenth's chamber and the Dragon Council gathering room. This arena was large enough to hold twenty dragons in the circular area with space for hundreds of man-sized creatures and even several giants. Before the Great War, the Dragon Council was composed of mostly gold and silver dragons, with a few bronze. Now there were only seven gold dragons and twenty-one silvers in all of the Alliance. Talinor Weir was currently commanded by Mkel's friend Dkert, with his copper dragon, Selenth, who he was looking forward to seeing, as well as his brother Bkert and friend Slidess.

After the Great War, the decision was made to consolidate most of the gold and silver dragons to the Capital Weir, except for the frontier Weirs of Draden, High Mountain, Eladran, and Ice Bay. This was to both cover for a wounded Michenth and to provide for a rapid and powerful reaction force until the metallics could recover their numbers. The bronze dragons had taken over all of the coastal Weirs—Ferranor, Denar, Rom, Rem, Atlean, Lancastra, and Machren—because of their affinity with the sea and ability to sustain a backup presence for the Alliance Navy. They were the only type of metallic dragon that could actually breathe underwater.

The hall was well lit with lighting crystals as they walked past the statues of dragons of all species and human leaders of the Alliance, like the Founding Council members Warrenton, Jefron, Jondam, and Befran, as well as elf and dwarf kings of note. Michenth was lying down at the far end of the hall with his head raised, conversing with Valianth, Falcanth, Draconth, and Strikenth. A huge mithril/silver-colored triangle showed brightly at the apex of the wall just below the ceiling, with a fifty-foot Alliance flag underneath. The great mithril dragon looked over to Gallanth as the other Capital Wing dragons turned their heads.

"Gallanth, Mkel, Master Wizard Jodem, you and your Weir are welcome," the arch dragon spoke out as his commanding voice echoed off the great hall's stone and marble walls. "It is good to see you, my friends, and my congratulations on your victory at Battle Point. Strikenth has told me of the fight you had and the foes you vanquished. You and your comrades saved many lives. We have much to discuss, for like you, my son Gallanth, I sense a dark storm rising. There are too many parts to this puzzle that are missing, so we must try to put them together. But that can be discussed later; now is a time of celebration, for the games have arrived, the harvest almost all across the breadth of the Alliance was excellent, and we still have the Creator's light shining upon us. I do trust that your injuries are healed?" the arch dragon asked.

"Yes, my Lord, we are fine, or at least no worse for wear," Mkel answered.

"We survived the encounter relatively unscathed; we have our friends, Strikenth and Talonth, to thank for that, my Lord Michenth," Gallanth seconded.

"Again, modesty is one of your more admirable traits, my son Gallanth. Master Wizard, you uncovered a few very interesting tales from the drow witch before the Shidanese assassin took her back to the underworld," Michenth said; he called Gallanth his son, as he considered all dragons his sons or daughters, for he was the father of all dragonkind. "We have the Alliance's best theorists, wizards, and the senior dragons trying to put all of this together, but many things do not make sense. Even I attempt to help when I am awake, in spite of my slowly healing wounds."

"We will find an answer, Lord Michenth," Jodem answered.

"I have faith, my wizard friend, I also understand that two dragonstones were successfully melded and Silvanth had her mating flight," Michenth continued.

"Yes, we have been fortunate in that regard, Lord Michenth," Mkel answered.

"This is indeed cause for a celebration; you better not let the Enlightened senators know about the mithril vein or they will call a vote to encourage the giving of a large portion of it for the common good, or at least for themselves as a giveaway to their greedy and gullible followers in exchange for votes in the next election," Michenth quipped; subtle humor was something he was known for, which was actually uncharacteristic for many dragons. "We will also debut the Avenger dragons during the games and the military demonstration for the public. Our first five Avengers are now of age; Darkenth, Vengenth, Bruntoth, and the female dragons Fellith and Liberth. They are proving very precocious but extremely motivated and anxious to prove themselves.

"How are their powers developing?" Jodem asked.

"They only have one breath weapon, a focused beam of sound or disruptive force," he explained, "which seems very effective against all types of targets and stone structures. They cannot use magic or cast spells but have a very powerful spell shield, and they are almost as strong as a red dragon even though they are the size of a bronze. They can also go into a fury like the Freiland raiders for short periods of time, which makes them as strong as a gold dragon. While they do not possess metallic dragon intelligence, they are still as smart as an average human, which is more than a typical Enlightened official." Everyone chuckled at that comment.

"The Avenger dragons can also apparently withstand a large amount of punishment and heal almost faster than we do. Our new brethren have very positive attitudes, with an almost fanatical admiration of the metallic dragons. They have the color of a brownish-gold hue with dull gold horns in the shape of a silver dragon's, and a sharp broadsword-like tail tip, which they have been training to use as a very effective weapon. So far they cannot soul bond with a human rider, but they seem to work well with the selected mithril knights that have been training with them.

They are powerful flyers with large ovoid-shaped wings but are not exceptionally fast, having the same aerial speed as a copper dragon, although still faster than most chromatics. Their wing fingers end in a short but strong talon, which makes strikes with their wings even more effective. We believe they can learn to teleport themselves and a rider, but they cannot mass teleport. We will see as they gain in experience and power. Likely, they will be our skirmish line, or breakers, aiding our forces against the chromatics and these new talon dragons, for presently we are spread too thin," Michenth added

"Yes, we must station dragons at Freiland, Ian, and Battle Point. The Capital Wing has been kept too busy, as well as all the Weirs. Captain Mkel, I know you and Draden Weir know this all too well," Becknor added to his dragon's narrative. Mkel smiled and nodded at that statement.

"Where are you keeping the Avengers, sir?" Toderan asked.

"We currently have them on the prison islands off the coast of Rom Weir," Becknor said. "Those islands are off limits to civilians and citizens, and Licanth and his other bronze dragons are keeping their part of the island surrounded in fog to limit the view from prying eyes. Since the POEs don't have any wizards with seeing eye spells, and the waters surrounding the island are patrolled by the Navy's swift sloops, latoucs, and the sea elves, we have maintained their secrecy."

"We look forward to seeing our new young friends in flight and by our sides in battle, should the need arise," Gallanth spoke up.

"And likely it will, my brother, but until then, we have a race to prepare for and our coordinated runs for the demonstration during the games," Falcanth added, to which Gallanth nodded.

"We also have something to show you, Colonel Wierangan, Captain Mkel," Colonel Therosvet said as he spoke into his seeing crystal. Several men then entered from the side of the hall connected to the laboratory areas deep within the Weir. Three were carrying a new type of crossbow, with others carting in a target and still three others pushing a small wagon that had no wheels; it was actually hovering three feet above the ground. "Captain Mkel, I know you love Markthrea as much as your wife, but if you would be so kind to put your crossbow down for a minute, you and Jodem could try out our new little inventions with your superior marksmanship."

Mkel and Jodem smiled as the men placed the targets at the far end of the hall, one hundred yards from the group, as they handed both he and Jodem one of the crossbows. It looked a lot like Markthrea but did not possess his dragonstone-powered sight, of course. Instead it had a graduated crosshair iron sight with the ability to adjust the point of impact. It had a mechanism to load a box with what looked like five bolts into the bottom of the stock; not the ten-round magazine that Markthrea had, but still not bad. It also had a similar type of cocking lever under the trigger guard.

"Fairly well balanced," Jodem said to Mkel.

"Yes, and the cocking mechanism looks surprisingly familiar, along with the dragon sinew string," Mkel replied.

"Very perceptive, Captain, our arms smiths copied your crossbow's style, function, and look for these weapons. If you two would please give them a try," the colonel asked.

Mkel cocked the lever below the stock forward and then back, which moved the first bolt into place, and pulled the string back. It was much stiffer than Markthrea, but then his bow was dragonstone powered. The bolts were also slightly longer and thinner than his. He then knelt down to take a kneeling shot. The metal sight was very finely made. *Good detail work,* he thought to himself, but still protected with a metal hood to keep it from damage under the harsh conditions of the field and in war. Jodem chose to take a standing shot.

Mkel smoothly pulled the trigger as he settled the main crosshair on the silhouette target, and the dragon sinew string snapped the bolt forward. It streaked toward the target with good speed and hit it just low and left of center. Mkel was surprised at its speed; while again not as fast as his bow, it was three or four times faster than a standard crossbow. He quickly cocked the lever, took quick aim, and fired another bolt, followed by the remaining three. Jodem fired his last shot just before Mkel was finished with his. *He always did have faster cadence,* Mkel said to himself, as he aimed up his last shot. He and Jodem had fairly tight groups on the silhouettes targets, which were set up one hundred yards away.

"Not bad craftsmanship, with excellent speed and accuracy," Mkel critiqued. "Good marksmen armed with these could be almost as efficient as elven archers. They are fast, accurate, and likely with at least a three-hundred-yard effective range, and an arching fire of at least three times that."

"Glad to hear you say that, and thanks to the over a dozen chromatics you killed, we have a lot of sinew to work with to make these bows. Draden Weir will get the first shipment of these, with the regiment getting them as well. We will have sixty ready for you both by the end of the games and the senate session," Becknor said with a smile. "You have some of the best marksmen in the Alliance. With these added to your men's shooting skills, it should make your next battle interesting."

"It will be a pleasure to distribute them among my sharpshooters. With these, my garrison's bowmen will almost match Dekeen's elven archers," Mkel answered, giving a wink to Dekeen, who snorted in a type of sarcastic gesture, but after which he quickly smiled. "Now sir, what of these new floating wagons?"

"These, gentlemen, are the result of our thunder giant allies finally revealing the secret of their cloud fortresses," Therosvet explained. "The thunder giant king, Golefad, has finally agreed to share their method of creating levitation crystals. It seems that the lighting crystals that the bronze dragons can create are not far from how they make these. Our most talented bronze dragon here at the Capital Weir has learned the technique. Zumanth and his mate Luminenth were the first to be able to create the levitation stones. It takes three small stones to provide lift for an average-sized wagon or six for a catapult base. What they do allow is for one horse to pull a fully loaded wagon over almost any terrain with little effort. Two good draft horses could pull a large catapult or its support wagon filled with ammunition and stones. We are also working on a way to have the wagons propel themselves, but that will take a little longer."

"Do these floating crystals have a recharge time?" Toderan asked.

"They can apparently operate for one to three days straight without shutting down," Therosvet answered. "Afterward they need six to eight hours to recharge. If not used continuously, they can go for almost a month without significant resting periods. We envision cargo wagons, armed wagons, and catapults able to maneuver and transport as fast and almost as freely as cavalry. We will start to field these to both Draden and Eladran Weirs and their supporting units as soon as possible. Draden is, of course, our strike legion, and Eladran is pure cavalry, but their support corps still has wagons, which they need for their logistics. You are only as fast as your slowest brother."

"I see a great potential for these, sir," Mkel commented, "but I think Battle Point could use them as much as the Weirs."

"You are right, and we are working to produce them as quickly as possible to fully equip that legion. The expanses they must control and patrol are vast, but we also have a surprise for them in that they will have at least one or two dragons soon. They are the first legion scheduled to have Avenger dragons assigned to them," Becknor said, answering Mkel's concerns.

"We believe that Battle Point will be calm for at least a short while," Michenth explained. "Strikenth, Talonth, and especially you all helped to see that all Morgathian forces in the area were eliminated. The horse clans of the Kaskar kingdom and the Southern Ontaror kingdoms will get the word of the Morgathian defeat soon, if they have not already, especially of the two wings of chromatics that were felled. This will keep them in line for a while, knowing that the Alliance will still back its far-off province city. However, we still are addressing General Daddonan's concerns."

"What of the Kingdom of Ian, Lord Michenth? I have heard from several Alliance naval wizards and Freiland raiders of chromatics flying within Shidanese lands," Jodem asked.

"I see the Wizard Council is up to date, Master Jodem. We are planning to send a makeshift wing of brass, copper, and Avenger dragons when they are ready, Michenth said, "which should be very soon. This will give them some degree of protection for their land dragons and keep their edge over the mongrel Shidanese."

"How many of these floating wagons do you think we will get by the end of the games?" Toderan asked.

"We will have enough levitating crystals for your support corps wagons and your catapult sections," Becknor said. "As for the regiment, you will have enough crystals to equip an integrated battalion with all of your combined arms sections. Colonel, this will give you at least a fully fielded strike battalion to work with until Licanth and Zumanth, with all of their subordinate bronzes, learn to create the new stones and increase our production rates. Once the rest of the republic learns about them, there will be a demand like we saw after the Great War for the heating, cooling, and lighting crystals."

"And the Enlightened senators will want their cut from the sale of these new crystals for the general fund coffers, which they can then dip into for their misguided projects," Tegent said with his normal poignant opinion.

"You are likely correct, Warrior Bard Tegent," Michenth said. "The trick will be to keep them in the dark as long as possible while we outfit the Weirs and our legions. While they will greatly enhance the quality of life and commerce in our Republic, there are other pressing issues that must be addressed first. The soldiers of the Alliance must always have an edge or measure of superiority over our adversaries. This is what we owe our young men and women who bear arms."

"Well, Captain Mkel, I know the marksmanship competitions start soon, and you and Jodem, as well as your archers, will want to get some practice in. It is always interesting to watch both the incredible accuracy of the dragonstone weapon competition and the traditional shooters display their skills. The wizards' demonstration this year will also be spectacular, won't it Jodem?" Therosvet inquired.

"Why yes, Colonel, as will the races, especially the Dragon Run," Jodem said with a smile, referring to the dragon race and the subtle competition between Gallanth and Valianth as the largest and fastest dragons in the Alliance. There were several silvers that had the ability, on a good day, to outdistance their gold cousins. This always made the race interesting, plus he liked to see the confident senior gold dragonrider placed slightly on the defensive. He heard Gallanth let out a slightly extra hard breath, akin to a muffled dragon chuckle.

"Yes, my good wizard, the races will be exciting as always. Gallanth, Mkel, again you and your men are welcome here as always, and again we thank you for your part in the Battle Point victory," General Becknor injected and motioned for the meeting to be concluded. Mkel and Toderan gave him a salute and Gallanth bowed his head to Michenth, after which they turned and began to walk back to the Weir landing and their guest quarters.

Several other Weir dragons began to arrive at the capital. Mkel wanted to see his friends from his original dragonrider training and his general studies at the university before he focused on his military education as an officer. Slidess from High Mountain Weir, Bkert from Atlean Weir, and his brother Dkert from Talinor Weir were all his close friends, with whom he shared many a youthful indiscretion. Their mounts, the silver Trikenth, the bronze Rapierth, and the copper Selenth, were all Weir lead dragons. Gallanth knew them all and was fond of them as well, even the mischievous copper.

Even as he thought about meeting them, he heard several greeting roars from dragons arriving over the bay through Gallanth's ears. He knew at least one was a silver and the other a bronze. Bronze dragons had a distinctly shrill but menacing roar, likely from their ability to breathe under water and from the electricity of their powerful lightning breath weapon. This one sounded especially deep, which told him it was likely Bkert on Rapierth, for he was one of the largest and most feared bronze dragons in the Alliance.

"It is Trikenth and Rapierth, my rider, and Selenth is teleporting in as I speak," Gallanth said to Mkel as he heard the gruff roar of a copper dragon. "Excellent, my friend, I look forward to seeing them, as I know you are happy to see their dragons," Mkel said out loud as they walked.

"They are early, especially for Bkert and his brother," Jodem said sarcastically, knowing of the sometimes flippant nature of the dragonrider brothers.

Bkert, whose family always had a love of the sea, was a natural rider for Rapierth. However, he was not an Alliance officer or even a member of the military. Rapierth took the lead in overseeing Atlean Weir, along with Shaltor, the Weir's lead wizard, who was one of the Wizard Council of Thirteen, along with Jodem. Bkert was content with just being Rapierth's rider and helping him in any fight and in their adventures under the sea as well. Bronze dragons were incredibly fast swimmers, having webbed claws and partially webbed forelegs. Their powerful tail fins extended or frilled up and were almost as well suited for propulsion in water as they were as a rudder for flight. As with all dragons, bronze dragon wings could be used to aid in swimming, but theirs were especially designed to do so, and their hide could force water over the surface as it did air, aiding their speed. The fastest bronzes could attain speeds that rivaled those of dolphins, or greater.

Like his brother, Dkert had a liking for the water, but he also had a love of the earth. This made him an ideal copper dragonrider, especially at Talinor Weir, which had a good-sized mountain lake beside it. He also did not choose to be in the military but preferred the simplicity of just being a dragonrider. His kidding and teasing nature was also a reflection of his copper dragon's style, for they were the most sarcastic of all dragons and also enjoyed a good joke. Talinor Weir, the only Weir located within the interior of the republic, was part of a large mountain chain along the Severic River; it was also the home of the second largest dwarven city. The Weir overlooked both the Severic to the north and the small mountain lake to the south, which spilled over as a spectacular waterfall; it was the headwater of the Missora River that flowed to Lancastra Weir.

"You are too critical, my friend," Mkel teased Jodem.

"I talk to their wizards, Mkel," Jodem answered.

"What of Slidess? He is also not an Alliance soldier, but a powerful wizard in his own right," Mkel quipped back.

"Kalger, the High Mountain Weir wizard, has a more favorable opinion of Slidess, but there is that wizard to wizard courtesy," Jodem answered with a smile.

Just then, Trikenth flew into the Weir interior, with Rapierth close behind. They both circled the inside of the Weir twice, descending as they glided, and landed a hundred yards from Gallanth and the Draden crew. Selenth then entered the Weir; his triangle-shaped tapered wings, with their copper and brownish hue, slightly twisted to make a tight curved circle before he landed. Coppers were ideal for sprinting flights but lacked the sustaining ability for great speed and distance. On short flights, however, coppers were very agile, especially in tight places. This ability, as well as their ground speed and jumping capability, made them particularly effective in ground and near ground flights. It allowed them to survive against and even win occasional fights with red dragons, which they took a particular joy in killing.

Slidess and Bkert dismounted as Selenth landed. Even though he was large for his species, Selenth was still visibly smaller than the silver and bronze dragons. Selenth's wingspan was just about fifty-five yards, and he was roughly thirty-three yards in length, being large for a copper dragon. His short but thick ribbed protruding eye horns were used as much for breaking rock as they were for weapons. His talons were also thick, being suited for digging and cracking rock as well as for grasping and rending. Their fiery acid breath weapon was similar to that of green and black dragons, but coppers had a longer range and a greater acidity, being iodine based. Selenth's deep copper and brownish tone almost blended in with the surrounding rock base of the Weir.

Slidess and Bkert waited for Dkert to dismount and then walked toward Mkel and Gallanth. They met at the midpoint on the spacious Weir grounds. The silver, bronze, and copper dragons bowed their heads to Gallanth, who returned the salute.

The three Weirleaders walked up to Mkel and all gave him a group hug.

"My friends, it's great to see you again," Mkel said with exuberance.

"Well, Mkel, glad to see you and Gallanth in one piece after the fight we heard you were in. You should have called on us to come and help," Slidess said.

"You know we always like a good fight, my brother," Bkert said with a big toothy smile. His greenish blue eyes always had life in them, which were accentuated with his long wavy blond hair.

"I know, but there were several other issues that had to be taken into consideration, plus I know all of you are busy as well," Mkel answered while still shaking his friend's hands in the traditional dragonrider lion's grip.

"I also heard that you and Jodem took out a company of drow on spiders, and you know how much Selenth likes his poisonous delicacies," Dkert said, referring to copper dragons' fondness of taking down poisonous creatures and then devouring them.

"It all happened very fast and furious but was handled nonetheless. In either event, I fear we will all be busy soon. But until then, we are all here now, for a couple of days, and we need to have ales together," Mkel replied.

"We also need to practice for the events of the games as well," Slidess stated, being the most serious of the group, likely from his discipline as a wizard. His tall lanky stature and short but well-kept dark hair and focused green eyes also added to this appearance. Slidess was a powerful wizard in his own right, with his dragonstone-powered wizard's staff that doubled as his quarterstaff in hand to hand combat. He was just shy of being a master wizard of Jodem's capability. The High Mountain Weirleader was also a very skilled monk, being deadly in hand to hand combat and wielding his staff with blinding speed and striking with magically empowered force. He frequently trained with his Draco Guards or the skilled bodyguards, who as a warrior caste were sworn to protect the dragons and especially their riders. Mkel and Lordan were the only dragonriders who refused to employ them.

Mkel's friend Bkert wielded a mithril alloy pole arm or short lance with a long mithril dual-edged main blade with smaller blades on each side. It was a very menacing weapon that he utilized in fights in the air, on the ground, or underwater. The emerald dragonstone imbedded in the center of the broadhead-like blade was empowered with the ability to fire powerful lightning bolts and deadly ice rays. He was a very skilled fighter in his own right but chose not to join the army or seek a commission.

Dkert was a cleric of notable piety and power, wielding a smooth ball mithril mace with an imposing pick on one side and a hammer on the other, powered by a dazzling green emerald dragonstone, surrounded by garnet. It was able to fire a disruption spell or ball of disruption energy, which was especially deadly against evil creatures. He had an amazing power to heal through his mace, along with a unique ability to manipulate rock and soil. The Talinor Weirleader also skillfully used his mace to aid the dwarves in their mining operations deep within the Talinor Mountain chain.

"Gallanth, I understand that the drow witch you captured mentioned a threat by sea," Rapierth said with a bronze dragon's businesslike, to the point, attitude. "That would make sense with the increase in enemy activity with bolder saragwin attacks and the Morgathian and Shidanese pirates."

"Yes, my brother, she started to allude to this but was killed by a Shidanese black scarab assassin before we could get more information from her," Gallanth answered.

"This could mean many things, Rapierth," Jodem said; "an all out war with the saragwin, the Shidanese, or a combination of these. Open war at sea will affect trade and commerce for the Alliance. The Freilanders are also experiencing this, as you know."

"Only a week ago, my rider and I had to respond to a distress call from a merchant convoy," Rapierth stated. "They were attacked by a whole tribe of saragwin and two kraken. We killed the evil beasts, but strangely they were uninterested in fighting the two Alliance warships defending the merchants. They just focused on sinking the unarmed vessels themselves, even though it was costing them lives from being exposed to the naval infantry's and Alliance ship's arrows and ballistae."

"What are the sea elves saying of this?" Dekeen asked.

"The normal skirmishes have escalated into full battles," Rapierth explained, "as the saragwin have been carrying greater and bolder incursions into sea elf territory. They have been reinforced by Shidanese ships ferrying orcs and other powerful sea creatures, including black and green dragons. All of the bronzes from the coastal Weirs, along with our supporting dragons, have been increasing our patrols of the sea lanes and experiencing ever intense fights.

"Yes, Rapierth, my Freiland friend had a saragwin hunting party attack his raider ships only a few miles from Sauric Bay," Mkel explained to the bronze dragon.

"The saragwin took us by surprise by being in Alliance waters," Lawrent stated, "but they mistook us for merchants at night and got more than they bargained for. They did have a sea witch of some power, though, and while my wizard slew her, he was taken by a lucky spear thrown by a saragwin chieftain."

"We knew of your fight after the sea elves found the saragwin bodies the next morning, but we assumed you handled it since we didn't get a call for assistance from you, and far be it from us to assume otherwise," Rapierth replied with a bronze dragon's usual sarcasm.

"We shall discuss this further and get the whole Wizard and Dragon Council to think this matter through, not to mention the senior Alliance military theory and strategy soldiers as well," Gallanth stated. "Until then we must always have a sense of caution but look to the games now, for the people of the republic want to view the competitions, and more importantly trust in the Alliance's might," Gallanth ended the conversation to focus everyone on the closer target, at which they acknowledged.

"My friends, before we start to practice for the games, I think we need breakfast; we have a lot to catch up on," Mkel corralled everyone up and ushered them to the dining hall of the Weir. He wanted to talk to his old friends before they got too serious into practicing for the games and the demonstrations.

After they had breakfast and talked for over two hours, they decided to fly the racing course, for Mkel did not want to shoot so soon after eating. They all mounted with Lordan and Talonth leading, as well as half the capital dragons including Strikenth, Falcanth, Draconth, Tigrenth, Lionoth, and several female dragons from the Capital Weir and other Weirs. Silvanth would occasionally fly the race, but now that she was nesting, she would not place the stress of a race on herself, for fear of losing the precious egg inside her.

Eighteen dragons gathered on the practice field in front of the Weir's north entrance, where the contests and the actual race would take place. Mkel stood up in his flying saddle as far as his riding straps would allow him, to view the other dragons. He sat the highest, as Gallanth's back was at least a foot higher than the next biggest dragon there, which was his older brother Falcanth. He enjoyed the view, for he rarely saw so many dragons this close together, being from Draden with only Gallanth and Silvanth there. Lloydell and Falcanth took charge, being the senior rider and gold dragon.

"All right, my friends, we will do a slow run around the flight course for the race. For the younger dragons, please keep an altitude of at least five hundred feet so as not to knock over any citizens or ships. During the actual run, we will fly lower to negotiate the sharper turns around the city, but today is just a familiarization run and to get the people of Draconia in the mood for the games. This as well gives all those of the Enlightened faith a little stomach ache," Lloydell said with a smile on his weathered face. "My brothers and sisters, you will follow my and Gallanth's lead and not pass us; keep an even pace," Falcanth stated to all dragons present. Falcanth had a great fondness for his younger but larger brother, as did Lloydell for Mkel, who he felt slightly responsible for; he was also proud of him for being the son of Jmes, an Alliance officer and a dragonrider. All dragons nodded an acknowledgment and began to move apart for room to spread their wings for takeoff. Mkel, Lordan, and the members of the Capital wing that were present gave Lloydell a salute, for he was a senior colonel, with only Therosvet and Becknor being higher in rank among the military officer dragonriders.

As soon as they were spaced well enough, Falcanth gave a signal bellow, which was then echoed by all dragons present. The earth shattering combined roars rumbled across the field and into the city. Falcanth took to the air, with Gallanth right on his tail. All the other dragons followed behind them. The rush of air from the push of so many massive wings almost seemed to flatten the already smooth parade ground. Mkel looked back at the crowd of dragons behind him. *An impressive sight*, he thought to himself, as if he could lead all these dragons and take on the whole Morgathian Empire. They rose quickly to the agreed altitude and soared east and then south to round the large

Weir Mountain toward Sauric Bay and the large port of Draconia. Sauric Bay was more like an inland sea, being over a hundred fifty miles long from its northern to southern shores and almost three hundred miles from the city to the ocean past Rom and Rem Weirs that guarded the choke point that separated the bay from the ocean. It provided a definitive buffer from the sea and a large source of income for the fishermen that inhabited the shores of the bay.

Mkel looked back to see Rapierth instinctively looking for large grouping fish in the waters of the bay. Bronzes were excellent large fish hunters, and he knew Gallanth wanted to look for some as well, an unusual treat for him. They began to cross over the edge of the bay and the Weir port. The ships were lined up to the docks by the hundreds, maybe thousands. The port of Draconia was very well thought out in its construction. The natural rise of the ground from the piers was reinforced by thick granite and dwarven concrete walls that shimmered in white and gray. Many cuts in the walls allowed for easy loading and unloading of the ships, but all could be quickly closed by carefully poised blocks in case of a hurricane storm surge or an invading seaborne assault. Attacking to the north would force an enemy army to move past or through the Capital Weir, and moving to the south they would have to cross over many small tributaries of the Severic River and well-placed swamps. These allowed for proper drainage from the city while also making an invading army get bogged down in the attempt.

The buildings and structures of Draconia were equally well made and sturdy. Dwarven concrete and brick were an extremely strong material, and when reinforced with steel rods, they made excellent structures. Most buildings in the city were constructed in this way, but the larger or taller ones were built in a pyramid-type of fashion for even greater strength. In the center of the city rose a great pyramid that reached a height of almost a thousand feet; this was ringed by four others that rose up to six hundred feet. The middle structure was the capital seat of the Alliance. It was the center of the government of the republic, and while holding all vital works and directorates, it was the home to no one. Its flat top mounted a massive mithril and gold triangular ovoid that showed brilliantly in the sunlight and also glowed in the focused lighting crystal illumination at night. All services were centered from here as well as the ringed Great Hall for the senate gathering arena. One of the two of the smaller surrounding pyramids that lay east and west of the main structure actually housed the senate chambers, with the other being the Grand Arbitrators Court and Council. The pyramid to the north was the premier's temporary home with all his staff and support, and the last structure to the south was the headquarters of the Alliance Army and Navy. This was the center of power of the Alliance, where all decisions and indecisions were made.

The huge Alliance flags were flying from atop all four of the smaller pyramid structures, and a gold and mithril coated triangle symbolizing the trinity of the universe and the Creator showed brightly from the outer face of all pyramids, as if to announce to all four corners of the world. The rest of the sprawling city surrounded the central government pyramids. Some of the housing and guild buildings rose up over two hundred feet, for Draconia was also the center of most of the major guilds in the Alliance. These ranged from the Wizards' Guild to the ship building guild, and everything in between. A great deal of merchants, businesses, and storage structures also dotted the city.

With Draconia being fully illuminated and powered by dragon-supplied lighting crystals, at night the capital almost glowed, being truly a city of light on the raised land above the bay. Mkel did notice only a few warships were docked, which was strange for the largest port in the Alliance and home to three fleets of the large galleys, warships, and support ships that made up the mainstay of the navy. *This must be due to the increased patrols and escort missions Rapierth was talking about,* Mkel thought to himself.

You are correct, my friend, Gallanth told him telepathically. *At any one time, the navy has well over half its warships out to sea. Their operational tempo is putting a strain on them and the coastal Weirs, according to Rapierth.* "I know the navy had decommissioned several older ships as part of the Enlightened downsizing plan after the Great War, but don't we still have enough warships for the job?" Mkel asked.

There are only about nine hundred ships in the entire Alliance Navy, and they have over five hundred to sea right now, Gallanth added. *The bronze dragons have been very busy, providing cover and fighting the many saragwin and their sea* monsters. *These belligerents have been mostly preying on merchant ships of all the Alliance allies, not to mention the pirates the Freilanders have been fighting.* They began to make the hard bank to the left toward the immense Befran Bridge.

Named after one of the Founding Council members, the stone, concrete, and steel bridge spanned the six-mile-wide mouth of the Severic River connecting the communities on the south shore to the city limits of Draconia. The bridge would not have been possible to construct without the combined knowledge of human, dwarf, and elf builders and strengthened by dwarven concrete and steel. It stood one hundred fifty feet above the water in its center, allowing all but the largest galleys and warships to pass. Gold, silver, and bronze dragons could even fly under its center portion between the largest supporting pillars. The brass and copper dragons could go under it closer to the shore, thus making a tighter turn and enabling the smaller dragons to gain on the faster larger dragons, all of which had to fly under the bridge as part of the race.

Mkel looked to his left at the docks and noticed that people were gathering to watch the makeshift wing of dragons flying past. Most of those he could see through his crossbow's sight were waving, for almost all of the usual flight paths for the Capital dragons were kept on the north side of the Weir and the city. This avoided any issues with wind wash of especially the bigger silver and gold dragons. Gallanth followed his brother, who slightly angled away from the docks and toward the center of the mouth of the mighty Severic and the Befran Bridge.

Falcanth descended to just seventy-five feet above the water, skimming the surface, with a large spray from the downdraft of his gold wings separating the water in his wake. A dragon, especially a bronze or larger, could capsize a small ship by flying over it from the wash of its wings. Gallanth lined up just on his brother's left while Talonth moved in on the right. The remaining dragons flew down and kept just behind the three leaders. Mkel could see the people on the bridge move to the side to see the wing approach and wave. The dragons split to miss a barge coming from up river. The barge captain looked very surprised, if not a little taken aback, by the number of dragons streaking by him, showering his craft with water spray.

Gallanth and Talonth started to fall back and line up behind Falcanth to go under the bridge. The center portion had the widest distance between its great supporting stone pillars and steel beams. Mkel looked back to see Selenth and several other copper and brass dragons shift to either side of the silver and bronzes behind him. The center span was barely a hundred yards wide, which while it could easily accommodate even Gallanth's or Michenth's wingspan, two dragons could not fly through it at the same time. The bottom of the bridge stood fifty yards above the water in the center to allow all but the tallest of ships to sail partially up the river, until the currents only allowed oar-powered or dragonstone-assisted vessels to proceed. It would be next to impossible for two dragons to fly under it at the same time. One flying directly over the other would create very unstable turbulence and likely cause both to crash into the water, or hit the bridge itself.

Mkel could feel the spray hit the crystal visor of his helmet and bead off of his dragon hide armor from the wash that Falcanth was making as he skimmed just over the water. He didn't want to turn his weapons' partial magic shield to block the wind or water, with his riding jacket being waterproof anyway. Since it was a nice day, he wanted to feel of the rushing air, but then Gallanth was not going nearly at full speed, which they would be flying at for the actual race.

Falcanth flew under the bridge first, with Gallanth right behind him and several dragons on each side. *This must be an impressive sight to see from the bridge,* Mkel thought to himself. He looked back to see the one-hundred-twenty-foot-wide bridge engulfed in spray as they sped away at over sixty miles an hour. *That will do us good in winning over support for the dragons among the civilians and citizens of Draconia,* Mkel said to himself.

Most of the people on the bridge were happy to see us fly, Gallanth said to him telepathically. *Those that prescribe to the POE propaganda would not have been swayed either way, my friend.*

"I know, it's just that the one thing that I loathe, besides missing Michen, is dealing with the Enlightened attitudes and false intellectual espousing," he replied. *Mkel, I think you will like this. Falcanth, guide us toward that pleasure barge with* the POE standards on it; I think they need a fly-over, Gallanth stated with an unusually mischievous tone in his voice.

Yes, my brother, a cleansing is what is needed here, Falcanth replied as he slightly veered toward the Enlightened senator's barge. This portion of the river was supposed to be clear of boat traffic, for the Capital Weir administrative personnel arranged it with the local naval and river patrols. This Enlightened senator seemed to think he was above the rules. Mkel could see the flamboyant rainbow-like flag that the Enlightened use as a makeshift standard, as well as several similarly dressed persons on the craft. He recognized it as one of Tekend's pleasure boats. Tekend, a very outspoken and overimbibed Enlightened senator from Ferranor, was also a habitual drunkard and former Alliance Navy arbitrator who did his minimum three years of service to allow him to hold office. His family controlled several shipping businesses and were either wealthy merchants or arbitrators that specialized in the sea trades. This included Shidanese and exotic wines and spirits, but other goods as well, especially those of questionable nature. Strangely enough, there had been almost no attacks against ships bearing their family standard, even in highly pirated waters, according to the Freilanders.

Falcanth and Gallanth moved next to each other, almost touching wingtips, with Talonth and Strikenth doing the same right behind them. Mkel could see them all on the deck, trying to wave the dragons off, but it was a fruitless attempt. Gallanth and Falcanth flew right over the ship, the wind wash from their immense wings sending a good-sized spray over the deck. All on board were either soaked or knocked down as the rush of water and wind rocked the boat violently. The two silvers then added insult to injury by performing the same maneuver, followed by ten other dragons. "This will be heard at the senate gathering," Mkel said to Gallanth telepathically. Let them bluster, he was in the wrong. As an arbitrator, he should have known the law, or at least known the consequences of disregarding it, Gallanth explained with a slightly disgusted tone to his mind voice. Mkel smiled, but he knew Tekend and his ilk were going to be very difficult to deal with, especially if he was called upon to testify on his initiative for veterans.

Falcanth rose in altitude and turned to the left after several miles to follow a tributary of the Severic to a small mountainous area just to the east of Draconia. This area was known as the Maiden Mountains because of the relatively small area the mountains encompassed; they were usually shrouded in a veil of fog and clouds. The race followed a series of shallow canyons in these mountains, requiring those flying through them to carefully navigate and make several tight turns. There were several paths through the mountains that different dragons found more suitable. The brass dragons took the shorter but more intricate path because of their smaller size and tight maneuverability. Copper dragons took these paths as well, being able to grapple and run along the canyon walls, for their legs were better suited for jumping, sprinting, and digging than other dragons. This enabled them to very effectively maneuver in tight places close to the ground.

The gold, silver, and bronze dragons were forced to take the longer way through, to accommodate their greater wingspans. Brass dragons, while not small by any standard, had an average wingspan of forty-five yards, which was over a third less than a gold. Copper dragons were only a slightly bit larger, but they had stubbier wings, limiting their air speed and flying endurance.

Once they rounded the small waterfall, the larger metallics veered right and the smaller ones went left. Gallanth followed Falcanth through the large canyon, making the turns and twists to avoid the rock walls but still trying to maintain good speed. Mkel was impressed at the maneuverability of the large gold and silver dragons in these relatively tight places. They emerged from the last turn over the forested area north of the mountains and immediately turned west back toward Draconia and the finish line at the Capital Weir.

The brass and copper dragons actually came out of the canyons way ahead of them, but they caught up quickly. The final leg of the race took them past the northern boundary of the city and then to the Weir, an almost straight shot to the training and parade grounds. Mkel could see hundreds of people lined up on the buildings, wall, and grounds to watch the dragons fly by. *If it weren't for the POEs, who insisted that the dragons not fly over the city to not offend anyone or scare young children, the citizens of Draconia would see more dragons in the air, and closer to them at that,* Mkel thought to himself. *You humans are confusing at times, my rider, but I guess that is what makes you so interesting,* Gallanth said, which made Mkel smile, although he felt that he would rather fight the chromatics again than have a verbal brawl with the Enlightened senators.

Falcanth and Gallanth, followed by the silvers and bronzes, overtook the brass and copper dragons just prior to reaching the parade grounds. They all streamed past the central section of the stone carved amphitheatre with several thousand waving and cheering people around the finish line. They then circled back up and into the Weir. *So much for the supposed hatred and fear of the dragons according to the Enlightened,* Mkel said to himself. As soon as they landed, he planned on going to the range to practice up for the archery competitions, also to give Gallanth time to talk to Falcanth and the other Capital dragons as well.

After they landed on the Weir grounds beside the immense lake, Mkel dismounted and slung Markthrea over his shoulder and started to walk to the northern entrance to meet with Jodem. All the dragons started to move to the back chamber to have an informal Dragon Council meeting with Michenth. He heard a voice yell to him from across the wide grounds of the Weir.

"Captain Mkel, wait up!" a figure shouted from several hundred yards away. He turned around to see who it was and recognized Scandalon, walking fast toward him, cradling his dragonstone crossbow. Scandalon was the rider of the brass dragon Krysanth, who was wingman to Selenth and Dkert. His crossbow was very similar to Mkel's, and he was also a master shooter. Scandalon used this skill to fly very effective cover for the copper dragon and his Weirleader, especially since Dkert's pick/mace was limited in its long-range capability. They served together on a few occasions and shot at several competitions as well.

"Well, my friend, nice to see you; will you join us for a little practice this afternoon?" Mkel called back to Scandalon as Jodem appeared from the opposite side of the Weir.

"Good to see you too, Captain, I've been waiting for a challenge since earlier this summer from the Talinor tournament," Scandalon stated as he walked up to Mkel and shook his hand.

"That was a good match, but if I recall, Jodem won the precision match and we tied for the long range," Mkel answered with a smile.

"Yes, and as I remember, you two only beat me at the six-hundred-yard match by a couple of points," Jodem said, weighing into the conversation as he approached.

"Master Wizard, honored to meet you again, and under happy circumstances as well," Scandalon said, greeting Jodem with a slight bow and handshake.

"Enough reminiscing on matches past, those are spent arrows; we have a tournament to shoot in tomorrow, so let us move on to the Capital's firing range," Jodem said as he turned toward the north entrance of the Weir. They all followed him out of the mountain, down the main foot path, and to the right, onto the half-mile-wide archery range next to the parade field. They decided to practice the precision shooting on the fifty- and one-hundred-yard range first, setting up in a prone position on the mats at the covered firing points. Archery had become a very popular sport in the Alliance, encouraged by the government, both for self-defense and for the defense of the republic itself in times of need, as well as if the government ever became too unjust.

A small group of engineers and master craftsmen, who had created the new repeating crossbows, came out to watch the three master shooters fire. "Dragonrider, Master Wizard, do you mind if we observe your practice? We want to see your techniques. Captain Mkel; we heard of your legendary speed and accuracy, and your compatriots' skill is also well known by us," one of the robed craftsmen stated.

"No problem here; we'll shoot a little at this course of fire and then go to the long range for our dragonstone weapons," Mkel answered. Jodem called for the targets; the halflings and workers in the pits raised the densely compacted hay bale target butts with the five circular targets printed on a thin sheet of paper. Each target was the diameter of a large grapefruit, with smaller concentric rings drawn inside, the center circle just thicker than the diameter of Mkel's bolts. All three settled down into their positions, tightening their slings around their nonfiring arms, which supported the weight of their crossbows. Mkel and Scandalon loaded a clip of ten bolts into their bows (Jodem had already loaded his).

Mkel looked through his special sight and settled the aiming crosshair onto the center of the target. The magnification of the dragonstone-powered sight brought the fifty-yard target so close and with such clarity he could count the veins on a fly's wings. He exhaled slowly and waited until the crosshairs settled inside the center circle of the target, and then he smoothly and slowly squeezed the trigger. The one pound of pressure that it took to fire the weapon crisply broke, and the bolt was sent sizzling toward the target. His first sighting shot went slightly high and right, which was typical of the practice bolts versus his masterwork quarrels with their deadly dwarven or mithril pointed heads or his explosive tips. They flew just slightly off. His sight automatically adjusted for the new projectiles, and his next four shots cut the center ring nicely. He then proceeded to fire at the record targets. Five shots per target, four targets per paper; after he completed firing, the pit crews dropped the target butts and replaced the paper.

This was a well-rehearsed process, and they had the target back up in moments. He fired each shot with great consistency, paying careful attention to the wind, for when shooting at a target so precise, any small draft could shift the strike of the bolt just enough to miss that center ring. After he shot the twenty record shots, he broke position and got to his feet, taking off his riding/armor jacket and glove he used to make himself steadier and dampen his pulse during precision firing such as this. He had missed just one center shot, Scandalon missed three, and Jodem missed one as well. "Not bad," he said to his two companions. "We did rather well."

"Yes, but even with a score of one point down, there will be stiff competition from the elves and the other dragonstone competitors," Jodem forewarned.

"Well, still, not bad; how about one or two more targets, and we'll proceed to the long range," Mkel commented.

"Sounds excellent," Scandalon replied as he began to prepare for another relay. The next round of targets had Mkel dropping only one point, Scandalon dropped two, and Jodem cleaned the target with a perfect score. They then moved to positions farther down the firing line, where the target berm was six hundred yards away and quickly set up again. Jodem spoke into the dragonstone gem on his staff to signal the crew to raise the targets up at the far distance. The frame holding the butts rose from behind the earthen mounds to reveal a large three-foot-diameter circle target that had a one-foot center ring, very difficult to hit especially in high wind.

The winds were fairly moderate and coming straight from the left. Mkel knew this would drive his bolts to the right and slightly down, as the small fletching made the bolts rotate in a clockwise direction to make them more accurate. His sight had already compensated by placing the aiming circle with an X to the left and slightly high of the center of the target. He let his sling take all the weight of the heavy crossbow and watched the sight reticule gradually go still as he slowed his breathing. He let out a final exhale, aimed, and smoothly squeezed the trigger, which was neatly tucked by the front pad of his trigger finger. The bow jumped slightly from the recoil but his sight picture instantly fell back on to his original aiming point. He held the position deadly still for at least two seconds and then looked for his bolt's impact. The bolt sank to the fletching at the bottom right of the center circle. He made a small but quick adjustment to his sight and proceeded to fire the next twenty shots.

Before his last shot, he had to adjust his shoulder position twice, taking him a little off his game, but he recovered quickly. He got up and placed Markthrea in the rack in back of the firing line. He had finished right after Jodem, who also stood up and leaned on his crossbow/staff, grumbling about losing two points of the possible two hundred.

"Don't feel bad, Jodem, I lost two points as well; this damned unpredictable sea breeze they have here," Mkel said with a smile.

"I know exactly what you mean, my friend, but this is what keeps us coming back; however, looking at all our groups, they would all have hit a man-sized target in the chest," the wizard answered.

"Gentlemen, a little tricky today, I even dropped one," Scandalon said as he got up from his mat.

"So says the brass dragonrider who only missed one point," Mkel jibed back with his normal smile. "We'll be neck and neck with each other tomorrow if we keep this up."

"That adds to the fun," Jodem added. "Gentlemen, do you have what you need for your production of those new repeaters?" he asked.

"We have a much better idea now, sir; we would like to see you at the snap or close quarter shooting range, if you dragonriders don't mind," the lead Capital Weir inventor said.

"You'll have to settle with just me; my friends don't indulge in the short range quick draw stuff. My elven brother and I will have to do," Mkel told the man as Dekeen walked up to them. "A little late, my friend," he asked.

"Sorry Mkel, I was slightly detained by King Denaris and Queen Eladra. They had several questions of me regarding our fight at Handsdown," the elf answered as he grasped Mkel's hand.

"Far be it from us to interfere in the matters of royalty," Mkel said with a smile, which Dekeen acknowledged.

"I will tell you of these matters later, but it will all come out at the Dragon and Wizard's Council tonight," the elf stated. "It is almost as if we were preparing for battle, not a senate session, but these are unique times we are heading into. I have never seen Queen Eladra as concerned as she is now, concerned and troubled. She told us that her powers of foresight have been clouded of late, but again this will be talked about this evening. Let us do simpler things like just enjoy the dynamics of shooting."

"I couldn't agree with you more, my pointy-eared friend; the simple act of sending a quarrel hurtling through the air and hitting your target dead center consistently is a satisfying part of life," Mkel answered.

Dekeen's eyes were able to estimate distance and adjust his arrow strike like Markthrea's sight, which could compute range estimates for moving targets and make automatic adjustments for quarrel strikes. He moved up to the firing line and nocked an arrow, drew, and then took careful aim. All elves, but especially Dekeen, were able to automatically ascertain distances and adjust for the arrow drop to hit their targets with amazing accuracy. Mkel saw him sighting in and scoped the target he was aiming at. Markthrea's sight read six hundred yards, a long shot, even for Dekeen. The elf steadied Elm and let the arrow loose. It streamed toward the target at unnatural speed, almost as fast as the three dragonstone crossbows. His arrow struck just low and left of center.

"Not bad for an elf," Mkel joked to Dekeen.

"I don't have a sight with the power of dragon vision," Dekeen quipped back with his usual half smile.

"It's all in the tools we have and how we use them; besides, with these new repeating crossbows, longbows will be obsolete soon," Mkel again teased his elf friend.

"I'll remind you of that during our next fight when you need backup fires from my elves," Dekeen answered.

"Just teasing, my friend; we will take a couple of more practice targets here at the long range and then move to the fast fire course," Mkel explained.

"Sounds like a plan," said Dekeen as he drew another arrow.

"Mkel, I will shoot with you until you move to the fast fire," Jodem said, "then I must retire to make ready for the council meeting tonight. Don't be too long, for we have to go over your speech one more time; I would guess that Michenth and Becknor as well as our arbitrators will want to read it as well to be able to plan our defense against the Enlightened's venom."

"Yes, Captain, that won't be a problem, never enough time when you're having fun," Scandalon stated as he got back into position. Mkel almost envied Scandalon at times. Just being a dragonrider and shooting, no other responsibility in the world, but he would never give up being Gallanth's rider and the command of Draden Weir and his infantry company, as well as the mixed battalion. He truly loved the men he commanded as well as his dwarf and elven comrades.

They shot at the long-range targets for another half hour, and then he and Dekeen went to the fast fire range, where the course of fire was rapid shots at twenty-five yards. Elves had a distinct advantage here due to their faster reflexes, but with Mkel's crossbow and its fast loading capability, it equaled the playing field. This course of fire was based on both time and accuracy. While not nearly the precision called for in the fifty- and hundred-yard course of fire, you still had to basically hit center mass on a man-sized target in seconds, and Dekeen was especially fast. After several runs at this range, Dekeen slightly edged out Mkel on points, especially on the last stage, where they had to engage four targets with six arrows in six seconds. They then both finished up at the fifty- and one-hundred-yard precision firing, which he liked the best.

After they finished, they walked back to the Weir and joined the rest of the Draden contingent in the dining hall for the evening meal. Everyone had a hard day of practice to prepare for their events, which would take place over the next several days, but the Dragon and Wizard Council meeting was the topic of discussion at the dinner tables. It was unusual and rare for the two councils to meet at the same time, but Mkel knew the importance of the matters of the time, both foreign and domestic.

While the food was good, it still fell a little short to Draden's halfling cooks at their Weir tavern. "Captain, how do you feel the senate will react to your motion for the veterans?" asked Gimbelon, one of Mkel's soldiers.

"Well, I hope I can make as good a throw at them as you do with your spear, my good corporal, but you are much better at that than I hope to be with the senate," Mkel said.

"Sir, you and Gallanth defeated a chromatic wing and helped destroy a whole Morgathian army; these POE senators don't stand a chance against you," Gimbelon said.

"Well, I wish I shared your confidence, but this is a different type of battle, and to be honest with you, I almost prefer to face the chromatics. At least they're honest in their evil," Mkel said back with a smile, reiterating what he had spoken earlier, but the words and sentiment still deemed true.

"Well sir, we all have faith in you, and I know you will come out ahead. You are fighting for veterans rights!" Gimbelon encouraged his commander.

"Thanks, it is really appreciated, especially from a troublemaker like you; I will need the support."

"Never a problem, sir," the young soldier replied. Mkel felt a sudden sense of pride and accomplishment at both his soldier's sentiment and his loyalty. This feeling was one that few would ever know, except those who successfully commanded an infantry or similar company or unit, and then only for the right reason. Personal glory was not an option but a detractor, for only a strong, cohesive, well-trained, combat-ready team was the true reward for a commander. Especially if that team knew their leader was looking out for them and truly cared about them, not just to enhance their own career. He did indeed love his men, but he also feared for them in that he and Gallanth couldn't protect them with the dark storm that he knew was coming. He hoped and prayed the Dragon Council could make sense of all this.

Dragons

<u>Amerenth</u> (am-ur-enth) — brass dragon and Alliance dragon ambassador along with his rider Canjon, Capital Weir

<u>Arathus</u> (ah-rath-us) — blue dragon at the battle for repatriation in the unsettled lands

<u>Asharanth</u> (ash-ur-anth) — female silver dragon and mate to Talonth

<u>Auroranth</u> (aw-roar-enth) — silver dragon, mate to Strikenth at Capital Weir, and fastest dragon in the Alliance, rider Andrace, wife of Padonan.

<u>Aventh</u> (ah-venth) — silver dragon in the Capital Weir wing, rider Jontzim

<u>Baranth</u> (bar-aunth) — young silver dragon at Eladran Weir, rider Altmed

<u>Batuul</u> (ba-tool) — black dragon at the battle for repatriation in the unsettled lands

<u>Breigor</u> (bray-gor) — land dragon in the Draden Weir garrison

<u>Bruntoth</u> (brun-toth) — Avenger dragon in Draconia

<u>Caraeyeth</u> (ka-ray-eth) — Female copper dragon originally from Eladran Weir, but eventually moves to Draden to be Gallanth's wing mate, rider Heathiret

<u>Darkenth</u> (dar-kenth) — Avenger dragon in Draconia

<u>Draconth</u> (drey-konth) — Silver dragon and member of the Capital Weir Wing, rider Senior Captain Gresson

<u>Doomshadow</u> (doom-sha-dow) — Black demon dragon of Tiamat's court and member of the Usurper Five

<u>Eagrenth</u> (e-grenth) — gold dragon of the Capital Weir, rider Willjon, a fearless warrior and veteran of the Great War

<u>Evtrix</u> (ev-trix) — demon blue dragon at the battle of Handsdown

<u>Falcanth</u> (fal-kanth) — gold dragon of the Capital Weir and Gallanth's brother, rider Lloydell, a friend and comrade to Jmes during the last Great Dragon War

<u>Fellith</u> (fell-ith) — female Avenger dragon in Draconia

<u>Fieranth</u> (fyr-anth) — large bronze dragon, wing mate to Talonth, at Eladran Weir

<u>Gallanth</u> (gal-onth) — largest and most powerful gold dragon in the Alliance and Draden, lead dragon, rider Captain Mkel

Glaiventh (glayv-enth) — bronze dragon and senior dragon of Machren Weir, rider Sighbolt

Groncelix (gron-sell-ix) — green dragon at the Battle of Handsdown

Havocfire (ha-vok-fyr) — lead demon red dragon of Dreadstone's Northern province of Morgathia

Hellstrafe (hell-straif) — lead red dragon of the central province under Talon sorcerer Nozok

Infernex (in-fur-nix) — Ashram's lead demon red dragon of the Northwest Morgathian province

Kadanth (kay-danth) — female gold dragon, daughter of Gallanth and Silvanth, bonded with Vicasek

Kakol (kay-kol) — green dragon at the battle for repatriation in the unsettled lands

Kearideth (kir-ah-deth) — female brass dragon from Draden Weir, rider Crystinj

Killenth (kill-enth) — bronze dragon, wing mate to Talonth, at Eladran Weir

Klaxtor (klax-tour) — blue dragon at the battle for repatriation in the unsettled lands

Krekon (kray-kahn) — red dragon at the battle for repatriation in the unsettled lands

Krysanth (kry-santh) — brass dragon at Talinor Weir and wing mate to Selenth, rider Scandalon

Liberth (ly-berth) — female Avenger dragon in Draconia

Licanth (ly-kanth) — bronze dragon and senior dragon of Rom Weir, rider Keisem

Lionoth (ly-on-oth) — silver dragon in the Capital Weir Wing, rider Delker

Livoth (ly-voth) — female bronze dragon, mate to Nemareth, at Ice Bay Weir

Luminenth (loom-in-anth) — female bronze dragon, mate to Zumanth

Machrenth (ma-krenth) — gold dragon of fame at the battle off the Adelif Peninsula during the Great War and the namesake of Machren Weir; invented the V formation tactic

Magnanth (mag-nanth) — bronze dragon, wing mate to Glaiventh at Machren Weir

Michenth (my-kenth) — arch dragon, lord of the metallic dragons residing at the Capital Weir; also known as the mithril dragon, most powerful dragon in the world, rider General Becknor

Rapierth (ray-pierth) — bronze dragon and senior dragon of Atlean Weir, rider Bkert

Raptoth (rap-toth) — bronze dragon and senior dragon of Lancastra Weir, rider Turjon

Rexkald (rex-kald) — green dragon of Tiamat's court and member of the Usurper Five

Saarex (sahr-ex) — green dragon at the battle for repatriation in the unsettled lands

Sabrenth (say-brenth) — silver dragon in the Capital Weir Wing, rider Colonel Pikelar

Sallanth (sal-anth) — brass dragon, at Lancastra Weir

Savrenth (say-vrenth) — bronze dragon hatchling, at Ice Bay

Scimenth (sy-menth) — bronze dragon and senior dragon of Ferranor Weir, rider Hardren

Selenth (sel-enth) — senior copper dragon and lead dragon of Talinor Weir, rider Dkert

Shantor (shan-tour) — female land dragon in the Draden Weir garrison

Shenenth (sheh-nenth) — silver dragon, mate to Tyrenth, at Ice Bay Weir

Silvanth (syl-vanth) — female silver dragon, at Draden Weir, Gallanth's mate, with Mkel's wife Annan as her rider

Slyvar (sly-var) — black dragon from the battle for repatriation in the unsettled lands

Strikenth (stry-kenth) — silver dragon of the Capital Weir Wing, second largest silver dragon in the Alliance, rider Lieutenant Padonan

Strongst (strongst) — land dragon in the Draden Weir garrison

Taeranth (tear-anth) — large copper dragon, at the Capital Weir, wing leader of the third Capital Wing

Talonth (tahl-onth) — silver dragon, senior dragon of Eladran Weir, and largest silver dragon in the Alliance, rider colonel Lordan

Tiamat (tee-ah-mat) — evil queen dragon and leader of the chromatic dragons; volatile five-headed dragon deity with her power bested only by her former mate, Michenth

Tigrenth (ty-grenth) — silver dragon of the Capital Weir Wing, rider Bagram

Traxsus (trax-us) — lead blue dragon of the Southwest province of Morgathia under sorcerer Tbok

Tridenth (try-denth) — bronze dragon and senior dragon of Denar Weir, known for his ferocity in battle, rider Bristurm

Trikenth (try-kenth) — silver dragon, senior dragon of High Mountain Weir, rider Slidess

Turanth (tur-anth) — young but powerful and good-sized bronze dragon, at Freiland

Tyrenth (ty-renth) — silver dragon, senior dragon, at Ice Bay Weir, rider Vermax

Uthrex (ooh-threx) — demon red dragon of Tiamat's court and member of the Usurper Five

Valcurath (val-qur-ath) — female Avenger dragon at Battle Point, chosen rider, Decray

Valianth (val-ee-anth) — senior gold dragon of the Capital Weir, second lead dragon in all of the Alliance after Michenth; Valianth leads the Capital Weir Wing with his rider, Colonel Therosvet

Validenth (val-ah-denth) — strong and wise bronze dragon, lead for the Capital Weir's second wing

Valkuran (val-qur-an) — female land dragon in the Draden Weir garrison

Vengenth (ven-jenth) — Avenger dragon in Draconia

Voltex (vul-tex) — blue dragon at the battle for repatriation in the unsettled lands

Vorgash (vor-gash) — Talon sorcerer Marlok's lead dragon

Wvythresher (vy-thresh-er) — white demon/berserker dragon of Tiamat's court and member of the Usurper Five

Zalenth (zal-enth) — bronze dragon and senior dragon of Rem Weir, rider Grommel

Zumanth (zoo-manth) — young but talented bronze dragon, at Capital Weir for training

Zythor (zy-thor) — blue demon dragon of Tiamat's court and member of the Usurper Five

Dragon Alliance Terms of Interest

<u>Aloras</u> (ah-luhr-us) — An opaque cream derived from a particular plant that the elves harvest that acts as both an anesthetic and an antibiotic. Alliance soldiers and especially healers carry small jars or skins of the salve, which can instantly stop blood flow from a wound, stop all infection, and ease great pain at the same time. It also forms a protective type of second skin over a wound or burn.

<u>Articles of the Alliance</u> — the document created by the Founding Council that formed the Dragon Alliance and the laws on which the representative republic is based

<u>The Alliance Flag</u> — The Alliance national flag is a bold standard with a white background having an embossment of Michenth in a mithril gold color in the center, a green oak leaf symbolizing the elves in the lower right corner, a brown and black hammer symbolizing the dwarves in the upper right corner, and a deep blue square field in the upper left corner with a circle of twelve white triangles in a circle with one slightly larger white triangle in the middle, all representing the thirteen Weirs and states of the Alliance that protect and bind the republic together, forever linking dragon and mankind together.

<u>Drachlar</u> (drok-lar) — Alliance basic unit of currency, gold alloy piece, a little over an inch in diameter

<u>Drachmere</u> (drok-myhr) — silver alloy piece, worth one hundredth of a Drachlar; larger drachmeres are worth fifty and a hundred drachmeres

<u>Dragon Alliance Republic</u> — The nation comprised of thirteen provinces under the protection of the thirteen Weir fortresses that were united under the Founding Council as ratified by the Articles of the Alliance. Over three thousand miles across and over a thousand miles wide, the republic is a bountiful, productive land rich in farmland, mineral wealth, and resources. There are also separate independent kingdoms of dwarves and elves that reside within the Alliance borders in cooperation with the citizens and the metallic dragons of the republic. The capital of the Alliance, Draconia, sits at the end of the sizable Sauric Bay and is the shining city of light on the hill in its prosperity and well-being to its citizens.

Dramites (drahm-ites) — small insect-like creatures that the elves have engineered to heal internal injuries

Fenig (fenn-ig) — a copper alloy coin worth one hundredth of a drachmere

Ground Thunder game - — a rugby-like game where the dragons have a large rubbery ball that they must pass or run from one side or another, across a line, or throw over a goal that is defended or not; passing is done by the head or tail

Hand and Foot Game — a humanoid version of the Ground Thunder game

Interefron (in-tur-eff-ron) — A medicine developed by the elves that when mixed with a small amount of blood from the donor can then be introduced back through the skin or orally; increases the patient's own immune system by a thousandfold. The basic components of interefron are derived from several rare plants and from the feathers of the griffon.

Morgathian Empire (Mor-gath-ee-an) — The antithesis of the Alliance that lies many thousand miles to the east. Approximately three thousand miles long and wide, it is mostly mountainous to the north and west; 25 percent of its land mass is desert to the west and northwest. It is ruled with an iron fist by Tiamat, her Usurper Five, and the Talon Covenant.

Skort — Insect-like creatures the dwarves use to clean their underground dwellings. Resembling small headless armadillos, they silently creep along the ground, walls, and ceilings and eat small bits of organic matter such as hair, dust, bits of food, mold, and even small insects.

Talon Covenant — group of powerful sorcerers that control the Morgathian Empire in conjunction with Tiamat and her Usurper Five court

Talestra (tell-es-tra) — special bodyguards for Stalenjh and the Usurper Five, consisting of the toughest and cruelest of the death knights in Morgathia that don't have the intellect to secure their own lands

Geography and Location Key

Adelif Peninsula (a-dell-if) — the peninsula where Machren Weir is located, at the tip of the southeast portion of the Alliance

Allghren Forest (ahl-grehn) — central northern forest in Alliance territory, which is home to Denaris and Eladra, the elven monarchs

Ariana (air-ee-ahn-a) — desert kingdom of the Eastern Ontaror region, with very evil and aggressive tendencies; home of the extremist Kallysh religion

Aserghul (az-er-ghoul) — the Morgathian capital city and site of Tiamat's five-tower fortress

Askala Island (ass-kul-la) — A large island that lies just over a thousand miles off the northwest coast of the Alliance. It is now a territory of the republic but was once inhabited by large populations of white dragons, ice giants, and gnolls that plagued the small local communities who survived on fishing, small agriculture, and limited trading; now mostly cleared by the Alliance and the Weirs.

Atlean City (at-lee-un) — key port city on the Alliance west coast and second largest city in the entire republic

Battle Point — the original site of the final and massive battle of the last Great Dragon War, now the site of a large detached Alliance city right in the middle of the unsettled lands

Columbrian (kul-um-bree-han) — port town on the southwestern coast of the Alliance

Conesquen River (kon-es-kwin) — river on the extreme eastern border of the Alliance that creates the border between the Alliance and the Ismer Emirates

Dagrad (da-grad) — capital city of Shidan

Donlan (dahn-lan) — largest city in Freiland

Draconia (drah-kon-ee-a) — capital city of the Alliance, center of government, commerce, and culture to the republic

Draden (dray-den) — Midsized city and province on the eastern border of the Alliance, border city in the shadow of Keystone/ Draden Weir, and gateway to the unsettled lands by the only gap in the Gray Mountain chain. The city lies just to the north of Draden Weir along the Severic River.

Eresta Lake (air-es-ta) — Large lake that sits at the base of Eladran Weir and is the headwaters for the Conesquen River.

It is very deep and over fifty miles across. The lake is claimed by the bronze dragons that inhabit Eladran Weir. It is a prime trade route between Eladran and Machren Weirs as well as the cities and provinces that surround the Weirs.

Fathracia (fa-thray-sha) — port city on the southwest coast of the Alliance, no adjacent Weir

Ferran Mountains (fair-ahn) rugged mountain chain located on the northwest coast of the Alliance and home to the largest dwarf kingdom; also the source much of the iron and gemstones in the Alliance

Freiland (free-lend) — island kingdom located several hundred miles to the direct west of the Alliance and the closest ally of the Dragon Alliance Republic

Kestal Lake (kes-tull) — large mountain-fed lake to the direct east of the Ferran Mountains

Handsdown — trading village forty miles east of Battle Point

Hasera (ha-sahr-ah) — northern inland port city of Ariana

Imiana (ee-mee-ahn-ah) — City on the tip of the Adelif Peninsula that Machren Weir overlooks and protects. A vibrant port city renowned for its beaches, merchants, and parties, Imiana is the jewel on the end of the stick of the Adelif Peninsula, which takes trade in from the many coastal islands and from all over the Southern Sea.

Ian (ay-an) — small kingdom in the Southern Ontaror chain, has strong defensive ties to the Alliance but still remains very independent. The only free nation in the Southern Ontaror chain.

Ismer Emirates (iz-mehr) — a conglomerate of small independent kingdoms to the Alliance's southeast

Kaskar (kas-kar) — loosely held massive kingdom of northern nomadic horse clans, with Elsidor as its capital. Adept at provocation, they align with whoever is most beneficial, but can field massive armies, being the most powerful kingdom without dragons.

Lucian Forest (lu-shee-ahn) — sizable forest on the border of the southern portion of the Gray Mountain chain just north of Eladran Weir

Maiden Mountains — small mountainous area just to the east of Draconia; named for its usual state of being shrouded in fog or mist due to the small but focused waterfall

Milstra River (mill-stra) — river that flows around Battle Point through the unsettled lands and eventually empties into the massive inland Ontaror Sea of the center kingdoms

Minara (min-ah-ra) — dwarf underground portion of the capital city of Ferranor in the Ferran Mountains

Missora River (mis-or-ah) — river that flows from the Crystal Lake at Talinor to the sea at Lancastra

Naterah (na-tehr-ah) — capital city of Ariana

Northern Kingdoms (or Northern Ontaror Sea Kingdoms) — series of kingdoms that lie on the northern shores of the Ontaror Sea and southern end of the unsettled lands; these form the Northern Ontaror Confederation

Ontaror Sea (on-tehr-or) — great inland sea that lies east of the Alliance and separates the northern and southern kingdoms

Savegsol (sav-ug-sul) — oasis city in the desert plains between Lancastra and Eladran Weirs, basically in the middle southern portion of the Alliance; a renowned stop or way point for travelers traversing the southern breadth of the Alliance

Severic River (sev-er-ik) — main waterway that flows from east to west from High Mountain Weir past Draden Weir, past Talinor Weir, and to Draconia, emptying into Sauric Bay

Shanaris (shah-nahr-is) — drow capital underground city

Shidan (shee-dahn) — desert kingdom in the Southern Ontaror chain that borders the Ontaror straits and the Southern Sea; known for its treachery and assassin guilds, but especially the black scarab assassins

Southern Islands — A general term for the series of islands that stretch from off the southern coast of the Alliance Adelif Peninsula several thousand miles east to the Morgathian coasts. One of the larger islands is home to a settlement from Freiland from centuries ago called Southland to the almost continent-sized island pair call the Canaris Twins.

Southern Ontaror Kingdoms — several smaller kingdoms that are mostly comprised of emirates and Kallysh theocracies that lie between the southern shores of the Ontaror Sea and the Southern Ocean

Talinor (tal-in-oor) large dwarf city located in the center of the Alliance along the Severic River and the Talinor Mountains directly across from Talinor Weir

Weirs	Dragon/Weirleader	Symbol/Shield Standard
Draden/ Keystone	Gallanth/Mkel	Gold/Gold dragon head on red keystone
High Mountain	Trikenth/Slidess	Silver/White capped mountain on blue shield
Ice Bay	Tyrenth/Vermax	Silver/Lightning bolt on blue shield
Ferranor	Scimenth/Hardren	Bronze/Black anvil on gold shield
Denar	Tridenth/Bristurm	Bronze/Black hammer on gold shield
Rom	Licanth/Keisem	Bronze/Left facing halberd
Rem	Zalenth/Grommel	Bronze/Right facing halberd
Atlean	Rapierth/Bkert	Bronze/White wave on blue shield
Talinor	Selenth/Dkert	Copper/Dwarf head over crossed axes
Lancastra	Raptoth/Turjon	Bronze/Three-leaf plant over reeds
Machren	Glaiventh/Sighbolt	Bronze/Blazing orange sun
Eladran	Talonth/Lordan	Silver/Green oak leaf with crossed arrows
Capital	Michenth/Becknor	Mithril/White shining diamond over cross swords
	Valianth/Therosvet	Gold

Language Key

Draconic Words

Dacul (dah-kuhl) — fool

Dackesh (dah-kesh) — honored thanks

Nineyak (nein-yok) — no

Onaba ham (oh-na-ba-hahm) — the sacred Draconic word for honored friend and comrade, who is dedicated to fight evil (to Mkel, a standard dragonrider greeting)

Pogach (po-gosh) — one of the worst Draconic insults

Preitoras (pray-tour-us) — sentinel or guardian, name given to land dragons by the metallic dragons, who were once employed to guard dragon eggs on the hatching grounds

Rethem Sildelfis (reth-em-zee-del-fis) — translates roughly into "to always faithfully guide those we serve"

Salvach/selvach (sahl-vash) — lowly servant or indentured slave

Sapsprech (sop-sprek) — chromatic insult to humans, means "talking monkeys"

Scheilsach (shyl-sak) — Draconic word for excrement

Verstek (ver-stek) — vermin

Yahsesh (ya-sesh) — yes or affirmative

Yvonalch (yah-vulnch) — Draconic for witch

Dwarvish Words

Jevya (yev-ya) — the dwarvish word for God

Raproch (ra-prok) — trusted/honored comrade

Taloshj (tahl-oj) — dwarvish for cleric or holy man

Elvish Words

Mogra (ma-gruh) — tree from which the elves make a particularly useful sap

Rescula se Solrela (rez-kuhl-a zee-sul-rell-ah) — elf prayer for the soul of a vanquished drow, similar to the one metallics use for slain chromatics

Salinvesh (sal-in-vesh) — Elvish curse word in a drow dialect meaning scum or vermin; the actual elvish word is Salvesh (sal-vesh)

Character Listing

Ablich (a-blick) — senior lieutenant and executive officer of the Draden Weir's infantry company

Akiser (a-kyzer) — one of the platoon leaders in the Draden Weir garrison, lieutenant

Aleslade (el-a-slade) — sea elf king

Altmed (alt-med) — rider of the silver dragon Baranth of Eladran Weir, a very skilled shooter of his dragonstone-empowered crossbow.

Andellion (ann-dellion) — midlevel wizard assigned to the Battle Point legion

Andrace (on-drace) — rider of the silver dragon Auroranth, wife of Padonan, and midlevel lady wizard

Annan (ah-non) — half-elf wife to Mkel and midlevel healer, rider of the Draden Weir silver dragon Silvanth

Ashram (ash-rom) — Morgathian Talon sorcerer and Talon Covenant member, overlord of the northwest province of the Morgathian Empire

Bagram (bah-grum) — paladin rider of the silver dragon Tigrenth of the Capital Weir Wing and wielder of a holy sword

Beckann (bek-kan) — wife of the Draden elf clan leader Dekeen and powerful wizard

Becknor (beck-nor) — rider of the arch dragon Michenth, lord of the metallic dragons, senior dragonrider in all of the Alliance, carrying the rank of senior general, wielder of the most powerful dragonstone-empowered sword in all the world

Befran (beh-fran) — Founding Council member and founder of Keystone or Draden regiment, key architect of the Alliance treaties between the elves, dwarves, and human kingdoms to form the Alliance as well as the Articles of the Alliance

Bkert (bee-kurt) — Atlean Weirleader and rider of the bronze dragon Rapierth, former schoolmate and friend of Mkel, wields a powerful dragonstone lance

Bilenton (bill-en-ton) — former premier of the Alliance and high ranking member of the Enlightened movement

Bristurm (bry-sterm) — rider of the bronze dragon Tridenth and Denar Weirleader, strong dedicated fighter and proficient monk, wielder of a dragonstone-empowered axe and resolute friend to Mkel

Canjon (can-john) — rider of the brass dragon Amerenth and former Alliance dragon ambassador, friend to Mkel, wily negotiator

Cheyneck (shay-neck) — pro-Alliance senator from the mountain region between Ice Bay and Ferranor Weirs and provinces

Craigor (kray-gor) — commanding general of the combined Keystone, High Mountain, and Eladran legions

Crystinj (kryst-inj) — rider of the brass dragon Kearideth in Draden Weir, shooting pupil of Mkel

Dackner (dak-ner) — young hippogriff rider from Battle Point legion, rider of the hippogriff Bracks

Daddonan (da-dough-nun) — commanding general of the reinforced legion at Battle Point

Dalmach (dal-muck) — emir of Ariana, a self-centered, egotistical man whose only desire is to transform the world to the Kallysh faith, a master of lying and provocation

Dansar (dan-saar) — hippogriff battalion commander at Battle Point, colonel

Debesa (de-beh-sah) — civilian aid to Captain Hornbrag in overseeing the Weir's resupply transactions, wife to Sergeant Tarbelav

Decray (dee-kray) — leader of a strike ranger company of the Battle Point legion, wields the dragonstone-empowered long sword called Palador, the Anvil of Light

Dejent (de-jent) — pro-Alliance senator from Eladran province and fierce supporter of the republic and the Weirs

Dekeen (deh-keen) — leader of the elf clan of Draden Forest, friend to Mkel and wielder of the powerful dragonstone longbow Elm

Deless (dee-less) — elf ranger/wizard and second in command of the ranger platoon under Lieutenant Lupek

Delker (dell-ker) — paladin and rider of the silver dragon Lionoth of the Capital Weir Wing and wielder of a powerful holy sword

Denaris (dee-nawr-is) — elf king who resides in the largest elven kingdom located in Allghen Forest

Dkert (dee-curt) — Talinor Weir leader and rider of the copper dragon Selenth, former schoolmate to Mkel, wields a dragonstone pick/mace weapon

Dodem (dough-dem) — the Draden Weir's barber

Donhan (don-han) —hippogriff squadron leader in the Alliance aerial legion, senior lieutenant

Dorin (door-inn) — brother to Ordin, oversees the mining operations in the bowels of Keystone Weir

Dreadleg (dred-leg) — death knight overlord of an eastern province in the Morgathian Empire and wielder of a vampire blade

Dreadstone (dred-ston) — very powerful and evil Talon sorcerer of the Northwestern Morgathian province and Talon Council member

Drekar (dray-car) — dwarf overking, resides in the dwarf capital city of Minara in the Ferranor Mountains, wields a dragonstone-powered Urgosh axe hammer weapon, pure mithril; its dragonstone is a large diamond given by Michenth

Dunn (dun) — colonel in charge of Draden Weir's support corps company

Eladra (ee-lad-ra) — Elven queen who resides in the Allghen Forest elf nation

Eldir (el-deer) — Dekeen's best elf weapons smith, aids in the creation of all dragonstone weapons

Fellaxe (fell-ax) — death knight and second in charge of Ashram's army

Fogellem (foe-gell-um) —Draden Weir-assigned arbitrator and former heavy infantryman

Frankrest (frank-rest) — commanding general of the Alliance Army

Gemorg (ge-moorg) — venerable but deadly shooter from the 36th Legion, joins Draden Weir in Mkel's sharpshooter squad

Gimbelon (gim-bell-un) — soldier in the Draden Weir garrison infantry company, and expert spear thrower

Golefad (goll-fad) — thunder giant senior noble or king

Golfine (gul-feen) — Denar province Enlightened party senator

Gresson (gress-un) — rider of the silver dragon Draconth of the Capital Wing and one time instructor to Mkel and Lupek

Grey (gray) — commander of one of the cavalry mounted legions of the Alliance, colonel

Grommel (grom-el) — rider of the bronze dragon Zalenth and Weirleader of Rem Weir as well as the only native of Askala Island to be a dragonrider, he oversees the legions from both Rom and Rem Weirs because of his experience and formal status as a colonel

Guilored (gill-or-red) — mayor of the city of Draden

Gustoug (gus-tog) — senior platoon sergeant of the 3rd Platoon of the garrison's infantry company

Haldrin (hull-drin) — elven baron in charge of the clans in Lucian Forest

Hardren (har-dren) — rider of the bronze dragon Scimenth and Weirleader of Ferranor Weir, wields a dragonstone-empowered javelin

Harfrac (har-frak) — sorcerer apprentice to Stalenjh

Hartsean (heart-shawn) — second senior sergeant to Gemorg of the Draden Weir sharpshooter section

Heathiret (hee-thrut) — rider of the copper dragon Caraeyeth and wingman to Mkel and Gallanth at Draden Weir; she is a fierce warrior and excellent battle analyzer

Hestal (hes-tull) — Apex Wizard of the Wizard's Council, likely the most powerful wizard in the Alliance, resides at Capital Weir and direct confidant to Michenth and Becknor

Hilrodra (hill-rod-dra) — outspoken Enlightened senator from Atlean who vehemently opposes the Alliance military and the metallic dragons

Hornbrag (horn-brag) — the money tracker for Keystone Weir and friend to Mkel, manages all the Weir's financial transactions both in payment of the supplies and the sale of the heating and cooling crystals that Gallanth and Silvanth create

Howrek (how-wreck) — platoon leader in the Weir garrison infantry company, lieutenant

Ibliss (ib-liss) — radical and fanatical cleric king of the desert kingdom of Shidan

Janta (jan-ta) — Mkel's and Annan's female halfling nanny/ helper

Jeffron (jeff-ron) — Founding Council member, third premier, and renowned philosopher as well as the author of the Articles of the Alliance

Jennar (jenn-ahr) — the beautiful nymph that inhabits Draden Forest and former lover to Mkel

Jern (jern) — stable master and head butcher for Keystone Weir

Jmes (jay-mez) — father to Mkel and former rider of Gallanth

Jodem (jo-dem) — senior wizard and co-second command of Draden Weir, member of the Wizard Council of Thirteen and close friend and mentor to Mkel as well a master crossbow shooter

Jondam (jon-dam) — Founding Council member and second premier of the Alliance

Jontzim (jon-zim) — Rider of the silver dragon Aventh of the Capital Weir, wing mates to Gallanth's brother Falcanth of the Capital Weyr. He served with Mkel's father Jmes during the Great War.

Kalger (kal-gur) — senior wizard for High Mountain Weir, and member of the Wizard Council

Karnak (kar-nak) — Talon sorcerer and overlord of the southern Morgathian province, Talon Covenant member

Katsleez (kat-sleez) — Enlightened senator from the eastern portion of the city of Draden

Keisem (ky-zem) — rider of the bronze dragon Licanth and Weirleader of Rom Weir, he is a friend to Mkel and wielder of a dragonstone-empowered crossbow

Kerlaw (ker-law) — Lawrent's raider first mate and second in command of his Freiland raiders

Kerneg (kern-neg) — Weir field master cook/mess chief

Kushien (kush-y-en) — outspoken Enlightened senator from the High Mountain province

Lawrent (law-rent) — Raider leader and Freiland ambassador to Draden Weir. He commands a small squadron of fast strike ships and a company of berserkers. A friend of Mkel, he and his raiders are a powerful ally of Draden Weir. He wields a dragonstone-empowered frost sword.

Lenor (lay-noor) — leader of the heavy cavalry platoon and powerful paladin; wields a dragonstone-empowered holy sword and is a senior platoon sergeant

Lloydell (loy-dell) — rider of the gold dragon Falcanth (Gallanth's brother) of the Capital Wing, he fought beside Jmes during the Great Dragon War

Lodar (lo-dar) — Morgathian warlord and powerful death knight, second in command of Ashram's province and army in the northwest region of the Morgathia Empire

Lordan (lor-dan) — rider of the silver dragon Talonth and Weirleader of Eladran Weir. He is a formal cavalryman and also commands the mounted legion at Eladran. He wields a mighty dragonstone-powered spear/lance.

Lupek (lu-pek) — ranger platoon leader and high level ranger of Draden Weir; very close friend to Mkel and wielder of a dragonstone-powered lightning javelin; mounts the powerful griffon Razor Claw, senior lieutenant

Macdolan (mak-dol-un) — senior platoon sergeant of the first platoon of the Draden Weir's garrison infantry company

Machuen (ma-q-en) — young messenger boy for Draden Weir

Magallan (ma-gull-un) — infantry battalion commander at Battle Point, colonel

Marlok (mar-lock) — intelligent but cruel Talon sorcerer and overlord of the Southwestern province of the Morgathian Empire, member of the Talon Council

Masheam (ma-shay-em) — lowly but ambitious Enlightened senator from Ice Bay

Masone (ma-sohn) — Mkel's personal liaison

Mkel (m-kell) — rider of the gold dragon Gallanth and Draden Weirleader, he wields two dragonstone weapons: the crossbow Markthrea and the mithril sword Kershan

Molotoc (mul-ah-tok) — fierce Morgathian general under the Talon sorcerer Marlok

Murjath (mur-jath) — Enlightened senator from the area just west of Draden

Nebelon (neh-bell-un) — Enlightened senator from the southern portion of the Talinor Province

Nozok (nah-zock) — Talon Covenant sorcerer from the south central province; very much aligned with Prefect Stalenjh

Ordin (or-din) — clan leader of the dwarf clan that resides in Keystone Weir, Weir council member and wielder of the Donnac, a dragonstone-powered war hammer

Orhanch (or-hanch) — pro dragon senator from the Talinor province

Padonan (pa-do-nun) — rider of the Capital Wing silver dragon Strikenth and longtime friend to Mkel; wielder of a dragonstone-powered glaive weapon, senior lieutenant

Paloud (pa-laud) — infantry platoon leader in the Weir garrison, senior lieutenant with paladin training

Penseun (penn-shawn) — Enlightened party playwright

Philjen (fill-jen) — the female half-dwarf, half-human matron of the Draden Weir's tavern

Pikelar (pyk-lar) — Rider of the silver dragon Sabrenth of the Capital Weir Wing and wing man of Eagrenth. He is a very talented wizard and wields a unique short curved dragonstone staff that also conceals a pure mithril saber for close-in fighting.

Ponsellan (pahn-sell-un) — self-serving battalion commander in the Battle Point legion, colonel

Poteignr (pot-ay-jer) — crossbow soldier of the Draden Weir garrison

Proctern (proc-tern) — young platoon leader of the Weir garrison infantry company, lieutenant

Ragnarg (rag-narg) — Freiland ambassador to the Alliance

Rainebard (rain-bard) — young wizard apprentice to Lawrent and his raiders

Raytodd (ray-tod) — crossbowman of the sharpshooter section of Draden Weir

Reagresh (ray-gresh) — current premier of the Alliance Republic

Reddit (red-it) — cavalry battalion commander at Battle Point, colonel

Reigngrim (rain-grim) — Dreadstone's overlord death knight, matches his master's cruelty and wields a dark crystal-powered vampire axe

Reigor (ray-gor) — crossbowman of the sharpshooter section of Draden Weir

Remsin (rem-sin) — Terrjok's dark crystal-wielding sorcerer

Reshdon (resh-dun) — the head monarch of the loosely held nomadic horse clans of the north of plains areas, the Kingdom of Kaskar

Richion (rich-ion) — Freiland monarch and former successful raider

Ritheud (rith-y-ud) — king of the dwarf clans in the Talinor mountains, wields a pure mithril double-bladed hand axe that can be thrown like Padonan's glaive and a studded mace in his off hand

Ronson (ron-son) — land dragon battalion commander at Battle Point, colonel

Santoric (san-tor-ic) — pro-Alliance/pro-dragon senator from the Draden Province

Scandalon (skan-dell-un) — brass dragonrider of Krysanth at Talinor Weir and shooting friend of Mkel

Shaltor (shal-tour) — senior wizard for Atlean Weir, member of the Wizard Council of Thirteen

Sheer (sheer) — infantry battalion commander of the Battle Point legion

Shumec (shoo-mek) — arrogant Enlightened senator from Atlean

Sighbolt (cy-bolt) — rider of the bronze dragon Glaiventh and Weirleader of Machren Weir; this very seasoned dragonrider is a veteran of the Great War and former mentor of Jmes before his death

Slidess (sly-dess) — rider of the silver dragon Trikenth and Weirleader of High Mountain Weir, a high-level wizard and monk

Stalenjh (stahl-enj) — head sorcerer of the Talon Council, and very powerful, evil, and cruel leader/prefect of the Morgathian Empire under Tiamat

Sternlan (stern-lan) — supply sergeant of Draden Weir and decorated veteran of the last Great Dragon War

Sykes (sykes) — chief of staff of Battle Point legion, senior colonel

Tabellen (tar-bell-un) — squad sergeant in the Weir garrison's infantry company

Taylag (tay-log) — senior cleric for the Capital Weir

Tbok (tow-bock) — Talon Covenant sorcerer and overlord of the Morgathian Empire's easternmost province

Tekend (ta-kend) — outspoken Enlightened party senator from Ferranor

Telenkis (tell-en-kis) — drow sorcerer at the battle of Handsdown

Terrjok (tear-jok) — wealthy Enlightened senator from Denar

Therosvet (ter-os-vet) — Rider of the gold dragon Valianth, senior rider in the Capital Wing, and second in command of all Draconic forces, General Becknor's executive officer. Therosvet wields a mighty dragonstone-empowered mithril mace and holds the rank of senior colonel.

Toderan (tow-der-in) — senior Weir sergeant and paladin and second in command of Keystone Weir as well as close friend and confidant to Mkel

Tomsfred (toms-fred) — pro-Alliance/pro-dragon senator from the Eladran province

<u>Tomslan</u> (toms-lan) — support corps commander for Battle Point, colonel

<u>Turbic</u> (tur-bick) — Enlightened party senator from Ice Bay

<u>Turjon</u> (tur-jhan) — rider of the bronze dragon Raptoth and Weirleader of Lancastra Weir. Uniquely known as the "gentleman dragonrider," very intelligent, unique as a human in being a fighter and a wizard. His slightly curved thin rapier dragonstone weapon also doubles as his wizard's staff.

<u>Tylorn</u> (ty-lorn) — son of the slain senior legionnaire and Debesora at Handsdown

<u>Vasterlan</u> (vast-er-lan) — Talon sorcerer, member of the Covenant, and overlord to the central province of the Morgathian Empire

<u>Vaughnir</u> (vahn eer) — senior platoon sergeant of the second platoon of the garrison's infantry company

<u>Vermax</u> (vair-max) — rider of the silver dragon Tyrenth and Weirleader of Ice Bay Weir. A hardened fighter, he wields a powerful dragonstone broadsword and a medium-sized mithril-lined shield with a centrally mounted dragonstone that adds to the magic shield power of his sword, capable of projecting a magic barrier.

<u>Vicasek</u> (va-kay-sek) — female captain of the Weir's support corps company and savvy fighter in her own right, wielding a dragonstone polearm.

<u>Vorgalla</u> (vor-gall-ah) — high priestess and powerful drow cleric captured at the battle of Handsdown

<u>Vorten</u> (vor-ten) — Stalenjh's apprentice, ruthless but cautious sorcerer, and courter of his master's daughter

<u>Warrenton</u> (wahr-en-ton) — Alliance's first premier and one of the Founding Council members

<u>Watterseth</u> (wa-ter-seth) — senior and very powerful cleric of Draden Weir; spiritual head of the Weir, wields a powerful dragonstone-imbedded holy mace

<u>Willjon</u> (will-john) — rider of the gold dragon Eagrenth of the Capital Weir Wing

<u>Wheelor</u> (wheel-or) — leader of the Draden Weir's land dragon platoon, lieutenant

<u>Willaward</u> (will-a-word) — the catapult section leader for Draden Weir, senior lieutenant

Xylest (zyl-est) — Yveshra's consort, high-level drow sorcerer/fighter

Yveshra (ya-vesh-ra) — powerful female drow cleric and countess to the drow queen Lolth, represents the drow at the Talon Covenant

Zewal (ze-wall) — high admiral of the Alliance Navy

Zelmellor (za-mell-ur) — pro-Alliance senator from the Atlean area

Zitron (zy-tron) — officer candidate at Draden Weir

CPSIA information can be obtained at www.ICGtesting.com
Printed in the USA
BVOW032053070513

320129BV00001B/99/P